MONSTERS, ANIMALS, AND OTHER WORLDS

Translations from the Asian Classics

MONSTERS, ANIMALS, AND OTHER WORLDS

A Collection of Short Medieval Japanese Tales

EDITED BY

KELLER KIMBROUGH AND
HARUO SHIRANE

TRANSLATIONS AND INTRODUCTIONS BY

David Atherton, Paul S. Atkins, William Bryant, Kelley Doore,

Raechel Dumas, Matthieu Felt, Keller Kimbrough,

Melissa McCormick, Rachel Staum Mei, Laura K. Nüffer,

Kristopher L. Reeves, Haruo Shirane, Tamara Solomon,

Sarah E. Thompson, and Charles Woolley

Columbia University Press   *New York*

We are thankful to the Shincho Foundation for the Promotion of Literature for their generous support of this book.

Columbia University Press wishes to express its appreciation for assistance given by the Pushkin Fund in the publication of this book.

Columbia University Press
Publishers Since 1893
New York   Chichester, West Sussex
cup.columbia.edu

Library of Congress Cataloging-in-Publication Data

Names: Kimbrough, R. Keller, 1968– editor. | Shirane, Haruo, 1951– editor.
Title: Monsters, animals, and other worlds : a collection of short medieval Japanese tales /
edited by R. Keller Kimbrough and Haruo Shirane.
Description: New York : Columbia University Press, 2018. | Series: Translations from
the Asian classics | Includes bibliographical references.
Identifiers: LCCN 2017022738 | ISBN 9780231184465 (cloth) | ISBN 9780231184472
(pbk) | ISBN 9780231545501 (e-book)
Subjects: LCSH: Otogi-zōshi. | Japanese fiction—1185–1600. | Japanese prose literature—1185–1600.
Classification: LCC PL777.3 .M66 2018 | DDC 895.63/208—dc23
LC record available at https://lccn.loc.gov/2017022738

COVER IMAGE: Having transformed into a demon, a *tanuki* runs away from a dog that has seen through its disguise. Detail from *Jūnirui kassen* (*The War of the Twelve Animals*), seventeenth century. (Photo courtesy of the Chester Beatty Library, Dublin, and the HUMI Project, Keiō University. © The Trustees of the Chester Beatty Library, Dublin, and the HUMI Project, Keiō University. All rights reserved)

COVER DESIGN: Milenda Nan Ok Lee

For Tokuda Kazuo, a friend and an inspiration to us all

一樹の蔭一河の流れも他生の縁

ichiju no kage ichiga no nagare mo tashō no en

Contents

vii

INTERSPECIES AFFAIRS

Contents

Acknowledgments

This book was first inspired by the "International Symposium on Monsters and the Fantastic in Medieval and Early Modern Japanese Illustrated Narratives," held at Columbia University on November 1, 2013, and co-sponsored by the Donald Keene Center for Japanese Culture, the Department of East Asian Languages and Cultures at Columbia University, and the National Institute for Japanese Literature. The scope of the project and the roster of contributors have changed over the years, but we are grateful to everyone—paper presenters, discussants, graduate-student assistants, and audience members—who participated in that initial gathering. Since then, we have received extraordinary assistance from numerous individuals and institutions, without whose help this book would not have been the same.

We would like to begin by thanking the seventeen institutions that allowed us to use their images in this volume, including Akita Prefectural Library, The British Library, The British Museum, The Chester Beatty Library, Eisei Bunko Museum, Gakushūin University Department of Japanese Language and Literature, The Harvard Art Museums, Jissen Women's University Library, Keiō University Library, Kōsetsu Museum of Art, Kyoto University Library, The Museum of Asian Art (Berlin), Nezu Museum of Art, Suntory Museum of Art, Tokyo National Museum, Tōyō University Library, and University of Tokyo Library System. We owe many thanks to the Shincho Foundation for support for the many illustrations included here; to Tokuda Kazuo for his inspiration and help over the years; to Eiko Kimbrough for expertly, tenaciously, and tirelessly securing images and publication permissions; to Saitō Maori and Ishikawa Tōru for their help in obtaining publishable images for *The War of the Twelve Animals*; to Paul Swanson and the *Japanese Journal of Religious Studies* for allowing us to reprint *The Tale of the Fuji Cave* and *The Tale of the Handcart Priest*; to Elizabeth Oyler, Michael Watson, Mai Shaikhanuar-Cota, and the Cornell University East Asia Program for allowing us to reprint *Little Atsumori*; to our three outside anonymous reviewers for Columbia University Press; to Irene Pavitt, our editor; to Milenda Lee, our book designer; and to Keller Kimbrough's students at the University of Colorado, Boulder (particularly Madeleine Crouch) for their proofreading skills. Finally, we would like to thank Jennifer Crewe at Columbia University Press for her unflagging support, even in the face of our sometimes unreasonable requests.

MONSTERS, ANIMALS, AND OTHER WORLDS

Introduction

Borders loomed large in the imagination of the medieval Japanese—borders of the country, the capital, and the rural village; the gate of a home; the foot of a mountain; and the edge of the sea—for it is at borders where one might encounter demons, monsters, serpents, dragons, gods, and the spirits of the dead, as well as anthropomorphized animals, birds, and plants. Border crossings form a critical element of a large body of Japanese vernacular fiction called *otogizōshi*, or Muromachi tales (named after the Muromachi period, 1337–1573), a genre of four to five hundred relatively short stories that were written from the fourteenth through the seventeenth century. The term *otogi* (companion; *zōshi* or *sōshi* means "booklets") comes from *Otogi bunko* (*The Companion Library*), a box set of twenty-three Muromachi tales printed by the Osaka publisher Shibukawa Seiemon in the Kyōhō era (1716–1736). These *otogizōshi*, while coming to the fore in the fourteenth and fifteenth centuries, continued to be written, illustrated, and printed well into the early modern period (Edo period, 1600–1867) and have even made a lasting mark on contemporary Japanese popular culture in the form of animation, films, and manga.

Early *otogizōshi* were for the most part written by aristocrats (many of whom had fallen on hard times) and Buddhist priests, the scholars and educated elite of the day. *Otogizōshi* differed from aristocratic court tales (*monogatari*) of the tenth through thirteenth centuries in that many of their subgenres derived from the culture of the roadside and of itinerant storytellers. For example, the *honji-mono* (stories of the human lives of gods and buddhas before they became deities), a number of which are translated in *Monsters, Animals, and Other Worlds*—including *The Origins of Hashidate* (*Hashidate no honji*) and *The Origins of the Suwa Deity* (*Suwa no honji*)— probably began as stories about the origins of gods and buddhas narrated by itinerant performers, likely for the purpose of temple or shrine fund-raising. Similarly, the many accounts of the warrior hero Minamoto no Yoshitsune (1159–1189)—such as *The Palace of the Tengu* (*Tengu no dairi*) and *Yoshitsune's Island-Hopping* (*Onzōshi*

1

shima-watari), both translated here—show the impact of semi-oral circulation: the wide range of textual variants, the use of contemporary vernacular, the storytelling conventions (repetition of set phrases, familiar motifs, and established plot patterns), and the content, much of which derives from either folk literature or short anecdotal stories.

Journeys to other worlds in these vernacular stories must be understood, at least partly, in the wider Buddhist context of belief in karmic rebirth in the Six Realms (*rokudō*)—the realms of hell (*jigoku*), hungry ghosts (*gaki*), animals (*chikushō*), warriors (*ashura*), humans (*ningen*), and gods/devas (*ten*)—into which humans were believed to be born and through which their spirits would wander until they could be enlightened or saved, hopefully to be reborn into the Pure Land (Jōdo). After death, during a forty-nine-day "interim time-space" (*chūu*), the spirit of the deceased was thought to be judged by the Ten Kings (*jūō*), or judges of hell, particularly King Enma, who, looking into a mirror that reflects all past actions, determines the person's fate, sending those who had sinned to appropriate realms of punishment. The medieval period (1185–1600) also saw the emergence of a "*Tengu* (Goblin) Path" (Tengudō), a dark wandering into which a person could fall while still alive.

As would be expected of literature frequently written by Buddhist priests, the narratives are often religious and pedagogical, describing the nature of the Six Realms and the various hells that await sinners. An *otogizōshi* such as *Isozaki*, which probably was written by a Buddhist priest and is translated here, was likely aimed at female audiences, to teach them the dangers of jealousy, excessive attachment, and the fate of women who do not abide by Buddhist laws. Many of the *otogizōshi*, which include "tales of spiritual awakening," were written or recited orally to guide the audience to a higher moral path or to a monastic order. For example, the author of *Little Atsumori* (*Ko-Atsumori*) took an earlier narrative found in *The Tale of the Heike* (about the slaying of a young and cultivated Heike warrior/aristocrat by a Minamoto warrior) and transformed it into a kind of Buddhist parable.

Otogizōshi and Media

These border-crossing stories are often richly illustrated in a painted-scroll format that foreshadows today's world of manga, anime, and science fiction. At the end of *The Tale of the Fuji Cave* (*Fuji no hitoana sōshi*), which is translated in this book, the protagonist, after his visit to various hells and the Pure Land, is asked to relate his experiences so that people can learn about what they cannot see. As this passage suggests, one of the key functions of Muromachi tales was to enable readers to experience what could not be directly accessed in everyday life. The images in the painted scrolls and illustrated books were a vital means in that process, functioning as a kind of virtual reality, and increasingly these tales came to portray other worlds, including those of anthropomorphized animals, plants, and monsters.

The *otogizōshi* represents a major turning point in the history of Japanese literature, bringing together many narrative types from the earlier traditions—court tales, military tales, anecdotal literature, and stories about the divine origins of shrines or temples (*engi-mono*). These various genres, most of which had existed independently of one another, intersected in the Muromachi period. The bundling effect is apparent in the wide assortment of subgenres of *otogizōshi*: tales of aristocrats, of warriors, of commoners, of Buddhist priests, and of relations with other species—to name only the most prominent.

There was also an unprecedented degree of interaction among different media and performance genres—fictional texts, painting, picture-telling (*etoki*), storytelling, preaching, and theater (such as *kōwakamai* and noh). For example, the interspecies tale *Lady Tamamo* (*Tamamo no mae sōshi*), which is translated here, focuses on a beautiful imperial consort who turns out to be a bewitching old fox and is hunted down and killed. The same story appears as a noh play, *Sesshōseki* (*Killing Stone*), and, as with *Killing Stone*, *otogizōshi* probably were the sources for many noh plays.

INTERACTING MEDIA

The *otogizōshi*, like many Muromachi genres, stands at the intersection of the book, the parlor, and the roadside. The book genres range from the court tale (*monogatari*) and the literary diary (*nikki*) to the scroll painting (*emaki*), the book with hand-painted illustrations (*nara ehon*), and various illustrated print genres in the Edo period. The parlor, by contrast, is highlighted by the screen painting (*byōbu-e*), the wall and sliding-door painting (*fusuma-e*), and later, in the medieval period, the hanging scroll (*kakejiku*). The culture of the roadside begins with itinerant storytellers, traveling preachers, and street performers, who often carried portable scroll paintings or hanging scrolls and who were frequently loosely associated with temples and shrines. In the late medieval period, the culture of the book and of the parlor, both of aristocratic origin, directly interacted with the culture of the roadside, which had more popular roots.

The increased presence of visual, oral, and corporeal media—specifically, the large rise in the use of scroll paintings and the spread of oral-performance genres—was a response to the needs of a broader audience, which expanded beyond aristocrats and priests to include elite warrior leaders, provincial daimyo families, wealthy townspeople, and even farmers. This new audience, unlike the educated aristocrats of previous eras, needed education; the *otogizōshi* became an important means of learning, providing both practical knowledge and moral education as well as delivering, particularly to women (who made up a large percentage of the audience), the essentials of cultural literacy (such as poetic composition), often with visual aids.

TEXT–PICTURE DYNAMICS

Most of the tales translated in *Monsters, Animals, and Other Worlds* appear as painted scrolls, and the best examples from the scroll paintings (and, in a few cases, printed illustrations) have been chosen to accompany the texts. The *emaki* is viewed not open fully, as in a museum exhibition, but between the hands of the viewer, who unrolls the scroll with the left hand while rolling it up with the right—a process that also creates a sense of suspense. The horizontal format is ideal for the narrative form; the eye moves from right to left, following the unfolding action and creating a sense of passing time. For example, in an image in *Ōeyama ekotoba* (*Mount Ōe in Pictures and Words*, late fourteenth century [Itsuō Art Museum]), a narrative *emaki* of the legend of Shuten Dōji, the drunken demon is shown lying asleep on the right and then being decapitated on the left, both in the same scene.

The first and most traditional *emaki* format, such as that found in most, if not all, extant versions of the scrolls of *The Tale of Tawara Tōda* (*Tawara Tōda monogatari*) and *The Tale of the Mouse* (*Nezumi no sōshi* [Harvard Art Museums]), is a sectional, horizontal scroll in which the text and the paintings alternate. A section of text is followed by a painting, allowing the viewer to understand the painting based on his or her knowledge of the text, and vice versa.

The second type of *emaki*, which became prominent in the *otogizōshi* genre, is sectional, with alternating text and paintings, but also has text embedded inside the paintings (see figure on pages 330–31). These so-called words in the painting (*gachūshi*) appear briefly in *setsuwa* scrolls of the Kamakura period (1185–1333), but they do not make a full appearance until the advent of illustrated *otogizōshi*. The "words in the painting" have various functions:

- As narrative text
- As a short explanation of the painted scene
- As identification of a painted figure
- As the speech or thoughts of the painted figures, much like the speech or thought balloons in modern Japanese manga

The dialogue inscribed in these paintings does not function simply to mirror the written text. The versions of *The Tale of the Mouse* in the Suntory Museum of Art, which is translated here, and the Spencer Collection in the New York Public Library, for example, have extensive dialogue among the mice that does not appear anywhere in the main text (see figure on page 281). The added dialogue and painted scenes often appear to have educational or humorous value. The kitchen painting in *The Tale of the Mouse*, for example, taught the viewer about cooking and preparing for a wedding; the painted scenes, which include the figure of the great tea master Sen no Rikyū, provide visual knowledge about various arts, from tea ceremony to noh theater, musical performance of *The Tale of the Heike*, and *kyōgen* (comic drama). The *gachūshi* also include a number of *waka* (classical Japanese poems), a staple of women's education, that do not appear in the main text. The paintings thus created a space for play in which the artist could improvise and add elements outside the narrative.

The *gachūshi* in these *otogizōshi* often are written in spoken vernacular (as opposed to the classical Japanese of the story), which creates a sense of performative immediacy. As one scholar has indicated, the main text in the picture scroll *Chigo ima mairi monogatari* (*The New Lady-in-Waiting Is a Chigo*) uses the literary auxiliary verb *haberi*, which indicates politeness, while the same speech in the *gachūshi* uses the auxiliary verb *sōrō*, which is common in spoken Japanese.[1] In other words, the same story is presented simultaneously from three perspectives: as narrative text, as visual representation, and as spoken drama.

The third type of scroll painting consists of paintings with only embedded text, or "words in the painting," without alternating sections of text. A prominent example is *Fukutomi zōshi* (*The King of Farts*). The combination of painting and embedded dialogue rapidly moves the action forward like an illustrated film script.

In the fourth type of *otogizōshi emaki* (such as the *Little Atsumori* picture scroll in the Spencer Collection, which has no alternating text and paintings, and *The Chrysanthemum Spirit* [*Kiku no sei monogatari*] picture scroll in the collection of the Harvard Art Museums), the text is sprinkled with painted figures, objects, or parts of landscape, usually below or above the lines (see figure on page 302).

The fifth type of *monogatari emaki* contains no text at all—only paintings—as in the *Hyakki yagyō emaki* (*Night Parade of a Hundred Demons*) and *Urashima myōjin engi emaki* (*Origins of the Urashima Deity*, first half of the fourteenth century [Urashima Shrine]). *Origins of the Urashima Deity*, a horizontal scroll that depicts the story of the fisherman Urashima and his visit to the Dragon Palace as well as the

1. Minobe Shigekatsu, "Otogizōshi hyōgen no shikumi," in *Chūsei denshō bungaku no shosō* (Tokyo: Izumi Shoin, 1988), 214–15.

activities of the shrine dedicated to the deity, is thought to be missing a separate text that was used for storytelling and preaching by picture-tellers (*etoki*) related to the shrine. A vertical hanging scroll (*kakejiku*; 168 cm [66 in.] × 140 cm [55 in.] [Ura Shrine, Kyoto]), with the same title and similar content, also exists. Separated into four horizontal panels, this hanging scroll allows the audience to see the entire painting at one time. In contrast to the small horizontal hand scrolls, which can be shared by only a handful of viewers, usually kneeling and leaning over the scrolls, the large *emaki* and the hanging scrolls can be seen by a larger number of people and were employed by picture-tellers, who narrated the stories depicted in the paintings using a feathered stick as a pointer. The *etoki* also enacted the speech of the figures in the paintings, much like the *benshi* (oral storyteller) did with early silent films. The picture-teller tradition survived in the form of the *kami-shibai* (literally, "paper drama") practiced in the first half of the twentieth century, in which an itinerant storyteller used rectangular pictures on a portable screen.

We thus have two fundamental paradigms of reading/viewing/listening: one in which an audience views a painting (usually a large hanging scroll or a large horizontal scroll) while being told about the content (as in the *etoki* performance), and the other in which an audience reads or hears the text while viewing the painted scroll. The *otogizōshi* were closely linked to both of these practices.

In the late Muromachi period, *otogizōshi* also took the form of the hand-painted book, or *nara ehon* ("Nara picture books," although the connection to the city of Nara is tenuous at best). In some *nara ehon*, the text appears inside or on top of the paintings, but generally speaking, like the narrative picture scrolls from which they are largely derived, the *nara ehon* alternate text and paintings, with the paintings occupying less space than the text. The *nara ehon* normally had one painting filling a whole page (or filling facing pages [see figure on page 238) for every six to ten pages of text. The picture books were constructed in three basic formats: the large vertical format (30 cm [12 in.] × 22 cm [8.6 in.]), the standard vertical format (23 cm [9 in.] × 17 cm [6.6 in.]), and the horizontal format (18 cm [7 in.] × 24 cm [9 in.]). The large vertical format, a kind of luxury book with color paintings, appeared from the late Muromachi to the early Edo period, and then again in the Kanbun era (1661–1673).

The typical *nara ehon* painting is in the style of the Tosa school, with open-roof perspective (*fukinuki yatai*), but the visual focus tends to shift to the figures and action rather than to the landscape, which the *emaki* excelled in. In a convention inherited from the *emaki*, the *nara ehon* paintings are almost always blocked off on the top and bottom by clouds (see figure on page 222), which became a highly decorative feature, and were often sprinkled with gold flake (similar to the gold decoration in Momoyama paintings). The *nara ehon* were bought or commissioned by either daimyo or wealthy urban commoners from illustrated-book stores (*ezōshiya*) in Kyoto, and the deluxe editions seem to have been sometimes commissioned by daimyo families as wedding gifts for their daughters.

In the early Edo period, with the rise of print culture, some *otogizōshi* took the form of *tanrokubon* (red-green books), with black-and-white printed line drawings enhanced with hand-daubed washes of color. Hand-painted *nara ehon* continued to be produced until at least the middle of the eighteenth century, but the *tanrokubon* allowed for greater reproduction and distribution and foreshadowed the printed, illustrated books of the mid-Edo period. Edo-period prose fiction can be divided into two fundamental types by their text–picture formats: (1) genres in which the text and picture are juxtaposed either horizontally or vertically (as in illustrated *ko-jōruri* playbooks, *ukiyozōshi*, *hanashibon*, *dangibon*, *sharebon*, and *ninjōbon*), and (2) genres in which the text is placed in the image or the image in the text (as in the broad genre of *kusazōshi*, which includes *akahon*, *kurohon*, *aobon*, *kibyōshi*, and *gōkan*). The illustrated *otogizōshi* and *nara ehon* provided the foundation for both of these book formats, and the use of the *gachūshi* foreshadowed the integration of text and dialogue in the *kusazōshi* genre as well as in modern manga.

Exploring Hells

Buddhist paintings of hell and the Pure Land, influenced by *Ōjōyōshū* (*Essentials of Salvation*, 985) by Genshin (942–1017), became extremely popular in the medieval period, particularly as a result of the spread of Pure Land Buddhism. These paintings played a crucial role in showing audiences the underworld (*meido*), where the spirits of the dead, during the forty-nine-day "interim time-space" (*chūu*), were judged by the Ten Kings of hell. Audiences looked at these paintings and were reminded to pray for their deceased family members and to think about their own futures. At temples and shrines and on the streets, itinerant performers used scroll paintings and portable hanging scrolls that illustrated the lives of Shakyamuni and various Buddhist saints as well as stories of miraculous occurrences of gods and buddhas.

Many illustrated *otogizōshi*, often written by Buddhist priests or commissioned by temples, had a similar function, showing readers worlds that they could not normally view. A good example is *Chōhōji yomigaeri no sōshi* (*Back from the Dead at Chōhōji Temple*, fifteenth–early sixteenth century), which depicts diverse aspects of hell in especially gruesome detail. Sometimes the Buddhist worlds, particularly that of the Land of the Dead (Yomi) and hell (*jigoku*), are relativized, are tempered, and even become a source of entertainment. In *The Tale of the Fuji Cave*, the warrior Nitta, in the year 1201, is sent down to the caves beneath Mount Fuji, where he meets a serpent (the god of Mount Fuji), visits the Six Realms, talks to King Enma, and then finally goes to the Pure Land. The story, which became very popular in the early Edo period, suggests that hell had become a place to visit on the way to paradise.

In *The Palace of the Tengu*, the young Yoshitsune, wishing to meet his father, Yoshitomo, in the Pure Land, travels beyond the human realm with the guidance of a *tengu* goblin (normally regarded as an enemy of Buddhism); he visits 136 different hells, as well as the realm of hungry ghosts and the *ashura* realm (a place of never-ending combat), before arriving at the Pure Land, where he discovers that his father has become the Cosmic Buddha (Dainichi Nyorai). In *Yoshitsune jigoku yaburi* (*Yoshitsune's Wreaking of Hell*), an *otogizōshi* that appeared in the early Edo period, Yoshitsune and his retainers go even further by destroying the demons and occupying hell, suggesting that hell is no longer a place to be feared.

The Three Countries

Various foreign countries appear in court tales of the Heian period (794–1185), including Hashi, or Persia, during the Sassanian period (third–seventh centuries). In *Utsuho monogatari* (*The Tale of the Hollow Tree*, tenth century), for example, the protagonist Toshikage makes a visit to Hashi. However, in almost all Heian vernacular tales, the main foreign country is Tang China, which is the setting for such works as *Hamamatsu chūnagon monogatari* (*The Tale of the Hamamatsu Middle Counselor*, eleventh century) and *Matsura no miya monogatari* (*The Tale of Matsura*), both examples of late-Heian court fiction. This binary worldview of China and Japan expanded into a Three-Country (Sangoku) worldview of India, China, and Japan, which first appears in full form in *Konjaku monogatari shū* (*Tales of Times Now Past*, early twelfth century) and which became the topographic foundation for late-medieval discourse.

Buddhism celebrated India as the birthplace of Shakyamuni and the home of deities such as the Cosmic Buddha (Dainichi Nyorai). A number of the stories in this anthology take place in India. *The Tale of the Clam* (*Hamaguri no sōshi*), an interspecies Buddhist tale, is set in the Indian kingdom of Magadha, where the historical Buddha lived and taught for many years. The center of the Buddhist cosmology was Shumisen (Mount Sumeru), a tall mountain surrounded by four great landmasses, the southernmost of which was Nansenbu-shū (Senbu, also Nan'enbudai or Jambudvipa), where India, China, and Japan were located. In the large hanging scroll

Gotenjiku-zu (*Map of Five Regions of India*, 1364; 170 cm [67 in.] × 166.5 cm [65.5 in.] [Hōryūji Temple, Nara]), India is divided into five regions—east, south, west, north, and central—while China exists in a small corner in the northeast and Japan appears as a small island in the sea. When viewed from India, China seems to be as small a country as Japan. Both existed on the "far edge" (*hendo*), on the east side of Nansenbushū. The islands of Japan are often described as resembling "scattered millet" (*zokusan*).

The Japanese view of the world had always come from China, which regarded itself as the Central Kingdom (Chūka), placing Japan in a low peripheral position. The introduction of India as the homeland of Buddhism, however, had the unexpected benefit of placing Japan and China in the position of equals. Part of the "three world" cosmology was the association of each of the three countries with a specific set of beliefs: Buddhism (India), Confucianism and Daoism (China), and Shinto (Japan). Even more important was the notion that all three worlds—Buddhist, Confucian and Daoist, and Shinto—were one at base. The belief in *honji-suijaku* (original ground and trace), according to which Indian Buddhist deities manifested themselves as native Japanese gods, and the idea of *shinbutsu shūgō* (the unity of Buddhist and Shinto gods) united India and Japan, even as Japan was connected to China, the center of Confucianism and Daoism. Japan and India thus coexisted in the same Buddhistic cosmology, with Shumisen at the center. The Buddhist notion of *mappō* (Latter Days of the Law) and the spatial notion of *hendo* (the far edge) placed Japan on the periphery, but as a result of *honji-suijaku* belief, Japan became bonded to the center.

Otogizōshi such as *Kumano no honji* (*The Origins of the Kumano Deity*), based on the "Avatars of Kumano" story in *Shintōshū* (*The Collection of the Way of the Gods*, ca. 1360);[2] *The Origins of Hashidate*; and *The Origins of the Suwa Deity* take place in different parts of India and Japan. These tales lean heavily on the genre of *honji-mono* (origin tales), which describe in detail a Japanese deity's earlier life as a human being in this world (often in India), dwelling on the suffering that motivated the protagonist to become a merciful, benevolent deity of Japan. The protagonist usually undergoes terrible experiences, having his or her mother and father killed, being torn away from a husband or wife, or being tortured by a jealous stepmother. Having understood human pain, the protagonist then emerges as a deity, vowing to save humans from similar distress. Popular narratives such as these brought India and Japan onto the same stage, spanning vast distances and time.

9

2. Anne Commons, trans., "The Avatars of Kumano," in *Traditional Japanese Literature: An Anthology, Beginnings to 1600*, ed. Haruo Shirane (New York: Columbia University Press, 2007), 887–900.

Other Worlds

The late medieval period also witnessed the expansion of "other worlds" (*ikai*). From the ancient period (to 784), the Japanese believed in Tokoyo (Everlasting Land), a realm of immortality somewhere in the sea, and in Hōrai (Penglai), a Chinese-derived, Daoist-inspired island of the immortals. There was also a belief in other worlds at the bottom of the sea, the most powerful and recurrent symbol of which was the Dragon Palace (Ryūgū), which appears from the ancient period in *Nihon shoki* (*The Chronicles of Japan*, 720) and *Kojiki* (*Record of Ancient Matters*, 712) and blossoms in the late-medieval imagination. In *The Tale of Tawara Tōda*, the Dragon Palace is said to lie at the bottom of Lake Biwa and overflow with jewels.

In these *otogizōshi*, other worlds also frequently exist beneath the surface of the earth, much as they do in the legends, paintings, and proselytizing traditions of Mount Tateyama and other sacred sites.[3] In *The Tale of the Mouse*, for example, a mouse dwells inside a wide burrow that closely resembles the Pure Land. In *The Origins of the Suwa Deity*, a vast other world appears underground, accessible through a deep hole. This place was sometimes associated with Yomi, the Land of the Dead, thus combining Buddhist and ancient Japanese cosmologies. Likewise, *The Tale of the Fuji Cave* describes a dangerous and mysterious cavern that links the human and non-human realms. A similar subterranean world appears in *Mokuren no sōshi* (*The Tale of Mokuren*).[4] In short, the underground becomes an alternate imaginary space connected to our own world by dark caves and chasms.

From as early as the Heian period, the sky above the earth (*tenkai*) intrigued the Japanese cultural imagination, but in the Muromachi period, it became a vast highway that connected this world to other worlds. In *The Tale of Amewakahiko* (*Amewakahiko sōshi*, also *Tanabata* or *Tanabata no honji*), which appears in multiple painted-scroll versions and is translated here, a serpent demands that he be allowed to marry one of the daughters of a rich man. When the serpent's head is chopped off, a handsome young man appears, and he and the daughter live happily until the man (Amewakahiko [Young Man of Heaven]) has to return to the sky. The lady climbs to the heavens in search of her husband, and she learns of his whereabouts from various stars, constellations, and other celestial bodies (see figure on page 170).

---

3. Caroline Hirasawa, *Hell-bent for Heaven in Tateyama Mandara: Painting and Religious Practice at a Japanese Mountain* (Leiden: Brill, 2012).

4. For a translation of *Mokuren no sōshi*, see Hank Glassman, "The Tale of Mokuren: A Translation of *Mokuren-no-soshi*," *Buddhist Literature* 1, no. 1 (1999): 120–61.

In the end, the man and the woman are turned into stars that can meet only once a year, on the seventh day of the seventh month (Tanabata).

Many of these other worlds are marked by a four-seasons-in-four directions (*shiki-shihō*) garden, a symbol of utopian space and time. Japanese court poetry (*waka*) and Heian classical tales frequently revolve around the four seasons. In Muromachi tales, when the protagonist arrives at a utopian world, the four seasons appear simultaneously, in the four cardinal directions, indicating the transcendence of time. When the lady visits the underground residence of the mouse in many versions of *The Tale of the Mouse*, for example, she comes across a four-seasons-in-four-directions garden.

This explosion of other worlds can be attributed to a combination of factors: the continued growth of China in the popular imagination, the prominence of India as a new cultural topography, and the increasing popularity of Buddhist underworlds and hells. These other worlds existed primarily in the cultural imagination. India, for example, is depicted as if it were China, with residences that feature crossed tile floors and tile roofs (the visual code for "foreign"). While there was contact with the continent (such as the failed Mongol invasions of Japan in the thirteenth century and Toyotomi Hideyoshi's aborted invasion of Korea in the sixteenth), the limited information about these foreign lands meant that there was no limit to the writer's imagination when it came to describing them, leading to a vast and complex cosmology of other worlds.

Interspecies Affairs

Many of the stories translated in this book—*The Tale of the Mouse*, *The Chrysanthemum Spirit*, *The Tale of Tamamizu*, *The Tale of a Wild Goose*, *The Stingfish*, *Lady Tamamo*, *The Tale of the Clam*, *The War of the Twelve Animals*, and *The Sparrow's Buddhist Awakening*—focus on anthropomorphized animals (mouse and fox), birds (goose and sparrow), plants (chrysanthemum), and creatures of the sea (stingfish and clam) who become involved with human beings, sometimes bearing their children and usually having to separate from their human partners. The proliferation of the spirits of plants and animals in Muromachi popular literature can be traced, at least in part, to the increasingly widespread Buddhist belief that trees, grasses, and earth are all inherently enlightened. Instead of simply regarding plants and animals as occupying lower tiers of existence, much as they do in early *setsuwa* anthologies such as *Nihon ryōiki* (*Record of Miraculous Events in Japan*, ca. 822), advocates of this new Buddhist view maintained that according to the Tendai doctrine of "original enlightenment," plants and animals, like humans, were inherently imbued with the buddha-nature.

This idea overlapped with long-held indigenous folk beliefs in the spirits of trees, plants, and animals, many of which were locally worshipped or feared as gods (*kami*) and often served as intermediaries between the human and the spirit world. The capital-centered, *waka*-based, highly codified view of nature also transformed animals, birds, and plants into elegant figures, as in *The Chrysanthemum Spirit* and *The Tale of a Wild Goose* (*Kari no sōshi*). Similarly, continental beliefs in the ability of foxes to take human form, deceiving humans, are also evident in *The Tale of Tamamizu* (*Tamamizu monogatari*) and *Lady Tamamo*.

Farmers had to kill insects and other animals that harmed their rice fields, which led to the widespread ritual of praying for the spirits of slaughtered animals and insects. In order to eradicate insects that damaged the harvest, farm villagers lit pine torches and rang bells. This was followed by *mushi-kuyō* (offerings to the spirits of deceased insects). Similar offerings were made to whales, fish, boar, deer, and other hunted animals. Numerous Muromachi popular tales and noh plays reveal this fundamental conflict between the need to control nature—particularly the pressure to hunt, kill harmful animals, and clear forests for agriculture—and the desire to appease and worship nature, which was believed to be a realm filled with spirits. The sin of killing could be ameliorated, at least in part, by praying for the spirits of dead animals or by releasing captured animals, which are frequent motifs in early and medieval anecdotal literature. The awareness of the Buddhist sin of killing enhanced the sense of sympathy for the hunted animal or bird, an attitude evident in this anthology in *The Tale of a Wild Goose*. Following a prominent pattern in Buddhist tales, the killing of an animal results in religious awakening and conversion (*hosshin*), as we see in *The Sparrow's Buddhist Awakening* (*Suzume no hosshin*).

In the medieval popular imagination, two worlds coexisted: this world of human beings and the other world of the dead, gods, buddhas, demons, and monsters. The natural realm, with its animal and plant life, was linked to the other world, which could not only bestow great fortune, protection, and long life (with animals and birds being bearers of gifts), but also bring plague, natural disasters, and death. In the military tales, brave warriors protect humans from demons and monsters who invade this world. In the interspecies stories, by contrast, humans make harmonious links to the other world through marriage to an animal, a bird, a sea creature, or even a plant (as in *The Chrysanthemum Spirit*). However, the interspecies marriage is inevitably doomed, with the spouses parting sorrowfully, a reflection of the belief that the two worlds ultimately have to exist separately.

The animals in these interspecies stories are often cute, act like human beings, and become objects of sympathy, empathy, and humor. These tales frequently function as literary parody or as satire on social conventions and the foibles of human beings. *Jūnirui kassen*, translated here as *The War of the Twelve Animals*, can be taken as a parody of a military chronicle such as *The Tale of the Heike*. The *Stingfish* (*Okoze*), which depicts the relationship between a mountain god and a remarkably unattractive fish, can be appreciated as a spoof on the conventions of the love romance. These stories could also serve a pedagogical function, as in *The Tale of the Mouse*, which provides lessons in poetry composition. The interspecies tales were the most heavily illustrated of the various subgenres of *otogizōshi*. The portrayal of animals—particularly such appealingly depicted animals as birds, turtles, and mice—was no doubt attractive to a wide range of audiences and constituted an important selling point, as do children's books and folktales today.

Warriors, Monsters, and Peripheries

The cultural topography of Japan began to widen radically in the medieval period, resulting in three concentric circles. In the middle were the so-called Western Provinces (Saikoku), centered in Kyoto. On the eastern border were the "Eastern Provinces" (Azuma, present-day Kanto region), and on the western border lay southern Kyushu. (Azuma and southern Kyushu had been under the jurisdiction of the Ritsuryō state, established in the ancient period, but they were distant from the capital.) A second periphery emerged in the medieval period: the farthermost borders of Japan, marked by Sotogahama (Outside Beach) on the northern tip of Honshū and by Kikaigashima (Island of Demons) in a nebulous zone to the south of Kyushu. Even farther out, beyond the country's borders, were Ezogashima (Island of the Ezo, present-day Hokkaido) to the north and Ryūkyū (Okinawa) to the south.

In *otogizōshi*, legendary warriors like Minamoto no Yorimitsu (Raikō; 948–1021) defended the inner circle (marked by mountains such as Ōeyama and Ibukiyama, which suggested the borders of the greater capital), while others like Minamoto no Yoshitsune (to the north) and Minamoto no Tametomo (1139–1170) (to the south) defended the second, outer circle. The third periphery appears in stories such as *Yoshitsune's Island-Hopping*, which centers on Ezo. In contrast to earlier military stories, such as *The Tale of the Heike*, which were created soon after the wars described, these demon-quelling warrior narratives take place hundreds of years earlier, often in the mid-Heian period. At least two major types appear: those that depict figures such as Yoshitsune from the Genpei (Genji–Heike) War in the late twelfth century, and those that center on warriors from the ninth and tenth centuries, such as Fujiwara no Hidesato, Minamoto no Raikō, and Fujiwara no Toshihito, who engaged in conquering barbarians or rebels to the northeast. Yoshitsune fought in the Genpei War, but he differed from his counterparts in that he led the last and most crucial stage of his life in Michinoku (present-day Tōhoku region), which had been the location of the Chinjufu, the military headquarters for subjugating the northern barbarians.

Mythic histories of different warrior lineages also emerged. *The Tale of Tawara Tōda*, for example, fuses various legends associated with Fujiwara no Hidesato (tenth century), one of the founders of the Fujiwara line. Hidesato meets a beautiful woman—a manifestation of a great snake—who asks him to kill the centipede that is terrorizing the area around Lake Biwa. Hidesato also defeats Taira no Masakado (903–940), a powerful warrior rebel whose exploits are recorded in *Shōmonki* (940s?). Here the warrior hero does more than fight rival clans; he vanquishes a monster or demon who brings chaos to the land. The same is true of the Shuten Dōji stories—*The Demon Shuten Dōji* (*Shuten Dōji*) and *The Demon of Ibuki* (*Ibuki Dōji*)—the former of which focuses on Minamoto no Raikō and his retainers and implicitly celebrates the military power of the Seiwa Genji (a branch of the Minamoto to which the Kamakura, Ashikaga, and Tokugawa shoguns traced their origins) and their ability to eradicate any threat to the state. The word *tsuchigumo* (dirt spider) appears in *The Chronicles of Japan* and one or more *fudoki* (gazetteers) as a general term for rebels against the imperial court. In *The Tale of the Dirt Spider* (*Tsuchigumo zōshi*), which is translated here, the *tsuchigumo* myth emerges in a new form: as a legend about the demon-quelling warrior Minamoto no Raikō, who conquers the *tsuchigumo* and brings peace to the land.

The demons and other monsters vanquished by these warriors represent a variety of evils:

- Rebels against the state
- Barbarians or foreigners
- Carriers of plague and pollution
- Enemies of Buddhism and the native gods

All these evils appear on one of the many borders of Japan, which were, in turn, linked topographically to "other worlds" (*ikai*), which could also be the source of treasures or power. The demon usually lives on the outskirts of the capital, deep in a mountain (as in *The Demon Shuten Dōji*), or on a distant island such as Hokkaido (as does the demon king in *Yoshitsune's Island-Hopping*). This other world is often both a dangerous place *and* a utopian space. The residence of the demon king in *Yoshitsune's Island-Hopping*, the home of the Dragon King under Lake Biwa in *The Tale of Tawara Tōda*, and the mountain hideout in *Shuten Dōji* are beautiful palatial residences, often depicted in Chinese style. As we see in a picture scroll of *Shuten Dōji* (sixteenth century [Suntory Museum of Art]) (in the Ibukiyama textual line), the monster lives in an opulent mansion with a four-seasons-in-four-directions garden. Demons were regarded as a part of the wilderness, with a stress on the baser parts of the body associated with eating and procreation. At the same time, they were only a single step away from the divine. Ritually, the triumph over the demon restores order to the state (exorcising danger) and reinvigorates the state (bringing treasures from the other world). The ferocious warrior, however, is usually able to do this only with the aid of the gods or buddhas, who are the higher protectors of the state.

These *otogizōshi* derive in part from the tradition of the Heian *monogatari* (court tales), with their focus on love rather than battle. Even when there is a fight, it tends to be a display of the martial arts (*gei*) rather than a physical conflict. Heian warrior leaders were simultaneously aristocrats, which gave them access to the "arts" (*gei*) that later warrior elites so admired and that often play a major role in these warrior stories. The narratives of the demon-quelling warrior thus combine warrior culture and court culture, as suggested by Yoshitsune's prowess with the elegant flute, which helps him overcome the demon king of Hokkaido.

Last but not least, the tales of demon-vanquishing warriors had great entertainment value, particularly in visual and dramatic media, so that in the Edo period, these superhuman figures and their dramatic encounters with the Other continued to be popular in an age of peace. In the early eighteenth century, when Shibukawa Seiemon printed *Otogi bunko* (the box set of twenty-three Muromachi tales), *The Demon Shuten Dōji* was added, with illustrations, to the other non-military tales, such as *Issun bōshi* (*The One-Inch Boy*), *Monokusa Tarō* (*Lazybones Tarō*), and *Urashima Tarō*. At this point, the tale of Shuten Dōji had become a part of urban popular culture, was enjoyed as an entertaining and felicitous story, and had spread into theater and ukiyo-e warrior prints (*musha-e*). In other words, a legend appropriated by the ruling military clan in the late medieval and early Edo period had been absorbed by the mid-Edo period into popular culture. In the Edo period, the ferocious warriors of medieval fiction became the rough equivalents of the pop icons of comic book and film culture in modern America, similar to Superman, Batman, and Spiderman.

The Translations in and Organization of This Anthology

Almost all the texts translated in *Monsters, Animals, and Other Worlds* appear in multiple variants, often differing widely in detail. The variants that appear in this book were selected not just for their content but because of the illustrations or paintings that accompanied them and that played a major role in the reception of these tales. The two editors take full responsibility for the accuracy of the translations.

For the convenience of the reader who wants to browse, the translations have been divided into three broad categories ("Monsters, Warriors, and Journeys to Other Worlds"; "Buddhist Tales"; and "Interspecies Affairs") that overlap to a great extent. The introduction to each translation provides historical context and indicates thematic interrelationships with other stories in the anthology.

HARUO SHIRANE

MONSTERS, WARRIORS, AND JOURNEYS TO OTHER WORLDS

Haseo and the Gambling Stranger

Haseo and the Gambling Stranger (*Haseo sōshi*) is not a tale for the faint of heart. The historical Ki no Haseo (845–912) was an aristocratic scholar known throughout the Heian court for his literary and artistic achievements. In 876, at the age of thirty-one, he assumed a position in the Faculty of Letters at the university. In 898, he participated in an imperial procession to Yoshino (Nara) headed by Retired Emperor Uda (867–931, r. 887–897). Haseo is believed to have forged an intimate friendship with Sugawara no Michizane (845–903), a leading scholar-poet and one of the most influential politicians of his time. The two would have traveled to China as imperial emissaries had the practice not been abolished in 894.[1]

Although previously thought to be a product of the fifteenth century, this tale is now believed to have been composed around the end of the Kamakura period (1185–1333), in the late thirteenth or early fourteenth century,[2] making it one of the earliest texts in this anthology. A slightly older version of the story is included in a treatise on court music, *Zoku kyōkunshō* (*Abridged Teachings, Continued*, 1270). That, in turn, seems to have been based on even earlier accounts in a number of twelfth- and thirteenth-century commentaries on *Wakan rōeishū* (*Chinese and Japanese Poems to Be Sung*, ca. 1012). A comparison of *Haseo and the Gambling Stranger* with these older texts suggests that it was derived from the commentaries on *Chinese and Japanese Poems to Be Sung* (or some related work) rather than from the more

---

The translation and illustrations are from the *Haseo sōshi* picture scroll (late thirteenth or early fourteenth century) in the collection of the Eisei Bunko Museum, typeset and photographically reproduced in Komatsu Shigemi, ed., *Haseo sōshi, Eshi sōshi*, Nihon emaki taisei 11 (Tokyo: Chūō Kōronsha, 1977), 2–39, 117–19. The translator also consulted the annotated version of a later manuscript of *Ki no Haseo* in the National Diet Library, in Kuwabara Hiroshi, *Otogizōshi* (Tokyo: Kōdansha, 1982), 242–56.

1. Murashige Yasushi, "*Haseo sōshi* no seiritsu to sakufū," in *Haseo sōshi, Eshi sōshi*, ed. Komatsu, 76.
2. Kuwabara, *Otogizōshi*, 243; Tokuda Kazuo, "*Haseo sōshi*," in *Otogizōshi jiten* (Tokyo: Tōkyōdō Shuppan, 2002), 391.

contemporaneous *Abridged Teachings*.[3] This is significant insofar as the story can be understood to have roots in both *setsuwa* (anecdotal literature) storytelling and traditional poetic discourse.

Considering its brevity and early origin, which comes before the rise of the *otogizōshi* in the Muromachi period (1337–1573), *Haseo and the Gambling Stranger* may be best understood as an illustrated *setsuwa* in picture scroll (*emaki*) format, in the manner of the *tengu* tale *Zegaibō emaki* (*The Tale of Zegaibō*) and some other early works, rather than a typical *otogizōshi*, which are generally longer.

Middle Councilor Haseo, prolific in learning and skilled in all manner of arts, was a man of high renown. One evening on his way to the palace, he was approached by a stranger whose crafty gaze suggested that he was no ordinary man.

"Having nothing much to do," the stranger began, "I thought it might be nice to play a little backgammon. It occurred to me that you're the only one I could play, so I came over." Haseo, finding this rather suspicious, was nevertheless intrigued.

"What an entertaining proposition!" he replied. "Where shall we play?"

"It's no good here. Come to my place."

"Fine," he said. And with neither carriage nor servant, Haseo followed the lone stranger until they came to the foot of the Suzaku Gate.[4]

"Climb up to the top of this gate," the stranger instructed. Haseo did not see how it was possible, but with the stranger's help, he went right up. Producing a backgammon board,[5] the stranger faced Haseo and said, "I wonder what I should wager? If I lose, I will give you a woman to satisfy your every desire in looks, form, and disposition. What will you give me if *you* lose?"

"I will give you every last treasure in my possession," he said.

"Splendid!" the stranger replied. As they played, Haseo won one round after another. The stranger appeared to be an ordinary man for a while, but as he continued to lose, he clutched at the dice and racked his brains, and as he did so, his true form emerged: that of a terrible demon. Haseo was terrified, but he thought to himself,

3. Tokuda, "Haseo sōshi," 391; Harada Kōzō, "Haseo-kyō no sōshi," in *Nihon koten bungaku daijiten* (Tokyo: Iwanami Shoten, 1984), 5:72.

4. The Suzaku Gate was the southern entrance to the imperial palace complex.

5. The passage reads はむてうと々り, which Kuwabara renders as *ban chōdo tori* (taking [out] a board and pieces), in *Otogizōshi*, 245. Komatsu interprets this as *hanchō to tori* (taking odds and evens), in *Haseo sōshi*, in *Haseo sōshi, Eshi sōshi*, ed. Komatsu, 117.

Haseo and the stranger play backgammon in the Suzaku Gate. (From *Haseo sōshi*, courtesy of the Eisei Bunko Museum, Tokyo)

"Still, if I can only win, he'll be no more than a mouse." With this one thought in mind, he continued to play, until he finally came out on top.

Assuming his former human guise, the demon said, "There's no point in saying it now, but still, I really thought . . . And what a wretched loss! I'll settle up on such-and-such a day." With that, he put Haseo back down on the street.

Haseo was filled with dread, but the appointed day soon arrived, and he prepared a suitable room and awaited his guest with anticipation. As the night grew deep, the stranger appeared with a woman of shimmering beauty, whom he presented to Haseo. The Middle Counselor could hardly believe his eyes. He asked, "Can I have her, just like that?"

"Naturally," replied the stranger. "Seeing as how I lost to you, you don't have to give her back. But you must wait one hundred days from tonight before indulging your desire. If you lay hands on her before a hundred days, things won't go at all as you wish."

"I shall do just as you say," Haseo replied, and seeing off his guest, he kept the woman behind. When he saw her in the light of dawn, he could not believe his eyes and wondered with utter astonishment how such a fair creature could appear in this world.

As the days passed, he grew ever fonder of the woman. He did not want to leave her side for even a moment. Eighty days came and went, whereupon he thought to

Haseo and the Gambling Stranger

Haseo's "prize" melts away. (From *Haseo sōshi*, courtesy of the Eisei Bunko Museum, Tokyo)

himself, "It's been a long time already. Surely the stranger didn't mean one hundred days exactly." Unable to restrain himself any longer, he pulled her close. The woman instantly turned into water and trickled away. Haseo lamented what he had done a thousand times over, but all in vain.

Three months later, as Haseo was leaving the palace in the dead of night, the stranger approached him on the road. Striding up from the front of Haseo's carriage, he said, "You failed to keep your word! It's despicable!" His expression souring, he continued closing in on the Middle Counselor. "Oh, god of Kitano Shrine," Haseo prayed in his heart, "save me, please!" whereupon a voice echoed in the sky, "Worthless pest! Be gone from here!" No sooner had Haseo heard this furious command than the stranger vanished into the air.

This man was the demon of Suzaku Gate. The woman had been pieced together from the finest parts of various corpses, and after one hundred days had passed, she would have become a real woman with a soul of her own. However, much to his chagrin, Haseo forgot his promise, and because he touched her, she melted away and disappeared. How he must have regretted it all!

TRANSLATION AND INTRODUCTION BY KRISTOPHER L. REEVES

The Tale of the Dirt Spider

The Tale of the Dirt Spider (*Tsuchigumo zōshi*), which exemplifies the complementary roles of text and image in medieval Japanese tales, is one of a number of fictional works that illustrate the exploits of Minamoto no Yorimitsu (948–1021), better known as Raikō, the Sinified reading of his personal name. The historical Raikō was a Kyoto bureaucrat who served as the governor of several provinces near the capital, but the legendary Raikō, aided by his four samurai retainers, the so-called Four Heavenly Kings, was a fearless warrior best known in the medieval (1185–1600) and Edo (1600–1867) periods for slaying the demon Shuten Dōji (as depicted in *The Demon Shuten Dōji*). In *The Tale of the Dirt Spider*, Raikō destroys a giant man-eating arachnid, or *tsuchigumo*, endowed with shape-shifting powers. The word *tsuchigumo* (earth, or dirt, spider) appears in ancient texts like *Kojiki* (*Record of Ancient Matters*, 712), where it refers to rebels against the throne, and it probably derives from *tsuchigomori* (dirt dweller), in reference to the pit housing in which those rebels may have lived.[1] By the early medieval period, the term had reverted to its literal meaning of "earth spider." Versions of the story appear in the "Book of Swords" chapter of *The Tale of the Heike* (thirteenth century), in the prints of Utagawa Kuniyoshi (1797–1861) and Tsukioka Yoshitoshi (1839–1892), and, in the modern period, in the collection of Japanese fairy tales published by Lafcadio Hearn (1850–1904).

This translation is based on the exquisite *Tsuchigumo zōshi* picture scroll (designated as an Important Cultural Property) in the Tokyo National Museum. An eighteenth-century certificate attributes the artwork to Tosa Nagataka (late Kamakura period)

The translation and illustrations are from the *Tsuchigumo zōshi* picture scroll (early fourteenth century) in the collection of the Tokyo National Museum, typeset in Komatsu Shigemi, ed., *Tsuchigumo zōshi, Tengu zōshi, Ōeyama ekotoba*, Zoku Nihon no emaki 26 (Tokyo: Chūō Kōronsha, 1993), 129–30.

1. Basil Hall Chamberlain, trans., *The Kojiki: Records of Ancient Matters*, 2nd ed. (North Clarendon, Vt.: Tuttle, 1981), 107n.2.

and the calligraphy to Priest Kaneyoshi (Yoshida Kenkō; 1283–1352), the latter of whom was well known in the Edo period for *Tsurezuregusa* (*Essays in Idleness*, ca. 1332). However, there is no proof for either claim. The work probably dates from the early fourteenth century,[2] which makes it very early for an *otogizōshi*. At some point, the pictures and text were cut apart and reassembled out of order, and some pieces are missing. The translation puts the events in their most plausible order. The text is also damaged and illegible in some places; words in brackets reflect a best guess at reconstruction. The superb detail and high quality of the scroll's illustrations set this work apart from other pieces that tended toward simpler expression, and it is an outstanding example of Kamakura-period *yamato-e* (native style) Japanese painting. Considering its early-fourteenth-century provenance, *The Tale of the Dirt Spider* was a pioneer in the *otogizōshi* picture-scroll genre, which was to reach full maturity only several centuries later.

Minamoto no Raikō [was] a descendant of the [Seiwa] emperor and a warrior of great courage. Shortly after the twentieth day of the tenth month, he traveled to the Kitayama area and came to the Rendaino Cemetery.[3] He had one retainer, Tsuna,[4] who was an exceptional man in his own right, and because this Tsuna was a clever warrior, Raikō took him along. Raikō carried a three-foot sword, and Tsuna, [wearing] an armored corselet, followed with a bow and quiver in his right and left hands.

As they were biding their time in the cemetery, a skull [appeared] in the sky. They watched it move along with the wind until it disappeared behind a cloud. Raikō discussed it with Tsuna, and when they went to see where the skull had gone, they came to a place called Kagura Hill. But the skull was nowhere to be seen.

However, there was an old house. They pushed their way through the front of a wide garden that was so overgrown they had to wring the dew from their sleeves. They saw that the gate was blocked and partially hidden under creeping vines. The house seemed to have been the residence of an old aristocrat. The mountains to the west [were covered] in a crimson brocade, and to the south there was a pond of

---

2. Komatsu, introduction to *Tsuchigumo zōshi*, in *Tsuchigumo zōshi, Tengu zōshi, Ōeyama ekotoba*, ed. Komatsu, unnumbered page.

3. Kitayama is in northern Kyoto, and the old Rendaino charnel grounds are in the present-day Kita district of Kyoto.

4. Tsuna is Watanabe no Tsuna (953–1025).

purest blue. The garden had become a field of blue spirea, and the gate a dwelling place for birds and beasts.

The two men passed through the middle gate. Raikō posted Tsuna outside the house as he looked back to his left and right.

[*There is a missing passage here. The accompanying image shows Raikō entering a building. A skeleton with the long black hair of a woman sleeps under a robe in a back room, and a pair of severed human heads litters the foreground. There is a sunken fireplace in the middle of the room, and to the side is a kitchen knife resting on a cutting board. Raikō, sword drawn, enters the room from the garden.*]

From behind the paper doors of the kitchen, Raikō heard the loud labored breathing of an old woman. When he rapped on the sliding partition, it opened. "Who are you?" Raikō asked. "I can't make any sense of things."

The woman replied, "I am an old person of this place. I am 290 years old, and I have served nine generations of lords." Raikō watched as she spoke. Her hair was white and bound together. Using a *kujiri*,[5] she peeled open her left and right eyes and then pulled the upper eyelids over her head like a hat. Then, with something that looked like a hairpin, she pried open her mouth and tied her lips to the nape of her neck. She stretched out her breasts, left and right, as if to rest them on her knees.

"Although spring goes and autumn comes," she said, "my heart is not [renewed]. Years come and years go, and the only thing I really feel is bitterness. This place [conceals] an evil lair, and all human traces have disappeared. Youth may leave us, but our aged selves remain, which is truly awful! The bush warblers of the palace are gone, and I lament the absence of the swallows in our rafters.[6] Seeing you, my lord, makes me feel like a singing girl from Chang'an meeting Bai Letian of the Yuanhe era.[7] People and places may change, but they share an origin, and whenever I see the moon floating atop the waters, tears of grief soak my pillow. But now I've met you, the dharma companion I was meant to know![8] I ask that you kill me, please. After completing ten recitations of the *nenbutsu*, I'll be received by Amida and his two attendants.[9] Could I ask any greater favor of you than this?"

Raikō thought that it would be useless to continue questioning someone like this, and he left. Tsuna came into the kitchen and surveyed the scene.

25

5. A *kujiri* is a pointy tool for untying knots.
6. Bush warblers and swallows are traditionally associated with spring.
7. Bai Letian is another name for the Tang poet Bai Juyi (772–846). The singing girls from Chang'an appear in the poem "Chang'an" by Lu Zhaolin (636–689).
8. A dharma companion (*zenchishiki* [abbreviated here to *chishiki*]) is a being who leads one along the path of the Buddha.
9. The *nenbutsu* is the ritual invocation of the name of Amida (Skt. Amitābha) Buddha. Amida is frequently depicted with the bodhisattvas Kannon (Skt. Avalokiteśvara) and Seishi (Skt. Mahāsthāmaprāpta).

As night fell, the sky took on an unnatural air. The wind howled, and the tree leaves, which were nearly invisible in the darkness, blew about in a fury. The heavens were thick with thunder and lightning, and the men doubted if they could survive. "If a bunch of monsters should appear," Tsuna thought, soaked by the rain and wilting in the wind, "then by staying here, we could catch them between us and cut them down from the ten directions. But if we were to be surrounded, that would be the end, which is why we should keep apart. We shouldn't run away, either. People say that the loyal retainer serves no two masters, and that the filial daughter attends without being seen. So how could I turn my back on my charge and forsake my duty?"

Inside, Raikō stilled his heart and listened. He heard footsteps like the beating of drums, whereupon an uncountable mass of indescribably strange creatures came walking toward him. Keeping a pillar between himself and them, Raikō watched as they all sat down. They had multifarious forms. Looking in the direction of the lamp, Raikō saw that their eyes shone like the stone between the eyebrows of a Buddhist statue. All the creatures roared with laughter, after which they opened the sliding paper door and departed.

Then a nun came in. She looked like a commoner from Daozhou.[10] She was three feet tall; her face was two feet long, and below that, only a foot. It was strange to think how short her lower body was! When she approached the base of the lamp and reached to put it out, Raikō glared at her, and she flashed him a smile. Her eyebrows were painted thick, her lipstick was red, and her two front teeth were blackened. She wore a purple hat and long crimson trousers, but she wore nothing else at all. Her arms were thin, like strands of string, and as white as snow. She faded away, disappearing like clouds or mist.

At the hour when the *keijin* announces the dawn,[11] when loyal retainers await the morning, Raikō was wondering what would happen next. Just then, he heard suspicious footsteps. The sliding screen in front of him [opened] about six inches, revealing occasional, partial glimpses of [a woman's face]. Her appearance was more elegant than a spring willow tussled by the wind. Raikō watched intently as she stood up, opened the screen, and walked in. She sat down on a mat, appearing unapproachable, her robes alluringly spilling out around her. Her beauty rivaled that of Yang Guifei and Li Furen,[12] leading Raikō to suppose that she was the mistress of the

---

10. Daozhou is in present-day Hunan Province, China.
11. The *keijin* (literally, "chicken person") was the person who announced the hours.
12. Yang Guifei (719–756) was a consort of Emperor Xuanzong of Tang (685–762, r. 712–756). Li Furen was a consort of Emperor Wu of Han (156–87 B.C.E., r. 141–87 B.C.E.). Both are immortalized in Chinese poetry and recognized as supreme beauties.

Raikō encounters a huge-headed nun. (From *Tsuchigumo zōshi*, courtesy of the Tokyo National Museum. Image: TNM Image Archives)

house who had happily come out to greet him. A cold wind began to blow, and as the space between them lightened, the woman suddenly stood up as if to go. She combed her hair toward the front, and her eyes, staring at the lamp, shone like polished lacquer glinting in the light of a fire.

As Raikō watched, unnerved by the woman's appearance, she kicked up the hem of her trousers and [shot] ten white clouds like *kemari* balls at him.[13] Although Raikō was blinded, he managed to pull her four or six yards toward him, but, unable to seize her, he drew his sword and slashed out ferociously. When he did, she vanished without a trace. His blade had cut through the wooden floor and nearly split one of the foundation stones in half.

The monster retreated, whereupon Tsuna came in, saying, "Well struck! But could it be that the tip of your sword is broken?" They pulled the sword from the floorboards and checked, and it was indeed chipped. Looking around, they found a huge pool of white blood, none of it draining. The same white blood was also on Raikō's sword.

13. *Kemari* is a traditional Japanese ball sport originally played by courtiers, wearing sophisticated attire, in the Heian and medieval periods.

The Tale of the Dirt Spider

Raikō slashes a mysterious woman with his sword. (From *Tsuchigumo zōshi*, courtesy of the Tokyo National Museum. Image: TNM Image Archives)

The two went looking for the creature and came to the room where Raikō had met the old woman the day before. There was white blood there as well, and the woman was nowhere to be seen. Thinking that she had already been eaten in a single bite, they continued tracking the monster, pushing their way to a cave in the far-off mountains to the west. When they looked inside, they saw white blood flowing out like a thin river coursing through a valley.

"When I saw the broken tip of your sword," Tsuna said, "I was reminded of the supreme filial piety of Mei Jian Chi of Chu, and this is no different from when he broke off the tip of his sword.[14] I suggest we cut some wisteria and creeping vines and make a dummy. I'll take off my hat and robe and clothe it in them. Then we can hold it in front of us as we proceed." The two of them completed these preparations together.

After going only a quarter of a mile or so, they reached the end of the cave, where there was an old building that seemed to be some kind of storehouse. Pine trees [sprouted] from the roof tiles, moss covered the hedge, and there was no sign of human habitation. When they looked inside, they saw a two-hundred-foot-long creature, the head of which appeared to be swathed in brocade. As they approached

14. Tsuna refers to the legend of the swordsmiths Gan Jiang and Mo Ye, which appears in various Chinese and Japanese sources. In the version of the story in *Taiheiki* (*Record of Great Peace*, late fourteenth century), Mei Jian Chi (J. Bikanshaku, also Mikenjaku), the son of the swordsmiths, breaks off the tip of his sword and uses it as a projectile to avenge his father's death.

Raikō and Tsuna drag the dirt spider from its cave. (From *Tsuchigumo zōshi*, courtesy of the Tokyo National Museum. Image: TNM Image Archives)

it from the front, they saw a mass of legs beyond counting. Its eyes shone like the light from the sun and moon. It let out a great scream: "Oh, how helpless we are! How is it that our injured body suffers so!"

Before the creature had finished speaking, a single strangely glowing object shot out of a white cloud, just as Raikō and Tsuna had expected. It hit the dummy, whereupon the doll collapsed. When he took out the projectile, Raikō saw that it was his broken sword tip. "It happened just like Tsuna said," Raikō thought. "He's no ordinary fellow." The creature was not making any sound, so they immediately went up to it and, with their strength combined, dragged it out.

It was strong—strong enough to move boulders—and it tried to wound them. Raikō prayed to Amaterasu and Shō Hachiman,[15] "Our country is a divine land protected by the gods, and the emperor rules through his ministers. I am his vassal and descended from kings, born into a house blessed with the imperial lineage. Looking at this creature, I can see that it's a beast. Animals are unrelentingly evil, and it's because they shamelessly broke the Buddhist precepts in their former lives that they have been born into that realm.[16] What's more, they harm the people and inflict calamity on the state. I am a warrior who protects the emperor, and a shield for those who rule. Won't you accede to my request?"

15. Amaterasu is the goddess of the sun in Japanese mythology. Shō Hachiman is a god of warriors and the patron deity of the Minamoto.
16. Along with the realms of hell and hungry ghosts, the animal realm is traditionally counted as one of the Three Evil Realms (*san akudō*) of existence.

The Tale of the Dirt Spider

Raikō and Tsuna slaughter the dirt spider. (From *Tsuchigumo zōshi*, courtesy of the Tokyo National Museum. Image: TNM Image Archives)

The two men pulled with all their might, and though the creature was of a mind to fight back at first, it soon submitted and fell over, face up. Raikō drew his sword and severed its head. When Tsuna went to cut open its belly, he found a deep slash in its midsection, from when Raikō had cut through the floorboards. When they looked to see what kind of creature it was, they realized that it was a mountain spider. Nineteen hundred and ninety severed human heads tumbled out from Raikō's laceration. They quickly cut apart the monster's side, whereupon innumerable small spiders the size of seven- or eight-year-old children began running about in a frenzy. Then, when they cut open its belly, they found a mere twenty more heads. They dug a hole and buried them, after which they set fire to the house and burned it down.

When the emperor heard of their deed, he was impressed. He appointed Raikō governor of Settsu Province and promoted him to Senior Fourth Rank, Lower Grade. As for Tsuna, he gave him the province of Tanba and promoted him to Senior Fifth Rank, Lower Grade.[17]

TRANSLATION AND INTRODUCTION BY MATTHIEU FELT

17. Settsu Province corresponds to eastern Hyōgo and northern Osaka prefectures. Tanba Province overlaps with central Kyoto and northern Hyōgo prefectures.

The Demon Shuten Dōji

As one of the most famous, influential, and widely reproduced works of medieval Japanese fiction, *The Demon Shuten Dōji* (*Shuten Dōji*) tells how the great Heian-period warrior Minamoto no Yorimitsu (948–1021), better known as Raikō, and his small band of samurai took on the rapacious demon Shuten Dōji in his remote mountain fortress. Like Minamoto no Yoshitsune (1159–1189), a hero of the Genpei War (1180–1185), both Raikō and Shuten Dōji are staple characters in medieval and early modern Japanese fiction and drama; for example, Raikō and his retainer Watanabe no Tsuna figure in *The Tale of the Dirt Spider*, and Shuten Dōji's human youth and demonic transformation are the subject of *The Demon of Ibuki*.

Although the earliest recorded version of *The Demon Shuten Dōji* is preserved in *Ōeyama ekotoba* (*Mount Ōe in Pictures and Words*, late fourteenth century), the early-Edo-period base text of this translation closely follows the medieval painter Kanō Motonobu's *Shuten Dōji* hand scrolls (ca. 1522), which, unlike the earlier *Mount Ōe in Pictures and Words* and other manuscripts in the Mount Ōe textual line, locates Shuten Dōji's cavern-palace on Mount Ibuki rather than Mount Ōe. Shuten Dōji's mountain home is a magical, otherworldly domain that stands in direct contraposition to the human emperor's palace in the city; and like Raikō, who commands a small cohort of principal retainers known as the Four Heavenly Kings, Shuten Dōji oversees his own Four Heavenly Kings: a handful of devoted demon lieutenants whom he dispatches to the human capital to kidnap beautiful young noblewomen for his sensual and gustatory delight.

Like Tawara Tōda Hidesato in the final part of *The Tale of Tawara Tōda*, Raikō and his men employ strategy and deception, rather than relying on their own brute

The translation and illustrations are from the five-scroll *Shuten Dōji e* picture scrolls (ca. Kan'ei period [1624–1644]) in the Mount Ibuki textual line, in the collection of the Tōyō University Library, typeset and annotated in Ōshima Tatehiko and Watari Kōichi, eds., *Muromachi monogatari sōshi shū*, Shinpen Nihon koten bungaku zenshū 63 (Tokyo: Shōgakukan, 2002), 268–325.

force of arms. They disguise themselves as mountain ascetics in the Shugendō Buddhist cult, whose legendary founder is reported in early Japanese sources to have subjugated demons, and they show that, ultimately, religious devotion may be the greatest weapon of all. Raikō and his retainers are the putative heroes, but they behave in some seemingly less-than-heroic ways, complicating readers' sympathies for Shuten Dōji and the men who defeat him. They may win in the end, but as characters they lack Shuten Dōji's power and charisma—his ability to capture the medieval imagination—and it is surely no accident that their story, like the older *Tale of the Dirt Spider*, came to be named after the monster they slay rather than themselves.

Japan, the Islands of Autumn Harbors, is a divine land. In the age of human sovereigns following seven and five generations of heavenly and earthly deities, Prince Shōtoku bestowed his mercy by becoming a mother of the country, nurturing the people so that he might introduce Buddhism to our land.[1] From that time until the age of Emperor Shōmu and the Engi lord,[2] Japan thrived with the Buddhist and Kingly Law. The righteous rule of the emperors as they conferred their merciful compassion excelled even the ancient reigns of Tang Yao and Yu Shun.[3] Thus the winds blew gently without making the branches creak, and the rains fell softly, leaving the clodded earth unbroken. The land was at peace, and pleasant prosperity extended to the population at large.

In particular, despite their being in this latter age, the years leading up to the era of Emperor Ichijō were ones in which the Kingly Law was all the more distinguished and the Buddhist Law flourished again, as it had before.[4] Since the realm was spared the ravages of wind and rain, the five grains ripened in abundance, and the entire country knew well-being. And since the realm was spared the calamity of fires, the capital filled with houses with little space between them. It was thus that some remarkable people, including the loyal retainers of warrior houses, nobles, and even

1. Prince Shōtoku (Shōtoku Taishi; 574–622) was the founder of Hōryūji Temple in Nara and an early champion of Buddhism in Japan.
2. Emperor Shōmu (701–756) reigned from 724 to 749. The emperor of the Engi era (901–923) was Daigo (885–930, r. 897–930).
3. Yao (traditionally ca. 2356–2255 B.C.E., r. 2333–2234 B.C.E.) and Shun (traditionally ca. 2294–2184 B.C.E., r. 2233–2184 B.C.E.) are two fabled emperors of ancient China renowned for their benevolent rule.
4. Emperor Ichijō (980–1011, r. 986–1011) is best known today for presiding over the court in which the authors and poets Murasaki Shikibu, Sei Shōnagon, Izumi Shikibu, and Akazome Emon served.

physiognomists gifted in the arts of divination, came to be assembled in this world. No one had ever imagined the likes of them, not in ancient or recent times. With all under heaven enjoying wealth and success, the people would say of the days in which they lived, "Never would I have thought that I'd see an age like this!"

Yet strange things were happening in the capital. Beautiful women were disappearing at random, and in large numbers. At first, when only five or ten of them had vanished, people thought that the women themselves must have been at fault, or that perhaps they had run away to take Buddhist vows. Families grieved among themselves, but it was not enough to raise a general alarm. Still, the cases continued, and as more and more women disappeared, the realm became ridden with anxiety and the people lamented in a way that was beyond expression. Whoever was abducting them, even if it was some demonic being—if they could only find that out, then they might make sense of it as a kind of Buddhist lesson! But without that knowledge, the people could only grieve and wonder what to do. Thus, as the situation surpassed the powers of the ruling authority and the strength of the warrior houses, there was nothing to be done.

Now there was a man known as the Ikeda Middle Counselor Kunikata.[5] He was beloved by the emperor, and being fabulously wealthy, everything went as he wished. He had a single daughter who was beautiful of face and form, and since she had such a marvelously excellent disposition, he doted on her with the utmost care, as if there were no one like her in all the world. However, one night she disappeared in the midnight hour. Her parents and nursemaid were extraordinarily grieved. They turned their faces to the heavens and lay on the ground, writhing and pining, but it was all for naught. Due to the intensity of their anguish, perhaps, they visited celebrated temples and shrines, made a variety of vows, and demonstrated their devotion in disparate ways as they supplicated in sorrow. It is the nature of people high and low to fret for a child, and even for those with five or ten children, the heartache can be severe. So how much worse it must have been for Kunikata and his wife to have lost their one and only daughter! Their distress was beyond reason.

At that time, there was a master diviner by the name of Seimei.[6] He could show auspicious signs as if he were pointing at his own palms, and when he divined with

5. The woodblock-printed *Shuten Dōji* (ca. 1716–1729) published by Shibukawa Seiemon identifies him as Kunitaka, rather than Kunikata. See Ōshima Tatehiko, ed., *Otogizōshi shū*, Nihon koten bungaku zenshū 36 (Tokyo: Shōgakukan, 1974), 444; and, for a translation of Shibukawa's edition, R. Keller Kimbrough, trans., *The Demon Shuten Dōji*, in *Traditional Japanese Literature: An Anthology, Beginnings to 1600*, ed. Haruo Shirane (New York: Columbia University Press, 2007), 1123–38.

6. Abe no Seimei (921–1005) was a yin-yang master who became legendary for his feats of wizardry. He appears as a character in numerous tales and is cited, in this volume, in *The Tale of the Mouse* and *Lady Tamamo*.

The Demon Shuten Dōji

divination cards, he was never mistaken. Regarding evil spirits and malevolent beings, he was not even slightly wrong.

Lord Kunikata summoned him and said, "I was born into affluence, I have known a surfeit of glory, and I have attained rank and position as I saw fit. I have never lacked for anything I desired. But even so, I have an only child who means more to me than myself and all my precious treasure, and though I wanted to shield her from every hardship—even the gusting wind—she has been missing like this, vanished into darkness, since the night of the first of this month. It's terribly mysterious. Recently many women have been disappearing from the capital, and when I think that the same thing may have happened to my own daughter, it leaves me sad beyond words. If you can, please divine for us, summon her with your cards, and let us see her one more time! If you do, I'll be happy to give you endless treasure in reward. First, let me give you something to use for the ritual." With that, Lord Kunikata presented Seimei with an assortment of precious gifts.

Seimei divined for seven days and seven nights, whereupon he presented his findings to Lord Kunikata. Seimei's letter read: "There is a rocky cavern at a place called Hundred Mile Peak at Ibuki to the north of the capital.[7] It is a demon's lair. That demon is the one who took your daughter. She is still alive. I inscribed the monster with my divination cards, so she has escaped being killed in his evil cavern. She will have the joy of seeing her parents again."

Being a great favorite of the emperor, Lord Kunikata would bring all manner of things to his attention. He therefore took Seimei's divination letter and presented it to His Majesty. The nobles held a meeting, and they received reports from various houses. One minister spoke, saying, "I have heard that this kind of thing happened in the past. Many people were abducted in the age of Emperor Saga,[8] causing unspeakable lamentation in the land. At that time, the emperor commanded Kūkai to enact a curse,[9] and it was thanks to that, perhaps, that people stopped disappearing. There is no monk in the land today who is capable of invoking such a spell. Upon careful consideration, it seems to me that we might start by having Raikō launch an attack.[10] Why? Because Raikō is a descendant of Emperor Seiwa and the chief of the warrior clans. He's stronger than everyone, and no one is as brave. Not even Fan Kuai could have compared.[11] Raikō's eyes flash with a fearsome light, he commands

7. Mount Ibuki, the central peak of the Ibuki Mountains, stands at the border of present-day Shiga and Gifu prefectures. According to Shibukawa's *Shuten Dōji* and other sources, Shuten Dōji's palace was on Mount Ōe in Tanba Province rather than on Mount Ibuki in Ōmi.

8. Emperor Saga (786–842) reigned from 809 to 823.

9. Kūkai (Kōbō Daishi; 774–835) was the founder of the Shingon school of Japanese esoteric Buddhism.

10. Raikō is the sinified reading of the personal name of Minamoto no Yorimitsu (948–1021).

11. Fan Kuai (J. Hankai) was a celebrated Chinese warrior of the third and second centuries B.C.E.

miraculous powers, and he can see the good and bad in himself and others as clearly as his own hands. That's why even the gods protect him. Evil beings probably fear him, too. If he is awarded an imperial edict, he's sure to destroy any enemy he faces. He's a warrior for the ages." All the other nobles agreed, and they summoned Raikō to the palace.

Wearing only light armor over a *hitatare* of red-backed brocade and attended by his Four Heavenly Kings—Tsuna, Kintoki, Sadamitsu, and Suetake—Raikō made his way to the Southern Hall.[12] Lord Kunikata bore the emperor's instructions, and descending the stairs to the courtyard, he announced: "It is a certain fact that countless times in this present reign, Our subjects have been called upon by their Sovereign to subdue the enemies of the court, enact Our glory throughout the realm, and extend Our authority to all places near and far. This time, We call upon you for the sake of the warrior houses, the state, and the people. As the Master of all the land and the four seas, We are the mother and father of the masses. We therefore feel compassion for the realm and bestow Our mercy on it. As We were wondering what to do, these things occurred in this present age, and We have become concerned for the lamentations of the people. There is a demon at a place called Hundred Mile Peak at Ibuki, and he is Our bitter enemy. He has abducted any number of Our citizens! Therefore, being a matter of critical importance to the realm, and that demon being an unparalleled enemy of the people, you shall make haste to that place, destroy the evil fiend, quell the outrage in Our state, and safeguard the people in their grief. For Us, your deed shall be an act of unrivalled loyalty, and for you, it shall be a credit to your name. Now go, without delay, and slay the demon!"

Without probing into the particulars of the matter, Raikō gave his humble assent and withdrew. He immediately returned to his lodgings, where he discussed the situation with his Four Heavenly Kings. "Giving it some thought," Raikō said, "it seems to me that we can't succeed by ordinary human power. We should entreat the buddhas and deities for their aid. Since it will be for the state and ourselves, why wouldn't they deign to help?"

The men agreed to offer prayers to their individual clan deities. Raikō made a pilgrimage to Yawata Shrine,[13] where he ensconced himself for three days and three nights. He received a miraculous dream, and he sponsored services in thanks. Then he went back home. Tsuna and Kintoki visited Sumiyoshi Shrine, and Sadamitsu

35

---

12. The Southern Hall is another name for the Shishinden Ceremonial Hall in the Imperial Palace in Kyoto. The Four Heavenly Kings were Raikō's four most trusted retainers: Watanabe no Tsuna, Sakata Kintoki, Usui Sadamitsu, and Urabe Suetake.

13. Yawata Shrine is another name for Iwashimizu Hachiman Shrine on Mount Otoko near Kyoto.

The Demon Shuten Dōji

and Suetake traveled to the mountains of Kumano,[14] where they pressed their heads to the ground in reverent supplication and sponsored prayer rites.

Later, Raikō addressed his men, saying, "I have an idea. It won't do for us to enter in large numbers, so I should take you four alone. We ought to have Hōshō join us, too."[15] Each of the six warriors prepared for the journey and donned a wooden pack. In his own pannier, Raikō had placed a scarlet-laced corselet along with a helmet known as the Lion Lord. He also carried a pair of swords called the Cloud Cutters, as well as a two-foot, one-inch sword named Blood Sucker. Hōshō had packed a purple-laced corselet and a short halberd called Stone Cutter. The halberd was a little more than two feet long, with a shaft finely wrapped in horsetail hair and cut off at a length of three fists. Tsuna had packed a corselet with yellow-green lacings, and a two-foot-plus striking sword named Demon Slasher. Each of the others packed their own accoutrements as they saw fit. In addition, the men cut lengths of bamboo into

14. Sumiyoshi Shrine is in present-day Osaka. The Kumano mountains are the site of the Kumano triple shrine complex on the Kii Peninsula.

15. Hōshō is the sinified reading of the personal name of Fujiwara no Yasumasa (958–1036).

Raikō receives an imperial command to slay the demon Shuten Dōji. (From *Shuten Dōji e*, courtesy of the Tōyō University Library)

what are known as "decanter tubes," filled them with saké, and strapped them to their packs.

Setting out from the capital, Raikō and his companions traveled through Ōmi Province. When they came to Ibuki, they sought out the great mountain, asking everyone they met how to get to Hundred Mile Peak. However, the people only answered that they did not know. Crossing an endless succession of ridges and plains, the men fell into a daze, unsure of what to do. With their eyes and hearts wavering, suffering in body and mind and broken to the marrow, and with vast distances spreading out before and behind them, they greeted the night in mountains and fields as they made their way forward. They came to a broad moat, and when they approached it for a look, they saw a country dwelling. There were three men standing there, two of whom were over the age of fifty and one of whom was a *yamabushi* mountain ascetic.

"Those fellows look like the demon's retainers," Tsuna said. "Let's grab them and make them talk."

"No, we mustn't do that," Raikō replied. "It won't help us if we set them on their guard. First, we should draw them to us, make their acquaintance, put them

The Demon Shuten Dōji

in a good mood, and then ask them about the fortress and what to expect as we go."

Raikō and his companions approached the three men and spoke: "We are ascetics on a journey through the provinces, but we have lost our way and come here. What is this place called? And can you please tell us how to get to a major road?"

"Oh, how dreadful!" the three men exclaimed. "What kind of people are you to visit such a remote place? This is the famous Hundred Mile Peak, the site of the demon's stony cavern. Ordinary people never come this way. Look over there—that mountain across the moat is the peak. It's a hard place even for birds to fly. The demon's den is on the other side. Since it's so near, the monster's retainers are always coming out to cavort. You should go back! And don't be thinking that we're that demon's attendants—someone dear to us, too, was abducted, and we're here to seek revenge. But we can't do it by our powers alone, so we've spent months and years by the mountain. Don't be reserved with us! Looking at you all, we can see that you're not average men. Come in here! We'd like to have a word." With that, they invited Raikō and his companions inside.

As the three men drew their guests closer, they all relaxed and began to converse. "We would like to offer each of you a drink," Raikō said, taking out a decanter tube of saké. Seeking to ingratiate himself with his hosts, he offered one to the apparent leader of the group, an old man sitting in the seat of honor.

The old man set down the cup and spoke: "Now that I've had a better look at you all, I can see that you've invoked great long-standing vows. Don't hold back—tell us everything! We'll do our best to help. What's more, we know all about the demon's lair, and we'll give you the details. Even if you were to attack him with a thousand or ten thousand riders, it wouldn't be enough. But with the aid of the gods and a clever plan, you'll see him destroyed."

Because the old man spoke with such obvious sympathy, Raikō and his men took his penetrating perception and candid compassion to be nothing short of miraculous. Suspecting that their hosts were mountain gods or their own clan deities come to lend them their strength, they placed their trust in them and spoke freely of what they intended. The three men likewise showed extraordinary consideration. Raikō was deeply moved, and he said, "Well, then, I shall be pleased to join you, too."

The old man sitting in the seat of honor spoke: "Those monsters love saké, and they don't realize that drinking it ruins them. It loosens them up and makes them talk." He brought out some wine and poured it into the men's empty decanter tube. "You should make them drink as much of this as you can. But you must be extremely careful not to take the slightest sip yourselves. It's poison." Next, the old man took out a cap-helmet and offered it to Raikō.[16] "You should wear this under your cloth cap. The demon has supernatural sight, and when he stares at people, he can see what's in their minds. But if you wear this helmet—even just this—he shouldn't be able to see your thoughts. He makes various vows, uses different tricks, and puts people to the test, so if you are going to beat him, you can't be afraid." The old man told them all about these and other things that were likely to happen.

"Well, then, let's be off!" the three men exclaimed. Raikō and his companions stood up and set out with their hosts leading the way. They were nine in all. They approached the moat and saw that it was big, broad, and too deep to see the bottom. "This will be difficult for you to cross," the three hosts said, whereupon they leaped over the chasm, picked up an enormous fallen log, and placed it over the moat as a bridge. "Quickly, cross this," they said, and the six men did.

Looking up at Hundred Mile Peak, they saw huge rugged rocks trailing clouds in the sky. There were chilly crags blue with lichen, and there was no path. As the men were wondering what to do, their three hosts stepped onto the sheer stone slope, leading the way. They put handholds and footholds into the rock, and when the way became too steep, they pulled the men up by hand. Thus by various and sundry means, the men scrambled up cliffy formations that even birds were hard put to ascend.

The group came to the mouth of a rocky cave. The three guides acted unlike any mortal men, and since they behaved in the manner of demons or gods, Raikō and his companions felt all the more encouraged. When they stepped inside the cavern, they could not see a path anywhere. The place was frightening beyond expression. As the men were wondering what would become of them now, their three hosts stepped forward to lead the way. They continued on, but there was still no trail. It dawned on the men that things could hardly have been worse for even Holy Teacher Yixing when he bore the punishment of exile and headed down the Dark Tunnel Road.[17]

After they had walked for what seemed like about a mile, they came upon a path in the cave. A single valley stream was flowing there. The three guides spoke: "You should follow this creek upstream. We will join you again inside the fortress, where we will be pleased to lend you our strength. We are true manifestations of the Hachiman, Sumiyoshi, and Kumano deities." And with that, they vanished without a trace.

---

16. A cap-helmet (*bōshi kabuto*) is a simple round helmet without a visor or a decorative crest.
17. According to *The Tale of the Heike* (thirteenth century), Yixing was an eighth-century Chinese monk who was made to walk to the land of Kara on the Anketsu (Dark Tunnel) Road. See Helen Craig McCullough, trans., *The Tale of the Heike* (Stanford, Calif.: Stanford University Press, 1988), 61–62.

The Demon Shuten Dōji

Raikō and his men encounter a young woman washing a blood-stained robe. (From *Shuten Dōji e*, courtesy of the Tōyō University Library)

Raikō and his men took heart, and with their newfound strength, their fighting spirits soared. They proceeded upstream until they found an eighteen- or nineteen-year-old girl. She was exceptionally beautiful, and she was washing something at the side of the creek. "Who are you?" the men asked as they approached. The young lady did not say a word; she only cried. After a while, she stifled her tears and said, "Oh, how dreadful! What kind of people are you to visit this place? No one normal ever comes here."

The young lady seemed to be so frightened that the men imagined her to be one of the demon's retainers, changed into human form in order to deceive them. All of them were agitated at the thought. Tsuna stepped forward and spoke: "Who are you? And what is this place called? Tell us the truth. If you don't, we'll kill you on the spot."

"I am from the capital," the young lady explained through her tears. "I was taken in the spring of last year. The demon should have devoured me already, but for some strange reason my life lingers on. There have been more than thirty other women kidnapped from the capital. My dear friend, the daughter of Lord Kunikata, has been here, too, since the first of this month. The demon keeps us captive like this; loves us as he will; and then, when he grows tired of us, puts us in a place called the 'people pen,' where he squeezes us for our blood. He calls it saké and drinks it. When he has killed us, he cuts away our flesh for food. Two or three years ago, he abducted the daughter of a certain Minister of Central Affairs from around Eighth Avenue, and he just squeezed her for her blood today. When she stopped breathing, he used some medicine to keep her alive. Since it was my turn to be on duty today, he sent me here to wash her robes. When I think that the same thing is probably going to happen to me sometime, I don't feel like I can take it anymore!" The young lady writhed on the ground in tears, and the men felt very sorry for her.

"You say you're from the capital," Raikō inquired, "so who exactly are you?"

"I am the daughter of Hanazono from near the Great Middle Gate.[18] There are other ladies here like me with whom I am close. We catch one another's eyes, but everything's so frightening that we don't put it into words or show it on our faces. Nobody speaks. If we're ever overcome with sorrow and weep, the demon glowers at us with his huge eyes. It's a shock, and it puts a chill in our bones. If we could just die, then we wouldn't have to suffer those awful stares! But our fleeting lives go on, and they're indescribably horrid and sad. If it's possible for you men to return to the capital, then please take a message for me. Tell my mother and father that I miss them so much, I don't know what to do!" And again, she was convulsed with grief.

"Oh, you poor girl!" Raikō exclaimed. "Who do you think we are? We've come here under imperial command. Tell us everything you know about the demon's dwelling and the inside of his fortress. If you do, we'll destroy him, wreck his stronghold, and escort you and the other ladies back to the capital."

Raikō spoke with such confidence that the woman was overjoyed. Letting down her guard, she said, "At the head of this stream, there is a stone wall with a large gate defended on the inside and out by twenty or thirty terrible guards. Behind that is an elevated foundation of layered rocks on which there is an encircling stone wall with an iron gate. Inside, the four sides and four corners are planted to show each of the four seasons. The spring is set with willows. If you open the east–west doors, you can hear birds chirping freely in their branches. The willow fronds appear to flutter and pull in subtle ways while a gentle breeze wafts among the flowers, spreading what seems to be the scent of plum blossoms planted near the eaves. On the summer side, a pond has been dug and filled with water. It is stocked with fish, and birds are made to float on its surface. It is called the Cool Chalice. If you open the door on the south side, there are jeweled pillars inlaid with silver and gold, and you can see the cool pond in the garden. The shadows of the pillars fall at the water's edge,

---

18. The Great Middle Gate (Naka no Mikado, also Taikenmon) was a central gate on the eastern side of the greater palace compound.

looking like water birds and floating logs. The autumn side is planted with myriad trees sporting autumn leaves. It is called the Spread of Broken Branches. If you open the door to the west, there is a bamboo grove fine enough to commune with Meng Zong.[19] In the clear light of an ample moon, you can find yourself pining for someone there. At the cries of the insects, we shed tears of longing for the capital, and they vie with the dew on the grasses in drenching our sleeves.

"There is a place called the Chamber of Wives, and that's where the demon has the women who live here take turns caressing and massaging him through the night in groups of more than ten while he rests with nothing on his mind. He has his retainers dance and play throughout the day and night, and they look after him with the utmost care. They feast on a cornucopia of delicacies of the land and sea, such that even the pleasures of the heavens could not compare.

"The demon has four retainers named Gogō, Kiriō, Ahō, and Rasetsu, and they are called his Four Heavenly Kings. Fleet of foot and deft of hand, they dash across oceans and rivers and smash boulders and stones. He also has two youths named Kanakuma Dōji and Ishikuma Dōji.[20] They're a pair of monsters with tremendous strength. The two of them stick close to their master, and whatever happens, they're the ones who serve him. At night, they keep a stern lookout over the entrance to the chamber. They may be demons, but to human eyes they look pale and plump, like magnificent, handsome, overgrown adolescents. Their master is named Shuten Dōji. He is immensely powerful and majestic.

"What with those gates and stone and iron walls and ramparts, and in the midst of all those retainers, I don't know how you'll ever break in! Moreover, the demon has posted guards everywhere. So how could you possibly slay him? It's hard to imagine, even for the fiercest sort of demon-god. And for you all to have thought to do this as a group of only six ... how strange! Still, since you're here under imperial command, Hachiman and the Sun Goddess Amaterasu may indeed protect you, and if they do, then why wouldn't the emperor's edict have its effect? For one, you have your luck as warriors, and if the buddhas' and gods' vows to help sentient beings are true, then there's no reason why they wouldn't grant you their protection. In that case, how could you have any problem breaking into the fortress and killing Shuten Dōji? It's really quite hopeful ..." The woman told them everything she knew as she

---

19. Meng Zong was one of the so-called Twenty-Four Exemplars of Filial Piety. He is known for having dug up bamboo shoots, which sprouted in the winter snow as a result of his tears, for his old and ailing mother.
20. "Youth" (*dōji*) is a term for a child or a sacred being with cropped and unbound hair in the manner of that of a boy before his coming-of-age ceremony, but it was also frequently used in the medieval period to signify demons (*oni*) with similar hairstyles.

led them along the path, through a succession of gates, and up to the demon's stony lair. Then, she went on her way.

The men followed the creek upstream until they came to a great roofed wall. There was an iron gate, to the front of which, on either side, stood some strange, misshapen beings. When the men took them to be demons, they looked like people, and when they took them to be people, they looked like demons. Some horrifying ones with big eyes and long noses caught sight of the men, whereupon they all rushed out and surrounded them, apparently intending to devour them where they stood. The men's courage fled. Their valiant hearts were turned upside down, and in any event, there was nothing they could do. But then one of the monsters addressed his fellows, saying, "Take it easy, you lot! To have such rare and wondrous visitors . . . we can't just finish them off on our own! We have to tell the master first and see what he decides. It wouldn't be right for us to dispose of them here." With these words, the demons settled down.

When the demons told Shuten Dōji the news, he was overjoyed. "How marvelous!" he exclaimed. "Just the other day, I was thinking about how we keep only women around here for our wine and food. It's a comfort, but it's not so special anymore. Men, on the other hand, have strong bones, firm flesh, and some interesting bits. These ones must have been terrified by your appearance, in which case they'll be wasting away, their meat thinning and their blood drying up. Do whatever you can to fool them and win their favor. And if they come from the capital, ask them how things are there, and find out if they know of any beautiful women. But first, bring them inside. Then from tomorrow you should put them in the people pen one at a time, fix them up nicely, and serve them to me."

Having received their instructions, the demons ran back outside the gate. Although they had previously scrambled over one another to seize the men, they now seemed to treat them with humble deference and good will. It was wholly unexpected. The men entered through the gate, whereupon the demons installed them in what seemed to be a guardhouse.

"I think I'll meet with them, too," Shuten Dōji announced, heading outside. "I can fool them while I see what kind of men they are and ask about the capital. Of course, if they shrink and tremble in fear of my authority, I'll truss them all up and put them in the people pen, one by one. In any case, I'm going to meet with them now."

Shuten Dōji stepped outside with more than ten retainers who looked like forerunners assigned to clear the way. They were unlike any normal attendants, having long noses and three eyes each. In fact, they were freakishly frightening sorts of creatures. The men were waiting deferentially in a courtyard when they felt a shaking

from deep inside the fortress, and a strong, warm wind begin to blow. It made their hair stand on end and their blood run cold.

After a while, Shuten Dōji emerged like the sun. Staring at his shining, sparkling figure, the men took him to be around ten feet tall. He was pale, portly, and handsome, and he wore his hair loose and bobbed in the manner of a child. He seemed to be about forty years old, and he sported a woven small-sleeved robe with a red *hakama* trouser-skirt, the trailing ends of which he tread on as he stepped. Leaning on the shoulders of his two youths, he surveyed his surroundings like a stag on a stroll, occasionally shading his eyes with an open hand at his brow. His power, presence, and sweeping magnificence as he swaggered out before the men exceeded everything they had heard. He was terrifying beyond description. Nevertheless, the six men did not appear agitated in the least.

Raikō and his men join Shuten Dōji for a bite to eat. (From *Shuten Dōji e*, courtesy of the Tōyō University Library)

Shuten Dōji sat down on his knees, facing sideways, about six feet from his guests. He smiled. He and the men caught one another's eyes as they sat, wondering what to do. "Well," Shuten Dōji said, "what business brings you here? These mountains are deep and craggy, and I don't see how you could have lost your way on the road when there isn't even a road." He glanced all around, periodically shading his eyes with a hand, frightening beyond words. After a while, he turned to his attendants and said, "Anyhow, these are some rare itinerant priests, so bring them a drink!"

Having received their charge, Shuten Dōji's retainers put some saké in a large vessel and brought it into the room. Looking at the so-called drink, the men saw that it was human blood and that it had stained the vessel black. Shuten Dōji took a sip first and then set the bowl before Raikō. This is the origin of what is known as

The Demon Shuten Dōji

"demon-sipping."[21] Raikō immediately picked up the bowl and drank, no less eagerly than his host. Next, the bowl was placed before Hōshō, who also drank. After that, it was Tsuna's turn. Without the slightest trepidation, they all received the brimming, sloshing bowl and drank.

"Do we have any special nibbles?" Shuten Dōji cried. Taking this as his cue, Kiriō produced a pale, beautiful, bloody thigh—freshly cut, it seemed—and set it out with a bit of salt. "Prepare that and serve it to the men," Shuten Dōji said, where-upon Raikō stepped over, unsheathed the dagger at his waist, and casually shaved a strip of flesh from the limb. He added salt and ate it. "A rare treat!" he exclaimed. "How excellent!" Tsuna ate some, too, every bit the equal of his master. The other men did not partake, claiming to be *yamabushi* mountain ascetics who were main-taining vows of monastic purity.

Shuten Dōji was so surprised by Raikō and Tsuna's behavior that he stared at them and said, "You gentlemen certainly enjoy our kind of saké! You're no ordinary fellows. Please accept our hospitality." In order to plumb the men's hearts, he enter-tained them in the most extraordinary ways. But neither Raikō nor his men were carried away with drink, and undaunted by the demon's power, they showed not the slightest sign of fear. For this reason, Shuten Dōji began to look annoyed.

"In order to honor the mendicant monks we meet," Raikō said, "it's our practice to carry what we call 'decanter tubes.' So what could be the harm? We'd like to offer you a drink." Shuten Dōji was pleased. "I was just wishing for some saké from the capital," he said, cracking a smile, "so how nice of you to offer!"

Raikō took out the saké and let him drink. Tsuna poured. After imbibing two or three times, Shuten Dōji was in high spirits. Tsuna therefore added more of the poi-soned wine to the vessel, and he pressed it on him so congenially that the demon drank and drank, indulging a full ten times. In an excess of glee, perhaps, Shuten Dōji said, "There are some women I adore above all the others. I'll call them here for a taste of your saké from the capital." With that, he summoned the daughters of Lord Kunikata and Hanazono and had them sit to his left and right.

Now the saké that he was drinking was poison. As Shuten Dōji became increas-ingly drunk, his mind reeled and he became befuddled. He put down the wine bowl and spoke: "I am truly glad that you all have made your way here. I'd like to put you up and entertain you." He paused. "Who do you think I am? I've lived in this place since long ago. I have my retainers bring me fine ladies from the capital for my plea-sure, and I have them fetch me all manner of precious things. I drink, eat, and enjoy myself beyond words. There's absolutely nothing that I lack! That said, there was

21. Demon-sipping (*oni-nomi*) is the practice of taste-testing saké and other beverages for poison.

once an imbecile by the name of Kūkai who put a curse on me, driving me out of this place to wander. I was always looking over my shoulder in the directions of Ōmine and Katsuragi,[22] constantly wondering how I might survive. But that scoundrel sealed himself up in a place called Kōya,[23] and since then there haven't been any villains like him around, which is why I've been living here now for more than a hundred years.

"I don't want for anything at all. In my splendor, I summon delightful people from the capital to indulge my fleshly pleasures. And when I'm bored, I have whatever I want—anything ever seen or known to man—brought to me for my diversion. These ladies, too, have recently joined me from the capital. I have lots of women here, but these are my favorites, and we're sure to be pledging our troth until the end of time.

"Looking forward, there's nothing that worries me at all. However, in the capital, there's a rat by the name of Raikō. Whether in the past or the present, there's never been a warrior like him. He's righteously inclined, and he protects the realm. He's stronger than other men, and his eyes flash with light. He's never failed to destroy an enemy of the court who's dared to take him on. Lately my retainers have been talking about him a lot, and it's a sure thing, I suppose, that he'll be causing us some trouble. Still, we've been taking powerful precautions, and since I have my minions keep a strict guard, he won't be able to break into this fortress, no matter what kind of evil demon-god he might be. Look around, you men! The fortifications of this place—"

Shuten Dōji stopped, and then he spoke: "When I take a good look at you all, you look like that Raikō and his men. Oh, how dreadful!" Raikō was wearing the cap-helmet, and so although Shuten Dōji tried to peer into his mind, his vision was obscured. "So this is why the old man gave it to me," Raikō thought to himself.

"Well," Raikō said, "what kind of man is that Raikō? This is the first I've ever heard of him. I haven't got wind of anyone like that, but the capital's a big place, so perhaps it's true. We are *yamabushi* mountain ascetics from Haguro in the province of Dewa, and we passed the New Year at Kumano. We visited the capital for our first time, and we were heading home now, but we lost our way and ended up here." He spoke with an earnest tone.

"It may be true that I'm addled by the saké," Shuten Dōji replied, "and that I got carried away in the moment. But I have penetrating sight, and when I look at someone, I'm not the least bit mistaken. You've got a light in your eyes, and I can see that

22. Mount Ōmine and Mount Katsuragi in Nara Prefecture are important sites in the Shugendō cult of Buddhist mountain asceticism.
23. Mount Kōya is the site of Kongōbuji Temple, headquarters of Kūkai's Shingon school of esoteric Buddhism. In 835, Kūkai is said to have entered a state of prolonged meditation on Mount Kōya that will continue until the advent of Miroku (Skt. Maitreya), the Future Buddha.

The Demon Shuten Dōji

each of you is hiding something. Even your traveling companions look like what I hear are Raikō's Four Heavenly Kings. Especially that one there," he said, pointing at Tsuna, "—the ferocity of his countenance is extraordinary."

The six men maintained their composure. "It's probably true," Shuten Dōji continued, his senses scattered by the wine. "But why should those men come here? Just drink more saké! We'll have a good time." And saying such things, he doted on his guests as he did before. He had been suspicious like that, probing the men's intentions, because he had remembered how Kūkai had once punished him so severely. It had occurred to him that some such swine might have come here now, which is why he said what he did.

Because of his intemperance, perhaps, Shuten Dōji lost all sense of shame, and he let slip some secrets. He revealed his heart so plainly that the men knew just what they faced. "Let's have a piece of entertainment," he cried, "for these marvelous men from the capital!" Gogō leaped up and sang:

miyakobito	Oh capital men—
ikanaru ashi no	on what sorts of feet
mayoi nite	do you wander lost,
sake ya sakana no	to become our
ejiki to wa naru	chow of nibbles and drink?

He danced to this verse two or three times. With the word "chow," he meant that he would turn the men into tidbits and wine. Listening to Gogō's song, the men were amused.

"That's just what a nasty lout would say," Tsuna thought. "Shuten Dōji's raving drunk, and now he seems to be out of his mind. If that's how it's going to be, I'll stab him through the middle, and when he shrinks and cowers, I'll chase him down and cut off his head. If I do, none of the other brutes will give us any trouble. I'll settle this here in the reception hall." Tsuna ground his teeth in fury; his cheeks tightened, and his eyes filled with blood. When Raikō saw Tsuna's veins bulge, and when he saw him place his hand on his two-foot, one-inch striking sword, he understood. He shot him a calming glare, and Tsuna relaxed.

Kintoki was famous in the capital for his dancing, and grasping the situation, he pushed himself forward and said, "Why shouldn't we provide you with a bit of entertainment, too?" He jumped up beside where Shuten Dōji sat and began to dance:

toshi wo furu	Spring has come
oni no iwaya ni	to the old demon's

haru no kite	stony lair.
kaze ya yo no ma ni	The wind, it seems, shall
fukiharau ran	sweep it clean in the night.

He danced to this verse two or three times, moving in ways that were beyond the mind to conceive or words to express. Shuten Dōji listened intently, but perhaps because he was so inebriated, he did not pay any mind to the song. He simply watched with pleasure, entranced by Kintoki's steps and the lovely sound of his voice.

Shuten Dōji's Four Heavenly Kings on the wide veranda, and even his retainers sitting in the courtyard below, all got the gist of Kintoki's verse. They even muttered among themselves about the look of determination in Tsuna's eyes. However, not wishing to oppose their master, they pretended not to notice. "Take good care of our guests," Shuten Dōji instructed. "I am extremely drunk from your saké. In return, I'll leave these two women with you. Ladies, pour the men some wine and treat them well." He withdrew inside.

Now Gogō, Kiriō, and Shuten Dōji's other Four Heavenly Kings, as well as Shuten Dōji's closer retainers, showed no signs of warming toward the men. But not wishing to act against their master's directions, some of them brought out saké and side dishes, and they entertained the men in assorted ways. It was a moment that would seal their fate. Taking all of Shuten Dōji's lackeys to be scoundrels, Raikō and his men produced the poisoned wine from before and variously pressed them to drink. And how could even a single drop fail to lay them low? Thus, although they intended to drink only once, the demons never left their seats—they were soon rolling on the floor in a drunken daze. Others cradled their heads in their arms and fled, until in the end the only ones who remained behind resembled the dead. Whatever might happen, they did not look like they would get up again.

By and by, the women spoke: "The Horie Minister of Central Affairs was awash with riches; he didn't want for anything at all. He had a beloved daughter, and he took a son-in-law. Three years later, she was carried off to this rocky cavern. It's been another three years since then. She stopped breathing when the demons squeezed her for her blood, but they used some medicine to bring her back to life. That was two or three days ago, and they served her leg and arm for today's nibbles. Among all the women here, it was her turn this time. How sad to become a side dish!"

Raikō beckoned the two women and questioned them carefully about the series of fortress doors and the layout of the lair. "The demon-retainers were saying that Shuten Dōji let down his guard," the women explained, "and that he revealed things he should have kept secret. They said, 'He told you things he shouldn't have, and it's

The Demon Shuten Dōji

no small matter. He lost himself in that saké, which is sure to bring us grief, too. Once the night's grown late, those men are certain to be passed out drunk. We'll sneak up and slaughter them, one after another. If we don't, they'll be too much for us to handle, which would be awful.' Then they were whispering various things about what might happen to them in the end. Oh, please be careful!"

"What could they possibly do?" the men replied. "Even if it's true that Shuten Dōji is a formidable foe, the rest of them don't amount to much." The men asked the two women who they were, and if they had been in this terrifying place for long.

"I am the daughter of the Ikeda Middle Counselor Kunikata," one of the women said. "Because I am an only child, my parents loved me especially dearly. I had never been away from my mother. For whatever blessed reason, she raised me with the utmost care. But then late one night, I heard a voice saying that she was calling, and thinking it was my nursemaid speaking, I went right out. Someone grabbed me on the way. 'Who are you?' I demanded, but there was no one to stop him. I was brought here in the night. Since we're so close to the capital, I can't imagine that my family would have given up the search, but it's been thirty days already. When I think about how much my mother, father, and nursemaid must be mourning and grieving, I don't feel like I can stand it. There's nothing more hateful than being a woman! If I were a man, I'd find some way to escape, and then why shouldn't I be able to return to the capital? I've seen terrible things these days—things I'd never seen before—and without a guardian or a nursemaid to comfort me. How my mother and father must miss me! The demons are fast asleep tonight, so if you can, please take us back to the capital!" She fell to the floor in a spasm of despair.

"We've come on the emperor's orders," Raikō explained. "We didn't have any particular plan, but we were able to get inside and meet with Shuten Dōji. We got his retainers drunk, just as we had hoped. Please hold on until later in the night. Once we get through the run of fortress doors and into his den, we should be able to cut him down, whatever kind of demon-god he might be." He spoke with such reassuring indifference that the two women exchanged joyful glances. "Then you really are Raikō, aren't you?" they said. "What heartening news! In that case, please be on your way. We'll lead you to his lair."

The night deepened, and all the demons were sunken in their cups, dead to the world. Now that everything was quiet, each of the six men clad themselves as they saw fit. Raikō wore a scarlet-laced corselet and the cap-helmet that the old man had given him; he fastened the cords of his five-plated helmet, the Lion Lord, on top of that, and he carried the two-foot, eight-inch sword known as Blood Sucker. Hōshō wore a purple-laced corselet, and he armed himself with a striking sword by the name of Stone Cutter.[24] Each of the others donned their own particular armor, whereupon the two ladies led them through the series of fortress doors.

The stone walls and iron gates were usually closed up tight, but because Shuten Dōji's retainers had passed out drunk on the evening wine, not a single passage was secure. Even Shuten Dōji's most vigilant retainers had been overcome by the poisoned saké, and they seemed to be utterly unable to rise. Thus, with no one to challenge them, the men passed through a number of stout doorways. Climbing to the top of a stone bridge, they saw a gated iron enclosure. But the portal was open, and the men proceeded inside. There they saw a massive iron cell, the great doors of which were sealed shut from the inside with wooden stoppers and a crossbar. To all appearances, not even the most powerful demon-god could break his way in.

Peering into the cell, the men could see lamps burning brightly at the four sides of the room. There was a large battle-ax by Shuten Dōji's pillow, placed there, it seemed, in case of attack. At his feet were a studded iron club and a row of huge halberds. Gazing at Shuten Dōji where he lay, the men saw that he was completely changed from the day before—a demon now from head to toe. His hair was like a tangle of gooseberry bushes, and his eyelashes bristled like lines of needles. He also sprouted hair from his arms and legs, like a bear. Before, he had looked to be about ten feet tall, but now he appeared to be more than twenty. He was lying face-up with his arms and legs stretched out in the four directions while more than ten ladies stroked and caressed him. Snoring peacefully on his high pillow, he seemed utterly unaware of his surroundings.

Spying the men outside, the ladies in the cell were overjoyed. They wished to open the doors at once, but because they were cast of iron, to do so would have been beyond the strength of even a hundred men. For women, it was impossible. The ladies simply clamored for help, utterly dejected.

The doors were shut fast, and having no way to get inside, the six men wracked their brains wondering what to do. Suddenly, they saw their three guides from before: the old men and the *yamabushi*. Handing the men four lengths of iron chain, the guides said, "Wrap these tightly around Shuten Dōji's arms and legs and attach them to the pillars at the four sides of the room. Five of you should set on him from the left and right, whereupon Raikō should cut off his head." The three men then stepped forward and opened the iron doors, and they did it with such force that the crossbar broke and the wooden stoppers shattered. "Now go inside," they said. "You'll fail if you don't pull yourselves together and give it all you've got." With that, they vanished into the air.

24. Previously, Stone Cutter was described as a short halberd rather than a striking sword. Likewise, Blood Sucker was said to be only two feet, one inch long.

The Demon Shuten Dōji

Having reverted to his demonic form, Shuten Dōji receives a massage in his private chamber. (From *Shuten Dōji e*, courtesy of the Tōyō University Library)

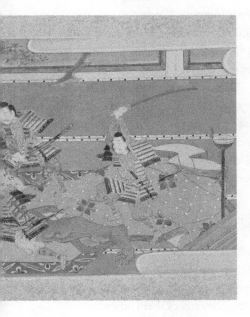

Raikō and his men attack Shuten Dōji as he sleeps. (From *Shuten Dōji e*, courtesy of the Tōyō University Library)

The men were elated, and rushing in together, they bound Shuten Dōji's arms and legs with the chains. But the monster only slept on like he was dead. Taking heart, Tsuna and Kintoki leaped on him while Raikō, approaching from behind, struck at his neck with Blood Sucker. Shuten Dōji neither woke at the first strike nor flinched at the second. But then shouting, "There, I knew it!" he sat up with a start. The men continued hacking, and with his third strike, Raikō lopped off his head. The body tried to rise, snapping two of the iron fetters. The fortress was a strong one, but it shook to its foundations as if it were going to collapse. The gods themselves had provided those chains, but Shuten Dōji easily pulled them apart. Wondering in dread at the extent of his power, the five men cut his struggling carcass into shreds.

Shuten Dōji's arms and legs were chopped into pieces, but his head rose up in the air and vomited poison on the men below. As the head ran out of bile, it seemed to have exhausted its strength. After a while, it came down on Raikō's helmet, biting hard. Without his inner helmet-cap, Raikō might have lost his life. The head bit through the Lion Lord and clenched so tightly that it left teeth marks in the cap. The deity had told Raikō that he would probably not survive if he failed to wear it, and now, at last, Raikō understood. Truly, it was an excellent prediction.

Having taken Shuten Dōji's head, the men set out to slay his demon-retainers. Tsuna picked up the battle-ax that Shuten Dōji had kept at the ready and stepped outside. The demons around the great courtyard wielded studded clubs and striking swords, and raising a mighty cry, they attacked. Raikō and Hōshō watched from a high place, leaving the fighting to Raikō's Four Heavenly Kings.

Tsuna held his ground, standing and battling at the base of the stone bridge. He had the strength of thirty men, and sparks flew as he fought. His opponent, Gogō, was fast, deft, and strong. Leaping and hopping in and out, he fought such that neither he nor Tsuna could immediately win. Tsuna kept a close eye on him and then seized him with all his might. The two grappled and rolled. Then something must have happened, because Tsuna found himself pinned. Just as he was about to meet his end, Sadamitsu rushed over and hewed off Gogō's head.

Suetake swung a club, and lightning flashed as he fought. Kiriō was a skilled fighter of tremendous strength, but as Suetake rained a torrent of blows on his head, leaving him no chance to breathe, something must have happened, for Suetake knocked him down on his back. Without allowing him a moment to regroup, he pinned him to the ground and cut off his head. Two remaining monsters stormed toward the men, and eventually spying Raikō and Hōshō, they flew at them headlong. They seemed to be more than the six men could handle. But because things could not go on in this way, the men encircled them and attacked, and without giving them time to find their footing, they struck them down.

"These brutes are stronger than I thought!" Raikō exclaimed. "If things go on like this, my Four Heavenly Kings are sure to be killed." He ran into the great courtyard and looked around. All the creatures who had seemed so ferocious the evening before were passed out drunk. He therefore went around stabbing and slashing them as he saw fit, and because none of them arose, he slaughtered them all.

Now the demons who had been outside the great gate had not drunk the saké, and upon hearing the commotion, more than twenty of them came rushing in. They were strange, misshapen beings, and their shrieking cries as they charged were like the simultaneous peal of a hundred thousand bolts of thunder. The Four Heavenly Kings burst into their midst, slashing all around in spider-leg, ribbon-knot, and criss-cross patterns. Raikō and Hōshō, too, battled with reckless disregard for their own lives. Shouting at the monsters to stand and fight, the six men cornered the remaining fiends and put them to the sword. Thus in no time at all, the demons were destroyed.

The men thought that they should spend the day searching Shuten Dōji's abode, and when they did, they found thirty female captives. Upon realizing that Shuten Dōji was slain and that his retainers were defeated, the women had been frightened witless that the mountain and the cavern would collapse. But when they caught sight of the men, they felt like sinners in hell who encounter the bodhisattva Jizō: joyful beyond compare.[25] Even in their jubilation, they were utterly choked with tears. With these women showing the way, the men opened up the second and third floors and looked around. The rooms in which the demon had stayed were inlaid with gold and silver and adorned with a webbing of precious stones. The men beheld a profusion of jewels and treasure, and then, in an instant, it disappeared. The views of the four seasons and the magnificent ornamentation of the four sides were likewise reduced to a useless stack of boulders.

Looking around a broad open space in the cavern, the men found thousands upon thousands of human skeletons, some old and some new. There were people pickled in vinegar, and others drying in the sun. There were also the dismembered heads, arms, and legs of beautiful ladies. Taking in the sight, the men pitied Shuten Dōji's captives even more than they had before.

"This here is the daughter of the Horie Minister of Central Affairs," the women explained. "Over the last two or three days, the demons squeezed her for her blood. She was still just breathing, but then they served her as yesterday's snack, and this is what happened."

25. The bodhisattva Jizō (Ch. Dizang) is widely revered for rescuing sentient beings who have fallen into hell. See, in this volume, *The Tale of the Fuji Cave*.

"How awful!" everyone exclaimed. "Out of all the people here, it was her turn to be butchered. If she had survived, why couldn't she have returned to the capital and seen her mother and father? But it's hard to escape your karma."

"The retainers also had dwellings," Raikō said. "Please help us to search those, too."

"Certainly," the women replied.

As they examined various rocky dens, one after another, they came upon the two youths Kanakuma Dōji and Ishikuma Dōji, each of whom was a match for a thousand. They were fleet-footed fiends, skilled with arms and enormously strong. Having been forced to drink the poisoned wine, they had vomited bile and passed out in their lair, just like they were dead. When they awoke and heard what was going on, they cried out in chagrin that they had seen it coming. They donned their armor and barricaded themselves inside their hollow. Now, upon seeing that Tsuna and Kintoki would force their way in, they stayed put and fought off the intruders six or seven times.

"Pretend to retreat," Raikō commanded. "Draw them out and then surround them and strike!" When the men fell back, the demons dashed outside to press their advantage. Choosing to rely on their strength, they threw away their armor and rushed at the men with open arms. Tsuna and the other Four Heavenly Kings grappled with them, held them down, and managed to take them alive. Because the demons were so strong, the men bound them with seven ropes, forcing them to their knees.

Although it goes without saying for Shuten Dōji, his retainers, too, possessed supernatural powers, allowing them to run on broad oceans and rivers and to pulverize solid boulders. They were accomplished with weapons and fast on their feet. Nevertheless, they were defeated by the might of martial strategy, which was amazing indeed!

Because Shuten Dōji had the all-powerful virtue and authority of a demon-god, he had turned great boulders and the grottoes here and there into tall, stately halls, just as he saw fit. The beautiful views of the four seasons were also visible from his home. But after he was destroyed, his palace, stately halls, and gardens of the four seasons all disappeared, becoming the caverns they had been before. Moreover, his demon-retainers lost their extraordinary powers. They could neither rise into the sky nor fly like birds, and each and every one of them was pitifully slaughtered. It was hard to imagine that a mere six men, even with the superhuman powers of the most ferocious demon-gods, could so easily subdue them. That they promptly quelled such wicked fiends was a rare and marvelous thing, and it was sure to become a fine story for future generations.

Shuten Dōji's lair was destroyed, and after demolishing all of the demon-retainers' quarters and executing some of the captives, the Four Heavenly Kings set out from the mountains bearing Shuten Dōji's head and the heads of his principal lieutenants. Each of the more than thirty ladies seemed to be happier than the rest, and they all departed together with the men. Still, they grieved the death of the Horie Minister's daughter, and cutting off a bit of her sidelocks, they carried it with them to present to her parents. Upon descending Hundred Mile Peak, the women felt as if they had entered another world.

There was talk in the capital that Raikō and Hōshō would be arriving with the demon's head, and all those who heard the news, not to mention the men's own retainers, came out to greet them. In addition to the major territorial lords, ten thousand riders were reported to have gathered for the warriors' entrance to the capital. It was not the first time, but on this occasion everyone from the emperor to all his many subjects praised the men not only for securing the safety of the realm, putting an end to the people's sorrow, and easing their sovereign's fury, but also for accomplishing an incomparable feat of martial valor.

When the men entered the city, the streets from the Fourth Avenue riverbed to the grand Third Avenue thoroughfare were thronged with palanquins, carriages, and thousands of spectators of all social stations. "No one ever achieved anything like this in ancient times," the people said, "nor will they in ages to come."

Word spread that the daughter of the Ikeda Middle Counselor Kunikata had returned, and Kunikata and his wife and the girl's nursemaid were overjoyed. The people who went out to receive her spruced themselves up and waited. It was also rumored that among the more than thirty rescued women, the daughter of the Horie Minister, too, had returned. The people from her household asked after her until one of the ladies told them that she had died. They went home in tears, their grief now a deeper hue than it had been before.

The Horie Minister of Central Affairs summoned one of the women who had been close to his daughter, and he questioned her about what had happened. She told him in detail, recounting everything that had occurred from beginning to end, after which she took out his daughter's talisman and sidelocks and offered them to him.[26] "Although we had lost her," the minister said, taking in the sight, "we always hoped that she might yet come home. But now . . . these keepsakes won't do us any good! The year may end and the days may pass, but how will I ever see her again except in a dream?" He twisted and writhed in anguish. Later, he is said to have built a buddha hall at Suzaku,[27] to have constructed bridges, and to have engaged solely in the performance of various Buddhist practices.

---

26. The type of talisman (*mamori*) that the young woman carried is unclear.
27. Suzaku is in the central part of Kyoto, south of Fifth Avenue and west of Nishi Honganji Temple.

The Demon Shuten Dōji

Previously, when Raikō received the imperial edict, he visited his clan deity at Hachiman Shrine and prayed for assistance. Other people, too, said, "Except for the protection of the gods, there was nothing he could really count on, and it was because he prayed to them that he'll leave a great name for future ages. It was an extraordinary thing." Furthermore, in regard to Seimei and the accuracy of his divination, everyone from the emperor on high to the myriad people below happily praised him as a most rare and remarkable physiognomist, whether in their own or ancient times.

One person said, "Emperor Ichijō is a manifestation of Miroku, and Raikō is an incarnation of Bishamon.[28] The emperor appeared in order to spread the dharma and to save sentient beings. Raikō came to defend against the bitter foes of Buddhism and to protect the state; he is the chief of the warrior clans. He is here, marvelously, wholly for the deliverance of the multitude of living beings in accord with his great merciful vow. Shuten Dōji was the Evil King of the Sixth Heaven. Scorning the majestic laws of sagacious sovereigns, he became an enemy of Buddhism and obtained the life span of a demon-god. All these things are explained in the holy teachings."

Indeed, even in ancient ages, the likes of these men's deeds were largely unknown. The men were an ally of the nobility, and among warriors they were supreme. Their

28. The bodhisattva Miroku is prophesied to appear in this world as the next human buddha after Shakyamuni. The heavenly king Bishamon (also Bishamonten, Skt. Vaiśravaṇa) is a Buddhist guardian deity.

Raikō and his men return to the capital with Shuten Dōji's head. (From *Shuten Dōji e*, courtesy of the Tōyō University Library)

martial feats were outstanding. Along with the diviner Seimei, they were the most extraordinary heroes. For this reason, the state has prospered, city and country flourishing without calamities of wind and rain and without fear of conflagration. Because these men so clearly displayed the virtue and authority of mantra kings,[29] it stands to reason that the people would maintain among themselves that they were manifestations of bodhisattvas.

Now in all the past, the life span of demon-gods has not been fixed. Yet in these times in which the buddhas bestow their blessings, the reduction of the human life span has occurred faster than the turn of a heel![30]

TRANSLATION AND INTRODUCTION BY KELLER KIMBROUGH

---

29. Mantra kings (*myōō*) are emanations of buddhas and bodhisattvas in particularly fearsome forms, taken on in order to subdue and save sentient beings who are especially resistant to Buddhism.
30. According to traditional Buddhist calculations, the human life span fluctuates between ten and eighty thousand years in an endless cycle repeated every twenty *kalpas*. First, in the course of ten "decreasing *kalpas*" (*gengō*), the human life span decreases by one year every hundred years until it has fallen from eighty thousand to ten years. Then, over ten "increasing *kalpas*" (*zōgō*), it increases by one year every hundred years until it has again reached eighty thousand. See Sawai Taizō's explanation in *Ibuki Dōji*, in *Muromachi monogatari shū jō*, ed. Ichiko Teiji et al., Shin Nihon koten bungaku taikei 54 (Tokyo: Iwanami Shoten, 1989), 203n.12. A *kalpa* is a measurement of time that Nāgārjuna (ca. 150–250) described in *Daichidoron* (*Commentary on the Great Wisdom Sutra*) as being greater than the time that it takes for a heavenly being to wear away a forty-*ri* (hundred-square-mile) rock by brushing it with a delicate sleeve once every hundred years.

The Demon Shuten Dōji

The Demon of Ibuki

There are few fictional or historical figures who captured the medieval and early-modern imagination to the extent of Shuten Dōji, the charismatic antihero of *The Demon Shuten Dōji*. As a late-medieval prequel to that work, *The Demon of Ibuki* (*Ibuki Dōji*) borrows plot elements from *Benkei monogatari* (*The Tale of Benkei*) to recount Shuten Dōji's human childhood and demonic transformation, exploring the dramatic implications of an excessively meaty and alcoholic diet.

The Demon of Ibuki survives in numerous illustrated versions, the contents of which—unlike the variants of *The Demon Shuten Dōji*—tend to differ from one another to a remarkable degree. For example, unlike the three-scroll *emaki* in the British Museum on which this translation is based, a three-scroll *Ibuki Dōji emaki* in the Tōyō University Library and a single-scroll *Ibuki Dōji emaki* in the British Museum maintain that Shuten Dōji's father, Ibuki no Yasaburō, was born as a result of his father's prayers to the Great Ibuki Deity.[1] That deity was, in fact, a reincarnation of the notorious Yamata no Orochi, the eight-headed serpent in *Kojiki* (*Record of Ancient Matters*, 712) that was slain by Susano'o no Mikoto because of its taste for live young women. Alternatively, according to a manuscript of *Ibuki Dōji* in Yokoyama Shigeru's former Akagi Bunko archive, Yasaburō was himself the Great Ibuki Deity in a human incarnation.[2] Yet, in either case, as a direct or an indirect descendant of

The translation and illustrations are from the three-scroll *Ibuki Dōji* picture scrolls (sixteenth or seventeenth century) in the collection of the British Museum, typeset and annotated in Ichiko Teiji et al., eds., *Muromachi monogatari shū jō*, Shin Nihon koten bungaku taikei 54 (Tokyo: Iwanami Shoten, 1989), 186–213.

1. The three-scroll *Ibuki Dōji* in the Tōyō University Library is typeset in Shimazu Hisamoto, ed., *Zoku otogizōshi*, Iwanami bunko (Tokyo: Iwanami Shoten, 1956), 152–63. The single-scroll *Ibuki Dōji* in the British Museum is typeset and photographically reproduced in Tsuji Eiko, ed., *Zaigai Nihon emaki no kenkyū to shiryō: zoku-hen* (Tokyo: Kasama Shoin, 2006).

2. The *Ibuki Dōji* in the Akagi Bunko, which differs radically from the Tōyō University Library, British Museum, and National Diet Library *Ibuki Dōji* texts, is typeset in Yokoyama Shigeru and Matsumoto Ryūshin, eds., *Muromachi jidai monogatari taisei* (Tokyo: Kadokawa Shoten, 1974), 2:357–78.

Yamata no Orochi, Shuten Dōji is shown to have inherited his appetite for women rather than to have simply acquired it on his own.

Although the unknown author of the Akagi Bunko *Ibuki Dōji* asserts that Shuten Dōji's metamorphosis resulted from his drinking, the illustrator of the three-scroll British Museum *Ibuki Dōji emaki* seems to have been inspired by the cannibalistic feast in *The Demon Shuten Dōji* to portray the story of Shuten Dōji's youth as a cautionary tale against the inordinate consumption of meat. Hamanaka Osamu has speculated that *The Demon of Ibuki* was composed in the vicinity of Mount Hiei, because of the work's preoccupation with the role of Tendai Buddhism as a guarantor of imperial authority and the safety of the state.[3] Since it is Saichō, the founder of Enryakuji Temple, who drives Shuten Dōji away from Mount Hiei at the climax of the story, we might read the three-scroll British Museum *Ibuki Dōji* as a kind of painted Tendai parable of the vegetarian Saichō's triumph over the carnivorous forces of evil.

Long ago in Ōmi Province, there was a powerful man by the name of Ibuki no Yasaburō. His father was a certain Lord Yatarō, from an old line of masters of Mount Ibuki. In that same province, there was a prominent person by the name of Lord Ōnogi, and he had a beloved daughter. Because she was very beautiful, Yasaburō took her for his wife, and they loved each other dearly.

Yasaburō was a man of clean good looks and a strong, sturdy build, but he loved saké from his youth and drank a great deal. The older he grew, the more he drank, so much so that he came to be perpetually drunk. His mind raving, he would spew the most unreasonable abuse and perpetrate the most horrible deeds. "Ah, if only I could drink my fill!" he would cry to his retainers. A provincial highway lay nearby, so he took to plundering the stocks of passing merchants and guzzling those.

It was Yasaburō's practice when he drank to eat all manner of meat, including boar, deer, monkey, rabbit, and raccoon. He would rend the animals' bodies and devour them just as they were. Because he killed three or four creatures every day, the mountains and forests were soon depleted, without a single bird or beast left to hunt. Yasaburō then took to seizing and devouring the horses and oxen that people had raised in their homes. He was terrifying to behold.

3. Hamanaka Osamu, "*Ibuki Dōji* kō: Eizan kaisōdan to jishujin," in *Muromachi monogatari ronkō* (Tokyo: Shintensha, 1996), 91.

Yasaburō feasts on a shank of meat. (From the three-scroll *Ibuki Dōji emaki*, courtesy of the British Museum. © The Trustees of the British Museum. All rights reserved)

In the past, there was a great serpent known as the Giant Eight-Forked Snake in a place called Hinokawakami in Izumo Province.[4] Every day, it ate living people who were offered to it in sacrifice. It also drank an inordinate amount of saké. It once drank itself drunk on eight-brewed saké from eight wooden bowls, whereupon the deity Susano'o no Mikoto put it to death. The serpent then transformed and became a god: the Great Ibuki Deity of today. People therefore shuddered to think that it was perhaps because Yasaburō oversaw the Great Ibuki Deity's mountain that he loved to drink saké and eat living things.[5] Even travelers came to avoid passing through the place, and the surrounding towns and villages fell to ruin.

Lord Ōnogi heard of these events, and he was immensely surprised. "Yasaburō is not acting like any human being," he thought, "but like some kind of demon! If the years go by and he attains supernatural powers, then he'll obliterate the people and rain calamity on the world. Somehow or other, I have to cut him down." Setting a

4. In Japanese, the serpent is called Yamata no Orochi. According to *Record of Ancient Matters* and *Nihon shoki* (*The Chronicles of Japan*, 720), it had eight heads and eight tails.
5. According to a manuscript of *Ibuki Dōji* in the Tōyō University Library, Yasaburō was born as a result of his father's prayers to the Great Ibuki Deity. See Hamanaka Osamu, ed., *Shinchū Muromachi monogatari shū*, Daigaku koten sōsho 8 (Tokyo: Benseisha, 1989), 122.

Lord Ōnogi stabs his son-in-law with a sword. (From the three-scroll *Ibuki Dōji emaki,* courtesy of the British Museum. © The Trustees of the British Museum. All rights reserved)

secret trap, Lord Ōnogi invited Yasaburō for a visit. However, Yasaburō was ashamed of his strangely changed appearance, and he declined. Lord Ōnogi therefore prepared a sumptuous feast, which he brought to him instead. Yasaburō greeted him warmly. He had various delicacies prepared, and hosted his guest in regal fashion. Lord Ōnogi took out the saké that he had brought, much to Yasaburō's delight. Since saké was the very thing that Yasaburō constantly craved, he accepted cup after cup, downing a prodigious amount, until he had quaffed all that Lord Ōnogi had brought—around seven horse loads, or so people said.

Being the drunkard that he was, and consuming the stupendous amount that he did, Yasaburō managed to drink himself senseless. Oblivious to his bed, he passed out flat where he fell on the matted floor. His luck had run out, sad to say. Heartened by the thought that his ploy was succeeding, Lord Ōnogi approached Yasaburō where he lay and ran him through with his sword, piercing him below the armpit from one side to the other. Then he returned to his own estate.

Although the daughter and her father were naturally close, the daughter never once suspected what her father had done. Assuming that Yasaburō was passed out drunk as usual, she covered him with a robe and left him alone.

Three days passed, and awaking from his sodden stupor, Yasaburō arose. Much to his surprise, he found that he had been stabbed below the armpit. "I've been deceived by that Ōnogi!" he shouted in chagrin. He hopped up with a start, but because he had been stuck in his vitals, his senses reeled and he eventually died.

The Demon of Ibuki

Yasaburō's widow dotes on her young son. (From the three-scroll *Ibuki Dōji emaki*, courtesy of the British Museum. © The Trustees of the British Museum. All rights reserved)

The local people were relieved to hear of Yasaburō's demise, and the entire region prospered.

Now the daughter, having lost her husband, was inconsolably grieved. "This is all my father's fault," she brooded. "How heartless of him!" But there was nothing she could do, and as time passed, she was soon heavy with child. Safely loosening the birthing belt,[6] she bore a strikingly, nobly handsome baby boy. She raised him with delight, treasuring him as a remembrance of her husband. The boy grew, and people began to say that he looked just like his father.

Word of this reached Lord Ōnogi, and he sent a message to his daughter: "It is certainly reasonable that you would cherish the boy as a memento of his father, but if he closely resembles him, then he is sure to take up evil ways. Please dispose of him somehow before he matures."

"You may be my father," she replied, "but you are a cruel man! It was awful, despicable enough that you betrayed Yasaburō—I couldn't forget it for a moment—but now, just when I happen to have found a parent's joy in this newborn child, this son in whom I was hoping to take some comfort in my constant sorrow, you have decided

6. This is an expression for childbirth, because it refers to the supportive sash typically worn by a woman during her pregnancy.

MONSTERS, WARRIORS, AND JOURNEYS TO OTHER WORLDS

The child Shuten Dōji drinks saké in the presence of his mother. (From the three-scroll *Ibuki Dōji emaki*, courtesy of the British Museum. © The Trustees of the British Museum. All rights reserved)

to bring me to grief again, saying these things!" She ranted with such bitterness that Lord Ōnogi was moved to compassion. "She cherishes her child like any parent would," he thought to himself, and after that he left her alone.

The days and months passed by, and the little boy quickly came of age. Like his father, he drank saké all the time. For this reason, everyone called him Shuten Dōji, "the saké-drinking boy." Now Shuten Dōji was constantly drunk and deranged, and his spirit was ferocious. He would abuse innocent people, and dashing through the mountains and fields, he would thrash the horses and oxen that he found there. When the local people saw how he devoted himself to evil so inappropriate to his youth, they remarked that he was indeed Yasaburō's son and that this time for certain it would be the end of mankind.

Hearing such things, Lord Ōnogi sent a message to his daughter, asking, "Why have you not followed my advice? Your son will soon bring ruin to the land." He spoke with such reproach that the daughter replied, "Your words are hard to ignore. Indeed, the people around here are frightened and dismayed, so it would be inappropriate for me to shelter him myself." Thus she abandoned her boy in a valley on the northern side of Mount Hiei. Shuten Dōji was seven years old at the time.

The Demon of Ibuki

"I am despised by those who should love me," the boy fretted, "and shunned by the peasants who ought to serve me. To make my home in this deep valley, the bottom of which lies who-knows-where . . . I'll surely lose my life in this very spot, mauled by some tiger, wolf, or fox!" But the boy showed no signs of languishing, and he did not appear to grieve. In fact, he grew stronger with the passing days and months, until he had lost his usual appearance and taken on a frighteningly terrible form. At first, he had lived by gathering fruits and nuts, but people say that later he took to eating all manner of birds and beasts.

After that, Shuten Dōji moved to Little Hiei Peak and lived there for a while.[7] But when the Second-Shrine Deity descended from the heavens to rebuke evil demons and malevolent gods, Shuten Dōji fled from that peak as well. Now this Second-Shrine Deity is a guardian deity of Japan. Long ago, when the Sun Goddess Amaterasu pushed open the stone door of heaven and probed the blue sea plain with the heavenly jeweled halberd, she struck something there. "What's this?" she inquired.

"I am a guardian deity of Japan," a voice replied, and it was Kuni-no-tokotachi no Mikoto. In his original form, he is Yakushi Buddha, lord of the Eastern Lapis Lazuli Realm. He once explained to Shakyamuni Buddha that he had been the lord of that place since the beginning of the age of the twenty-thousand-year human life span.[8]

To its east, Mount Hiei is succeeded by a range of steep, craggy peaks. Thinking that this would be a fine place to live, Shuten Dōji carved himself a grotto and made his home there. He seems to have attained miraculous powers, for he used them to summon and engage a horde of frightening retainers from wholly unknown places. However, because his cave was on a pure, sacred site known as Golden Rock, the children of the Sun Goddess descended from the heavens, manifesting in their godly forms, and harried him, saying, "Get out of here, you foul spirits and demons!" Shuten Dōji and his followers fled. The place that we call Hachiōji is where this happened.

7. Little Hiei Peak is the site of the Ninomiya "Second-Shrine" Hall of the Great Hie Shrine in the eastern foothills of Mount Hiei.

8. According to traditional Buddhist calculations, the human life span fluctuates between ten and eighty thousand years in an endless cycle repeated every twenty *kalpas*. First, in the course of ten "decreasing *kalpas*" (*gengō*), the human life span decreases by one year every hundred years until it has fallen from eighty thousand to ten years. Then, over ten "increasing *kalpas*" (*zōgō*), it increases by one year every hundred years until it has again reached eighty thousand. The age of the twenty-thousand-year human life span corresponds to the ninth decreasing *kalpa*. See Sawai Taizō's explanation in *Ibuki Dōji*, in *Muromachi monogatari shū jō*, ed. Ichiko et al., 203n.12. A *kalpa* is a measurement of time that Nāgārjuna (ca. 150–250) described in *Daichidoron* (*Commentary on the Great Wisdom Sutra*) as being greater than the time that it takes for a heavenly being to wear away a forty-*ri* (hundred-square-mile) rock by brushing it with a delicate sleeve once every hundred years.

Shuten Dōji moved on to Great Hiei Peak. It was here, in the past, in the age of Kuruson Buddha, that the voice of the waves on the spreading sea could be heard to recite, "Sentient beings all possess the buddha nature; buddhas abide constantly, forever unchanging."[9] In seeking the waves' destination, Shakyamuni found an island that had formed around the leaves of a single reed. This is the place called Hashidono, or "Waves' End." Shakyamuni said that Buddhism should be spread there, and that the site should be made a restricted space for religious practice. Yakushi replied by promising to become king of the mountain and defend Buddhism there for the latter five hundred years.[10] Yakushi and Shakyamuni then parted ways, one heading east, and the other, west. Yakushi quickly manifested as the Second-Shrine Deity, descending from the heavens to Little Hiei Peak. Shakyamuni manifested as the Great Shrine Deity, and he descended to the Shiki district of Yamato Province.[11] Then, appearing as an old man, he moved on to Great Hiei Peak.

Shuten Dōji was filled with fear, and he immediately abandoned Great Hiei Peak and moved to Nishizaka on the western slope. The site was defensibly steep. He logged the deep valley and set its great trees in rows; quarrying massive boulders, he constructed a fortress-cavern hundreds of yards across. He took up residence there, and commanding his many minions, he sent them scurrying about the surrounding regions, seizing people's treasures and heaping them up into a mountainous hoard. He would also fly around the mountains and fields, capturing and collecting the birds and beasts on which he constantly fed. He was terrible beyond description.

Now in the Shiga region of Ōmi Province, there was a man by the name of Mitsu no Momoe who had a single son. The boy was naturally intelligent, and at the age of twelve he took monastic vows. His Buddhist name was Priest Saichō.[12] He studied and trained for several years, but thinking that he wished to further "polish the rare and wondrous jewel," he traveled to China, where he plumbed the depths of the exoteric and esoteric schools of Buddhism and received instruction in the deepest teachings. Then he returned to Japan. He is the person known as Dengyō Daishi.

9. This is a verse from the Nirvana Sutra. Kuruson (Skt. Krakucchandha) was the fourth of six buddhas to appear in the world before Shakyamuni.
10. The latter five hundred years refers to the fifth of five five-hundred-year periods after the death of Shakyamuni.
11. This is the site of Ōmiwa Shrine in the city of Sakurai.
12. Saichō (767–822) was the progenitor of the Tendai school of Buddhism in Japan, and the founder of Enryakuji Temple on Mount Hiei.

The Demon of Ibuki

Shuten Dōji's demon-retainers bring him a variety of meaty treats. (From the three-scroll *Ibuki Dōji emaki*, courtesy of the British Museum. © The Trustees of the British Museum. All rights reserved)

Around that time, the Kashiwabara emperor moved the Nara capital to the Otagi region of Yamashiro Province—what is now the blessed vicinity of our present Heian capital.[13] Saichō addressed the emperor, saying, "Please allow me to construct a temple to the northeast of the imperial city, for the protection of the state.[14] I will guard the land and pray for your auspicious reign." The emperor was pleased, and because he and Saichō were of one mind on the matter, he instructed him to build his temple. Saichō climbed up Mount Hiei and looked around for a pure, sacred spot. He heard a voice in the wild chanting the Lotus Sutra, and when he sought it out, he found that it was emanating from deep within the earth. "This is where I should build my temple," he thought, making up his mind.

Shuten Dōji saw what was afoot. "If a temple is built here and this becomes a restricted Buddhist space," he thought, "then I won't be able to live on this mountain anymore. I'll have to put a stop to it somehow." Shuten Dōji had previously

13. The Kashiwabara emperor was Emperor Kanmu (737–806, r. 781–806). The Otagi region of Yamashiro Province comprises the northern and northeastern areas of the Kyoto valley.
14. Saichō asks to be allowed to construct a temple in the *kimon* (demon's gate). According to traditional yin-yang thought, demons and other malevolent beings infiltrate human habitations from the northeast, which is why the northeastern corners of cities, parks, buildings, and other public and private spaces are known as "demon gates."

attained supernatural powers, so in the course of a single night, he transformed into a cedar tree dozens of arm spans around and planted himself on the chosen site. Many woodcutters tried to cut him down, but their efforts were for naught. Saichō paid obeisance to the ten directions and intoned the following verse:

anokutara	You Buddhas
sanmyaku sanbodai no	of Most Perfect
hotoketachi	Enlightened Wisdom—
waga tatsu soma ni	bestow your silent protection
myōga arasetamae	on this forest that I fell![15]

The cedar dwindled and disappeared like frost in the morning sun.

Saichō built a temple in that place and designated it the "Konpon Chūdō" central hall. He enshrined a statue of Yakushi, the Medicine King Buddha, and brought the Tendai teachings there. In its three pagodas, the mountain manifests the three monastic pursuits of righteousness, serenity, and wisdom; in its three thousand priests, its members evince the principle of "three thousand in a single thought."[16]

Later, Saichō lived in solitude at the top of Little Hiei Peak, where he composed:

Hamo-yama ya	Ah, Mount Hamo!
Obie no sugi no	The wind blows cold
hitori-i wa	and no one comes to call
arashi mo samushi	at a hermit's cedar dwelling
tou hito mo nashi	on Little Hiei Peak.[17]

When he recited this verse, the three lights of the sun, the moon, and the stars appeared in the sky. Saichō contemplated them intently as they transformed into images of Shakyamuni, Yakushi, and Amida, and then merged into a single whole and revealed a variety of propitious signs. From before, Saichō had revered the god of

15. This is poem 1920 in *Shinkokin wakashū* (*New Collection of Ancient and Modern Poems*, 1205) and appears in numerous other sources.
16. "Three thousand in a single thought" (*ichinen sanzen*) is a fundamental Tendai Buddhist concept, according to which all phenomena (represented by the number three thousand) are contained within the single human heart-mind.
17. This is a variant of poem 2107 in *Fūga wakashū* (*Poetry Collection of Elegance*, 1344–1346), attributed to "the guardian deity of [Mount] Hiei."

this mountain as the Sannō Deity, recognizing it as a wondrous manifestation of neither-one-nor-three Middle Path Ultimate Reality.[18]

Mount Hiei, written with the characters for "imperial compare," is so-named because the emperor compared his heart to Saichō's. The temple itself is called Enryakuji. It propagates the Tendai Mahayana traditions in this Latter Age of the Law, and its monks have always prayed for a long imperial reign. Their efforts are truly auspicious.

As for Shuten Dōji, because he was despised by the buddhas of the three ages and detested by the deities of the seven shrines, it became impossible for him to continue living in his fortress-cavern. He ran away to Tanba Province, where he found a grotto in a place called Mount Ōe. His home was dreadfully imposing. It was surrounded by towering, craggy peaks over which not even the birds could fly,

18. Neither-one-nor-three Middle Path Ultimate Reality is the penultimate reality of this world, in which all phenomenon both exist and do not exist, and in which the three Tendai truths of emptiness (*kū*), provisionality (*ke*), and the simultaneity of the two (*chū*) are neither a single truth nor three separate truths.

Shuten Dōji drinks saké with a bevy of abducted noblewomen at his palace on Mount Ōe. (From the three-scroll *Ibuki Dōji emaki*, courtesy of the British Museum. © The Trustees of the British Museum. All rights reserved)

and in the deep valley below, there was not even a winding road upon which a traveler might pass. He carved boulders out of that most treacherous place and piled them up for a stone wall. He built a stone gate and set his demon-retainers to guarding it night and day. Toward the back, he built a vast stone palace and took up residence there. He would fly all around, extorting treasure, and he would abduct beautiful noblewomen and make them serve him like his wives and palace attendants. Reveling in his glory, he wallowed in extremes of pleasure unheard of in previous ages. His palace was known as the "demon castle."

TRANSLATION AND INTRODUCTION BY KELLER KIMBROUGH

The Demon of Ibuki

The Tale of Tawara Tōda

Among the many legendary warriors of Japan in the Heian (794–1185) and medieval (1185–1600) periods, few have been more widely celebrated in literature and art than Fujiwara no Hidesato, more commonly known by his sobriquet of Tawara Tōda Hidesato. His most enduring legacy—the medieval *Tale of Tawara Tōda* (*Tawara Tōda monogatari*)—survives in a plethora of illustrated books and picture scrolls from the sixteenth through twentieth centuries. *The Tale of Tawara Tōda* was cobbled together from a large number of preexisting textual sources, including the martial chronicles *Taiheiki* (*Record of Great Peace*, late fourteenth century), *Genpei jōsuiki* (*The Rise and Fall of the Minamoto and Taira Clans*, late fourteenth century), and *Heiji monogatari* (*The Tale of Heiji*, 1221?); the *setsuwa* anthology *Kojidan* (1212–1215); and various other works. Nevertheless, the stitching was generally good, and except for a few loose threads, the story holds together as a sensible whole. The tale is particularly well known for several major events: Hidesato's encounter with a dangerous monster, his subsequent journey to the palace of the Dragon King at the bottom of Lake Biwa, and his battle with the supernatural Taira no Masakado, the infamous rebel who has six body doubles. So while it bears some resemblance to medieval military tales, it also depicts a journey to another world.

In the textual line translated here, from the early Edo period (1600–1867), which contains a longer and more developed version of the story than the Konkai Kōmyōji picture scroll, from the Muromachi period (1337–1573),[1] *The Tale of Tawara Tōda* presents its protagonist as an unscrupulously ambitious young man with a profound

The translation and illustrations are from the three-scroll *Tawara Tōda monogatari* picture scrolls (early Edo period) in the collection of the Department of Japanese Language and Literature at Gakushūin University, typeset and annotated in Ichiko Teiji et al., eds., *Muromachi monogatari shū 2*, Shin Nihon koten bungaku taikei 55 (Tokyo: Iwanami Shoten, 1992), 87–139.

1. Matsumoto Ryūshin, "Zōtei Muromachi jidai monogatari-rui genzonbon kanmei mokuroku" [classification of manuscripts], in *Otogizōshi no sekai*, ed. Nara Ehon Kokusai Kenkyū Kaigi (Tokyo: Sanseidō, 1982),

concern for etiquette. Despite his obviously heroic qualities, which are particularly apparent in the first part of the tale, Hidesato seems to be marked in the latter half of his story by a surprising moral ambiguity, confounding the usually clear-cut distinction between hero and villain in medieval Japanese fiction. For someone who will later fight for the court against the heinous Masakado, he displays an astonishing willingness to depose the emperor if it might result in his own personal gain; and it is only after observing Masakado's unkempt appearance and poor table manners that he actually resolves to oppose him. Masakado, however, may appear to some contemporary readers as a relatively sympathetic figure, suggesting a complexity of characterization that would indicate that in some *otogizōshi*, at least, the line between hero and villain may be less than clearly drawn.

The Tale of Tawara Tōda may be unique in its sectarian orientation: unlike most works of medieval fiction, which tend to champion Pure Land Buddhist doctrine (and, somewhat more rarely, that of the Zen sects), Hidesato's story displays an unusual affinity for the Tendai-*mikkyō* esoteric tradition and the cult of the Future Buddha, Miroku Bodhisattva.

In the age of Emperor Suzaku there was a famous, valiant warrior by the name of Tawara Tōda Hidesato.[2] He was the eldest son of Murao Ason of the Junior Fifth Rank, Upper Grade, and a fifth-generation descendant of Minister of the Left Lord Kawabe Uona, who was descended from Supreme Minister Kamatari of old. Murao Ason lived in Tawara Village, which is why Hidesato took the name Tawara Tōda at his donning-of-the-cap ceremony at the age of fourteen.[3] He was summoned to the palace in his youth, and he served there for many years.

One time, Hidesato visited his father at home. Murao Ason was in an especially good mood, and meeting with his son, he pressed him with wine and said, "As a parent, it would be laughable of me to sing the praises of my own child. However, you outshine other men's sons, and you cut an awfully fine figure with a sword at your side. Indeed, you look like a man who's bound to uphold the honor of his ancestors. Speaking of which, we have a wondrous sword in our family that's been passed down

---

103b. The Konkai Kōmyōji *emaki* is photographically reproduced in Okudaira Hideo, ed., *Otogizōshi emaki* (Tokyo: Kadokawa Shoten, 1982), 66–77.

2. Tawara Tōda Hidesato was born Fujiwara no Hidesato (d. 958?). Emperor Suzaku (also Shujaku; 922–952, r. 930–946) is traditionally counted as the sixty-first emperor of Japan.

3. The name Tōda indicates that he was a first-born son of the Fujiwara clan.

through the generations since the time of Minister Kamatari.[4] I am too old to keep it anymore, so I'll pass it on to you now. Take this blade and earn yourself a marvelous reputation." The father produced a gilded long sword—more than three feet in length, it seemed—and set it before Hidesato. In his joy, the son reverently raised it to his head three times and then humbly withdrew.

After inheriting the sword, Hidesato was all the more emboldened. Everything went as he wished. Whether with a blade or a bow, no one could compare. He was granted lands in Shimotsuke Province as a reward for his outstandingly faithful service to the emperor, and it was happily decided that he would make his way there.[5]

Now around that time, there was a great dragon-snake sprawled across Seta Bridge in Ōmi Province,[6] obstructing the way for rich and poor alike. Thinking this suspicious, Hidesato went to have a look. The serpent indeed seemed to be some two hundred feet long, and it was lying spread atop the bridge. Its two eyes shone like a pair of suns in the sky, and its twelve horns bristled like the spiky treetops of a withered winter forest. It seemed to be spitting flames as it flicked its crimson tongue between its overlapping iron fangs. If any ordinary people were to see it, they would likely lose their wits and fall dead on the spot. But because Hidesato was such a great strong man, he paid it little mind. Blithely stepping on the monster's back, he crossed over and continued on his way. The dragon-snake did not appear to be the least bit surprised, and Hidesato, too, left it far behind without once looking back.

From there, Hidesato set out on the Eastern Sea Road. As the sun set behind the western mountains, he took lodging in the great main room of an inn. The night grew late, and as Hidesato was adjusting his pillow for a light, dreamless sleep, the innkeeper announced, "I don't know who she is, sir, but there's a weird woman standing by the gate who says she wants to see you."

"Well, that's unexpected," Hidesato replied. "I wonder who she could be, saying she wants to see me! I can't begin to imagine. But she must have something on her mind to have come all this way. If she's got something to ask, then show her inside."

The innkeeper reported this to the woman. "Oh, it's nothing serious," she said. "I come from around the capital, and there's a little thing I'd like to request. I'm really very sorry, but could he please come out here instead?"

Since he could not very well refuse, Hidesato immediately got up and went outside the gate. Looking around, he saw a lady in her early twenties standing by herself. Her face was so lovely that it lit up the space all around. The clean sweep of

4. Fujiwara no Kamatari (614–669) was the progenitor of the Fujiwara.
5. Shimotsuke Province (present-day Tochigi Prefecture) lay in the eastern part of Japan, far from the Heian capital (Kyoto).
6. Seta Bridge spans the Uji River at the southern tip of Lake Biwa, immediately to the east of Kyoto.

Hidesato steps over the great dragon-snake at Seta Bridge. (From *Tawara Tōda monogatari*, courtesy of the Gakushūin University Department of Japanese Language and Literature)

her hair was exquisite, as if she were from another world. It was utterly uncanny. "Excuse me," he said, abashed at the sight, "but it's unsettling that a total stranger should take the trouble to seek me out so late at night."

The lady sidled up to Hidesato. "Indeed," she said in a low voice, "it stands to reason that you wouldn't recognize me. I am not a regular sort of person. I am a female transformation of the dragon-snake you met today at Seta Bridge."

"I knew it!" Hidesato thought, and he asked, "So what brings you here like this?"

"You must have heard of me from before," she said. "I live in the lake in Ōmi.[7] I've made my home there since the ancient opening of the shining realm of heaven, the jelling of the ore-rich earth, and the creation of these isles of Japan. In all the seven times that the lake has turned to mulberry fields and back again, I have never shown myself to people. But in the reign of Empress Genshō, forty-fourth human sovereign, the secondary *inko* deity of Japan descended from the heavens to the peak of Mount Mikami beside my lake.[8] A centipede appeared on the mountain, and in all the years since then, it has been devouring the animals of the mountains and fields

7. Lake Biwa, in present-day Shiga Prefecture, is the largest lake in Japan.
8. Empress Genshō (680–748) reigned from 715 to 724. The meaning of *inko* is unknown. Mount Mikami stands to the east of the southern tip of Lake Biwa, near Seta.

The Tale of Tawara Tōda

and the fishes of the rivers and bays. Sometimes it eats my kind, too. Thus, in addition to suffering the Three Burning Torments,[9] my fellow dragon-snakes and I are beset with constant sorrow. Even if we were to devise a plan somehow to destroy our enemy and restore the security of the past, it would be hard for creatures like us to carry out. I thought that if there were a human who was up to the task, I could ally with him and ask his help. I therefore lay across Seta Bridge to test the people as they passed. But in all the time I was there, no one would come near! Then, today, the way you behaved . . . it was almost too brave to bear! Since you are the only one who can wreck our enemy, I have come here with my hopes set on you. The safety of my realm depends on your reply alone."

The woman was persuasive. Having listened carefully to her request, Hidesato thought, "What a dilemma! While it would be shameful for me to refuse such an extraordinary creature when it has come here counting on my help, it would be a disgrace to my ancestors and a dishonor to my own descendants if I were to take on the task and fail. But still, it's really thanks to the favor of my patron deity that this thing has come here to ask me, out of everyone in the sixty-plus provinces of Japan. And most of all, how could I object when I hear that it's because the Dragon Palace and Japan are joined lands of the Diamond and Womb Realm Mandalas that the Sun Goddess Amaterasu both conceals her true form in the august image of Dainichi Buddha and reveals her manifest form as a dragon deity of the great blue ocean?" Having thus made up his mind, Hidesato said, "Let's not wait. We should go tonight to destroy your enemy." The woman was overjoyed, and she disappeared without a trace.

Not wishing to be late, Hidesato put on his heirloom sword. He took up his rattan-wrapped bow—the one that never left his side and that required five ordinary men to string—and strung it with a silk-wrapped and lacquered bowstring. Placing it under his arm, he hurried off for Seta with only three great arrows in hand. They were fifteen handbreadths and three fingers long, carved from three-year-old bamboo and with elongated heads extending past the midpoint of their shafts.

Hidesato peered out over the edge of the lake. When he looked up at Mount Mikami, he saw repeated flashes of lightning. "That must be the monster coming," he thought as he stared. After a while, amid a ferocious flurry of wind and rain, he saw two or three thousand blazing torches coming down from the tall peak of Mount Hira, rolling and swaying like the mountain itself was astir. The noise as it shook the heights and rang through the valleys was like a billion peals of thunder, frightening beyond expression.

9. The Three Burning Torments are three special agonies that snakes and dragons are said to suffer in the animal realm.

Hidesato slays the centipede. (From *Tawara Tōda monogatari*, courtesy of the Gakushūin University Department of Japanese Language and Literature)

Nevertheless, being such a famously brave warrior, Hidesato was not troubled in the least. Deciding that this must be the enemy of the Dragon Palace, he notched an arrow and waited for the monster's approach. When it was in range, he drew his bow to the full and shot for what seemed to be the middle of the creature's forehead. The arrow bounced off the beast with a clang as if it had hit an iron plate.

Hidesato anxiously strung a second arrow. Aiming for the same spot, he drew his bow to the full, held it for a while, and then let his missile fly. But that one, too, simply ricocheted off without penetrating at all.

Of his three arrows, Hidesato had now lost two. All his hopes were pinned on the third. He racked his brains, wondering what to do if this one, too, should fail. He spit on the point, fit his arrow to his bow, and prayed in his heart to the great bodhisattva Hachiman. Aiming again for the same spot, he pulled back on the string and sent his shaft whizzing through the air. This time, the arrow seemed to land with a thud, whereupon the two or three thousand torches that he had seen all went out at once. The great thunderous noise, too, was suddenly squelched.

Thinking that the monster must have been destroyed, Hidesato had his attendants light torches. Having a good look at the creature, he saw that it certainly was a centipede. The noise of a billion thunderclaps had been the sound it made against

The Tale of Tawara Tōda

the earth, and the two or three thousand torches appeared to have been its legs. Its head was like that of an ox-headed demon, huge beyond compare. Hidesato's arrow had pierced it through the center of its forehead and come straight out below its throat. Even if it were natural that the beast would die from such a wound, it was a testament to Hidesato's prowess as a warrior that he was able to crush such a massive creature with a single piercing shaft.

Now the first two arrows had been deflected as if they had been shot into iron. But the third one penetrated because its point was daubed with saliva, which is generally poisonous to centipedes. Since the monster had been such a mighty one, Hidesato wondered if it might not yet seek revenge. He therefore hacked it to pieces and threw them in the lake, after which he returned to his inn.

The next night, the same lady appeared as before. This time, she immediately entered the great main room, saying, "I'd like to see Master Tōda, please." Hidesato met with her at once. In a cheerful voice, she said, "Thanks to your great strength, our long-standing enemy has been subdued and an age of peace achieved. Very well done! I'm so happy, I don't know how to repay you. I thought I might begin by offering you at least some personal items, which I've brought here now." Gazing at the gifts laid out before him, Hidesato saw two rolls of silk, a straw *tawara* rice sack sewn shut at the top, and a single crimson-copper pan.[10]

He immediately bowed his head and said, "How thoughtful of you! But it was thanks to divine intervention that I was able to achieve such a great feat of arms, to say nothing of your own happiness. Could there be any equal glory for my family? And then, to receive these treasures to boot . . . it's a joy on top of a joy."

The lady, too, was pleased. "Well then," she said, "I should return home tonight. But rest assured that I am not alone in my delight. You have benefited ten million beings, and we will repay you for even more." With that, the woman returned to an unknown place.

Hidesato took out the rolls of silk that he had received and began to make a robe. But however much he cut, he never ran out. Then he opened the straw *tawara* rice sack. He scooped out rice, but the sack, too, was never depleted. This is why he came to be called Tawara (Rice Sack) Tōda.[11] Finally, the pan would well up with whatever food Hidesato wished, which was especially miraculous.

Thinking that he might yet witness some miracle, Hidesato waited. Sure enough, as the moonlit night deepened, the lady visited him again. Hidesato hurried out and invited her in through the middle gate. Taking in her appearance, he saw that she

10. Crimson copper (*shakudō*) is an alloy of copper and gold comprising 3 to 6 percent gold.
11. Previously in the tale, Hidesato is said to have received his name as a result of his father living in Tawara Village.

was even more beautiful than before. People speak of Princess Yaśodharā of India, or Xi Shi and Li Furen of the Tang,[12] but how could even they have compared? Hidesato simply stared in wonder as if she were some celestial nymph descended from Śakra's palace in the Trāyastriṃśa heaven.

The Dragon Lady spoke: "As I explained before, our entire clan is overjoyed that you were able to destroy our longtime enemy with such ease. Many of my people have come to me wishing to repay our debt, and although that might seem simple enough, you may find it an inconvenience. So, although I hate to trouble you, I have come to ask if you will allow me to take you back with me to my home. After the kindness you've shown us already, there's no need for you to feel any reserve. Please come with me now."

"Since she's treating me with such consideration," Hidesato thought, "it couldn't be so bad," and he hurried off with her toward the Dragon Palace.

The Dragon Lady led Hidesato into the brimming, boundless lake. He looked straight down, but the bottom was nowhere in sight. After pushing through smoky waves from unseen depths, they encountered churning, cloudy waves. Forcing their way through those, they came to the end of the Water Wheel plane. Passing through that, they reached the rim of the Metal Wheel, after which they neared the edge of the Wind Wheel.[13] Then they emerged into a land like our own.

"This is where I live," the woman said. When Hidesato looked up, he saw a great golden gate and a seven-jeweled palace soaring some fifty feet in the air. The buildings sparkled all around. The Dragon King's retainers—all manner of scaly, non-human creatures—were bustling about the gate and other structures, each according to its duty. They were no different from the palace gate guards in our own sunlit realm.

When the Dragon Lady led Hidesato through the gate, all the dragon deities bowed their heads in salutation. Inside the palace grounds, various kinds of trees stood with blossoms abloom. Each of the blossoms overflowed with seven-jeweled fruit, just like in the paradise world.[14]

After passing through the great gate, Hidesato and the woman clambered up a jeweled ladder so fragrant that it perfumed their very feet. At the top was a huge decorated palace building reminiscent of the Shishinden Ceremonial Hall.[15] The

12. Princess Yaśodharā was the beautiful wife of Prince Siddhārtha before his enlightenment as Shakyamuni Buddha. Xi Shi (seventh–sixth century B.C.E.) and Li Furen (second century B.C.E.) were famous beauties of ancient China.
13. According to traditional Buddhist cosmology, the earth is undergirded by three "wheels" or planes: the Metal Wheel (*konrin*), the Water Wheel (*suirin*), and the Wind Wheel (*fūrin*). In this story, the order of the first two planes is reversed.
14. The paradise world is the Pure Land Paradise of Amida (Skt. Amitābha) Buddha.
15. The Shishinden Ceremonial Hall is another name for the Great Throne Hall in the Imperial Palace in Kyoto.

Hidesato (*right*) visits the underwater palace of the Dragon King. (From *Tawara Tōda monogatari*, courtesy of the Gakushūin University Department of Japanese Language and Literature)

courtyard was strewn with an endless supply of crushed lapis lazuli and pearl sand, and the golden pillars, jeweled rafter caps, seven-jeweled railings, and jeweled stone floors gave the building a warm sensation. The resplendent, majestic beauty of the palace hall was of a sort never heard of, much less seen, before.

The Dragon Lady held Hidesato by the sleeve. "Here," she said, seating him in a jeweled liturgist's chair that she had placed in the center of the main room. After a while, some musicians began to play. Then Sāgara Dragon King, the first of the Eight Great Dragon Kings,[16] entered with his eighty-four thousand attendants and sat on a jeweled throne. The Dragon Lady likewise perched on a throne. After taking their respective seats, they exchanged elaborate greetings. A dragon woman with her hair twisted into buns on either side of her head emerged, bearing a tray of assorted delicacies. She placed it first before the Dragon King, then Hidesato, and then the Dragon Lady. The food and drink were extraordinary—pleasant to taste and fragrant beyond compare.

Some time passed, after which an attendant brought out a golden plate bearing a goblet of ambrosial dew and a silver flagon full of heavenly wine. These, too, were

16. According to the Lotus Sutra, Sāgara is actually the third of the Eight Great Dragon Kings. He is also the father of the eight-year-old dragon girl who attains enlightenment in the "Devadatta" chapter of the sutra.

MONSTERS, WARRIORS, AND JOURNEYS TO OTHER WORLDS

served first to the Dragon King, who drank from them three times. Then they were served to Hidesato, who likewise drank three times. Their flavor was that of sweet celestial nectar, impossible to describe. People believe that it was thanks to the virtues of these wines that Furan and Udraka Ramaputra lived for eighty thousand years.[17]

The formalities of the banquet were different from those of Japan; rather than passing the cup or pouring for others, everyone simply drank as much as they pleased. Rare fruits from the land and sea were heaped up like Mount Hōrai. In addition, Hidesato was fêted with gifts in the most splendid style. He wondered in his heart how even the glories of King Bonten's palace might match the pleasures here.[18]

"Is there any suffering in such an excellent land as this?" Hidesato inquired.

"Of course," the Dragon King replied. "That goes without saying. Whether it's the Five Dilapidations of the Heavenly Realm, the Eight Agonies of the Human Realm, or the Three Burning Torments of the Dragon Palace, there's no place at all without pain. In particular, we suffered an awful scourge here for many years, but thanks to you—wielding your wondrous powers to destroy our foe with such ease— it's the same as if we were saved by the buddhas and deities. We are deeply grateful. When people speak of the joy of ten thousand births from a single death, this is what they mean. It will be hard to pay you back in full, and we may never succeed. We'll always be thankful to your descendants for what you've done."

The Dragon King presented Hidesato with a golden suit of armor and a matching long sword. "Wear this armor and bear this sword," he said, "to serve as general and defeat the enemies of the court." Next, the Dragon King had his retainers bring out a crimson-copper temple bell. "As for this bell," he said, "long ago, when the great sage Shakyamuni Buddha appeared in central India, a wealthy man named Sudatta built Jetavana Temple and offered it to him. At that time, this bell was cast to reproduce the sound of the Jetavana infirmary bells, and for that reason it rings with the impermanence of all things. To hear it is instantly to dispel the darkness of delusion and arrive at the shore of enlightenment. Because this bell is such a great mysterious treasure, we have kept it here for many years. But I present it to you now as one of our gifts. Please make it a treasure of Japan."

"The armor and the sword will be true family heirlooms," Hidesato replied. "As for the bell, since I am a warrior, it is not something that I particularly desire. However, now that I have heard its history, I cannot think of any greater treasure for my people in the ages to come. I am especially grateful. Still, how can I take such a heavy object back with me? It's a problem."

81

---

17. Udraka Ramaputra was an ascetic and one of Siddhārtha's teachers. Furan is unknown.
18. Bonten (Skt. Mahābrahman) is a Hindu god incorporated into Buddhism as a Buddhist protective deity. He appears, in this volume, as a character in *The Origins of Hashidate.*

The Dragon King smiled. "How right you are! Although we may not rival your kind in our ability to take up arms and destroy our foes, our retainers are used to handling things like this. Please give it no concern." The king spoke to his fishy attendants, who pulled the bell off into the water.

Time was quickly passing. Hidesato recalled how once long ago, the son of someone named Urashima of Mizunoe in the Yoza region of Tango Province had met a woman named Otohime and inadvertently come to this eternal land.[19] He had been immersed in pleasures like these, whereupon he forgot about the past and the future and let three years go by. Missing his home one time, he took leave of Otohime and returned to Mizunoe. But when he looked around, he saw that his old hometown was changed and that there was no one there he knew. Wondering how this could be, he asked all around. Someone told him that he spoke of a time more than three hundred years before. What a surprise! People say that in the end he died. Hidesato took this as a warning. "I serve the emperor," he thought, "and I have an elderly father and mother back at home, so I'd like to keep an eye on the time."

Hidesato asked to take his leave, and because his request had come so soon, the dragon deities were all the more sad to see him go. In their grief, they sought to amuse him with every manner of diversion.

Now the Dragon Lady looked after Hidesato and entertained him in various ways, but because the time was quickly passing, he took his leave of the great king and set out from the Dragon Palace. He seemed to walk in the water for just a moment, whereupon he arrived at Seta Bridge. From there, he went to see his father, Murao Ason, to whom he recounted everything that had happened from beginning to end. Hidesato's father and mother were amazed and exceptionally pleased.

"The Dragon King's presents include a golden sword, a golden suit of armor, and a crimson-copper temple bell," Hidesato explained. "Since the sword and armor are precious treasures for a warrior, I'll pass them on to my descendants. The bell belongs at a temple, so it's of no use to a layman. I should offer it to the Three Jewels.[20] Maybe I'll give it to a temple in Nara, or maybe I'll give it to Enryakuji Temple on Mount Hiei."

"Indeed," the father replied, "these are all truly priceless treasures. And among them, that bell! It would be marvelous to donate it to a temple in supplication for our coming meeting with the Future Buddha.[21] It may be true that the inner realizations of

---

19. Hidesato remembers the legend of Urashima Tarō, the famous fisherman whose story is told in an *otogizōshi* bearing his name.

20. The Three Jewels (or Treasures) of Buddhism are the Buddha, the dharma (teachings of the Buddha), and the sangha (monastic community).

21. The Future Buddha is presently the bodhisattva Miroku (Skt. Maitreya), who is prophesied to appear in the world as the next human buddha after Shakyamuni.

the many buddhas and bodhisattvas are actually a single expedient means,[22] but even so, please offer your bell to the principal image at Mii Temple.[23] I'll give you some reasons why. For one, it's in our province. Also, the guardian deity of Mii Temple is Shinra Daimyōjin, a god of warriors to whom we should pray for the martial skills of our descendants. Finally, the principal image at Mii Temple is Miroku Bodhisattva. By means of the merit you'll accrue, you'll be able to seal a karmic bond to see him and hear him preach at the Dawn of the Three Assemblies when he appears in this world 5,670,000,000 years after the death of Shakyamuni. What's more, Nara and Mount Hiei already have bells. But at Mii Temple, nothing rings at all these days. Now hurry and make up your mind."

"In that case," Hidesato said, having taken in these particulars, "I should give it to Mii Temple." And with that, he sent a message to the temple.

Chitsune traveled to Mii Temple,[24] where he met with the superintendent and explained his father's intentions. The superintendent was immensely pleased; he convened an assembly of monks from throughout the temple complex and engaged them in a lively discussion. "Since the founding of our institution," he said, "we have prospered with the help of great patrons. And because we are a principal center for Buddhist practice, we have entrusted the ringing of bells to the heart alone. But insofar as this is a bell that was brought back from the Dragon Palace, it is incomparably precious and will be an honor for us for ages to come. Rather than debating this matter any further, we should simply accept the offering." The entire assembly of monks agreed.

"Choose an auspicious day," the superintendent instructed Chitsune, "and please give us your bell. You should present it to the temple right away." Then he sent him back.

Upon hearing the decision, Hidesato traveled to Karasaki Beach.[25] When he looked around, he found the bell. It seemed to have been brought up from the Dragon Palace in the night. "It won't be easy to pull to Mii Temple without a lot of workmen," he fretted. Then, the night before the ceremony, some small snakes crawled out of the lake,[26] took the bell's dragon-headed crown loop in their mouths, and pulled it

83

22. In other words, the diversity of enlightenment among buddhas and bodhisattvas is in fact a single instrument for guiding and saving sentient beings. According to this logic, no particular buddha or bodhisattva should be preferable to another.

23. Mii Temple (more formally known as Onjōji) is a Tendai institution in present-day Ōtsu City, at the southern tip of Lake Biwa. Its principal image is a statue of Miroku supposedly imported from Baekje, one of the Three Kingdoms of Korea, during the reign of Emperor Yōmei (518–587, r. 585–587).

24. According to the genealogy *Sonpi bunmyaku* (*Blood Lineages, High and Low*, late fourteenth century), Chitsune was Hidesato's fifth son.

25. Karasaki Beach lies on the southwest shore of Lake Biwa in Ōtsu City.

26. Or, "a single small snake." The number of snakes here is unclear.

The Tale of Tawara Tōda

with ease into the courtyard of the Great Lecture Hall. Afterward, they vanished into the air, leaving the superintendent and his monks amazed.

Now the people of the various provinces had heard for some time that a bell would be coming up from the Dragon Palace and that its dedication ceremony would be held on this day at Mii Temple. Thus from distant provinces—to say nothing of those nearby—men and women, lay and monastic, vied to make the pilgrimage. Because the capital was especially close, high and low and young and old flocked from there in droves. The current chancellor, ministers of state, senior nobles, senior court ladies, imperial havens, consorts, and intimates all came to the temple in creaking carts in the hope of sealing a karmic bond for Miroku's Dawn of the Three Assemblies. Packed toe-to-heel before the principal image, they scattered the clouds of the Five Obstructions.[27]

The time soon arrived, whereupon the offering ceremony began in a stately way. The Mii Temple superintendent is reported to have served as the officiant, and the Tendai prelate as the invocator.[28] In addition, several thousand famously virtuous scholar-monks from various temples occupied the assembly seats.

The officiant ascended to his dais. He rang his supplication bell, saying, "In return for these good roots that he has planted, may Master Hidesato enjoy unparalleled pleasure in the present life and Pure Land rebirth on an upper-grade lotus platform in the world to come.[29] In addition, may his ancestors to the seventh generation be immediately released from the painful cycle of rebirth in the Three Worlds and achieve the pinnacles of delight in the heavenly realm.[30] And may all sentient beings everywhere equally receive the benefits of the Buddha, escaping the cycle of birth and death and achieving instant enlightenment." Grateful for the priest's distribution of merit, the people all wept with emotion. Lay and monastic alike shed tears of joy.

How glorious, that bell! Because it rings with the four-verse notes of the Jetavana Temple infirmary bells—that "all things are impermanent, as those that rise will also fall; when rising and falling themselves have ceased, that quiet extinction produces joy"[31]—everyone who hears it awakens from the dream of the long, dark night,

27. According to the Lotus Sutra, the Five Obstructions are five forms of rebirth precluded to women because of their gender, including, most importantly, rebirth as a buddha.
28. The Tendai prelate (zasu) was the superintendent of Enryakuji Temple, headquarters of the Tendai school of Buddhism.
29. According to the Visualization Sutra (Kanmuryōjukyō), there are three grades of rebirth (upper, middle, and lower) in Amida Buddha's Pure Land Paradise. Each of them is divided into an additional three grades, for a total of nine grades of Pure Land rebirth.
30. The Three Worlds are the worlds of desire, form, and non-form. They constitute the three realms of delusion through which sentient beings transmigrate according to their karma.
31. This is a famous verse from the Nirvana Sutra, widely reproduced in Heian-period and medieval Japanese sources.

realizes a desire for the dharma, and achieves the shore of enlightenment. Truly, it is a wondrous miracle of this latter age.

Now if you ask about the origins of Mii Temple, they date to the ancient age of Emperor Tenji, our thirty-ninth human sovereign,[32] and his relocation of the capital to Ōtsu near this lake. Because of a revelation in a dream, the emperor instructed his son Prince Ōtomo to secure a sacred site at the rippling-water Shiga Flower Garden,[33] build a temple, and enshrine a sixteen-foot statue of Miroku Bodhisattva. The temple was named Shūfukuji. Later, after Prince Ōtomo met with misfortune and passed away, his son Prince Yota spoke with the emperor, moved the temple to the site of his father's home, and renamed it Onjōji. There was a pure spring well among the rocks nearby, and because its water was used for the first baths of three generations of newborn sovereigns—Emperor Tenji, Emperor Tenmu, and Empress Jitō—the temple was also called Mii, or "Three Wells," Temple.

Two hundred years eventually passed. At that time, there was a famous, virtuous scholar-monk by the name of Enchin.[34] He was a nephew of Kūkai and the son and heir of Ienari, a resident of the Naka district of Sanuki Province.[35] From childhood, his features were superior to others, and he had two pupils in each of his eyes. He entered the capital at the age of fourteen; at the age of fifteen, he ascended Mount Hiei and shaved his head as a disciple of the Tendai prelate Gishin Kashō.

In the practice hall for melding with the Three Mysteries, Enchin plumbed the depths of the ultimate teachings of the Single Vehicle.[36] Later, in the autumn of Ninju 3 [853], he traveled to China to further seek the dharma. As he was on his way, a sudden, evil wind began to blow. Just as his ship was on the verge of capsizing, Enchin struggled to the gunwale, bowed one time in each of the ten directions, and recited a prayer-vow. The Mantra King Fudō Myōō, divine protector of Buddhism, appeared in a golden incarnation and stood on the ship's prow. Moreover, the Great Mantra Deity Shinra Daimyōjin appeared on the stern before everyone's eyes and took the helm of his own accord. As a result, the ship arrived safely at the port in Ming Province.

---

32. Emperor Tenji (also Tenchi; 626–672, r. 661–671) is traditionally counted as the thirty-eighth emperor of Japan.
33. The Shiga Flower Garden was the name of Tenji's palace at Ōtsu. "Rippling-water" (*sazanami*) is a poetic epithet that normally accompanies the place-name Shiga.
34. Enchin (Chishō Daishi; 814–891) was the fifth prelate of Enryakuji Temple and the founder of the Jimon faction of the Tendai school, headquartered at Onjōji Temple.
35. Kūkai (Kōbō Daishi; 774–835) was the founder of the Shingon school of Japanese esoteric Buddhism.
36. The Three Mysteries (*sanmitsu*) are the body, speech, and mind of the Buddha; in the Tendai-*mikkyō* esoteric tradition, the practitioner seeks to attain union with them through contemplating images, chanting mantras, forming mudras, and the like. The Single Vehicle (*ichijō*) refers to the single unified teaching of the Buddha.

During the six years that he was in China, Enchin studied the profound principles of the exoteric and esoteric teachings under such famous, distinguished monks as Wuwai of Guoqing Temple, Liangxu of Kaiyuan Temple, Dade of Qinglong Temple, and Zhihuilun of Xingshan Temple. Having explored the deepest doctrines, he returned to Japan in Ten'an 2 [858].

As his teachings spread, Enchin became indispensable at court and trusted throughout the land. Because he safeguarded the imperial reign, the emperor declared that he should head Mii Temple. When he entered there, an old monk emerged and identified himself, saying, "I am Kyōdai Kashō. I have been living in this place and waiting for you for more than two hundred years." He handed Enchin a deed to the temple precincts and flew off into the air.[37] Enchin was astonished. Later overseeing the institution, he led it in practicing the secret esoteric teachings.

The temple includes a great lecture hall, forty-eight feet on four sides; a single three-story pagoda; an Amida hall, forty-two feet on four sides; and a four-legged, single-ridged treasury hall containing a sub-shrine to the Sannō Deity.[38] The China Hall houses a Chinese edition of the sutra canon, including more than seven thousand scrolls. In addition, the temple contains an Ima Kumano shrine; a prayer hall to the benevolent guardian deities; a Fugen hall; a Qinglong "Blue Dragon" hall; a pagoda to the Venerable Star King, Myōken Bodhisattva; a great treasury hall; a four-sided ambulatory; and a seventy-two-foot Hall of the Five Elements. In total, the temple comprises more than 630 larger and smaller buildings and two thousand buddha images.

Since it was a holy place of steadfast purity, Enchin scooped the temple's well-flower waters as an offering to the Buddha in the ritual of the Three Part Consecration.[39] Some people say that it was because he awaited Miroku's Dawn of the Three Assemblies in this way that the temple came to be called Mii, or "Three Wells," Temple.

But for whatever reason, such an excellent practice center eventually burned. It happened like this: after Enchin's death, the community of monks at Mii Temple petitioned the authorities to construct an ordination platform. The monks of Enryakuji protested and appealed, and donning their priestly robes of meekness and forbearance,

37. According to a related account (11:28) in *Konjaku monogatari shū* (*Collection of Tales of Times Now Past*, early twelfth century), the old monk was a manifestation of Miroku. The name Kyōdai 教待 is written with characters meaning "wait to teach," a sentiment appropriate to the Future Buddha. Kashō is a monastic title.
38. The Sannō Deity is venerated as the guardian god of Enryakuji Temple on Mount Hiei. A four-legged hall is constructed with four subsidiary pillars in addition to its central two.
39. Well-flower waters (*seika no mizu*) are waters drawn from the temple well for Buddhist practices in the pre-dawn hours. The Three Part Consecration (*sanbu kanjō*) is an esoteric rite in the Tendai-*mikkyō* tradition.

they rushed out to attack at Shiga and Karasaki. Some were struck and killed, while others grappled and fell. Drenching the temple in blood, they turned it into an *ashura* battlefield[40]—a deplorable contribution to the destruction of the dharma.

Now Tawara Tōda Hidesato was living in Shimotsuke Province. Having pacified the area, he held sway in the neighboring provinces as well.

Around this time, there was a man named Masakado in the Sōma district of Shimōsa Province.[41] A descendant of Emperor Kanmu, he was the son of General Yoshimasa of the Northeast Pacification Headquarters and a fourth-generation scion of Prince Kazurahara.[42] In the second month of Shōhei 5 [935], Masakado killed his uncle, Deputy Governor Kunika of Hitachi Province. Having come to wield power in eight regions, he built a castle at Isohashi in the Sōma district, styled himself the New Taira emperor, and employed a multitude of officials. Among his younger brothers, he had Mikuri no Saburō Masayori appointed governor of Shimotsuke Province, Ōashiwara no Shirō Masahira appointed deputy governor of Kōzuke Province, Gorō Masatame appointed governor of Shimōsa Province, and Rokurō Masatake appointed governor of Izu Province. In addition, he had Tajimi no Tsuneakira appointed deputy governor of Hitachi Province, Fujiwara no Harumichi appointed governor of Kazusa Province, Fujiwara no Okiyo appointed governor of Awa Province, and Fun'ya no Yoshikanu appointed governor of Sagami Province.[43]

Declaring that he would raise a great army, march on the capital, and become the lord of Japan, Masakado set about making the necessary preparations. Hidesato listened intently to the news. "Indeed," he thought, "in addition to being such a strong, courageous warrior, Masakado commands a ferocious force. I'd like to join him in taking over the country, one half each." And with that, he set out for the Sōma district.

Upon arriving, Hidesato sent a man to the castle with a message: "Tawara Tōda Hidesato, a resident of Shimotsuke Province, has traveled here to meet and speak with the master." A samurai gate guard conveyed the message to Masakado, who at the time happened to be combing out his unbound hair. What could he have been thinking? With his hair disheveled and wearing only an informal white under-robe,

---

40. The *ashura* are a race of supernatural warriors who engage in constant, bloody battle. They occupy the *ashura* realm, one of the Six Realms of unenlightened existence.

41. Taira no Masakado (d. 940) was the notorious leader of a rebellion against the court in 939/940.

42. Prince Kazurahara was a child of Emperor Kanmu (737–806, r. 781–806). The Northeast Pacification Headquarters (Chinjufu) was a military office charged with subduing the Emishi of Michinoku and Dewa provinces.

43. Tajimi no Tsuneakira, Fujiwara no Harumichi, Fujiwara no Okiyo, and Fun'ya no Yoshikanu were four of Masakado's most trusted non-familial retainers.

The Tale of Tawara Tōda

Hidesato (*center*) meets with Masakado (*upper right*) for the first time. (From *Tawara Tōda monogatari*, courtesy of the Gakushūin University Department of Japanese Language and Literature)

he immediately went out to the middle gate and met with Hidesato. Hidesato had always had an eye for detail, and taking note of the lord's appearance, he marked it as a sign of weakness.

Seeking to be hospitable, Masakado set out a tub of rice and urged his guest to dig in. As Masakado ate, he spilled bits of the food that he was chewing on his trouser-skirt and brushed them away with his hand.[44] "This man behaves like a wretched peasant!" Hidesato thought to himself. "Since he's such a dolt, it's unthinkable that he should become the ruler of Japan." And having had a change of heart at their first meeting, he kept his proposal to himself and left in disgust.

From there, Hidesato set out for the capital, traveling day and night. Visiting the palace, he informed the emperor, saying, "Kojirō Masakado of Sōma is plotting an insurrection. He has seized the eight eastern provinces, and what's more, he's raising an army to march on the imperial palace. You should send an envoy to strike him down at once. If you don't act now, it's sure to be a disaster for the court. I myself may be lacking, but if you were to appoint me commander, I could

---

44. Masakado apparently donned a trouser-skirt (*hakama*) before the meal. Or, alternatively interpreted, he may have spit flecks of food on Hidesato's *hakama* instead.

MONSTERS, WARRIORS, AND JOURNEYS TO OTHER WORLDS

probably find a way to effect his execution." The emperor was alarmed, and summoning his senior and junior nobles, he debated the proper course of action with them.

Meanwhile, an additional message arrived from the eastern provinces regarding Masakado's rebellion: "There is no time for delay. Since Hidesato knows his way around the east, it might be best to send him first and then send a large punitive force after that." Everyone agreed that this was an excellent idea. Hidesato was quickly summoned to the palace, where he was presented with an imperial decree: "Regarding the pursuit and punishment of this heinous rebel, His Majesty places his entire trust in your devices. Make your way from here at once. Use every means at your disposal to destroy the traitor, ensure the prosperity of your sovereign, and put the people at ease. Your reward will depend on your achievement. We will be sending additional forces behind you. You must travel day and night with all possible speed."

"What equal honor could there be for a warrior?" Hidesato replied, and emboldened by his charge, he withdrew. Saying that there was no time to waste and that he should be on his way, he set out from the capital before dawn. He passed through Shirakawa and Awataguchi, and as he climbed Hinooka Pass, the sky began to lighten. With sidelong glances toward the Shinomiya Riverbed, he made his way along the Ausaka Barrier mountain road and came to Mii Temple.

Hidesato bowed his head before the lecture hall and prayed: "Hail the great bodhisattva Miroku! If I am to be struck down by my enemy this time, then in return for the single-minded trust that I have placed in you, please spare me from rebirth in the Three Evil Realms."[45] Then visiting the shrine of Shinra Daimyōjin, he prayed, "You most venerable Great Mantra Deity, I ask that you aid me in my plan, let me subdue my enemy with ease, ensure the prosperity of my sovereign, allow the people to thrive, and forge an everlasting reign of peace throughout the land. If you will, then my entire clan and I will be your devoted parishioners for years to come, bowing our heads in reverent obeisance." He prayed for a while with such exceptionally earnest devotion that the deity must have heard his pleas. The inner shrine curtain swayed without a breeze to blow, and the stone-carved lions and guardian dogs that greet supplicants to the left and the right of the shrine hall were seen to stir. Hidesato bowed his head again in grateful adoration, after which he whipped his horse on to the eastern provinces.

Back at the palace, the senior nobles convened a council. Concluding that Masakado's insurrection could not be promptly put down without entreating the buddhas and deities for their help, they requested the virtuous scholar-monks of various

45. The Three Evil Realms (*san akudō*) are the realms of hell, hungry ghosts, and animals.

temples and sacred mountains to perform a subduing curse. First, the Tendai prelate Son'i Sōjō, Esoteric Master of the Hosshōbō Cloister, erected a platform on Mount Hiei and conducted the rite invoking the Mantra King Daiitoku. Next, Jōzō Kisho of Ungoji Temple set up a platform at Yokawa and performed the rite invoking the Mantra King Gōsanze. Then the virtuous scholar-monks at the Konpon Chūdō Central Hall at Enryakuji Temple performed a *goma* fire ritual, and Meitatsu of Mimasaka erected a platform at Jingūji Temple and conducted the rite invoking the Four Heavenly Kings. As these were all royal, virtuous scholar-monks known for the efficacy of their invocations, the court was heartened to think that every one of their ceremonies would succeed and that the enemy would certainly be destroyed.

Now the punitive force to the eastern provinces included men from the Minamoto and Taira clans chosen for their skills in both the literary and the martial arts. Declaring his intent to appoint a supervising general and grant him a Sword of Commission, the emperor first summoned Uji Minister of Civil Affairs Fujiwara no Tadafun. Then, because Taira no Sadamori of Hitachi, the first son and heir of General Kunika of the Northeast Pacification Headquarters, was a warrior like his father and oversaw an especially large number of retainers, the emperor summoned him to be lieutenant general.

Since there was an established ceremony for the supervising general to receive the Sword of Commission and set out for the provinces, the emperor proceeded to the Shishinden Ceremonial Hall. The chancellor went to Lord Ononomiya.[46] Ministers of state, including the Ninth Avenue Lord and other Major Counselors,[47] as well as Middle Counselors, consultants, controllers, and representatives of the Eight Ministries and assorted bureaus, took their places on the steps of the Shishinden, where, at the mid-level banquet-ceremony,[48] the Sword of Commission was produced. The supervising general and lieutenant general entered the palace in the proper way, paid their respects, and received the sword, after which they made a magnificent exit through the small gate to the south of the Archery Hall. They looked splendid.

It was the hour of the horse on the eighteenth day of the first month of Tengyō 3 [940], during the reign of Emperor Suzaku.[49] Because word had spread that on this day the commanders would be leaving for the eastern provinces to vanquish the enemies of the court, hordes of people had come from near and far to see. Men and

---

46. Due to an apparent mistranscription, the meaning of this is unclear. Lord Ononomiya was an alternative appellation for Fujiwara no Saneyori (900–970).
47. The Ninth Avenue Lord was Fujiwara no Morosuke (908–960), although at this time he was still only a Provisional Middle Counselor.
48. Mid-level banquet-ceremonies (*chūgi no sechie*) were attended by courtiers of the sixth and higher ranks.
49. The hour of the horse is approximately 11:00 A.M. to 1:00 P.M.

women, lay and monastic, high and low alike—everyone who had heard the news had gathered side by side along the city streets. Since the transfer of the capital to the city of Heian,[50] there had never been a disturbance like this in all the land. The warriors might as well have forgotten how to wield their bows. But now, with this first strange movement of arms, the men set out with their horses and armor and with long and short swords sparkling and shining in a grand spectacle.

Meeting no obstacles along the way, the party galloped over a slew of perilous passes, eventually arriving at the Kiyomi Barrier in Suruga Province at the beginning of the second month. General Tadafun rested there for a while, taking in the views of fabulously scenic Mount Fuji, the Miho Inlet, and Tago Bay. A poet and deputy commander by the name of Kiyowara no Shigefuji recited a verse at the sight of the bay:[51]

> The cold light of the fishing-boat fires burns the waves;
> A post-road bell echoes through the mountains at night.

The general and his men were moved to weep. They soaked their sleeves in tears of joy.

Lieutenant General Taira no Sadamori summoned his kinfolk and retainers and spoke: "What do you all think? If we spend days on the road in this manner, like a big army, we're bound to miss out on the action. In addition to being a foe of the court, that Masakado was the mortal enemy of my father. For that reason, we have to get to him first and settle this before anyone else. Hidesato is a clever strategist, and he's in the vanguard. If he gets all the glory, it'll be a disgrace to us as warriors. Then our regret won't mean a thing. So how about it? Shall we race out of here, ride day and night, and join up with Hidesato's bunch?" "Yes, right!" the men exclaimed. Spurring their horses forward, they galloped up and down the steep mountain roads of Ashigara and Hakone through the misty moonlit night.

With his two thousand–plus imperial riders, Taira no Sadamori crossed the Ashigara and Hakone mountains before dawn, arriving at the Musashino Plain on the thirteenth day of the second month of Tengyō 3. Joining with Hidesato's forces for a total of more than three thousand riders, his men crossed the Tone River and pitched camp at Isohashi in Shimōsa Province on the fourteenth day of the second month at dawn. Masakado heard reports, and concluding that he could not allow

---

50. The capital was moved from Nagaoka to Heian in 794.
51. Kiyowara no Shigefuji is misidentified here as a supervising general. I have corrected his title based on a related passage in the "Gosechi Dances" section of book 5 of *The Tale of the Heike* (thirteenth century). The verse that he recites is a transliteration of a Chinese couplet by Du Xunhe (846–904), reproduced as poem 502 in *Wakan rōeishū* (*Chinese and Japanese Poems to Be Sung*, ca. 1012).

The Tale of Tawara Tōda

the enemy to breach his stronghold, he immediately sent his brothers Shimotsuke governor Masayori and Ōashiwara no Shirō Masahira with a force of more than four thousand Kazusa and Hitachi riders to a place called Kitayama in the Kōshima district, where they encamped at the hour of the horse on the same day.

Galloping toward the enemy position, Sadamori raised a mighty cry, shouting, "Who do you think I am, charging at you now? Have a look with your eyes, you men nearby, and listen to my words, you all far away! I am Taira no Sadamori of Hitachi, first son of Taira no Kunika, general of the Northeast Pacification Headquarters and a descendant of our fiftieth human emperor. By our lord sovereign's command, I have come here now to put down your heinous rebellion. Since even the earth and trees fall within our emperor's domain, where could wicked villains like you ever find a home? Hurry up and throw down your bows, take off your helmets, and come to your lord!"

Hearing these words, Masayori roared with laughter. "What?" he cried. "Do you think it would be loyal for a man to abandon his brothers for the sake of the emperor? The rank of king might have meant something in the old days of excellent reigns, but in the face of Masakado's power, how could even a Lord of the Ten Virtues compare? In any case, you can have an arrow as an offering to the God of War!" He took out a shaft that was fifteen handbreadths long and polished like a sword. Fitting it noisily to his five-man bow, he let it fly with reckless imprecision. The bowstring seemed to catch on his breastplate and the arrow missed its mark, plunging instead into Sadamori's horse's rump and passing straight through. The horse collapsed like an overturned folding screen, and Sadamori leaped onto his reserve mount.

Perturbed at having squandered an arrow, Masayori drew his three-foot, ten-inch sword and charged at Sadamori. Among the imperial forces were Sadamori's brothers Muraoka no Jirō Tadayori and Saburō Yoritaka, as well as Yogo no Koremori and Koremochi and the like, each of whom was a warrior worth a thousand. More than three hundred of them rushed in to attack. From the other side, Hitachi governor Tsurumochi, Musashi governor Okiyo, and Sakanoue no Chikataka stormed forward with a thousand-plus riders, shouting, "Don't let them kill Masayori!"[52] The mountains, rivers, grasses, and trees all swayed with their ferocious fight. It was a terrible sight to see.

Receiving news of the battle, the New Taira Emperor Masakado exclaimed, "To have dogs like that invade my realm and kick my men around with their horses hooves . . . it's intolerable! I'll cut off every one of their heads and throw them all away!" He donned his chieftain armor, mounted his dapple-gray horse, and whipped

---

52. Previously in the tale, Fujiwara no Okiyo is said to have been the governor of Awa, rather than Musashi, Province.

Masakado and his six shadow-warriors stand ready for battle. (From *Tawara Tōda monogatari*, courtesy of the Gakushūin University Department of Japanese Language and Literature)

it forward. His appearance was truly extraordinary. He stood more than seven feet tall, and his entire body was golden. He had two pupils in his left eye, as well as six body doubles who looked identical to himself. Hence, no one could tell which one was the real Masakado.

When Masakado launched his attack, Masatake and Masatame rallied around him with more than a thousand of their warriors and plunged, without a moment's hesitation, into the middle of their assailants' ranks. Masakado was more frightening than Lu Yang beckoning back the setting sun or King Xiang subduing the three generals, and not one of the enemy would face him.[53] Thus from the hour of the sheep until the hour of the monkey,[54] more than eighty members of the imperial army lost their lives, and hundreds more were injured. Half of the remaining forces fled. Because he had no way left to fight, Sadamori retreated to Musashi Province that night to await reinforcements. Masakado was arrogant by nature, so he looked down on

53. During a battle with the Han in the Chinese Warring States period (403–221 B.C.E.), Lu Yang of Chu is said to have used his spear to reverse the course of the setting sun. King Xiang (Xiang Yu; 232–202 B.C.E.) is said to have beheaded three enemy generals in the Battle of Gaixia in 202 B.C.E.
54. The hour of the sheep is approximately 1:00 to 3:00 P.M., and the hour of the monkey is approximately 3:00 to 5:00 P.M.

The Tale of Tawara Tōda

the imperial army and dismissed it as a threat. Choosing not to pursue the fleeing forces, he let out a great war whoop and returned to his castle.

Having seen Masakado in action, Hidesato thought, "The way he acts, he's hardly human! Even if everyone in all the provinces joined together to take him on, they couldn't hope to win. But people say that he lacks wisdom, and that he has always been weak on strategy. I'll have to come up with a plan to trick him and cut him down." Hidesato discussed the matter with Sadamori and then set out alone for Masakado's Sōma castle.

Masakado met with Hidesato and entertained him warmly. Hidesato flattered him, saying, "When I look at you, you're mightier than the Four Heavenly Kings! What's more, since you're a descendant of Prince Kazurahara, there's no reason why you shouldn't become emperor. It won't be long before you've subdued the entire realm. I don't have many retainers, but if I can be of any use, I'd be honored as a warrior to serve at your side."

Hidesato spoke so convincingly that Masakado was foolishly pleased. "With the help of each of my allies," he replied, "I intend to conquer the entire land for the greater glory of my ancestors. As for you, when I asked around I heard that you're descended from Lord Tankai![55] Once I've restored the peace, we'll govern as master and minister, in perfect accord." Masakado spoke over several cups of wine. His nonchalance was reasonable, perhaps, insofar as his entire body was made of gold. Since he was not frightened to meet with an enemy, it goes without saying that he had no reservations about Hidesato's visit. But considering that this would be his undoing, he cut a sad figure indeed.

Hidesato was given charge of the castle's southern compound, from which he set out daily to serve. One time when he was going to the guardroom, he saw an exquisitely beautiful young woman—about twenty years old, perhaps—through the blinds of the western hall. With one look, he was overcome, and feeling dazed, he returned to his room and collapsed in a stupor. "Truly," he thought, brooding in his bed, "my feelings are like those of the summer insects drawn to a flame. It's a pointless obsession." But try as he might, he could not forget the face he had glimpsed, and in his torment, he thought that he would not mind dying if he could only tell her how he felt.

There was another woman who came and went from the castle, and her name was Shigure. She visited Hidesato's room and said, "Judging from your appearance, this is serious. If you have something on your mind, then tell me, please. I'll help you if it's in my power. Don't hold anything back." The woman spoke with deep consideration.

94

55. Lord Tankai (Tankai-kō) is the posthumous name of Fujiwara no Fuhito (659–720), the second son of Fujiwara no Kamatari.

Hearing this, Hidesato thought, "How nice of her to ask! But who knows what's in the cloudy depths of another person's heart? If I were to disregard all that and confess to something so absurd, destroying myself for an impossible love, I'd be a laughingstock for ages to come." But then he reconsidered. "Still, is there anyone who lives past the age of one hundred? In this life as fleeting as dust or dew, even the autumn stag approaches the hunter's horn because of his love for his mate. I shouldn't begrudge my own life, either, if I'm throwing it away for my darling."

Having made his decision, Hidesato sat up. "How embarrassing!" he whispered. "This must be what people mean when they speak of a person's feelings showing through. So what sort of thing do you think has been bothering me? The other day, when I was on my way to see the master, I caught sight of a lady standing behind a blind in the women's apartments. I've been sick with love ever since! Who'll show me any sympathy in this state I'm in, hovering between life and death?" And he dissolved into tears.

Sensing the truth of Hidesato's love and pitying him for it, Shigure replied, "Well, then, it's just as I suspected! The lady is Kozaishō, the child of my master's former wet nurse. It's the way of the world that people fall in love. If you have something to say, then please write it in a note. I'll see that it's delivered."

Hidesato was overjoyed. On a slip of thin purple paper, the scent of which seemed to rub off on his hands, he simply wrote:

koishinaba	To die of love
yasukarinubeki	would be easier indeed,
tsuyu no mi no	but I'll linger on
au wo kagiri ni	in this dew-like body
nagarae zo suru	until the day we meet.[56]

He folded his message in a knot and handed it to Shigure.

Shigure took the letter to Kozaishō. "Here," she said, "I picked this up someplace. Read it, please." Unsuspectingly, Kozaishō spread out the paper and had a look. "It's a poem," she replied, "written on the topic of 'hidden love.'"

Shigure drew near. "I can't be keeping secrets," she apologized. "A certain gentleman asked me to give you this and then get your reply. I couldn't very well refuse, so I've taken the liberty of bringing it here. But what could be the harm? Why don't you take a short little moment to show him some compassion?" Kozaishō blushed,

56. This is a slight variation on poem 1337 in *Shin shūi wakashū* (*New Collection of Gleanings*, 1364), attributed to the thirteenth-century poet Go-Fukakusa-in no Ben-no-Naishi.

The Tale of Tawara Tōda

the guilt

lost for words. Shigure continued: "If the man dies of unrequited love, with his fierce heart set on you like that, it's bound to haunt you for ages to come. Don't you know about Śubhakara of India? He fell in love with an empress and then burned up in the flames of his own passion."[57]

Shigure spoke at length on the man's behalf, and not being made of stone or wood, Kozaishō wondered sadly what might become of her if the gentleman's feelings were to weigh on her after his death. She therefore wrote a little line at the edge of the paper, which she folded back into a knot and returned to Shigure.

In her happiness, Shigure immediately went to Hidesato's room and handed him the letter. Receiving it with shaky hands, he opened it and read:

hito wa isa	How is it with people,
kawaru mo shirade	so unaware of changes?
ikabakari	For however long
kokoro no sue wo	our love may endure,
togete chigiran	I'll pledge my troth to you.

excuse me? you don't know who he is; there is no "our love"

Hidesato was pleased to no end. From then on, he began to visit her in secret, and they came to share an extraordinary bond. Because they took pains to keep their love concealed, no one in the castle knew of their affair.

Now the New Taira Emperor Masakado had his eye on this lady, and because he, too, was smitten, he would visit her apartments from time to time. On one such occasion, Hidesato happened to discover him there. Being suspicious, Hidesato peered through a gap, whereupon he saw seven identical men in formal attire seated in exactly the same way. Thinking this strange, he returned to his room for the night. He went to see Kozaishō again on the following evening, and after exchanging various pleasantries of love, he said, "Last night I heard someone in here, and since I wondered who it was, I stepped up and peeked through a gap. There were some very dignified-looking men in your room. Who were they?"

"That was Lord Masakado," Kozaishō replied. "Did you mistake him for someone else?"

"If that was the master," Hidesato said, "then he should have been alone. It was certainly odd to see seven gentlemen all dressed in the same way."

"But didn't you know? My lord is superior to ordinary men. He has a single form, but he casts seven bodily shadows, which is why the world sees him as seven people."

---

57. According to various Buddhist and literary sources, the fisherman Śubhakara (J. Jutsubaka) fell in love with an Indian princess and then burned to death in the flames of his unrequited longing.

so many snitches

Hidesato was astonished. "Then is there any way to recognize the real Masakado?"

"It's an absolute secret," the lady replied, "but you, I'll tell. You can't reveal it to anyone, not even if you think it's trivial. Masakado may appear as seven men, all of whom behave in just the same way, but only the real one casts a shadow when he faces the sun or the light of a torch. The other six don't. Furthermore, even though people say that his entire body is golden, the *komekami* rice-spot beside his ear is actually made of flesh and blood."[58] *men dog and his pressure points*

Hidesato listened closely. "Yes!" he thought. "Now I've heard something important. This must be a divine revelation from the Great Mantra Deity back home." And in deepest gratitude, he bowed down and prayed in the direction of his birth province.

Concluding that he could indeed take down Masakado with a single arrow as he had hoped, Hidesato secretly took to carrying a bow under his arm and peeking in on Kozaishō's apartments when he visited her every night. As he had anticipated, Masakado returned to the lady's chambers, where Hidesato found him relaxing and engaging her in small talk. Peering in through a gap, he saw that in the lamplight, six of the figures really did cast no shadow. Heeding what he had heard and staring hard at the one whom he took to be the master, he saw the rice-spot move from time to time. "I've got him!" he thought. He notched his arrow and sent it whizzing. Being an excellent archer, he surpassed even Yang You's skill at a hundred paces,[59] and in this case his target was close. So how, then, could he have missed? The shaft pierced Masakado's head at what seemed to be the base of his ear and ripped through to the other side. The almighty Masakado fell flat on his back and died, and the remaining six figures vanished in a sudden flash of light.

Now that Masakado was destroyed, Sadamori and Hidesato were all smiles. Bearing the heads that they had taken and leading their living captives, they marched for the capital in a boisterous and magnificently powerful procession. Being so far away, the people at the palace had not yet heard what had happened, and amid rumors that the imperial army had been defeated in battle and that Masakado was now launching his attack on the capital, the emperor was alarmed. He sent emissaries to various temples and sacred mountains, instructing them to perform quashing curses with all their might.

Among those he contacted, Jōzō Kisho of Yasaka Temple replied,[60] saying, "The rumors about Masakado marching on the capital are an utter fabrication. If they

58. The *komekami* (rice-spot) is the part of the temple that flexes when a person chews rice.
59. Yang You (also Yang Youji) was a famous Chinese archer of the Spring and Autumn period (770–403 B.C.E.).
60. This is presumably the aforementioned Jōzō Kisho of Ungoji Temple. Yasaka Temple (Yasaka-dera) is another name for Hōganji Temple, in the eastern hills of the Kyoto valley.

The Tale of Tawara Tōda

Hidesato slays Masakado with a single arrow. (From *Tawara Tōda monogatari*, courtesy of the Gakushūin University Department of Japanese Language and Literature)

aren't, then all our rites have been for naught. More likely, his head is on its way." And, indeed, on the twenty-fifth day of the fourth month, Sadamori and Hidesato entered the capital carrying Masakado's head. Thanks to this, the emperor's concerns were relieved, his ministers were reassured, and the hearts of all the people were set at ease.

The imperial police were dispatched at once, and taking charge of Masakado's and his minions' heads, they paraded them along the avenues and then hung them in a tree outside the eastern prison gates. Masakado's head alone remained bright-eyed, its color unchanging, and from time to time it would gnash its teeth in anger. It was terrifying. A man of the arts happened to see it, and he composed:

not a brilliant poem, but silly

Masakado wa	Masakado
komekami yori mo	was shot
irarekeri	through the <u>rice-spot</u>—
Tawara Tōda ga	all according to
hakarikoto nite	"Rice Sack" Tōda's plan.

People say that the head roared with laughter, after which its color changed and its eyes closed.

Now the senior and junior nobles gathered at the palace to dispense rewards for the subjugation of the wicked rebels. Among all the many monks who had prayed, Son'i Sōjō and Jōzō Kisho were granted special honors. Their rewards excelled those of the warriors. Among the emperor's soldiers, Taira no Sadamori was promoted from no rank to Senior Fifth, Upper Grade, and recommended for general by imperial decree; Fujiwara no Hidesato was promoted to Junior Fourth, Lower Grade, and granted the two provinces of Musashi and Shimotsuke. Both Sadamori and Hidesato were summoned to the palace to receive their commendations. The ceremony was truly splendid—a warrior's honor for generations to come.

Having accepted his edict, Tawara Tōda Hidesato picked up his entire clan and moved to Shimotsuke Province, secure in the confirmation of his lands. His prosperity grew with the days and months, such that there was no place to hitch a horse outside his gate and no day on which a banquet was not held inside.[61] Among the people of the province, those who showed him loyalty were rewarded beyond their desserts without even asking, while those who committed offenses were swiftly punished. Because of the justice of his sanctions and rewards, the people admired and obeyed him to no end. In addition, his descendants were exemplary, and they later became generals in their own right. He had dozens of sons, including Oyama no Jirō, Utsunomiya no Saburō, Ashikaga no Shirō, and Yūki no Gorō, adding to the majestic glory of the clan.

The fact that Hidesato was able to destroy Masakado and wield power in the eastern provinces was thanks entirely to the support of the dragon deities. And how could this be? Dragon deities manifest as women, which is why Kozaishō and Shigure felt sorry for Hidesato in the cloudy depths of their hearts and gave him such vital information, allowing him to achieve the pinnacle of fame. If we think about it long and hard, it seems that the dragon deities may have entered into these women's hearts. Mysterious indeed! Moreover, it was thanks to the profound blessings of Miroku Bodhisattva, the principal image at Mii Temple, that Hidesato's descendants inherited his prosperity. In the sixty-plus provinces of Japan, among the many warrior houses that take the name Fujiwara, all are likely descended from him. What an extraordinary example from the past!

TRANSLATION AND INTRODUCTION BY KELLER KIMBROUGH

61. There was no place to tether a horse because of the large number of visitors to his estate.

The Tale of Tawara Tōda

The Origins of Hashidate

According to the model of the world inherited from Buddhist cosmology, the Japanese islands constituted a peripheral realm scattered like tiny millet seeds at the edge of an enormous continent. This continent itself was merely one part of a vast cosmology that encompassed a range of heavens and hells, and was populated by an assortment of buddhas, guardian deities, and demons. The differences of scale between this broader Buddhist cosmology and the Japanese realm at its periphery are put to striking narrative use in *The Origins of Hashidate* (*Hashidate no honji*), also known as *Bontenkoku* (*The Land of Bonten*), probably composed sometime in the late Muromachi period (1337–1573). The hero of the story is a talented young courtier whose filial heart and otherworldly flute-playing skills earn him a powerful father-in-law: Lord Bonten, a Buddhist guardian deity derived from the Hindu creator god, Brahma. The envy of the Japanese emperor, jealous that his subordinate has been granted the hand of this powerful deity's daughter in marriage, sets the plot in motion.

Two hierarchies are thus placed in conflict: the political order of Japan, in which the emperor is the supreme figure, and the cosmological order of Buddhism, in which the emperor is little more than a peon ruling over a trifling realm. The effect is a satirical relativizing of traditional structures of Japanese authority. It is no coincidence that the tale originated during the late medieval period, a time when the traditional order was collapsing and the Japanese sovereign was little more than a symbolic figurehead. Real power rested with violent warlords whose armies wreaked havoc

The translation and illustrations are from the two-scroll *Hashidate no honji* picture scrolls (seventeenth century) in the collection of the Harvard University Art Museums, typeset and annotated in Ōshima Tatehiko and Watari Kōichi, eds., *Muromachi monogatari sōshi shū*, Shinpen Nihon koten bungaku zenshū 63 (Tokyo: Shōgakukan, 2002), 175–224. The translator also consulted the variant text published as *Bondenkoku* in Shibukawa Seiemon's anthology *Otogi bunko* (early eighteenth century), typeset and annotated in Ichiko Teiji, ed., *Otogizōshi*, Nihon koten bungaku taikei 38 (Tokyo: Iwanami Shoten, 1991), 265–88.

and destruction as they battled for advantage. Such figures of dangerous and violent power may be reflected in King Haramon, the demon king who presents a much greater threat to the hero and his wife than does the petty, self-centered emperor.

The Origins of Hashidate falls into the category of didactic, religious "origin tales" (*honji-mono*), but the emphasis in the tale is not on religious edification. Rather, the landscape of the Buddhist cosmos becomes the exotic setting for an exciting quest narrative, as the hero rides a flying horse to visit otherworldly realms in an attempt to appease the emperor and, later, to rescue his wife from the demon king. Even the religious figure Bonten is depicted less as a deity intended for veneration than as a narrative character: a (very powerful) father who desires a good son-in-law and who dotes on his daughter.

Elements of the narrative are familiar from other works of medieval short fiction: the birth of the talented protagonist to a childless couple through the intercession of a divinity, the series of seemingly impossible challenges set to the hero, and the journeys to other worlds. Many such tales feature strong female protagonists, and that aspect is particularly pronounced here in the figure of Bonten's daughter. She openly scoffs at the emperor's pettiness, disparages Japan as a "land of bandits," and steps in, time and again, to come to the aid of her frequently hapless husband. Even when it is the hero's turn to rescue his wife from the demon king, the rescue would be impossible without her own quick thinking and decisiveness.

With the exception of his childhood, when he is known as Tamawaka, the protagonist of *The Origins of Hashidate* is referred to throughout the text only by his court titles, progressing from Chamberlain to Middle Captain to Middle Counselor, and this approach has been followed in the translation.

Long ago, during the reign of Emperor Junwa, there lived a man known as the Great Minister of the Left Takafuji of Fifth Avenue.[1] Handsome in appearance and exceedingly learned, he had erected forty thousand storehouses in the four directions and wanted for nothing in all matters. However, human longing is never exhausted, and although over the age of fifty, he was still without a filial child to call his own.

Brooding over the matter, he concluded that his lack of a child in the present life was perhaps the result of a sin committed in a previous existence. "Even if I live to be one hundred," he thought, "this is not a world in which one can linger forever. After

---

1. Emperor Junwa (786–840, r. 823–833) is more typically known as Emperor Junna.

I am gone, who will pray for my repose? From ancient times to the present, people have made requests of the gods and buddhas, and surely there are examples of requests such as mine being granted." So thinking, he made his way to Kiyomizu Temple. There he confined himself for seven days, pressing his body to the ground and offering 3,333 obeisances.[2] With all kinds of prayers, he entreated, "Please grant me a filial child of my own—it does not matter whether a boy or a girl. If my wish is granted, I will make an offering of thirty-three flower-shaped sacred mirrors of gold and silver every month for three years. I will have a multitude of votive lamps lit every month for three years. I will offer up sevenfold brocade altar curtains for three years. I will assemble one hundred monks and have them devote themselves to the recitation of the Lotus Sutra with single-minded concentration and without cease for a period of three years. I will see to it that 3,303 copies of the Kannon Sutra are written out, inscribed in gold ink." In this way, he offered up all kinds of prayers.

Just before dawn at the end of the seven days, he heard an imposing voice addressing him, saying, "Approach." Entering a small, ten-foot-square room, he encountered an aged monk of impressive mien wearing a robe and surplice of light red tinged with ocher. Takafuji realized that the small chamber contained thirty-six thousand altars, like the fabled room of Vimalakīrti, and he was filled with deep reverence.[3] He was uncertain where to stand, but the monk addressed him again, saying, "Right there, right there." When Takafuji had arranged himself properly before the aged priest, the monk spoke: "So then, you have requested a filial child of your own. It is fitting that your wish be granted." He produced a polished jewel. Just as Takafuji observed it pass into his own left sleeve, he awoke. Not long after that, a noticeable change came over his wife's condition, and before long she gave birth to a son. They named him Tamawaka: Youth of the Jewel.

Tamawaka grew day by day, and his father the minister raised him with great care, never parting from his side for even a moment. When Tamawaka reached the age of five, Takafuji began taking him along on his visits to the imperial palace. Word of these visits reached the emperor. "This is without precedent," he said. "There have been instances of children of seven years being permitted to ascend to the Courtiers' Hall, but for a five-year-old to do so is unheard of. However, seeing as how it is Takafuji's child . . ." The emperor treated Tamawaka with exceptional kindness and

2. The number thirty-three (or 3,333) is significant for its correspondence to the thirty-three manifestations of Kannon (Skt. Avalokiteśvara), one of which is the principal image at Kiyomizu Temple.
3. In the Vimalakīrti Sutra, the layman Vimalakīrti's ten-foot-square room miraculously expands to accommodate seats for thirty-two thousand Buddhist disciples, bodhisattvas, and other beings who come to hear him debate the bodhisattva Mañjuśrī (J. Monju). The reference to thirty-six thousand may be a mistranscription of "thirty-two thousand."

favor, and soon announced that they should commence the ceremony of investiture. The Minor Controller of the Left prepared the ceremony. Tamawaka was made a Chamberlain of the Fourth Rank and was permitted to sit among the highest courtiers. His ascension to the high ranks would not be complete without a concrete token of his new status, and so he was granted the provinces of Tajima and Tango to govern. Takafuji devoted himself all the more to the careful fostering and advising of his son. The young Chamberlain turned six, then seven. He surpassed all others in learning, and he also became adept at playing the flute.

Around this time, his mother was summoned away by the winds of impermanence, and she faded from this world like the fragile dew at sunrise. Takafuji passed the days and nights with the young lord as his only source of consolation. Then, when his son had reached the age of thirteen, Takafuji, too, passed from this world. The young Chamberlain's grief was beyond words. To pray for his father's repose, he had a large tower built, one thousand yards high, and seated himself atop it. For seven days, he gave himself wholly to playing upon his flute. He offered the music to the deities Bonten and Taishaku, and prayed with all his heart from the four corners of his square tower, imploring them to look after his father in the afterlife.[4]

At noon on the seventh day, purple clouds trailed across the sky and then descended from the heavens. Out of them emerged sixteen heavenly youths, bearing a jeweled palanquin and wearing jeweled caps.[5] They carried the gold palanquin on their shoulders, bearing down from the heavens a magnificent official, who faced the young Chamberlain with tears in his eyes, and said, "For seven days, you have played upon your flute, until the music reached unto the heavenly kingdom of Bonten. Your filial intent, which is without compare, has been recognized by those in the highest realms of paradise above, and in the realm of the dragon deities below. I have a daughter; it is fitting that I bestow her upon you. On the approaching eighteenth day of the month, purify this dais, burn incense, and compose yourself. Play your flute and wait. Know this: I myself am none other than Lord Bonten." With that, purple clouds enveloped the entourage and vanished into the sky. The Chamberlain could not tell whether it had been real or all a dream. He descended from the tower, entered his private chapel, and, opening the Lotus Sutra, began to recite, now on behalf of his mother's rebirth in paradise.

Soon the appointed day arrived. Although he found it difficult to believe any of it to be real, the Chamberlain purified the tower, burned all variety of incense, and,

---

4. Part of the text is unclear here; the meaning as presented is a conjecture. Bonten corresponds to the Indian deity Brahma, and Taishaku to Indra. Originally Hindu gods, both entered into the Buddhist pantheon of guardian deities.
5. The text appears to be somewhat garbled here and has been slightly amended to render it comprehensible.

The Origins of Hashidate

Lord Bonten descends from the heavens to speak with the thirteen-year-old flute-playing Chamberlain. (From *Hashidate no honji*, courtesy of the Harvard Art Museums)

composing himself, began to play upon his flute. It was the eighteenth of the month, and the moon arose pure and bright, illuminating the landscape for a thousand leagues all around. Everything shone. There was not a single cloud in the sky, but the breeze carried a wonderful fragrance. Before long, a gathering of purple clouds descended. From among them emerged a large number of people, wearing all manner of dress and riding in fleet chariots. Among them, sixteen youths bore a jeweled palanquin down from the heavens and up to the porte-cochère of the Chamberlain's mansion. The personage who alighted from the palanquin could not have been more than fourteen or fifteen years old. Upon her head, she wore a jeweled crown. Her body was adorned with dangling ornaments, while her feet were clad in golden slippers with upward curving toes. Mere words could not do her justice. "This way," the Chamberlain summoned her forward, and, bringing her in among his standing curtains, he seated her on a mat of brocade. She did not resemble a person of this world.

The two gave themselves to each other with the deepest vows, and time went by. However, in this world in which vile rumor will spread even about matters of no consequence, word soon began to circulate. "It is said that the Chamberlain of Fifth Avenue has received a bride from none other than Lord Bonten himself," the rumor went. "Truly, she is of no ordinary appearance, but appears to glow with beauty." This gossip soon reached the ears of the emperor. "I possess the Throne of the Ten

Virtues, and the Four Seas lie as though in the palm of my hand," he lamented. "Why was I not made son-in-law to Lord Bonten?"

Not long thereafter, the Chamberlain was promoted to Middle Captain. Word came from the palace that he should call at court at once. The order from the emperor was as follows: "You must have your wife present herself to me at the palace for a period of seven days. If you will not do so, then you must instead present the birds known as the kalavinka and the peacock, and have them dance at the palace for seven days. In that way, I will console my lovesick heart.[6] If you cannot accomplish this, the land of Japan will hold no place for you."

"You have spoken," said the Middle Captain, and he returned home.

Meeting the princess, he explained to her the august order he had received from the emperor. "Why are you so distressed?" she said. "Why, at the pond in the gardens of my palace, there are numerous peacocks and kalavinkas. Shall I just summon a pair of them? Then again, they are heavenly birds: this tiny country will be far too small for them. In that case, how about if I simply summon their spirits? First you must procure the Five-Virtue Brocade, a treasure of the Kamo Shrine."[7]

"That is an easy matter," replied the Middle Captain. He brought five bolts of Five-Virtue Brocade, of both red and green ground, and presented them to the princess. From the brocade, she crafted a three-foot version of each of the birds, the kalavinka and the peacock; placed one in a gold box and the other in a silver box; went out onto the southern veranda; and in a voice as beautiful as that of the kalavinka itself, called out, "Kalavinka of Bonten's realm! Peacock of Bonten's realm!" When she opened the boxes again and looked inside, there were the two birds, preening themselves. "Quickly, take them to the palace and present them to His Majesty," she said.

The Middle Captain, riding in an ox-drawn carriage emblazoned with the Eight-Leaf Crest, rode up to the palace.[8] "Never before have I heard their voices—I have only seen their appearance in pictures," said the emperor. "Nothing could be more wondrous!" The emperor and empress, as well as the chancellor and nobles from the highest and middle ranks, gathered together, whispering among themselves.

105

---

6. The kalavinka is a mythical creature with the head of a beautiful woman and the body of a bird, said to dwell in paradise. It was believed to have a particularly beautiful voice, used for the propagation of Buddhist doctrine. The peacock, while not imaginary, was considered highly exotic and, like the kalavinka, said to live in paradise.

7. The precise meaning of the text is unclear here. The referent of *kamo no miya*, translated as "the Kamo Shrine," is uncertain. The meaning of Five-Virtue Brocade is also unknown. There are multiple interpretations of the term "five virtues" (*gotoku*), which may refer, for example, to the five fundamental natural elements (wood, fire, earth, gold, and water) or to the five cardinal virtues of Confucian thought.

8. Carriages marked with the Eight-Leaf Crest, a pattern of eight-petaled lotuses, were reserved for courtiers of high rank.

The Origins of Hashidate

The emperor (*upper left*) enjoys the singing and dancing of the peacock and the kalavinka. (From *Hashidate no honji*, courtesy of the Harvard Art Museums)

The lids of the boxes were opened in the outer corridor of the Throne Hall, and the peacock and the kalavinka leaped out and began to frolic about. Their singing was captivating, and soon the two birds joined together in a tumultuous dance. This must be what it is like at the Pool of the Seven Treasures in paradise, thought everyone present, and they watched with tears rolling from their eyes, feeling as if they had been awakened from the slumber of worldly desires. When seven days had passed, the birds were returned to their boxes.

Before another seven days had passed, the Middle Captain was summoned once more to the palace. "I have heard it said that the demon's daughter Jūra is comparable in beauty to Bishamon's sister, the heavenly maiden Kichijō, and to Lord Bonten's daughter," said the emperor.[9] "Is it true? Summon the demon woman Jūra and have her present herself at the palace for a period of seven days. I want her to bring solace to my heart. If you are unable to summon her, then you must present your wife instead."

"You have spoken," said the Middle Captain, and he returned home.

9. The text gives the demon woman's name as Jūra, although in other variants her name more frequently appears as Jūrō. It is unclear which demon's daughter she is meant to be. Bishamon (also Bishamonten, Skt. Vaiśravaṇa) is an important Buddhist guardian deity. The heavenly maiden Kichijō (Skt. Lakṣmī or Mahādevī), referred to here as his sister, is more commonly considered his consort.

He faced his wife: "I have been given an order that makes me ashamed. Here is what happened . . ." But the princess just laughed when she heard. "Why, that's a mere trifle!" she said. "She is a servant in my father's household. I will summon her myself." And so saying, she called out, "Lady Jūra!" The woman appeared instantaneously. "The heart of the ruler of this Land of the Reed Plains has fallen from the right path, and he has announced his desire to enjoy your looks for seven days' time.[10] Quickly, go up to the palace. Do not disobey the sovereign's wishes in the slightest. Entertain him for seven days, and when the seven days are up, take your leave and return home." The Middle Captain accompanied her to the palace.

"Well, well, this is remarkable!" said those at the palace, both high and low, as they crowded around to see her. No one could tell when or how she did it, but she kept changing her attire as she played all variety of music for seven days, leaving nothing out. And when the seven days were up, she disappeared as though vanishing into thin air.

The emperor thought to himself, "I had heard the two women compared to each other. But if Jūra is actually no more than a servant woman, how I long to have a glimpse of her mistress—Lord Bonten's own daughter! I will order the Middle Captain to complete some impossible task, and then exile him to Silla or to the Demon Islands and take the princess all for myself."[11] He summoned the Middle Captain: "Having seen Jūra the demon's daughter, I find myself in even deeper longing. Summon the thunder gods of the heavens, who are said to shatter feelings of longing, and have them beat upon their drums here at the palace.[12] I wish to console myself."

"You have spoken," said the Middle Captain, and he returned home. It was such an impossible task that he was unable even to get the words out, but the princess approached him and asked, "Is it another order? I should hear it for myself." And so he told her the whole thing in all its details.

"Why, that's a mere trifle," the princess replied. "In the Land of the Reed Plains, they may be known as the Thunders of the Southern Heavens, but in my father's

---

10. Land of the Reed Plains (Ashiharakoku) is one variant of an archaic name for Japan.
11. Silla was a Korean kingdom, traditionally said to have been founded in 57 B.C.E., that lasted in various forms until 935 C.E. The Demon Islands (Kikaigashima) is a general term for the islands reaching from the south of Kyushu to Okinawa.
12. This may be an oblique or a garbled reference to the unattributed poem 701 in *Kokin wakashū* (*Collection of Ancient and Modern Poems*, ca. 905):

Ama no hara	Throughout Heaven's Plain
fumitodorokashi	the god of thunder's stride resounds;
naru kami mo	and yet even he
omou naka wo ba	could never split asunder two
sakuru mono ka wa	who love each other as we do.

The Origins of Hashidate

realm they are servants—mere low-ranking enforcers! A trifle!" She went out onto the southern veranda and *tap-tap-tap*ped with her fan. "Dragon King Nanda! Dragon King Batsunanda! Dragon King Hatsura!"[13]

As the saying goes, around a flame things are dry; near water they are damp: it would be foolish to bother describing the power of the Eight Dragon Kings. Seemingly out of nowhere, a great umbrella-shaped cloud appeared to soar from the peak of Mount Atago and whirl down before the princess. "Now, then," she addressed the Eight Dragon Kings, "the heart of the ruler of the Land of the Reed Plains has fallen into excessively improper ways, and he has summoned you gods of thunder to calm his lust. Quickly! Make your way to the palace, and for seven days show him how you can roar. On the seventh day, roar with the strength of deva kings. And don't simply return home after that: starting from the southwest, shoot red and white flames and reduce the palace to smoke. Then you may return. Well, how long are you going to stand there? There's nothing stopping you!" The princess spoke with truly bitter rancor.

Crying, "Everyone, this way, this way!" the Eight Dragon Kings transformed themselves into devils and bounded off toward the main hall of the palace. The Middle Captain made to go too, but the princess tugged at his sleeve and produced a jeweled crown. "Wear this today," she said. "Otherwise, your eardrums will burst, and the flashes of lightning will make your eyes fall right out of your head."

At first, there were two or three rumbles of thunder, which by themselves were enough to frighten a person out of his wits. The thunder rumbled four times, then five. Soon balls of light the size of umbrellas—one or two hundred of them—came flying about. After that, there were one thousand flashes of lightning, then two thousand more. And not only thunder and lightning: the wind blew hard enough to kick up waves, and the rain fell as thick as axle rods. From the empress down to the courtiers, countless numbers cowered in fear. As for the emperor, his words to the Middle Captain were like sweat: once out, they could not be put back in. "All I need to do is wait out the seven days," he said at first, thinking to be strong. But soon he found his feelings in turmoil and his imperial heart in deep distress. He threw his robes over his head and lay cowering.

On the seventh day, flames rained down from the sky, and the palace was burned to ashes in an instant. The Middle Captain's ears heard nothing; no harm befell him at all. He did not feel it appropriate, however, to live in the emperor's realm and yet cause so much anguish to the imperial heart. "Eight Dragon Kings," he said, "now be

13. These are three of the Eight Dragon Kings, Buddhist guardian deities associated with rain. Their Japanese names are derived from Sanskrit: Nanda, Upananda, and Utpalaka.

still!" And with that, the thunder ceased, the dark clouds vanished, and the sky turned blue. The Middle Captain returned home.

After that, the Middle Captain was promoted to Middle Counselor.

Fifty days went by, and the Middle Counselor was summoned once more to the palace. When he arrived, there was a new order from the emperor: "You did indeed produce the kalavinka, the peacock, Jūra the demon's daughter, and even the gods of thunder and lightning. These are impressive acts, and most marvelous. You have excelled at following my orders. However, there is one final thing. I wish you to bring me the imprint of Lord Bonten's own personal seal. If you can accomplish this task, I will ask of you nothing more."

"You have spoken," said the Middle Counselor, and, returning home, he told the princess everything. Tears flowed from her eyes. "This is a truly difficult task. Even for me, it is no easy thing to return from the Land of the Reed Plains to my father's realm. And if you, my husband, are to go on that long and arduous journey to Bonten's kingdom, what ever will I do in your absence?" She threw herself down, sobbing.

"If I do not present you to His Majesty," the Middle Counselor said through his own flowing tears, "I will be exiled to Silla or Baekje and ultimately end my days there. The thought of it is too miserable! Please—just go to the palace."

"This Land of Reed Plains, Japan, is a land of bandits," the princess replied. "The people's hearts are not those of sages. They think nothing of leaving one place and going off to another, pledging themselves to as many people as they please. In the heavenly realm, we say that a wise man does not serve two lords, and a chaste woman does not take more than one husband.[14] Once a woman has touched a man's skin, never will she promise herself to another. If a man and a woman are called by the name of husband and wife—even if the two have never met and then spend their lives on different paths—neither the man nor the woman will ever sin against the other. How much more so for us two, who have grown so close! And now you tell me to go to the palace. How dreadful, my husband, that you are able to utter such heartless words. I am prepared to follow you even to the most distant wilds, to the deepest mountain recesses, to the fields where tigers make their homes—even into the midst of the flames or the depths of the waters! Now listen closely, and do just as I say. Starting this very day, spend seven days purifying yourself, and perform sevenfold ablutions. Then climb to the peak of Mount Atago. There you will encounter a narrow path heading off toward the northwest. Follow it for seven leagues and look

14. The word translated here as "heavenly realm" (*tenjiku*) is intended in this context to refer to Bonten's realm; its more typical meaning is "India."

The Origins of Hashidate

The Middle Counselor rides into the heavens on a flying horse. (From *Hashidate no honji*, courtesy of the Harvard Art Museums)

around. You should find eight enormous trees, and at the foot of them, three horses. Choose the lankiest one among them, and lead it back here."

The Middle Counselor did just as he was told. He climbed to the top of Mount Atago, and indeed there he found six paths. He chose the one leading to the northwest and followed it for seven leagues, and when he looked about, there were the enormous trees, and at the foot of them the three horses: one dappled white, one dappled cream, and one dappled gray. Among them, the white one looked as thin as if it had been pressed between two planks. He led it back home.

The princess looked it over. "We won't be able to do anything without feed."

"What kind of grass does it eat?" her husband asked.

"It usually takes about thirty *ryō* of gold," the princess replied.

"That's no trouble," her husband replied. Opening up his northern storehouse, which was always full of gold, he took out thirty *ryō* and fed it to the horse. He then had water brought from the falls at Kiyomizu Temple, and let the horse drink about 150 gallons. After the horse had fed and watered, it rolled about on its back to the right and to the left, shook itself all over, and stood up.

The princess gave her husband detailed instructions: "Ride the horse over to the end of Fifth Avenue Bridge and face east. After a while, the horse will shake itself and paw the ground; when it does this, close your eyes as tightly as you can. Do not open your eyes, whatever happens. Once the horse comes to a stop and shakes itself, then you can open them and look around."

The Middle Counselor did as his wife instructed him. He took his leave of her, led the horse to Fifth Avenue Bridge, pointed it toward the east, and calmly mounted. After a while, the horse shook itself, looked up to the sky, and pawed the ground. The Middle Counselor closed his eyes as tightly as he could, and at a swift touch of his whip, the horse leaped right up into the heavens. After some time, the horse touched down on what seemed to be land and shook itself three times. Opening his eyes, the Middle Counselor saw that they had arrived on a boundless expanse of sand. When he dismounted and looked around, the horse whinnied three times, as though bidding farewell in the manner a human. It then galloped off into the sky. The Middle Counselor gazed after it into the distance with a heavy heart. For a while, it looked like a bird flying across the sky, and then it vanished altogether.

Soon the Middle Counselor found himself following a narrow road, and before long he encountered a person. "Please tell me," he asked, "what is the name of this realm?" The man replied, "This is Bonten's kingdom."

"Which way leads to Lord Bonten's palace?"

"Follow this road to the south and look about; it will lead you to the palace."

The Middle Counselor proceeded with buoyed spirits. The land around him was vast and flat, with no fields, no mountains, and no end in sight. Gradually, the color of the sand turned completely golden. Before long, he came across a silver gate inset with a golden door. Beyond it, sands of pure gold spread for one hundred yards in all directions. Adorned with the seven treasures, the place looked no different from descriptions he had heard of paradise.[15] Passing through the gate, he discovered a set of jeweled steps leading up to a jeweled hall hung with jeweled blinds. Never in his life had he seen a place so wondrous.

Before long, a heavenly being, bejeweled with dangling ornaments and looking to be about thirty years of age, approached him and pointed to the south, as though instructing him to proceed in that direction. Doing so, the Middle Counselor beheld a palace hall. It appeared to be equivalent to the Throne Hall of the Japanese palace, only this one was fronted with two or three seven-foot pillars of lapis lazuli. Inside, upon matting of pure gold, was a raised platform covered in jewels, and facing it was a seat of silver. This seat appeared to be for guests, and so the Middle Counselor placed himself there. A heavenly maiden of twenty-four or -five years of age appeared, bearing silver decanters and a square golden tray with a lapis lazuli cup on it. She placed these items before him

---

15. The seven treasures as described in the Lotus Sutra are gold, silver, lapis lazuli, seashell, agate, pearl, and carnelian. See Burton Watson, trans., *The Lotus Sutra* (New York: Columbia University Press, 1993), 170.

The Origins of Hashidate

and departed without uttering a word. The Middle Counselor recalled having heard that among the ways of heaven, there was no custom of urging a guest to eat or drink; one should simply partake of as much or as little as one liked. He tasted a small sip from the cup: it was delightfully fragrant and tasted of heavenly ambrosia. He poured himself cup after cup, drinking four or five in all. Then he returned the cup to the tray.

Next, a maiden of thirty-four or -five years of age appeared, bearing a covered bowl of lapis lazuli. It contained beautiful white rice piled nearly a foot high. The Middle Counselor lifted his chopsticks and was just about to partake, when he happened to glance into the next room. He was shocked by what he saw there. Bound with chains in all directions was a being—neither man nor demon—that looked like a withered skeleton.

"Oh, how cruel!" it cried in a doleful voice. "Won't you give me just one bite of that rice? I have been starved for food, and my life has nearly reached its end. How I wish to live on, even if for no more than only a few moments."

The Middle Counselor was a man of the utmost compassion. "This being must be a prisoner," he thought, "just as we imprison people who commit offenses in Japan. He must indeed be starving—how he must suffer!"

Pitying the creature, he said, "Put out your tongue."

The creature was overjoyed. It strained at all its chains to get as close as possible, and then thrust out its tongue, which unraveled like a large pair of crimson trousers nearly ten feet long. "How horrible!" thought the Middle Counselor. "The size of its tongue does not fit its withered body. Clearly this is no ordinary creature." His hair stood on end, but he scooped up some rice and tossed the being a mouthful.

Immediately, the creature ripped out all of its chains and demolished its iron bonds. It seized the rest of the rice and devoured it, and then set about smashing the jewel-like palace hall. At last, it called down rains and wind, and leaped off into the sky.

The maiden from a moment before came rushing in. "How dreadful!" she cried, and with a reproachful tone added, "You really are a man of ill fortune, aren't you?" She gathered up the bowl and left.

The Middle Counselor remained seated, with a stunned and agitated heart. Soon Lord Bonten himself, the very deity whom his flute had once summoned down from the heavens when he was only thirteen years old, appeared before him, dressed in proper courtly robes and cap. He seated himself on the jeweled platform.

"I understand," said Lord Bonten, "that you have come all this way to seek an imprint of my own personal seal. I also understand that you were ordered to do so by the ruler of the Land of the Reed Plains, who desires my daughter the princess. The seal, however, would be of use to you only if my daughter were still *in* the Land of the Reed Plains.

In the palace of Lord Bonten, the demon King Haramon of Rasen devours a bowl of magical rice as the Middle Counselor looks on. (From *Hashidate no honji*, courtesy of the Harvard Art Museums)

"What do I mean by this? The being you saw imprisoned here is King Haramon of Rasen, the demon realm that lies to the south of the northerly kingdom of Kiman.[16] When my daughter was five years old, I learned that he had plans to kidnap her and make her his primary queen. I consulted with the Four Heavenly Kings, and together we pursued him through the Nine Mountains and the Eight Seas as he fled among Mount Shumi, Mount Miro, Mount Makamiro, and the Great Encircling Iron Mountain.[17] We finally caught him and bound him with those iron shackles.

16. The realm of Kiman (Kimankoku) is unattested, but the word has an Indic sound in Japanese. The land of Rasen (Rasenkoku) appears to be a corruption of Rasetsukoku, a realm of man-eating demons, or *rasetsu* (Skt. *rākṣasa*). King Haramon's name, oddly, may stem from Baramon, another Sanskrit-derived appellation for Bonten (Brahma). More commonly, however, *baramon* appears as a transcription for "Brahman," a member of the Hindu priestly class. In Buddhist literature and folklore, Brahmans not infrequently appear as antagonists.

17. The Four Heavenly Kings (*shitennō*) are four deities, originally of Hindu origin, who were incorporated into Buddhism as guardian gods of the four cardinal directions. They are said to dwell on the middle slopes of Mount Sumeru, the mountain at the center of the world in Buddhist cosmology. Bishamon guards the north; Zōjōten (Skt. Virūḍhaka), the south; Jikokuten (Skt. Dhṛtarāṣṭra), the east; and Kōmokuten (Skt. Virūpākṣa), the west. They are frequently depicted as fierce and powerful warrior-like figures. Mount Shumi, Mount Miro, and Mount Makamiro are most likely variations of Sanskrit names for Mount Sumeru, which in Buddhist cosmology is surrounded by concentric seas and landmasses known as the Nine Mountains and Eight Seas. The Great Encircling Iron Mountain may refer to the chain of mountains said to enclose the entire cosmos.

The Origins of Hashidate

We planned to hold him for one thousand days without feeding him anything. Then, following the customs of this land, once one thousand days had passed, we would have had him torn to pieces. How deplorable—tomorrow was the thousandth day, and today he has escaped!

"The food you gave to him is no ordinary rice. It is grown at the edge of the Pool of Seven Treasures to the south and then offered up to us.[18] Eating just one grain will give you the strength of one thousand men and allow you to live for one thousand years. I had presented it to you as an honored guest—how terrible that you allowed him to eat it! By now, he must already have stolen away the princess and taken her to Rasen. By eating the rice, he instantly acquired divine strength and was able to shatter all of his iron fetters." Lord Bonten, august being though he was, became choked with tears and could say no more.

The Middle Counselor felt as though his very soul had left his body. He could not hold back his own tears. Finally pulling himself together, he said, "Even if things are as you say with the princess, please do grant me the imprint of your seal. After I have presented it to the emperor, thereby leaving a name for myself in the world, I intend, one way or the other, to take the tonsure."

Replying that it was an easy request to grant, Lord Bonten used his golden seal to make an imprint on a silver card, which he gave to the Middle Counselor. He then called out for someone to come and conduct the Middle Counselor back to the Land of the Reed Plains. Reflecting that he was in the home of his wife's own father, the Middle Counselor found the thought of leaving unbearable. If only the princess were at home waiting for him! Then he would not feel weary at all, even after the long and arduous journey back to Japan. With these thoughts, he gazed at Lord Bonten's face and soon succumbed to tears. Lord Bonten pitied and sympathized with him. "If the princess still lives," he said, comforting him, "sooner or later she will find a way to get word to you." The courtiers all went together to see him off at the gate.

The Middle Counselor had not expected the dappled white horse to be anywhere nearby, but it appeared right before him and whinnied. Just as he had the first time, he mounted and closed his eyes tightly. They soared off into the sky, and after what in Japan would have felt like a journey of about ten leagues, the horse touched down on solid ground. Opening his eyes and looking about, the Middle Counselor saw that he was back in Japan's blossom-like capital, at the eastern end of Fifth Avenue Bridge. He dismounted, and the horse went off to the peak of Mount Atago.

18. The Pool of the Seven Treasures was said to be in the Pure Land Paradise.

The Middle Counselor proceeded to Fifth Avenue. There he came across two or three children playing. The most forward among them came up to him and said, "The capital has been in a huge uproar."

"And why is that?" asked the Middle Counselor.

"The Middle Counselor of Fifth Avenue vanished, making everyone in the realm, right up to the emperor, terribly distressed. As for the heavenly lady, something seems to have stolen her away. A large black cloud covered up their mansion, and she disappeared without a trace. Everyone has been thinking of how upset the Middle Counselor will be, and the whole realm is in an uproar. Hadn't you heard?"

Well, then, it had happened. Shedding tears, he proceeded straight to the palace without returning home. Alas, overcome by his feelings, he presented the imprint of Lord Bonten's seal without even requesting a direct audience with the emperor. The seal was regarded as a wonder of the realm and placed for keeping in the storehouse of the Imperial Building Bureau.

The Middle Counselor then returned to have a look at his home. Thinking he might return, the servants had left everything untouched. The blinds of the southern hall had not been replaced, and the marks of King Haramon's visitation were still plainly visible, left just as they were. When the ladies and nursemaids saw the Middle Counselor, they plunged into deeper sorrow, throwing themselves to the floor and rolling about in grief. In the princess's room lay the same pillow and the same bedding just as before. Dust had accumulated on the bed, and the bedroom felt desolate. The Middle Counselor felt as though he had been awakened from a splendid dream.

It happened to be the middle of the eighth month. At some point, the reeds of the garden had begun to rustle; the wind blowing over them felt chill on his skin. Insects' cries rang out clearly, and, adding to the sadness of the old poem that asks, "What is the color of autumn?" he reflected that this was an "autumn for himself alone."[19] The flood of his tears dripped down on the pillow together with the dew. The night was long, and since he could not fall asleep, he could not glimpse her even in his dreams. The bamboo leaves rustled; if he could rest for only a moment, he thought, the sky would soon grow light. He heard the restless voice of a lone crow and the cries of birds as they left their groves: faintly, dawn was beginning to break. He cut off his topknot and made his way to Kiyomizu Temple, where he prayed with flowing tears. "Ever since I was a child, I have come each month to pay my respects here. Please, allow me to glimpse the princess once more in this lifetime. We were

19. The narrator appears to refer to poem 367 in *Shinkokin wakashū* (*New Collection of Ancient and Modern Poems*, 1205), attributed to Saigyō (1118–1190), and then to poem 193 in *Kokin wakashū*, attributed to Ōe no Chisato (ninth–tenth centuries).

The Origins of Hashidate

forced to part from each other without wishing it to be so. And if such a meeting is impossible, then I request that you take my life and help me to meet her in the life beyond."

Although it was not yet daybreak, an old monk who looked to be about eighty years of age appeared before him. "If you wish to know the whereabouts of the princess," he said, "set forth on a pilgrimage. Proceed to the port of Hakata in Tsukushi and seek passage on a ship.[20] Once one hundred days have passed, you will learn where she is without fail." Coming to himself, the Middle Counselor could not tell whether it had been a dream or reality, but he decided it must have been a revelation from the compassionate and merciful bodhisattva Kannon. He proceeded at once to Tsukushi.

He found passage on a Chinese vessel and set out over the waves of the vast blue sea: toward what destination he did not know, and he felt troubled at heart. Thirteen days after leaving land, a great gale arose. The waves grew rough; lightning flashed all around. The ropes binding the thirty boats of the flotilla snapped in the gale, and the boats went off in all directions. The Middle Counselor's boat, however, was not blown into oblivion, but bore its way over the many waves, past the land of Kiman, and finally to the shores of Rasen, the demon realm.

The Middle Counselor, having survived all of this, made his way ashore and looked in all directions. The sea appeared no different from the sea in Japan. He went looking here and there, feeling hopeless, and then began to play upon his flute. Large numbers of tall, dark, frightening creatures with hair that stood straight up came running to him. "What a marvelous melody!" they exclaimed. "You must be from the Land of the Reed Plains, of which we have heard tell."

"What place is this?" the Middle Counselor asked.

"This is none other than the realm known as Rasen. Our lord is King Haramon. One year, he journeyed to Lord Bonten's realm with a plan to steal away the princess of that place and make her his primary queen, but he was captured and bound by the Four Heavenly Kings and locked away in an iron prison. But then he managed to eat some of the rice that had been offered up to that great king, and it instantly gave him divine strength. He broke out of his prison, went to the Land of the Reed Plains, and stole away the princess. And now he worships and waits on her as his number-one queen.

"However, the princess, thinking to fool him, told him that she wanted to pray for her dead mother's repose by reciting sutras for one thousand days. She asked that a

20. Tsukushi is another name for the island of Kyūshū. Hakata is an important port city in the northern part of the island.

separate palace be built for her where she could pray morning and night. Once one thousand days are up, she said, she would do whatever he asked, but until then she requested that he spare her. King Haramon, overcome by the beauty of his queen, did just as she said. He had a separate palace built, and he treats her with the greatest care. Three times a day, he goes onto the veranda and gazes at his queen, but then he returns to his own palace. He has announced that people from the Land of the Reed Plains are enemies, and he has issued a promulgation stating that Japanese must not be allowed into the realm. Be on your guard, monk, and tell no one that you are from Japan!" Thus they explained everything to him in great detail.

"Come home with us tonight," one of them said to him, "and let's hear some interesting things." There were two of them, an old woman and an old man. He went to their home, and they looked after him and listened to what he had to say.[21] Then the old woman spoke up: "I am originally from Tango Province in Japan, but I was captured and taken off to the realm of Kiman. Grandpa here is from Tajima.[22] It is a wonder to us that we have ended up dwelling here in this land. We are now over two hundred years old, and we haven't returned to our homeland once. How we have missed our fellow Japanese!"

That was what she told him, but the Middle Counselor, suspicious that they might actually be followers of the demon king, felt frightened. Yet he could not very well leave it at that, so he said, "I come from Tsukushi. Because I am an ascetic who has renounced the world, I make my way in life by playing my flute. Sometimes people let me stay in their homes. When they don't, I find lodgings in places that aren't really lodgings at all, such as old temples and shrines. How many times I have awoken from my dreams in such places! And that is how I know that this life is no more than a dream or an illusion: it is the life to come that is our final home. Be that as it may, while I am here, I would like to have a closer look at King Haramon's palace."

"Why, that's easy!" the old woman replied. "My daughter, Lady Shakotsu, attends upon the queen. There are many women who wait on her: Lady Hiwa, Lady Haraki, Lady Uwa, Lady Hōtō, Lady Yashiya, and Lady Akutoku.[23] King Haramon has great affection for all of them. Go to the palace and present yourself."

Just then, a messenger arrived from King Haramon: "A peculiar melody was carried on the wind this evening. Send the one who played it to the palace."

"Whatever happens," the old woman told the Middle Counselor, "do as you are told. It should not amount to anything serious."

21. The original text appears to be missing one or two lines here, and has been amended to make sense.
22. Tango and Tajima are the provinces granted by the emperor to the Middle Counselor to govern when he was still the child Tamawaka.
23. The provenance and significance of these unusual names are unclear.

The Origins of Hashidate

Dressed as a monk, the Middle Counselor plays the flute for his wife (*upper left*) in the palace of King Haramon. (From *Hashidate no honji*, courtesy of the Harvard Art Museums)

The Middle Counselor proceeded to the palace. When King Haramon saw him, he said, "Play the piece you played this evening." The Middle Counselor took out his flute and played; it was a melody of interest beyond compare. "The queen suffers and longs for the Land of the Reed Plains morning and night," King Haramon said. "Go and offer her solace with the sound of your flute."

He had the ascetic sent to the Myōken Hall, which was as close to the princess as he was allowed. When he began to play his flute, the princess recognized it at once. "He must somehow have found a way to reach this land," she thought. A hundred, a thousand times she felt the urge to rush tumbling from her room and clasp him in her arms, but she knew that would spoil everything. And so she sat, listening forlornly.

Lady Shintsū, one of her attendants, spoke up in an indignant tone: "Ever since this ascetic appeared, a change appears to have come over our lady."

Lady Shakotsu was among the attendants. "There is nothing peculiar in that," she said. "In the Land of the Reed Plains, even the humblest people pursue the Way of music, and the flute is considered the most important of all instruments. What's more, the birds that frolic at the lakeside in the palace of great Lord Bonten—the mallards and geese, the mandarin ducks, the kalavinka, peacock, and phoenix—all sing with voices that imitate the sounds of music. Just now, our lady heard the sound of the flute, and how she must have missed her parents and her homeland! It is only natural that a change seemed to come over her."

"Truly," agreed all the women. Standing on the white sands of the inner courtyard, the Middle Counselor played all through the night.

At that time, the neighboring kingdom was ruled by a king known as Celestial King Ryūkyū. He sent a messenger to Haramon's court: "The lions and elephants in my realm are so numerous that they are eating too much and causing great suffering to the people. I invite you to visit for a hunt." King Haramon consented. Accompanied by over one thousand horsemen, he mounted his Flying Chariot of Three Thousand Leagues. "Let the queen have the ascetic play his flute for her, and in that way she may console herself," he said. "I shall return on the fiftieth day." He then addressed the queen's ladies: "Be good companions to her and offer her comfort. If her spirits seem any lower on my return, I will have you all torn to pieces." As swiftly as a gust of wind, he flew from Rasen and proceeded to the kingdom of Keishin.

After he had gone, the princess said to her ladies, "The ascetic always plays his flute while standing on the sands of the courtyard—he must be chilled to the bone! Have him play while standing in the middle gate gallery."[24] The Middle Counselor moved to the gallery and continued playing. After that, she summoned him to a seat within the mansion itself. Now only a papered sliding door separated them.

The princess addressed her ladies: "For the sake of my mother's repose in the afterlife, I would like to have this ascetic play his flute for seven days as an offering to the gods and buddhas. All of you should listen together, as with one heart—your sins and hindrances will vanish away."

During the seven days, she plied them with saké, until the ladies became drunk and flopped down to rest. Although the princess recognized the Middle Counselor, she wanted to catch a glimpse of him with her own eyes. Just as she was wondering how she might do so, a powerful gust of wind lifted her blinds, and their eyes met. There was nothing they needed to say aloud. Understanding that the critical moment was upon them, the princess continued to urge saké on her ladies for those seven days. For seven days, the ladies had not had even a moment's sleep. Being drunk on the saké, they could not recognize their own beds, but finally just toppled over here and there.

At last, when the night had grown late, the princess thrust open the sliding door. "Quickly!" she said. "Take me with you, and let us flee!"

119

24. In classical aristocratic architecture, the middle gate stood between the front gate and the main house. It was connected to the main house by a narrow gallery that ran along the edge of the inner garden.

The Origins of Hashidate

"If I could do as my heart wished, I would flee with you," the Middle Counselor replied, "but we could not escape even if we tried. We would simply be taken back and made to suffer all the more. I don't care what happens to me, but how I would grieve for you! Let us keep on forever just as we are. I will serve you and play my flute."

"Just take me with you, and let us flee!" she replied. "There is a vehicle known as the Flying Chariot of Three Thousand Leagues, but King Haramon took it with him. However, there is also a Flying Chariot of Two Thousand Leagues. Let us use that to escape!" The princess and the Middle Counselor went to the porte-cochère of the palace and mounted the chariot.

Although it was said to be a chariot that could fly of its own volition, it must have felt some concern for the feelings of its owner, King Haramon. It hardly flew at all. While it should have been able to soar well beyond the two thousand leagues of its name, the two escapees found themselves asking what was wrong with it before it had made it even that far.

Among the princess's attendants, there was one called Lady Sara, who was tall, red-faced, and with hair like that of a giantess. While the other ladies had finally fallen asleep, she had not even dozed, and she now noticed that the sound of the flute had stopped. With an uneasy heart, she wondered what had become of her ladyship. Leaping up, she ran out to look: just as she had suspected, neither the queen nor the ascetic was anywhere to be seen.

Lady Jintsū, Lady Akutoku—two or three attendants in all—also awoke. The moon was lovely: Perhaps their lady had gone to view it from the Southern Palace? They ran about to the palaces of all four directions, and then they saw that the flying chariot was also missing. The women were mortified. "How furious King Haramon will be!" they cried. "Surely we will be made to suffer for this—how miserable!"

Lady Yashiya went running from the group. A system of signal drums existed in case anything should happen, with one drum positioned at every league. She struck the first drum. The sound was heard at the next drum, which was then struck, and the sound of that drum was heard at the next, and so on. The Keishin kingdom was over five hundred leagues away, but the distance could be covered with only four or five hundred drumbeats.[25] The sound of the drumbeats reached Keishin in an instant.

King Haramon heard the sound. "What has happened in Rasen?" he said. "The signal drums are sounding!" Mounting the Flying Chariot of Three Thousand

---

25. The original text says that the distance could be covered "with only four or five drumbeats," but since the drums are positioned at one-league (ca. three-mile) intervals, "four or five hundred drumbeats" seems intended (and appears as such in the *Otogi bunko* variant).

Leagues, he was back in his kingdom in less time than it takes to snip a single hair. Lady Yashiya came out to meet him and told him everything just as it had happened.

King Haramon's temper flared. "That ascetic must have been the Middle Counselor of the Land of the Reed Plains. No matter: they escaped in the Flying Chariot of Two Thousand Leagues, so pursuing them will be easy. All those who consider yourselves worthy, come with me!" His wrathful appearance gave truth to the expression "as furious as King Haramon," which is used to describe someone who is frightfully angry. The hair on his head pointed straight up to the sky, and his glaring eyes were as large as carriage wheels. He gnashed his teeth and leaped up and down again and again in fury.

In no time at all, he had overtaken the princess's flying chariot and reached out to grab hold of it. "I have already told you," the Middle Counselor said to his wife, "that I don't care what happens to me, and I don't begrudge my life. But how wretched it makes me feel to think of the suffering you will face!"

"Now that we've come to this," the princess replied, "there is no point saying any more. They say the bond between a husband and a wife lasts for two lifetimes. Rather than be cloistered away in a demon's castle, I would rather plunge with you beneath the waves to the bottom of the sea. Let us die together!"

Just at that moment, two birds appeared: the kalavinka and the peacock, the very two that had danced at the palace. The kalavinka came up swiftly and gave King Haramon's chariot a sharp kick, sending it flying ten leagues away. Meanwhile, the peacock gave a swift kick to the princess's chariot, propelling it ten leagues forward. Then the two birds joined as one and began kicking King Haramon's chariot this way and that. They kicked in the wheels and then smashed the rest of the chariot to pieces. And with that, King Haramon himself plunged straight down into the depths of hell.

The two birds then managed to grasp the princess's chariot under their wings and flew off with it to the palace in Bonten's kingdom. For the princess and the Middle Counselor, who felt as though they had just escaped from the crocodile's jaws, the journey was like a dream. When Lord Bonten saw them, he too could hardly tell whether he was dreaming or awake, and his happiness surpassed all bounds. "My princess, how is it that you are here?" he said, clutching his daughter's sleeves. "I had thought it impossible for us to meet again in this lifetime. I am overjoyed!" His delight was almost more than he could bear, and he treated the two of them with exceptional care. He would have liked to keep them there with him forever.

"But the ruler of the Land of the Reed Plains must miss you," he said to the Middle Counselor. "Return home. I no longer have any regrets, for this life or the next.

With the aid of the peacock and the kalavinka, the Middle Counselor and his wife escape from King Haramon in a flying chariot. (From *Hashidate no honji*, courtesy of the Harvard Art Museums)

But what kind of person are you, really? How is it that you were able to return here safely? Surely you are no ordinary man!"

Then he called out, "Someone—escort these two back!" The two birds appeared again, lifted the chariot, and soon deposited it on Fifth Avenue Bridge, known throughout the Land of the Reed Plains, right in the heart of the blossom-like capital.

The Middle Counselor and the princess proceeded together to the Fifth Avenue mansion. At some point, it had fallen into terrible disrepair. There were gateposts but no gate, an earthen wall but no roof tiles. The garden showed not a human trace; ivy and morning glory had climbed up to the eaves. "Remembrance grass" and "forgetting grass" grew rampantly together, and in the pines the wind sighed as though waiting for no one. The lonely feeling of the place only grew and grew. In fits and starts, forgotten water flowed among the rocks, but not a person showed his face to scoop or staunch the flow. The blinds were lifted by the wind, letting in the moon, but the mansion had no master to gaze upon its glow. Their sense of lonely desolation growing all the more, they wandered here and wandered there, unstopped by anyone.

After a while, however, a man who appeared to be of the Sixth Rank emerged from the depths of the mansion. With a look of suspicion, he called to them to stop and then gazed at them with an expression of disbelief.

"Ah, aren't you the courtier Chikamitsu?" asked the Middle Counselor. "I have something to say to you!" At the sound of his voice, the man dropped to the ground in astonishment and crawled over to him. The Middle Counselor became choked with tears and could not get out any words.

"After you took the tonsure," Chikamitsu said, "all of us at the court, right down to such a lowly one as myself, searched for you throughout the realm. Among its paltry sixty-six provinces, there was not a single place we did not look. And now— where have you appeared from?"

"No, no," the Middle Counselor replied, "there is no need for explanations just now. First I must visit the palace." He mounted his carriage and proceeded to the palace. The emperor, observing him, said, "Remarkable! Retaining the form of a human being of this sullied world, you visited Lord Bonten's palace and the Rasen kingdom—this is truly marvelous! Because they were once your own lands, I once again grant you the provinces of Tajima and Tango."

Not wishing to remain for long in the capital, with its unpleasant memories, the two hurried to Tango, where they built a new mansion and passed their days telling each other all kinds of stories from their times of hardship. Their former servants learned of their return and went to join them there.

And so, when she reached eighty years of age, the princess transformed into the Kannon of Nariai Temple, and the Middle Counselor transformed into the Monju of Kusenoto.[26] They employed many highly effective means for the salvation of all sentient beings. There was not a single person who did not consider their great vow of boundless compassion to be supremely powerful and wondrous. The old woman and old man from whom the Middle Counselor had borrowed lodgings in Rasen became the gatekeepers of Nariai. From that time until today, the Kannon of Nariai and the Monju of Kusenoto have been greatly popular. It is to our great fortune that the story of the origins of these sacred sites of Hashidate has been handed down for all to hear.

TRANSLATION AND INTRODUCTION BY DAVID ATHERTON

---

26. Nariai Temple, famous for its image of the bodhisattva Kannon, is located at the northern end of Ama no Hashidate (Heaven's Bridge), a large, visually arresting sandbar in Miyazu Bay north of Kyoto, in what was once Tango Province. Kusenoto (also Kusedo or Kireto), now part of the city of Miyazu, is located at the southern end of Ama no Hashidate. The image of the bodhisattva Monju at Chion Temple there has traditionally been considered one of the most famous and important depictions of Monju in Japan.

The Origins of Hashidate

The Palace of the Tengu

Demonic, avian, anti-Buddhist *tengu* are ubiquitous in the world of medieval Japanese fiction, including *The Tale of the Handcart Priest*, as is Minamoto no Yoshitsune (1159–1189), a hero of the Genpei War (1180–1185) and the protagonist of *Yoshitsune's Island-Hopping*. *The Palace of the Tengu* (*Tengu no dairi*) brings them together in a single story, recounting Yoshitsune's teenage education by *tengu* at their hidden palace on Mount Kurama, just to the north of Kyoto. The *tengu* in this tale are seemingly benevolent: their leader, the Great Tengu, entertains Yoshitsune in a grand style before leading him on a fantastic journey through the realms of hell, hungry ghosts, and *ashura* (a terrible land of constant, endless violence), followed by a visit to the Western Pure Land to see the boy's late father (now Dainichi), who died as a result of his participation in the Heiji Rebellion against the ruling Taira clan.

In the diverse genre of Muromachi fiction, extraordinary, supernatural, or otherwise improbable journeys are the norm. But even so, Yoshitsune's otherworldly odyssey is a strange one. It seems to function allegorically, both as an extended tour of other worlds and as a metaphorical tour of Yoshitsune's psyche, allowing the troubled youth to reach a decision about whether to take monastic vows or to take up arms and fight the Taira. The fact that a *tengu* leads him on this peculiar peregrination is intriguing, because *tengu* are best known in medieval sources for misleading people—particularly through conjuring visions of other worlds—rather than guiding them or helping them on their way. The supposedly natural antipathy that *tengu* feel toward Buddhism often leads them to attack Buddhist practitioners (as in *The Tale of the Handcart Priest*), and insofar as the Great Tengu's guidance ultimately results in Yoshitsune's abandonment of the monastic path, he seems to succeed where so many other *tengu* in other tales fail.

The translation and illustrations are from the two-scroll *Tengu no dairi* picture scrolls (sixteenth century) in the collection of the British Library, typeset in Tsuji Eiko, *Zaigai Nihon emaki no kenkyū to shiryō* (Tokyo: Kasama Shoin, 1999), 353–70.

The Palace of the Tengu dates from around the early sixteenth century. Little is known about its origins, but based on the language of its earliest versions, scholars agree that the story circulated orally before it was transcribed. Shimazu Hisamoto proposed in 1928 that the tale is an adaptation of book 6 of Virgil's *Aeneid* (in which Aeneas travels to the underworld and meets his dead father, Anchises, who prophesies his future), but while it is true that the two works share similar plots and narrative structures, the question of influence remains unresolved.[1]

Minamoto no Yoshitsune came to live at Kurama Temple from the age of seven. He studied there, and because he had been the Heavenly King Bishamon in a former life, he learned the full eight fascicles of the Lotus Sutra before the year was through.[2] At the age of eight, he learned the six hundred fascicles of the Greater Prajñāpāramitā Sutra, the thirty fascicles of the *Abhidharma Discourse*, and the fourteen fascicles of the Nirvana Sutra. Among literary works, he read *The Tale of Genji*, *The Tale of Sagoromo*, *Furōei*, the twenty-scroll *Hichūda*, *The Broken Inkstone*, *Furōenshu*, *Kokinshū*, *Man'yōshū*, and *The Tales of Ise*. He studied over a hundred volumes of plant-matching poems; eighty-two volumes of insect-matching verse; *The Book of a Thousand Islands*, which demons read; *The Cedar Palace*; *The Kirise Courtyard*; and the like.[3] In all, he read some 2,424 scrolls of literary texts.

Yoshitsune thought to himself, "I'd like to experience a bit of that thing that people call 'enlightenment,'" and thus, from the age of ten, he took up a course of Zen Buddhist study. Before the end of his thirteenth year, he had fathomed the 1,700 koan.

Bored by the rain one day, he paid a visit to the temple's southern courtyard. Gazing at the blossoms, he saw that they were a little beyond their prime. "Indeed," he thought, "it's true that flowers bloom for just a little while. It's like that for people, too. My father was cut down when I was young, and how bitter it would be if I were to meet my end without having avenged his death! Actually, I've heard that our ancestor Hachiman Tarō Yoshiie left home when he was fifteen and made a name for himself in the world.[4] It may be presumptuous of me, but I ought

---

1. Shimazu Hisamoto, *Kinko shōsetsu shinsan* (Tokyo: Chūkōkan, 1928; repr., Tokyo: Yūseidō, 1983), 609–15.
2. Bishamon (also Bishamonten, Skt. Vaiśravaṇa) is a guardian deity of Buddhism. At Kurama Temple, located in the mountains north of Kyoto, a statue of Bishamon is enshrined as the principal image.
3. *Furōei*, *Hichūda*, *Furōenshu*, *The Book of a Thousand Islands* (*Chishima no fumi*), *The Cedar Palace* (*Sugi no miya*), and *The Kirise Courtyard* (*Kirise ga tsubo*) are unknown.
4. Hachiman Tarō Yoshiie (Minamoto no Yoshiie; 1039–1106) was a particularly famous warrior in the Seiwa branch of the Minamoto clan.

The Palace of the Tengu

to follow in his footsteps and run away when I'm fifteen. I'm already thirteen, and I've just been wasting my time on this mountain! Whether or not it's true, I've heard that there's a *tengu* palace in these hills. I've never seen it, but I'd love to get a look somehow."

On rainy nights and dry days, windy or calm, Yoshitsune combed the forests and fields searching for the palace of the *tengu*. But because *tengu* are naturally endowed with supernatural powers, he could not find it. "Since I was a small child," he thought, "I've always entreated Bishamon for his help. I should pray to him now to help me find the palace." After performing thirty-three sets of cold-water ablutions, he entered the Kurama Bishamon Hall, rang the sacred summoning bell, and prayed with all his might: "Hail Great Merciful Tamonten![5] In return for all the times I've visited you over the months and years, please allow me to meet the *tengu*."

The night grew late, and when Yoshitsune dozed off for a little while, Bishamon graciously appeared before his pillow as an eighty-year-old monk. "Hello, Ushiwaka," the deity said.[6] "If you wish to visit the palace of the *tengu*, then wait at the foot of the temple slope as dawn breaks in the fifth hour of the night. I will be sure to instruct you then." Yoshitsune awoke. Feeling confirmed in his faith, he repeatedly bowed down in reverent thanks. As the sky began to lighten, he set out for the temple slope, where he waited impatiently to receive his reward.

Bishamon manifested as a twenty-year-old monk, awesome to behold. He wore a figured gossamer surplice over his priestly robes and a pair of *kenjushō* shoes.[7] Fingering a pure crystal rosary, he stood before Yoshitsune and spoke: "Hello, Ushiwaka, listen. If you wish to visit the palace of the *tengu*, you should climb the mountainside from here. If you search, you will find five earthen walls, each of a different color. Keeping the white wall on your left and the red wall on your right, you should tread the single path of the blue, black, and yellow walls, recognizing the dust-like instability of the Three Worlds.[8] Then, you will be certain to find the palace." The deity vanished without a trace.

Yoshitsune was deeply grateful. Making his way along a steep mountain path, he soon saw the five colored walls. He was overjoyed. "I've been searching everywhere these days," he thought, "but until now I couldn't find a thing. What a miracle!" Hurrying along as he had been instructed, he did in fact arrive at the eastern gate of the *tengu* palace.

---

5. Tamonten is another name for Bishamon.
6. Ushiwaka (also Ushiwakamaru) is one of Yoshitsune's childhood names.
7. The meaning of *kenjushō* is unknown.
8. The Three Worlds are the worlds of desire, form, and non-form. They constitute the three realms of delusion through which sentient beings transmigrate according to their karma.

First examining the outer wall, he saw that it was built of boulders to a height of more than eight hundred feet. There was a great stone gate, inside of which was an iron wall built to a height of more than six hundred feet. It was attached to an iron gate, inside of which was a silver wall built to a height of four hundred feet. The silver gate was erected to reflect the evening sun. Inside that was a golden wall built to a height of more than three hundred feet. Its golden gate was erected to reflect the morning sun. The pebble courtyard was paved with golden sand.

Yoshitsune walked in without any fear. Gazing at the palace buildings, he saw that they seemed to be adorned with all the seven jewels, and he doubted if even the Pure Land Paradise of which he had heard could surpass what he saw here.[9] He climbed thirty or forty feet up a Chinese wooden staircase and stared into the room beyond, where he saw counselors, ministers, and other lesser palace personnel dressed in fine robes and court caps and seated in tight, orderly rows. Catching sight of Yoshitsune, all the *tengu* began to clamor, "Hey, everyone, humans have never visited the palace, not in ancient or recent times. That's peculiar!"

"Who are you?" someone inquired.

"I am a child," Yoshitsune replied, "and I have been studying on this mountain. Out of all the seventy-five acolytes at my temple, it was my turn today to gather the offertory flowers. I was out looking for blossoms when I found this place. I think if we're in the east, this must be the Pure Land of Yakushi Buddha, and if we're in the south, then it must be Kannon's Immaculate Realm. Since I have come all this way, please tell your emperor that I'd like to meet him."

Hearing this request, the *tengu* realized that their visitor was not an ordinary sort of person. "Deliver the message," one of them said. A *tengu* set off for the Shishinden Ceremonial Hall, where he informed the Great Tengu of the boy's desire. Having supernatural powers, the Great Tengu said, "Yes, yes, he's all right. His name is Lord Ushiwaka, and he's an orphan of the Minamoto clan. He was sent to live on this mountain. He goes by the name Lord Shanaō these days, taking the character *sha* from the 'sha' in 'Bishamon.' Don't be rude—invite him in here!"

The Great Tengu immediately got up from where he had been sitting and donned a set of seven-layered robes. He put on a left-folded cap, but then, thinking that it might in fact be impertinent to wear such headgear in the presence of a Minamoto, he exchanged it for a fine cherry-folded one instead.[10] He sauntered into the inner

9. The Pure Land Paradise is the immaculate, sacred realm of Amida (Skt. Amitābha) Buddha.

10. According to volume 22 of *Genpei jōsuiki* (*The Rise and Fall of the Minamoto and Taira Clans*, late fourteenth century), in a section subtitled "Ōtarō eboshi no koto," left-folded *eboshi* caps had been worn by the Minamoto since the time of Hachiman Tarō Yoshiie.

The Palace of the Tengu

reception hall, and peeking through a gap in a sliding paper door, he saw that his guest looked even more appealing than usual. He was pleased to no end.

"Hurry up and decorate the hall," the Great Tengu commanded. Hundreds of *tengu* gathered in a squawking multitude, starting with an albatross *tengu*, the twelve *tengu*, the seven *tengu*, *tengu* children, and a priestly *tengu*.[11] They cleaned the verandas, washing rather than wiping them down, and set up a number of decorative folding screens. They covered the floor with woven reed mats, the edges of which were sealed with a single-colored trim of light and dark hues, Korean brocade, and a purple and indigo rub-dyed trim. They laid out piles of leopard and tiger skins fringed with silver and gold, wrapped the pillars in damask and gold brocade, and decorated the ceiling with gold and Chinese brocade. They stacked seven reed mats at the place of honor, where they also set up a silver liturgist's chair.

The Great Tengu threw open the sliding paper doors between himself and Yoshitsune and announced, "Your visit is like a vision or a dream come true! Please enter in here." The Great Tengu led Yoshitsune to the seven straw mats piled up at the place of honor, while he withdrew to a lower seat with only three mats. Pressing his palms together, he bowed three times in reverent salutation. Then he summoned a single lesser *tengu* and said, "Take a message to Tarōbō of Mount Atago, Jirōbō of Mount Hira, Saburōbō of Mount Kōya, Shirōbō of Mount Nachi, and Buzenbō of Mount Kannokura. Tell them that I have an unusual guest with me, and that they should come and enjoy themselves here."

"Yes, sir," the messenger replied, and he immediately left the room. A moment later, he rushed back inside. "The five *tengu* are on their way," he said, whereupon the five *tengu* arrived on the front veranda with their own entourages of other *tengu*. As soon as he saw them, the Great Tengu invited them in, saying, "Hello, everyone, listen. There's a Minamoto lord here, which is why I've called you all over. Come this way, come this way."

"Yes, yes," the *tengu* all exclaimed. Entering the reception hall, they pressed their palms together and bowed as one. Then, from among themselves, they produced three thousand *ryō* of gold.[12] Piling it on a golden tray, they heaped it in the shape of an orange blossom and presented it to Yoshitsune. As the wine cup made its rounds, the *tengu* doted on their special guest, offering him an assortment of delicacies from the land and sea. After they had drunk about half the wine, the Great Tengu again summoned a lesser *tengu* and said, "Go tell Hōkōbō of China and Nichirinbō of India that I am hosting an unusual guest, and that they should come, too."

11. The meaning and significance of these varieties of *tengu* are unclear.
12. In the Muromachi (1337–1573) and Edo (1600–1867) periods, one *ryō* equaled about four or five *monme* (depending on the time and place), or approximately one-half ounce.

MONSTERS, WARRIORS, AND JOURNEYS TO OTHER WORLDS

"Yes, sir," the messenger replied, hopping down to the pebble courtyard. In an instant, he came rushing back, saying, "Right now those two *tengu* are playing *sugoroku* on Mount Hiko in Tsukushi, but they're on their way."[13] Meanwhile, the two *tengu* arrived on the front veranda accompanied by hundreds of their own attendants. As soon as he saw them, the Great Tengu said, "Hello, you two *tengu*! We've got a Minamoto lord in here! Come this way and meet him."

"All right," the two *tengu* replied and went inside to see Yoshitsune. They were enormously pleased. Everyone joined in the banquet, indulging themselves in the pleasures of the celebration. As the wine cup passed from hand to hand, the Great Tengu sprang to his feet and cried, "Hey, you two *tengu*! The party's getting dull; why don't you amuse us with one of your ancestors' supernatural skills?"

"That's easy enough," the two *tengu* replied, and they dashed into the adjoining room. Hōkōbō of China slid open a paper-door partition and shouted, "Watch this!" As Yoshitsune stared, a vision of Jingshan Temple in China appeared. The temple bell hung by a lamp wick, and he saw a person strike it with a Korean bell hammer. Then Hōkōbō entertained him with a scene of someone setting fire to Nankai Hall, which burned up in an instant. Next, Nichirinbō of India pushed open another paper-door partition and cried, "Look here!" Yoshitsune did, whereupon Nichirinbō ran a rope through the mist, created a bridge between the clouds, floated a ship in the distant mountains, and clambered up and away as freely as he pleased. It was utterly amazing.

The Great Tengu turned to the other five *tengu* and said, "Each of you can delight us with one of your martial skills."

"Certainly," they said, jumping down to the pebble courtyard, where they demonstrated for Yoshitsune all manner of secret techniques. Because Yoshitsune had long had an interest in the martial arts, he strolled out to the broad veranda to watch from nearby. He was exceptionally pleased.

The Great Tengu spoke: "We've shown you the two *tengu*'s supernatural powers and the five *tengu*'s martial skills, and, for your entertainment, we could show you more of the same, but it wouldn't be very interesting. So let me display for you the five regions of India instead. Come this way!"[14] The Great Tengu led Yoshitsune into a sumptuous chamber, where he began by slipping open the sliding paper door

129

13. *Sugoroku* is a backgammon-like board game. Tsukushi is an old name for the island of Kyūshū in the southwestern part of Japan.
14. In the manuscript of *Tengu no dairi* (ca. 1504–1528) in the Keiō University Library, the Great Tengu warns Yoshitsune that upon his return to the human world, he will suffer divine punishment—including death—if he reveals any of what he is about to see. See Yokoyama Shigeru and Matsumoto Ryūshin, eds., *Muromachi jidai monogatari taisei* (Tokyo: Kadokawa Shoten, 1981), 9:558. All subsequent references to *Tengu no dairi* (ca. 1504–1528) are to this typeset edition.

Yoshitsune and the Great Tengu observe a martial arts demonstration at the palace of the *tengu*. (From *Tengu no dairi*, courtesy of The British Library. © The British Library Board, No. Or. 13839)

to the east. In a single glance, Yoshitsune took in the 760-plus provinces of eastern India, which the Great Tengu then reproduced in a hundred sheaves of Chinese paper. The Great Tengu opened the sliding paper door to the south, whereupon Yoshitsune saw each and every person's house in all the 760-plus provinces of southern India. This, too, the Great Tengu replicated in a hundred sheaves of Chinese paper. When the Great Tengu opened the sliding paper door to the west, Yoshitsune saw the mountains and forests of the 700-plus provinces of western India before his very eyes. The scene looked absolutely real. It was beyond depiction, but the Great Tengu was able to capture it. On more than five hundred sheaves of paper, he reproduced all the features of the five Indian regions, including the running waters of northern

MONSTERS, WARRIORS, AND JOURNEYS TO OTHER WORLDS

India, and central India, too. Yoshitsune was overjoyed at the thought of preserving the paintings as a treasure for future generations.

Later, the Great Tengu received a message from his wife. Wondering what she wanted, he withdrew to his inner rooms. "Is it true?" she asked, clinging to her husband's kind sleeves. "I hear that there's a young lord who's come here from the human realm! I'm from there, too, and I miss the place. It seems like just the other day that I left it behind and tied the knot with you here, but it's been seven thousand years already! For the love that I've shown you all these months and millennia, won't you please give me leave for a little while? I want to go and meet our guest!"

The wife pleaded, and although the Great Tengu wondered what might come of such a meeting, he was not made of stone or wood and gave his consent. "Yes, indeed," he said, "whether in China, India, or Japan, the young lord has no equal, so it's only natural that you might want to see him. Go on then and meet him for yourself."

The wife was delighted, and she changed into a set of twelve-layered robes. Treading on the train of her scarlet trouser-skirt, she put on a protective charm of the Mantra King Aizen. Then, with a Buddhist chant on her lips, she set out with a bevy of female attendants who were no less attractive than herself. With her bejeweled locks and her seductive, flowery face, her appearance was like that of the autumn moon rising over distant mountains and shining down on a lake. When Yoshitsune saw her, he recognized at once that she was the Great Tengu's wife. He invited her in, saying, "Truly, my lady, you are all too resplendent! Come in, come in."

Taking a seat in the room, the wife peered intently at Yoshitsune. After a while, she spoke: "It embarrasses me to speak in this way, but I should tell you about my family background. I, too, am a person of the human realm. I come from Two Bridges in Kai Province, where there once lived a wealthy man by the name of Kokin Chōja. I am his only daughter, Lady Kinuhiki. In the spring of my seventeenth year, I went on a trip to Mount Hanazono, where I was playing music with some others. My instrument was the koto, and I was thinking to myself that the sound of my plectrum on the strings was the most marvelous that anyone had ever heard. There was no one in Japan who could compare—no one who could match my playing that day! As I was thinking such arrogant thoughts, a divine wind began to blow, and just like that a *tengu* lured me away and brought me here to the palace.

"It seems like it was just the other day, but when I count the months and years, it's been more than seventy centuries! But even though I've lived all this time, it hasn't been much fun. Still, there's one thing that I do enjoy: once, and sometimes two or three times a month, I hold services for my dead parents in the afterworld. That's my one-and-only pleasure. You lost your father when you were only two years old, so

The Palace of the Tengu

you must miss him terribly. My husband, the Great Tengu, flies through the 136 hells and the Pure Land of Nine Grades every day.[15] Your father, Yoshitomo, has achieved the rank of Dainichi Buddha in the Pure Land. Don't tell my husband that I told you, but if you beg him with all your might, he'll surely see that you two meet." The wife was so sympathetic, and she spoke with such warmth and ease, that Yoshitsune was elated. "Even so," he replied, "it's certainly a marvel!"

Having spoken her mind, the wife turned to her attendants and said, "Serve our guest some auspicious wine!"

"Yes, ma'am," the young ladies replied, and standing up to pour, they each pressed Yoshitsune to drink.

"I have nothing for your entertainment," the wife said, joining in the drinking, "so I'll tell you about this wine. Amazingly, it was produced as a powerful medicinal libation by infusing it with the merit of the 69,384 characters of the Lotus Sutra. One cup, and you will be loved and revered by the people; two cups, and you will be envied by others; three cups, and you will achieve your desires; four cups, and you will attain a fortune; five cups, and your five bodily components will manifest the Five Elements;[16] six cups, and you will voice the tidings of the Six Realms;[17] seven cups, and you will achieve a buddha's name; eight cups, and your eight-leaved lotus blossom will bloom;[18] nine cups, and you will become a ruler of all the land. Since we're having this wine in celebration, drink nine cups, if you will." After the wine had made its rounds, the wife took Yoshitsune's cup. "To many happy months and years!" she cried, and served him another. Then saying farewell, she withdrew deep inside the palace.

Yoshitsune addressed the Great Tengu, saying, "The hospitality you've shown me has been beyond all expression. It can't be put into words or conveyed with a brush. If my debt to you were a mountain, it would be greater than Mount Sumeru,[19] and if it were an ocean, it would be deeper than the deep blue sea. How could I ever forget? But even so, there's one more wish inside my heart. Whether or not it's true,

---

15. The Pure Land of Nine Grades is the Western Pure Land of Amida Buddha. Devotees may be reborn there in any one of three grades (upper, middle, and lower), each of which is divided into an additional three grades.

16. The Five Elements are earth, water, fire, wind, and air; according to one interpretation, the five bodily components are sinew, pulse, flesh, bone, and hair. The esoteric Buddhist concept of *gorin jōshin* (corporeal attainment of the Five Elements) holds that when practitioners manifest the Five Elements in their five components, they possess the bodies of buddhas.

17. The Six Realms (*rokudō*) are the planes of existence through which unenlightened sentient beings transmigrate according to their karma: the realms of heaven, animals, humans, *ashura*, hungry ghosts, and hell. *Ashura* are a race of superhuman beings who engage in constant, bloody battle.

18. Because of an omission in the British Library manuscript, I have translated the eighth sip from *Tengu no dairi* (ca. 1504–1528). In the esoteric Tendai (*taimitsu*) tradition, an eight-leaved lotus blossom is believed to open in the practitioner's heart as a result of his or her devotional practice.

19. According to traditional Buddhist cosmology, Mount Sumeru is a great towering mountain at the center of the universe.

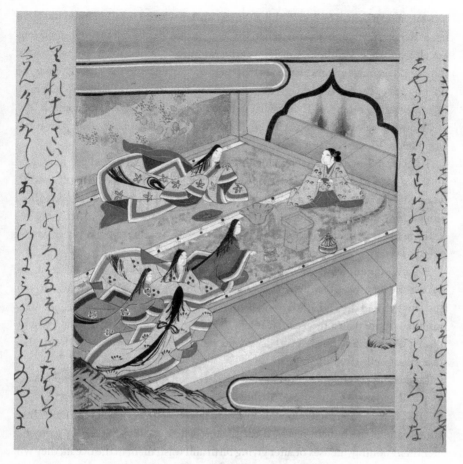

With saké cup in hand, Yoshitsune speaks with the human wife of the Great Tengu. (From *Tengu no dairi*, courtesy of The British Library. © The British Library Board, No. Or. 13839)

when I was in the human world I heard that you fly through the 136 hells and the pure lands of the ten directions. I lost my father, Yoshitomo, when I was two, and I desperately want to see him. I'm begging you, please!"

"What you say may be true," the Great Tengu replied, "but in this case, it's out of the question. Nevertheless, your visit here is utterly amazing. Do you know what it means to hold a dialogue with yourself? Speak now, I'm listening!"

"I came to Mount Kurama at the age of seven, and since then I have studied the sutras, the commentaries, the sacred teachings, and the writings of China and Japan. I have learned all that I could about music and Chinese and Japanese verse. I have

The Palace of the Tengu

also taken up a course of Zen Buddhist study, during which I have explored the 1,700 koan. According to one of those, when the heavens, the earth, and the four directions are all iron walls, you hold a dialogue with yourself.[20] When we hear that the ten thousand teachings are one, it means that there are no fences in the Three Worlds, no boundaries to the Six Realms, no two dharmas within the dharma, and no two buddhas among the buddhas. That is what it means to hold a dialogue with yourself."

"How marvelous!" the Great Tengu exclaimed. "In that case, I shall be your travel companion. Please come this way!"

The Great Tengu ushered Yoshitsune deep inside the palace, where he placed him on a jeweled pedestal. He stripped Yoshitsune of the small-sleeved robe and *hitatare* that he had been wearing since coming from the human realm and clothed him in a woven robe of Chinese scarlet and Japanese lotus thread.[21] After tying Yoshitsune's hair with a hair cord, he lifted the thirteen-year-old boy in his arms and quickly set out for the afterworld.

Passing sometimes along mountain roads and sometimes along an ocean shore, Yoshitsune and the Great Tengu toured the 136 hells, seeing what there was to see. They first visited the Hell of Burning Flames, which was truly terrifying. There was a mountain more than a thousand feet tall. It was suddenly swept with flames, whereupon it was instantly burned and destroyed, reduced to dust and gritty ash that flew up and out in the four directions.

Looking in another place, they saw a lake of blood some eighty thousand *yojanas* deep and wide.[22] "What is this?" Yoshitsune asked.

"This is the Blood Hell into which women fall," the Great Tengu replied. "When women are in the human realm, if they take off their clothes and other garments after their monthly menses or after giving birth and wash them in the ocean, they will suffer the wrath of the Dragon King. If they wash them in a lake, the lake deity will reproach them severely. If they scoop up water and wash them in that and then pour the water out, it is like piercing the bodies of the great Buddhist guardian deities with a sword. If they wash them in a river, when sentient beings of the Three Worlds unknowingly draw that water and offer it to the Buddha or as alms for the clergy, they will be committing a defilement.

20. Yoshitsune seems to allude to the preface of the fifty-seventh case in *The Blue Cliff Record* (J. *Hekiganroku*, early twelfth century), a Chinese collection of koan. Thomas Cleary and J. C. Cleary's translation of the relevant passage reads, "Before you have penetrated, it all seems like a silver mountain, like an iron wall. When you have been able to penetrate, from the beginning it was your self that was the silver mountain, the iron wall" (*The Blue Cliff Record* [Boulder, Colo.: Shambhala, 1977], 2:378).

21. A *hitatare* (also *yoroi hitatare*) is a kind of loose-fitting shirt-and-pants set worn by both warriors and courtiers in the medieval period as everyday attire.

22. One *yojana* equals approximately seven or nine miles, depending on the interpretation.

Yoshitsune and the Great Tengu visit the Blood Pool Hell. (From *Tengu no dairi*, courtesy of The British Library. © The British Library Board, No. Or. 13839)

"As for the punishments of this hell, there is an iron cable over the Lake of Blood. Five demons appear in five different colors, and they goad women out over the lake. 'Cross the cable!' they shout. But the women lose their footing before they even reach the center, and they fall in with a splash. Their bodies sink below, while their long hair floats on the surface like duckweed. When they try to rise, the demons push them back down with iron rods. The women's anguished cries are thinner than a spider's thread. 'It's your punishment for the crimes you committed in the human realm!' the demons shout, their voices echoing everywhere. 'So don't blame us!'"

"How can a woman avoid these punishments?" Yoshitsune asked.

The Palace of the Tengu

Yoshitsune and the Great Tengu visit the realm of hungry ghosts. (From *Tengu no dairi*, courtesy of The British Library. © The British Library Board, No. Or. 13839)

"Well," the Great Tengu replied, "if a woman in the human realm keeps 133 copies of the Blood Bowl Sutra, or if she recites the *nenbutsu* and prays to be reborn in a favorable place, then she can go straight to the Pure Land.[23] But if she fails to do good and loves evil with a misguided heart, remaining ignorant of the buddhas and the dharma, then this will be her punishment when she dies."

Leaving the Lake of Blood behind, Yoshitsune and the Great Tengu came to the hellish realm of hungry ghosts. As they drew near, Yoshitsune saw countless crowds

---

23. The Blood Bowl Sutra is a short apocryphal scripture imported from China to Japan around the late fourteenth or early fifteenth century. The *nenbutsu* is the ritual invocation of the name of Amida Buddha.

of hungry ghosts, including those called "well-to-do ghosts," "indigent ghosts," and "*chikuren* ghosts."[24] There were places where some of them were stacking rocks, while others were picking flowers. One particular ghost was dancing, prancing, and laughing for joy. Yoshitsune was intrigued. "You must be pleased about something," he said.

"Yes," the ghost replied, "I'm overjoyed! One of my seventh-generation descendants is in the human realm now, and he's going to become a monk! I'm rejoicing because I'll finally be released!"

"Indeed," Yoshitsune thought, "the Buddha explains that when a person takes monastic vows, nine generations of his ancestors will attain the heavenly realm. Now I finally understand what that means. I've also heard that if a single person takes vows, then even his family's oxen and horses will achieve buddhahood. If that's a lie, then so is the idea of becoming a buddha." He suddenly realized his plight. "I was intending to become a warrior, but when I think about it this way, I can't decide what I should do. My entire family was killed during the Hōgen and Heiji conflicts,[25] and if I want to pray for their enlightenment, I'd do well to become a monk. Still, if I want to fulfill my original intention to avenge my father, then I should take up arms and do my filial duty." With these thoughts, Yoshitsune was overcome with silent tears.

Because they could not very well remain in the realm of hungry ghosts, Yoshitsune and the Great Tengu moved on to the hellish *ashura* realm.[26] Drawing near and staring hard, Yoshitsune first saw a person who seemed to have died without avenging his father's death in the human realm. He was cutting and stabbing himself as a horrific punishment. Looking around, Yoshitsune saw warriors striking signal drums and gongs and blowing on great conchs and the like, just as they did in the human realm. They rushed together in a great slashing melee. The losers fled in retreat, while the winners raised a victory shout. Their battle cries and archers' yells shook heaven and earth.

"So, how can a person avoid this punishment?" Yoshitsune asked.

"During a battle in the human realm," the Great Tengu replied, "if warriors imagine that the enemy whom they strike is a bell, and their sword, a wooden clapper, keeping in mind that the present is what it is because of the karma of the past, and that in the future, they and their enemy will attain buddhahood together, then they are sure to obtain release."

137

---

24. Hungry ghosts are miserable, pitiful beings who suffer constantly from hunger and thirst. Among them, "well-to-do ghosts" (*uzai gaki*) are those who can eat and drink, while "indigent ghosts" (*muzai gaki*) cannot. The meaning of "*chikuren* ghosts" is unclear.

25. As a result of the Hōgen and Heiji rebellions (1156 and 1159), Yoshitsune lost his father, his paternal grandfather, and most of his brothers. In addition, he was consigned to a childhood at Kurama Temple.

26. The *ashura*, or "warrior," realm is a cruel world of constant, never-ending battle.

Yoshitsune and the Great Tengu visit the *ashura* realm. (From *Tengu no dairi*, courtesy of The British Library. © The British Library Board, No. Or. 13839)

Leaving the *ashura* realm behind, Yoshitsune and the Great Tengu visited countless hells, all of which were extraordinarily bad. The cries of sinners being tortured were terrifying, utterly beyond the power of written words to describe.

Next, Yoshitsune and the Great Tengu visited the Pure Lands of the Ten Directions. After observing the misery of hell, the magnificent glory of the buddhas was marvelous beyond compare. And to see them in person and hear them preach! Among those Pure Lands, the most wonderful one of all was the Nine-Grade Pure Land Paradise World of the West. It was without rival. And it was in just this Pure Land of Nine Grades that Yoshitsune's father, Yoshitomo, had become Dainichi Buddha, blessedly enshrined as the central sacred figure.

The Great Tengu approached the Pure Land from the north. He called out for Miroku Bodhisattva, and after paying him his respects, he and Yoshitsune proceeded inside.[27] The place was astounding. The ground was strewn with lapis lazuli sand, and the entry steps were lined with golden rails. The garden trees sparkled and shone, and lotus blossoms bloomed on the seven-jeweled lake, their fragrance wafting through the air. The light of heavenly nymphs at play glinted in the colors of the flowers, while the twittering cries of birds mixed with the sounds of waves.

There was a gate adorned with all the seven jewels. "What is that?" Yoshitsune asked.

"In the human world," the Great Tengu explained, "if people plant good roots and recite the *nenbutsu* with a pure and earnest heart, then when they die and come to the Pure Land, this gate swings open. The sound that it makes rings as music throughout China, India, and Japan."

Yoshitsune and the Great Tengu passed by palace buildings and pagodas, but there were always more; and travel as they might through groves of kaido crab apple trees, these, too, were without end. Sounds of music rang in the sky, and Yoshitsune wept tears of joy to find himself in a place decorated with banners, wreaths, and garlands of jewels.

"You wait here," the Great Tengu said. He made his way to the Great Audience Hall and addressed Dainichi Buddha, saying, "By some strange connection, your son Ushiwaka in the human realm has accompanied me here. He says that he would like to pay his respects to you one time."

"That's too bad," Dainichi replied. "Teacher and student are bound for three generations, husband and wife for two, and parent and child for one. It's not going to happen."

"The boy will surely accept your decision," the Great Tengu persisted, "but he has attained cognizance of the Three Worlds. So please meet with him anyway."

"What is the crossroads of the dharmic Three Worlds' reward?" Dainichi inquired.

"Though I may say, 'Whether in heaven or on earth, only I myself am the exalted one,'[28] not a single sutra is lacking," the Great Tengu replied.

"How wonderful!" Dainichi exclaimed. "In that case, bring him here."[29]

27. The bodhisattva Miroku (Skt. Maitreya) is prophesied to appear in the world 5,670,000,000 years after the death of Shakyamuni Buddha as the next human buddha after Shakyamuni.
28. Like all other buddhas before him, Shakyamuni Buddha is said to have uttered these words at the time of his birth.
29. In *Tengu no dairi* (ca. 1504–1528), Dainichi sends the famous Maudgalyāyana (J. Mokuren) to bring Yoshitsune inside.

139

The Palace of the Tengu

Yoshitsune sat in an honored seat, while Dainichi Buddha sat on a lotus. Yet the poor boy! Although he had attained cognizance of the Three Worlds, because he was still human he was enveloped in clouds of delusion, allowing him to hear his father's voice but obscuring him from view.

"So, Ushiwaka," Dainichi asked, "what would you judge to be the essence of the Lotus, the first among the many sutras?"

"It is the mysterious teaching, referred to by the character *myō*, meaning 'mysterious,' that the sutra explains: that there are neither two nor three—only a single vehicle of the dharma.[30] This is how I understand it."

"What about travelers passing through the coalescence of heaven and earth?"

"As for that," Yoshitsune replied, "in the heavens there are 9,008 worlds and seven streams, and on earth there are also 9,008 worlds and seven streams. In the heavens, there is an expulsion of forty-eight heavenly clouds, and on earth there is an emplacement of forty-nine shallows-barriers. Travelers passing through the coalescence of heaven and earth are like 'each venerating the feet of the Buddha, withdrawing and taking a seat to the side.'"[31]

"What about the three barriers of Tosotsu?" Dainichi inquired.[32]

"As for those," Yoshitsune explained, "pull together the mountain-frost-mountains and bind them up to make a brushwood shack; when they come apart, they are the fields that they were before. This is my understanding of the heart of attachment."

"What is the heart of *vajra*?" Dainichi inquired.[33]

"I understand it to be the buddhas of the Three Ages and the Ten Directions in the character *A*; all the many bodhisattvas in the character *mi*; all the eighty thousand sacred teachings in the character *da*; and all of these together in the buddha Amida."[34]

Dainichi asked another question: "What is the true form of *vajra*? Tell me, quickly."

"All right, then. The true form of *vajra* enters wood by the gift of wood; fire by the gift of fire; water by the gift of water; metal by the gift of metal; and earth by the gift of earth. Cutting without being cut, burning without being burned, being unheld and unseen, simply as it is in its true form."

30. *Myō* is the first character in the name of the Lotus Sutra (Myōhō rengekyō).
31. Yoshitsune quotes a passage from chapter 1 of the Lotus Sutra describing how King Ajātaśatru and his followers paid obeisance to the Buddha and then sat to hear him preach. See Leon Hurvitz, trans., *Scripture of the Lotus Blossom of the Fine Dharma* (New York: Columbia University Press, 1976), 3.
32. In Buddhist cosmology, Tosotsu (Skt. Tuṣita) is the fourth of six heavens in the heavenly realm.
33. *Vajra* (J. *kongō*) is an indestructible diamond-like substance, frequently employed in Buddhist discourse as a metaphor for the wisdom of the buddhas.
34. The British Library text contains an omission in Yoshitsune's explanation that I have remedied from two texts of *Tengu no dairi* (ca. 1504–1528 and 1659). For the latter, see Shimazu Hisamoto, ed., *Kinko shōsetsu shinsan* (Tokyo: Yūseidō, 1983), 273.

"When you were born from this soil into the human realm," Dainichi said, "there were five things that you borrowed. What did you borrow and from which buddhas did you borrow them when you were born into that world?"

"Right. As for the five borrowed objects, I received my bones from Dainichi, my flesh from Yakushi, my blood from Kannon, my sinew from Amida, and my vital force from Shakyamuni. I was born into the human realm, and when my connection to it expires and I come to the Pure Land, those things will be settled as earth, water, fire, wind, and air."

Dainichi pressed him on this point: "When your connection to the human realm expires and you come to the Pure Land, how will you return those five things you've borrowed?"

"Well, by the virtue of wood, I will return them to wood; by the gift of fire, I will return them to fire; by the gift of earth, I will return them to earth; by the gift of metal, I will return to metal; and by the gift of water, I will return to water. When I return wood to wood and fire to fire, a wind will blow up and they will become clods of earth as they were before. This is my understanding."

"Tell me, Ushiwaka," Dainichi inquired, "what do you make of the *kenninjō* verse?"[35]

"Yes. Regarding the *kenninjō* verse—when the winter's blanket of snow disappears, it melts and becomes the same valley-river water. The river runs in five streams, and its waters in five hues."

"Then what are the differences among the five precepts?"

"The five precepts are proscriptions against killing, stealing, licentiousness, lying, and drinking. The first—the precept on killing—includes the killing of people, of course, but it also pertains to killing animals, birds, and insects. There is a poem that explains it like this:

mukūbeki	Do they seek the seeds
tsumi no tane wo ya	of the offenses
motomuran	for which they must pay—
ama no shiwaza wa	those deeds of the fishermen
ami no megoto ni	in every eye of their nets?

"The precept on stealing has to do with taking other people's things. For example, if you take even a scrap of paper or a strand of filth from someone without his permission, that is stealing. There is a poem that reads,

footnote
35. The meaning of *kenninjō* is unclear.

The Palace of the Tengu

ukikusa no	Even if it's just
hitoha naritomo	a leaf of floating grass,
iso kakure	don't set your heart
kokoro na kake so	on hiding it in the rocks,
okitsu shiranami	you thieving white ocean waves![36]

"The precept on licentiousness concerns adding extra blankets, or bedfellows, to your own.[37] On the whole, the rule prohibits violating other people's spouses. There is a poem that puts it this way:

sanaki dani	The covers are
omoki ga ue no	heavy enough already
sayogoromo	without piling more on.
waga tsuma naranu	Add no new blankets (no new lovers)
tsuma na kasane so	that are not now your own.[38]

"The precept on lying has to do with saying things that aren't true and deceiving people with sweet talk. There is a poem that goes,

hana yuki wo	People gaze
kōri to hito no	at a snow of blossoms
nagamuru wa	as if it were ice—
mina itsuwari no	and they all become
tane to naru kana	the seeds of lies!

"The precept on drinking forbids the consumption of alcohol.

sake nomu to	When you drink,
hana ni kokoro wo	don't give your heart
yurusu na yo	to the flowers!

36. This is poem 1962 in *Shinkokin wakashū* (*New Collection of Ancient and Modern Poems*, 1205), attributed to Jakuren Hōshi (d. 1182). The word *shiranami* (white waves) can also signify "thief" or "pirate."
37. Like the next poem that he cites, Yoshitsune puns on *tsuma* (blanket-skirt) and *tsuma* (husband or wife).
38. This is a slight variation on poem 1963 in *Shinkokin wakashū*, attributed to Jakuren. It depends for its effect on a pun on *tsuma* 褄 (blanket-skirt) and *tsuma* 妻 (wife), as well as on the phrase *tsuma na kasane so*, which can mean both "add no [new] blankets" and "sleep with no [new] partner." This poem also appears, in this volume, in *Isozaki*.

yoi na samashi so	And don't sober us up,
haru no yamakaze	you spring mountain breeze.

These are the five precepts."

"What does it mean for 'the paper candle to wane and go out'?" Dainichi inquired.

"'I saw Torch-Bright Buddha, and his former auspicious portent-ray was just like this,'" Yoshitsune replied.[39]

"Then what about the unattainability of the Three Ages of past, present, and future?"

"The good roots that we planted in the past have become the blessings of the present," Yoshitsune explained. "This is the unattainability of the first age. In the present, we initiate our enlightenment in a later life; by turning our hearts to the Way, we will attain buddhahood in the future. This is the basis of my practice."

Flowers bloomed at the sound of Yoshitsune's words, and he spoke with such impeccable purity that Dainichi Buddha was overcome with jubilation. Dainichi threw his fan into the sky, whereupon the clouds of delusion blessedly cleared and the father and his son were left gazing into each other's eyes. Whether in ancient or present times, in the human world or the world to come, the bond between parent and child is close indeed! "Oh, how you've grown!" Dainichi exclaimed, weeping for joy. "My extraordinary Ushiwaka!" Unable to tell if he was dreaming or awake, Yoshitsune, too, wept a torrent of tears.

"Come here, boy, come here!" Dainichi declared. Throwing deference to the wind, Yoshitsune went to his father, who gently smoothed back his son's stray locks and said, "There there, Shanaō. There there, Ushiwaka."

After a while Dainichi spoke, and his complaints were moving to hear! "My poor unfortunate child! If I were still alive in the world today, I wouldn't let you suffer such hardship. In the past, I did a poor job of upholding the precepts and performing my Buddhist practices, which is why I died so young. How pitiful you were after that, wandering from place to place with only your helpless mother to rely on! But even so, from my grave I stuck to you like a shadow, protecting you and keeping you from harm. You didn't have the faintest idea. Now, like a white spindle bow, you should pull back and win the land for the Minamoto."

39. Yoshitsune quotes from chapter 1 of the Lotus Sutra. See Hurvitz, trans., *Scripture of the Lotus Blossom of the Fine Dharma*, 21. An auspicious portent-ray (*kōzui*) is a ray of light that issues from between the eyebrows of a buddha immediately before he bestows a revelation.

The Palace of the Tengu

Yoshitsune is reunited with his father in the Western Pure Land. (From *Tengu no dairi*, courtesy of The British Library. © The British Library Board, No. Or. 13839)

Yoshitsune spoke through his tears: "However that may be, since you've become a buddha like this, are you in any great pain?"

"I don't suffer any particular anguish," Dainichi said, "but there is one thing that's weighed on my mind. I feel ashamed whenever I see the Taira in the capital doing wicked deeds, and in that state I can't escape the torments of the *ashura* realm. I don't need a thousand or ten thousand copies of the sutras—just avenge my death!"

"I've been at Kurama Temple since the age of seven," Yoshitsune said, "studying hard and chanting the sutras every day for the sake of your enlightenment. But if that's what you want, then from now on I'll give up my goal of becoming a monk. I'll head out to Michinoku Province, gather together our vassals and retainers, and see

you avenged. Please be my protective deity and shower me with martial blessings."
Yoshitsune spoke admirably indeed.

Dainichi was delighted. "In that case," he said, "I should tell you generally about
your past and your future. Listen closely. First of all, our family is descended from
Emperor Seiwa. Our ancestor Hachiman Tarō Yoshiie left home at the age of fifteen
and made a name for himself subduing the eastern barbarians. You, too, will travel to
the northeast at the age of fifteen, and when you come back, it will be without incident. But first, you will be fourteen next year, and in observance of the thirteenth
anniversary of my death, you must set out to slay a thousand men at the Fifth Avenue Bridge. After you have killed the first 999, Musashibō Benkei, the heir of the
Kumano Shrine intendant Tanzō, will come.[40] Don't kill him—save his life and
make him a retainer. He will serve you for a very long time. After that, go back home
and hold a blood celebration.

"Later, when you ask Kichiji for his help and travel to the eastern provinces, you
will encounter a person named Sekihara Yoichi, from Mino Province, at Jūzenji
Komatsubara.[41] He will be riding to the capital with thirty-six mounted men, and
when he meets you, he will treat you rudely. Even if you think it's only a little thing,
as a Minamoto away from home you must be sure to cut him and every one of his
men down from their horses. If you strike them on the left, I'll strike them on the
right.

"Now there's something important here. When your mother, Tokiwa, hears that
you've left for the eastern provinces, she will come after you, trying to chase you
down and make you stop. At a place called Yamanaka at the border of Mino and
Ōmi provinces, she'll be wounded and killed by the night bandit Kumasaka and his
rotten gang. But there's nothing you can do about it; it's her karma from a previous
life.[42] Nevertheless, you should see that she's avenged right away. To do so, stay at
the house of a certain Chūkōbō at the Takai Post Station in Mino Province. The night
bandits will break in there to steal Kichiji's treasures. Because it's your mother you
will be avenging, be sure to kill them all and be done with it. Don't spare anyone or let anybody escape. Do what you set out to do and then hold a blood
celebration.

"As you travel east from there, you should stay at the house of a man named

40. The story of Yoshitsune's battle with Musashibō Benkei (1155–1189) at Fifth Avenue Bridge is preserved in *Gikeiki* (*The Chronicle of Yoshitsune*), the *otogizōshi Benkei monogatari* (*The Tale of Benkei*), the
noh play *Hashi Benkei* (*Benkei on the Bridge*), and other sources.
41. Kichiji is identified in various medieval sources as a wealthy gold trader. Dainichi alludes to a story
preserved in the noh play *Sekihara Yoichi* and the *kōwakamai* (ballad-dance) *Kurama ide*.
42. The story of the murder of Yoshitsune's mother is preserved in the *kōwakamai Yamanaka Tokiwa*
and other sources.

The Palace of the Tengu

Fujiya Dayū at the Banba Post Station in Suruga Province. Oh, how awful! You'll be beset by a mysterious illness, and since you won't know up from down, Kichiji will abandon you and continue on his way. Fujiya will be a kind fellow, but his wife is an evil, horrible woman, and she'll leave you at Six Pines at Fukiage Shore. You'll be in a dreadful state there, hovering on the verge of death, but you'll summon Lady Jōruri from Mikawa Province, and she'll tend to you with care.[43] You'll recover right away.

"After that, you'll make your way to Michinoku Province without any problems. You should entreat Hidehira and the Satō brothers for their help.[44] Later, in Sanuki Province in Shikoku, Hōgen will have an heirloom scroll titled *Ishitamaruta Supernatural Powers*.[45] You'll pledge vows of love with his only daughter, Minazuru-onna, and then steal the scroll and leave.

"Now there is an island of demons to the northeast of Japan known as the Land of Ten Thousand Devils. The demon general there is called the Great Eight-Faced King, and he owns the forty-two-fascicle *Tiger Scrolls*.[46] You will sail to the island; become the Great King's son-in-law; seal a bond with his only daughter, the Asai Heavenly Maiden; take the scrolls as a wedding present; and then return home.

"When you are eighteen, you should lead Hidehira's five hundred thousand riders toward the capital. As you do, your older brother Yoritomo, who is at Hōjō Hiru-ga-kojima in Izu Province, will also raise an army and set out. Putting your minds together in perfect accord, you will advance on the capital, whereupon the Taira are sure to fall. You should chase them out to the western sea, and at Dan-no-ura at Yashima, you should spur each other's forces on.[47] At that time, the Taira general Noto governor Noritsune will encounter you and make you a target. Be sure to take his arrow without flinching. I'll make it fly astray. Nevertheless, Satō Motoharu of Michinoku Province has two sons, the elder of whom, Tsuginobu, is going to step in and take your place. He will be struck by the arrow and die. This, too, is his karma from a previous existence, and his life will end there.

43. Lady Jōruri was the daughter of the governor of Mikawa Province. In the *otogizōshi Jōruri monogatari* (*Jōruri jūnidan sōshi*), Yoshitsune summons her with a letter.
44. These men are Fujiwara no Hidehira (1122–1187), Satō Saburō Tsuginobu (1158–1186), and Satō Shirō Tadanobu (1160–1186). The text simply says "Satō" (rather than "the Satō brothers"), but I have taken it this way because both Tsuginobu and Tadanobu famously supported Yoshitsune.
45. Hōgen is Ki'ichi Hōgen (also Oni'ichi Hōgen), a legendary warrior and divination master. His and Yoshitsune's story is recounted in *The Chronicle of Yoshitsune* and the *otogizōshi Hōgan miyako-banashi* (*The Tale of Yoshitsune in the Capital*).
46. The *Tiger Scrolls* (*Tora no maki*) is a legendary martial-arts treatise described in *Yoshitsune's Island-Hopping*, translated in this volume, and other sources.
47. Dainichi conflates the battles of Yashima and Dan-no-ura, which took place many miles and weeks apart.

"Later, when you are twenty-one, the Taira will have been destroyed and you will rule the realm. Yoritomo will build a palace in the east, where he will be lionized as the Kamakura lord. You will be revered as the lord of the Horikawa Palace in the capital, and at that time you won't have any troubles. However, Kajiwara will slander you to Yoritomo, and you and your brother will become estranged.[48] I should explain to you why this is so.

"In a previous age, there were three holy men by the names of Raichō, Jishō, and Keijibō. Raichō was the present Yoritomo, Jishō was Hōjō Shiro Tokimasa, and Keijibō was Kajiwara. You were a mouse living in a shrine in Yamato. You jumped into an itinerant's backpack, and because of the merit that you achieved by visiting the sixty-plus provinces, you attained rebirth in the present life as Ushiwaka. Being a mouse, you nibbled on the characters of a sutra, and because of Keijibō's bitter resentment against you for it, he will cast aspersions on you.

"You will die at Takadachi in Michinoku Province on the twenty-ninth day of the fourth month of your thirty-second year. Just like that, the karma from your previous lives will run its course, like a wheel turning in a garden. By no means should you reproach yourself or anyone else for what will transpire. Now I will let you venerate the Pure Land, to which you will come when you die."

With those words, Dainichi slid open a sliding paper door. "There, pay your respects!" he said, presenting Yoshitsune with a view of paradise. It was a blessed sight! The grounds were spread with gold and silver, lapis lazuli, and all the seven precious stones, and were decorated with garlands of jewels. The twenty-five bodhisattvas and their heavenly hosts played music in the sky in magnificent manifestations. "Oh, I'd like to stay here, even if it meant never again returning to the human world," Yoshitsune thought, which was truly excellent.

Dainichi spoke: "Your connection to the human realm has not yet expired. Go home, Ushiwaka. Be sure to cherish your enlightenment in the next life, and don't forget the *nenbutsu*, not even for a moment! You should embrace the sincerity of devotion, the profundity of faith, and a determination to pass your own Buddhist merit on to others.[49] As a parting present, I will show you the unenlightened realm."

Dainichi opened a sliding paper door, revealing the great trichiliocosm, the third-order thousand great thousand-fold universe. It contained everything from all times, but Yoshitsune saw it all in a single glance, just like his own reflection in a

48. Kajiwara is Kajiwara Kagetoki (d. 1200). The story of his slander is recounted in *The Tale of the Heike* (thirteenth century) and many other sources.
49. These are the "three minds" (*sanshin*) identified in the Visualization Sutra (Kanmuryōjukyō) as an assured means of attaining the highest rank of the highest grade of rebirth in the Pure Land. See Hisao Inagaki, trans., *The Three Pure Land Sutras: A Study and Translation* (Kyoto: Nagata Bunshodo, 2000), 339.

The Palace of the Tengu

mirror. Indeed, such miracles are the province of buddhas and bodhisattvas who have attained the six supernatural powers, so there is no point in speaking of them.

It was hard for him to take his leave, but Yoshitsune said goodbye and headed for the gate. Dainichi watched him go for a while, and they both wept uncontrollably. Together with the Great Tengu, Yoshitsune returned to the palace of the *tengu*. They made their way deep inside the Shishinden Ceremonial Hall, where Yoshitsune addressed the wife, saying, "Thanks to your advice, I was able to meet my father. I am boundlessly grateful. Goodbye, Great Tengu. And goodbye, ma'am." With that, Yoshitsune headed for the front.

"Farewell, you dear child!" the Great Tengu and his wife exclaimed.

"I'll come again," Yoshitsune replied. "I promise to be your pupil from now on."

The Great Tengu and his wife accompanied Yoshitsune as far as the golden gate. Yoshitsune thought to say goodbye, whereupon he found himself back in the reception room of the Eastern Light Cloister.

Hearing such a story, we must realize that as long as we are in this world, we should cultivate humanity, righteousness, propriety, wisdom, and integrity on the outside while on the inside praying for enlightenment in the life to come.[50] Thanks to this, it seems, the Minamoto would enjoy a hundred generations of prosperity.

TRANSLATION AND INTRODUCTION BY KELLER KIMBROUGH

---

50. Humanity, righteousness, propriety, wisdom, and integrity are the five principal Confucian virtues.

MONSTERS, WARRIORS, AND JOURNEYS TO OTHER WORLDS

Yoshitsune's Island-Hopping

Yoshitsune's Island-Hopping (*Onzōshi shima-watari*) is a traveler's tale about Minamoto no Yoshitsune (1159–1189), a hero of the Genpei War (1180–1185), and his mission to steal a set of precious military scrolls from a notorious demon king on the far island of Ezo. If Yoshitsune's historical life was one of danger and daring, then his fictional adventures are even more so, having been a favorite subject for generations of storytellers and dramatists from the thirteenth century onward. In *The Palace of the Tengu*, the thirteen-year-old Yoshitsune learns the secrets of the god-like *tengu* at their secret mountain lair; in *Yoshitsune's Island-Hopping*, which takes place some two or three years later, he not only departs from Japan but charts a course through a geography of the imagination where each island is more fantastical than the last.

Yoshitsune's Island-Hopping calls to mind Jonathan Swift's *Gulliver's Travels* (1726, 1735), which it predates by more than a hundred years. In a delightful synchronicity, both Gulliver and Yoshitsune encounter island races of horse-men, giants, and miniature "Lilliputians." Of the many islands that Yoshitsune visits, only one bears the name of an existing place: the island of Ezo, which was once the common name for Hokkaido and points north. In this tale, it is identified as the home of demons. Another one of the places that Yoshitsune visits is the storied Island of Women, long identified with Japan and even included in early maps of the Japanese archipelago.

Yoshitsune's Island-Hopping survives in multiple manuscript and woodblock-printed editions. This translation is based on an exquisite large-size picture scroll (*ōgata emaki*). Throughout the island scenes, Yoshitsune is positioned in the foreground with his back turned toward the reader, encouraging viewers to see through his eyes. He

The translation and illustrations are from the *Onzōshi shima-watari* picture scroll (seventeenth century) in the collection of the Akita Prefectural Library, typeset and annotated in Ōshima Tatehiko and Watari Kōichi, eds., *Muromachi monogatari sōshi shū*, Shinpen Nihon koten bungaku zenshū 63 (Tokyo: Shōgakukan, 2002), 91–118.

rejoins the action when he reaches the land of demons, charming his suspicious hosts with flute playing and mudra magic.

Once when Minamoto no Yoshitsune was staying at the Satō family manor, Terui no Tarō approached Fujiwara no Hidehira and said, "Excuse me, my lord. Please listen to what I have to say. By whatever means, I would like to see young master Yoshitsune become ruler of the realm."[1]

"What an excellent thing to suggest!" Hidehira exclaimed. "In my own heart of hearts, I have not been without similar inclinations. I think that you are absolutely right."

Hidehira abruptly left the room and appeared before Yoshitsune. Seeing his guest, Yoshitsune said, "Hidehira, what a surprise! Come in, come in." Hidehira knelt down before him and said, "Excuse me, my lord. As you know, military hand scrolls are indispensable for warriors like ourselves. The island of Ezo lies to the northeast. It is the home of demons, the king of whom is said to possess the *Tiger Scrolls*—the greatest of all his treasures.[2] I hear that they're a true marvel, and that the light they shine serves as the sun and moon of the demon-land. Sail to that island, find some way to get the scrolls, and come back home! Then, if you do, my lord, you should circulate an appeal through the fifty-four districts of Michinoku Province, raise a cavalry at least one hundred thousand strong, ride on the capital, and establish Minamoto rule."

"Oh, what an awful thing to propose!" Yoshitsune thought, feeling that now at last he understood what it meant "to be rained upon under a sheltering branch." What was he to do? Fretting and agonizing, he drifted off to sleep. At that time, his father, Yoshitomo, who had perished in Owari, drew near his pillow and spoke: "My son, Ushiwaka.[3] You should honor Hidehira's words as though they were mine, and Overseer Satō's as though they were your mother Tokiwa's words. If you do, in

1. Yoshitsune is in hiding at the home of Satō Motoharu, overseer of the Shinobu district in Michinoku Province in the far north of Japan. Terui no Tarō was a retainer of Fujiwara no Yasuhira (1155–1189); Fujiwara no Hidehira (d. 1187) was general of the Northeast Pacification Headquarters (Chinjufu), a military outpost established to suppress the Emishi of Michinoku and Dewa provinces.
2. In the Shibukawa text of *Onzōshi shima-watari* (early eighteenth century), Hidehira explains that the capital of the demon island is called Kikenjō (the name of the palace of the Buddhist guardian deity Taishakuten, and a euphemism for any paradise world). See Ōshima Tatehiko, ed., *Otogizōshi shū*, Nihon koten bungaku zenshū 36 (Tokyo: Shōgakukan, 1974), 129.
3. Ushiwaka (also Ushiwakamaru) was one of Yoshitsune's childhood names.

three years' time you shall bring the realm under the rule of the Minamoto. Take this to heart." Then, being a ghostly phantasm, he vanished without a trace.

The poor boy! Awaking from his dream and startled by his vision, he wept bitter tears. "If that's how it is," he thought, "I suppose I'll do as my father says and sail to the island of Ezo." He summoned Hidehira and said, "If I am to do what you suggest, I will need a boat. Do you have a vessel that I could manage on my own?"

"We have several highly regarded ships here, such as the *Kite*, the *Sparrow*, the *Wave-Skipper*, and the *Little Hawk*," Hidehira replied. "Among them, the *Little Hawk* is unique: Bishamon stands at its prow; the Great Kasuga Deity occupies its middle; and Shō Hachiman, the tutelary deity of the Minamoto, stands at its stern. Thus, although it might rain, you won't get wet, and although the sun might shine, you won't be burned. And even without oarsmen, it travels its captain's course."

The young master was utterly delighted, and he boarded the *Little Hawk*. After having a thousand bolts of silk loaded up, he headed out toward the harbor. The feelings in his heart were moving indeed!

The days passed as Yoshitsune sailed anxiously on, and on the seventeenth day he reached a certain island. He rowed his boat to the shore, where he found the islanders all standing in a line, naked. Seeing this, Yoshitsune said, "Excuse me, you islanders. What is the name of this place?"

"Well," the people replied, "long ago we ran out of hemp seed, and having none, we all live naked. This place is therefore called Naked Island, Young Sir from the Capital."

"But don't you get cold when the wind blows?" Yoshitsune inquired. A particularly clever fellow composed the following in reply:

kaze fukeba	When the winds blow
samusa zo masaru	our chills do grow—
hadaka-shima	on Naked Island,
asa no koromo mo	in hempen raiment
mi ni mo matowade	we swathe ourselves not.

But one the islanders dissented, saying, "No, no—the line 'we swathe ourselves not' makes it sound like we have hempen robes, but just don't wear them. That's no good at all." He revised the second part as follows:

asa no koromo no	our hempen raiment
taete nakereba	exhausted, we have none.

Yoshitsune's Island-Hopping

Yoshitsune gives bolts of silk to the inhabitants of Naked Island. (From *Onzōshi shima-watari*, courtesy of the Akita Prefectural Library)

Yoshitsune was moved to find such refined souls among these islanders. Unloading three hundred bolts of silk from his vessel, he gave it to them, saying, "Please, wrap yourselves in this." Henceforth, the people of the island have always worn clothes.

After he left Naked Island, the days passed quickly as the young master pressed on, until on the eighteenth day he reached yet another island. He rowed his boat to the shore, where he found beings who resembled horses from the waist down, and men from the waist up. Seeing this, Yoshitsune said, "Hey, hey, you islanders—what's the name of this place?"

Yoshitsune visits Horse-Man Island. (From *Onzōshi shima-watari*, courtesy of the Akita Prefectural Library)

"Well," the people replied, "a human and a horse who indulged in lovemaking were exiled to this island from Japan, and since both their human form and their equine shape survive in us, this place is called Horse-Man Island, Young Sir from the Capital."

After he left Horse-Man Island, the days passed quickly as the young master pressed on, until on the twenty-fifth day he reached yet another island. He rowed his boat to the shore, where he found that he had come upon an island of people who were a full hundred feet tall. Each and every one of them had a drum strapped on, and they were all standing in a line. Seeing this, Yoshitsune said, "Excuse me, you islanders. What is the name of this place?"

"Well," the people replied, "from long ago, our height has been fixed at one hundred feet, three-tenths of an inch. This place is therefore called Tall Island."

"What are the drums fastened to your waists for?" Yoshitsune inquired.

"Once we've fallen over, getting ourselves back up is impossible. So we beat on these drums, and all the other islanders gather around to heave and ho us back to our feet, Young Lord from the Capital."

Yoshitsune visits Dwarf Island. (From *Onzōshi shima-watari*, courtesy of the Akita Prefectural Library)

Shortly thereafter, the young master left Tall Island. He pressed on, and soon, on the thirty-second day, he reached a certain island. He rowed his boat to the shore, where he found that he had come upon an island of people who were no more than one foot tall. Sitting in a large circle, they were diverting themselves by reciting poems, composing Chinese verses, or taking turns in linking stanzas. Seeing this, Yoshitsune said, "What is the name of this place?"

"Well," they replied, "from long ago, the height of our people has been fixed at one foot, two-tenths of an inch. This place is therefore called Dwarf Island. However, since on this island we spend our days reciting poems, composing Chinese verses, and taking turns in linking stanzas, it is also called Bodhisattva Island or Linked-Verse Island, O Lord from the Capital."[4]

After learning this, the young master left Linked-Verse Island. The days passed quickly as he pressed on, until on the thirty-fifth day he reached a certain island. He rowed his boat to the shore, where he found that he had come upon an island populated entirely by women, without so much as a single man.

"What is the name of this place?"

"Well," they replied, "from long ago, there have been no men on this island, only women. This place is therefore called the Island of Women."

"But what do you do for men's seed?" Yoshitsune inquired.

"Well," they began, "we take the southern wind that blows from Japan as the 'male wind' and love it dearly. When one of us dies, another is born, and when another is born, one of us dies, so people say that the number of women on the island is 108,000. As for men like you who have been blown here by distant winds, we truss them up right away, carve off their flesh, and offer it to the palace. We make a broth from the bones, and those of our station receive it to drink." Turning to one another, the women said, "Now, grab that man!" and swarmed toward him.

Forming the Mist Mudra, Yoshitsune cast it in their direction, scrambled aboard his boat, and pushed out to sea. On the island, the women gathered about, complaining to one another with visible disappointment: "What kind of devil was that who landed here? And what on earth did he set on fire? The smoke still hasn't cleared! It's as hard to see around here as on a hazy night—I can't tell one thing from another!"

The days passed quickly as the young master pressed on, until on the forty-second day he reached a certain island. He rowed his boat to the shore, where he found that he had come upon an island of people no more than an inch tall. They

4. In the Shibukawa text, the islanders explain that "the island is called Bodhisattva Island because the twenty-five bodhisattvas come from the Southern Paradise World three times every evening and three times every day, playing music and manifesting with a wondrous fragrance, falling petals, and drifting purple clouds" (*Onzōshi shima-watari*, in *Otogizōshi shū*, ed. Ōshima, 136).

Yoshitsune's Island-Hopping

ねうご志ま

Yoshitsune visits the Island of Women. (From *Onzōshi shima-watari*, courtesy of the Akita Prefectural Library)

had fastened threads to a single reed, which a full thousand men were tugging along, heave-hoing all the way. Seeing this, Yoshitsune said, "Excuse me, islanders. What is the name of this place?"

"Well," the people replied, "from long ago, the height of our people has been fixed at one and one-tenth inch. This place is therefore called Biting Midge Island."

"So, what are you going to do with that reed?" Yoshitsune inquired.

"Well," the people replied, "construction is being done at the palace, and we've been tasked with presenting reeds to our lordship in teams of one hundred, Young Lord from Japan."

Yoshitsune thought the people of this island honest and straightforward and, imagining he would like to question them about his destination, asked, "Excuse me, islanders, but how far is it to the island of Ezo from here?"

"From here to the island of Ezo," they replied, "it would take twenty days on your current course. On the way there is a treacherous place called the Kanbuttō Strait, which is eighty thousand *yojana*s deep and eighty thousand *yojana*s wide.[5] We hear that its currents run as fast as a three-feathered battle arrow, and that its waters are even colder than seven winter streams combined in your Reed Plain Country. With favorable winds, you can reach it in three days. But if they are bad, it will take you twenty."

Yoshitsune was impressed by their earnest instruction. To reward them, he carried as much wood to the palace as would have taken them four or five years on their own and piled it up in one great heap. When they beheld this feat, the islanders were overjoyed at being delivered from their long, arduous toil, and they praised him as the "Ushiwaka Buddha."

"Whatever far-flung fields, deep mountain passes, and treacherous sea straits might await," Yoshitsune thought, "I'll have to make my way through." With such thoughts in mind, he put Biting Midge Island behind him. And by what places did he pass? Beginning with Dog-Man Island, China-Cat Island and Monkey Island, Ox-Demon Island, Ebisu Island and Daikoku Island, he bypassed a total of thirty-three islands until he arrived at the rumored strait.

Yoshitsune peeked out over the waves, but what he saw was almost too much to bear! He purified his hands with water from the sea and bowed down in the direction of Japan, and then entreated the gods, saying, "Hail Great Compassionate Tamonten and Shō Hachiman,[6] tutelary deity of the Minamoto! If it would please you this once to see the realm fall under Minamoto rule, then allow me safe passage across this sea." Ah, the feelings in his heart as he made his way forward! Truly, it must have been because of the gods' and buddhas' vows that he made it safely across.

When the young master came ashore on the island of Ezo, the demons were at play, lifting up boulders and climbing old trees. However, the moment they caught sight of Yoshitsune's splendid figure, they leaped down from their perches. Thinking to make a meal of him, they grabbed their red-hot iron cudgels, huffed flaming breath, curled their crimson tongues, and headed straight for him. "These brutes are a bit worked up," Yoshitsune thought. Climbing to higher ground, he pulled out his

---

5. One *yojana* equals seven or nine miles, depending on the interpretation.

6. Tamonten is another name for Bishamon (also Bishamonten, Skt. Vaiśravaṇa), the Buddhist guardian deity of whom Yoshitsune himself is said to be a reincarnation in *The Palace of the Tengu*.

Yoshitsune plays his flute for some of the demons of Ezo. (From *Onzōshi shima-watari*, courtesy of the Akita Prefectural Library)

flute, Broken Cicada, and slipped off its brocade cover. From all the many airs, he performed "Hitchi," "Snake-Catcher," "Myriad Autumns," "Ōshōkai," and then "Sōfuren" two and three, and then four and five times.

"What wonderful sounds come from that bamboo!" the demons exclaimed. "We were just going to grab him and eat him up, but he's so good at tooting that stalk . . . let's have some fun playing one, too." They each pressed on the joints of some island bamboo, but blow and blow as they might, they could not make a sound.

From among them, a demon by the name of Diamond Devil came forward and said,[7] "Excuse me, you all. Rather than keeping such entertaining music to ourselves, we should make haste to tell the king and present this whelp to him." They discussed the matter with Yoshitsune, whereupon they went to the palace.

When Yoshitsune saw how the palace was put together, he found that the outer gate was built of cast iron and set within a cast-iron wall eighteen *chō* around.[8] The middle gate was built of silver and set within a silver wall seventeen *chō* around. The inner gate was built of gold and set within a golden wall sixteen *chō* around. The great king of this realm had an unlimited supply of gold, and he was therefore called King Kanehira, or "King Gold-Leaf."

Diamond Devil approached the great king and said, "Excuse me, my lord. A gentleman has just arrived from Japan. He's a famous bamboo player. Please have him play something for you."

"Have you all been taken in by this Japanese?" roared the king. "I'll snatch him up and make a meal out of him!" How his body rocked and heaved as he came out! If one were to compare, it would be like Mount Fuji in the Reed Plain Country uprooting and turning itself over. He was sixteen-times-ten feet tall and had sixteen noses and sixteen eyes, sixteen mouths, and eight heads. His voice at a whisper was like thunder, and when he was angry, it was like the peal of a hundred thousand million bolts of lightning, enough to fell mountains and rend the earth. Nevertheless, he did not ordinarily take this form, appearing instead like other *dōji*.[9]

The great king rushed through the outer gate and cried, "You, Young Sir—why have you come here? What is the meaning of this?"

"If what I have heard is true," Yoshitsune replied, showing not the least bit of fright or surprise, "I understand that you possess the *Tiger Scrolls*. I would like to see them, even if only once, which is why I have come all this way."

The great king took in Yoshitsune's words. "Oh, what a fine young man!" he exclaimed. "Truly, how excellent your determination, to have come this far on rumors heard in Japan! Please, come inside." With that, he invited Yoshitsune into the palace.

Looking around, Yoshitsune saw that the courtyards were strewn with gold and silver sand. Everything shone and glittered, and myriad flowers bloomed in all their fragrant glory. The splendor of the place was without limit. The king ushered the

---

7. In Japanese, his name is Kongō Yasha (Skt. Vajrayakṣa), which is also the name of one of the Five Mantra Kings dedicated to protecting the Buddhist Law.

8. One *chō* equals 119 yards; eighteen *chō* is approximately 1.2 miles.

9. *Dōji* (youth) is a term for a child or a sacred being with cropped and unbound hair, and in medieval fiction it is also commonly used to signify demons.

young master into a particular room, where he set out rare delicacies from the land and sea, along with fruits of the realm, and offered him all sorts of wine. When they had finally finished drinking, the king said, "I have heard, Young Sir, that you are a famous bamboo player. Please let me hear a strain."

"Certainly," Yoshitsune replied, "by all means, listen." He pulled out Broken Cicada, which, of course, he had acquired from Midajirō.[10] "This bamboo belonged to Kūkai, who is famous throughout Japan and who was the great founder of the Shingon school of Buddhism. While he was in China, he traveled to Sacred Eagle Peak in India. He passed the Pamir peaks, and on the far side of the River of Flowing Sands, he came upon a waterfall. This bamboo was growing at its base. Thinking it a remarkably good stalk, Kūkai drew the sword that he was carrying beneath his robes, cut three lengths from it, and set them afloat on the Flowing Sands, certain that he would find them again in Japan if karma allowed. They drifted to our realm, where Kūkai found them right away, and as he lifted up the shoots, he spoke with them as though they were living people. What wondrous bamboo!" Yoshitsune then played the piece called "Blue Sea Waves" as though to shake the heavens with the sound.

"How delightful the sound made by this bamboo!" the king bellowed. "But rather than keeping such refined music all to myself, I should have my daughter Asahi come listen." With that, he sent a messenger to the young lady's quarters. Asahi agreed, and as she made her way out, her gently swaying figure, draped in a twelve-layered robe, was radiantly beautiful.

To think that so incomparable a woman could be found on an island such as this! On seeing her, the young master was lost in his own thoughts for a while. "But no," he suddenly realized, "what should become of me if these feelings were found out? I'll try to play even better than before." And out of all the many airs, he performed "Shishi" and "Toraden"—songs about a boy longing for a girl—two or three times in a row. The king, being a keen observer,[11] noticed that the sound of the flute was somehow different from before, and he thought it curious how the young man's eyes would fall on Asahi. In sum, the king realized that the young man had set his heart on her.

"I can see from your face, Young Sir, that you pine for my daughter. That being the case, let's have a contest of talents! We'll leave the matter to sport. If you lose, I'll snatch you and eat you. And if I lose, I'll give you Asahi."

---

10. The identity of Midajirō is unknown.

11. Literally, the king is said to be cognizant of the Four Aspects of Phenomenal Existence (*shisō*), which, in other words, means that he was perceptive.

"What a happy proposition!" Yoshitsune thought. Concluding that this princess would now be his to do with as he pleased, he agreed to the king's conditions.

"What, then, is your pleasure?" Yoshitsune asked.

"O ho! The young man from the capital asks me my pleasure? What heartening words! Come, let us decide the matter with our swords."

"Very well," Yoshitsune replied.

The king took the offensive, his Taniyama-forged sword five feet, eight inches long, while the young master was forced on the defensive with his sword, Companion Cutter,[12] which was two feet, eight inches. They countered and parried back and forth until—how unfortunate!—the king somehow failed to deflect Yoshitsune's blade and had a great tuft of hair shorn from his left temple. Dabbing away the blood from his wound, the king brought the match to an end.

Nevertheless, the king was not deterred. "Let's see who can jump higher!" he cried, and he leaped ten feet into the air. Yoshitsune formed the Small Hawk Mudra and jumped a full thirty feet. As soon as he saw this, the king said, "Well, let's play a game of *go*!" But having been raised a scholar at Kurama Temple, the young master won the first six rounds.

As soon as he saw this, the king proclaimed, "In that case, let's wrestle!" Hearing this, the young master considered: "All the contests so far have favored my abilities, but this is a test of strength. This king is famously strong, and I've always been a weakling. I'm sure to meet my end here." Poor Yoshitsune! Prostrating himself in the direction of Japan, he made his supplications, saying, "Hail the All-powerful Tenjin of Kitano;[13] the Great Compassionate Tamonten of Kurama; Shō Hachiman, the tutelary deity of the Minamoto; and all the greater and lesser *tengu* on whom I always call: if it would please you this once to see the realm fall under Minamoto rule, then let me win this wrestling match."

As the referee, Diamond Devil set Yoshitsune opposite the king, whereupon they grappled. Truly, he looked like a small bird perched on some great tree. For a while, the outcome seemed uncertain, until, somehow, the king lost hold with one of his hands. The young master seized him, and the king was thrown. Letting out a great sigh, the king exclaimed, "This young man can't be human! The Great Tengu from the Land of Reed Plains must have come here as a man in order to put an end to me! What do you all think?"

12. Companion Cutter (Tomokirimaru, formerly Higekiri) was a famous Minamoto family sword, so-named because it is said to have once cut one-quarter of an inch from its companion blade.

13. Tenjin is the divine manifestation of the courtier Sugawara no Michizane (845–903), who is enshrined at Kitano Shrine in Kyoto.

Yoshitsune plays *go* with the demon king of Ezo. (From *Onzōshi shima-watari*, courtesy of the Akita Prefectural Library)

The king did not go back on his promise, and he thus moved Yoshitsune into his daughter Asahi's quarters. The twenty-one days of feasting that followed were truly delightful. "We have to have some venison at such a splendid feast," the king declared. "Let's go hunt some deer!" And with that, he took a great number of demons, red-hot iron cudgels in hand, to Tenken Mountain in pursuit of their quarry.

When the young master looked about the palace, he could not find a single demon, and thinking that this was the perfect time, he summoned his wife, Asahi, and said, "Where is the cavern? Please tell me."[14]

14. Although it has not been mentioned before, the *Tiger Scrolls* (*Tora no maki*) are kept in a secret cavern on the island.

Yoshitsune wrestles the demon king of Ezo. (From *Onzōshi shima-watari*, courtesy of the Akita Prefectural Library)

"Before visiting the cavern," Princess Asahi immediately replied, "one must perform ablutions in the Kanbuttō Strait seven times a night and seven times during the day for one hundred days and one hundred nights—only then can one hope to look upon the scrolls. Whatever you do, it can't be done."

"That's a custom of this island," Yoshitsune began, "because you're impure of body. I am Japanese, and moreover, from the age of seven, as a student at Kurama Temple, I did nothing but pray morning and night, from dawn to dusk. So what could be the problem? When strangers on the road take shelter together from a

Yoshitsune's Island-Hopping

sudden rain, or when two people put their pillows together for a night, it's because of the karma they share from former lives. Considering the love that you've shown me, please tell me plainly."

Asahi, being an honest and straightforward woman, took him at his word, and pulling on the young master's flowery sleeve, she showed him to the cavern. Yoshitsune was overjoyed, and on looking around, he found that the scrolls were sealed within a stone coffer. There seemed to be no way of opening it, so he formed the Great Stone Mudra and struck it, whereupon the stone coffer shattered in three and revealed the scrolls.

After he had stolen the scrolls, Yoshitsune approached the princess and said, "Do you have any idea who I am? I am Ushiwakamaru of the Minamoto—famous throughout all of Japan—the ninth son of Minamoto no Yoshitomo and a descendent of Emperor Seiwa.[15] Hearing rumors of these *Tiger Scrolls*, I came to this island. And now, thanks to your kindness, I have achieved my goal. Although I would like to take you back with me, too, you're such a stunningly beautiful woman that the dragon deity would surely set his eye on you. And if that happened, I doubt that either of us could return to Japan. So even though I'm quite fond of you, there's nothing I can do. In any case, I'll be sure to send someone for you next spring. Please wait until then."

Having deceived her so completely, Yoshitsune set out, feigning tears. He climbed aboard the *Little Hawk* and cast off to sea.

Now because these scrolls had provided light to the sun and moon on the demon island, the sky was swept with an icy rain and the seething of the heavens knew no bounds. Seeing this from Tenken Mountain, the king exclaimed, "What, has the man from the capital visited the cavern? Let's go and see!" And with that, he put the mountain behind him. When he saw the state of the cavern—the stone coffer shattered in three and the scrolls missing—he had the palace searched. His men looked high and low, even breaking open carriage axles and peering inside, but the young master was nowhere to be found.

Putting two and two together, the king ordered boats prepared, and he set out in pursuit toward Japan. Seeing this, Yoshitsune cast the Mist Mudra, but it proved useless. He tried the Wind Mudra, the Fire Mudra, and innumerable others, but as his pursuers were demons, the signs had no effect. The young master pulled out the scrolls and quickly spread them open, finding the *Sassatsu* Mudra. He formed it and cast it out, whereupon seven mountains of salt, each of which was a thousand leagues high and a thousand leagues around, rose out of the sea.

15. Emperor Seiwa (850–881, r. 858–876) was the fifty-sixth emperor of Japan.

"How long would it take to sail around such mountains?" the king cried, taking in the sight. "Turn back, men, it's hopeless." And with that, they all returned home.

Two hundred and ten days later, having escaped the proverbial jaws of the crocodile, Yoshitsune arrived at the harbor from which he had first set out. As soon as Hidehira heard the news, he came to greet him with a retinue of more than three thousand horsemen, and he moved him into the Willow Palace.[16] Day in and day out, Yoshitsune was on duty with barely a moment to spare. His good fortune waxed by the month and improved by the day, such that words can hardly measure.

TRANSLATION BY CHARLES WOOLLEY; INTRODUCTION BY KELLEY DOORE

16. The Willow Palace was the residence of the powerful warlord Fujiwara no Kiyohira (d. 1128) in Hiraizumi.

Yoshitsune's Island-Hopping

The Tale of Amewakahiko

The Tale of Amewakahiko (*Amewakahiko sōshi*) is one of a substantial number of Japanese fictional works that recount the legendary origins of the Tanabata Festival, an annual observance rooted in the Han dynasty myth of the star-crossed lovers Zhinü (Weaver Girl) and Niulang (Cowherd), the stars Vega and Altair, respectively. Since the eighth century, the festival has been observed in Japan, where the lovers are commonly referred to as Orihime and Hikoboshi. The title character is also deeply entrenched in Japanese mytho-history. Amewakahiko appears in *Kojiki* (*Record of Ancient Matters*, 712) and *Nihon shoki* (*The Chronicles of Japan*, 720) as a deity who is entrusted with the task of traveling to earth in order to pacify the lands and retrieve Amenohohi, a child of Amaterasu, the goddess of the sun, and Susano'o, a god of storms and a brother of Amaterasu. After shooting Nakime, the pheasant that has been dispatched to ascertain his plans, Amewakahiko is killed by the same arrow. Amewakahiko appears also in the fragmentary gazetteer of Settsu Province (*Settsu no kuni fudoki*), in *Utsuho monogatari* (*The Tale of the Hollow Tree*, tenth century), and in *Sagoromo monogatari* (*The Tale of Sagoromo*, early eleventh century). He is the subject of several works of medieval and early modern fiction, including a considerably longer Muromachi-period (1337–1573) version of the story than the one presented here and an early-Edo-period (1600–1867) illustrated manuscript. These later narratives diverge from earlier representations of Amewakahiko to varying degrees while maintaining a focus on one of this figure's most remarkable features: his ability to transcend the boundary between heaven and earth.

The translation of Part One is based on a handwritten transcription, in the collection of the Tokyo National Museum, of the textual portions of the *Amewakahiko sōshi* picture scroll (fifteenth century) in the Museum of Asian Art, Berlin. The translation of Part Two is based on the incomplete *Amewakahiko sōshi* picture scroll, only the second scroll of which now survives, in the Museum of Asian Art, Berlin; the illustrations are from the same source. Both parts are typeset and annotated in Matsumoto Ryūshin, ed., *Otogizōshi shū*, Shinchō Nihon koten shūsei (Tokyo: Shinchōsha, 1980), 77–85.

The calligraphy in the scroll on which the translation of Part Two is based is attributed to Emperor Go-Hanazono (1419–1471, r. 1428–1464), and the images to the court painter Tosa Hirochika (ca. 1439–1492). This version of *The Tale of Amewakahiko* is characterized by the brevity of its textual passages; by comparison, some other renditions of the story are approximately four times as long.

Part One

Long ago, there was a woman washing clothes in front of the residence of a wealthy man. A large serpent appeared before her and said, "Won't you listen to what I have to say? If you do not, I will crush you!"

"What can I do for you?" the woman replied. "As long as I am able, I will be happy to listen."

The serpent spat out a letter. "Take this to the wealthy man inside," he instructed. The woman departed with the letter. Presently, the wealthy man opened it and read: "Give me your three daughters.[1] If you do not, I will kill you and your wife! You are to make a dwelling in preparation for our union. Construct a pavilion in front of the pond at such-and-such a place, and know that even a building that's a hundred feet wide will be difficult for me to enter." Reading this, the father and mother wept to no end.

The man sent for his eldest daughter and spoke with her. She replied, "This is preposterous! I refuse to do this even if it means we will die!" When the man spoke with his middle daughter, she gave the same reply. Sobbing, the man summoned and spoke with the youngest and most beloved of his three daughters, who said, "Rather than allow the snake to take my two sisters, let it take me: whatever happens to me will happen." Weeping the entire time, her parents prepared for her departure—a moving sight!

The man built a house in front of the pond described by the serpent, and they all set out. The father left the young woman in the house by herself, and he and his attendants returned home. That night, around the hour of the boar,[2] the wind suddenly picked up, rain began to pour, and thunder crackled as lightning bolts

---

1. In a variant of this story—the *Tanabata no honji* picture scroll in the former Akagi Bunko archive—the snake instructs the man and his wife to give him the kindest of his three daughters. See Yokoyama Shigeru and Matsumoto Ryūshin, eds., *Muromachi jidai monogatari taisei* (Tokyo: Kadokawa Shoten, 1980), 8:493.
2. The hour of the boar is approximately 9:00 to 11:00 P.M.

flickered across the sky. Great waves began to rise from the center of the pond, and the young woman wondered whether she was alive or dead. She found the scene so frightening that she seemed to be hardly of this world. A snake that would indeed have filled a hundred-foot house appeared and said, "Do not be afraid of me! If you have a sword, cut off my head." Saddened in the midst of her fear, the young woman easily decapitated him with the blade of a fingernail clipper. A strikingly handsome man in casual court attire sprang from the serpent's body. He peeled off the snake's skin, rolled it up, and placed it in a small Chinese chest. He and the young woman then lay down together. Their fears forgotten, they lay in amorous embrace.

While living together and sharing love, the two enjoyed a wide assortment of items from the chest. They took out whatever they needed, and lacking nothing, they enjoyed endless prosperity.[3] Having amassed a great number of vassals and retainers, the man said, "In truth, I am a Dragon King of the ocean, even though I also traverse the skies. I have to go somewhere soon; sometime tomorrow or the day after, I will ascend to the heavens. I'll be back in seven days. If I do not return as planned, wait for two weeks. If I don't come back then, wait three weeks. If I still fail to come, you will know that I will never be back."

At these words the young woman said, "If this happens, what shall I do?"

"There is a woman in the western part of the capital," the man explained, "and she has something called a single-night gourd. Give her something for it, and ascend to the heavens.[4] This is a great undertaking, and the climb will be most difficult to achieve. But if you do ascend, ask those you encounter along the path where you might find the dwelling of Amewakahiko, and come to me." He continued: "As for the Chinese chest, whatever might happen, do not open it by any means—if you do, I will never be able to return." And with that, the man rose up into the sky.

Presently, the older daughters came to their sister's dwelling to have a first-hand look at her new prosperity. In the midst of such opulence, the sisters lamented, saying things like "Because of our own wretched karma, we thought he was frightening!" As they went around prying into everything, they discovered the chest that the young woman's husband had told her not to open. "Open it!" they demanded. "Let's have a look! Let's see!"

"I don't know where the key is," the young woman said.

3. The *Tanabata no honji* picture scroll explains that they amassed great wealth, including and beyond the seven jewels and myriad treasures. See Yokoyama and Matsumoto, eds., *Muromachi jidai monogatari taisei*, 8:497.

4. Judging from illustrations of the scene, the woman is to plant the gourd and, as it grows, walk along its vines to ascend to the sky.

MONSTERS, WARRIORS, AND JOURNEYS TO OTHER WORLDS

"Just take it out! Why would you want to hide it?" the older sisters shouted, and they began to tickle her. The key was tied to the waist of the young woman's trouser-skirt, and it knocked against a standing blind. Hearing the sound, the sisters said, "Ah, look! Here it is!" and immediately opened the chest. There was nothing inside, but a wisp of smoke came out and rose up into the sky. With that, the sisters returned home.

After waiting twenty-one days and seeing no sign of her husband, the young woman went to the western part of the capital, as he had instructed. There she met with the woman and gave her something for the single-night gourd. Riding the gourd up into the heavens, she thought of how her parents would grieve at word of her disappearance and grew forlorn. "It seems I will never again see my home," she thought, glancing back again and again.

au koto mo	Knowing not whether
isa shirakumo no	I will find my love within
nakazora ni	the white-clouded sky,
tadayoinubeki	I must drift about here—
mi wo ika ni sen	What will become of me?[5]

Part Two

As she ascended to the sky, she encountered a beautiful man garbed in white hunting robes. "Where might I find Amewakahiko?" she asked, and he replied, "I don't know. Ask the person you will encounter next," and continued on his way. "Who are you?" she called out, and the man replied, "The Evening Star."[6]

Next, someone holding a broom appeared, and when again she asked the same question, this person replied, "I don't know. Ask the one you will meet after me. I am called The Comet," and with these words he continued on.

Subsequently the young woman encountered a cluster of people. When she made the same inquiries, they answered as the others had, adding, "We are the Pleiades."[7] And they continued on their way.

Since everyone answered in the same way, the young woman wondered how she might ever find her husband. She felt helpless and forlorn. But as it would not

5. This poem pivots on the phrase *isa shira[zu]* (not knowing) and *shirakumo no* (white-clouded).
6. The Evening Star (Yūtsuzu) is the planet Venus. In Greek mythology, it is known as Hesperus, and its Latin name is Vesper.
7. The Pleiades (Subaru hoshi), or Seven Sisters, is a star cluster in the constellation Taurus. Owing to its proximity to the earth, it is the most visible cluster to the human eye.

The Tale of Amewakahiko

The young woman travels through the sky, asking directions of those she meets on her way. (From *Amewakahiko sōshi*, courtesy of the Museum of Asian Art, Berlin, and Art Resource, NY)

do for her to indulge in such thoughts, she pressed on. She encountered a person riding in a splendid, jeweled palanquin. The young woman asked the same questions as before, and the person instructed her, "As you travel farther on, you will find a jeweled mansion built on a bed of azure stone. Go there, and ask for Amewakahiko." The young woman resumed her journey. Upon finding her husband, the young woman told him of her sadness as she wandered lost through the empty sky. Deeply moved, Amewakahiko replied, "I have been constantly dejected, not knowing what to do; yet even then, I waited and took comfort in the thought that you might come looking for me as we had agreed. And to think that you felt the same— oh, how moving!" Whispering sweet nothings, they shared a bond that was profound indeed.

"There's something that worries me," Amewakahiko said, "and I'm wondering what to do. My father is a demon. I am afraid of what he'll do to you when he finds that you are here." Although she was shocked to hear this, the young woman thought to herself, "Come now—since it's my lot in life to meet endless hardship, I must accept it. It may be distressing, but I can't very well go back; I'll just have to let things take their course."

After a number of days had passed, the man's father arrived. Amewakahiko transformed the young woman into an armrest, and the father leaned on her. For Amewakahiko, it was difficult to watch. "I smell someone from the human realm," the father cried, rising to his feet. "It's rancid!" The father would come again from time to time, and each time Amewakahiko transformed the young woman into fans and pillows and the like, continuing to deceive him.

Seeming to have found her out, the father returned again. With silent footfalls, he arrived stealthily. Amewakahiko was napping, and, because he was unable to conceal her, the young woman remained visible. "Who is this?" the demon father demanded. Because there was no hiding her now, Amewakahiko candidly explained the situation. His father replied, "In that case, she's our bride! And since I don't have anyone to serve me, I'll put her to use."

"As you wish," Amewakahiko replied, forlornly. It would not do to refuse his father, so he handed over the young woman.

The demon father led the girl away, saying, "I have several thousand cattle in the field. You will care for them morning and evening. Send them outside in the daytime and put them in the barn at night." The young woman discussed this with Amewakahiko, asking, "How am I to do this?" whereupon he detached his sleeves, handed them to her, and said, "Say 'Amewakahiko's sleeves' and wave them." When she waved them,

Amewakahiko (*center*) speaks with his demon father about his wife (*right*). (From *Amewakahiko sōshi*, courtesy of the Museum of Asian Art, Berlin, and Art Resource, NY)

The Tale of Amewakahiko

the cows went out to pasture in the early morning and returned to the barn in the evening. The thousand cows yielded to her will. "How amazing!" the demon exclaimed.

"Transport a thousand measures of rice from my storehouse here to my storehouse over there, right away!" the demon said. "And do not drop a grain." Again, the young woman waved the sleeves and spoke, "Sleeves, sleeves," whereupon a great number of ants appeared and, in a short period of time, relocated the grains of rice. Upon seeing this, the demon pulled out a calculating device and, noticing that a single grain was missing, grew ill-spirited and said, "You'd better go and look for that grain!" Judging by his face, it appeared that this would be the young woman's end. He was frightening beyond measure. "I'll certainly have a look," the young woman said, and spied an ant that was bent over at the waist and unable to carry its grain of rice. Delighted, she picked it up and took it away.

Next the demon said, "Lock her up in the centipede storehouse!" and he sealed her inside a building with iron reinforcements. Although he used the word "centipede," these were no ordinary centipedes. They were a little over a foot in length, and there were four or five thousand of them swarming together. They opened their mouths to devour her. Swooning in fear, the young woman again waved her sleeves, saying, "Amewakahiko's sleeves," whereupon the centipedes retreated to a corner and did not approach her. After seven days had passed, they opened the door and looked in: nothing had happened to the young woman.

Again she was placed in confinement, this time inside a castle of snakes. And, just as before, not a single snake had drawn near her. They waited seven days and looked

The young woman helps an ant with its grain of rice. (From *Amewakahiko sōshi*, courtesy of the Museum of Asian Art, Berlin, and Art Resource, NY)

Amewakahiko's father sends the young woman into a room full of snakes. (From *Amewakahiko sōshi*, courtesy of the Museum of Asian Art, Berlin, and Art Resource, NY)

in again: as before, she was still alive. She appears to have been too much for her father-in-law to handle!

"It seems that this is as it should be," the demon said, "so you can meet with my son like you did before, once each month." The young woman misheard and asked, "Did you say once a year?" The demon replied, "Yes, in that case, once a year!" He then picked up a handful of wild rice and flung it at her, whereupon the grains transformed into the Milky Way. Now the two lovers, called Vega and Altair,[8] are reunited once every year on the seventh day of the seventh month.

TRANSLATION AND INTRODUCTION BY RAECHEL DUMAS

8. In the original text, Vega and Altair are referred to as Tanabata and Hikoboshi. Tanabata is one of several names for Orihime.

The Tale of Amewakahiko

The Origins of the Suwa Deity

As a classic *honji-mono* (origin tale), *The Origins of the Suwa Deity* (*Suwa no honji*) reflects the complex intertwining of Buddhism and native Japanese beliefs. Origin tales relate the former human lives of buddhas, bodhisattvas, and deities, frequently recounting the struggles and hardships that led to their manifestation as divine beings. *The Origins of the Suwa Deity* concerns the former human lives of the gods of Suwa Shrine in Nagano Prefecture, one of the oldest shrine complexes in Japan.

The *honji-mono* were closely linked to the belief in *honji-suijaku* (original ground, manifest traces). In its simplest form, *honji-suijaku* maintains that the Japanese gods are actually manifestations of Buddhist divinities. In order to aid the multitude of sentient beings, buddhas and bodhisattvas would manifest themselves in this world as humans. Suffering the vicissitudes of karma, they would ultimately become native deities and offer guidance to enlightenment. The *honji* (original buddha or bodhisattva) and the *suijaku* (manifest deity) formed two parts of an inseparable whole and generated a cosmology that directly linked Japan to India, the origin of the Buddhist divinities.

The narrative appeal of *The Origins of the Suwa Deity* comes both from its journeys to other worlds and countries and from its story of the estrangement and reconciliation of a family. The protagonist, Kōka no Saburō Yorikata, undergoes an inner journey of intense and sometimes contradictory emotions. When he resides in the Land of Yuiman, he longs for his homeland, but he is also reluctant to leave his new family; after returning to his homeland, he finds his former residence strange and unfamiliar.

One of the more interesting aspects of *The Origins of the Suwa Deity* is its emphasis on mercy, even though the Suwa Deity tends to be known as a warrior god.[1] The

---

The translation is from the unillustrated *Suwa no honji* manuscript (Tenshō 13 [1585]) typeset and annotated in Matsumoto Ryūshin, ed., *Otogizōshi shū*, Shinchō Nihon koten shūsei (Tokyo: Shinchōsha, 1980), 251–87.

1. Nogami Takahiro, "Suwa Shinkō," February 24, 2007, in *Encyclopedia of Shinto*, http://eos.kokugakuin.ac .jp/modules/xwords/entry.php?entryID=1080.

gratuitous violence that can sometimes characterize medieval prose fiction is conspicuously absent here. Instead, the heroic deeds by which conflicts are resolved are, in fact, acts of restraint. For example, Kōka no Jirō Yoritada's retainer defies his master's execution order; Lady Kasuga challenges the logic of vengeance and persuades her father not to go to war; and Yorikata eventually chooses to forgive his treacherous brother.

The Origins of the Suwa Deity survives in numerous manuscripts that are conventionally divided into two textual lines. In one, the protagonist's name is given as Kaneie, and in the other, he is known as Yorikata. This text is derived from the Yorikata line, which is traceable to *Shintōshū* (fourteenth century), a collection of tales on Shinto shrines.

South of the world mountain Sumeru lies Jambudvīpa, where humans live. There, in the first days of the great land of Japan, dwelled the god Kunitokotachi. After seven generations of celestial gods and five generations of terrestrial gods, a divine prince appeared named Unoha Fukiawasezu. For 836,042 years, he will maintain the rule of all under heaven. The line of human emperors began when this prince took the name of Emperor Jinmu, who reigned for 127 years. During his time, Jinmu pacified the land and established the imperial way; he cleared the fields of reeds and raised up the imperial palace. Three generations of sovereigns lived there after him: Emperor Suizei, Emperor Annei, and Emperor Itoku.[2]

In the reign of Emperor Kōshō,[3] in the district of Kōka in Ōmi Province, there lived a man—a fifth-generation descendant of Chinkyū—called the Provisional Governor of Kōka. This man had three sons. His eldest was named Tarō Yorinori, his second was Jirō Yoritada, and his third was Saburō Yorikata. They were blessed with the emperor's favor in all matters, and did not want for anything.

In the spring of a certain year, Lord Kōka stepped out from his southern estate. As he gazed into the distance, a strange wind blew through his body and he collapsed. He incurred a severe illness, and he was dead within a week. In his final hour, he called for his three sons and spoke: "Tarō, since you have built your house by the Eastern Gate, I will name you the Eastern Lord. Jirō, since you have built your house by the Western Gate, I will name you the Western Lord. As for Saburō, you moved

175

---

2. The legendary emperors Suizei, Annei, and Itoku are said to have reigned from 581 to 477 B.C.E.

3. Emperor Kōshō (507–393 B.C.E., r. 475–393 B.C.E.) is traditionally counted as the fifth human emperor of Japan. The identity of Chinkyū is unknown.

into our house, you have kept your mother company, and you have been diligent in court service. As the Central Lord, you must take good care of your mother.

"Now for territory. Tarō, you will be the master of the three provinces of Shimotsuke, Michinoku, and Hitachi. Jirō, the three provinces of Wakasa, Hida, and Echizen are yours. You will be the clan head, Saburō, so you must maintain a good relationship with your brothers and treat the people with compassion. You shall rule the seven provinces of Ōmi, Mino, Owari, Shinano, Mikawa, Tōtōmi, and Iga." With these words, he passed away.

On the thirty-fifth day after his death, Lord Kōka's wife, in her grief, also fell terribly ill. She handed over her property to her children, and asking that they diligently pray for her rebirth, she died. The three children, with sadness piled upon sadness, grieved endlessly. From the first seven days after their parents' death until the third year, they did not neglect to perform memorial services.

Now it came to pass that in the spring of the fourth year, Saburō Yorikata went to the capital and met with the emperor. "You should stay in the capital for a while," the emperor said. Yorikata did and resided there for three years. Day and night, he served the emperor. Then, in the second month of his fourth year, he took leave and set out from the capital, whereupon he was appointed governor of Yamato Province and granted authority over the Hokuriku region.[4] Yorikata was overjoyed. Thinking that he would visit the northern provinces later, he proceeded to Yamato, where the Provisional Governor of Kasuga put him up in his mansion and treated him with great hospitality.

To celebrate his receipt of the province of Yamato, Yorikata visited Kasuga Shrine and sponsored a seven-day sacred dance. One of the shrine maidens, a daughter of Lord Kasuga, was Lady Kasuga; she was seventeen years old and skilled in poetry and music. She had a soft lotus gaze, indigo-painted eyebrows, ruddy cheeks, and fair snow-white skin. There was no beauty in the three thousand worlds who could match her.

"Who is that lady?" Yorikata asked, to which Lord Kasuga replied, "She is my child." Yorikata was immensely pleased, and he asked for her hand in marriage. They then returned to his mansion in Kōka. Each day on which he did not see her felt like a hundred or a thousand.

Five years thus passed. During the third month, a seven-day circle-hunt was held on Ibuki Peak.[5] Yorikata took along his wife, and he built a temporary lodge and

---

4. The Hokuriku region includes the seven coastal provinces of Wakasa, Echizen, Kaga, Noto, Etchū, Echigo, and Sado along the Japan Sea.
5. A circle-hunt was an event in which many hunters surrounded a site and advanced inward, trapping game. Mount Ibuki stands at the border of Shiga and Gifu prefectures; in the medieval period, it was rumored to

installed her there. He and his men would drive the deer down before her and shoot them before her eyes. His brothers Yorinori and Yoritada accompanied them as well. All told, they were a force of over a thousand horsemen. Each and every one of them came to please Lady Kasuga and to earn the admiration of the Yamato governor Yorikata. The hunt went on for seven days, after which Yorikata said, "That's enough—let's return home." Just then, seven or eight large deer made their way down from the upper reaches of the mountain, so the men decided to stay an extra day, making it an eight-day hunt.

Yorikata climbed to the top of the mountain to look around, when suddenly a whirlwind blew three beautiful books into Lady Kasuga's quarters. When she picked one up and looked at it, the books transformed into three young boys. They seized Lady Kasuga and disappeared to the southeast. The warriors who saw this went pale and fell into complete disarray. When they informed their master, Yorikata, he hurried down the mountain and searched around the lodge, but he did not see her anywhere. "Our eight-day hunt has come to nothing!" he cried. "What do I have to live for now?" He writhed and wailed, but it was all for naught. Finally he said, "I will search for my love for as long as I live," and he headed back to Lord Kasuga's residence to explain.

At first, Lord Kasuga made no reply, but simply wept. At length he said, "Search every mountain and every valley. She must be somewhere."

"I shall," said Yorikata. "Nor will I search only in Japan. I will search as far as China or India, or the Korean kingdoms of Silla, Baekje, and Goryeo. I will search for her for as long as I live." Upon hearing these words, Lord Kasuga took heart.

Later, Yorikata purified himself by undergoing a period of abstention and visited Kasuga Shrine,[6] where he sponsored a seven-day sacred dance. He earnestly prayed: "Even if she was taken by the King of Demons himself, please watch over my lady and keep her safe."

The Great Kasuga Deity heard his prayers and replied, "Bestow unto Saburō Yorikata the Gem of Sustenance, which will allow him to go without food." There was much celebration, and the item was given to him.

Later, Lord Kasuga addressed Yorikata, saying, "During the seven days of your circle-hunt, how many deer did you bring back?"

"Only around two or three hundred," Yorikata replied.

"Among you three brothers, who has the strongest bow-arm?"

---

be the home of the demon Shuten Dōji and other malevolent deities. See, in this volume, *The Demon Shuten Dōji* and *The Demon of Ibuki*.

6. During his abstention, Yorikata would have avoided speaking taboo language, performing ritually defiling activities, and eating fish or meat.

The Origins of the Suwa Deity

Yorinori, hearing this, said, "I use a two-man bow with thirteen-handbreadth arrows, and Jirō uses a three-man bow with fourteen-handbreadth arrows. But when Saburō draws his bow, he is the strongest archer among us. Moreover, during the seven days of our hunt, it was Saburō's arrows that found the most deer." Yorinori thought very highly of his brother.

As the night gradually gave way to dawn, Yorikata gathered up his gear. "I want you to know that when I return, it will be with your daughter," he told Lord Kasuga and took his leave. He visited Kasuga Shrine and then turned to his older brothers, saying, "I am very grateful that you two have come this far with me. But you should go home now. I will be back soon, and we'll see one another then." However, his older brothers insisted that no matter how far his journey might take him, they would help. So they set out with more than five hundred horsemen.

Yorikata circled around the great peak of Mount Hiei in Yamashiro Province, Mimuro Peak in Yamato Province, and Inata Peak in Kawachi Province. He searched the great peak of Mount Fuku in Izumi Province, and Mount Kinpu and Yoshino Peak in Kii Province. He went to Suzuka Peak in Iga Province, Aitsu Peak in Ise Province, and Hikone Peak in Tsukushi, but he did not find his beloved.

Thinking that they should visit the eastern Kantō district, Yorikata made his way to the Hokuriku region, where he searched Mount Yura in Kaizu in Echizen Province, Mount Haku, and Mount Tateyama in Etchū. On the island of Sado, he searched the peak of Mount Hoku, and in Echigo Province, he searched the Tatsu-koku Grotto. He went to Tsukuba Peak in Hitachi Province, Mount Nikkō in Shi-motsuke Province, the peaks of Akagi and Ikao in Kōzuke Province, and Asama Peak in Shinano Province. He circled and circled around, visiting the great peaks of Nishina, Myōken, and Mount Hikaru; Shirone Peak in Kai Province; the peaks of Izu, Hakone, and Makata in Sagami Province; the great peak of Mount Kara in Izu Province; and Fuji no Takane in Suruga Province. But no matter where he looked, his beloved was not to be found.

The task was beyond his power. As Yorikata wondered bleakly where he ought to search next, his tutor, the Court Inspector of the Third Rank, came to him and said, "I don't know if this is true, but according to what I have heard, in the province of Shinano there is a frightful mountain known as Tadeshina Peak. To the south of the mountain, there are three camphorwood trees. At the base of those trees, there is a very deep hole. It seems quite ominous."

Yorikata was pleased. "In that case," he said, "we shall cross over to Shinano." And with that, they went to Tadeshina Peak. When Yorikata saw the hole, it looked truly frightening—certainly not a place to which humans ought to come. He had his warriors lay out a pile of wisteria and weave it into a basket. Then he had them attach seven or eight ropes. Yorikata got into the basket, and assigning three hundred men to the ropes, he started to descend. "Even if it takes a few days," he instructed, "when I shake this rope, hoist the basket up." The men gave their word.

In his right hand, Yorikata gripped his sword, Kentōba—the foremost sword in Japan. In his left hand, he held the Gem of Sustenance, which he had been granted by Kasuga Shrine. This gem had five properties: first, its bearer is never hungry, even if he eats nothing; second, he is never cold, even if he wears nothing; third, he is never hot, even in fire; fourth, he is never wet, even in water; fifth, he will not be discovered, even if he encounters the King of Demons. All these powers were contained within this gem, and because of this gem, Yorikata passed through the hole with ease.

The hole turned out to be around thirty-four or -five *chō* deep.[7] At the end of his descent, Yorikata landed on flat paved stone. Although it was dark, the light of his gem and sword illuminated his surroundings. Straining his eyes, Yorikata could see a road off to the east. He stepped out of the basket, and after walking some two leagues, came to the road. Crossing a bridge and looking around, he saw a large lake lined with pines and cedar. In the middle was a great buddha hall, enshrining nine sixteen-foot-high buddha statues, and a Threefold Prabhūtaratna pagoda.[8] There was also a bamboo grove. Following a narrow road through the bamboo, Yorikata found an eight-ridged mansion thatched with cypress bark.

He stepped up on the veranda and looked around, but nobody challenged him. He entered the foyer from the direction of the guardhouse, but he saw no one there. Thinking it strange, he opened the sliding paper door to the western room, and when he peered inside, he saw Lady Kasuga sitting there, weeping and reciting a sutra. Yorikata rejoiced and hurried to her side. "It's me," he said, "Yorikata! I've come!"

The young lady jumped up, and clinging to her husband's sleeves, she exclaimed, "Am I dreaming or awake? It seems so unreal!" She wept and wept. Yorikata could not hold in his tears either, and the two of them were overcome to the point of collapse.

After some time, Yorikata spoke: "What is the name of this place? And where is the master?"

"This place is called Onki, the 'Land of Demons,' or something like that. Right now, the master is off in China. Since the daughter of Emperor Zhou is said to be beautiful, he's gone to seize her."

"Then this is a good chance," said Yorikata. "We should go quickly," and he hoisted her onto his shoulders. They returned to the road from which he had come,

7. One *chō* is approximately 119 yards; thirty-five *chō* is just under 2.5 miles.
8. A two-story Threefold Prabhūtaratna pagoda is dedicated to the Threefold Prabhūtaratna Buddha.

The Origins of the Suwa Deity

and on the same stone paving as before, Yorikata shook the ropes attached to the basket and had his men pull them up.

Back above ground, Yorikata told everyone of the strange things that he had seen in the depths of the cavern when Lady Kasuga unhappily said, "We were in such a rush to leave that I forgot to bring my gold-lettered Yakushi Sutra; my copy of *A Dalliance in the Immortals' Den*, which is well loved in China; my precious Chinese mirror; and a book called *Omokage*, which I received from my father.[9] What should we do?"

"That's simple enough," said Yorikata. "Lower me down in the basket, just like before." With that, he went back down the hole.

Jirō Yoritada started thinking to himself, "The three of us are children of the same man. So how could Saburō have surpassed us so much in the world? It's maddening." While he was musing, he glanced at Lady Kasuga, and, as such matters had been on his mind for some time now, he began to think that this was a good chance to do away with Saburō and take the lady for himself. He met with his older brother, Yorinori, and said, "This has been on my mind for a while. I cannot abide how much Saburō has surpassed us. Now is a good chance for us to do away with him."

Yorinori said, "As you are both my younger brothers, I won't favor one of you over the other. If you are serious about this, I am going back to my estate in Michinoku," and he left.

Yoritada cut off the head of Yorikata's tutor. Yorikata's subordinates said, "Since the two of you are lords of the same household, we might as well follow you instead." They cut down the seven or eight ropes holding up the basket, and Yoritada went home with Lady Kasuga.

Now Yoritada met with Lady Kasuga and said, "From today, you must forget about that Saburō and swear to me, Yoritada, that you will be my wife."

"What a heartless thing to say!" the young lady replied. "Since it is the way of the world for peoples' hearts to change, I might warm to you if I were someone else. But because I know you to be so cruel, I could never love you. I cannot even count the number of books I have read; I am a devotee of the Way of letters. You, however, know nothing of such things. It is written that 'a wise man does not serve two masters, and a virtuous woman does not see two men.'[10] What's more, since you've killed the man I love, why should I feel anything for you?" She thus refused to obey him.

Yoritada became angry. "This must be what people mean when they speak of a fruit that looks nice but has no taste," he said, sending her away. "Take her to Mino'o

9. *A Dalliance in the Immortals' Den* (*You xianku*) is a Chinese romance attributed to Zhang Zhuo (ca. 657–730). The book *Omokage* is unknown.
10. Lady Kasuga quotes from *Records of the Grand Historian* (*Shiji*, first century B.C.E.), by the Han dynasty official Sima Qian (ca. 145–ca. 85 B.C.E.).

Bay and put her to the sword." Under his master's orders, a man named Yamada no Sakon Ienari set out with Lady Kasuga. The young lady did not weep at all.

Begging a brief leave of the warriors, Lady Kasuga recited half of the sixth scroll of the Lotus Sutra. Holding back her tears, she said, "You know, it goes without saying that reading or reciting just one passage or one verse of the Lotus Sutra bestows tremendous blessings. And since people say that even a person who hears it fiftieth-hand will receive joyous merit, I'll have no doubts about the afterlife, though I am to die at the point of a sword." She faced the west and prayed: "Please take me to the Pure Land together with my husband, Saburō Yorikata, Lord of Kōka, who ventured into that deep hole."

Ienari took up his sword and circled behind her. Just then—perhaps because she was under the protection of the Ten Rakshasa Daughters of the Lotus Sutra—a man by the name of Yoshida no Hyōe Ienaga approached with a force of more than three hundred riders.[11] "Who is it that would take my lady's head?" he demanded. Swiftly dismounting, he asked, "Do you kill her to avenge your parent or your child?"

"I am not a heartless man either," Ienari responded. "It is only that I cannot refuse my master's orders."

"My lady has done nothing wrong," Ienaga rejoined. "Furthermore, in wit and beauty, she is outstanding among humankind—a gem under heaven." After discussing the matter, they decided to help her, and they took her to the mansion of her father, the Provisional Governor of Kasuga. Because the entire household was of like mind to protect her, when Yoritada heard of this, he was angry but had no recourse.

Lord Kasuga said, "Truly, this is a horrible thing. So he's made himself the enemy of my son-in-law. In that case, how could I not attack him?" With that, he gathered together a force of over a thousand horsemen.

However, Lady Kasuga addressed her father, saying, "Even without this added burden, it is said that women are deeply sinful. To kill many people for the sake of one—and life being as uncertain as the dew on the tips of leaves, or the droplets at our feet—how could I bear such wicked karma? I simply wish to pray for my husband's enlightenment."

"What you say is true," said her father, moved by her sad words, and he relented.

From that day, Lady Kasuga confined herself in Kasuga Shrine and prayed, "Please let me meet Saburō Yorikata just once while I yet live." For that reason, perhaps, her life was to be a long one—and it was truly wondrous that they did meet again!

11. The Ten Rakshasa Daughters appear in chapter 26 of the Lotus Sutra, where they swear to "shield and guard those who read, recite, accept, and uphold the Lotus Sutra and spare them from decline or harm" (Burton Watson, trans., *The Lotus Sutra* [New York: Columbia University Press, 1993], 310).

As for Saburō Yorikata, upon returning to the stone paving at the bottom of the hole, he saw that the ropes attached to the basket had been cut down. "How can this be?" he cried, staring up at the sky and falling to the ground, wailing endlessly. Eventually, as there was no sense in going on like this, he went to the buddha hall and made invocations, praying for a good afterlife. "A man should never lose his heart to a woman!" he thought, lamenting. "She must have fallen in love with Jirō or Tarō and thrown me away." But then he reconsidered: "No, that can't be. Jirō must have fallen in love with her and arranged for this to happen."

Then, since there was nothing else to do, he walked aimlessly toward the east and looked around. He saw a road leading off to the southeast. When he followed it, he came upon a large hole, which he entered. Proceeding some ten *chō*, he saw a country there. It seemed to be summertime, and there was a person weeding the fields. "What country is this?" Yorikata asked.

"This is the Land of Kōin," the person replied. "You should go on to the east."

Yorikata went to the east, as he had been told. It looked to be around autumn, as in this land the people were reaping grain. "What country is this?" Yorikata inquired.

"This is the Land of Kōchō," he was told.

He turned toward the north and found a road that he followed until he came to another large hole. Making his way through it some forty or fifty *chō*, he emerged in a land where people were planting rice seedlings. "Where is this place?" he asked.

The people stared at him and said, "To come to this land, a person from Japan would have to change his form. To have come here without doing so is exceedingly strange! You are no ordinary man. Move on quickly."

In this manner, Yorikata passed through seventy-two holes and came to a very large country. Looking around, it seemed to be autumn. The treetops had turned a light crimson, and the cries of the deer and the buzzing of the insects filled Yorikata's own heart with lonely sorrow, with everything bringing him grief. Contemplating the impermanence of things in the world, he moved on. He came to a small deer hut in the middle of the mountain fields, where an old man, no doubt more than eighty years of age, saw him and said with surprise, "Where did you come from? It's certainly strange."

"I am a person from Japan," Yorikata replied.

"Well, then, you must be a troubled man. There are no more lands beyond this point. Even if there were, you could not reach them without changing your form. Stay with me for a while and take your time." That night, the old man took Yorikata to his lodgings, where he warmly entertained him.

Later, the old man said to his wife, "This man has deep spiritual power and knows propriety. Shall we take him for our son-in-law?"

"I was thinking the very same thing," his wife replied.

When the next night came, the old man summoned his three daughters. They served Yorikata and poured saké for him until dawn. Afterward, the old man said, "For your wife, please take whichever daughter catches your eye and live with us here." Now the eldest daughter was eight thousand years old, the middle was five thousand, and the youngest was two thousand. Yet the eldest sister looked to be thirty, the middle looked to be twenty-five, and the youngest looked to be twenty. Each one was wearing colorful garments. Moreover, they were extraordinarily beautiful, far surpassing the usual run of women, such that it was impossible to judge among them. Nonetheless, Yorikata chose the youngest with whom to seal his vows.

The old man said, "Even though my daughter is two thousand years old, you will find her to be a woman of twenty." Yorikata said that he was thirty years of age.

The two of them grew close—their vows were by no means shallow. One day, the maiden asked him, "How long has it been since you left Japan?"

"Because I have been traveling," he replied, "I have been unaware of the passage of months and days."

"What a pity!" his wife said. "How Lady Kasuga must grieve. Still, it must have been some fleeting karmic link between us that brought you to this land. It has been twenty years and six months since you left Japan. You should forget about Japan and obey my father. If you do, he will surely allow you to return home."

Yorikata was shocked, thinking, "How strange! How does she know so much about Japan?" But he was also happy, and he felt his bond with her grow ever deeper. In that land, year after year passed until it had been another nine years and seven months.

One night at around dawn, Yorikata remembered his homeland, and he wept until his pillow seemed to float in a pool of tears. His wife was surprised. "What's wrong?" she asked.

"The truth is," Yorikata explained, "I saw Lady Kasuga of my homeland in a dream."

"I thought it was something like that," she said. "Women's hearts are all the same. Just as I love you, so too must she. You must ask leave of my father. This land is called the Land of Yuiman. All the lands you passed through on your way here pay a tribute to us once every ten years. Likewise, the lands along the road you will follow to return home all pay tribute once every three years. My father is called Old Man Kōbi of Yuiman. My name is Lady Yuiman. Without my father, you may never return to Japan, even if a thousand or ten thousand years should pass. I, too, would regret our parting, but it would be unreasonable for me to keep you here just because of that."

The Origins of the Suwa Deity

When he heard his wife's words, he found himself at a loss. While he longed for his homeland and Lady Kasuga, he also thought that it would be difficult to leave Lady Yuiman. Nevertheless, if he were to remain here, he would miss his homeland. He thus grieved like one who was utterly lost.

"If you wish to go back to Japan," Lady Yuiman said, "tell my father, 'I miss my homeland very dearly. I would like to take my leave,' and no matter what, don't make him angry. When you say that, the old man will respond, 'It would be easy enough to send you home, but I don't know what my daughter would think.' When that happens, I will take care of things." Yorikata was overjoyed.

Now Old Man Kōbi had decided that the next day they should amuse themselves by holding a hunt. Assembling his best retainers, he said, "Assemble the forces of Yuiman: tomorrow we will hunt!"

"Right away," his men replied, and immediately they took off, racing around the country like a flash of lightning. It is recorded that more than seventeen thousand horsemen set out to join the hunt, each following his own intentions. A crowd of them assembled, bearing bundles of miraculous humming-bulb arrows on their backs. Yorikata, too, stood among them. Hoping to earn the old man's favor, he comported himself with loyalty. Vast as the Land of Yuiman was, it seemed that there was nowhere among its peaks and valleys that one could not find the men. In the end, they spent three weeks hunting, after which Old Man Kōbi recorded his hunters' feats in shooting deer. He gave all of them gifts. Yorikata was singled out for honor due to his prowess with the bow. In sum, the number of deer he brought back over the course of those three weeks was set down as 1,371. It was the custom of this land for the people to make their living by hunting, and in this land they ate the heads of deer.

Yorikata addressed Old Man Kōbi, saying, "I would like to take my leave, that I may return to Japan." The old man nodded his head. "I thought that might be on your mind, but because it's hard to know my daughter's heart, you must ask her instead."

Yorikata went home and told his wife. "That is a simple matter," she said and took Yorikata along to see her father. "My Lord Kōka has been miserable, longing to return to his homeland. Seeing him like this is heart wrenching—please, let's send him home immediately."

When the night grew late, Old Man Kōbi spoke: "If you are to return to your homeland, Lord Kōka, then first let me show you a secret place within our realm." He led Yorikata some fourteen *chō* into the bamboo forest to the west, where they came upon an iron wall with a copper gate. "Open!" the old man said, and the gate opened from within. Stepping inside, Yorikata saw fourteen or fifteen ladies who looked to be thirty-four or -five years of age; they seemed to be watch-women.

Farther on, they came to a copper wall with a silver gate. When the old man said, "Open!" it opened from within. There were ladies who seemed to be twenty-seven or -eight years old, whom Yorikata took for watch-women. Passing through, they came to a silver wall with a golden gate. When the old man said "Open," it opened from within. There were ladies whom Yorikata took to be twenty-four or -five. Continuing farther on, they came to a wall of lapis lazuli with a gate adorned with garlands of jewels. "Open!" the old man said. Inside, there was a row of seven eight-ridged palaces thatched with cypress bark.

Looking around outside the palaces, Yorikata saw many pines and cedars growing there. To the south, he could see a mountain so vast that it could have been Mount Potalaka, the Pure Land of the Bodhisattva Kannon. To the east, there was a tall mountain, and at its foot was a shrine. To the west, there was a buddha hall and a Threefold Prabhūtaratna pagoda. It was a truly auspicious place.

They entered one of the palaces. The ceiling was swathed in light-blue-grounded brocade, and the pillars were wrapped in brocade with a dark-blue ground. There was sandalwood incense, and the floor was covered with tatami fringed with red-grounded brocade. The old man seated Yorikata and Lady Yuiman on the tatami, where a set of covered drinking vessels had been placed. A seventeen- or eighteen-year-old lady came out bearing an assortment of side dishes, and she waited on them hospitably.

As the night gradually gave way to dawn, the old man said, "When you return to Japan, Lord Kōka, you will encounter many hardships. Even so, if you do exactly as I say, without erring in the slightest, you should arrive in the realm of Japan without any particular problem." He explained in detail every hardship that Yorikata would face. Then he took the kneecaps of a thousand deer and ground them as if they were *mochi* rice. He presented Yorikata with enough for 1,100 days, together with a great number of jewels in a knotted sack. "Eat one portion of bone meal every day," he said. "Should you eat even two, you will never reach Japan. Take heed and do not doubt my words."

Yorikata was elated. "I understand," he said. He accepted the numerous jewels and returned to his lodgings to prepare for his journey.

Both Yorikata and his wife were terribly pained at the prospect of his parting. Finding himself unable to leave, Yorikata wrung tears from his sleeves. Nonetheless, as it would not do to go on like this, he set out. His wife spoke between sobs: "I will never forget the terrible sorrow of our parting. Although I am to lose you now, our bond will remain unbroken. Now go! I will see you off."

They left Mount Yuiman and forded a river named Chigirigawa, the "River of Vows." There, his wife composed a poem:

The Origins of the Suwa Deity

kono higoro	We have grown so close,
nareshi nagori no	day after day these past years—
oshikereba	in this pain of parting,
sakidatsu mono wa	that which departs from me first
namida narikeri	must certainly be my tears![12]

In response, Yorikata composed:

nise made to	You must not forget
chigirishi koto wo	the vows we made for this life
wasurezu wa	and also for the next.
tazunete mo koyo	Come and find me, if you will,
akitsushima made	on Autumn-Harbor Island.[13]

They wept together in sorrow over their premature parting.

Eventually, Yorikata took his leave. Scrupulously following the old man's instructions, he overcame one hardship after another. The days passed until he had used up all the bone meal, and he emerged in Japan, at the foot of Mount Ōnuma, west of Asama in the district of Saku in Shinano Province. Yorikata immediately made for Tadeshina Peak in the same province, but it looked different. He had been on the road for a thousand days already. He thought that he had spent nine years and seven months in Yuiman, but in fact three hundred years had passed, and the old trees from before had rotted away.[14] Recalling the past as if it were before his very eyes, Yorikata was overcome with loneliness and sorrow.

Yorikata placed his knotted sack in the mouth of the hole and built a hermitage. For three thousand days, he drew water, purified himself through a period of abstention, read the sutras, and prayed to the gods and buddhas, entreating them with regard to Lady Kasuga: "I beseech you, please allow me to meet my beloved wife just one more time while I am alive."

After the three thousand days had passed, Yorikata traveled to his homeland, the district of Kōka. He saw the Shakyamuni Buddha Hall that his father had built, but

12. In his modern Japanese translation, Matsumoto suggests that this poem could be taken to mean that whenever Lady Yuiman tries to speak, her tears "depart from her first" (*Suwa no honji*, in *Otogizōshi shū*, ed. Matsumoto, 273n.11). The verb *sakidatsu* ("to set out" or "to depart") also suggests Yorikata's departure, which comes after her tears.

13. Autumn-Harbor Island (Akitsushima) is a poetic term for the islands of Japan.

14. The narrator may be referring to the three camphorwood trees that were at the mouth of the hole into which Yorikata was lowered. It is a convention in medieval Japanese fiction that in different worlds, time may pass at different speeds.

the pillars and ridgepoles had rotted away; and the great hall had been reduced to a cavern. "How many years could I possibly have spent in Yuiman?" he thought. "If this is how things are, I should have never left that place!" Sadly wondering what had become of Lady Kasuga, he wept until he had to wring his sleeves dry. He entered the buddha hall, threw himself on the devotional dais, and made invocations.

Now it so happened that it was the twentieth day of the seventh month, and a large group of parishioners had gathered for a sermon. The children went first into the buddha hall to play, but when they saw Yorikata they shouted, "Look out! There's a huge snake in here!" Hearing this, the adults, too, became frightened.

"Well, this is upsetting!" Yorikata thought. "So it seems that my body has become that of a serpent. How sad." Weeping, he hid himself under the altar.

After some time, the service concluded and the parishioners went out, still gossiping about the earlier incident: "But that was one big snake! I wonder if somebody was turned into a serpent."

"What can I do?" Yorikata thought, and he listened, forlorn, to the temple bells as the day grew dark. In the tall grass, pine crickets, bell crickets, and katydids were raising their voices, as if in season. It seemed to Yorikata that the insects were crying for him.

When evening came, a large number of monks visited the buddha hall to perform a reading of the Lotus Sutra. As the night grew late, the sutra reading came to an end, and the elder priest in the seat of honor said, "Since we've nothing much to do now, somebody tell us a story of times gone by."

"Someone tell us what became of the three sons of the Provisional Governor of Kōka, the former master of this place," said a priest seated in the midst of the group.

Another priest, thirty-four or -five years of age, in the row to the right, spoke up: "Any of you could tell it, but I know it especially well." He began, "During the reign of Emperor Kōshō, the fifth in the line of human emperors, there lived a man in this very place called the Provisional Governor of Kōka. He had three sons. His eldest was Tarō Yorinori, his second was Jirō Yoritada, and his third was Saburō Yorikata. As he had three sons, when the time came, he left his territory to the three of them and passed away. Their lamentations were without limit; until the third year, they did not neglect their filial duties, and when the fourth year came, Lord Saburō, as the clan head, went to the capital to serve the emperor . . ."

The priest related how Yorikata served assiduously at court, burning the midnight oil,[15] and he described the Land of Yuiman exactly as it was. "I thought he

15. Literally, Yorikata would "dispel the midnight mist and fix his gaze upon the Three Stars constellation," a conventional phrase for diligent effort.

The Origins of the Suwa Deity

would be here by today or tomorrow," the priest went on to say, "so it's curious that we haven't seen him yet." Yorikata was truly frightened.

When he heard this, an old priest sitting to the left said, "That snake that frightened the pages today at noon—could that be him?"

"That may well be the case," said the priest who had told the story.

"But how could that be?" another said. "Saburō Yorikata is a human, isn't he? Why would he appear as a snake?"

"Because he donned the garb of Yuiman. He would certainly look like a snake."

Another old priest said, "Is there a way that he could shed those clothes and turn back into a man?"

"He must submerge himself in a pond where the calamus plant grows," the storyteller priest explained. "When the morning sun comes out, he must face the east and chant three times the words, 'Blue color, blue light, dawning eastern sky.' Then he must bow seven times in prayer. After that, he must turn to the west and chant forty-eight times, '*Kyōkyō kōsai*, O Buddha of Infinite Life.' Then he must bow forty-eight times in supplication. After that, he must turn to the north and chant seven times, 'I prostrate myself before you. Bring peace to my family, Vajrayakṣa.'[16] He must bow his head to the ground three times. After that, he must face south and chant seven times, '*Nanshu taishō, chaku tansha*' and bow seven times in prayer. If he then casts off and abandons the garb of Yuiman, making himself naked, he will become a man as he was before." Yorikata was glad to hear this, and he waited impatiently for the break of dawn.

When the sky eventually brightened, Yorikata went out through the main temple gate, and looking around, he saw a pond in which calamus plants grew. Joyfully, he submerged himself in the water and awaited the morning sun. When the sun came out, he chanted the spell just as the priest had said the night before, and, removing his clothes, he transformed back into his original form. Then he went back to the great hall.

"Look!" said one of the old priests from before. "It's Saburō Yorikata."

"We've prepared clothes for you," another old priest said, and he dressed him in a dark-gray small-sleeved under robe.

The first priest spoke again, saying, "We've prepared this for you as well." He presented him with a *hitatare* with a mulberry-leaf design and a silk *hakama*.[17]

---

16. Vajrayakṣa (J. Kongōyasha) is one of the Five Mantra Kings, venerated as guardian deities of Buddhism.

17. A *hitatare* (also *yoroi hitatare*) is a kind of loose-fitting shirt-and-pants set worn by warriors and courtiers in the medieval period both under armor and as everyday attire. *Hakama* are loose-fitting trousers worn over a robe.

"Take these, too," said a priest sitting to the right, and he added to the gifts an *eboshi* cap and a side sword. The priest who had told the story said, "And these, also," and he gave him a great sword and a bow and arrows. Then, since it was already late morning, the monks scattered and dispersed, leaving only the one who had told the story.

Holding back his tears of joy, Yorikata asked, "Excuse me, but who are you venerable monks who reside in this place?"

The priest explained: "To utter the words is awesome indeed! The elder monk who sat in the seat of honor dwells in Ise Grand Shrine.[18] The first monk to the left was the Kumano Avatar. The second was the Great Kamo Deity. The first to the right was the Great Umeda Deity, and the second was the Great God of Hirano. As for myself, I am the Great Ōharano Deity, who has thrice witnessed Lake Ōmi transform over a thousand years into mulberry fields, and over another thousand years into a lake. Because of your deep love for your wife and your marvelously rare faith in the gods and buddhas, we accompanied you to the Land of Yuiman and protected you from harm. Furthermore, the one who called himself Old Man Kōbi is, in fact, in his original form, Dainichi Buddha, who dwells in the womb realm Garbhadhātu. Now, you must make a pilgrimage to Kasuga Shrine. Lady Kasuga still lives on, cloistered within." Having said this, he vanished.

189

"As I suspected," thought Yorikata, "they were no ordinary men." Marveling at what had transpired, he immediately went to Kasuga Shrine, where his wife was making invocations and weeping. He drew near to where she was reciting the Lotus Sutra and said, "Your husband, Yorikata, has arrived!" His wife, stunned, was speechless. She took him by the sleeves, and doubting her senses, fainted straight away.

Some time later, the two shared their feelings and told each other of things past and present. Lady Kasuga spoke of how she had earned Yoritada's ire, how she was taken to Mino'o Bay, and how Yoshida no Hyōe had saved her when she was about to be executed, whereupon she had returned to her father's side; how her father had set out to take vengeance on the enemy of his son-in-law, and how she herself had stopped him in the end. She recounted how she had spent her days and nights on the road, sleeping alone in humble huts, and she wept for her previous sadness and her present joy.

Yorikata told her of the grief he had felt when he came to the bottom of that hole, of his faltering journey to the Land of Yuiman, and of his journey home—the difficulties he had encountered during his 1,100 days of hardship, the pains he met on the

18. Although not identified by name, considering subsequent events, this deity may be the god Tejikarao (Strong-Armed Man) of Ise Shrine.

The Origins of the Suwa Deity

way, his arrival in Japan, what he saw in the Shakyamuni hall in Kōka, and his strange transformation.

"I hate Jirō," Yorikata later said, "because he made me live in that miserable country." Yorikata and his wife discussed the matter, and seeking out a fast ship, they crossed over to the Land of Hezei in eastern India.[19] Three years passed until the god Tejikarao arrived, bearing a message from Ise Grand Shrine: "The time has come for you to return to Japan, realize the dharma of godhood, and manifest as deities to bestow your blessings on the people."

Giving their assent, they again boarded their fast boat and crossed to the Land of Tensō, where they presented themselves to Prince Hayanaki and received the dharma of the gods along with the sacred invocation, "The gods alight on the High Plain of Heaven."[20]

They boarded a swift heavenly chariot and flew back to Japan, where they set about crushing their enemies and repaying their debts of gratitude. Jirō Yoritada hid himself in the province of Hitachi, since it was his land. He, too, had become a god, but his divine power was not yet like Yorikata's. In the district of Okaya in Shinano Province, Yorikata and his wife built a ridgepole palace and made their home there. As his name was Yorikata, this place came to be known as the district of Suwa— "Suwa" being an alternative reading of the characters in Yorikata's name.

In time, Yoritada put his hands together and begged for amnesty, pleading to the Great Kasuga Deity that he might receive the dharma of godhood from Suwa. Struck by the intensity of his lamentations, the Great Kasuga Deity reported this news to the Southern Hall of Suwa Shrine.

"It's unthinkable!" Yorikata replied. "He has bound himself to me with bonds of enmity. I would never grant such a request."

"Then your grace is not so wide-reaching after all."

Yorikata saw the truth in this. "It is as you say," he said, and he granted Yoritada the dharma of godhood. Yoritada rejoiced to receive this divine power.

Yorikata wandered underground during the reign of Emperor Kōshō. He spent 69 years beneath the earth, emerging only when the emperor was 125 years old.[21] Kōshō's heir, Emperor Kōan, lived for 104 years. His son, Emperor Kōgen, lived to be 72, followed by Emperor Kaika, who lived to be 150; Emperor Sujin lived to 120; Emperor Suinin lived to 30; and Emperor Keikō lived to 106. Over the course of these eight generations of emperors, 806 years passed.[22] As a god, Yorikata is known as the Great Suwa Deity. His father later became known as the Great Kōka Deity of Ōmi Province. His mother is known as the avatar of Mount Nikkō in Shimotsuke. Tarō Yorinori of Kōka is known as the Inner Uchita Deity. As for Yoritada, he is known as the Great Tanaka Deity of Hitachi Province. Although he made peace with his brother, Yoritada remained shy in his presence, which is why, of his two annual festivals, his spring festival is celebrated at night.

Lady Kasuga is the deity of Lower Suwa Shrine. In her original form, she is the Thousand-Armed Kannon. Yorikata is the deity of Upper Suwa Shrine. His original form is the bodhisattva Fugen. Because of what Yoritada did to Lady Kasuga, her shrine maintains a particularly strong prohibition against sexual pollution. Furthermore, because she herself had been unable to fulfill her filial duties for so long, she forbid those who came before her from visiting her shrine during the first month after the death of a parent so that they would be diligent in performing the appropriate rites.

In addition, while Lady Kasuga had been on her way to the Land of Hezei with her husband, she once found herself fatigued in the kingdom of Silla. A woman emerged from a maternity hut and presented her with an offering of rice cakes to ease her exhaustion. Because of this debt, Lower Suwa Shrine does not deeply eschew the pollution of childbirth. Although the woman was poor, her compassion was deep, and so her descendants prospered.

Furthermore, because of Yorikata's misery from the hardships on the road home from Yuiman, he drove horseflies, mosquitoes, snakes, centipedes, and all manner of poisonous vermin into the valleys. For this reason, the region came to be known as the Abuka Valley, the "Valley of Mosquitoes and Horseflies."

The queen of Yuiman yearned after the departed Yorikata and appeared on Asama Peak in Shinano Province. Like him, she manifested great virtue and influence, and is now enshrined as the Great Sengen Bodhisattva.[23] Saburō Yorikata of Kōka swore to guide the multitude of sentient beings to his pure land.

Mysterious happenings transpired. In eastern India, there was a place called the Land of Kurubei, and there was a rich man there called Chikurui Chōja. He had a daughter of superior beauty named Lady Chikuchō. She was the loveliest maiden in India. The king of their country, a monarch by the name of King Sonata, asked for

---

22. This list omits Emperor Kōrei (342–214 B.C.E., r. 290–215 B.C.E.), who succeeded Kōan (traditionally 427–291 B.C.E., r. 392–291 B.C.E.). Furthermore, the years do not add up to 806, possibly due to this omission.
23. Sengen is an alternative reading of the characters for "Asama." The Great Sengen Bodhisattva (Great Asama Bodhisattva) is Nitta no Shirō Tadatsune's guide to the afterworld in *The Tale of the Fuji Cave*, which is included in this volume.

her to be his queen, but because her father had hoped for her to marry a greater king—the lord of the Land of Shatō—the father did not respond. The king's messengers came repeatedly, but to no avail. The king was furious, and one night he attacked Chikurui Chōja with a force of more than a thousand horsemen. Fleeing from the night attack, Lady Chikuchō took her father's jeweled pike and planted it head-first in the Ganges River. She made her home atop the shaft. When King Sonata heard of this, he declared that that place was still within his realm.

"As long as I remain in this land, I will continue to hear such things," she said, and following the king's edict, she once more took up the pike and boarded a swift heavenly chariot. She flew over the Taklamakan Desert and the Pamir Mountains to Baekje, and from there she boarded a swift heavenly boat and crossed over to Japan. She arrived in Itsutsu in Tsukushi, and drawn by the eastern advance of the dharma, moved to Mount Aichi at the border of Shinano and Kōzuke provinces.[24] She filled a crater in the mountain with water and turned her heavenly boat upside down, vowing that when a rain of fire should fall on the world, she would quench it with that water. She constructed a shrine on top of the upside-down boat and made her residence there. The helmsman of the boat, a person named Somekura no Tsūshi, dwelled in the shrine along with her. For this reason, the god of the shrine is known as the Arafune, or "Wild Boat," Deity.

Now the Great Suwa Deity often traveled to see his mother, the Nikkō Avatar, and because the Arafune Shrine was on his way, he began a love affair with the Arafune Deity. When Lady Kasuga heard of this, she was incensed.

"It's only natural that she would feel that way," the Arafune Deity said. Saying "I can't stay here," she constructed a shrine in the village of Ozaki in the district of Kanra in Kōzuke Province and made her home there. Today, this is known as the First Shrine of Kōzuke. Because she drew her pike from the Ganges River and descended from the heavens, she is also known as Hokonuku-no-kami, or "Lance-Drawing God."

The reason that buddhas and bodhisattvas dwell in our land is so that they may bring salvation and guidance to suffering beings. Like us, they meet with anguish, and they appear as gods to aid the people. Because of the blessings they bestow by dimming their brightness and manifesting as gods, they dote, as they would on a child, on even those with anger in their hearts.

Once, the holy man Kūya secluded himself in Suwa Shrine and challenged the god, saying, "Your original form is that of a great bodhisattva. For what reason, then,

24. Tsukushi is an old name for Kyushu. The Buddhist teachings are believed to have spread eastward in a linear progression from India to Japan, and then, in this case, from the western to the eastern regions of Japan.

MONSTERS, WARRIORS, AND JOURNEYS TO OTHER WORLDS

should we slaughter the beasts of the mountains and fields and offer them to you?"[25] At dawn on the fifth day, the shrine was filled on all four sides with a multitude of two- or three-inch buddhas. After a while, the door to the inner sanctuary opened. Clad in a mulberry-leaf *hitatare* and bearing a sword and a rod, the Great Deity faced the holy man and spoke: "You are a fool. Animals, subject to the vicissitudes of karma, become the food of useless, wicked men. They die in futility and are born in futility. In order to show them pity in their transmigration, I bind them to myself for a time that I may aid them in the next world:

> Deep in karma, sentient beings:
> though set free, they cannot live.
> Yet dwelling within humanity,
> they likewise obtain the fruit of the buddha.[26]

What this means is: even if you set them free, these sentient beings that are mired in karma cannot live. For this reason, I take them to reside within myself that I may bring them buddhahood."

We must take these words to heart. Moreover, we should not distinguish between Buddhist and secular writings, for they are the same path. Thus it is written: "Even if the sins of a sage are great, the sage will not fall into hell; even if the sins of a fool are slight, the fool will fall." You must heed this carefully. Have faith in the buddhas and gods, revere the Three Treasures,[27] abide in mercy, be correct in the rites, and pray for your wishes in this world and the hereafter. Those who read this secret account of Suwa, and those who hear it told, must purify themselves through a period of abstention. An impure heart will avail you nothing.

TRANSLATION AND INTRODUCTION BY TAMARA SOLOMON

193

25. Kūya Shōnin (903–972) was an itinerant Buddhist monk known for building roads and temples, working with the sick and the poor, and advocating the practice of the *nenbutsu*, the ritual invocation of the name of Amida (Skt. Amitābha) Buddha.

26. This passage is written in classical Chinese in the form of a sutra verse; its origin is unknown. Because it is held that one can obtain enlightenment from only the human realm, by joining with the human body (being eaten), animals may gain the possibility of buddhahood.

27. The Three Treasures are the Three Treasures (or Jewels) of Buddhism: the Buddha, the dharma (teachings of the Buddha), and the sangha (monastic community).

The Origins of the Suwa Deity

BUDDHIST
TALES

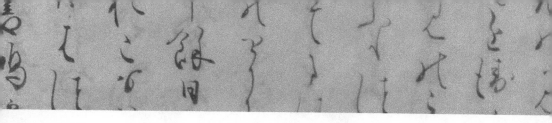

The Tale of the Fuji Cave

As the ghastly story of one man's tour of hell, *The Tale of the Fuji Cave* (*Fuji no hito-ana sōshi*) appears to be a relic of the vanished and largely undocumented world of late-medieval street-preaching and popular Buddhist entertainment. Nishino To-shiko has proposed that the story circulated in the medieval period (1185–1600) in the oral repertoires of *zatō* (blind minstrel priests), who are specifically praised within the work, and *etoki bikuni* (picture-explaining nuns), some of whom are known to have preached using elaborate paintings of heavens and hells, and who may have been married to *zatō*.[1] Koyama Issei, on the contrary, has argued that the *Fuji* narrative was recited by medieval *yamabushi* (mountain ascetics) and, possibly, mendicant *miko* (shamanesses, or shrine maidens) from the Fuji mountain region.[2] In either case, scholars agree that *The Tale of the Fuji Cave* is rooted in a medieval Buddhist storytelling and proselytizing tradition, as its vituperatively didactic contents so clearly suggest.

The story either was inspired by a set of entries in the historical chronicle *Azuma kagami* (*The Mirror of the East*), compiled in the late Kamakura period (1185–1333), or shares a source with it. According to these records, the second Kamakura shogun, Minamoto no Yoriie, sent his retainer Wada no Heida Tanenaga to explore a "great cave" in a place called Itōzaki in Izu Province in the sixth month of 1203. Heida Ta-nenaga returned on the same day, after slaying what he said was a huge snake that tried to swallow him whole. Two days later, Yoriie gave Nitta no Shirō Tadatsune a precious sword and sent him to explore a different cavern, this one located on the

---

The translation is from an unillustrated *Fuji no hitoana sōshi* manuscript transcribed by Priest Dōkyō, who is otherwise unknown, in the fifth month of 1603, typeset in Yokoyama Shigeru and Matsumoto Ryūshin, eds., *Muromachi jidai monogatari taisei* (Tokyo: Kadokawa Shoten, 1983), 11:429–51.

1. Nishino Toshiko, "*Fuji no hitoana sōshi* no keisei," *Ōtani joshidai kokubun* 1 (1971): 42a–43b.
2. Koyama Issei, *Fuji no hitoana sōshi: kenkyū to shiryō* (Tokyo: Bunka Shobō Hakubunsha, 1983), 38, 48–50.

side of Mount Fuji in neighboring Suruga Province. Tadatsune led a party of six men, including himself; only two survived. As Tadatsune explained upon his return, after contending with darkness, bats, wet feet, and a passage "too narrow to turn around in," the party came to a raging underground river, where they saw a mysterious apparition in the light of their torches. Four of Tadatsune's men dropped dead, and Tadatsune himself managed to escape only by sacrificing his new sword, which he claims to have thrown into the river in response to the apparition's demand.

For modern readers, *The Tale of the Fuji Cave* is intriguing both as a samurai adventure story and for the light it can shed on late-medieval conceptions of sin, death, and karma, as well as the cults of Jizō and the Great Asama Bodhisattva in the sixteenth and early seventeenth centuries. In its central section, the tale constitutes a veritable catalog of contemporary social transgressions and their imagined punishments, emphasizing, in particular, the sins and sufferings of women and bad priests. Its religious and social message is conservative, and like *The Tale of the Heike* (thirteenth century), which chronicles the downfall of Taira no Kiyomori and his clan, it proclaims the fleeting nature of wealth, power, and worldly fame. Taking up where the *Heike* epic leaves off, it describes the fall of the Genji, embodied in the figure of Minamoto no Yoriie, Yoritomo's eldest son and heir, by attributing it to Yoriie's own arrogance and recklessness: his purportedly disastrous obsession with the sacred Fuji cave.

On the morning of the third day of the fourth month of Shōji 3 [1201], the shogun Yoriie summoned Wada no Heida Tanenaga and spoke: "Listen, Heida. People are always talking about the Fuji cave, but no one's ever seen it. I want you to explore it and tell me what sorts of mysteries you find."[3] Heida took in his master's words. "My lord," he replied, "if it were some bird of the sky or beast of the earth, I could catch it easily enough. But your request leaves me at a loss. Still, to disobey your instruction would be to invite the wrath of heaven. So for you I'll give my one and only life."

Leaving the shogun, Heida immediately went to see his uncle Yoshimori, to whom he explained what had occurred.[4] "You see," Heida said, "our lord has given

---

3. Minamoto no Yoriie (1182–1204) was the second Kamakura shogun. Wada no Heida Tanenaga (1183–1213) was the son of Wada Yoshinaga.
4. Wada Yoshimori (1147–1213) was a close personal retainer of the first Kamakura shogun, Minamoto no Yoritomo (1147–1199). The words "his uncle" are interpolated from the *Fuji no hitoana sōshi* text of 1607, typeset in Yokoyama Shigeru, ed., *Muromachi jidai monogatari shū* (Tokyo: Inoue Shobō, 1962), 2:318–37.

me this most unusual command." Yoshimori was incredulous. "Since I am to explore the Fuji cave," Heida continued, "it's uncertain if I'll ever return to Fukazawa. So this is my last chance to see everyone—until we meet in the world to come, that is." He woefully prepared to take his leave.

Yoshimori wept. "I am especially sad for you," he said, "because I raised you on my knee from when you were a little boy. But since it's not my decision, there's nothing I can do. Go get yourself some glory and come back soon!"

Heida stood to go, his eyes welling with tears. Asaina no Saburō Yoshihide saw what was afoot, and taking up his great sword, Teimaru, he drew it two or three inches from its sheath and glared at his cousin, Heida.[5] "You stupid fool!" he said. "Getting all weepy-eyed in the presence of Japanese samurai—it's a disgrace! Having someone like you in the family makes cowards of us all. If that's what you are, then stretch out your neck and let me kill you myself!"

"I'm no coward," Heida shot back. "Stone, boulder, dragon's or tiger's lair, I'll smash it open and stroll inside once or twice! There's nothing weak about me. So long, Asaina." Heida started to leave. Asaina laughed at the sight of his cousin. " 'Spur a running horse,' " he said, "or 'dye a robe that's been dipped a thousand times to make it redder still!' I'd like to join you myself, but since you've been given the job alone, there's nothing I can do. Go get yourself some glory and make the family famous!"

Heida's attire that day was extraordinarily splendid. He wore a small-sleeved robe of Chinese brocade over an unlined inner garment loosened at the sides. The sleeves of his mist-patterned *hitatare* were hitched back at the shoulders,[6] and on his head he wore a court cap tied securely under his chin. He carried a gilded fan together with a one-foot, six-inch sword mounted with silver clasps. His other sword was adorned with copper-gold alloy fittings and a hardened leather guard. With the two blades at his side and a porter bearing a bundle of sixteen torches, he declared, "I'll be back in a week," and entered the Fuji cave.

"There's nothing sadder than the plight of a warrior," everyone said as they saw him off, and they all wept.

Some hundred yards into the cave, Heida came upon a mass of striped snakes with mouths as red as if they had been daubed with paint. The scene was terrifying to behold. Being under orders, Heida had no choice but to proceed, and thus leaping this way and that over the heads of the serpents, he made his way another five hundred yards. He came to a place where a fishy stench wafted through the air,

5. Asaina no Saburō Yoshihide (b. 1176) was the third son of Wada Yoshimori. The word "cousin" is interpolated from the 1607 *Fuji* text.
6. A *hitatare* (also *yoroi hitatare*) is a kind of loose-fitting shirt-and-pants set worn by warriors and courtiers in the medieval period both under armor and as everyday attire.

The Tale of the Fuji Cave

frightening beyond measure. Pressing farther on, Heida saw a young woman, seventeen or eighteen years old. Dressed in twelve-layered robes and a long crimson trouser-skirt, she bore the thirty-two marks of perfect feminine beauty. Her locks were as delicate as the wings of a cicada, as richly hued as flowing ink. Perched at the foot of a silver loom, she wove with a golden shuttle. "Who are you to visit my abode?" she asked in the voice of a heavenly bird.[7]

"I am a retainer of the Kamakura shogun," Heida replied. "My name is Wada no Heida Tanenaga of the Miura clan."

"I don't care whose servant you are," the woman said. "I won't let you pass. And if you try to force your way through, I'll take your life in an instant."

Heida thought to himself, "There's no point in doing something stupid. After all, what good is all the land in Japan if you're dead?"

"You are eighteen years old this year," the woman said. "In the spring of your thirty-first year, you will be killed fighting Izumi no Kosaburō Chikahira of Shinano Province.[8] Now leave here at once!" Heida was bitterly disappointed at not having seen the inner reaches of the cave, but given the woman's words, there was nothing he could do.

Returning to the capital, Heida appeared before the Kamakura shogun and recounted the mysteries he had observed. Yoriie listened. That no one had plumbed the depths of the cave weighed on his heart, and he made a further declaration: "I have four hundred *chō* of open land.[9] Anyone who aspires to a domain should explore the Fuji cave." The samurai of the various provinces grumbled among themselves, saying, "Only the living want land. What good is it when you're dead?" and no one volunteered.

At that time, there was a resident of Izu Province by the name of Nitta no Shirō Tadatsuna, a twelfth-generation descendant of the Kamatari Minister and a thirteenth-generation descendant of the Shirotsumi Middle Counselor.[10] "I have sixteen hundred *chō* of land," Nitta thought to himself. "With the shogun's four hundred, I could have two thousand, and then I'd be able to leave one thousand each to my sons Matsubō and Okubō." Nitta thus made his way before the shogun and

---

7. The woman speaks in the voice of a kalavinka, a Himalayan bird renowned for its exquisite song. In the Pure Land Buddhist tradition, the kalavinka is depicted with the face of a beautiful woman and is said to reside in the Pure Land.
8. Heida was indeed killed at the age of thirty-one as a result of his involvement in the Izumi Chikahira Disturbance—a failed attempt in the second month of 1213 to install the late Yoriie's orphaned son as shogun—but he was Chikahira's ally rather than his opponent.
9. Four hundred *chō* is approximately 980 acres (397 hectares).
10. "Tadatsuna" is likely a mistake for Tadatsune. The historical Nitta no Shirō Tadatsune (d. 1203) is best known for his role in the assassination of Yoriie's father-in-law, Hiki Yoshikazu, in 1203. The Kamatari Minister is Fujiwara no Kamatari (614–669), founder of the Fujiwara clan.

announced his intention to explore the Fuji cave. Yoriie was exceptionally pleased, and he granted Nitta a deed for the four hundred *chō*.

After taking his leave, Nitta summoned his two children, Matsubō and Okubō. "Listen, boys," he said. "I'm off to explore the Fuji cave for our Kamakura Lord. I'm doing it because I love you. The shogun's given me a deed for four hundred *chō*, so now I can leave you one thousand each."

The boys tried to dissuade their father. "One thousand or ten thousand," they said, "we don't want it if it's going to cost your life."

"I'm not likely to die just by entering the Fuji cave," Nitta said, comforting his sons, "not without some sign, at least. So take it easy. But if I do die, I don't want you to grieve for me. Be good brothers and always get along. Stick together, no matter what, and serve your lord and keep up the family name." As there was nothing that they could do, the boys withdrew.

"All those samurai must hate me now!" Nitta mused. "But there's nothing for it— every father loves his sons. It's for them alone that a man bothers to plant pines and cedars. There's an old poem that goes,

> | *hito no oya no* | Though a parent's heart |
> | *kokoro wa yami ni* | may not be mired |
> | *aranedomo* | in darkness, |
> | *ko wo omou michi ni* | one still wanders lost |
> | *mayoinuru ka na* | on paths of love for a child."[11] |

Such were Nitta's thoughts.

Nitta's attire that day was exceptionally grand. He wore an unlined inner garment with a lattice design, loosened at the sides, and a finely woven silk *hitatare* with the sleeves hitched back at the shoulders. On his head he wore a court cap, laced on tight, and at his waist he carried a great Mōbusa sword, a short sword in a white ribbed sheath, and a crimson-edged fan. The Kamakura shogun assigned him a retainer: a certain Kudō Saemon no Suke, whom Nitta had carry a bundle of sixteen torches. After declaring his intention to return at noon, seven days later, Nitta and his man entered the cave.

Nitta walked some hundred yards, but there was nothing to be seen, no lady weaving at a loom. Drawing the great sword from his waist, he brandished it in the

11. This is a slightly alternative version of poem 1102 in *Gosen wakashū* (*Later Collection*, 951), attributed to Fujiwara no Kanesuke (877–933). According to section 45 of *Yamato monogatari* (*The Tales of Yamato*, tenth century), Kanesuke composed it out of concern for his daughter's fortunes at court.

The Tale of the Fuji Cave

four directions and continued on his way.[12] After what seemed like six or seven hundred yards, Nitta came to a place where the moon appeared in the sky, just as in Japan. A multi-hued pine forest of blue, yellow, red, white, and black spread across the land. There was a small stream with footprints in the bed, from which Nitta surmised that someone had recently made his way across. Nitta traversed the stream, and he saw a succession of nine eight-ridged palaces with cypress bark roofs.

Nitta entered the palace grounds. Water dripped from the eaves with a sound like that of *ge-ke-shu-jō*—"the salvation of all sentient beings"—played upon a lute, and the rustling sound of wind in the pines was such as to awaken a person from the cycle of birth and death. Proceeding farther inside, Nitta saw hanging strands of threaded jewels. Night and day were as one, distinguishable only by the periodic opening and closing of lotus blossoms. In one place, Nitta found a lute left standing as if it had just been played. The ceilings were draped with sheets of red-ground brocade, and the pillars were wrapped in similar bolts of blue. The red and blue brocade was, in turn, adorned with gold and silver. When Nitta and his companion spoke, their voices echoed like the bells of Gion Shōja,[13] beyond the heart to fathom or words to express. Supposing that he had arrived in the Pure Land, Nitta was overjoyed.

Exploring a road that ran to the northeast, Nitta found a lake with an island. There was a palace there that glowed with the radiant light of Jambu River gold.[14] A bridge with eighty-nine sections connected the island to the shore, and for the eighty-nine sections there were eighty-nine bells. The first bell rang the name of the Lotus Sutra, after which the others rang out every syllable of the twenty-eight chapters of the eight-fascicle Lotus. In addition, the eighty-ninth bell rang the following prayer: "Tamon, Jikoku, Zōjō, Kōmoku, and you Ten Rakshasa Daughters: by the power of the Lotus Sutra, lead all sentient beings to the Pure Land of Nine Grades."[15] It also rang, "May this merit be spread equally so that all alike will aspire to enlightenment and achieve rebirth in the Land of Tranquility and Bliss."[16]

12. It was believed that by brandishing a sword, a traveler could expose hidden malevolent spirits.
13. This is a reference to the legendary bells at the Indian temple where Shakyamuni Buddha is said to have preached.
14. The Jambu River runs through the great mango forest in northern Jambudvipa, which, in Buddhist cosmology, is the island-continent at the foot of Mount Sumeru that is inhabited by human beings. The Jambu River is known for its purple gold. The word "palace" is interpolated from the 1607 *Fuji* text.
15. Tamonten (also Bishamon and Bishamonten, Skt. Vaiśravaṇa), Jikokuten (Skt. Dhṛtarāṣṭra), Zōjōten (Skt. Virūḍhaka), and Kōmokuten (Skt. Virūpākṣa) are the Four Heavenly Kings (*shitennō*). Together with the Ten Rakshasa Daughters, they are divine protectors of Buddhism. The words "eighty-ninth bell" are interpolated from the 1607 *Fuji* text.
16. This is a passage from the preface to Shandao's *Commentary on the Visualization Sutra* (seventh century). The Land of Tranquility and Bliss is the Pure Land.

There was an eight-petaled lotus in the five-colored water of the lake. Nitta was enthralled, and when he approached it for a closer look, he noticed that the eastern garden of the palace was paved with silver. A husky voice called out from inside: "Who are you to visit my abode?" It was a snake with eyes like the sun and the moon, and a mouth so red that it seemed to have been daubed with paint. A full twenty fathoms long, it had sixteen horns and a hundred and eight eyes. Its flaming breath rose up a thousand feet in the air.[17] The sight of it flicking its scarlet tongue was enough to make Nitta's hair stand on end.

"Nitta," the snake said, "who do you think I am? I am the Great Asama Bodhisattva of Mount Fuji. Luck has run out for the Kamakura shogun Yoriie, ruler of Japan, now that you, his servant, have found me here. It causes me shame, but I'll confess: my six sensory organs are wracked with pain three times every night and day.[18] Please feed me your sword."

"Certainly," Nitta said, and he drew his four-foot, six-inch Mōbusa sword and offered it to the serpent. The bodhisattva took the weapon and swallowed it point-first.

"Your short sword, too," the creature said. Nitta proffered his short sword, and the bodhisattva swallowed that as well.

After a while, the bodhisattva spoke: "In exchange for your swords, I will show you the Six Realms and then send you home."[19] Changing his appearance to that of a seventeen- or eighteen-year-old boy, the bodhisattva explained: "The people of Japan say that hell is frightening, but no one who's been there has ever returned. And they say that paradise is wonderful, but no one's ever seen it. So I am going to show you hell, and then send you back."

Taking Nitta under his left arm, the bodhisattva declared that first he would reveal the Children's Riverbed Hell. "Listen, Nitta," the bodhisattva said. "The magistrates of hell are as follows: first, there's the Hakone Gongen; second, the Izu Gongen; third, the Hakusan Gongen; fourth, me; fifth, the Mishima Gongen; and sixth, the Tateyama Gongen of Etchū Province. We are the six magistrates of the 136 hells, and we are all manifestations of Kannon. If you disregard us, you're doomed.[20] Now look here at the Children's Riverbed Hell."

17. The words "hundred and eight eyes" and "flaming" are interpolated from the *Fuji no hitoana sōshi* manuscript (sixteenth century) in the Keiō University Library, typeset in Ishikawa Tōru, "Keiō gijuku toshokan-zō *Hitoana sōshi* kaidai, honkoku," *Mita kokubun* 26 (1997): 31–44.
18. The six sensory organs (*rokkon*) are the eyes, ears, nose, tongue, body, and mind. The term is often employed as a synonym for the body as a whole.
19. The Six Realms (*rokudō*) are the planes of existence through which unenlightened sentient beings transmigrate according to their karma: the realms of heaven, humans, animals, *ashura* (a world of never-ending battle), hungry ghosts, and hell.
20. This and the preceding three sentences are translated from the Keiō text, which contains a clearer explanation of the six magistrates of hell than does the 1603 *Fuji* text. *Gongen* (avatar) is a term for a buddha

Seven- and eight-year-old children held hands with three- and four-year-olds, all of them stricken with inexpressible grief. "What's the meaning of this?" Nitta asked, taking in the sight. The bodhisattva explained: "These are children who died without compensating their mothers for the pain they caused them during their nine months in the womb. They're to suffer on the riverbed like this for nine thousand years." A blazing fire swept the expanse, and the stones all burst into flames. As the children had nowhere to run, they were burned up until only their ashen bones remained. Soon, a number of demons arrived. Shouting "Arise! Arise!" and beating the ground with iron staves, they restored the children to their former selves.

Looking toward the west, Nitta saw the Sanzu River, ten thousand *yojana*s deep and wide.[21] An old woman was stripping passing sinners of twenty-five robes in accord with their twenty-five types of sin. Those without robes were stripped of their skin, which the old woman hung on the limbs of a *biranju* tree and made into celestial feather gowns. The old woman was a manifestation of Dainichi Buddha.[22]

Crossing the river, Nitta and the bodhisattva arrived at the Mountain of Death.[23] When the dead receive memorial services on the anniversaries of their passing, spirits come here to report it. Avoiding the mountain, they call out, "People are praying for you on your death day! Quick, tell the birth companion deities!"[24] The birth companion deities receive the dead and seek to extirpate their eight billion *kalpas* of sin by interceding with Taishaku.[25] They record the news of the services in their "good" tablets, enabling some of the dead to proceed to the Pure Land of Nine Grades.

To the side, Nitta saw demon wardens flogging a sinner who was burdened with a heavy stone. With cries of "Climb! Climb!" demons were hounding countless others up the jagged sides of iron boulders. The bodhisattva explained: "These are people who overloaded horses in the course of doing business. They reveled in their profits and callously worked their animals to death. They'll suffer constantly like this

---

or bodhisattva who has taken on a temporary manifestation as a Japanese deity in order to save sentient beings.

21. One *yojana* equals seven or nine miles, depending on the interpretation.

22. The old woman is Datsueba 奪衣婆, whose name is written with the characters for "clothes-snatching hag." The *biranju* is a kind of marmelo native to India.

23. The Mountain of Death (Shide no yama) is a place through which all the dead must pass.

24. Birth companion deities (*kushōjin*) are pairs of Buddhist deities who affix themselves to a person's right and left shoulders at the time of the person's birth and then record his or her good and bad deeds on "good" and "bad" tablets throughout the person's life. When the person dies, the deities report their findings to Enma, the king and judge of the afterworld.

25. A *kalpa* is a measurement of time that Nāgārjuna (ca. 150–250) described in *Daichidoron* (*Commentary on the Great Wisdom Sutra*) as being greater than the time that it takes for a heavenly being to wear away a forty-*ri* (hundred-square-mile) rock by brushing it with a delicate sleeve once every hundred years.

for eighteen thousand years. Nitta, tell everyone in the human world: never over-load a horse just because it can't speak. You'll go to hell if you do."[26]

Nitta saw some sinners being skewered on the points of blades. With shouts of "Climb! Climb!" demons were chasing them up the Mountain of Swords. Their flesh fell in pieces like shreds of deep-dyed crimson cloth. "These are people who didn't repay their obligations to their masters and parents in the human world," the bodhisattva explained. "This is their punishment for failing to settle down, and for speaking badly of their masters and parents."

To the west, Nitta saw a place where demons were forcing people through tower-ing waves of fire and water. The demons were affixing iron shackles to the people's wrists and ankles, and in one place, they were pounding nails into each person's forty-four joints, eighty-three bones, and nine hundred million hair follicles. "What's this?" Nitta asked, to which the bodhisattva replied, "These are the punishments for judiciary officials. They're doomed to suffer like this without relief. If there's anything that a person should avoid, it's becoming a judge."

There was a high place to the east, and the bodhisattva led Nitta there for a look. They could see a road running eastward to the Crossroads of the Six Realms, where a lone priest stood dressed in a monastic stole. A crowd of sinners had gathered before him. "Save us, Buddha!" the people cried in their despair. Demon wardens seized them and declared that they would drop them into the Hell of No Respite.[27] "Who is that priest?" Nitta asked.

"That's Jizō Bodhisattva of the Six Realms," the bodhisattva explained. "He doesn't help those who were interested in only fame and fortune in their former lives, and who didn't chant his name, even if now they beg to be saved. Tell everyone back in the human world."

The bodhisattva further explained: "Those who want to go to the Pure Land should wash their hands at dawn every day and chant Jizō's name one or two hundred times. Now listen closely, Nitta: the Six Realms are the realms of hell, hungry ghosts, ani-mals, *ashura*, humans, and heavens. First, I'll show you the animal realm."[28]

The bodhisattva led Nitta to a place where there were three snakes. Two of them were female, and together they wound around a third snake, which was male. The

26. The abused horses will themselves become demons and torture their former owners in hell, according to the Keiō text and the woodblock-printed *Fuji no hitoana sōshi* (1627), typeset in Yokoyama and Matsu-moto, eds., *Muromachi jidai monogatari taisei*, 11:452–75.

27. The Hell of No Respite (Muken jigoku, Skt. Avīci) is the deepest and worst of the eight burning hells, where evildoers are tortured constantly without interruption.

28. According to the Keiō and 1607 *Fuji* texts, the bodhisattva says that first he will show Nitta the hell realm. "Animal realm" (*chikushōdō*) may be a mistake here, considering that Nitta and the bodhisattva are again said to visit the animal realm later in the tale.

The Tale of the Fuji Cave

females sucked on the male's eyes and mouth; their breath rose up a thousand feet in the air. "What's happening here?" Nitta asked.

"The snake in the middle was a man who kept two wives in the human world, enraging them both. They'll suffer together like this for 7,300 years."[29]

Looking in another direction, Nitta saw demons taking hold of a sinner, stretching his tongue out twelve feet, and pounding it full of nails. Other demons were gouging out people's eyes, and in one place, iron dogs and crows were devouring mounds of flesh. "What's this?" Nitta asked, to which the bodhisattva replied, "These are punishments for people who spoke badly about their masters, parents, and teachers."[30]

There was a woman being sawn in half at the crotch. "This is a woman who fell in love with a man when she was already involved with another," the bodhisattva said. "She'll be tortured like this without reprieve for 405,000 years."

In another place, Nitta saw a woman in twelve-layered robes standing on top of a boulder. She began ripping apart her own flesh, which several demons messily devoured. Her screams were terrible beyond belief. "That woman was a prostitute in her former life. She spent her days lusting after men, which is why she fell into the animal realm."[31]

There was a woman beside a standing oil lamp. Demons were peeling the skin from her face and dripping oil on the flesh underneath. "Now this woman was naturally ugly, but because she wanted to be attractive to men, she tried to improve her looks. Such efforts are bound to fail. And even if they do succeed for a while, their consequences for the next life are severe. When a woman like this ends up distributing talismans and the like, people simply say, 'How sad!' and don't pay her any mind. This is the punishment for people like her who make up their faces with rouge and white foundation that they bought in secret from men. They're bound to suffer in this way for fifty thousand *kalpas*."

Farther on, Nitta saw a sinner being pulled toward him by thirty sets of iron chains. Looking closely, he saw that it was a disheveled nun. Nitta asked the bodhisattva to explain. "This is the nun Usui from the Akatsuka estate in Kōzuke Province. She envied others when they prospered, and rejoiced at their misfortunes. She was born the mistress of a wealthy house with as many as three hundred retainers.

29. The words "7,300 years" are from the 1607 *Fuji* text. The 1603 text states, "ten thousand three hundred, four thousand years," which is an apparent copyist's mistake. According to the Keiō and 1627 *Fuji* texts, the three snakes would suffer for 1,300 and 300 years, respectively.

30. The word "teachers" is interpolated from the Keiō and 1607 *Fuji* texts. According to the Keiō text, people can also have their eyes gouged out for stepping over their parent's pillow.

31. In the 1607 *Fuji* text, the bodhisattva gives Nitta the additional instruction to "tell the women of the human world never to take up prostitution. It has deep karmic implications."

She wouldn't feed them even salt or miso, but when it came to herself, she had them serve her lovely meals every morning and evening. In short, she had no compassion for those in her employ. Worse still, she didn't make any offerings to monks or priests. Since she didn't give the slightest bit of charity to anyone, the Ten Kings had nothing to say on her behalf.[32] 'Drop her right into the Hell of No Respite!' they declared. So now she's going to be pushed down to the bottom of a boiling pot.

"Listen, Nitta. It's true that both men and women fall into hell, but many more women do than men. Women's thoughts are all evil. Still, women are forbidden to approach men on only eighty-four days a year.[33] Women don't know their own transgressions, which is why they fail to plant good roots. It's a shame, you know."

Nitta saw another woman being pulled toward him by thirty iron chains, and he asked the bodhisattva to explain. "This woman was the master of an estate. She abused innocent farmers, causing them considerable consternation. Women like her will have nails pounded into their chests, and their breath will rise up a thousand feet in the air. They'll all fall into hell for a very long time."

Looking to the side, Nitta saw some demons hunting sinners with a pack of iron dogs. Calling the sinners "game" and "prey," they set the dogs to chasing after them and devouring their flesh. "What kind of karma causes that?" Nitta asked.

"That's the punishment for people who don't like to farm, yet who envy others for the things that they produce. They'll be tortured like that for five hundred thousand *kalpas*.

"Listen closely, Nitta. Commoners should tend to their fields, pay their annual levy, and then use what remains to support their families and make offerings to monks and priests. If they do, they're unlikely to fall into hell."

Horse- and ox-headed demons had placed a sinner in a flaming carriage, where they were beating him with iron cudgels. After forty-four years, he would be put in a stone cell from which there would be no release—not even if people in the human world prayed for him there. "Who's that?" Nitta asked. The bodhisattva replied, "He was a priest of Sodeshi Shrine in Tōtōmi Province. He managed the shrine lands, and he lavished their income on his own wife and children, rather than using it to perform services for the deity. He also failed to abstain from the proscribed foods or to read the Heart Sutra, which is why he's being punished like that. He'll spend a long time passing through the eighty thousand different hells. If there's one thing that a person should never become, it's a *kannushi*, a Shinto priest. Even those who associate with them will fall into hell."

32. The Ten Kings (*jūō*) are the ten judges of the dead.
33. Women cannot approach men during the seven days of the menstrual cycle, repeated twelve times a year, for a total of eighty-four days.

There was a woman screaming as her tongue was being pulled out, and there was a woman upon whom demons were piling thirty iron round weights. "These women made false accusations against their servants, causing them terrible distress. They'll suffer constantly like this for seven thousand *kalpas*."

Several demons were stuffing a seven-foot priest into a "dragon-mouth" water-spout.[34] They squeezed six and a half quarts of greasy fat from his body in a single day. "This man became a priest, but he couldn't read and he knew nothing of the sutras and sutra commentaries. He never offered incense or flowers to the Buddha; instead, he spent his life caring for his own family alone. People like him are doomed to suffer in this way for nine thousand years."

Nitta saw a priest with robes around his waist. He was running around the perimeter of the Hell of No Respite. "This man also became a priest in his former life, but he was like an ocean fish that absorbs no salt; his Buddhist devotion was only for show.[35] His heart was full of filth and desire, and he did nothing for the sake of others. Avaricious priests like him are bound to suffer in this way. Still, as a result of having taken holy vows, they'll be spared from falling into the Hell of No Respite."

In another place, Nitta saw demons pounding nails into a woman's hips. They were also cutting her open with a sword. The woman's belly was swollen like the Four Great Seas.[36] "In the human world, this woman pretended to be young in order to make herself more attractive to men. Then, when she became pregnant, she caused herself to miscarry. She'll suffer like this without relief for one hundred thousand *kalpas*."

A man who looked like a master was piling iron round weights on a servant and pushing him into the Hell of No Respite. "This is the punishment for people who sell themselves into bondage and then run away without honoring their contracts. They'll suffer constantly like this for eighty thousand *kalpas*. Nitta, tell everyone when you get back home: if you put something in writing, you can't just ignore it and behave as you will. It's a terrible crime if you do. It's also a crime if you don't return a contract when its term has expired."

Looking up into the sky, Nitta saw a woman with beautiful hair riding in a finely ornamented carriage. Golden flags fluttered in the merciful breeze. Twenty-five

---

34. The metal "dragon-mouth" spout (*tatsu no kuchi*) is cast in the shape of a dragon's head, so that water appears to pour from the dragon's mouth.

35. Like a fish that swims in brine yet remains sweet to the taste, the priest remained unaffected by his monastic environment.

36. In Buddhist cosmology, the Four Great Seas (Shidaikai) surround Mount Sumeru at the center of the world.

bodhisattvas played music, and Kannon and Seishi accompanied her as well. Nitta asked the bodhisattva to explain. "She's a woman from the Kikuta district of Hitachi Province. She was born into a wealthy family, and because of her kindness, she made offerings to monks and priests and looked after those who were alone in the world. She gave clothes to people who were cold, and in particular she favored zatō, blind minstrel priests.[37] Thanks to the goddess Benzaiten's compassion, her wealth increased day by day, year after year. You see, zatō are different from ordinary people, which is why Myōon and Benzaiten protect those who treat them kindly. This woman was always thinking of others, from the time that she was a child. There's a poem that goes,

hotoke to wa	Of the Buddha,
nani wo iwama no	what shall we say?
koke mushiro	As a mat of moss in a rocky cleft
tada jihishin ni	cannot be "spread,"
shiku mono wa nashi	his compassion is beyond compare.[38]

Such was the depth of her compassion. Taishaku was informed, and Kannon and Seishi came to lead her to the Pure Land of Nine Grades. Nitta, spread the news in the human world: if you show wholehearted compassion to everyone—man, woman, and beast—then you're sure to attain the Pure Land."

Looking to the side, Nitta saw some sinners who were bound with an iron cable. A demon held them fast, torturing them all the while. Pressing against the cord, the sinners cried with endless grief. "This is the punishment for people who kill all kinds of living things. They'll suffer like this for five million *kalpas*."[39]

In another place, Nitta saw a hundred demons piling and pressing rocks on the chests of sinners. "These are people who ate baby birds in the human world. People who selfishly eat whatever they please will suffer in this way for sixty thousand *kalpas*."

There was a Buddhist priest hanging upside down, and demons were cutting strips of flesh from his head. Nitta asked the bodhisattva to explain. "This one put on holy airs, but his heart was full of filth and greed. He thought nothing of the gods

---

37. Zatō are the blind *biwa*-playing raconteurs of *The Tale of the Heike* and other popular medieval narratives. They are traditionally associated with the goddess Benzaiten and the bodhisattva Myōon.
38. The poem depends for its effect on the double meaning of *shiku* ("to spread" and "to be the equal of") and on the overlapping syntax of *nani wo iwa* [*mu*] (what shall we say?) and *iwama no koke mushiro* (a mat of moss in a rocky cleft).
39. According to the Keiō and 1607 *Fuji* texts, the people were hunters and trappers in their former lives.

and buddhas. He never offered incense or flowers, and he didn't even recite the *nenbutsu*. For him, being a priest was just for show."

There was a demon stabbing a sinner in the eyes with an awl. "In the human world, this person hoodwinked and robbed other people. He's bound to suffer like this for five million *kalpas*. Listen, Nitta. Those who read the founder Shakyamuni's sutras are close to being buddhas. If you speak badly of a person who knows even just a little of a sutra, you're sure to fall into the Hell of No Respite. And to know nothing of the sutras is the same as being blind. What's more, people who expose their bellies to the sun or the moon, or who take off their clothes to be naked, are sure to fall into the Hell of No Respite."

There were shivering sinners in the ice of the Crimson and Great Crimson Lotus hells.[40] "These people were burglars, thieves, bandits, and pirates in their former lives. They robbed others and stripped them of their clothes. Their punishment is to be locked in ice like this for thirty-five thousand years."[41]

Next, Nitta saw a nun. She had shorn her hair when she was in her prime, and then later come to regret it. "If only I had my tresses," she thought, "then a man might take me by the sleeve!" The sight of women who were loved by men made her rue the day that she took holy vows. Filled with envy, she longed for the past, murmuring her regrets at the sounds of the wind and the waves as if she were reciting poetry. Forgetting that she was a nun, she took leave of her senses, found a man, became pregnant, and gave birth to a child. Now a demon was pounding nails into her hips and cutting her apart with a sword. Blood poured from her eyes and nose. To regret her deeds at this point would do her no good. Dropped into the animal hell, she was being tortured without respite.

Some demons had bound a woman with an iron cable. "You were crazy about men in the human world," they said. "Let's see how many!" They piled approximately three hundred iron round weights on the woman's body. "You can try to lie about the number of your lovers," they taunted, "but nothing's a secret from the Ten Kings!" The woman would suffer like this for fifteen thousand years.

Nitta saw a demon pushing a woman's face into an iron kettle. The kettle burst into flames, and the woman's head was burned. The bodhisattva explained: "In her former life, this woman would be chagrined to see a stranger approach at mealtime. She would turn red in the face and take her indignation out on some blameless

40. The Crimson and Great Crimson Lotus hells (Guren jigoku and Dai guren jigoku) are the seventh and eighth of the eight freezing hells. They are named after the splotchy red appearance of their inhabitants' frostbitten skin, which is said to resemble the blossoms of a crimson lotus.

41. According to the Keiō and 1607 *Fuji* texts, sinners carry their clothes with them into the Crimson and Great Crimson Lotus hells, but when they try to put them on, the clothes burst into flames.

servant or child. Women like her will be burned and charred in this way for four hundred thousand *kalpas*.[42] If someone comes at mealtime and you give them food, it's the same as making a Buddhist offering. You'll earn enormous merit and become rich in the present life."

Looking in another direction, Nitta saw a woman with hair that was three hundred yards long. Demons were setting fire to the ends and burning it all up. "What's this?" Nitta asked.

"When she was in the human world, she used to wish for a thousand new strands of hair for every strand that she lost. Now she'll spend nine thousand years having her forehead burned with hot iron round weights.[43]

"It's an infinitely terrible sin for a woman to be childless, and it's a horrible sin for a woman with only one child not to bear any more. Also, it's very bad for a woman not to have her period. If such women become wealthy and still fail to plant good roots—if they want more than what they already have, or want to wear more robes than they're already wearing—then when they die, they'll be like leaves blown from a tree. If you have wealth like that, your first thoughts should be for the next life, and you should plant good roots. People with children are likely to receive some benefit in the world to come, although it depends of course on the children. And even so, there aren't many children who pray enough to get their parents out of hell."

Nitta saw a demon hacking off a man's arms and legs with an adze. "That man cut down trees and grasses for no reason at all, and he let them wither and die. He'll be tortured to no end."

Saying that he would show him the realm of hungry ghosts, the bodhisattva led Nitta farther on. The sinners there had bellies as vast as oceans, necks as thin as threads, and heads as large as Mount Sumeru.[44] There was food before them, but when they tried to eat it, it burst into flames. Unable to consume a single thing, they were tormented by hunger, day and night. "These people were wealthy in their former lives, but they didn't share their riches with others, or even allow themselves to eat. They reveled in their coins and grain, forcing themselves all the while to endure hunger and cold. People like them will fall into the realm of hungry ghosts, where they'll suffer without cease for five hundred thousand *kalpas*.

42. The 1607 and 1627 *Fuji* texts explain that the woman would ignore visitors by hiding her head in her kettle, which is why she is punished in the way that she is.
43. According to the Keiō and 1607 *Fuji* texts, nails are being pounded into the woman's forehead. The 1607 and 1627 *Fuji* texts explain that her punishment is for the sin of envying the length of other women's hair.
44. This and the following two sentences are translated from the Keiō *Fuji* text, which in this part is more complete than the 1603 *Fuji* text.

"Nitta, tell everyone back in the human world: whether you're rich or poor, you'll find wealth if you clean your rooms, maintain your clothes, prepare proper food, feed others, and also feed yourself. The world is no more than what we see in a dream. If you failed to plant good roots in the past and resent rich people in the present, you'll fall into the realm of hungry ghosts."[45]

There was a hungry ghost who was giving birth to children and then ripping them apart and eating them. "This is the punishment for people who feed themselves by selling adolescent children, and for people who abandon their babies. They'll suffer like this continuously for three million *kalpas*. No matter how much trouble children are, it's forbidden to sell or abandon them."

Nitta saw a demon stuffing a sinner's mouth with rice. Blood gushed from the sinner's maw, and he was unable to eat.[46] "Now this person, he hated giving things to others. People like him will all fall into the realm of hungry ghosts for a very long time."

Nitta and the bodhisattva came to a crossroads where they saw a man with Jizō and Taishaku. "That's the Hirata Priest, otherwise known as Myōshinbō, from the Hirata district of Mikawa Province. He and his wife didn't have any children in the human realm, so they decided to renounce the world and pray for their lives to come. They took holy orders, and now they're on their way to the Pure Land of Nine Grades. The buddhas of the three ages have all gathered there to build them a golden hall."[47]

Examining the animal realm, Nitta saw all the birds of the sky and beasts of the earth spliced together in disturbing combinations. "This is what happens to children who lust after their own parents, and to people who lust after their stepmothers or stepchildren. They all fall into the animal realm."

Nitta looked into the *ashura* realm. He saw tremendous flames rising up into the air, and warriors armed with bows and blades engaged in ceaseless fighting. "People who die in battle fall into the *ashura* realm, where they suffer for 2,300 years."

After showing him the Six Realms of hell, hungry ghosts, animals, *ashura*, humans, and heaven, the bodhisattva took Nitta under his arm and led him to Enma's court. There was a golden palace hall there where the Ten Kings dwelled. Birth companion deities had recorded the deeds of the righteous in tablets of gold, and those

45. The Keiō *Fuji* text alternately explains: "People who were born poor because they failed to plant good roots in their previous lives, who envy the rich because they themselves do not succeed, and who long to possess everything they see—they are the hungry ghosts of this present [human] world."
46. According to the 1607 *Fuji* text, the demon is also sewing the sinner's mouth shut with iron thread, pounding nails into his cheeks, and piercing his throat with needles.
47. The three ages are the past, the present, and the future.

of the wicked in tablets of iron. There were demons shouting, "Look here, sinner! I'll show you all the crimes you committed since you were seven!" They were forcing sinners to gaze on the iron tablets. When the sinners protested that they were not guilty of so many crimes, the demons declared, "Then we'll weigh you on the karma scale!" and they did just that. For sinners who continued to protest, the demons offered to show them the Jōhari Mirror, which reveals all of a person's crimes and transgressions from the age of seven. Before the mirror, the sinners were unable to argue any further. Falling to the ground, they pressed their faces to the earth and cried, "Save me, Buddha, please!"

The Ten Kings would ask, "Did you have a child in the human world?" Those who answered yes would be taken from the demons and set to the side; those who answered no would be dropped right down into the Hell of No Respite.[48] "Listen, Nitta," the bodhisattva said. "Read *dharani* and the sutras, recite the *nenbutsu* with unwavering concentration, and avoid hating or envying others without good cause. And always show compassion. The Ten Kings revere those who do."[49]

Nitta saw some sinners being mashed up in an iron mortar. He also saw the Ten Kings rising from their seats to pay homage to a *nenbutsu* practitioner and send him on to the Pure Land. There were also demons using iron bows to shoot a priest full of arrows, one after another, with a cruelty that was difficult to watch. "That man pretended to know a sutra that he didn't. Priests like him who eat offerings, accept alms, and allow themselves to be honored will be made to suffer in this way."

The bodhisattva addressed himself to the people at large: "Listen, sinners. If no one in the human world prays for you on any of the seventh, fourteenth, thirty-fifth, forty-ninth, or hundredth days after you die . . ."[50]

"We'll drop you into the Hell of No Respite!" the demons shouted.

Hearing these words, the Ten Kings wept and spoke: "See here, demons, at least wait until the third year!"

"If no one prays for them by then, we'll take them and dump them into hell!"

"Then wait until the seventh year," the Ten Kings said. "And if they don't receive prayers by then, then wait until the thirteenth year." The kings agreed that if by that time the sinners had still not received any prayers, they would release them to the

213

---

48. The 1627 *Fuji* text explains that because sinners with children might receive prayers from the human world, the Ten Kings delay their judgment until such prayers have (or have not) been received.

49. The bodhisattva's advice is interpolated from the 1607 *Fuji* text. In the 1603 text, the bodhisattva simply advises Nitta to always show compassion. *Dharani* are magical Buddhist incantations, and the *nenbutsu* is the ritual invocation of the name of Amida (Skt. Amitābha) Buddha.

50. Due to an apparent textual corruption, the bodhisattva's sentence is left unfinished. In the other early *Fuji* texts, the bodhisattva makes no such statement.

The Tale of the Fuji Cave

demons, who, sad to say, would drop them into the Hell of No Respite. Turning back to the Ten Kings, the sinners cried, "Oh, Ten Kings, please save us!"

The bodhisattva spoke: "Well, Nitta, that's pretty much the gist of hell. Shall I show you some of the better places now?" The bodhisattva led Nitta to the west. They came to a place where there were four bridges. "Those are for buddhas, bodhisattvas, and venerable people to cross over into the Pure Land of Nine Grades."[51]

Radiating a brilliant light, Amida Buddha was awesome to behold. Around the lake, the wonderful cries of ducks, geese, and male and female mandarin ducks rose up from among the waves.[52] Golden flags fluttered in the merciful breeze, and twenty-five bodhisattvas played music and danced for joy. Flowers rained from the sky, beyond the heart to fathom or words to explain. Nitta wished to stay, but the bodhisattva, saying that he would show him where the buddhas and bodhisattvas dwelled, led Nitta on and made him pray.

They visited the abodes of Jizō, Ryūju, Kannon, Seishi, and all the buddhas of the three ages. Among them were places where the inhabitants engaged in seated meditation, places where they meditated on the Lotus Sutra, places occupied by esoteric practitioners, and places inclined toward righteousness. There were also places where ignorant people, beset with desire, had nails pounded into their six sensory organs.

In one place, Nitta saw a woman screaming as she was being eaten by a venomous snake. The bodhisattva explained: "This woman failed to give up her attachments to men. She'll suffer constantly like this for fifteen thousand years." Nitta also saw a woman who had flushed with anger when her husband sought to plant good roots. "This life is all that's important," she had thought to herself. "Who cares about the next? My husband and his damned 'good roots.' He should be worrying about my clothes!" The woman was impaled on the point of a sword. Her punishment would last for fifty million *kalpas*.

The bodhisattva spoke: "Husbands and wives should always encourage each other to plant good roots. The present life is just a dream within a dream. Still, some people think that they'll live for a thousand or ten thousand years, and in their wickedness, they want more than what they already have, and wish to wear more than what they're already wearing. They should simply accept the world as it is.

---

51. The Keiō *Fuji* text explains that of the four bridges, the first three were made of gold, silver, and copper, and they were intended for those who would achieve the upper, middle, and lower ranks of Pure Land rebirth. The fourth bridge, which was made of iron, was for the use of evildoers. According to the 1607 *Fuji* text, the iron bridge leads to the Hell of No Respite on Mount Tateyama in Etchū Province.
52. According to the Visualization Sutra, all the ducks, geese, and male and female mandarin ducks in the Pure Land expound the dharma.

"The present life lasts a mere fifty or sixty years, but the future is long. Those who don't know that they should seek to be reborn in the Pure Land and then enjoy themselves there are truly ignorant. It's extremely important that people tend toward goodness, and that they not obstruct, mislead, or interfere with others who do so, too. They'll achieve glory in the present life and attain the Pure Land in the next."

After a while, the bodhisattva continued: "There were many things that I wanted to show you, so I'll outline them here and then send you home." The bodhisattva fashioned three golden scrolls. Handing them to Nitta, he said, "Listen. Don't tell anyone about me or about the hells and paradise you've seen. You should tell the shogun and others after three years and three months have passed, but not before. Otherwise, I'll take your life and the shogun's, too. Then you could move to hell—how does that sound? I'll return you to your own world now."[53]

The bodhisattva led Nitta down a road that ran to the east. "Whatever you do," he warned again, "don't tell anyone about me." Then he disappeared.

Nitta returned on the seventh day after his departure. He appeared before the shogun and explained his injunction. Yoriie listened, exceptionally pleased. Various provincial lords said that they wished to hear Nitta's tale, and soon they and many others, humble and noble alike, had crowded the shogun's abode. They filled the upper and lower verandas and the open space outside. The shogun wore a hunting robe of blackish-green. "Come now, Nitta," he said from his elevated seat, "tell us what mysteries lie within the cave."

Nitta pressed his face to the floor. "I could describe them easily enough," he said, "but to do so would bring you immediate harm. You'd surely lose your life. Your order therefore leaves me at a loss."

"Tell us now," the shogun insisted, "even if it brings me harm."

Nitta sat up straight and began to speak. He explained in detail about the cave, the Six Realms, the Four Types of Beings,[54] hell, and the Pure Land Paradise. All those who heard him were spellbound and amazed. His story brought to mind the sermons of Pūrna, Shakyamuni's disciple,[55] awakening its listeners from the cycle of birth and death. But before Nitta had finished, in what was then his forty-first year, his life disappeared like the early-morning dew.

---

53. In the 1627 *Fuji* text, the bodhisattva states that the scrolls contain painted representations of hell and the Pure Land. According to the Keiō, 1607, and 1627 *Fuji* texts, Nitta should use them to preach. In the 1607 *Fuji* text, the bodhisattva explains that "most people are unimpressed by hell because they can't see it with their own eyes. You should show these scrolls to them."

54. The Four Types of Beings (*shishō*) are designated according to the ways in which they are born, whether from a womb, from an egg, from moisture (insects, for example), or from nothing at all (those who spontaneously appear in heaven or hell as a result of their karma).

55. Pūrna (J. Furuna) was one of Shakyamuni's ten principal disciples. He is renowned for his eloquence.

A voice called out from above: "You made him speak of me, Yoriie, so there's nothing that can save you now, either. I'm taking Nitta's life." Hearing these words, the provincial lords were frightened beyond compare.[56]

Nitta's body was sent to his family in Izu. Matsubō, Okubō, and Nitta's wife and his men took in the sight. "How can this be?" they cried, utterly distraught. They later cremated him, gathered up his ashen bones, and performed memorial services on his behalf. Matsubō and Okubō went on to enjoy the greatest prosperity; their descendants flourish to this very day.

All those who see this scroll should pray to the Great Asama Bodhisattva of Mount Fuji. Those who read it or hear it should devote themselves to the Way, listen closely, recite the *nenbutsu*, pray for the next life, and chant *Namu Fuji Asama Daibosatsu*, "Hail, Great Asama Bodhisattva of Mount Fuji," one hundred times. If they do so, they are unlikely to fall into the three evil realms. This is *The Tale of the Fuji Cave*.

Faithfully copied by Dōkyō on an auspicious day in the fifth month of Keichō 8 [1603].

TRANSLATION AND INTRODUCTION BY KELLER KIMBROUGH

---

56. The historical Minamoto no Yoriie was in fact assassinated by agents of the regent Hōjō Tokimasa (1138–1215), Yoriie's maternal grandfather, on the nineteenth day of the seventh month of Genkyū 1 (1204). He was twenty-three years old.

Isozaki

Along with *The Tale of the Handcart Priest*, *Isozaki* is one of only two *otogizōshi* in this volume with an explicitly Zen Buddhist orientation. Named after the bigamous husband in the tale, *Isozaki* tells of a vicious murder and the religious awakenings that it inspires. Insofar as it relates how even the most heinous acts may lead to the best spiritual results, it demonstrates the principle of non-duality, according to which delusion and enlightenment, samsara and nirvana, and good and evil are all ultimately the same. In the frequently hyperbolic realm of medieval Buddhist discourse, women are known to be especially prone to hatred and jealousy, and it is against these tendencies, in particular, that the author of *Isozaki* warns. Nevertheless, the husband in the story does not escape censure, suggesting that men, too, may bear some of the blame for the resentments and animosities that can arise in the domestic sphere.

Although *Isozaki* is pungently didactic and more than a little misogynistic—its author takes an unusually heavy-handed approach to storytelling—it employs poetry, allusion, and metaphor in some interesting ways. For example, after the first wife murders her rival, her sudden inability to remove her demon disguise suggests the inner, psychological transformation that has occurred in her as a result of her crime. Likewise, her eventual ability to remove the demon mask—her re-attainment of humanity as a result of her son's Buddhist preaching—suggests her internal spiritual redemption. The means of that redemption, as the author is so careful to point out, is not prayer to a bodhisattva, recitation of the *nenbutsu* or the Lotus Sutra, or any other popular devotional practice, but rather a concentrated session of seated meditation. In addition to being deeply moralistic, *Isozaki* is highly literary, invoking

The translation and illustrations are from the *Isozaki* picture book (*nara ehon*) (seventeenth century) in the collection of the Keiō University Library, typeset and annotated in Ōshima Tatehiko and Watari Kōichi, eds., *Muromachi monogatari sōshi shū*, Shinpen Nihon koten bungaku taikei 63 (Tokyo: Shōgakukan, 2002), 328–53.

references to famous poets and anecdotes of the past, chapter titles from *The Tale of Genji*, and a range of traditional and spuriously attributed verse.

Isozaki seems to date from around the second half of the sixteenth century; it survives in numerous picture scrolls and *nara ehon* picture books, as well as in a woodblock-printed edition published in Kanbun 7 (1667).

A lifetime is but a dream within a dream. Who among us can live for a hundred years? All things are empty, yet why then do we believe that they abide unchanging? The pine may survive for a thousand years, but when it finally rots its glory is more fleeting than that of a rose of Sharon, blooming and withering in a single day. Cherry blossoms and autumn leaves last for only a little while, lingering in the hours when the wind does not blow. And although we are as short-lived as they, when our companions neglect us we may feel as bad as the wretched reeds at Naniwa Bay. At such times, we must remember that other people's hardships are sorrows of our own, and that to engage in jealousy and hatred is despicable indeed.

At the foot of Mount Nikkō in Shimotsuke Province, there was a samurai by the name of Lord Isozaki. During the reign of Yoritomo,[1] a year or two passed without his receiving an official confirmation of his lands. He therefore took up residence in Kamakura in order to seek legal redress. In his absence, his wife attended to everything. One time, she sold a mirror to provide clothes for her husband in the capital, and morning and evening she diligently prayed to the buddhas and deities of the house that their lands might be finally, officially confirmed. As a result, perhaps, her husband eventually received his confirmation and returned to Shimotsuke. But having a man's vile heart, he brought back another wife. He built a house for her beyond the moat, and calling it the New Manor, he installed her there.

"Oh, how maddening!" the first wife thought. "I took care of everything while he was in Kamakura, and all for nothing! How heartless of him to go and do something like that!" She brooded and complained throughout the day and night.

Her husband spoke, saying, "It's not just me. This kind of thing happens with the rich and poor alike. Even in the tales of old, the major captain Genji sought out his

1. Minamoto no Yoritomo (1147–1199) reigned as shogun from 1192 to 1199.

'Lavender' link.[2] With the fleeting evening smoke of the 'Paulownia Pavilion,' he was smitten by the dew on the 'Evening Faces' in the course of the 'Broom Tree' night-time conversation. In the deeply fragrant 'Festival of Autumn Leaves,' he heard the chirp of the 'Empty Cicada' decrying the hollowness of the world. He slipped his love a leafy branch of the 'Sacred Tree,' and with no thought for the world to come, he set his heart on the 'Village of Falling Flowers.' Trapped at the bay of 'Suma,' wandering in the cycle of birth and death, he exhausted himself in untold heartache among the 'Channel Buoys' of 'Akashi,' bay of the four-fold bright and perfect wisdom.

"What's more, I've heard that Ariwara no Narihira slept with as many as 3,734 women![3] Even if their ranks and looks were varied, their hearts were all second-to-none. So come now, give it up. Back in Kamakura, that woman showed me the deepest affection, and since I couldn't very well abandon her, I brought her here with me. It's not right for a man to take a woman's love when he's down on his luck and then to drop her when he's back on his feet. There's a saying that goes 'Never forget your friends from when you were poor, and never turn out a wife who saw you through hard times.' I've also heard it said that you should 'never abandon a woman and her father from the days when you were broke.'

"You know, people say that the daughter of Ki no Aritsune pushed so much burning jealousy down inside her chest that when she put a pot of water on it, it boiled.[4] She wrote a poem about it, and that, too, became a dream:

tsurenaku mo	For your cruelty,
hisage no mizu no	the water in the kettle
wakikaeri	seethes and boils.
mune no keburi wa	Does smoke rise from my breast
tatsu ya tatazu ya	or does it not?

In any case, please just let me be." With that, her husband clasped his hands in earnest appeal. But having a woman's fickle heart, the wife could not turn a blind eye.

2. Genji is the amorous protagonist of *The Tale of Genji* (early eleventh century). In his speech, Lord Isozaki puns on several chapter titles from *Genji*, each of which I have indicated with single quotation marks. Some of the chapter titles are also the names of prominent female characters.

3. Ariwara no Narihira (825–880) was a poet and the purported protagonist of *The Tales of Ise* (ca. tenth century), which was long believed to document his personal sexual exploits.

4. This is according to a story in section 149 of *Yamato monogatari* (*The Tales of Yamato*, tenth century) and other sources. The daughter of Ki no Aritsune was married to Ariwara no Narihira. In the *otogizōshi Koshikibu*, she is said to have placed the pot of water on her chest in order to soothe her smoldering heart. See R. Keller Kimbrough, trans., *Koshikibu*, in *Preachers, Poets, Women, and the Way: Izumi Shikibu and the Buddhist Literature of Medieval Japan* (Ann Arbor: University of Michigan Center for Japanese Studies, 2008), 288.

She brooded constantly, thinking to herself, "However that may be, I still want to have a peek at that woman from Kamakura, just to see what she looks like."

One time, the husband traveled to Kamakura on business. While he was away, a *sarugaku* performer by the name of Kuraichi Taifu happened to arrive in the area,[5] and he came by the house to pay his respects. The wife sent out a servant to tell him, "My husband is in Kamakura, but he should be back soon, so please stay around for a while." She had him served saké and the like and then sent him on his way. Later, she sent a man to his lodging with a message. "There's a child that I need to frighten a little bit," she wrote. "Please lend me a horrible demon mask with a set of matching trouser-pants and a red demon wig." Kuraichi thought that this was inappropriate for a lady, but because he could not very well refuse, he sent them to her anyway.

Night soon fell, whereupon the wife donned the wig and trouser-pants. She crept out of her house with a hammer-staff in hand.[6] All alone, she made her way to the other woman's house, where she stealthily opened the gate and slipped inside. She paused for a while, but as the night deepened and the house grew quiet, she peered in through a window. There she saw a young lady, seventeen or eighteen years old, with free-flowing hair as long and lustrous as the wings of a river cicada. The wife could barely make out a set of beautiful black-painted eyebrows amid the lady's rich tresses. With her crimson outer robe cast off to the side, the young lady was perusing a written work in the dim light of an oil lamp. A faint scent of incense hovered in the air, highlighting the extraordinary beauty of her visage.

"She's so beautiful," the wife thought, "lovelier than Mount Mubasute and the Kiyomi Barrier combined, or a plum-scented willow branch with cherry blossoms abloom. Even in the past, how could the empress of Emperor Wu of Han or Yang Guifei or Li Furen have surpassed her?[7] Is there any man at all, however unfeeling, who could look at her without losing his composure, without falling in love? Next to her, I'm middle-aged. My skin is dark, my hair is reddish, and I've got kids! Oh, how awful!" But then the wife reconsidered: "Still, however beautiful she might be, what right does she have to steal another woman's husband? It's so hateful, so heartless!"

Just at that moment, the young lady summoned her maid, Kiritsubo. "Somehow or other," she said, "I feel more alone tonight than usual. I can't stop thinking about

---

5. *Sarugaku* was a theatrical forerunner of noh, but here the term likely refers to noh.

6. A hammer-staff (*uchizue*) is a kind of rod with a head shaped like a wooden bell hammer. It is typically carried by demons in noh.

7. Yang Guifei (719–756) was a consort of Emperor Xuanzong of Tang (685–762, r. 712–756). Li Furen (second century B.C.E.) was a consort of Emperor Wu of Han (156–87 B.C.E., r. 141–87 B.C.E.). They were legendary beauties of ancient China.

In her demon disguise, the first wife peers through a window at the second wife and her maid. (From *Isozaki*, courtesy of the Keiō University Library)

his Lordship. Oh, I wish he'd come back soon! Until he does, it's just too lonely waking up by myself in the mornings." Then she recited a poem:

yamadori no	Clouds above the ridge
o no e no kumo wo	like a mountain pheasant's tail
hedatete mo	may hold us apart—
kokoro wa kimi ni	but there is never a time
sowanu ma zo naki	when my heart is not with yours.

"His Lordship will be back soon," Kiritsubo replied. "And when he comes, he's bound to show you even more consideration than usual."

Hearing this, the first wife must have been all the more enraged. "How maddening!" she cried. "Well, I'll take her life and go!" With that, she burst through a sliding paper door and rushed inside. The young lady screamed in terror. Staring at the intruder, she took her to be a demon. She had never actually seen one, but she had heard them described. As for the wife, to say that she was frightening could hardly do her justice; the young lady was scared out of her wits. The wife pummeled her with her hammer-staff, bludgeoning her to the point of death. "Help!" the woman cried, "I'm being beaten!" Her agony was horrific, and because she was still so very young, she quickly died.

Isozaki

The first wife murders the second wife as the maid, Kiritsubo, runs from the room. (From *Isozaki*, courtesy of the Keiō University Library)

"Now I feel better!" the wife exclaimed. "Where's Kiritsubo?"

"Help! A demon!" Kiritsubo cried, running from the room.

The Buddha explains about this. When he says that "women are bodhisattvas on the outside and demons within," he means that although they may be beautiful on the surface, resembling even bodhisattvas, in their hearts they are more wicked than devils. There is a poem by the monk Saigyō that also tells of the perversion in the female heart:

yo no naka ni	If the hearts of
nyōshō no kokoro	the women of the world
sugu naraba	were righteous,
meushi no tsuno ya	then the horns of heifers
jōgi naramashi	would be as straight as rulers.[8]

There is truth in Saigyō's verse.

8. Saigyō (1118–1190) was a poet. This verse is cited in several other late-medieval and Edo-period sources, including the poem-tale anthology *Ochikochigusa* (ca. 1580), in which it is attributed to the monk Gyōgetsu (Reizei Tamemori; 1265–1328).

The Buddha himself once lodged in an ordinary woman's womb, and there are venerable learned monks and holy men who, though they themselves were born of women, yet remonstrate against women for their wickedness. Some people wonder how this could be, and they, too, seem to be right. This is why a certain sutra says that "people have the characteristics of buddhas, so they rank as buddhas."[9] On the other hand, the sutras also explain that "women are the servants of hell; they stamp out the seeds of the buddhas."[10] By tearing out her rival's hair, stomping on her chest, and briskly beating her to death, the first wife was assuredly stamping out the seeds of the buddhas.

The wife returned home, but when she tried to remove her mask, she found that it was affixed more firmly than if it had been chained or nailed into place. Even if she twisted off her head, it was unlikely to budge. In addition, she could not let go of the hammer-staff in her hand. Truly, she had become the demon of her wicked, brooding heart. "Oh, how horrible!" she lamented. "What could have happened? And what will become of my poor, wretched self?" Ashamed at the prospect of being seen and feeling that she was neither dreaming nor awake, she passed the night in tears.

The day had dawned, and since it would not do for her to be seen, the wife crept out into the back mountains and sat at the base of a large tree. How frightening! Since she had become a demon in outward form, had her heart, too, turned demonic?

"Oh, I hope someone will come along," she thought to herself. "I'd like a bite to eat to stop this hunger for a while." Besides this, she could think of nothing else. She wanted to visit the town, but clearly it was impossible. She could only hide in the trees like the forest guard of Mount Ōuchi, neither scattering with the autumn leaves of Tatsuta and Hatsuse nor disappearing with the dew in the Miyagino and Musashino fields. With her worthless life dragging ever on, she soaked her sleeves in tears as miserably shallow as the mountain stream in which the forlorn buck, bugling restlessly in the night, could scarcely dip his hoofs.[11] She was boundlessly chagrined.

9. This quotation is obscure. According to an *Isozaki* manuscript in the Iwase Bunko archive, people rank as buddhas because they possess the buddha-nature. See Ōshima and Watari, eds., *Muromachi monogatari sōshi shū*, 337n.10.

10. This is another quotation of unknown origin, but is frequently misattributed to the Nirvana Sutra. It is also usually combined with the preceding passage about women being bodhisattvas on the outside and devils within.

11. This sentence contains puns on *ukine* (sad cry) and *ukine* (restless sleep), and on *asashi* (shallow) and *asamashi* (miserable). The forlorn buck is a staple figure in Japanese court poetry.

The wife weeps as her son preaches to her about Buddhism. (From *Isozaki*, courtesy of the Keiō University Library)

Now the wife had a son who was an acolyte. He was a student at the temple on Mount Nikkō,[12] and he had an outstanding reputation. Hearing what had happened, he hurried down from the mountain. "Oh, how awful!" he thought. "What will become of my mother? I'd like to see her one time, even if she's in a hopeless state." He searched here and there until he heard some people carrying on about a terrifying creature in the back mountains. Intrigued, he went to take a look.

The son found a demon-like person hiding at the base of a large tree. "You there," he called out, "who are you?" The demon wept and replied, "Oh, for shame! To be seen this way, not yet vanished like the dew on the grass!"

"Well, then, are you my mother?" And lamenting, he exclaimed, "Ah, what's to become of you in such a condition? How horrible!" With that, the demon told him exactly what it had done.

"You may be my mother," the boy said, "but who knew you had such an evil heart! Oh, how awful! Shall I try to pull off the mask somehow?"

"It won't budge, even if you twist my head off."

The son spoke: "This has happened because of your wickedness, and for that reason neither the gods nor the buddhas are likely to intercede. Whether or not

12. This is Rinnōji Temple, in the city of Nikkō in present-day Tochigi Prefecture.

the mask and hammer-staff will fall away depends on your heart alone. You must forget your hatred, be unaware of your own personal sorrow, forget yourself, be unaware of others, and simply sit in silence. When we hear of the multitude of conditioned phenomena,[13] although they may be hard to tell from a vision or a dream, it is when we cannot tell them from phantasms that there is no self and there are no others.

"Even now, the Three Buddha Bodies—the so-called buddha-nature of the three ages—reside within your breast. When you do good, you are a buddha incarnate; and when you do bad, the Three Buddha Bodies become three demons and punish you. Judging from your appearance, there's no doubt about it. The Buddhist Law isn't far; it's actually close, inside your heart. Universal Truth is none other than this. The buddhas despise it when we seek outside of ourselves.[14]

"Speaking of unconditioned existence,[15] you should understand that there will certainly come a time when you will attain buddhahood as yourself. The eight schools, nine schools, twelve schools, Shingon, Tendai, Kusha, Hossō, and Sanron schools of Buddhism all appear within this realm. Incanting *dharani*, invoking the seven hundred–plus sages of the Kongōkai Mandala and the five hundred–plus sages of the Taizōkai Mandala, forming mudras, ringing handbells, clutching single-pointed *vajras*, and chanting: these are all practices of conditioned existence. To perform them is like setting your heart on a woman in a picture. Rather, it is the Way of Zen to abandon the single-pointed *vajra* and the handbell and to meditate on the character *A*.[16] That is why there is a poem that says:

aji yori mo	Beginning with *A*,
aji ni tomonau	all those who proceed with
hito wa mina	the character *A*
mata tachikaeri	will return to the hometown
aji no furusato	of the character *A*.[17]

As the verse explains, returning to the hometown of *A* is meditation.

13. The multitude of conditioned phenomena (*issai uihō* 一切有為法) includes all things that are constantly rising, changing, and disappearing according to the principle of karma.

14. I have translated this sentence from an *Isozaki* manuscript in the collection of Ishikawa Tōru, which in this case is clearer than the Keiō text. See Ōshima and Watari, eds., *Muromachi monogatari sōshi shū*, 342n.7.

15. Unconditioned existence (*muihō* 無為法) refers to a state of being free from the changes wrought by karmic causality, hence, nirvana.

16. *A* (*a* 阿) is the first letter of the Sanskrit alphabet. In esoteric Buddhism, it is taken to signify the beginning and totality of all things.

17. Variants of this poem appear in the Lotus Sutra commentary *Hokekyō jurin shūyōshō* (*Gathered Leaves of the Lotus Sutra from a Grove on Eagle Peak*, 1512) and other sources.

Isozaki

"In the practice of the *nenbutsu*,[18] too, we abandon the bell and the mallet and face the wall, whereupon:

tonafureba	When we chant the name,
hotoke mo ware mo	both the Buddha and the self
nakarikeri	no longer exist.
namu Amida-bu no	There is only the voice saying
koe bakari shite	'Hail Amida Buddha.'[19]

When this happens, there is no buddha and there is no self; there is only a voice. And whose voice is it? It is the manifested form of meditation.

"How sad that you have squandered this precious life, when human form is so difficult to attain! Women, in particular, suffer from the thick clouds of the Five Obstructions, never clearing.[20] In this world of dreams and visions, you must forget your hatred!

"Long ago, there was someone like you. When the wife of Mibu no Tadayoshi in Awa Province became especially jealous, she sprouted scales on her back and a single horn from her brow. Her mouth split open from ear to ear, and she actually became a serpent in this very life. A venerable monk was passing by, and when he heard about her, he said, 'Ah, how pitiful! I'll teach her about the dharma and save her.'

"'Oh, give it up,' the snake-woman said. 'I don't need your instruction. Even just hearing about the Buddhist Law makes me sad. All I want is a way to take that hateful man and woman in each hand and drag them down into hell. It hurts me even just to hear about the Buddhist Law, so I'm hardly going to join you in it. Listen, priest, in all your time in the world, if you've ever learned a secret rite for killing people you despise, I want you to teach it to me now.'

"'That's easy enough,' the monk replied. 'I'll show you a secret way of making those you hate disappear. Can you do as I say?'

"'Certainly,' the snake-woman said. 'If it'll finish off my enemies, then I'll do just as you say, even if I fall into hell as a result.'

"'In that case, I'll teach you. First, you must sit in mindless contemplation for one or two weeks, being unaware of yourself and forgetting those you despise. Then,

---

18. The *nenbutsu* is the ritual invocation of the name of Amida (Skt. Amitābha) Buddha, the first character of whose name is also *a* 阿.
19. This poem is traditionally attributed to Priest Ippen (1234–1289), the founder of the Jishū sect of Pure Land Buddhism. According to *Ippen Shōnin goroku* (*Record of Ippen*) and other sources, Ippen composed it when he studied Zen under Hottō Kokushi.
20. According to the Lotus Sutra, the Five Obstructions are five forms of rebirth precluded to women because of their gender, including, most importantly, rebirth as a buddha. The clouds of the Five Obstructions obscure the light of the moon, which is a traditional symbol of Buddhist Truth.

as you do, your enemies will vanish and you will be restored to your former self. But if any other thoughts arise in that time, you aren't likely to succeed.'

"'All right,' the woman agreed, 'if it will only rid me of those awful people,' and for three weeks she sat single-mindedly facing a wall. People say that over the course of those three weeks of sitting without thought, she was restored to her former self.

"At times when we've been unaware of ourselves, where were the people we despised? When the wind calms, the waves become still, and in a cloudless sky the moon shines clear.

sakuragi wo	Split the cherry tree
kudakite mireba	and look inside—
hana mo nashi	there are no blossoms there.
haru koso hana no	It is the spring itself
tane wa mochikure	that brings the seeds of blossoms.[21]

As the poem explains, the seeds of the blossoms are not inside the tree.

"What we call 'demons' don't exist apart, in some other place; depending on the inclination of our hearts, we ourselves are the demons of this world. So when it comes to engendering a single-minded desire for enlightenment, good and evil are one and the same. After all, what is delusion? And what is enlightenment? If you hate and envy others, then you'll become a demon or a snake in this very life. Likewise, if you earnestly turn your heart toward enlightenment, then why wouldn't you become a buddha? People say that a single session of seated meditation can erase the sins of countless ages. If you can become unaware of yourself as yourself, then those you despise will also disappear. And when that happens, the mask should fall away." The son thus delivered his ardent instruction.

The wife must have been persuaded, because she withdrew to the base of the tree and sat in silence for a while. Then, in the dead of night, she was surprised to feel the biting chill of the dawn wind. She stood up and looked around, whereupon the mask and hammer-staff mysteriously fell from her face and hand. "Oh, how wonderful!" she cried. "And how marvelous that it happened just as my son explained! The moon reflects in the waters of a marsh, illuminating them to their depths, and my heart, too, is dispelled of darkness!" She composed a poem on this very thought:

shizuka naru	The clear moon
kokoro no uchi ni	that dwells

21. Variants of this poem are in the Zen treatises *Ikkyū gaikotsu* (*Ikkyū's Skeletons*, 1457) and *Ikkyū mizukagami* (*Ikkyū's Water Mirror*, sixteenth century).

The wife's demon disguise falls away. (From *Isozaki*, courtesy of the Keiō University Library)

sumu tsuki wa	in a still heart
nami mo kudakete	is smashed by waves,
hikari to zo naru	becoming shards of light.

In comparison, how could even Prince Siddhārtha's enlightenment, which he attained long ago upon glimpsing the morning star after six years of solitary meditation, have exceeded her own?

"Still, how horrible!" the wife thought. "Though I was born a phantasm in a world of dream, with my vile heart I murdered a lady who was beautiful beyond anything that anyone could ever paint. It was I, but it was heartless what I did." She blamed herself, yet it was all for naught. She therefore cut off her hair, threw it away, and exchanged her clothes for the ink-dark robes of a nun. Then praying for the lady she had killed, she wandered the sixty-six provinces of Japan. Sometimes pursuing the path of enlightenment through seated meditation and sometimes composing poetry and reciting the *nenbutsu*, she constantly strove for her victim's salvation.

Lord Isozaki later returned from Kamakura, only to discover that one of his wives had left him in death and the other one in life. And he realized that the hardship of that separation—both in death and in life—was due entirely to his own offense. There is a poem that warns,

The wife wanders the provinces as a Buddhist nun. (From *Isozaki*, courtesy of the Keiō University Library)

sanaki dani	The covers are
omoki ga ue no	heavy enough already
sayogoromo	without piling more on.
waga tsuma naranu	Add no new blankets (no new wives)
tsuma na kasane so	that are not now your own.[22]

If we disregard this advice and behave as we will, then the teachings of the Buddha will do us no good. Lord Isozaki took inspiration from these events, and cutting off his topknot, he immediately abandoned his warrior household and set out to wander the provinces and pray for his dead wife. People say that he, too, became a buddha.

Three people attained buddhahood because of the one wife's wicked deed. When we think about this, how can we have any doubt that delusion is itself enlightenment, that the cycle of birth and death is nirvana, and that good and evil are actually one? If we consider the forms of evil deeds, we cannot go so far as to say that they are the doings of originally enlightened beings. It is rather a matter of good atop of evil.

---

22. This is a slight variation on poem 1963 in *Shinkokin wakashū* (*New Collection of Ancient and Modern Poems*, 1205), attributed to Jakuren Hōshi (d. 1182). It depends for its effect on a pun on *tsuma* 褄 (blanket-skirt) and *tsuma* 妻 (wife), as well as on the phrase *tsuma na kasane so*, which can mean both "add no [new] blankets" and "sleep with no [new] partner." This poem also appears, in this volume, in *The Palace of the Tengu*.

Isozaki

Those who see or hear of such things should never be jealous of others. There is a poem by Gyōgetsu that says,

waga tsuma wo	Even if other men
hito no toru tote	sleep with my wife,
hitogoto ni	why should I care?
heranu mono yue	There'll be just as much of her left
nani oshimuran	after they've all had their turn.[23]

It may be a funny example, but it is also true.

In addition, the Lotus Sutra speaks of women facing the Five Obstructions and the Three Obediences.[24] Men around the world have all lost their positions and their homes because of women. First, there are examples from foreign lands. People say that King You of the Zhou dynasty met his end because of a consort, and that Emperor Xuanzong's longing thoughts strayed as far as Japan because of Yang Gui-fei. Then, in this country, the holy man of Shiga Temple fell in love with an imperial consort, and because she kindly allowed him to touch her hand, his sixty-plus years of Buddhist practice were all wiped out and he cycled through the Three Worlds of Delusion after death. There was also the Fukakusa Lesser Captain, who fell in love with Ono no Komachi.[25] His resentment at failing to meet with her after traveling to her abode for a hundred nights came to bear on her in the end. Her looks went to ruin, and she became the old woman of Seki Temple. People say that she suffered a horrible transformation in this very life.

The Blood Bowl Sutra is a savior of women,[26] and as it, too, reveals, if at the time of her menstruation a woman spills blood on the ground, the deity of earth will mourn. Or if she releases blood in a river, the deity of water will suffer. As women's menses and parturition blood accumulate, they become the Blood Pool Hell, eighty thousand *yojanas* deep and wide.[27] Upon falling into this boiling lake of blood,

23. According to an anecdote in *Ochikochigusa*, Gyōgetsu composed this verse after discovering his wife *in flagrante* with another man.

24. The Three Obediences are specific to women and hail from Confucian rather than Buddhist philosophy. Confucian tradition holds that a woman must obey her father as a girl, her husband after she has married, and her son after she has been widowed. Although the Lotus Sutra describes the Five Obstructions, it contains no mention of the Three Obediences.

25. Ono no Komachi (ca. 825–ca. 900) was a poet. The story of her unfortunate affair with the Fukakusa Lesser Captain is recounted in the noh plays *Sotoba Komachi* (*Komachi on the Stupa*) and *Kayoi Komachi* (*The Courting of Komachi*).

26. The Blood Bowl Sutra (Ketsubonkyō) is a spurious sutra imported from China to Japan around the late fourteenth or early fifteenth century.

27. One *yojana* equals approximately seven or nine miles, depending on the interpretation.

women are tortured by demons who shout, "It's blood from your own bodies, so drink it all up!" Although a woman may feel remorse, it will have no effect, and although she may have children, they will do her little good.

The wife of Lord Isozaki became a murderous demon because of her single-minded resentment. And in this, she was not alone. If you indulge in envy and hatred, then even if you do not kill anyone, those feelings will build up and eventually turn you into a demon or a snake. What doubt could there be? Simply put, there is nothing as frightening as the feelings in a person's heart.

Once in the past, the daughter of a rich man of Komuma fell in love with a *yamabushi* mountain ascetic who was on a pilgrimage to Kumano. "I beg of you," she said, "please allow me to fulfill my yearning for you." The ascetic replied, "I have given up desire and entered the Buddhist path. It's my whole-hearted wish to leave this world of delusion, and I value my reputation. I made a great vow to visit Kumano, and since I'm on my way there now, I can't possibly consider your request." With that, he set out on his way. The daughter chased after him longingly, nearly catching up. The ascetic ran inside Kanemaki Temple,[28] shouting "Help me, please!" whereupon a priest hid him under a bell. The daughter made her way to the base of the bell, and suddenly transforming into a giant snake, she wrapped herself around it and sank into the earth.

Both the woman and the ascetic fell into hell because of the woman's single-hearted desire, but people also say that it was because of the ascetic's stupidity. Nothing like this would have happened if she had been allowed to achieve her small aspiration. It would have been like drinking water when you are thirsty. The Buddha, too, was once a layman. Water may be muddied, but it will become pure again.

Indeed, people say that because Ariwara no Narihira secretly appeared to married and unmarried women alike and fulfilled their desires, all 3,333 of them attained buddhahood.[29] He was like the wind sweeping a bank of clouds away from the moon, allowing its original light to shine through again. The monk Saigyō, too, loved an imperial lady, and he awakened to a desire for the Way when she graciously showed him a little kindness.[30] He wandered the provinces purifying his practice, after which he is said to have saved her and to have achieved buddhahood for himself, too.

In this world in which we somehow live out our lives, even good and evil exist within a dream. Udraka-Ramaputra once had eighty thousand years of life, but now

231

28. Kanemaki Temple is an alternative name for Dōjōji Temple in contemporary Wakayama Prefecture.
29. Previously in the tale, Lord Isozaki claims that Narihira slept with 3,734 women. The number 3,333 suggests the thirty-three manifestations of the bodhisattva Kannon (Skt. Avalokiteśvara), of which Narihira is sometimes said to have been a human incarnation.
30. According to an account in volume 8 of *Genpei jōsuiki* (*The Rise and Fall of the Minamoto and Taira Clans*, late fourteenth century), a consort of Retired Emperor Toba subtly admonished Saigyō for his love, whereupon he took Buddhist vows.

he has none.[31] Dongfang Shuo's nine thousand years have also disappeared, and the man survives in name alone.[32] Even the thousand years of Uttara-kuru will eventually come to an end.[33] How much more uncertain is this world of ours, in which young and old may perish like the dew on the grasses of the Adashino Plain![34] We may survive the morning, but the evening we cannot. No one remains young for long, and since we all grow old in the end, can either children or the elderly endure? This is why we should never drink, view the blossoms, and harbor wicked thoughts when we are young.

kokoro ni wa	The youthful winds
waka no urakaze	of Waka Bay
otozurete	blow into my heart,
sugata ni yosuru	drawing to my visage
oi no shiranami	the white waves of age.

Will we ever again see the moon reflected in the water, or an image in a mirror? To be born in human form is as rare as a one-eyed turtle finding a floating log. We must treasure our lives. Using our best judgment, we must show compassion for others and always avoid jealousy. I have written this story for the sake of women.

kimi ga yo wa	The reign of our lord
matsu no uwaba ni	shall shine everlasting,
oku shimo no	till the frost that gathers
tsumorite yomo no	in the upper branches of the pines
kage zo hisashiki	fills the oceans all around.[35]

TRANSLATION AND INTRODUCTION BY KELLER KIMBROUGH

31. Udraka-Ramaputra (J. Utsutsura) was one of Shakyamuni's early teachers. He is said to have attained a life span of eighty thousand eons in a later rebirth.
32. Dongfang Shuo (J. Tōbōsaku) was a literatus of the Western Han dynasty (206 B.C.E.–9 C.E.). In the noh play Tōbōsaku, he appears as a nine-thousand-year-old man.
33. In traditional Buddhist cosmology, Uttara-kuru (J. Hokkurushū) is the great continent to the north of Mount Sumeru. Its inhabitants are said to have life spans of one thousand years.
34. Adashino was a famous charnel ground at the eastern edge of Kyoto, the capital of Japan.
35. This is a variant of poem 311 in Kinyō wakashū (Collection of Golden Leaves, 1127), which supplies the crucial last line: yomo no / umi to naru made (fills the oceans all around). The poem is attributed to Minamoto no Toshiyori (d. 1129). It is included in only two of the many extant Isozaki manuscripts, suggesting that it is a later addition to the narrative, according to Watari Kōichi, in Ōshima and Watari, eds., Muromachi monogatari sōshi shū, 353n.22.

The Tale of the Handcart Priest

The Tale of the Handcart Priest (*Kuruma-zō sōshi*) is the fantastic tale of an eccentric Zen Buddhist practitioner who is said to have wandered around Japan in a rickety two-wheeled cart. It survives in a single manuscript: a colorful, likely seventeenth-century *nara ehon* picture book, the pages of which were unbound at an unknown time and mounted to form an exquisite hand scroll. The story is based in part on the noh play *Kuruma-zō* (*The Handcart Priest*), the first recorded performance of which was held in Nara in 1514, but its narrative extends far beyond that of the older play. Like its source drama, *The Tale of the Handcart Priest* concerns a day in the life of an itinerant "handcart priest," a type of low-level Buddhist renunciant of whom little is now known, but who Tokue Gensei argues was a relatively common figure in late-medieval Japan.[1] Tokue posits that these mendicant beggar-priests employed their carts as both rolling homes and platforms from which to preach, and that in their sermons, they expounded on the metaphorical implications of their carts as vehicles of Buddhist Truth.

In *The Tale of the Handcart Priest*, the Handcart Priest confronts a succession of hostile *tengu* (anti-Buddhist, supernatural bird-men) who challenge him on the significance of his cart and seek to punish him for his pride.[2] Like many *otogizōshi*, which are often concerned with otherworldly creatures, magical settings, and improbable events, the work can be seen to function on a symbolic level by depicting Buddhist and psychological abstractions as external, concrete phenomena, allowing audiences the

---

The translation and illustrations are from the *Kuruma-zō* picture scroll (seventeenth century) in the collection of the Kyoto University Library, typeset in *Kuruma-zō sōshi* (Kyoto: Kyoto Teikoku Daigaku, 1941), 2:15–34, and in Yokoyama Shigeru and Matsumoto Ryūshin, eds., *Muromachi jidai monogatari taisei* (Tokyo: Kadokawa Shoten, 1976), 4:273–81.

1. Tokue Gensei, "*Kuruma-zō no shusse*," *Nihon bungaku ronkyū* 21 (1962): 64–70, and "*Matsuhime monogatari kō*," in *Miryoku no nara ehon, emaki*, ed. Ishikawa Tōru (Tokyo: Miyai Shoten, 2006), 127–90.
2. Their ringleader, Tarōbō of Mount Atago, also appears, in this volume, in *The Palace of the Tengu* and *The War of the Twelve Animals*.

privilege of visualizing the invisible, or seeing the unseen. The story's rich and sustained use of symbols invites a variety of interpretations, concerning both the contested meanings of the Handcart Priest's cart and the significance of the many *tengu* in the tale, whether as fanciful representations of *yamabushi* mountain ascetics or as externalized projections of the priest's own inner demons. Thus considered from a loosely allegorical perspective, *The Tale of the Handcart Priest* may challenge our conceptions of the *tengu* motif in popular medieval discourse, as well as our notions of the broader possibilities for psychological realism in the world of medieval Japanese fiction.

At a time in the not-so-distant past, there was once a venerable Zen priest. Following in the steps of the reverend Bodhidharma, patriarch of the west,[3] he passed more than thirty years in diligent study, straining his eyes by the light of fireflies and the snow. He eventually awoke to the nature of the individual's and the Buddha's body, the non-transmitted teachings of the buddhas and the patriarchs, the extra-scriptural instructions, and those truths that are not expressed in words. He began to feel a little pride because there was now nothing, he thought, that weighed on his mind.

The priest pondered: "To take monastic vows means 'to leave the home.'[4] So if the three worlds are our home from the start,[5] then it won't do for me to live in any one place, or to bother with what other people think." Having thus made up his mind, he built himself a small cart in which to ride. He would wander where his two wheels took him, and when night fell he would sleep where he parked. Because he lived in his cart, people called him the Handcart Priest.

Once when there had been a lovely snowfall, the Handcart Priest rolled his cart to the Saga Plain. As he was gazing on the surrounding scene, Tarōbō of Mount Atago saw him and thought, "This person looks a little happy with himself! I might as well fool with him a bit." Manifesting as a fellow priest, Tarōbō descended Mount Atago and approached the edge of the plain. "Hello there, Handcart Priest!" he shouted. "I'd like to have a word."

"Who are you?" the priest replied. Without the slightest explanation, Tarōbō intoned:

3. Bodhidharma is traditionally recognized as the founder of the Zen school of Buddhism. Here, "west" means west of China—that is, India and Central Asia.
4. The word for becoming a monastic, *shukke* 出家, is written with characters that mean "to leave the home."
5. The Three Worlds are the worlds of desire, form, and non-form. They constitute the three realms of delusion through which sentient beings transmigrate according to their karma.

The *tengu* Tarōbō approaches the Handcart Priest on his cart. (From *Kuruma-zō sōshi*, courtesy of the Kyoto University Library)

ukiyo wo ba	Why do you roll
nani to ka meguru	around this world of sorrow,
kuruma-zō	you Handcart Priest?
mada wa no uchi ni	You look to be caught up still
ari to koso mire	in the cycle of wheels.[6]

"A delightful turn of phrase!" the Handcart Priest replied, and he said:

6. Tarōbō equates the Handcart Priest's rolling progress with the plight of sentient beings who revolve in the endless cycle of birth and death.

The Tale of the Handcart Priest

ukiyo wo ba	I do not revolve
meguranu mono wo	in this world of sorrow!
kuruma-zō	The Handcart Priest
nori mo urubeki	could ride in a cart (receive the Law) only
waga araba koso	if there were a self (if there were wheels).[7]

Tarōbō took in the priest's response. "He's a wily one," he thought. Drawing closer, he spoke: "How about it, Handcart Priest? To which school's teachings do you subscribe?"

The Handcart Priest stared. "What a lot of nerve!" he thought. "He must have come to disturb me because he thinks I'm full of pride." The Handcart Priest replied: "Well, sir, since the tenets of my school are transmitted outside the scriptures and not set down in words, they cannot be spoken or explained. We reject the various sects because they point to written words to teach. Just consider the course of the breeze that flutters a single leaf—now that is intriguing!"

"Then what is the message of the Buddha?" Tarōbō inquired.

"To abstain from all evil deeds and to perform every goodness."

"Then why are there dharma companions in hell?"[8]

"Because if people like me didn't venture into hell," the Handcart Priest said, "then how would wicked people like you who are sunken down in the evil realms ever obtain release?"

"Well, as the Founder said, 'It is easy to enter the world of the buddhas, but difficult to enter that of evil.' So enter an evil realm for a while—come over to where I live!"

"Where you live? You're that Tarōbō who lives on the peak of Mount Atago!"

"And where's your home?"

"No one place."

"Then what's that cart of yours?"

"The carriage of the burning house."[9]

Tarōbō was defeated. "I need to take this up with the twelve *tengu*," he thought to himself, and he replied: "It's as you say, Handcart Priest. I live on Mount Atago.

7. The Handcart Priest's poem is a knot of complexity, due to the double meanings of *nori* ("Buddhist Law" and a form of the verb *noru* [to ride]) and of *waga araba / wa ga araba* ("if there is a self" and "if there are wheels"). The verse seems to suggest that as there is no self, there is also no cart upon which to ride, and thus, by extension, no world in which to revolve and no dharma to obtain, according to Sanari Kentarō, *Yōkyoku taikan* (Tokyo: Meiji Shoin, 1942), 2:966.

8. A dharma companion is a being who leads others to the path of the Buddha. Tarōbō suggests that dharma companions go to hell in spite of their good deeds.

9. "The carriage of the burning house" is a metaphor for the Single Vehicle of the Dharma, as described in the parable of the burning house in the Lotus Sutra.

There's no carriage road, but do come. I'll be waiting." A single black cloud streaked across the sky and tumbled to the ground. Tarōbō stepped on it and vanished without a trace.

"I was ready to leave," the Handcart Priest thought, "but maybe I'll stay. The way that fellow was talking, it sounds like he may come back. If he does, then I'll catch him and make him do some magic, come what may." Clearing his mind, the Handcart Priest gazed out on the surrounding scene.

Now around this time, the tree-leaf *tengu* who live here and there heard news of Tarōbō's encounter with the Handcart Priest, and they gathered together to consult. "Listen, everybody," one of them said, "it seems that our Tarōbō ran into some scoundrel known as the Handcart Priest at Saga Plain. The priest was clever or something, and Master Tarōbō flew back to Atago to discuss it with the twelve *tengu*. That's what I heard. So why don't we go to Saga and try to shake him up a little?" The tree-leaf *tengu* all thought that this was a fine idea, and flocking together like clouds or mist, they made their way before the Handcart Priest.

Seeing the tree-leaf *tengu*, the priest thought, "Whatever they are, they've surely come to meddle with me." He carefully cleared his mind. The tree-leaf *tengu* spoke as one: "Hello, Handcart Priest! You've gotten so proud of yourself, why don't you step into our world for a while?" They flew this way and that before his very eyes, demonstrating all their supernatural skills, but the Handcart Priest meditated upon the surrounding scene and was not perturbed in the least.

The *tengu* drew closer, wondering what to do. They took hold of his carriage shafts and began to climb on board. "Little pests," the priest growled, and swinging his *hossu* flapper,[10] he struck one *tengu* hard on the wings. The *tengu* tumbled to the ground. "You hateful Handcart Priest!" the remaining *tengu* cried, and they fell upon him in a swarm. The priest chanted an invocation to Fudō,[11] sweeping clear all the surrounding space. Frightened by the priest's power, the tree-leaf *tengu* scattered and disappeared.

Tarōbō returned to Mount Atago to gather the twelve and eight *tengu*. Each of them appeared at his home in an instant. Tarōbō was overjoyed, and he came out to greet them. "I've invited you all here to discuss a certain scoundrel known as the Handcart Priest," he said. "He's got himself full of pride at Saga, where he's meditating on the views." Tarōbō explained everything from beginning to end. The other *tengu* were incensed. "That Handcart Priest!" one of them exclaimed. "However strong his Buddhist powers are, we should be able to obstruct him if we choose. Let's go get him!"

10. A *hossu* is a Buddhist ritual implement that resembles a wooden-handled hemp or horsehair duster.
11. Fudō Myōō is the leader of the Five and Eight Mantra Kings.

The Tale of the Handcart Priest

The Handcart Priest fends off a horde of tree-leaf *tengu*. (From *Kuruma-zō sōshi*, courtesy of the Kyoto University Library)

The *tengu* were all eager to set out, when Jirōbō from Mount Hira spoke: "It's certainly strange that Sōjōbō from Mount Kurama isn't here. His peak is right nearby." "Indeed," everyone agreed, "Sōjōbō is a match for a thousand. Why didn't he come? Let's send a messenger, quick!" A tree-leaf *tengu* was instructed to ask Sōjōbō to appear at once. Having received his charge, the messenger departed for Mount Kurama, where he met with Sōjōbō and delivered his appeal.

Sōjōbō spoke: "Yes, well, I recently met that scoundrel, the Handcart Priest, at the Ichihara Plain. He shattered my wings, and I may not survive. So you'll have to excuse me this time."

"But Master Sōjōbō," the messenger said, repeating his request, "we'll never succeed without you. Please come!"

Sōjōbō was enraged. "How dare you speak such nonsense! Can't you see that I'm hovering between life and death? And yet you still request my presence? It's incredible! Hurry back and give them my reply."

The messenger quickly returned and related his conversation. "What?" the various *tengu* exclaimed. "If the Handcart Priest can do that to the likes of our Sōjōbō, then he's no ordinary man. You should give up your plan this time, Tarōbō, and wait for a proper opportunity." The *tengu* all wagged their tongues in dread, suddenly disenchanted with their task.

Sagamibō of Mount Shiramine stepped forward and spoke: "What happened to Sōjōbō happened because he was alone. And it was probably his own fault. With this many of us, it should be easy to corrupt that priest!" "Yes, yes, that's true, too!" the many *tengu* cried, and they all clamored to take up the fight.

The sun slowly dipped behind the western mountains. The Handcart Priest watched as cawing crows sought out their nests, and he thought to himself, "There's no use in spending a snowy night like this in such a forlorn field. I suppose I'll make my way toward some village." He was redirecting his carriage shafts when he heard a voice from the sky:

"Hello, Handcart Priest! Where are you going? As they say, 'There's no path through the snow,' so you've got no way to return! You're so conceited, imagining that there's no one as lofty as you, but do you think your pride won't leave a trace? Will that non-attachment-desire-for-the-dharma business push or pull your cart? Turn your heart toward evil! Good and bad are like the two wheels of your cart: if there's the Buddhist Law, there's the worldly law; if there's delusion, there's enlightenment; if there are buddhas, there are non-buddhas; and if there's the Handcart Priest, then there's Tarōbō the ascetic. Conjure if you will, and I will too. You can use your magic powers, but mine are just as strong! How about it, priest—shall we test our skills for fun?"

Startled by the voice, the Handcart Priest gazed up toward Mount Atago. He saw a black cloud trailing in the sky. It contained Tarōbō and a multitude of other *tengu*, too numerous to count. The priest had been expecting them, however, and he was not disturbed in the least. "You can't move my heart," he said, "no matter how much you try. So just go home."

The *tengu* replied: "Say what you like, but we can take you if we want!" They all jumped down on the snow and began to lash the priest's cart with switches. The priest watched and then exclaimed: "What an amazing bunch of creatures! Do you think the cart will move if you thrash it? Why don't you whip the ox instead?"

"True," the *tengu* said, "the cart has no mind." They wished to strike the ox, but there was none to strike. "Just beat the cart," they cried, the same as before. They flogged it mercilessly, but the cart refused to budge. The priest watched. "Stupid fools on the path of man and ox!" he said. "Why don't you strike the ox that you can see? Or are you blind to the man-ox before your eyes? Get away from there!"

The *tengu* were enraged. "So if we beat you," they said, "then the cart will move?" "Of course!" the priest replied. "Now I'll show you how I strike the white ox of the

The Handcart Priest flies through the air on his cart. (From *Kuruma-zō sōshi,* courtesy of the Kyoto University Library)

open space.[12] Watch this!" The Handcart Priest raised his *hossu* flapper and struck the air. Strange to say, the cart, which until now had seemed to be a rickety contraption, wobbled forward with neither an ox nor a man to pull and instantly flew up into the sky. It circled around the mountains and rivers of Saga, Ogura, Ōi, and Arashi before returning. The *tengu* were stunned as they took in the sight.

"So, how about your miracle?" the Handcart Priest inquired. The many *tengu* jostled and clamored that they, too, would show him a marvel, whereupon they split apart the earth in a rush of flames, revealing the realms of hell and eternal

12. The Handcart Priest again refers to the parable of the burning house in the Lotus Sutra.

The *tengu* conjure a vision of the *ashura* realm of eternal carnage. (From *Kuruma-zō sōshi*, courtesy of the Kyoto University Library)

carnage. Before their very eyes, they saw a Lord something-or-other face off against a Lord this-or-that and declare their names, ready to fight. The lords grappled and fell heavily between their horses, where one took the other's head and the other had his taken.

There were still others in retreat, sorely wounded, and others setting fires and battling as if this were their last. To the side, there was a warrior declaring his name. He shouted, "Watch and learn how a fearless fighter ends his life! Take this as your model!" He slashed open his belly and pulled out his entrails. Other warriors could be seen locked in mortal combat, until flames again erupted from the earth and the snowy plain became as it was before.

"This is amazing, fascinating!" the Handcart Priest thought to himself, his mind slightly shaken. The *tengu* realized that they were succeeding. "Listen, priest," they said, "we can show you sights like these for a hundred days and a hundred nights, if we choose."

The Handcart Priest quickly regained his composure. "Once will be enough," he said. "From now on, I'll use my Buddhist powers to keep you from performing such feats."

The Tale of the Handcart Priest

"But they're easy to do!" the *tengu* shot back. "Shall we show you a vision of the paradise world this time?[13] Here, take a look!"

The Handcart Priest pressed his palms together, bowed once to the open air, and recited a demon-quelling spell. Miraculously, purple clouds spread from the surrounding mountains, though the sky until then had been clear. First the Mantra King Fudō, then Kongara, Seitaka, the Twelve Guardian Deities, and a host of other demon-quelling gods and buddhas appeared from within the clouds. They compelled the free-flying *tengu* to kneel before the Handcart Priest and swear that they would never again perform their evil deeds. With shamefully drooping wings, the great and small *tengu* took an oath, saying, "You awesome Handcart Priest, we humbly promise never again to play our wicked tricks on you."

"If that's so," the Handcart Priest said, "then I'll forgive you. Now get out of here!" The many *tengu* withdrew. Escaping into the clouds and mist, they all flew off toward Mount Atago.

It was because the Handcart Priest was so deeply versed in the Way of the Dharma that he evinced such miracles from time to time. His feats were made possible by the conquering power of the Buddhist Law. Have faith, have faith! The Buddhist Kings will defend the Buddhist Law.

242

TRANSLATION AND INTRODUCTION BY KELLER KIMBROUGH

13. The paradise world is the Pure Land Paradise of Amida (Skt. Amitābha) Buddha.

Origins of the Statue of Kannon as a Boy

Origins of the Statue of Kannon as a Boy (*Chigo Kannon engi*) tells the story of an aging holy man living near Nara who wishes for a disciple to care for him in this life and pray for him in the next. He prays before a statue of the bodhisattva Kannon (Skt. Avalokiteśvara) at the nearby Hase Temple, and, after more than three years of monthly pilgrimages, his hopes are realized when a very attractive teenage boy appears mysteriously out of the morning mist, playing a flute.

As the title suggests, *Origins of the Statue of Kannon as a Boy* was written to explain the provenance of a specific statue, no longer shown to the public, that depicts Kannon in the form of a *chigo* (boy).[1] More specifically, the Japanese term *chigo* refers to boys who served Buddhist monks and abbots or court nobles as personal assistants. They are portrayed in paintings as having feminine features—long black hair, white skin, and red lips. *Chigo* were made much of at the temples where they lived, often occupying the highest seats at banquets. In return for room, board, and, typically, an education in music, poetry, and the Buddhist scriptures, the *chigo* entertained the monks and their guests and provided companionship, including sexual services, to their masters. *Origins of the Statue of Kannon as a Boy* is but one example of a small subgenre of medieval Japanese short stories about the *chigo*. Often, a cherished and coveted *chigo* meets an untimely death due to suicide or murder but, in the end, is revealed to be the manifestation of a higher being. *Origins of the Statue of Kannon as a Boy* is somewhat atypical in this regard.

The translation and illustrations are from the *Chigo Kannon engi* picture scroll (ca. early fourteenth century) in the collection of the Kōsetsu Art Museum, transcribed and photographically reproduced in Komatsu Shigemi, ed., *Taima mandara engi, Chigo Kannon engi*, Nihon emaki taisei 24 (Tokyo: Chūō Kōronsha, 1979), 37–72, 156–59.

1. Tagawa Fumihiko, "Jisha engi no saiseisan to sono hen'yō: *Chigo Kannon engi* o megutte," *Indogaku Bukkyōgaku kenkyū* 52, no. 1 (2003): 234.

A contemporary proverb held that parents and children spend but a single lifetime together; husbands and wives, two (the current one and the one to come); but teachers and students, like lords and vassals, are joined by karma in three lifetimes: this life, the previous one, and the next. At the very end of the tale, Kannon himself reveals the depth of his relationship to the holy man through an allusion to this belief.

Long ago in this realm of Japan, in the province of Yamato, not far from Hase Temple, there was an extremely distinguished holy man. At his window of contemplation, he never neglected to perceive myriad phenomena in a single ordinary thought; on his cot where he attained the five phases of buddhahood, he accumulated the merit of practicing the Buddhist dharma through years of devoted practice. He was more than sixty years of age.

Yet he lacked a disciple to serve him closely in this world, to follow his footsteps in the Buddhist teachings, and to pray that he should gain the virtuous fruits of enlightenment in the next life. Deeply, indeed, did this holy man rue the skimpiness of the good karma he had accrued in the past, and so he decided to make a pilgrimage to the Kannon at Hase every month for three years.

"Grant me a disciple fit to serve me closely in this world, to whom I can bequeath my place in the dharma," he prayed.

Three years passed, but still no wondrous boon came to him.

Although he resented the Kannon, the holy man kept up his pilgrimages for another three months. Yet even after the passage of three years and three months, there was no miraculous sign. Then, resenting his poor karma, he said, "The great holy one, the revered Kannon is the crown prince of the Pure Land Paradise, the master of the Potalaka realm. His solemn vow of compassion is profound. Nevertheless, his promise to treat all equally as his own children has omitted me, and reveals partiality. Though the moon may illuminate a thousand rivers without discrimination, it does not let its light float upon muddy waters. And while the moon of Kannon's compassion may be pure and bright, he does not send that light to dwell in the clouded minds of sentient beings. Such is beyond my powers to change."

The persistence of his sins and karmic obstructions, like so many stubborn clouds, had brought the holy man nothing but grief, but the next morning, as he made his way home in tears, he was passing the foot of a mountain called Obuse when a boy of thirteen or fourteen, refined in appearance, with a face as lovely as the moon and a figure as pretty as a blossom, appeared before him. The boy wore a purple under-robe with narrow sleeves under a white silk jacket and an elegant pair of divided skirts dyed russet brown. With a melancholy air, he played a flute made of Chinese bamboo. His long hair was gathered in a ponytail that hung down his back. It was dawn on the eighteenth day of the eighth month. Wet with dew, the boy seemed even more lovely than a willow in spring blowing wild in the wind.

The holy man beheld him, with a sense of utter unreality. He thought the boy must be some sort of evil being that had transformed itself. Nevertheless, he approached and asked, "Here you are, with the night still dark, in this mountain meadow, all by yourself. That seems unusual. What sort of person are you?"

The boy replied, "I was living near Tōdaiji Temple, but the other day I grew angry with my master, and I ran away, walking all through the night, wherever my feet would take me. Where do you live? I know that monks are very compassionate. Take me with you, and make me your page boy. Please, I beg you."

Delighted, the priest said, "There must be more to the story than this. But it can wait for later; right now, I shall take you with me," and he left, bringing the boy with him back to his cloister.

The priest was overjoyed. Days and nights passed with no one coming to inquire about the boy's whereabouts. Nothing he did displeased the holy man. The boy was without peer in poetry and music. Years and months went by, as the holy man rejoiced in the generosity of Kannon. Then, as the spring of the third year came to a close, the boy suddenly fell ill. His body grew weaker with each day, and he drew near to death. The boy rested his head in the holy man's lap as they held hands, face to face, and each bade the other farewell. The boy's last words were especially poignant: "For the past three years, I have spent my days in your cloister of compassion, and my nights under your quilt of forbearance. In what lifetime could I possibly forget the lessons you taught me morning and evening? Although it is the way of the world that the old do not always depart before the young, I had hoped to outlive you so that I could pray for you as a son after your passing. But now my wishes have come to nothing, and I regret only that I must go on before you. They say that the bond with one's teacher lasts three lifetimes, so we will meet again in another life.

"After I have taken my last breath and passed away, do not bury me in the earth, or turn me into smoke to rise above the fields, but rather lay my body in a coffin, place the coffin in the memorial chapel, and, after five weeks have passed, open it and see—" he said, and before he could finish he breathed his last.

The boy's spirit departed, as evanescent in its vanishing as the dew in a graveyard.

The holy man was completely bereft. When birds are about to die, they chirp softly; when humans part ways, their words touch the heart. Realizing that these

Origins of the Statue of Kannon as a Boy

words are the last someone will ever say, one pleads with the dying one about the past and the future, and it is all the more poignant and sad. The misery and pain of being separated from a loved one is something that all experience, but this grief was one that had few precedents.

He who gazes at the blossoms on a spring morning laments their scattering; and he who chants poems under the moon on an autumn evening resents the cloudy sky.

The holy man's affection was unparalleled, as he felt the boy was a reward for the pilgrimages that he had made to Hase Temple for three years and three months. And for three years and three months, they had grown used to each other when, all of a sudden, they were parted. His grief was extraordinary.

That face like the moon—which cloud was hiding it now? That blossomy complexion—what sort of breeze had lured it away? His sleeves were soaked in

The holy man encounters a beautiful flute-playing boy. (From *Chigo Kannon engi*, courtesy of the Kōsetsu Museum of Art)

tears at the thought of the youth who had passed away before an aged man—when would they ever dry? And the master's grief at being separated from his disciple—when would the day come for it to end?

How poignant it was! The old one remained behind, while the young one had gone away. It could be compared to the scattering of dayflowers or to the heartlessness of falling colored leaves. It was like a drop of water slipping off the root of a plant, like a bead of dew evaporating from the tip of a leaf.

The holy man could not go on weeping forever, so he laid the boy in his coffin. In accordance with the boy's last words, they placed him in the memorial chapel and did not neglect to perform the rites. Worshippers gathered from the nearby villages and the distant hills, and then they copied the Lotus Sutra in a single day and held a memorial service, offering the sutra on behalf of the boy's enlightenment.

Origins of the Statue of Kannon as a Boy

The holy man weeps over the boy as he dies. (From *Chigo Kannon engi*, courtesy of the Kōsetsu Museum of Art)

After he delivered a sermon at the service, the holy man was so overcome by grief that he lifted the lid of the coffin and peered inside. A strange fragrance of sandalwood and aloeswood filled the room. The boy had changed his alluring appearance of times past and appeared now as Kannon, with eleven golden faces. His eyes shone clear like green lotuses; his lips were majestic, like cinnabar. Smiling, he spoke with a voice like the kalavinka bird and said to the holy man: "I am not a being of the human world. They call me the Master of the Potalaka Realm, the great holy one, the revered Kannon. That is who I am. For a while, I dwelled in the foothills of Onoe on Mount Hase in order to rescue a sentient being with whom I had a karmic bond. You were kind enough to make pilgrimages there for many years, and so, of my thirty-three manifestations, I assumed that of a boy, and joined with you in a pledge to last two lifetimes.

"Seven years from now, in autumn, on the fifteenth day of the eighth month, I will come for you. We shall be reunited on a lotus pedestal in the ninth level of paradise." Then he released a burst of light like a bolt of lightning and ascended into the sky, vanishing among purple clouds.

The boy emerges from his coffin as the bodhisattva Kannon. (From *Chigo Kannon engi*, courtesy of the Kōsetsu Museum of Art)

This is the Boy-Kannon currently located at the Bodai-in Cloister in Nara. Kannon really did appear as a boy to bestow blessings on someone who had made a vow before him and accumulated merit by making pilgrimages. When the people from nearby villages and the distant hills gathered to make a copy of the Great Vehicle that is the Lotus, Kannon appeared before them immediately in his original form, to show them the blessings of interior enlightenment. Apparitions in this world of the buddhas of the past, present, and future are blessings of interior enlightenment from the great holy one, the revered Kannon.

TRANSLATION AND INTRODUCTION BY PAUL S. ATKINS

Origins of the Statue of Kannon as a Boy

Little Atsumori

In the second month of 1184, the ruling Taira clan suffered a crushing defeat at the battle of Ichi-no-tani in the Genpei War (1180–1185). Among the many casualties was a youth by the name of Atsumori, purportedly beheaded on the beach by the Minamoto warrior Kumagai no Jirō Naozane before he could make his escape. His story came to be included in *The Tale of the Heike* (thirteenth century), from which it was later singled out for re-telling in numerous works of medieval fiction, painting, and drama. Atsumori himself came to be celebrated as a kind of medieval cult figure, and his flute, which Kumagai is said to have taken from his corpse, was enshrined at Suma Temple from at least the early fifteenth century.

Little Atsumori (*Ko-Atsumori*) dates from the fifteenth or sixteenth century. Although it was inspired by its related episode in *The Tale of the Heike*, it focuses less on the death of Atsumori than on the resulting havoc wrought in the lives of those he left behind. It explores the physical and psychological consequences of war, describing the ways in which three characters—Atsumori's widow, the warrior Kumagai, and a posthumous son (Little Atsumori, from whom the work takes its name)— come to terms with the shared tragedies of their past. Although the war haunts each in a different way, all find solace in the healing powers of truth, fidelity, and Pure Land Buddhism. Even Little Atsumori, an unwitting victim of a conflict that was over before his birth, finds a way to make peace with a ghost from his past: the father he never knew. Marked by the miraculous revelations, fantastic coincidences, and didactic and emotive narrative style that are so characteristic of the *otogizōshi* genre, his story captures, in microcosm, the struggles of thirteenth-century Japanese society to overcome the crippling wounds of war.

The translation and illustrations are from the *Ko-Atsumori* picture scroll (sixteenth century), in the "old picture scroll" textual line, in the collection of the Keiō University Library, typeset and annotated in Matsumoto Ryūshin, ed., *Otogizōshi shū*, Shinchō Nihon koten shūsei (Tokyo: Shinchōsha, 1980), 305–27.

Scholars have traced *Little Atsumori*'s roots to the oral proselytizing traditions of the wandering holy men of Mount Kōya (Kōya hijiri) and a variety of Tendai and Pure Land Buddhist preacher-entertainers; the earliest datable reference to the tale is contained in a diary entry from the fourth month of 1485.[1] The account of Atsumori's death in *Little Atsumori*, which the work re-creates in its first part, is clearly based on one or more *Heike* manuscripts in the *yomihon* (readerly) textual line, rather than on the better known Kakuichi manuscript in the *kataribon* (recited) line of texts. As a result, it plays down the significance of music in the tale and instead emphasizes the importance of Atsumori's revelation of his name to Kumagai in the moments before his death—a scene that is eerily reenacted at the climax of the story when Atsumori's ghost demands that Little Atsumori, too, tell him his name.

In the face of their defeat at the battle of Ichi-no-tani, the young emperor, the Lady of Second Rank, and all the Taira forces dashed to their ships and fled.[2] From among them, Atsumori was somehow left behind.[3] He was riding toward the shore, chasing Lord Munemori's boat, when a warrior by the name of Kumagae no Jirō Naozane appeared. Kumagae wore a dark-blue *hitatare*,[5] a suit of armor with shaded-green lacing, and a three-plated helmet pulled down low on his head. Sporting a protective cape with a two-bar design, he rode a dark-chestnut steed and carried a bow in one hand, an arrow notched at the ready. "Just once I'd like to wrangle with some fine opponent," he was brooding, when he spotted Atsumori, a lone warrior riding out from the direction of Ichi-no-tani.

Atsumori wore a *hitatare* embroidered with ferns and forget-me-nots, a suit of armor with shaded-purple lacing, and a helmet of the same design. On his back, he bore twenty-five dyed-feather arrows, and in his hand, he held a rattan-wrapped lacquer bow. His mount was a gray-dappled roan. The saddle was adorned with a

1. The reference is in *Shaken nichiroku*, the diary of the Zen priest Kikō Daishuku (1421–1487), discussed in Minobe Shigekatsu, *Chūsei denshō bungaku no shosō* (Osaka: Izumi Shoin, 1988), 106–9.
2. The young emperor was Antoku (1178–1185, r. 1180–1185), who later drowned at the battle of Dan-no-ura. The Lady of Second Rank (Taira no Tokiko; d. 1185) was his grandmother, the wife of Taira no Kiyomori (1118–1181), previous head of the Taira clan.
3. Taira no Atsumori (1169–1184) was the third son of Kiyomori's younger half-brother Tsunemori (1124–1185).
4. Lord Munemori (Taira no Munemori; 1147–1185) was a son of Kiyomori and Tokiko. Kumagae (usually Kumagai) no Jirō Naozane (Taira no Naozane; 1141–1208) allied himself with Minamoto no Yoritomo (1147–1199), the first shogun, after the battle of Mount Ishibashi in the eighth month of 1180.
5. A *hitatare* (also *yoroi hitatare*) is a kind of loose-fitting shirt-and-pants set worn by warriors and courtiers in the medieval period both under armor and as everyday attire.

Little Atsumori

circular crest of eulalia and mistletoe design and was inscribed, in metal, with the character for "wind." His eyes were fixed on a noble's ship in the offing, and he spurred his horse into the sea and pressed it to swim, plunging and bobbing in the surf. Kumagae watched.

"You there, adrift in the shallows," Kumagae shouted, "you look to be a commander in chief. It's a disgrace to show your back to an enemy! I am Kumagae no Jirō Naozane, a resident of Musashi Province and the fiercest warrior in Japan. Come back and fight!" Atsumori was not flustered in the least. Pulling his horse back by the reins, he headed for the shore.

From the moment his horse found its footing, Atsumori brandished his weapon and lumbered to the beach. Kumagae observed his opponent. "Just the sort of adversary I was looking for," he thought, and drawing his great sword, attacked. Atsumori raised his blade, and after exchanging two or three blows, grappled with Kumagae from atop his steed. They fell to the ground between their horses. Kumagae was a man of prodigious strength, and Atsumori, just a youth. After pinning him down, Kumagae cast away his long sword and drew the short one at his waist. Ripping off Atsumori's helmet, he seized the boy's disheveled hair and wrested back

Kumagae charges Atsumori on the beach at the battle of Ichi-no-tani. (From *Ko-Atsumori*, courtesy of the Keiō University Library)

253

his head. He saw a young fighter, *just a baby* sixteen or seventeen years old, with a lightly powdered face, eyebrows plucked and painted high on his forehead, and blackened teeth.[6] Kumagae was at a loss where to strike. He hesitated before cutting off his head. "Who are you?" he demanded. "Give me your name!"

"You call yourself the fiercest warrior in Japan," Atsumori replied, "but you make a foolish request! What kind of man would give his name when he's held down by a foe? When a warrior gives his name, he gives a trophy to his enemy—a battlefield honor for him to pass on to his heirs. That's what it means to give your name! Now hurry up and take my head, and ask someone else whose it is." *silly baby*

Kumagae spoke: "What you say is true, but this morning, at the Ichi-no-tani fortress gate, my son Kojirō Naoie died at the hand of the Noto Lord.[7] You look to be about his age, and it makes me sorry. I'll pray for you when you're gone, so tell me your name."

6. Atsumori's make-up suggests his gentility and refinement.
7. Taira no Noritsune (1160?–1185?) was known as the Noto Lord because he was appointed governor of Noto Province when Kiyomori seized power in 1179.

Little Atsumori

"I'd rather not," Atsumori said. "But, then, to think there's someone as sensitive as you among the Eastern warriors . . . and what have I got to hide? I am Atsumori, sixteen years old, holder of fifth court rank with no official post. I am the third son of New Middle Counselor Tomomori. My father is the son of Master of the Office of Palace Repairs Tsunemori, who was himself a younger brother of Chancellor Kiyomori, an eighth-generation descendant of Emperor Kanmu.[8] This was my first battle. Please . . . if any of my family survive, give them this flute and *hitatare*." He took from his waist a flute in a rosewood case and handed it to Kumagae. "Now get it over with—hurry up and take my head!"

Kumagae was bewildered, powerless to strike. "Alas!" he thought, "there's nothing so wretched as the life of a warrior. I saw my son Kojirō take a grievous blow by the Ichi-no-tani fortress gate, but we were separated by fighting enemies and allies, and I lost track of him after that. It was the last time I saw him alive. Noble or humble, all parents love their children—it's an unchanging rule. The Master of Palace Repairs Tsunemori must be waiting anxiously for his son on his ship in the offing. He'll be devastated if he hears he was struck down on the beach. The boy's the same age as Kojirō, and the poor man will suffer like me. If only I could help him get away . . ."

254

Brushing the dust off the boy's armor, Kumagae set him on his feet. He had him put on his helmet while he himself looked around for a way to escape. He saw a group of thirty riders—what looked to be the Kodama League, flying a banner of a battle-fan design—assembled on the ridge above. To the west, he saw what looked like the Hirayama warriors lined up on their horses, bridles in a row. Others were there, too, countless as the mist. There was nowhere to run. The boy would be unable to make it west to Ogura Valley or Akashi, or east past the harbor at Suma. It was hopeless. Kumagae made up his mind: rather than let him die at someone else's hand, he would kill Atsumori himself, take Buddhist vows, and then conduct rites for him and Kojirō.

Kumagae urged the boy to invoke the name of Amida Buddha for his last ten times. Atsumori turned to the west and recited the *nenbutsu* as he was told.[9] "Do it now, quickly," he said. Kumagae was overwhelmed. He closed his eyes. Then, through his tears, he cut off Atsumori's head.

Stripping off Atsumori's armor, Kumagae found a scroll wedged in a space between the plates. He took it out and saw that it was a collection of a hundred poems.

8. Atsumori was actually the son of Tsunemori, not Tomomori (1152–1185). Also, Kiyomori was a twelfth-generation descendant of Emperor Kanmu (737–806, r. 781–806), not an eighth.

9. The *nenbutsu* is the ritual invocation of the name of Amida (Skt. Amitābha) Buddha.

He picked up Atsumori's head, and when he took it to Lord Yoshitsune,[10] he showed him the scroll. Yoshitsune examined the document. "What a pity to have killed a man as refined as this!" he declared, and weeping, he explained: "The poems are in the hand of the wife of the governor of Echizen. She composed a hundred of them to while away the hours." Everyone wept when they saw or heard of their commander spilling tears on his armored sleeves.

Kumagae had lost his son, and since taking Atsumori's head, he had come to understand the futile inconstancy of the world. "A man's life is uncertain," he reflected; "it can be gone before the evening sky. The darkness of the long night ahead is all that really matters." The land was at peace, but Kumagae had no worldly ambition. Having set his heart on the Buddha, he ascended Mount Kōya and shaved his head in the manner of a priest. Later, he became a disciple of Priest Hōnen and took up the *nenbutsu* with single-minded, unwavering devotion—wonderful indeed![11]

Now there was a lady by the name of Ben no Saishō, daughter of Tōin, the grandson of Lesser Counselor Novice Shinzei, and she was known as one of the most beautiful women in the capital.[12] Atsumori had set his heart on her, and because her feelings had been the same, they had been wed. Atsumori soon had to flee the capital; his grief-stricken appearance at that time was desolate beyond compare. "If I should be killed in the coming battle," he had teased, "you'll probably take up with some Easterner and never think of me again." Although the parting had been bitter, from amid their tears they had said farewell. As remembrances, Atsumori had left with her an Eleven-headed Kannon protective charm and a sword with a rosewood hilt.

From that day forward, Atsumori's wife had been mired in sadness. She had worried constantly for her husband's fate, until at last she heard people say that he had been struck down by Kumagae at the battle of Ichi-no-tani. "Is this a dream?" she cried. "If he had survived, we might have met again . . . at least that's what I had hoped. But what's to become of me now?" Pulling a robe over her head, she collapsed in a fit of grief. To see her like that was all the more affecting!

Their love had been brief, but as is the way with husbands and wives, the lady was with child. The months passed, and she gave birth to a beautiful baby boy. Although she wished to raise him in some deep mountain dwelling or cliffy crag—to keep him

255

10. Lord Yoshitsune is Minamoto no Yoshitsune (1159–1189), a hero of the Genpei War and the protagonist of two other stories in this book, *The Palace of the Tengu* and *Yoshitsune's Island-Hopping*.
11. Hōnen (1133–1212) was the founder of the Pure Land sect of Japanese Buddhism, which advocates the sole practice of the *nenbutsu* to achieve rebirth in the Pure Land.
12. Lesser Counselor Novice Shinzei (Fujiwara no Michinori; 1106–1159) was a scholar and a close attendant of Emperor Go-Shirakawa (1127–1192, r. 1155–1158). His grandson Tōin is unknown, as is Ben no Saishō.

Little Atsumori

The monk Hōnen finds Little Atsumori while his mother watches from a distance. (From *Ko-Atsumori*, courtesy of the Keiō University Library)

as a memento of her husband—the Genji were slaughtering all the Heike children, no matter how young, searching them out even in the womb. Fearing that she, too, would come to grief, she wrapped her baby in a white, lined robe; placed the sword with the rosewood hilt at his side; and left him, in great despair, at a place called Shimomatsu.

At that time, Hōnen had taken Kumagae and his other disciples on a pilgrimage to Kamo Shrine. He heard a baby crying at Shimomatsu, and bringing his palanquin near, he found a beautiful, abandoned little boy. The holy man spoke: "He's surely not a commoner, left wrapped up in a robe like that with a sword at his side. Someone must want him saved. Either that, or he's a gift of the Kamo Deity." The holy man picked him up and took him home, gave him a wet nurse, and raised him as his own.

The months and years passed by, and the boy was soon eight. He was more mature than the other children at the temple, and far more intelligent. Once when Kumagae was stroking the boy's hair, Kumagae remarked, "Of all people, this child looks just like that Atsumori I killed at the battle of Ichi-no-tani! It's like he's right here before me," and time and again he wept.

The boy was playing bows-and-arrows with some other children, and he got into an argument over who had won. "You motherless, fatherless orphan," another child railed, "how dare you talk to me like that! You act that way because the holy man

BUDDHIST TALES

Little Atsumori cries when another child calls him a "motherless, fatherless orphan." (From *Ko-Atsumori*, courtesy of the Keiō University Library)

took you in." Dejected and chagrined, the boy threw away his bow and arrows and cried.

Although the boy wept for his parents, the other children continued to tease him. He became all the more depressed. Visiting the holy man, he said, "I don't have a mother or father, do I? Oh, how I miss them!" He threw himself to the ground and wailed in sorrow. Hōnen was touched, and he shed tears on the sleeves of his priestly robes. "Poor boy," he said. "You were an abandoned child, without a mother or a father. But I brought you up, so think of me as your mother and father instead." The boy gave it some thought: "The other children sometimes receive visits and letters from their parents and siblings. Why don't I have a mother and father, too?"

Morning and evening, he pined. He stopped eating, and he refused to drink water, hot or cold. After seven days, he appeared on the verge of losing his senses, as if his life was near an end. Hōnen and the others were alarmed. Summoning his disciples, the holy man spoke: "Look here, everyone. This poor child is dying from longing for his parents. If you've seen or heard anything relating to his family, please say so now." Kumagae raised his voice: "Our poor boy! I do remember one thing. A very pretty lady, about twenty years old, comes to hear your sermons on the six abstinence days

Little Atsumori

every month. She brushes the child's hair when she thinks no one's looking and then cries her heart out. If there happen to be many people around, she goes home like she doesn't care, but she still acts suspicious." "Well, then," the holy man said, "we'll hold sermons from today and see who comes!"

Hōnen soon began to preach. Toward the middle of his address, he pressed his sleeve to his face and wept. "Dear audience," he said, "still your hearts and listen. One year when I went to visit Kamo Shrine, I found a baby by Shimomatsu. I've brought him up, and now he's eight. Recently, he's been yearning for his parents. He mourns and cries, he won't eat or drink, and now his life is in danger. Does anyone here know his family? He won't come to any harm, even if he's a Taira. I've raised him myself, and I'll make him a priest. I'll go to Rokuhara and beg for a pardon if I have to. But if things go on like this, the poor boy is sure to die!" The holy man broke down in tears. Everyone wept, whether they knew the child or not.

An exceptionally beautiful woman stepped forward from the audience. She wore a trouser-skirt and a twelve-layered robe. Without a word, she set the boy on her knee and began to sob. The poor little child—his handsome features were stretched with sorrow! He looked up at the lady with his sunken, listless eyes, and together they cried. Seeing them, the holy man stumbled down from his seat; his own tears were moving to behold! All the people wet their sleeves with emotion.

After a while, the lady turned to Hōnen and spoke: "I am Ben no Naishi, a relative of the late Lesser Counselor Nobukiyo.[13] From the time that Atsumori was thirteen and I, fourteen, we shared a fleeting love. Later, in the first year of Genryaku [1184], Atsumori fled the capital. He was sixteen then, and he spoke of many things. Since his son looked just like him, I thought to hide him away as a token of our bond. But then I heard that the Genji were hunting down the Heike heirs—cutting off their heads, even searching them out in the womb. I couldn't stand the thought of suffering such misery again. I didn't know what to do; although it broke my heart, I decided to abandon my baby. I watched you pick him up and take him to your temple, and then I went home.

"In the eight years since then, I have come to all your sermons on the six abstinence days of every month. I have watched the boy, and I've seen how he's come to look more and more like his father. It makes me long for the old days, and I end up crying. I've suffered so much sometimes that I've been desperate to tell him who I am. But the world being what it is, I've always kept my secret to myself and gone home

---

13. There is a discrepancy in the text. Previously in the tale, the lady is identified as Ben no Saishō, not Ben no Naishi. Also, Nobukiyo is problematic. Matsumoto suggests that it is a Japanese reading of a mistranscription of the Chinese characters for "Shinzei," in Ko-Atsumori, in Otogizōshi shū, ed. Matsumoto, 317n.7.

in tears." The woman poured out her heart. All the people there were choked with pity. Hearing that this was his mother, the boy was neither happy nor sad—all he could do was cry.

In his free time, Kumagae had been in the habit of taking out Atsumori's silk *hitatare*, with the ink design, and the flute in the rosewood case. He would chant the *nenbutsu* and cry. The holy man had seen him and asked what he was always grieving about. Kumagae had replied: "One year during the Heike disturbance, I took the head of Atsumori, the youngest child of the Kadowaki Lord, at Harima Beach in Settsu Province.[14] He told me to pass these keepsakes on to his relatives, if any of them survived. But I haven't heard of any family, so I've been carrying them around with me ever since." The holy man had taken a look. "How sad!" he had exclaimed, shedding copious tears.

Hōnen now remembered their conversation. "Where's brother Kumagae?" he asked, and summoned him at once. "You know those relatives of Atsumori's you mentioned," he said, "well, the boy who's been with us all these years—he's his son! And that lady over there is his mother! Those relics of Atsumori's you said you wanted to give his family—you can surrender them now." Kumagae was delighted. Producing the flute and *hitatare*, he explained in detail Atsumori's final moments. Weeping, he presented the objects to the wife and son. The little boy and his mother passed them back and forth, entranced, and then dissolved into tears—most touching indeed!

After a while, the mother placed her hands on the keepsakes and spoke: "This *hitatare*—I made it for Atsumori when he left the capital. There are ferns on the left sleeve, forget-me-nots on the right, and on the skirt, there is an ink design of two ducks—a male and a female—drifting among the reeds of Naniwa Bay. There is also a poem here:

nagaraete	It wasn't for us
chigirazarikeru	to live on together
mono yue ni	pledging tender vows—
awazu wa kaku wa	yet if we'd never met,
omowazaramashi	we'd never have known such love.

It was his without a doubt. 'So hurtful now, these keepsakes—if not for them, sometimes I might forget.'[15] The way he looked that time . . . I wonder if I'll ever

14. The Kadowaki Lord (Taira no Norimori; 1128–1185) was a younger brother of Kiyomori. Atsumori was a son of Tsunemori, not Norimori.
15. The widow quotes the anonymous poem 746 in *Kokin wakashū* (*Collection of Ancient and Modern Poems*, ca. 905).

Little Atsumori

259

escape the memory!" The woman wept. The holy man and Kumagae were similarly overcome.

Kumagae spoke: "So that's why whenever I looked at the child, it was like Atsumori was right in front of me! It makes sense now," and he wept anew. The little boy stared at his father's souvenirs and longed for him all the more. He made a petition to the buddhas, gods, and Three Holy Jewels, and constantly prayed: "Please let me see my father—either his bones or his ghost!"[16] "It is all because of the Kamo Deity that the holy man took me in and brought me up like this," the boy once thought. "He must be my patron deity. I'll visit him and pray to see my father's ghost." The boy ensconced himself in Kamo Shrine for seven days. He paid obeisance 1,133 times a day, prostrating himself in supplication. The deity must have been moved, for on the final, seventh night, he appeared before the boy where he slept. "Among all the children of the world," he said, "there are few who feel deeply for their parents, even when they are alive. How moving, then, that you, who have never seen or known your father, should pray with all your heart for his remains!" The deity recited a poem:

sugisarishi	For love of
sono tarachine no	a parent departed—
koishiku wa	the dew and the frost
Koyano Ikuta-no-	of Ikuta-no-ono
ono no tsuyu shimo	on Koyano Plain.

"What joy!" the boy thought upon receiving the dream-revelation. "My father's bones must lie in Ikuta-no-ono field in Settsu Province!" Without a word to his mother or the holy man, he secretly set out. Although ignorant of the way to Settsu, he had heard that it was west. Rustling the dew from the grasses of an unfamiliar road, he wandered forth, pitiful to behold.

Tramping through fields of eulalia, pampas, and cogon grass; blind to the way ahead; pillowing his head some nights on frosty bunches of bamboo weed, he eventually came to what he thought was Ichi-no-tani. A thunderstorm was raging. The boy was endlessly forlorn. All he could hear was the lapping waves, the wind in the pines, seagulls in the offing, and beach plovers exchanging cries. Other than these, he was alone. As he drifted forward, lost, he noticed a glimmering light in the distance. Although it might belong to some goblin, he thought, he was so distressed

16. The Three Holy Jewels are the Three Jewels (or Treasures) of Buddhism: the Buddha, the dharma (teachings of the Buddha), and the sangha (monastic community).

that he did not care. Stumbling on, he soon observed the hulking frame of an old temple hall.

The boy approached, and in the dim light of a torch, he saw a stranger with painted eyebrows and a lightly powdered face. The man wore a soft pointed hat and paced the veranda in prayer.[17] "Excuse me," the boy called out.

"Who's there?" the man replied. "No one comes around here. Identify yourself!"

The boy wept and explained: "I am from the capital, and I'm searching for my father. I've been walking for the last ten days. But the rain is so heavy and the darkness so dark that I'm at my wits' end. Please give me lodging for the night."

"Who is your father?" the man asked.

The boy thought: "The Genji rule the land now, so what will happen if I give my name? But I'll tell him anyway, and if I lose my life, it will have been for my father, which won't be so bad." He spoke: "My father was a Taira by the name of Atsumori, third son of the Master of Palace Repairs. He was cut down at the battle of Ichi-no-tani. I wanted to find his bones, so I prayed to the Kamo Deity. I had a dream-revelation, and I've come here to search at the Bay of Suma." Without saying a word, the stranger broke down in tears.

After a while, the man took the boy by the hand, pulled him up to the veranda, and brushed the dew from his rain-soaked clothes. "This way," he said, beckoning him inside. "You must be exhausted, traveling at your young age. Rest here," and he set the child's head on his knee. Although no longer upset or tired, the boy drifted off to sleep. The man spoke, neither in this world nor in a dream: "How sad that you should yearn so for a parent you've never seen! It's because of your profound filial devotion that I have come to you now as an apparition. When you were still in your mother's womb, I was struck down by Kumagae here on the Harima shore. It was the spring of my sixteenth year. If you want to serve me in my grave, then study very, very hard; become a man of wisdom; and save sentient beings near and far. That will make me happy." He wrote a poem on the boy's sleeve:

koi koite	To the waking world
mare ni au yo mo	I cannot return—
yume nare ya	for love and longing,
utsutsu ni kaeru	a precious meeting this night
mi ni shi araneba	in a dream.

17. The stranger's hat was a *nashiuchi eboshi*, typically worn by a warrior under his helmet.

Little Atsumori

Little Atsumori speaks with his dead father. (From *Ko-Atsumori*, courtesy of the Keiō University Library)

The boy was overjoyed at meeting his father. "Oh, Papa!" he cried, grasping at the man's sleeves, and at that moment, awoke. His mind reeled when he looked around. Where he had seen the temple hall, there was only the wind in the pines; where his father had been, there was only a tangle of eulalia and cogon grass; where he had pillowed his head on his father's knee, there was only a mossy white thigh bone in a clump of weeds. The boy was overcome. "How cruel!" he cried. "Father, where did you go? Please take me with you! Why did you leave me here alone in the deep grass at the foot of a pine?" He sank into a slough of tears—truly most affecting!

Because the boy could not stay on in this way, he strung his father's bones around his neck and returned to the capital, where he interred each at a different temple or sacred site. Having thus come back to the city, he made his way to Hōnen's temple. The holy man and others had been worried. "We haven't seen our child for some time," they had said, and searched high and low. They were overjoyed now to hear that he had returned. The boy told Hōnen and his mother about all that had happened to him on his trip to Settsu Province.

"The child's still so young," people said, "—and to think of the hardships he's endured! His father, Atsumori, must have been moved by the filial piety in his heart,

Little Atsumori awakes in a field beside a pile of bones (*right*) and, with the bones around his neck, sets out for the capital (*left*). (From *Ko-Atsumori*, courtesy of the Keiō University Library)

and appeared to him as a ghost in a dream." Everyone wept at the thought. The months and years passed by, and the boy became a blessed priest.

The mother also became a nun at that time. She built a brushwood shack by the Kamo riverbed in the northern part of the capital, and planted morning glories for her fence. Watching her flowers wilt at the touch of the morning dew, she awoke to the fleeting nature of worldly affairs. At dusk, listening to the evening bell at Urin'in Temple, she would gaze at the sun as it set in the west and wonder that paradise was there. She chanted the *nenbutsu* day and night—so auspicious!—and plucking flowers and burning incense, she prayed for the enlightenment of the many Taira who met their doom at the western sea.[18] In particular, she mourned for Atsumori, and recalling their vow to share a lotus-seat in the Pure Land, she prayed for her own rebirth in Paradise.

She composed poems in her spare time:

shiba no to no	My heart
shibashiba isogu	often hastens
kokoro ka na	at my brushwood door

18. The western sea refers to the Inland Sea, to the west of the capital.

Little Atsumori

| nishi no mukae no | to see the western Pure Land welcome |
| yūgure no sora | in the sunset sky. |

kokorozashi	As salvation
fukaki ni ukabu	comes to those most
narai zo to	deeply mourned,
itodo mukashi no	all the more I pray for him
ato wo koso toe	who died so long ago.

Many years passed after the boy became a priest. In the course of his studies, he plumbed the deepest truths and came to be known as Priest Zen'e of the Western Mountain.[19] It was thanks to his profound sense of filial devotion that his sect of Buddhism flourishes in the present day. Those who read this tale should always be dutiful to their parents and teachers. It was a truly wonderful turn of events; we should all chant the *nenbutsu* for the sake of our departed.[20] Amen!

TRANSLATION AND INTRODUCTION BY KELLER KIMBROUGH

19. Zen'e Shōnin (Shōkū Shōnin; 1177–1247) was a disciple of Hōnen and the founder of the Seizan (Western Mountain) sect of Pure Land Buddhism. He was unrelated to Atsumori.

20. According to a *Ko-Atsumori* manuscript at Kōshōji Temple, we should all chant the *nenbutsu* for Atsumori's sake. See Tokuda Kazuo, "Otogizōshi *Ko-Atsumori* no Kōshōji-bon wo megutte," *Gakushūin Joshi Daigaku kiyō* 4 (2002): 50.

The Crone Fleece

The cult of the bodhisattva Kannon (Skt. Avalokiteśvara) has thrived in Japan since around the time of the introduction of Buddhism in the sixth century. Kannon is a staple figure in fiction and narrated genres of the late medieval period, and in *The Crone Fleece* (*Ubakawa*), the bodhisattva bestows its grace in a most unusual way: by granting the dazzlingly beautiful female protagonist a magical disguise—the eponymous crone fleece—to protect her from the depredations of covetous men. As a Cinderella-type love story with apparent connections to the *otogizōshi Hachikazuki* (*The Bowl Bearer*) and *Hanayo no hime* (*Lady Blossom*), *The Crone Fleece* invokes a range of social and sexual anxieties as it describes the travails of its tender young heroine, first at the hands of a cruel stepmother—another ubiquitous figure in medieval Japanese fiction—and later as a menial servant at the estate of Sasaki no Minbu Takakiyo in Ōmi Province, where her future is finally secured. The charm of the work lies in its dark humor, rooted in various characters' false impressions and misunderstandings. Having been placed in an omniscient position, the reader is free to enjoy the comedy in the reactions of Takakiyo and his household to the apparent willingness of Takakiyo's son to violate marital norms and social taboos, as well as the clever skill with which Takakiyo's son eventually attains his parents' consent to wed. Like most *otogizōshi*, *The Crone Fleece* ends auspiciously, and at its conclusion readers are urged to recite an incantation to Kannon, suggesting the story's likely origins in a late-medieval proselytizing tradition intended to encourage faith in the bodhisattva.

The translation is from a single-volume *Ubakawa* picture book (*nara ehon*) formerly in the collection of the Kannon Sengyōkai (Kannon Devotional Association), typeset and annotated in Hamanaka Osamu, ed., *Shinchū Muromachi monogatari shū*, Daigaku koten sōsho 8 (Tokyo: Benseisha, 1989), 13–21. The illustrations are from the *Ubakawa* picture book in the Jissen Women's University Library.

The Crone Fleece survives in at least four *nara ehon* picture books, indicating its popularity in or around the sixteenth and seventeenth centuries. Despite the apparent fictionality of its characters, the story is set in a specific historical period—the Ōei era (1394–1428)—which is unusual among *otogizōshi*.

In the Ōei period, there was a person called Left Palace Guard Naruse no Kiyomune in the village of Iwakura in Owari Province. He lost his long-time wife and had only a single daughter to remember her by. Because it would not do for him to live on in that way, he later took a second wife. His daughter was eleven years old. Before long, Kiyomune was required to travel to the capital to perform a period of guard duty there. Turning to his new wife, he said, "My daughter is still very young, so please bring her up as well as you can." He gave her detailed instructions and then set out for the capital.

Kiyomune entrusts his daughter to his second wife. (From *Ubakawa*, courtesy of the Jissen Women's University Library)

Thereafter, the stepmother resented the girl to no end. The daughter thought to herself, "None of this would be happening if my father were here." She pined for her father in the daytime and for her dead mother at night, leaving not a moment for her tears to dry. Because the girl lamented in this way, her stepmother hated her all the more, and she stopped feeding her and providing her with any other care. Thus in the spring of her twelfth year, the girl crept out of Iwakura Village under the cover of darkness. Because she had nowhere to go, she simply wandered where her feet led her until she came to the Kannon Hall of Jinmokuji Temple.

"This is the very buddha that my mother always used to visit!" she thought. "I hear that she used to make her way here on foot, night and day, to pray for my future. I hope that I'll starve soon and speed on to where she is."

Hiding from other people, the girl ensconced herself under the veranda of the inner sanctuary and prayed: "Truly, people say that your great compassionate vow is a vow to ensure peace in the present life and a happy rebirth in the next. I have nothing to ask for in this world, but please help me in the next." Then, without a moment's pause, she set about reading the Kannon Sutra, which her mother had always taught her.

On the third night at dawn, the bodhisattva Kannon appeared, awesome to behold, shining a golden light throughout the earthly realm. The bodhisattva stood at the sleeping girl's head and spoke: "How sad to see you lost like this, when your mother used to come here all the time to pray for your future! Since you are so exceptionally beautiful, someone somewhere is sure to steal you for himself. Put this on." Kannon gave her something that looked like a strip of tree bark. "This is called a 'crone fleece.' You should wear it and go where I tell you. Stand before the gate of Sasaki no Minbu Takakiyo of Ōmi Province." With these words, the bodhisattva disappeared without a trace.

"What a wonderful revelation!" the girl exclaimed, and she prostrated herself in prayer. As the sky lightened, she donned the crone fleece and crawled out from under the veranda. The people who saw her laughed and said, "What an ugly old woman!"

Doing as she had been told, the girl traveled to Ōmi Province. Because she resembled a horrible hag, no one gave her a second glance, even though she slept in the mountains and fields. She eventually wandered to the house of Sasaki no Minbu Takakiyo, where she rested beside the gate and reverently chanted a sutra.

Takakiyo's son, Sasaki no Jūrō Takayoshi, who was nineteen years old, happened to be lingering near the gate. He summoned a samurai and said, "I've noticed something strange. This old woman here is reading a sutra, yet in spite of her appearance, her

The Crone Fleece

Kannon grants the girl the protective crone fleece. (From *Ubakawa*, courtesy of the Jissen Women's University Library)

voice is majestic, like a heavenly bird.[1] We'd do well to keep an odd person like that around. Call her inside and have her tend the cauldron fire."

"Hey, old lady!" the samurai beckoned. "You can stay here and tend the cauldron fire." The girl entered and did exactly as she had been told.

It was just past the tenth of the third month, and the southern-front garden was planted with all kinds of flowers. When the cherry blossoms scattered, other bulbs were there to bloom. The willows by the waterside trailed yellowish-green fronds, and the moon at the mountain ridge in the deepening night vied with the flowers in their colorful beauty. Late in the night when the house had grown still, the girl went out into the garden to take in the blossoms and the moon. Wistfully thinking back on her past, she paused and recited,

> *tsuki hana no*   Though the colors
> *iro wa mukashi ni*   of the moon and the blossoms
> *kawaranedo*   remain unchanged,

---

1. Literally, a kalavinka, a Himalayan bird renowned for its exquisite song. In the Pure Land Buddhist tradition, the kalavinka is depicted with the face of a beautiful woman and is said to reside in the Pure Land.

waga mi hitotsu zo	this single body of mine
otoroenikeru	has gone to rack and ruin.

Jūrō Takayoshi knew a thing or two about poetry and music, and since he was a person of refinement, he, too, begrudged the setting moon. As he sat in the flower-viewing pavilion with the bamboo blind rolled up high, he spied a suspicious figure in the garden. Taking up his sword, he slipped in among the blossoms for a closer look. It was the old woman who tended the cauldron fire. "That old wretch," he thought, watching her quietly. "What's she doing here?"

Unaware that she was being watched, the girl stood facing the moon. She pulled back the edge of the crone fleece, revealing her lovely face. Then she recited,

tsuki hitori	You moon alone,
aware to wa miyo	look down on me with pity!
ubakawa wo	When might I ever
itsu no yo ni ka wa	shed this crone fleece
nugite kaesan	and give it back again?

The girl was so beautiful that she seemed to light up the space all around.

269

Takayoshi confronts the girl in the garden after she pulls back the crone fleece. (From *Ubakawa*, courtesy of the Jissen Women's University Library)

The Crone Fleece

"What's the meaning of this?" Takayoshi thought, and being a sturdy fellow, he readied his sword and strode over to the girl. "I recognized you as the old fire tender," he glowered, "but you're not her—you're a beautiful lady. You must be some evil deity. I won't let you escape!"

The girl stared. "Please settle down for a moment," she calmly replied. "I am no evil deity. I'll explain to you my appearance." With that, she recounted everything that had happened to her until then. Takayoshi listened intently. "So it's a miracle of Kannon!" he exclaimed, and he clasped his hands and wept for joy.

Because Takayoshi did not yet have a wife, his bedroom was a forlorn place where he slept and rose alone. But now taking the girl by the hand, he led her into the flower-viewing pavilion, pulled off the crone fleece, and gazed at her in the lamplight. She was like a heavenly being descended to earth, gorgeous beyond compare. Her beauty lit up the space all around. "You must be the daughter of Naruse no Saemon Kiyomune," he said, "the one about whom I've heard. It may be a hasty thing for me to say, but what problem could there be? Please marry me." He then spoke at length of their life to come.

"But my appearance—," the girl replied, "it's extraordinary! Your parents would be so angry if they heard. Please keep me in service here forever, and I'll tend the cauldron fire as an old woman."

"Now that I've met you like this," Takayoshi said, "I won't leave you for a moment, not at the ends of the fields or in the deepest mountains, not even if I'm to be disowned." He lay down beside her and wept, and since there was nothing else that she could do, she bent to his touch. Thus, beneath shared covers, they sealed a vow of eternal love.

Night eventually gave way to dawn, and bewailing the morning parting, Takayoshi and his darling shed endless tears. As it was already growing light, they could hear the lesser servants bustling about. Pulling the crone fleece back over her head, the girl set out to build the cauldron fire. Takayoshi held her by the sleeve and recited,

Kannon no	Thanks to Kannon,
on wo kitarishi	whose debt you bear,
ubakawa wo	the crone fleece
sue tanomoshiku	has served you ever well.
ware ya nugasen	Shall I be the one to strip it off?[2]

---

2. *Kitarishi* functions as a pivot-word between the phrases *on wo ki[ru]* (to owe a debt [to Kannon]) and *kitarishi ubakawa* (the crone fleece that [you] wore).

The girl replied,

ukikoto wo	Hardships I've borne,
kasanete kitaru	like robes on top of robes—
ubakawa wo	if you were not in this world,
kimi yo ni nakuba	could there be anybody
tare ka nugasen	to strip me of my crone fleece?

It was pitiful indeed how she composed these lines and then went off to build the fire.

Takayoshi's mother and father had previously arranged for their son to marry the daughter of the Kyoto Imadegawa Major Captain of the Left. They had the nursemaid Saishō deliver a message to their son explaining that they would send him to the capital. Takayoshi simply answered, "Although it is a terrible thing to disregard your will, my only wish is to take monastic vows. I cannot do as you advise."

"What's the meaning of this?" the parents wondered when they heard his reply. "Like other young people, he must have fallen in love. Get to the bottom of this, Saishō."

Saishō visited Takayoshi and said, "It's wrong of you to trouble your parents so! You're a young man, and even if you've set your heart on someone else, it's not very bad. If she's lowly, you'd still be within your rights as a lord to summon her here and make her your wife. That kind of thing happens all the time. Your parents wouldn't be particularly upset." She went on and on.

Takayoshi took in her words. "What do I have to hide now?" he said. "It may be beyond most people's imagination, but I want to marry the old woman who tends our cauldron fire." Saishō was utterly aghast. Without saying a word, she burst into tears and ran back to the boy's parents, to whom she reported the news.

"What's the meaning of this?" the parents exclaimed. "Has our son gone insane?" They each lay down where they were and cried. After a while, the father said, "A fine boy like our Takayoshi isn't prone to telling lies. This must be part of his plan to become a monk. Oh, how disturbing!" But then he said, "Well, at any rate, we'll let him take the old fire tender for his bride and see what he thinks about that!" He sent a messenger to his son, saying, "In that case, since tomorrow is an auspicious day, summon the old woman and make her your wife."

Takayoshi was overjoyed. He immediately prepared a wickerwork carriage and sundry celebrations. The people of the house were incredulous, but because it was their master's command, they all set to work.

The Crone Fleece

When the day arrived, Takayoshi summoned the old woman and ushered her into his personal quarters. The two of them dressed and adorned themselves together, in private. As the sky lightened, the girl pulled her head cloth down over her brow, stepped into the carriage, and went to see Takayoshi's mother. The men bore her carriage right into the reception hall, where the parents watched her emerge. She was not the same old woman as before.

"What's the meaning of this?" everyone exclaimed. The parents were dumbfounded. The family stared as the girl approached her father-in-law. She seemed to be of another world, as if a bodhisattva or some heavenly being had descended to the earthly realm. Someone so pretty was unheard of in the past. She looked to be thirteen or fourteen years old, with a fresh face and a figure so lovely that it could never be painted. Her beauty was beyond words to describe. Staring in astonishment, Takakiyo and his wife were infinitely pleased.

As his wedding present, Takayoshi was entrusted with the family fortunes.

Word of these events spread throughout the land. "So it was because Kannon brought them together that Takayoshi found a wife!" the emperor declared upon hearing the news. "Amazing!" He immediately summoned Takayoshi to the capital, where he designated him the Sasaki Right Commander of the Military Guards. He also granted him the provinces of Ōmi and Echizen, which was a splendid case of "stacking domains." Later, Takayoshi and his wife had many children, and they prospered for ages to come.

All of this was due to the compassion of the most merciful Kannon. Everyone who reads this story should recite three times, "Hail the Merciful Bodhisattva Kannon." Have no doubt that Kannon will grant us peace in this world and a happy rebirth in the next.

TRANSLATION AND INTRODUCTION BY KELLER KIMBROUGH

INTERSPECIES
AFFAIRS

The Tale of the Mouse

The Tale of the Mouse (*Nezumi no sōshi*) belongs to a subgenre that modern scholars call "interspecies" (*irui-mono*) tales, in which non-humans act and speak like humans and interact with human beings in this world. Contemporary readers would have understood the world to be divided into the Six Realms of heaven, *ashura*, humans, animals, hungry ghosts, and hell. The mice in this tale seek to escape from the realm of animals, and for a brief time they are able to transgress the boundary between the human and bestial realms.

Major highlights of the narrative are the wedding preparations and the wedding reception, which are described and painted in loving detail. The picture scroll consists of an erudite, humorous narrative that alternates with lavish illustrations of frolicking mice. Bits of text in the paintings (*gachūshi*) take the form of transcribed speech and labels identifying the characters or places. The contrast between the more serious tone of the main text and the irreverent chatter of the servants in the *gachūshi* is a part of the *otogizōshi*'s charm. The servant-mice in the painted images speak in an eastern dialect that is exaggerated for comic effect.[1] As they work, they sing songs, at least one of which is based on a song that would have been well known in the sixteenth century.[2] Most notably, the *waka* poems that the protagonist Gonnokami composes on the belongings that his human wife leaves behind overflow with allusions to famous poems from *The Tale of Genji* (early eleventh century), all of which were well known and would likely have been recognizable to an educated

The translation and illustrations are from the five-scroll *Nezumi no sōshi* picture scrolls (sixteenth century) in the collection of the Suntory Museum of Art, typeset and annotated in Ōshima Tatehiko, ed., *Otogizōshi shū*, Nihon koten bungaku zenshū 36 (Tokyo: Shōgakukan, 1974), 496–527. For the dialogue in the illustrations, the translator also consulted the modern Japanese translation in *Ehon Nezumi no sōshi* (Tokyo: Santorī Bijutsukan, 2007).

1. Izumo Asako, "Chūsei makki ni okeru tōgoku hōgen no isō: *Nezumi no sōshi emaki* no ekotoba wo megutte," *Kokugo to kokubungaku* 72, no. 11 (1995): 64–75.
2. Ono Mitsuyasu, *E no kataru kayōshi* (Osaka: Izumi Shoin, 2001), 36–41.

reader in the sixteenth and seventeenth centuries. Other sections of the story are also potentially didactic (probably intended to educate young readers): the discussion of the history of noh, the demonstration of different methods of divination, and even the comical conversation about the Five Precepts of Buddhism.

The lineage of *The Tale of the Mouse* to which the text translated here belongs includes the largest number of surviving manuscripts, and their words and images are nearly identical. It is widely believed that these illustrated manuscripts were produced by a picture-scroll studio in the late Muromachi (1337–1573) or early Edo (1600–1867) period. Some of the mice in the illustrations are named after recognizable public figures, including noh actors and the tea master Sen no Rikyū (1522–1591), which has helped scholars to date this group of scrolls.

Once upon a time, a venerable old mouse named Gonnokami lived near the Horikawa Mansion on Fourth Avenue in the capital. Perhaps due to this Latter Age of the Buddhist Law, when things have deteriorated, the mouse, in the tedium of a rainy day, summoned his retainer, Sakonnojō the Hole-Digger, Captain of the Left Inner Guards, and said, "What karma we must carry from our previous lives, Sakonnojō, that we were born not only as beasts, but as such small beasts! How vexing! But I have an idea. What if I were to wed a human so that my descendants would be liberated from this realm of beasts?"

"What a splendid idea!" Sakonnojō replied. "Please decide soon, and exchange vows with whomever you like. If you'll excuse my frankness, your appearance is no different from that of the Shining Genji of old when he lingered by Yūgao's lodging at dusk, or Commander of the Right Gate Guards Kashiwagi when he stood in the shadow of a cherry tree and set his sight on the cat's leash.[3] You would not even pale in comparison with the Fifth Rank Middle Captain Ariwara no Narihira when he gazed upon the cherry blossoms scattering like snow at dawn on the Katano Plain.[4] Why should a man as handsome as you settle for any ordinary woman? The daughter of the Yanagiya—a girl of seventeen or eighteen, I think—lives on Oil Lane

3. Sakonnojō compares Gonnokami with the classical romantic heroes Hikaru (Shining) Genji and Kashiwagi from *The Tale of Genji*. In *Genji*, Kashiwagi first glimpses Genji's wife, the Third Princess, when her cat inadvertently displaces her blind with its leash.

4. Ariwara no Narihira (825–880) was a poet and the purported protagonist of *The Tales of Ise* (ca. tenth century). In this sentence, Sakonnojō paraphrases poem 114 in *Shinkokin wakashū* (*New Collection of Ancient and Modern Poems*, 1205), attributed to Fujiwara no Toshinari (Shunzei; 1104–1204).

276

around Fifth Avenue, not too far from here.[5] For years, she has been on my mind, and I have peeked at her, through the hinges of folding screens, beneath verandas, through the holes that visiting crickets have chewed in the walls, through knotholes, and all sorts of nooks and crannies, and there is no maiden more beautiful than she. Her beauty is like a willow swaying in the breeze; like flowering crab apples in the garden smiling in the spring rain, announcing from the shade of the dormant cherry trees the coming of spring; or like the hazy moon emerging from the mist. She is beyond compare, bringing to mind the women of old of whom the poets wrote such things. I think that any woman other than this would be a poor match for your noble heart. However, it may be difficult to fulfill your wishes in the ordinary ways. From time immemorial, people have prayed for love at Kibune and Miwa shrines, to the Kamo Deity, and at Tadasu Shrine. The buddhas have made a vow:

nao tanome	Depend on me,
Shimejigahara no	o wild mugwort
sashimogusa	of Shimejigahara,
ware yo no naka ni	for as long as I live
aramu kagiri wa	in this world.[6]

The mugwort is written as 'all living things.' And you, it goes without saying, and even those such as I, are not excluded from the category of living things. If we trust in this vow, make a pilgrimage to Kiyomizu Temple and offer a prayer—why wouldn't your wish be granted? Please consider it." Thus advised by Sakonnojō, Gonnokami scurried off to Kiyomizu.

Meanwhile, the wealthy Saburōzaemon of the Yanagiya lived on Oil Lane around Fifth Avenue in the capital, where he passed the months and years in luxury. But there was one thing that weighed on his heart: his only daughter. Perhaps because of some punishment from a previous life, she could not find a suitable match and passed her days in fruitless sorrow. The age for an appropriate marriage had passed, and it became a constant sadness for Saburōzaemon and his wife. Although they prayed to myriad gods and buddhas, it was to no avail. One time, they sent their daughter with a maid named Jijū no Tsubone to Kiyomizu to make a prayer-vow and view the cherry

5. The Yanagiya was a famous saké store in Kyoto that may have been attractive to a mouse because of all the rice required to make saké, according to Saitō Maori, "Katami no waka: Nezumi no sōshi shichū," Kokubungaku kenkyū shiryōkan kiyō: bungaku kenkyū hen 37, no. 28 (2011): 97–99. Oil Lane is another reference to a favored food for mice; Gonnokami himself refers to snacking on oil later in the tale.

6. This is poem 1917 in Shinkokin wakashū, attributed to the statue of the bodhisattva Kannon (Skt. Avalokiteśvara) at Kiyomizu Temple. The word sashimogusa (mugwort) is written with the characters for issai shujō (all sentient beings).

Gonnokami (*center*) sits in his mansion with Sakonnojō and his other retainers. (From *Nezumi no sōshi*, courtesy of the Suntory Museum of Art)

blossoms. At the same time, Gonnokami was performing a twenty-one-day vigil before the altar at the same temple.

Kannon thought, "This mouse has put his faith in my declaration that all sentient beings should depend on me, and although he is a beast, his heart is sincere and the feelings with which he beseeches me are pitiful indeed! On the other hand, the Yanagiya maiden, perhaps because of some karma from a previous life, cannot find a partner in marriage, even though she has searched the mountains and seas. But if I were to match her with the mouse, I could sweep away the clouds in both of their hearts!"

In the first illustration, Gonnokami sits in his mansion, with Sakonnojō and seven other retainers on the veranda. The adjoining scene (not reproduced here) shows a procession of thirty-five mice on foot and horseback; some of the horses have distinctly mousey faces and feet. Gonnokami's retainers are identified with names like Saruchiyo the Beam-Runner, Tōbei the Bean-Lover, Bad Tarō the Glutton, Yoroku the Hem-Stabber, Shinnojō the Tailless, and Kuranojō the Rice-Chewer. Next to the image of Gonnokami is a cartouche containing a single line of dialogue: "Good weather, just as I thought!"

Just before dawn on the twenty-first day, Gonnokami had a wondrous vision. Kannon spoke to him in a miraculous dream: "Your plea has aroused my compassion. At dawn, there will be a group of women visiting my temple around the Otowa waterfall. I will give you one of them as your wife." In his joy, Gonnokami wondered whether he was dreaming or awake. Opening his eyes wide, he arose and performed thirty-three obeisances to Kannon.

INTERSPECIES AFFAIRS

As the night was late, Gonnokami watched the moon at the eaves of the Tamura Hall. The sky eventually lightened, whereupon he headed to the Otowa falls. Just as Kannon had said, a number of women from an unknown place had gathered around the waterfall. It must have been late in the second month, because the temple cherry trees were blooming in a snowy profusion. Among them was a woman holding a single spray of blossoms in her hand, and she was so lovely that it was hard to tell her apart from the cherry trees. Gonnokami thought happily that this must be the woman of his vision, and approaching Jijū, he addressed her, saying, "This is a brazen thing to say, but being as yet unmarried, I secluded myself in the temple and prayed for a part-

[handwritten: my girlfriend]

In the second illustration (not fully reproduced here), a group of human women are gathered at Otowa waterfall: the young lady, Jijū no Tsubone, and four other attendants. Jijū speaks to Gonnokami, who is accompanied by Sakonnojō and three other retainers. To the left, cherry trees in full bloom surround a temple building; there are seven human figures on the veranda, including pilgrims and priests. The following dialogue is inscribed:

SON'YA: I came with Lord Katsushiki. Ah, aren't these cherry trees lovely? How captivating!
TŌZAEMON: I live around here.
SENMATSU: I have come to see Kiyomizu's cherry trees.
TAMONBŌ: I often come here to serve the Buddha, but oh, how wonderful, how wonderful!
HIKONAI THE PILGRIM FROM KAZUSA: Ah, what a lovely time of year!

279

ner. I had a miraculous dream, according to which the first person to visit the Otowa waterfall today is to be my wife. Don't fuss now, just do as I say."

[handwritten: excuse me sir, let's not forget you are a mouse]

Gonnokami speaks with Jijū at Kiyomizu Temple (*right*). (From *Nezumi no sōshi*, courtesy of the Suntory Museum of Art)

The Tale of the Mouse

In the third illustration (not reproduced here), which depicts more than fifty mice and humans, the young lady's procession travels to Gonnokami's mansion. Sakonnojō and several other mice are on horseback, while the young lady, Jijū, and another female attendant ride in palanquins borne by mice. Many mice are on foot, bearing spears, halberds, bows, and swords; others carry luggage. At the end of the illustration, they arrive at the gates of Gonnokami's mansion, with cherry blossoms visible inside. The following dialogue is inscribed:

FUNSHICHI: It's hard leading this horse!
SAKONNOJŌ THE HOLE-DIGGER: What a splendid procession! Walk with care.
AKUBŌ: There are no attendants as great as we are!
SHINGO: If you're tired, switch shoulders.
HIKOZAEMON: How could I be tired already? Just watch me walk!
SKINNY HEITA: How heavy is the burden of our lord's love!
MAGOSHICHI OF THE BIG FIELD: We think so, too!
GENTA: What's inside these trunks? I want a peek.
SAKUZŌ: It's so heavy, I feel like my eyeballs are going to pop out!
YOSHICHIRŌ: If you say that sort of thing, it'll be your head!
NAISEN (*in charge of luggage*): The ladies-in-waiting disobey me because I'm just a spear-carrier.

"What an amazing thing for him to say!" Jijū thought. "How could such a thing happen? Still, given that my lady, too, has come here to pray for a match, this must be a revelation of the Kiyomizu Kannon." And she replied: "If this is Kannon's command, then how could I object? We will do just as you wish."

Gonnokami was beside himself with joy. "Well then, we will prepare many carriages, and I'll lead the way! As for your escort, I'll put Sakonnojō the Hole-Digger in charge of things. Off we go!" he said, setting out.

Sakonnojō gathered the young lady's belongings, omitting nothing, and fully dressed in finery, he rode his horse beside her to Gonnokami's residence.

Believing Kannon's instructions to be true, Jijū accompanied her charge to this unknown place. Looking around the parlor, she saw that it had many sliding paper doors and gold folding screens; gazing out over the front gardens, she noticed that they were planted with a mix of willow and cherry reminiscent of decorative brocade. In the *kemari* field,[7] the cherry trees bloomed in wild profusion, in no way inferior to the springtime dawn in the capital. A servant escorted the young lady to a room deep inside the mansion, pulled a small screen beside her, and offered her an armrest, which she leaned against as delicately as the tendril of a willow, lovely beyond compare. The night grew late, and when the time was right, Gonnokami appeared. They began the three-rounds-of-saké nuptial ceremony, and

7. *Kemari* is a traditional Japanese ball sport originally played by courtiers, wearing sophisticated attire, in the Heian and medieval periods.

Gonnokami and his bride celebrate their wedding. (From *Nezumi no sōshi*, courtesy of the Suntory Museum of Art)

went all the way to eleven rounds![8] After that, they dimmed the lanterns, whereupon the lady-in-waiting Ayame no Mai took charge and led the visitors to their rooms, starting with Jijū.

Perhaps because there was no hiding the news of this marriage, all ranks of blind musicians in the capital, from the highest to the lowest, representing the Myōkan, Shidō, Tojima, and Genshō factions of the Ichikata school and the Ōyama and Myōmon factions of the Yasaka school—friends and foes alike—pushed forward eagerly to perform at such an auspicious occasion.[9] They hurried along with their lutes slung over their backs, their canes clicking along the ground as they went. From the shadows of a thicket, a tiger-striped dog ran out, but before they could see it a great many other dogs heard it barking at the musicians toward the back and ran out from all four directions, howling at the men in a noisy pack. The sight of the blind musicians picking up their canes and turning to flee—even in a picture, one could hardly do it justice!

Behind them, there was the lovely sight of the four schools of noh actors arriving: the Kanze, the lively Konparu, the Kongō, and the Hōshō. The origins of noh lie with a teacher of the Tang emperor Xuanzong.[10] This teacher taught the Dance of the Rainbow Skirt and Feather Robe to the emperor, and it became a consolation

---

8. It was customary for the bride and groom to exchange three rounds of saké (one round consisting of three cups), and this is likely a joke about the excessive consumption of alcohol at weddings.
9. The Ichikata and Yasaka schools were two of the major schools of blind minstrels (*biwa hōshi*).
10. The doomed love of Emperor Xuanzong of Tang (685–762, r. 712–756) for his consort Yang Guifei (719–756) is the subject of the famous Tang poem *Song of Everlasting Sorrow* (*Chang hen ge*, 806), by Bai Juyi (772–846).

In the fourth illustration, the wedding ceremony is performed. To the right, Gonnokami and his bride sit together, accompanied by a mouse monk, human attendants, and Ayame no Mai, who is portrayed as a mouse. Female mouse servants pull back a curtain and peek in on the proceedings. The bulk of the illustration (not reproduced here) is devoted to the servants and their many preparations for the wedding. The following dialogue is inscribed:

BEN NO TONO: Hey, Kodayū, let's peek in a little. Could there be anything so splendid in the whole wide world? Oh, what a beautiful bride!

SŌEKI (*in charge of water for the tea*): The water for the tea is ready. I, Sōeki, present it to you.[1]

MON'ICHI: However blind I may be, I can't grind tea all day long without some saké. Izumi, how cruel you are! Give me a cup. I'm thirsty!

IZUMI NO KAMI (*in charge of saké*): This is Milky Way. And this is high-grade Egawa!

KINZŌ: High-grade Egawa is excellent. For such a happy occasion, give me one cup after another! I'll drink twenty or thirty cups and my face will turn as red as Shuten Dōji's![2]

IYAROKU (*to Sakuzaemon, who is identified as being in charge of the food trays, including those bearing* tachibana-yaki *fish cakes and shrimp*): If there is a tray of food I should bring out, I'll take it.

KINNAI: Saemon, carving the swan is important! Please take care and don't damage it when you cut.

YASANZAEMON (*in charge of the knives*): This bird's bones are so tough that they're quite a chore to cut! I'm working this hard so that they'll give me a big knife in return.

ICHIROHYŌE (*in charge of the fish knives*): We might receive a bolt of fabric, too!

OKO: Oh Matsuko, the rice is getting a little soft. Chase off the flies quickly! When we receive our wedding favors, let's share them.

MATSUKO: They really should give us an obi, too. I wonder what they think about how hard I'm working, chasing off these flies? Please meow at those little mice behind us. They're so naughty that they might ruin the rice.

MATSUKO (*in charge of the bath*): Oh Matsukae, when I draw the water for his bath, the lord takes my hand and we have a little fun, but that's all over from tonight on, isn't it? But I won't be abandoned like this! My mind is made up, Matsukae!

to him in his constant pining for Yang Guifei. People say of noh, even today, that humming it allows you to forget your worries for the world to come—it is written in the *Song of Everlasting Sorrow* that "the players of the Pear Garden have new white hair."[11] In Japan, too, the Fujiwara and other special wards of the Kasuga Deity—the noh actors—are no ordinary people. This may be why, from just a moment of song and dance, or even from the turn of a dancer's sleeve, one may imagine the way in which Sayohime of Matsura Bay waved her sleeves in farewell.[12]

11. This is a quotation from the *Song of Everlasting Sorrow*. The Pear Garden (Liyuan) was a school established by Xuanzong for actors and musicians.

12. According to legend, when Sayohime's husband, Ōtomo no Sadehiko, departed for Korea, she waved goodbye to him from a mountaintop and then turned to stone. Her earliest literary appearance is in the poetry collection *Man'yōshū* (*Collection of Myriad Leaves*, ca. 785), and her ghost is in an eponymous noh play.

MATSUKAE: Matsuko, you have no business saying such things. The lord's made up his mind, too. Be kind to the new wife, and if you get that obi you want, then just put up with it. The lord might be up to something already. Oh, how vexing, how vexing!

KOROKU: The cooking is done, Magoemon. Give it a sip to taste. Should I add more salt? Or should I flavor it with some saké? It's up to you, 'Emon.

MAGOEMON (*in charge of the soup*): Add some shellfish. Without shellfish, how are you to know whether it's salty enough? The saltiness is just right, and the fragrance is excellent.

HIKOZŌ: In the market today, there were hardly any fish. In the end, this was all I could get. And I'll be scolded by my superiors for my lateness, but the road was so slow and I can't help being tired.

YONE: No matter how the children hurry ahead, with my back the way it is it's just no good.

NENE: Kōbai, the water is cloudy, and I can't draw it.

KŌBAI: It's cloudy because of the frogs. Oh, what shall we do?

ANEGO (*sings*): Tomorrow is the rice-pounding for our lord!

YONE (*sings*): Pull it up and push it down, pound, pound, let's pound this rice! This winnowing basket is new, and it's hard to fan it!

CHIYOTOMO (*sings*): "How I miss you, how I long to see you," reads the letter dropped off the long bridge at Seta. Alas, the heartless letter-bearer!

OTOME: I, too, lost my love letter somewhere. I'm just back from chopping cherry trees to be used as firewood for our splendid lord. Oh, I'm bushed!

MORIYAYAKO (*sings*): Sleep, sleep, little baby, don't cry and get caught by a cat!

HYŌBU NO JŌ (*in charge of wedding favors*).[3]

1. Sōeki was the Buddhist name of the famous tea master Sen no Rikyū.
2. Shuten Dōji is a saké-loving demon who appears in numerous *otogizōshi*, including, in this volume, *The Demon Shuten Dōji* and *The Demon of Ibuki*.
3. There is some additional text here, probably a line spoken by Hyōbu no Jō, that is partially illegible.

After the noh players, the masters of dance came along, with Yūgiri and Kōwaka leading the way. This being the capital, all sorts of famous people vied to attend; they rejoiced in the wedding favors and then returned home.

Having pledged their troth in this way, Gonnokami's love for the young lady was beyond compare. Spring being spring and fall being fall, Gonnokami brought the cherries of Yoshino and the maples of Tatsuta to plant in his garden and gaze upon. The bathhouse was modeled after the Huaqing Palace in China,[13] with hot-spring waters to caress the lady's snow-white skin.

One day, Gonnokami approached the young lady and said, "That I can share a love like this with you is a blessing from Kiyomizu. Since there's a vow that I made

13. The Huaqing Palace was built in the Tang dynasty, and Yang Guifei famously bathed there. This is another allusion to the *Song of Everlasting Sorrow*.

The Tale of the Mouse

when we met, please give me leave for a little while. I'm going on a pilgrimage to the temple. Whatever you do, be sure not to leave this room." With this earnest instruction, he departed.

The young lady summoned Jijū and spoke: "Lately, I've been looking around at the way things are here, and it's not like how most people live. What sort of unclean, evil magic has brought us here? It's horrible, like we've fallen into the realm of beasts! You know, there's something funny about the way my lord finishes his sentences. Let's peek through the slits in the screen to see what the servants are up to." And with that, she and Jijū listened in.

The young lady turned to Jijū and said, "It's just as I suspected—we've fallen into the realm of beasts! How awful! They come and go through a hole in the earthen wall. Perhaps if they are mice,

In the fifth illustration (not reproduced here), mouse musicians and actors come to the festivities. Nine blind lutenists walk with canes and hold one another's paws. The last two mice in the procession are turning around in alarm as two dogs bound toward them. They are followed by actors (wearing colorful, patterned clothes), musicians, and their attendants—eighteen in all.

In the sixth illustration, the young lady bathes in a tub, accompanied by several of her attendants. To the left, she and Gonnokami face each other while he tells her that he must go. The maid Chachako says, "She is taking quite a long bath."

284

The lady bathes (*right*) and then meets with Gonnokami (*left*). (From *Nezumi no sōshi*, courtesy of the Suntory Museum of Art)

The lady and Jijū (*right*) observe the mice in their true form. (From *Nezumi no sōshi*, courtesy of the Suntory Museum of Art)

we can catch them." She took a string from the koto that she often played, and tying it into a loose knot, she set out a trap. Perhaps Gonnokami had reached the end of his luck—before long, he was caught. He gave just a little squeak and soon was in a perilous state.

"Sakonnojō, are you there? I'm caught in a trap! Get me out before she sees," was all that he could say before losing consciousness.

In the seventh illustration, which contains no labels or transcribed speech, the young lady and Jijū peek through an open doorway at the mice; instead of the cute, anthropomorphized white mice portrayed in the majority of the pictures in the tale, they are depicted as animal-like gray mice on all fours. Most wear no clothes, and a few seem to be wriggling out of their robes. Their primary activities are eating and fighting over food.

Hearing this, Sakonnojō exclaimed, "What a dreadful state you're in! How can this be?" He gnawed at the trap, and performing a glorious feat with his two front teeth, well trained from splitting the hardest of walnuts, he immediately cut through the koto string. The young lady saw this, and abandoning everything, she pushed Jijū ahead of her, fleeing blindly from the mansion.

From the past to the present, whether of noble or low birth, a woman's heart is despicable. Even though she may think of the months and years that she spent with her spouse, and she may not think that they were disagreeable, her desire to look back on the one who would detain her is fleeting.

When the young lady finally emerged and looked around, she found that she had crawled through the crumbled opening of an old dirt burrow. In her anger at the Kiyomizu Kannon, she recited:

The Tale of the Mouse

Gonnokami lies ensnared in his wife's trap. (From *Nezumi no sōshi*, courtesy of the Suntory Museum of Art)

saki tatanu	An eight thousand–fold
kui no yachitabi	sadness over the regrets
kanashiki wa	I cannot undo—
Kiyomizu-dera no	that was my blessing
rishō narikeri	from Kiyomizu Temple.

Weakly mumbling these words, she headed for the capital. But not knowing the way, she felt as lost as a waterbird on land. After all she had been through, she gave up hope of returning home. She thought that she would become a nun and pray for enlightenment in the next life, and having heard of a place called Saga-no-oku, she set out on foot to find it.

In the eighth illustration, the young lady and Jijū sit inside the mansion. Gonnokami lies sprawled on the ground outside, presumably caught in a trap, with Sakonnojō beside him. His sword has fallen to his side, his clothes are in disarray, and his mousey body and tail are revealed. To the left (not reproduced here), the young lady, Jijū, and a human attendant are escaping.

Gonnokami had been saved by Sakonnojō, for which he squeaked with relief, but then lamenting the loss of his bride, he choked with tears morning and night. Now there was a fortune-teller who was said to be a descendant of someone connected to Abe no Seimei, about whom we hear in tales of old,[14] and as this person was truly talented with

14. Abe no Seimei (921–1005) was a yin-yang master who became legendary for his feats of wizardry. He appears as a character in numerous tales, including, in this volume, *The Demon Shuten Dōji*, and is cited in *Lady Tamamo*.

Gonnokami weeps as he ponders his wife's possessions. (From *Nezumi no sōshi*, courtesy of the Suntory Museum of Art)

divining rods, Gonnokami summoned him and asked him to divine where his wife had gone.

"She is seventeen," the fortune-teller explained, "and you are over one hundred. [*old mouse*] According to this reading, water is victorious over fire. The one you have lost had in-

tended to renounce the world and retreat deep into the mountains, but she
has exchanged vows with a man in the
capital, and they are like lovebirds with
wings entwined. She is now ashamed of
the time she spent here. She has a cat
called the Flute-Playing Cat Monk that
is famous in the capital for its quick
paws, good nose, and fast bite; and no matter how deep the hole, it will force its way
inside to catch a mouse. That being the case, you should be on your guard. Don't give
that lady a second thought." With that, he hurriedly put away his divining rods.

> In the ninth illustration (not reproduced
> here), Gonnokami and Sakonnojō consult
> Arimasa, the fortune-teller who uses
> divining rods, and Tsuruichi, the
> catalpa-bow medium. Gonnokami can be
> seen wiping tears from his eyes as the
> medium speaks.

In his sadness that the divination had come to nothing, Gonnokami called for a catalpa-bow medium and had her channel the spirit of his wife. The medium summoned deities, saying, "I pluck the bowstring, and here they are: Avatar of Mount Izu, Avatars of Ashigara and Hakone, and Great Deity of Mishima, listen to me now! Oh Kibune and Miwa Deities, foremost in matters of love, and you other gods of Japan, come here!"

Through the medium, the young lady spoke: "Husband, although I cannot forget your abiding love over the months and years, I am now bound to a prosperous man,

The Tale of the Mouse

In the tenth illustration, Gonnokami weeps as he looks over the young lady's abandoned belongings. A poem is written next to each abandoned object:

Sash:

uki koto wo	I think only of sad things
hitoe ni zo omou	when I gaze upon
mie no obi	her three-layered sash,
meguri awan mo	because I don't know
shiranu mi nareba	if we'll ever meet again.[1]

Koto:

ima to te mo	The wind through the pines
kawaranu niwa no	in the garden
matsukaze wo	is unchanging even now,
shirabeshi koto wa	but the koto that once harmonized with it
mukashi narikeri	is long gone.[2]

Hair tie:

nagaki yo wo	Every time I look at it,
musubi kometsuru	I weep:
motoyui wo	the hair tie
miru ni tsukete mo	that once bound together
naku namida kana	our fates!

Small box:

Urashima ga	Now I understand
sono inishie no	how Urashima Tarō
tamatebako	must have felt
akete no nochi zo	after opening
omoishiraruru	the jeweled box of yore.[3]

Futon:

tonikaku ni	I do nothing
naku yori hoka no	but weep
koto zo naki	each time I see
kono hitogara wo	the empty shell of her blankets
miru ni tsukete mo	without her.[4]

Folding fan:

kimi masade	Without my lady,
namida ni shizumu	I am so miserable
ukimi zo to	that I drown in tears;
ōgi no kaze yo	oh fan, may your breeze
fuki mo tsutaeyo	send word of this to her!

Comb:

nubatama no	Oh boxwood comb
sono kurogami wo	that once stroked
kakinadeshi	my darling's
tsuge no ogushi mo	raven hair—
ima wa nani sen	what do you do now?

Mirror box:

omokage no	Even if it were true
tomaru narai no	that it held
ari to seba	its owner's image,
kagami wo mite mo	gazing at your mirror
nagusamete mashi	would not console me.[5]

Fan:

tsuyu no ma mo	You were with me
wasuraregataki	as briefly as the dew,
omokage no	but I cannot forget you;
inochi no uchi wa	as long as we live,
mi ni soite mashi	we can never be together.[6]

Go board and *go* piece container:

midarego wo	You used to count
tō hata miso to	the game pieces:
kazoenishi	ten, twenty, thirty—
sono omokage no	how am I to forget
wasurarenu kana	the image of you back then?[7]

Inkstone case:

musubinishi	The water you scooped
kakei no mizu mo	from the pipe
ishi zo kashi	is now only stone.
kakitaete miru	No one writes with it;
katami bakari wo	it is just a memento to look at.

Lacquered brazier:

nurioke ni	I no longer know of you
kakarishi hito wa	who once warmed yourself
shiranui no	at this brazier.
Tsukushi no wata mo	What use now is the Tsukushi cotton
ima wa nani sen	to feed this will-o'-the-wisp's flame?[8]

Shell basket:

arasoite	We gathered shells
ware okureji to	together, competing
aioishi	not to fall behind.
kai no na kiku mo	Even hearing the word "shell"
uki katami nari	now is a sad reminder of you.

Incense burner and tongs:

mi wa kakute	Thus I am left
Fuji no keburi no	alone,
takimono no	like a wisp of smoke
hitori nokorite	rising from a lone fire
kuyuru narikeri	on Mount Fuji.[9]

(continued)

(continued)

Hair extensions:

asagao no	Your jeweled chaplet,
hana no yukari no	as lovely as
tamakazura	a morning glory;
kakete mo yoshi ya	but wear it though you may,
tsuyu no chigiri wa	our vows, as brief as the dew—

Washcloth and stand:

sakidatsu wa	It's my tears
namida narikeri	that come first,
kakeokishi	every time I look
kono tenugui wo	at your washcloth
miru ni tsukete mo	draped there.

1. There is a pun on the word *hitoe*, which means both "to think earnestly of" and "an unlined sash."
2. This poem may echo a poem from the "Akashi" chapter of *The Tale of Genji*: (*au made no katami ni chigiru naka no o no shirabe wa koto ni kawarazaranamu*) "This koto is yours, that you may remember me till we meet again,/and I hope you will not change the pitch of the middle string" (Murasaki Shikibu, *The Tale of Genji*, trans. Royall Tyler [New York: Penguin, 2001], 273).
3. This is a reference to the legend of Urashima Tarō, a man who, after returning to Japan from the underwater Dragon Palace, is said to have opened a forbidden box and suddenly grown old.
4. This poem refers to a poem in the "Utsusemi" chapter of *The Tale of Genji*: (*utsusemi no mi wo kaetekeru ki no moto ni nao hitogara no natsukashiki kana*) "Underneath this tree, where the molting cicada shed her empty shell,/ my longing still goes to her, for all I knew her to be" (Murasaki Shikibu, *Tale of Genji*, trans. Tyler, 52).
5. This poem is similar to a poem in the "Suma" chapter of *The Tale of Genji*: (*wakarete mo kage dani tomaru mono naraba kagami wo mite mo nagusamete mashi*). "Were it only true that the image may linger when the person goes,/ then a glance in this mirror would be comforting indeed" (Murasaki Shikibu, *Tale of Genji*, trans. Tyler, 233).
6. There is a pun on the word *uchiwa*: *inochi no uchi wa* means "as long as I live," and *uchiwa* means "fan."
7. The counting of *go* pieces alludes to a scene in the "Utsusemi" chapter of *The Tale of Genji*. The young lady played a game called *midarego* or *rango*, the rules of which are now unknown but which was once regarded as an elegant game for women, according to Saitō Maori, "Katami no waka: *Nezumi no sōshi* shichū," *Kokubungaku kenkyū shiryōkan kiyō: bungaku kenkyū hen* 37, no. 28 (2011): 110–12. By the Muromachi period, *midarego* had become a gambling game, the name of which appears in *renga* linked poetry.
8. This poem pivots on the word *shiranui*: while the phrase *hito wa shiranu* (I know not the person) suggests that the woman's whereabouts are unknown, *shiranui* signifies a "will-o'-the-wisp," or a kind of mysterious, flickering light associated with spirits.
9. There is a pun on the word *hitori*, which means both "alone" and "incense burner."

so please do not think of me any longer. If you have any feelings left for me at all, I'll set my cat on you." And the spirit departed from the medium.

Fortune-telling having proved to be fruitless, Gonnokami was simply dazed. In his despair, he gathered the twelve trunks that his wife had left behind, took out forty-two of her personal belongings, and gazed on them as mementos of her.

Having taken out the young lady's belongings, Gonnokami exhausted his store of words composing poems on them. Although he longed for times gone by, there was no returning to the past. So he called Sakonnojō and said, "I have been abandoned by my lady, and although I may weep and lament day and night, there is nothing to be done. If I do not clear away this darkness in my heart, I fear that I may not attain buddhahood. I think I shall pursue the Buddhist path and use this as an opportunity to take vows and pursue enlightenment. What do you think?"

"You are already more than twenty years past your hundredth birthday. Without this opportunity, you might not be able to enter the Buddha's path. Now is the time for you to make a decision."

Following this exhortation, Sakonnojō accompanied Gonnokami to his family temple, Sosei-ji. When they had finished explaining their intentions, the venerable priest put a razor to Gonnokami's brow and bestowed on him the Buddhist name Nen'ami. The priest lectured him strictly: "You must obey the Five Precepts. And what are those precepts? The first is to abstain from killing; the second, to abstain from stealing; the third, to abstain from lewd behavior; the fourth, to abstain from lying; and the fifth, to abstain from drinking. The first means that you should not take another being's life; the second that you should not take things from people; the third that you should not indulge in base desires; the fourth that you should not speak falsehoods; and the fifth that you should avoid alcohol."

To that, Gonnokami reverently pressed his palms together and replied, "How grateful I am for your teachings! I truly intend to obey the precepts. That said, please allow me a little leeway. As for the first one, not killing, please allow me to kill just a few shrimp, some little fish, and some grasshoppers and the like when I have a craving for them. As for the second one, not stealing, as you know, sacks of provisions lie in the corners of storehouses and other rooms, so please permit me to nibble on them and eat what spills out. Furthermore, if I live in a temple, allow me to steal the extra flour, chestnuts, persimmons, sweets, rice cakes, walnuts, *nattō*, pickles, and lamp oil. As for the third, not engaging in lewd behavior, you can rest easy. Since my wife left me, how could I? But please permit me to indulge just four or five times a month; I'll consult with you. As for the fourth, not lying, if I happen to meet with a cat monk, I might trick him. As for the fifth, not drinking, as you know, saké is all that keeps me alive! I don't plan on draining a whole saké jug or barrel and getting drunk, but please permit me to have ten cups or so, even if the cup isn't very big. If you allow me these things, then you have nothing to be concerned about; I will strictly observe the Five Precepts."

291

In the eleventh illustration (not reproduced here), Sakonnojō and Gonnokami are in the mansion, discussing Gonnokami's plan to become a monk. To the left, they journey on foot through a misty landscape to the temple, where a priest shaves Gonnokami's head while Sakonnojō looks on, weeping into his sleeves. Gonnokami is now labeled as Nen'ami, his new Buddhist name.

The Tale of the Mouse

After becoming a monk, Gonnokami encounters a cat monk. (From *Nezumi no sōshi*, courtesy of the Suntory Museum of Art)

After that, intending to make his way along the Buddhist path, Gonnokami headed for Mount Kōya shouldering a paper umbrella. As he was climbing, a dubious figure emerged from beside the road. To Gonnokami's shock, it was an old cat monk—more than two hundred years old, it seemed—wearing a yellow robe with a yellow surplice. In his panic, Gonnokami flung aside his umbrella and dove into the bushes.

The cat addressed him, asking, "Why have you become a monk?"

"My beloved wife has left me," Gonnokami replied, all atremble, "and as the world seemed hateful, I have become a monk."

The cat, tears flowing down his face, replied, "My wife left me, too, and that is why I became a monk and follow the Buddhist path. That being so, my former evil impulses are no more than dew and dust. Please do not fret, and let us be comrades as we aim for buddhahood." Thus the cat and the mouse ascended Mount Kōya together. Along the way, the cat recited this poem:

kamisori no	When they shaved my head,
tsuide ni tsume wa	they also
kiritaru yo	trimmed my claws.
ware osoruru na	Fear me not,
nezumi nyūdō	oh mouse priest!

INTERSPECIES AFFAIRS

In the final illustration, Gonnokami walks along and then falls over in surprise at the sight of the cat monk. To the left, Gonnokami and the cat journey to Mount Kōya, which has labels identifying some of its famous sites, such as Oku-no-in Hall, Shisho Myōjin Shrine, and the Sanko Pine.[1] The two animals pray together under a full moon and recite the following poems:

GONNOKAMI:

omoiki ya	Did I ever imagine
neko no obō to	that I would gaze
morotomo ni	upon the moon
Takano no oku no	in the depths of Takano
tsuki wo min to wa	together with a cat monk?

CAT MONK:

Nyūami yo	Oh meowse monk,
kakaru Takano no	look at the moon
tsuki wo miyo	above Takano.
akunen wa nashi	I have no evil intentions;
ware na osore so	fear me not.[2]

1. Kōya Shisho Myōjin is another name for Niutsuhime Shrine on Mount Kōya. The Sanko Pine is named after the *vajra* that, according to legend, Kūkai threw from Mañjuśrī's Pure Land to Japan.
2. The first line of the cat's poem seems to contain a pun on Nen'ami (Gonnokami's Buddhist name) and a cat's meow (*nyū . . .*). Likewise, both the *mi yo* at the end of the first line and the *miyo* (the imperative form of the verb "to look") in the third line suggest the voice of a cat.

293

Gonnokami immediately replied:

inishie no	I cannot forget
sono omokage no	the way you looked
wasurarede	in the past.
osore mōsu yo	I am still frightened,
neko no obō	oh cat priest!

Conversing in this way, they finally arrived at the Oku-no-in Hall.

TRANSLATION AND INTRODUCTION BY RACHEL STAUM MEI

The Tale of the Mouse

The Chrysanthemum Spirit

The Chrysanthemum Spirit (*Kiku no sei monogatari*), also known as *Lady Kazashi* or, literally, *The Girl with the Flower in Her Hair* (*Kazashi no himegimi*), recounts the love affair of a young lady whose intense longing for the quintessential autumn flower conjures up its manifestation in the form of a dashing courtier. Although the romance between the two ends tragically, the tale turns felicitous when a daughter born to the couple becomes an imperial consort and gives birth to descendants worthy of the Chrysanthemum Throne. The text, which was probably written in the middle to late Muromachi period (1337–1573), belongs to a long tradition of flower-spirit stories in East Asia, including ones of impregnation, but offers a new twist in its sustained treatment of a flower manifestation that is gendered male.[1] In the process, it provides a condensed lesson on life, love, and the poetic tradition.

A rich history of chrysanthemum symbolism structures the story and derives from ancient courtly associations established well before the flower became the official emblem of the imperial house in the nineteenth century. Legends that the chrysanthemum could bestow longevity on those who drink tea and wine made with its infusions, or water mingled with dew from its petals, originated on the continent and inspired the annual Chrysanthemum Festival on the ninth day of the ninth month in China and Japan. This led to associations of the chrysanthemum with the

---

The translation and illustrations are from the *Kiku no sei monogatari* picture scroll (late Muromachi period) in the collection of the Harvard Art Museums, typeset and annotated in Ichiko Teiji et al., eds., *Muromachi monogatari shū jō*, Shin Nihon koten bungaku taikei 54 (Tokyo: Iwanami Shoten, 1989), 291–309.

1. Stories in the poetic commentaries *Kokin wakashū sanjō shō* (*Third Avenue Notes on Kokin wakashū*) and *Rōeichū* (*Commentary on Wakan rōeishū*) include those of women who become pregnant after encounters with orchids, and in "The Cherry Tree Lover," a tale in *Ima monogatari* (*Tales of the Present*, ca. 1240), a lady famously uncovers her lover's floral identity when she stitches a thread to his sleeve, only to find that it has been sewn to a cherry in her garden. See Tokuda Kazuo, *Kazashi no himegimi*, in *Otogizōshi jiten* (Tokyo: Tōkyōdō Shuppan, 2002), 198–99.

longevity of the imperial line, as witnessed in the seventeen poems on the chrysanthemum in honor of Empress Shōshi (988–1074) and her imperial offspring in *Eiga
monogatari* (*Tale of Flowering Fortunes*, eleventh century). Japanese court poetry
also celebrated the white blossom's transformation to purple upon the first frost,
and likened its fading to the vicissitudes of love. *The Chrysanthemum Spirit* artfully
employs many of these tropes, along with puns on dewdrops; a description of the
man's purple robe in autumn, as if alluding to the flower's famous shifting of color;
and his "wilted" appearance on the eve of being plucked. Even the young woman's
name, Lady Kazashi, refers to flowers placed in the hair for adornment or in the
headdresses of court dancers as a part of courtly spectacle and ceremony.[2]

The small scroll in which this version of the story is recorded engages the reader
with nineteen colorful paintings and vibrant calligraphic texts while functioning as
something of a botanical primer in visual form.[3] The first painting in the scroll depicts
eleven varieties of autumnal flowers, including lantern plants with their papery orange
seed covers, bush clover, pampas grass, pinks, thoroughworts, and several varieties of
mums. The plants' charmingly anthropomorphized scale echoes the story's theme,
yet recalls flower-arranging manuals newly popular in the Muromachi period. As
both flower and pollinator, the personified chrysanthemum works didactically as
well. It provokes questions about the "birds and the bees," as when the flower-man
informs the lady that he has sown "a seedling in her womb," or in a conspicuous
birthing scene included among the paintings in the scroll. *The Chrysanthemum Spirit*
thus addresses readers on multiple levels, but first and foremost transforms a classical poetic trope on longevity into a spirited narrative tinged with the poignancy of
life's fleeting nature.

Long ago, in the vicinity of Fifth Avenue, there lived a man of great refinement
known as the Minamoto Middle Counselor. His wife was the daughter of the Lord

2. When Genji dances "Waves of the Blue Sea" before the emperor in the "Beneath the Autumn Leaves"
chapter of *The Tale of Genji* (early eleventh century), for example, a courtier places chrysanthemums in his
headdress to match his radiant face, creating an alignment among Genji, the chrysanthemum, and sover-
eignty that echoes the themes of *The Chrysanthemum Spirit*. *Kazashi no himegimi* is an alternative title for
this story in its other versions, but the title of the Harvard text seems to be the oldest, taken from the original label affixed to the mounting of the scroll.

3. The scroll in the Harvard Art Museums measures 17.2 centimeters (6¾ in.) in height and 748.7 centimeters
(294¾ in.) in length, small enough to fit comfortably in one's hands and short enough to be read in one
sitting. See Melissa McCormick, *Tosa Mitsunobu and the Small Scroll in Medieval Japan* (Seattle: University
of Washington Press, 2009).

Minister. They had one daughter, whose name was Lady Kazashi. She was a sight to behold with her lovely cascade of hair, beautiful brow, and shapely lips. In the spring, she spent her waking hours beneath the blossoming branches, and in the autumn, she spent her nights beneath the moon. She was forever composing poems and reciting verses on all sorts of flowers and grasses.

Above all, she adored the chrysanthemum. And during the ninth month, the "month of long nights," she found it nearly impossible to part from her garden. Indeed, this is how she spent the passing years.

Toward the end of autumn in her fourteenth year, the young lady felt an overwhelming sadness over the fading of the chrysanthemum flowers. In this melancholy state, she dozed off and beheld the dim outline of a man, no more than twenty years old, in a formal cap. He wore a pale-lavender hunting cloak and had a lightly powdered face, blackened teeth, and thickly drawn brows. The radiant bloom of

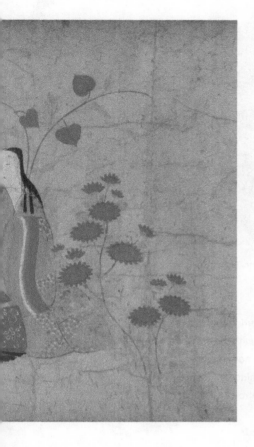

Lady Kazashi, accompanied by her attendant, visits her beloved chrysanthemums. (From *Kiku no sei monogatari*, courtesy of the Harvard Art Museums)

elegance about him was enough to make her think, "So this is what the famous Lord Narihira and the Shining Genji must have been like!"[4] He moved in close to embrace her. Was this dream or reality? The young lady no longer knew. As she got up with a start, the man held fast to her sleeve, saying, "Have you not one dewdrop of feeling for me?" He spoke tearfully, pouring out his heart, so that even the young lady could not remain unmoved.

Now deep in the night with their sashes undone, the man was elated. They talked until dawn about the events of the past and their future yet to come. When it became time to untangle their layered robes, he faced the young lady and tearfully pledged, "I will return another night":

4. Ariwara no Narihira (825–880) was a poet and the purported protagonist of *The Tales of Ise* (ca. tenth century). Like Genji of *The Tale of Genji*, he came to be recalled as a quintessential romantic hero.

The Chrysanthemum Spirit

A handsome stranger visits Lady Kazashi in the night. (From *Kiku no sei monogatari*, courtesy of the Harvard Art Museums)

uki koto wo	Enduring the pain of parting
shinobu ga moto no	beneath the grasses of remembrance,
asatsuyu no	the morning dew
okiwakarenan	forming and then leaving
koto zo kanashiki	is sorrowful indeed.

To which the young lady promptly replied:

sue made to	"Until the end of time"—
chigiri oku koso	to promise such love
hakanakere	seems fleeting indeed,
shinobu ga moto no	when I hear of the dew on chrysanthemums
tsuyu to kiku yori	beneath the grasses of remembrance.[5]

Having exchanged verses, the mysterious visitor left. He seemed to approach the chrysanthemums at the brushwood fence, whereupon he vanished without a trace.

The young lady felt increasingly unsettled, but there was no one reliable in whom she could confide. Despite her best efforts to overcome it, their bond formed on that first encounter proved far from shallow, and they continued to meet in secret. Night

---

5. In her response, the young lady posits that it is the man's vow as much as the dew that is unreliable. There is a pun on the word *kiku*, which means both "to hear" and "chrysanthemum."

The handsome stranger vanishes beside a bed of chrysanthemums. (From *Kiku no sei monogatari*, courtesy of the Harvard Art Museums)

after night they spent, until one day, the young lady ventured, "What is it that you conceal from me even now? Come, let me know your name." Seemingly flustered, the man replied, "In these parts, I am known as the Lesser Captain. In time, you will come to understand." Then he departed.

Around that time, it was announced that there would be a flower display at the palace. Various courtiers were summoned, and the young lady's father, the Middle Counselor, attended as well. Calling the Middle Counselor before him, the emperor said, "Bring me chrysanthemum flowers the likes of which are rarely seen in this world." The Middle Counselor, powerless to refuse an imperial command, replied that he would bring the chrysanthemums and returned home.

Toward the evening of the same day, the Lesser Captain, looking unusually withered, came to the west wing of the young lady's residence. He spoke on and on about the ephemeral things of this world and then burst into tears. Because he appeared so inexplicably anguished, the young lady was moved to ask, "What is tormenting you so? Open your heart and tell me everything." She implored him throughout the night, until he responded, "Why bother keeping anything from you now? Even my visits will end today. How sad to realize that what I thought should have endured for many lives to come has turned to naught!" Silently he wept. "How can this be?" exclaimed the young lady. "I have relied on you so completely; what will

The Chrysanthemum Spirit

The Middle Counselor presents his chrysanthemums at the palace. (From *Kiku no sei monogatari,* courtesy of the Harvard Art Museums)

become of me now? How can you say such things? You must take me with you, whether to the end of the fields or deep into the mountains!" There was an unrestrained sadness in her voice. "It is not as I would have wanted . . . ," said the Lesser Captain, who had run out of words.

A while later, the Lesser Captain choked back his tears and said, "I shall swiftly take my leave. Do not forget. Do not forget. As for me, how could I ever let the memory of your affections disappear?" Having said this, he cut off a side lock, pressed it into a delicate paper embellished with background designs, and wrapped it up. "Whenever you think of me, look upon this," he said, presenting it to the young lady. "And in the womb, I have left behind a seedling that you should raise ever so carefully. May the child remind you of me." With these words he departed, weeping as he went. The young lady moved quietly to the edge of the blinds to see him off, thinking that he might pause at the garden's brushwood fence. But she could see nothing.

And so night turned into dawn. The Middle Counselor presented the chrysanthemums to the emperor, who could not take his eyes off them.

The young lady waited until evening, but the Lesser Captain never reappeared, not even in her dreams. Oh, how woeful! Although the moon shone through the treetops against the clear midnight sky, tears clouded her heart. She spent night after long sleepless night, until one day she took out the keepsake the man had instructed her to use as a memento. Overwhelmed with emotion, she opened it and discovered a single poem:

nioi wo ba	The fragrance
kimi ga tamoto ni	on your sleeves
nokoshiokite	I left behind—
ada ni utsurou	how it withers in vain,
kiku no hana kana	the chrysanthemum flower!

What she had taken to be a lock of his black hair had all along been a wilted chrysanthemum flower. She felt more unsettled than ever, and thought to herself, "Then even the leaves of verse left behind were composed by none other than the spirit of the chrysanthemum."

Making her way into a garden of white chrysanthemums, she cried, "The poet wrote that 'the blossoms may scatter, but the roots will never die,'⁶ and thus your fate is known. Even if you are a chrysanthemum spirit, I beseech you to exchange with me your leaves of verse just once more." She appeared at her wits end, and the reason was all too clear. "If there had been no flower-gathering at the palace, then I would have no such despair. Whatever the case may be, I am not long for this world." To even contemplate such thoughts was excruciating.

"Hurry, hurry, come to me, Lesser Captain! In whose care will you leave me? Oh, where could you be? The sadness of our mortal lives! Although you said again and again that this was the end, I assumed you were just talking about the ordinary fleetingness of the world. How can this be? Oh, how wretched! Am I dreaming or awake?" She went on and on, bewildered, sinking to the ground in despair. He had left her with only instructions never to forget. Now it was clear that those had indeed been his final parting words. Distraught, she continued, "Alas, I will give my

6. This is a slightly garbled reference to poem 268 in *Kokin wakashū* (*Collection of Ancient and Modern Poems*, ca. 905), attributed to Ariwara no Narihira. The headnote reads, "A poem sent attached to chrysanthemums for a person's garden":

ueshi ueba	If firmly planted,
aki naki toki ya	only without autumn
sakazaran	will it fail to bloom;
hana koso chirame	the blossoms may scatter,
ne sae kareme ya	but the roots will never die.

The poem is the first of thirteen on the chrysanthemum in the Autumn section of *Kokin wakashū*. It also appears in section 163 of *Yamato monogatari* (*The Tales of Yamato*, tenth century) and in section 51 of *Ise monogatari* (*The Tales of Ise*, ca. tenth century).

The spirit medium divines. (From *Kiku no sei monogatari*, courtesy of the Harvard Art Museums)

life for that fragile vow! Let us see each other once more!" She was in a certain maternal condition and grieved ceaselessly the entire time. How sad her nurse must have been to see the young lady so distressed.

After the nurse told the young lady's mother the state of things, she and the Middle Counselor were beside themselves. They tried to help in whatever way they could, but to no avail.

The nurse sought the help of a spirit medium, saying, "My young lady, just fifteen years of age, has been ill ever since the evening of the last day of the ninth month. Just what should we do? Please perform a divination."

The spirit master spoke: "The divination you ask for is difficult to read. Could she perhaps be in a certain condition? However viewed, the signs suggest peril."[7] The nurse rushed back home with an eerie feeling and relayed all of this to the young lady's mother. The lady responded, "I, too, suspected that she might be in that way, but naturally I hesitated to speak up, assuming that you would know of such a thing. What if they meet again? Go question her thoroughly."

7. The diviner employs bundles of bamboo sticks laid out for the *bokuzei* method of divination based on the *Yijing*. The painting in the scroll clearly shows six bundles of three sticks arranged in a pattern on the ground.

Heeding her words, the nurse headed for the adjacent quarters and went straight to the young lady's side. "By the looks of you," she said, "you do not seem at all like your usual self. There must be something you are concealing from me." Continuing in a delicate whisper, she said, "Please, open up your heart." The young lady knew that it should remain a secret, but she longed to talk about it. Although deeply embarrassed, she recounted the affair from beginning to end, sparing no detail. The nurse was astonished.

The nurse and the young lady's mother approached the Middle Counselor to inform him of the situation. "This is an unthinkable disgrace!" he responded. "And just when I had been consumed with arranging her entry into court service! I have no desire to abandon that now," he said, and dropped the matter.

The days and months slowly passed, and the young lady grew ever weaker and more helpless. Then, with her own nurse and numerous ladies attending to the delivery, she bore a beautiful baby girl. The Middle Counselor and his wife felt boundless affection for the child. And yet the young lady seemed to be nearing the end.

The Middle Counselor and his wife were beside themselves with grief. The young lady had her mother and father brought near, and she tearfully addressed them, saying, "Take that truism to heart, that all living things must one day vanish, and do not lament my passing. What matters most is the little girl whom I leave behind in this world. Although I myself will have passed away, please do not forget her. I am overcome with regret that I must precede my mother and father on this journey. How wretched you must think me. It is excruciating indeed to leave behind so many people, but most of all my mother and father." Uttering these final words, she faded with the morning dew. The Middle Counselor and his wife were at a complete loss. The nurse, immersed in grief, swiftly took the tonsure. Such a profoundly moving thing is difficult to put into words.

Since they could not simply leave her as she was, they tearfully sent her remains to the moor, where the smoke from her pyre evoked the evanescence of this world. When they had completed her funerary rites, they turned their attention to the granddaughter and lavished her with care. With each passing year, she became more and more the living image of her mother. Cherishing her, they appointed a wealth of young women to her service. The days and months passed, and at the age of seven she donned her first trousers.[8]

---

8. She performed the *hakama gi* (donning of the trousers), a rite that marked the passage from toddler to young girl in which a child was first dressed in split, pleated trousers.

The Chrysanthemum Spirit

The years went by, and before they knew it, the girl turned thirteen. Her looks were exquisite. "Surely she would surpass the likes of Yang Guifei of Tang, Lady Li of Han, or, in our land, Princess Sotoori and Ono no Komachi!" the people all exclaimed.[9] Before long, word of her beauty had reached the ears of the emperor. By his order, she was made a consort. The Middle Counselor and his wife were overjoyed.

9. Yang Guifei (719–756), Lady Li (Li Furen; second century B.C.E.), Sotoorihime (Princess Sotoori; fifth century), and Ono no Komachi (ca. 825–ca. 900) were famous beauties of China and Japan. In particular, Sotoorihime is described in *Nihon shoki* (*The Chronicles of Japan*, 720) as having been so brilliant that her beauty shone through her clothes like light.

304

Lady Kazashi bears a child. (From *Kiku no sei monogatari*, courtesy of the Harvard Art Museums)

Rumor had it that the emperor loved her above all others. His feelings for her grew only deeper, and before long a prince and a princess were born in quick succession. Everyone remarked how truly fortunate this was.

Because this story is so unusual, I have recorded it for posterity.

TRANSLATION AND INTRODUCTION BY MELISSA McCORMICK

The Chrysanthemum Spirit

The Tale of Tamamizu

In Japanese and Chinese folklore, foxes are notorious for their shape-shifting powers and their penchant for deceiving and seducing humans. The carnal threat that they typically pose to unsuspecting men results from the danger implied by transgression of the bestiality taboo, which, if such stories are to be believed, frequently results in death, for either the man or the fox. In *Konjaku monogatari shū* (*Tales of Times Now Past*, twelfth century), for example, foxes can be good, bad, or simply mischievous, but in their personified forms they are usually depicted as attractive young women who engage with men.

In *The Tale of Tamamizu* (*Tamamizu monogatari*), a male fox falls in love with a young woman, but in order to insinuate himself into her world, he assumes the identity of a teenage lady-in-waiting—the lovely Tamamizu-no-mae, or simply Tamamizu—in an alluringly feminine form more usually associated with his vulpine kind. Like the malevolent Lady Tamamo in her eponymous tale, the gender-bending Tamamizu possesses superhuman erudition, but unlike his notorious counterpart, who sets out to seduce the emperor and destroy the state, Tamamizu wishes only the best for his love. Torn between his affection and his realization of the hazard that it implies, he finds himself trapped in his own web of lies, incapable of consummating the affair or admitting the truth. His plight is a poignant one, as he himself is all too aware. *The Tale of Tamamizu* survives in multiple illustrated manuscripts from the late medieval (1185–1600) and/or early Edo (1600–1867) periods, suggesting its popularity among readers of the age.

The translation and illustrations are from the two-volume *Tamamizu monogatari* manuscript (undated) in the collection of the Kyoto University Library, typeset in Yokoyama Shigeru and Matsumoto Ryūshin, eds., *Muromachi jidai monogatari taisei* (Tokyo: Kadokawa Shoten, 1980), 8:570–84.

It must have been some time ago when, in the area of Toba, there lived a man named the Takayanagi Captain. He had no children, despite being over thirty years of age. He wondered why this was so, and it grieved him. He prayed to the gods and buddhas, and perhaps as an answer to his prayers, his wife began to look pregnant. His joy knew no bounds. In due course, a daughter was born to them, around the beginning of the eleventh month. They treasured and raised her as though she were a jewel in their arms. Blessed with the twenty-five features of feminine beauty,[1] she was truly radiant to behold. *what are they*

The months and years passed until she was fourteen or fifteen years old. Setting her heart on the sweeping wind and the lapping waves, she composed Japanese and Chinese verse. Somehow, even the household was more refined by her presence, and in *me* their gratitude her father and mother thought the world of her. Cherishing her all the more, they thought that they might send her to serve at court. Because she had such a sensitive nature, she was captivated by the blooming and scattering of the flowers in her garden, as well as by the mist that spread over the mountains in all directions.

One evening, the young lady went out into her flower garden with a single attendant named Tsukisae, the child of her wet nurse. They amused themselves, taking pleasure in the flowers, without a care in the world.

Many foxes lived in this area, and on this occasion, one of them happened to be in the garden and gazed at the young lady. He thought to himself, "Oh, how lovely! If only I could see her sometimes, even from afar." Crouching behind a tree, his heart was all aflutter. He was frighteningly taken with the lady. Eventually she went back inside, and the fox, thinking better of remaining where he was, also returned to his den.

The fox reflected intensely on his situation: "For what sin in a past life have I been reborn like this, as an animal? Ever since I first saw that gorgeous lady, I've been wasting away from love. How sad that I am likely to fade away for nothing!"

As he lay brooding, weeping a torrent of quiet tears, he thought to himself, "If only I could change into a nobleman and meet with that lady!" But then he reconsidered: "If I were to meet with her, it would certainly mean her ruin. Her parents would grieve, and how sad to think that I would be the death of her unparalleled

---

1. The twenty-five features (normally thirty-two) are derived from the belief that a buddha has thirty-two distinguishing physical characteristics. In this case, the thirty-two features seem to have been conflated with the twenty-five bodhisattvas.

The Tale of Tamamizu

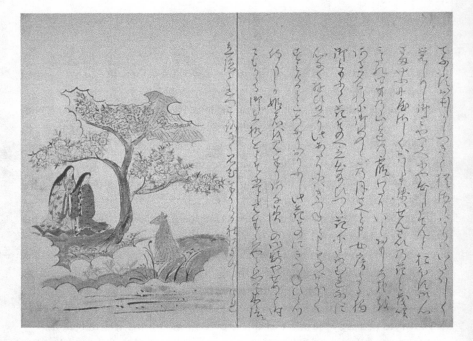

A fox spies the daughter of the Takayanagi Captain, together with her maid. (From *Tamamizu monogatari*, courtesy of the Kyoto University Library)

beauty!" His thoughts were in turmoil as he mulled the problem. Passing his days without a bite to eat, he lay in a state of utter exhaustion.

Thinking that he might see her again, he limped out to the flower garden. But someone saw him, and one day he was pelted with stones. On another day, someone shot at him with blunt wooden arrows. It was pitiful how his heart pined all the more. Unable to fade away like the dew or the frost, he wretchedly thought to himself, "Somehow, if I could just be by her side and see her morning and night, what a comfort it would be!"

There was a certain household that had many sons, but no daughters. Morning and evening, the master's wife lamented, saying, "If only I had just one girl among all these children!" Hearing this, the fox transformed into a lovely fourteen- or fifteen-year-old maiden. He went to the house and said, "I am from the area around the western part of the capital, but I've been orphaned, and without anyone to rely on, I took to the road. I've wandered all this way, and since I have no place to go, please take me in and let me be a part of your family."

The master's wife took one look at her and said, "Oh, dear, you're no ordinary girl at all! How on earth could you wander all this way? Please think of me as your mother. We have many sons, but no daughters, though I've wanted one day and night."

"That makes me so happy, since I have nowhere else to go!" the fox replied. The master's wife was overjoyed, and she took him in with kindness and consideration. "Now, if only I could introduce her to some man or other . . . ," she thought, and she busied herself with this goal in mind.

However, this new "daughter" showed no sign of settling in, and she would occasionally burst into tears. The master's wife tried to comfort her, saying, "Now, dear, if there's a man, you just tell me. Don't keep it to yourself."

"Oh, no, it's nothing like that at all," the fox replied. "I feel surprisingly wretched, and being depressed like this, it wouldn't do at all for me to be seen by a man. I would just like to serve at the side of a lovely young mistress."

Disguised as a young lady, the fox speaks with her adoptive human mother. (From *Tamamizu monogatari*, courtesy of the Kyoto University Library)

The Tale of Tamamizu

Her adoptive mother replied, "Well, I've often said that I'd like to set you up in a good household, and if you think so, too, I shouldn't oppose your wishes. Lord Takayanagi's daughter is very sweet and kind. My younger sister serves her as a lady-in-waiting, so I think I'll ask her about it. If there's anything on your mind, please tell me. I don't think I'd say no." When the fox heard this, he was very happy.

As they were discussing the situation, the mother's sister came over. When the mother had explained everything, she replied, "I'll bring it up with the household." She returned to the lord's mansion and asked the young lady's wet nurse, who answered, "Well, then, send her here as soon as you can!"

The fox was overjoyed, and he made himself up and left right away. He looked so beautiful that even his new young mistress was pleased, and she gave him the serving name Tamamizu-no-mae. Tamamizu was gentle and kind in whatever he did and was at his mistress's side day and night in all her amusements. He served her food and drink, and, just like Tsukisae, would lie down with her under her bedclothes, never leaving the young lady's side.

Now, whenever a dog came onto the grounds, Tamamizu would turn pale, and every hair on his—now her—body would stand on end. She would be unable to eat a thing and looked so pitiful that her mistress felt sorry for her and banned dogs from the household. There were doubtless others in the place who resented her, thinking, "She's such a pathetic coward! I wish the mistress thought of me like that."

Time passed, and around the middle of the fifth month, there was a night when the moon was especially, perfectly bright. The young mistress crept out to the edge of her blinds and gazed up at it. Cuckoos were singing, and it was so lovely that she composed the first part of a poem:

hototogisu	The cuckoo,
kumoi no yoso ni	out there among the clouds,
ne wo zo naku	calling out in song—

Tamamizu immediately capped the verse with the lines,

fukaki omoi no	I wonder if its longing
tagui naruran	is just as deep as mine?

She had suddenly given voice to the feelings that were in her heart.

"What do you mean?" the lady replied. "I'd like to know what you're thinking. Is it love or jealousy? It's so strange!" The mistress composed,

samidare no	In the season of
hodo wa kumoi no	the early summer rains,
hototogisu	you cuckoo in the clouds—
ta ga omoine no	whose love do you know,
iro wo shiruran	whose longing in the night?[2]

Tamamizu immediately responded with:

kokoro kara	Emerging from
kumoi wo idete	the clouds inside my heart,
hototogisu	the cuckoo—
itsu wo kagiri to	when, I wonder,
ne wo ya nakuran	will it stop singing its song?

Tsukisae composed:

obotsukana	Somehow or other
yama no ha izuru	it reaches from the moon
tsuki yori mo	as it crests the mountain's rim:
nao nakiwataru	the solitary cry
tori no hitogoe	of a bird.

They composed poems like this until the night grew late and the young lady went back inside. However, saying that the moon was still high, Tamamizu stayed outside. She thought deeply about her past and future: "I wonder when and how it will all come to an end for me?" Her tears spilled out unexpectedly, and she could only try to wring them dry. She composed:

omoiki ya	Could I have thought it—
Inari no yama wo	that I would be gazing out
yoso ni mite	at Mount Inari,[3]
kumoi haruka no	and at the distant moon
tsuki wo miru to ya	up there beyond the clouds?

2. The word *omoine* (longing in one's sleep) contains the word *ne* ("chirp" or "cry"), which suggests the cuckoo's song.
3. Foxes are traditionally associated with Mount Inari and its Fushimi Inari Shrine.

The Tale of Tamamizu

She composed another poem:

kokoro kara	Emerging from
kumoi wo idete	the clouds inside my heart,
mochizuki no	the full moon—
tamoto ni kage wo	I wish that somehow it could
sasu yoshi mogana	shine its light upon my sleeve!

And another:

kokoro kara	These tears of love
koi no namida wo	that pour from my heart:
sekitomete	to hold them back,
mi no ukishizumu	I'd bob and sink . . .
koto zo yoshinaki	and that won't do at all![4]

Tamamizu had been out for so long that Tsukisae became concerned. She went back outside and heard Tamamizu murmuring these things to herself. Thinking it strange, she inquired with a poem:

yoso nite mo	Even from afar,
aware to zo kiku	it makes me sorry for you!
tare yue ni	For whose sake
koi no namida ni	will you sink and drown
mi wo shizumuran	in tears of love?

Their mistress heard them and said:

ōkata no	Do you think that
aware wa tare mo	nobody knows what it means
shirazu ya to	to feel sorrow,
mi ni wa narawanu	though they may be unfamiliar
koiji naredomo	with the path of love?

4. The phrase *mi no uki* (wretched self) is contained within *mi no ukishizumu* (a body [would] float and sink), adding to the density of the verse.

The mistress said, "It's grown so late already! Do come inside." Tamamizu returned, weeping all the while, and together with Tsukisae she lay down beside her mistress. But perhaps because she had no way to express her troubled thoughts, she was unable to sleep.

The days passed until the eighth month arrived. The cries of the first geese echoed through the sky, seeming to pierce Tamamizu to the quick. She felt as if they were asking after her sorrow. Meanwhile, Tamamizu's adoptive mother sent her constant messages and doted on her more than even a real parent would. In addition to her regular attire, she sent her some lovely clothing. In one of her letters, she complained, "Why don't you come and see me sometimes? It would be a comfort. I lie awake at night thinking that you are treating me so coldly because I am not your real mother."

Tamamizu replied, "I, too, pass the time somehow or other, asking myself about the shallowness of my heart.[5] How sad it is to hear you say that it is because you are not my true parent!" Her adoptive mother saw this and realized that of course Tamamizu must feel that way, and she wept.

Three years later, in the eleventh month, many of the young lady's close friends came to visit. They decided to have an autumn leaf–matching contest. Thinking to find the most beautifully colored leaves for her mistress the next day, Tamamizu slipped outside in the dark of night and turned back into her—now his—original form. He went to the mound on the south side of the Toba mansion where his older and younger brothers lived. When they saw him, they were overjoyed and said, "Hey, where did you come from? We thought you were dead! It's been three years since we held services for you."

"I've been serving at the mansion," he explained. "Quiet down, and I'll tell you all about it. But first, there's something important going on tomorrow so I've come here to look for autumn leaves. Everyone, please help me find some."

"That's easy!" his brothers replied. "After all, is there anywhere in the mountains we haven't been?"

Tamamizu was delighted. "Great! Then please put them on the veranda on the south wing of Takayanagi's mansion."

"No problem. But are there any dogs there?"

"No, they don't have dogs. Don't worry about that." Having given those instructions, he returned to the mansion.

5. We have translated this and some subsequent passages from the two-volume *Tamamizu monogatari* in the collection of the Kyoto University Kokugogaku Kokubungaku Kenkyūshitsu, which in some cases seems to be clearer than the Kyoto University Library text. See Kyoto Daigaku Bungakubu Kokugogaku Kokubungaku Kenkyūshitsu, ed., *Kyoto daigaku zō Muromachi monogatari* (Kyoto: Rinsen Shoten, 2000), 12:375.

The Tale of Tamamizu

"Where have you been?" the young mistress and Tsukisae inquired, which was unusual for them. Jesting, Tamamizu smiled and replied, "Oh, I had a rendezvous with a dubious fellow this evening."

"Really? That might be so, since you were gone such a long time!"

They carried on in this way until her mistress teased Tamamizu, saying, "Well, if that's true, you must really hate me now! Since it's a fact that people's feelings change, I must be banished from your thoughts."

Tamamizu was overjoyed, but also disturbed. "Oh, no, how embarrassing," Tamamizu replied. "Although I am hardly a person fit to be in society, as for leaving your side and taking up with someone else, I could never do that!"

"Well, it's hard to tell . . . ," her mistress said, and the sight of her smile cut Tamamizu to the core. Tamamizu felt utterly dejected.

Meanwhile, Tamamizu's brothers had gone into the mountains looking for leaves. Among them, his next-younger brother found some six-inch branches, the five-colored leaves of which were all rubbed with the characters of the Lotus Sutra. They stood out brightly as if burnished into place.

At around noon the next day, Tamamizu went outside and discovered ten branches with leaves, which she brought to her mistress. "What's this?" the young lady exclaimed. "Could there really be such things in the world? I've never seen the like!" In her joy, she praised them to the stars. Others, too, offered her a multitude of leaves, but how could theirs have compared?

"Now, since everyone is required to attach poems to their autumn leaves," the young lady instructed, "Tamamizu, you'll have to compose some, too."

"But I thought you'd judge them as they are!" Tamamizu protested. Her mistress pressed the point, and Tamamizu thought, "In that case, I'd like to write out some poems for her to read. She's sure to correct anything that might be wrong."

Tamamizu took up her brush and began to write. The master, too, came over to see the leaves, and he was deeply impressed. After he left, his wife came over as well. Meanwhile, Tamamizu wrote out her verses and presented them to her mistress. Saying that they were all charming, the young lady attached the five poems to five of the branches.

On the branch with green leaves:

momijiba no	These autumn leaves
iro wa midori ni	have all turned green—
narinikeri	examples of things
ikuchiyo made mo	that never disappear
tsukinu tameshi ni	over many thousands of ages.

Tamamizu and her mistress prepare for the autumn leaf–matching contest. (From *Tamamizu monogatari*, courtesy of the Kyoto University Library)

On the branch with golden leaves:

ki naru made	The color of
momiji no iro wa	these autumn leaves, it seems,
utsuru nari	has turned to gold.
waga hito kaku wa	But my darling's feelings
kokoro kawaraji	won't change in this way![6]

On the branch with red leaves:

kurenai ni	By how many tides
ikushio made ka	must these leaves have been dyed
sometsuran	to turn scarlet?

---

6. The last two lines of the poem are ambiguous. Alternatively translated, they might read, "May my feelings for another not change like this!"

The Tale of Tamamizu

iro no fukasa wa	The depth of their color
tagui araji wo	must have no match!

On the branch with white leaves:

nobe no iro	Though the fields
mina shirotae ni	should all turn white
narinu to mo	as mulberry cloth,
kono momijiba no	the color of these autumn leaves
iro wa kawaraji	will surely never change.

On the branch with purple leaves:

ikushio ni	In how many tides
somekaeshite ka	must they have been soaked,
murasaki no	for all of the tips
yomo no kozue wo	of the purple branches
somewatasuran	to be stained through and through?

These were Tamamizu's poems; her mistress wrote the rest.

Finally, the day of the contest arrived. When they judged the leaves, taking a great deal of care in reading their poems and arranging their extraordinarily colored sprays, not a single one could compare with those of the young mistress. Even though they were matched five times, every time she emerged victorious.

Word spread, and it even reached the palace, from which came a summons for the leaves. Having no reason to refuse, Lord Takayanagi sent them right away. The emperor saw them and informed the regent that the young mistress should be sent to him immediately.

"Although he should, no doubt, be delighted to send his daughter to court," the regent replied, "the Takayanagi Captain is a man of limited means, and it may be difficult for him to do so." The emperor immediately understood, and he bestowed on him three estates. As this was something that Lord Takayanagi had wanted from before, his joy was boundless.

The preparations were splendid, and Tamamizu's feelings were beyond compare. The emperor granted her a place named Kakuta in Settsu Province as her own estate. "Being an orphan," she said, "how happy I am to be favored with your grace! It's beyond my wildest dreams." She expressed her thanks repeatedly, but people said spiteful things about her anyway. "In that case," she thought, "I'll give the property to my adoptive parents," and she did. Her mother and father were enormously pleased.

Sometime later, her mother fell ill, as if she were possessed. The family offered a multitude of prayers, but as the days and months passed, she seemed to grow only worse. Her father and her children were consumed with grief. "My daughter, serving at the Takayanagi mansion—," she said, "I'd like to meet with her just this once. I miss her all the time, and I really want to see her." Someone conveyed her request to Tamamizu, and feeling very sorry for her mother, she asked for some time away from her duties.

When Tamamizu arrived, her mother was delighted. "From what bond in a previous life does my heart ache for you alone, morning and night?" she exclaimed. "I fret about how long even your period of service will last! Thanks to you, I was able to get along with some peace of mind, and for that I am grateful and glad. But then, to suddenly come down with an ailment like this that almost no one survives! And the sadness of leaving you behind . . ." The mother stretched out a wasted hand, stroked her daughter's hair, and wept. The girl was at a loss for words. She could only cry. Since Tamamizu was by their mother's side, the other children felt free to rest for a while, and they took their ease.

In her more lucid moments, the mother would speak of how sad she was, but when her illness seemed to worsen from time to time, she would appear to be possessed, like someone not of this world. She grew worse, but then rallying a little bit, she said, "Being in such a state, I'm sure to die in the end. You poor thing! When I am no longer of this world, who will you have to be your mother? I have a mirror left to me by my own mother, and since I've been thinking these days that my time has come, I want you to take it as a keepsake." With that, she gave the mirror to Tamamizu. "Now get back to the mansion," she urged. However, Tamamizu could not bring herself to leave her mother, and before long she had been there for three days.

There was a letter from Tamamizu's mistress: "It must be painful for you, your mother being ill. But if she gets a little better, then please return at once. I need you to dispel the boredom around here. I feel dreadfully gloomy." The young lady had appended a poem:

toshi wo furu	When the aged leaves
ha wa sono kaze ni	(your elderly mother)
sasowareba	are beckoned by the wind,
nokoru kozue mo	What will become of the branches,
ika ni narinan	the child left behind?[7]

7. The poem contains puns on *haha* はは (mother) and *ha wa* はは (leaves + subject particle marker), and on *nokoru ko* (remaining child) and *nokoru kozue* (remaining tips of branches).

The Tale of Tamamizu

Tamamizu's mother perused the letter for a little while, and her spirits improved. "What a gracious thing for her to say!" she cried. "If it weren't for your service, how would she even know of my existence in the world? In any case, I'm deeply grateful. I think far more of you than any of the children I've borne myself." She was very pleased.

Tsukisae had also written out a poem:

hatsuhana no	In her suffering
tsubomeru iro no	for the tint
kurushisa ni	of the first budding flowers,
ika ni ko no ha no	how is it for the mother-leaf
iro wo mikiku ni	to hear of their hue?[8]

But even upon seeing these words, Tamamizu's mood did not brighten. In her reply, she wrote, "I could never fully express, or even put on paper, the gracious kindness of your letter. There is never a time when you are not in my thoughts, and although I would like to return to you, it would be too hard to abandon my mother. If she gets even a little bit better, I will return and tell you all these things myself.

chirinubeki	If the wind blows
oiki no hana no	through the fragile blossoms
kaze fukaba	of the aged tree,
nokoru kozue mo	even the remaining branches,
araji to zo omou	I think, will ill survive."

To Tsukisae, too, she likewise replied:

kage tanomu	When the moldering cherry
kuchiki no sakura	on whose shade they once relied

8. The word *ko no ha* (tree leaf) suggests the homonymic *ko no ha* (leaves of the child) and *ko no haha* (mother of the child). In the text of *Momiji awase* (*The Contest of Autumn Leaves*), a variant of *The Tale of Tamamizu* in the Kyoto University Library, Tsukisae's poem reads:

hatsuhana no	In her affinity
tsubomeru iro no	for the tint
yukashisa ni	of the first budding flowers,
ika ni kozue no	how she must hate to leave
yo wo oshimuran	the world of the branches!

As in her mistress's poem, the word *kozue* (tips of branches) contains the word *ko* (child). See *Momiji awase*, in *Muromachi jidai monogatari taisei*, ed. Yokoyama Shigeru and Matsumoto Ryūshin (Tokyo: Kadokawa Shoten, 1985), 13:195a.

kuchihateba	rots and disappears,
tsubomeru hana no	even the budding flowers' hue
iro mo nokoraji	will likely not remain.

She sent these back to the capital.

At around that time, the mother's affliction took a turn for the worse, and the family gathered together and grieved. But she soon seemed to rest a little easier, and everyone relaxed. As the night deepened and the house grew quiet, only Tamamizu remained awake. She suddenly saw a bald old fox, without a single hair, drawing near. Looking closely, she realized that it was her father's brother. She called it away from her mother, whereupon the ailing woman settled in her sleep.

"How strange!" they both exclaimed. "What are you doing here?" Being herself a young fox, Tamamizu said, "Due to a certain little circumstance, I've come to rely on this woman as my mother. So please stay away from her and stop this suffering!"

"Absolutely not!" the old fox replied. "The reason is this: her father killed my child, who I was depending on, for no particular reason. So why shouldn't I show him how it feels? I am going to break his heart by sickening his daughter and taking her life."

"That makes sense," Tamamizu said, "but being pulled by our karma,[9] we wander lost through the Six Realms of Darkness. Because of our transgressions, we return to the same old Three Evil Realms,[10] where flames erupt from our bodies. We are animals and therefore still remain mired in our karma. But even so, if we should plant good karmic roots, then why shouldn't we be reborn as humans next time? What's more, the human form is the form of the Buddha. So if our hearts don't stray, then why wouldn't we become buddhas the next time around? In this brief life of ours, if we let ourselves be pulled by a momentary thought—if you cause this woman's death—you'll have to bear both the sin of your deed and the weight of many people's grief. Everything has its consequences, and as a result you, too, might end up falling prey to a hunter. And even if you don't, see how quickly you return to the Three Evil Realms! Just leave this woman alone and save her life!"

The old fox glared and said, "It's for those who are born into the human realm to follow the teachings of the buddhas. That's why the buddhas, too, sometimes appear

319

9. Tamamizu recites what seems to be a garbled quotation from an unknown sutra, which we have glossed over in the translation.

10. The Six Realms of Darkness are the six planes of existence through which unenlightened sentient beings transmigrate according to their karma. They include the Three Evil Realms of animals, hungry ghosts, and hell.

The Tale of Tamamizu

in the world and snatch away people's lives. For me, this is no sin! People bring it on themselves, which is why it's no fault of mine. I could sit and meditate all day, but I wouldn't find any karmic seeds in my heart. By knowing moral principle, we take it to heart, and by taking the measure of principle and thinking it through, we make non-arising thought our principle. By sweeping away thought, we create virtue. Unless you understand this enemy, nothing you might believe will be of any use.

"The Engi emperor behaved with restraint until the end of his days, but because of the karma from his past, he fell to the depths of the Hell of No Respite.[11] His foremost prince, the holy man Kōya Shōnin, was a man who turned his back on worldly ways, and people say that, following a revelation in a dream, he used a pair of metal tongs to pluck his father's body—a thing like a large lump of charcoal—from the bottom of that abyss.[12] So not even such a splendid emperor could escape the karma of his previous lives.

"Then there was the great snake that lived on Mount Shosha in Harima Province. He heard someone chanting the Lotus Sutra when he went looking for baby sparrows, and because of that, he was reborn as the empress of Emperor Shōmu.[13] Now, if we dispel evil thoughts, cultivate a desire for enlightenment, and trust in the name of Amida Buddha, which guides even those sinners who are guilty of the ten wicked and five heinous crimes, then our rebirth in the next life will be ensured. Nevertheless, since you and I are both animals, we share the same karma and will experience the same effects. Which one of us, then, ought to preach to the other?"

"You know reason exceptionally well," Tamamizu replied. "But your shape-shifting plan to take on the powers of a buddha is a one-time trick. One of Hōnen's sayings sticks in my ears: that to learn and ask is to abhor neither good nor evil.[14] When it comes to sin, right and wrong play no part. It is precisely because Prince Siddhârtha, the son of King Śuddhodana, left the royal palace that he became Shakyamuni Buddha.

"To distinguish between good and evil requires the karma to do so. If you take revenge on the enemy of your child, that would be evil. If you save her, that would be good. To determine good and evil in this case, then consider: Is your desire to kill

---

11. The Engi emperor was Emperor Daigo (885–930, r. 897–930). The Hell of No Respite (Muken jigoku, Skt. Avīci) is the deepest and worst of the eight burning hells, where evildoers are tortured constantly without interruption.

12. According to *The Contest of Autumn Leaves*, it was Daigo's "only child, the holy man Hōin Shōnin," who plucked him out of hell. See *Momiji awase*, in *Muromachi jidai monogatari taisei*, ed. Yokoyama and Matsumoto, 13:196b.

13. Mount Shosha is the site of Enkyōji Temple. Emperor Shōmu (701–756) reigned from 724 to 749.

14. Hōnen (1133–1212) is traditionally recognized as the founder of the Pure Land sect of Japanese Buddhism. He appears, in this volume, as a character in *Little Atsumori*.

the woman beyond thought? Rather, it is an undispelled thought. But if you can give up these wishes, then that is enlightenment. And to attain buddhahood in this very body is desirable indeed. You shouldn't indulge in all the ten wicked and five heinous crimes and then seek to rely on Amida Buddha's teachings. If you don't resolve to do more, they will be of no avail."

The old fox hung his head and nodded. "To encounter such wondrous wisdom must be my good fortune from a previous life," he said. "Indeed, even if I were to kill this woman, it wouldn't bring back my beloved child. Please pray for my child now with all your heart! I am going to become a monk, hide away in the deep mountains, and recite the *nenbutsu*."[15] He left the sick woman and withdrew. The mother thought that her daughter had been speaking with a person all this time.

Soon the sick mother began to feel better, and she spoke. When she heard that something had taken hold of her, she said that she had seen her assailant, although the daughter in whom she confided was the same sort of beast. "Truly, such things do occur," Tamamizu replied, and she prayed for the dead fox that had been shot and performed all manner of services on its behalf. With her heart at ease, she left her mother and returned to the mansion.

The eleventh month had now arrived, and the ceremonies for the young lady's Procession to the Palace were magnificent to behold. Out of her mistress's thirty ladies-in-waiting and young attendants, Tamamizu was designated Lady Middle Captain, first among the women. But she was not particularly pleased, and when her mistress asked her about her persistent melancholy, she put her off, saying that she felt as if she somehow had a cold.

"You do seem to have something on your mind," her mistress maintained. "Why do you keep it to yourself when I hold you in such close regard? Tell me, please, and give me some relief!" Tamamizu wept and replied, "You will surely understand in the end, but I cannot tell you just now. Please think of me kindly, even after I am gone." Her mistress was most disturbed.

As the day of the procession drew near, Tamamizu thought long and hard: "Although I may be an animal, I'd like to approach my mistress and seal a lover's bond. But how sorry I would feel for her if I did![16] And yet to go on simply seeing her and being beside her like this . . . it would be only a fleeting comfort! I'd like to tell her this to her face, but considering that I've kept it a secret until now, she would be

---

15. The *nenbutsu* is the ritual incantation of the name of Amida (Skt. Amitābha) Buddha.
16. In *The Contest of Autumn Leaves*, Tamamizu reasons that it would be easy enough to consummate their relationship, but that it would cause her mistress's death if her mistress were to sleep with an animal. See *Momiji awase*, in *Muromachi jidai monogatari taisei*, ed. Yokoyama and Matsumoto, 13:198b.

The Tale of Tamamizu

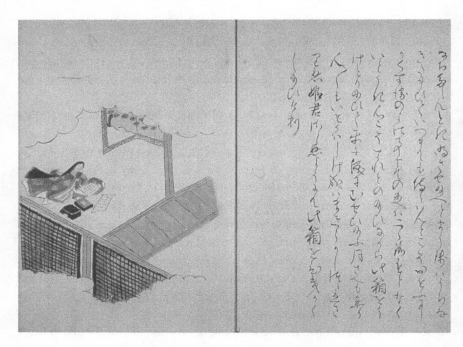

Tamamizu writes her confession. (From *Tamamizu monogatari*, courtesy of the Kyoto University Library)

utterly horrified. The Procession to the Palace—that's when I'll disappear! It's a wonder that I haven't been found out yet in this shape-shifting form."

Claiming to have a cold, Tamamizu shut herself up in her room and wrote down everything from the beginning: her condition when she first fell in love with her mistress, and all that had happened since. She collected the pages and placed them in a small box, which she took to her lady. "Lately," she said, "I've somehow come to realize that the world is pointless and fleeting. In my wretchedness, it occurred to me that I might even just vanish in the night. So I would like to offer you this box. If something should happen to me, then please take a look inside." She broke down and wept.

Her mistress thought this strange. "What could you be thinking to say such a thing?" she asked resentfully. "Perhaps you don't intend to see me to my new home."

"I'll almost certainly accompany you on your journey to the palace," Tamamizu lied, "but since I've been saddened by the thought that something might happen, I wanted to leave this box with you. It seems to me that at the time of the ceremony, there will be so many people watching that I might not be able to give it to you.

Please, please consider it to be a precious treasure. Don't even show it to your dear Tsukisae! There's a reason for all this, so you shouldn't show it to anyone else. Open the inner tray after some years have passed and you've come to brood on the world and think that you might leave it."

Her mistress wept and replied, "I had thought that we would always be together, but since you speak like this of the world to come, it leaves me uneasy. I am deeply distressed!" As she took the box from Tamamizu, they both were choked with tears. Tsukisae arrived, and amid the bustle of people coming and going, Tamamizu took her leave. The young lady acted as though nothing had happened and hid the box away.

Now in the confusion of the Procession to the Palace, as the young lady and her attendants were boarding their carriages, Tamamizu slipped away. The Takayanagi Lord thought that she had accompanied his daughter to the court, and at the palace, everyone thought that she had remained behind, given that she had often said that she felt ill. The young lady was grief-stricken, and in her desolation she wondered what on earth could have happened. Two or three days passed. When she heard that Tamamizu was nowhere to be found, she had her father search here and there, but to no avail.

Five and then ten days passed, but even so the young lady thought that she might hear word. She waited in the hope that Tamamizu would return from some distant place, but she never did. "Where could she have disappeared?" she wondered. "Could someone have spirited her away?" Thus, in the midst of her joy at moving to the palace, the gloom in her heart increased all the more. Her ladies-in-waiting in the Women's Quarters all wept and wailed together, and whatever they did, they thought, "If only she could be here with us!"

The Takayanagi Captain was promoted to Middle Counselor. "Tamamizu has become so famous that something terrible might have occurred," he thought. Wondering whatever could have happened, he grieved for her as well.

The young lady felt drawn to the contents of the box, but with the emperor constantly present she had no time to spare, and thus the days passed. On one occasion, His Majesty visited the Council of State, and taking this to be a good opportunity, the young lady surreptitiously opened the box and looked inside. The fox had written down everything, from beginning to end. "What is this?" she thought, her heart aflutter; she was both horrified and filled with pity. "To think that he transformed himself like that for my sake, passing the days without ever revealing what he had done . . . he may be an animal, but how sad! And to have done those things while showing me such consideration—it's so touching! What a noble heart!" As she

The Takayanagi Captain's daughter reads Tamamizu's parting epistle. (From *Tamamizu monogatari*, courtesy of the Kyoto University Library)

read on, her eyes welling with tears, she saw that there was a long poem at the end of the scroll:

tsuka no ma mo	Even though my mound,
sarigatakarishi	for even a moment, was
waga sumika	a dwelling difficult to leave,
kimi wo aimite	ever since that time
sono nochi wa	when I happened to see you
shizugokoro naku	I languished
akugarete	with an unquiet heart.
uwa no sora ni mo	And while my mind wandered
mayoitsutsu	in the vast, spreading sky,
hakanaki mono wo	my life, though fleeting,
kazu naranu	grew wretched
ukimi narikeru	with concerns beyond count.
mono yue ni	All because of this

suzuro ni mi wo ba	I fretted myself away,
tsukushibune	like a boat from Tsukushi:
kogiwataredomo	though rowing out upon the deep,
hare yarade	I was adrift upon the waves,
nami ni tadayou	with no clear sky in sight,
sasagani no	weaker and more frail
ito suji yori mo	than a single thread
kasuka nite	of spider's silk.
suginishi tsukihi	The days and months that passed—
kazoureba	when I counted them
tada yume to nomi	they seemed to have become
narinikeri	only a dream.
waga mi hitotsu wa	So what to do
ika ni sen	with this single life of mine?
kimi sae nagaki	To think that even you
urami wo ba	might bear
oinan koto no	a long-lasting grudge—
yoshinasa yo	how worthless it would be!
asa yū kimi wo	Even seeing you
miru koto mo	morning and evening,
mi no tagui zo to	"At least our bodies are alike!"
nagusamete	I comforted myself;
yume utsutsu to mo	and reality and dreams
wakigataku	were so hard to tell apart.
akashikurashitsu	This is how I spent my days.
omokage wo	Thinking through the night
itsu no yo made mo	that in whatever world to come
kawaraji to	my image of you
omoiakashi no	might remain unchanged,
ura ni idete	I walked out to Akashi Bay
shioi no kai mo	to gather seashells
hirou kana	from the shoreline.
ama no taku mono	And the evening smoke
yū keburi	of the fisherman's fire—
tanabiku kata mo	seeing how it trailed off,
natsukashi ya	I thought fondly of you.
shima-zutai nite	Though I am not
mirume karu	a fisherman's child

The Tale of Tamamizu

ama no kodomo ni	hunting for seaweed
aranedomo	from isle to isle,
kawaku ma mo naki	my sleeves still have no time to dry,
sode no ue ni	and even the wind
tobikuru kaze mo	that blows upon them
hoshikanete	can hardly make them so.
nabiku keshiki wo	When from afar
yoso ni mite	I see them trailing,
omoishirarenu	I feel that our lives,
mi no hodo mo	the span of which
tsui ni kainaki	we cannot know,
kokochi shite	are useless in the end.
tada hitofude wo	I can only ply my brush
susamioku	and set these things down.
tamazusa bakari	And with this letter alone
mi ni soete	to keep beside you
nagaki omoi no	as a witness of my
shirushi zo to	long-held affection,
tsune wa toburau	you must grieve, I think,
kokochi aran	with constant sorrow.
nochi no yo made no	Even if I should become
kakehashi to	a bridge for you
narite mo kimi wo	'twixt this life and the next,
mamoriten	I will protect you.
kakaru ukimi wo	I thought to keep my wretched lot
hito shirezu	unknown to others
toburawaji to wa	and unmourned by them,
Ono no yama	but my feelings color my face
mada aki naranu	like Mount Ono
iro ni idete	before autumn's arrival.
mada tameshi naki	Wishing that you
tagui wo mo	might remember
omoiideyo no	our unprecedented bond,
kokoro nite	I simply keep on writing,
tada kakisusamu	letting my brush run as before.
mizukuki no	More than the waters
iwane wo izuru	of the mountain stream
yamagawa no	gushing from the rocks,

tanimizu yori mo	these tears overflow
tokoroseki	my dewy sleeves.
tamoto no tsuyu mo	Might you never for a moment
kimi wa shiraji na	know such sorrow!
iro ni idete	May you come to know
iwanu omoi no	through these leaves of words
aware wo mo	the pathos of my feelings,
kono koto no ha ni	unspoken yet betrayed
omoishiranan	by my blushing face.
moreidete	Having leaked out,
mata kaeramu to	this jeweled water—this Tamamizu—
tamamizu no	longs to come back again
nigori naki yo ni	and protect you in the clear pool
kimi wo mamoran	of an unsullied world.

He had written this poem and appended two shorter verses at the end. He wrote of some other things in great detail, and these moved the lady to believe that his feelings were far from shallow: "Although the years may pass, this box, if not despised, will not grow old; because its love for the one who keeps it will increase, I present it to you. Just as I told you, do not open the inner tray while I am privileged to be near you; it is when you have come to brood on the world and wish to leave it behind that you must open it and look inside."

Although he may have been a beast, his heart was as gentle as these words, and it was to express the depth of his compassion that he wrote these things down.

TRANSLATION BY WILLIAM BRYANT AND KELLER KIMBROUGH;
INTRODUCTION BY KELLER KIMBROUGH

The Tale of a Wild Goose

In classical Japanese poetry, the sound of a wild goose's cry or the sight of a line of migrating wild geese suggests autumnal melancholy and loneliness. As Haruo Shirane has observed, wild geese are the second most frequently mentioned bird in poems from *Man'yōshū* (*Collection of Myriad Leaves*, ca. 785).[1] *The Tale of a Wild Goose* (*Kari no sōshi*) draws deeply on these poetic associations and frequently alludes to other poems, including two by Ono no Komachi (ca. 825–ca. 900). It is written in a highly literary style that is somewhat unusual in *otogizōshi*, thus fusing the *irui-mono* (interspecies) subgenre with the tradition of court poetry.

The *Kari no sōshi* picture scroll on which this translation is based consists of a single handscroll with monochrome ink illustrations of landscapes and interior scenes (with simply drawn human figures) that depict Ishiyama Temple, a house, its garden, and a nun's mountain retreat surrounded by rice paddies. In addition to the main text, there are some passage of dialogue, poetry, and narration that appear as *gachūshi* (words within the painting) in the illustrations. Although there is no evidence of wide distribution, this sole surviving manuscript probably is not the original; after the final ink illustration, a postscript by the calligrapher seems to mean "omissions possible," implying that the extant *Tale of a Wild Goose* was copied from another text. The postscript ends with "Brushed in Keichō 7 [1602], middle of the sixth month," indicating that any earlier versions would have been composed in or before that year. Both the author and the calligrapher are unknown; all that we can say for certain is that he or she must have been quite familiar with the classical poetic tradition.

The translation and illustrations are from the *Kari no sōshi* picture scroll (1602) in the collection of the Kyoto University Library, typeset and annotated in Ichiko Teiji et al., eds., *Muromachi monogatari shū jō*, Shin Nihon koten bungaku taikei 54 (Tokyo: Iwanami Shoten, 1989), 311–24.

1. Haruo Shirane, *Japan and the Culture of the Four Seasons: Nature, Literature, and the Arts* (New York: Columbia University Press, 2012), 41.

Near Horikawa, there lived a daughter of a minor nobleman. She went into service at the court, and when her parents, who lived in a rustic village of no account, retired deep into the mountains,[2] she had even less support than she did before. She thought about hiding her poor self among the blossoms in some distant vale, and while she sowed the seeds of these lonely thoughts, the days slipped by. How sad it would be to take that face of hers—now in the full bloom of youth, as she could see in the mirror—and shroud it in the black garb of a nun!

The woman was in the habit of visiting temples. Although she spent the months and days in the world, empty as the floating clouds in the sky, even the people in the palace thought only of their immediate diversions, and there was no one to whom she had truly pledged her troth. Thinking that Kannon might take pity on her lonely grief, she made a pilgrimage to Ishiyama Temple, intending to seclude herself there for seven days. To speak of her misery seemed pointless, even to herself, but because she had heard that the Kannon fulfilled people's wishes in various ways, she prayed: "As I have no one to rely on, I earnestly ask for you to keep me from wandering lost in this world of dreams, and to bestow on me a desire for the world to come." In time, without dwelling on her suffering, she read sutras and prayed day and night. In her anguish, as she gazed out at the horizon, she recalled the sentiments of the one who said long ago, "In the bright eighth month, I am sending my thoughts a thousand leagues away."[3]

She heard a flock of wild geese come flying through the sky. "Even winged creatures such as these share lovebirds' vows," she thought, gazing jealously at the geese in their unstraying formation. And what could she have been thinking then? "The vows of men are like the morning glory," she pondered, "not lasting long enough for the dew to linger. If even an ephemeral flying thing like this were to be my own true love, I would give my consent."

One of the wild geese she saw in the distance flew down. She thought that she would rest for a while, and she dozed a little. Suddenly, she was startled to see a person nearby; beside her was a man dressed shabbily in informal clothes; he did not seem to be from the capital.[4] Perhaps because her eyes were dazzled by the moonlight,

---

2. The implications of this passage are unclear. It could mean that they either took monastic vows or died.
3. This is an allusion to a poem by the Tang poet Bai Juyi (772–846).
4. The man is said to be dressed in *kari shōzoku* (hunting garb), which is a kind of informal court attire. The word *kari* (hunting) is a homophone of *kari* (goose).

The Tale of a Wild Goose

she did not seem to recognize him, and she thought that among the many noblemen she had seen in the court, a figure such as his was rare.

He approached with a familiar expression: "I happened to be going to the capital, and since it's on the way and I heard that this Kannon gives truly miraculous blessings, I came here. To meet you like this is surely not because of the vow of a single lifetime. If you will tell me exactly where you will be upon your return, and if there is no one standing in my way, I intend to stay in the capital for a while. So please prepare a travelers' bed for me."[5] He spoke with passion.

Because she, too, had decided to visit the temple out of her lonely grief, she believed with all her heart that this was in fact the doing of the bodhisattva. Nevertheless, not knowing where he was from, she felt adrift, and unable to speak to a man who had spoken to her so abruptly, she gave no reply.

"I will accompany you on your return from Ishiyama Temple," the man said. "I am Assistant Captain of the Guards Akiharu of the Koshiji Road."[6] Then he slipped away and disappeared.

Still unaccustomed to travelers' lodgings outside the capital, the woman felt somehow sad. By day the cicadas sang, and all night long the insects in the grass cried beneath her pillow. At dusk, the setting sun and the moon emerging from behind the mountains were clear and bright, and only those friends of hers in the sky remained unchanged. She felt the gloom of autumn in them, too.

---

5. This is a pun on the word *ukine*, which signifies both a temporary or an unsettled bed, and the floating sleep of a bird on the water.
6. The name Akiharu means "fall and spring," and it suggests the seasons of a goose's migration.

A flock of wild geese passes over Ishiyama Temple (*right*), and a mysterious man appears before the woman at Ishiyama Temple (*left*). (From *Kari no sōshi*, courtesy of the Kyoto University Library)

The unknown traveler came and said, "When you return from your pilgrimage, if you don't make sure to tell me where you are, I must inform you that I will bear eternal resentment and disappear like the dew." Night after night he came to ask, and because of his heartfelt, passionate pleas, the woman thought that perhaps indeed he had been sent by a bodhisattva. She vaguely hinted, "Truly, if you were to seek out this lovers' bond, then in Horikawa . . ."

Toward the left of the first illustration (not fully reproduced here), the following dialogue is inscribed:

MAN: Because of a long-standing vow, I have made a pilgrimage from the distant countryside, and drawn by the faintest glimpse of you, I have come here. This might seem rude, but please be my guide to the capital. I will accompany you on your return.

There is a little something I want to speak to you about.

WOMAN: Who are you? Perhaps you have mistaken me for someone else.

I am also a fisherman's child with no fixed abode,[1] and I don't know the capital.

1. The woman's words allude to the anonymous poem 1703 in *Shinkokin wakashū* (*New Collection of Poems Ancient and Modern*, 1205):

shiranami no	As I am a fisherman's child,
yosuru nagisa ni	passing my days
yo wo sugusu	by the shore, lapped by
ama no ko nareba	the white-capped waves,
yado mo sadamezu	I have no fixed abode.

After seven days had passed, she returned to the capital. The man found her some-how, and he visited night after night. Because he was from the country, she feared that he would be terribly rustic and rough, but he was in fact incomparably gentle and charming. Even had he not been, she would have been of a mind to go "like the float-ing weeds, should the water invite,"[7] so she earnestly rejoiced at Kannon's blessing. She stayed shut up in her home, and even neglected her court service. However, the man did not come to speak with her by day; he visited only at night. "Perhaps he lives near Katsuragi," she thought, completely failing to understand.[8]

Time passed one way or another, and perhaps because he was a man from the countryside, he sometimes brought her large gifts of rice from the autumn fields. This was a funny, countrified way of doing things, but maybe because she guessed at the sadness of his poverty, she did not seem to love him any the less for it.

The woman did not know precisely where in the capital the man was staying, so she sometimes resented him, think-ing, "He is as reserved from me as a re-mote mountain. Has the cruel autumn of his love arrived?"[9]

> In the second illustration (not reproduced here), the following dialogue is inscribed:
>
> WOMAN: You said that there's nothing separating us, so what should I say? We can't leave things as they are.
> MAN: Just because I don't say where I go, do you think that means I must be holding back from you? I'm a man who has a little something to hide, so what of it?
> SERVANT (*bearing a tray*): Since the lord happens to be resting now, please give him this.

"Ever since I was young," he said evasively, "I have been cautious of my parents' enemies, so even if you feel deeply for me, I am reluctant because of the people serv-ing around you."

The year ended, and the light of spring arrived at last. Even the poor plum trees at the fence of a humble dwelling blossomed as if they were smiling. For some reason,

---

7. This is an allusion to poem 938 in *Kokin wakashū* (*Collection of Poems Ancient and Modern*, ca. 905), attrib-uted to Ono no Komachi:

wabinureba	In my loneliness,
mi wo ukikusa no	like the rootless
ne wo taete	floating weeds,
sasou mizu araba	should the water invite me,
inamu to zo omou	I would go.

8. The woman alludes to the legend of Hitokoto-no-nushi, a deity associated with Mount Katsuragi who is said to have been so ashamed of his ugliness that he came out only at night.

9. This passage contains layered, poetic language. The phrase *kokoro wo oku* (to be reserved) connects to *okuyama* (remote mountain). In addition, there is a play on *aki*, which means both "autumn" and "to tire of."

with the arrival of spring, the man seemed to be lost in thought. He was unable to sleep at night, and in the morning he made uneasy vows repeatedly, saying, "If for some reason I should go far away beyond the clouds, I wonder what sort of men you will see! It worries me."

The woman did not know what to make of this. "Because he is a traveler," she thought, "perhaps he is considering returning to his hometown." She was endlessly forlorn, and her feelings were in complete disarray.

The cherry blossoms by the eaves were at their peak, and now would only scatter; gazing at them together in the moonlight, the man recited:

kokoro ni wa	Although my heart
kokoro wo sashite	does not hasten so,
isoganu ni	the flowers
kaeru to tsuguru	in the night breeze
hana no yūkaze	say I must return.

Despite the blossoms, the woman's spirits darkened, and she replied:

kaeru sa wo	Because he is
susumeba koso wa	so eager to return
furusato ni	to his hometown,
hana wo misutete	the traveler hurries,
isogu tabibito	overlooking the flowers.

On one night, around the middle of the third month, the man came to her and said, "Tonight is the last night that I can come here. At dawn, I will return to my hometown. It is not my wish, but I have been summoned and must go. If I live until then, I intend to return again next autumn. As long as the colors of your heart have not faded like a pale-indigo robe, I will definitely come. Please wait faithfully." He spoke falteringly, weeping heartfelt tears—how sad!

"Even if it is not your intention," the woman said, "if you are summoned by the snow and hail of Mount Arachi, I will not hold it against you."[10] She yearned to be with him, but because it could not be, she said, "If this is the end, when I receive word of you on the wind, I will surely write."

Speaking intimately throughout the night about what had passed and what was to come, they eventually parted in despair. Thinking that this was the end, she went

10. Mount Arachi lies on the border between Ōmi and Echizen provinces, to the north of Lake Biwa.

The Tale of a Wild Goose

The woman watches her husband fly off into the early-morning darkness. (From *Kari no sōshi*, courtesy of the Kyoto University Library)

outside to watch his departing figure in the darkness before dawn, whereupon, strange to say, the man seemed to disappear. A wild goose emerged from near the eaves and flew off, crying into the distant sky:

ima wa tote	Now is the end, you say;
isogu mo kanashi	how sad is the hurried parting,
wakareji no	with tears
namida ni kumorite	clouding the eyes
kaeru karigane	of the returning goose.

What a fleeting vow—she felt as if she were in a dream. Dwelling intently on this, she realized her wretched fate: she had confined herself at Ishiyama Temple and voiced her despair at not having anyone of her own, and because of some attachment from an unfortunate previous life, Kannon had matched her not with a human but with a bird. Still, the man had come night after night, regardless of the wind and rain. Even the traces of him lingering in the sky moved her, and remembering their parting words, she felt as if she were facing him now. Even though she regained her composure, she longed for him terribly.

INTERSPECIES AFFAIRS

With her old pillow as her companion, thinking all night that he might come to visit, if only in a dream, she wore inside out the raven robe of the night.[11] While she was half-dozing, half-dreaming, a wild goose flew through the sky and left a letter by her pillow. Thinking it strange, she looked at it in surprise.

Delighted that it was real, the woman quickly arose and read it: "How strange was our previous life, that because of some trivial fate I was born with these hateful wings, but without any way to escape the bonds of love. For eight months it was like a dream, our pillows side by side, rising and resting in the same bed with you, but the sky of my journeys was darkened by tears of rain. I rested by the side of the road, and without reaching my hometown, I disappeared at the tip of the arrow of a huntsman's catalpa bow. I promised to come again next autumn, but I have abandoned that as a dream for the distant future. Thus, as my intentions have not changed, I wish to be reborn in Amida's Pure Land with you. Please become a nun and help me in the afterlife."

The third illustration (not reproduced here) contains no text. In the fourth illustration, the following text is inscribed:

The woman watched his departing figure sadly, knowing that now the end had come. Because her eyes were blurred with tears, perhaps, she could not see where he went; and perhaps because of the mist, she could not see the road. It seemed strange, but there was only a wild goose flying away. She wept miserably, realizing that her husband had been the wild goose that she had heard on the Koshiji Road.

The letter continued with a poem:

akazu shite	Without tiring of you,
misutete ideshi	I have abandoned you
karigane no	and gone away;
hana yori saki ni	how sad for a wild goose to have fallen
chiru zo kanashiki	before even the short-lived blossoms.[12]

The woman dwelt intently on her strange vow: "In China, there was also such an example. The Han emperor attacked the Xiongnu barbarians and sent Su Wu to the

11. This is an allusion to poem 554 in *Kokin wakashū*, attributed to Ono no Komachi:

ito semete	When I long for you
koishiki toki wa	the very most,
mubatama no	I wear inside out
yoru no koromo wo	the raven robe
kaeshite zo kiru	of the night.

It was believed that wearing robes inside out would allow one to see a lover in a dream.

12. The word *karigane* (goose) contains the word *kari* (short-lived), which refers to the ephemerality of the blossoms.

The woman lives as a nun in a brushwood shack. (From *Kari no sōshi*, courtesy of the Kyoto University Library)

In the fifth illustration (not reproduced here), the following text is inscribed:

"Well, Sukedono,[1] you have been dreaming. You thought that he had come—you were about to say 'how wonderful'—but even to see him is pointless. You know that he is unhappy and imperiled. You were doubtful, and then because you were surprised to discover that that wonderful man of the Koshiji Road was perhaps only a dream, how strange that a real letter has arrived! Impatient to open it, you arise and look; how unreal it feels. Well, Sukedono, reading a letter from the man you love makes it feel as if he's really here."

1. The woman may be speaking to herself, or another woman may be addressing her.

distant border; fearing the barbarian forces, Su Wu fled, pointlessly prolonging his life. Trapped in a cave and having lost his leg, time passed in vain, and in his sadness he entrusted to a flock of wild geese a letter to his hometown. The wild geese dropped it in the garden of the Han emperor, and thereby Su Wu returned to his home.[13] Perhaps among birds, wild geese truly have a heart, and thus we sealed such a fleeting vow." Pitifully, she abandoned hope of even the man's promise that she should wait for the next autumn.

One evening, she summoned her nurse Chūjō and left in disguise, becoming a nun in a nearby temple. She decided to perform austerities wherever her feet might lead her, and since it was all the same, she departed toward the Koshiji Road. In a certain field, standing in the shadow of the reeds of Tamae of the

13. The story of Su Wu is recorded in volume 54 of *Han shu* (*The Book of Han*). The story of Su Wu and the goose is retold in Japanese in *The Tale of the Heike* (thirteenth century; Kakuichi text [1371], 2:17).

INTERSPECIES AFFAIRS

summer harvest, the woman felt the sadness of being without a sky to fly off into.[14] Traveling onward, she came to the Koshiji Road. She built a brushwood hermitage near a mountain rice paddy and spent the months and days there.

The end of her life neared, and in her final hour the woman attained rebirth in the Pure Land.

tanomitsuru	The leaves of rice
inaba no karete	that I had relied on
tsuyu no ma no	wither as briefly as the dew:
kakaru hakanaki	the fleeting night's dream
kari no yo no yume	of a wild goose.

[Colophon:]

Omissions possible.[15]

Brushed in Keichō 7 [1602], middle of the sixth month.

How awful! But we would all wish to be like this.

TRANSLATION AND INTRODUCTION BY RACHEL STAUM MEI

14. This is an allusion to poem 219 in *Goshūi wakashū* (*Later Collection of Gleanings*, 1086), attributed to Minamoto no Shigeyuki (d. 1000):

natsukari no	Trampling the reeds
Tamae no ashi wo	at Tamae of the summer harvest,
fumishidaki	the flocking birds
mureiru tori no	have no sky
tatsu sora zo naki	to fly off into.

15. These words appear to be a disclaimer added by the calligrapher.

The Stingfish

Popular wisdom tells us that love is blind—and if the *The Stingfish* (*Okoze*) is to be believed, this saying holds true not only across cultures, but across species. Bug-eyed, lumpen-faced bottom dwellers bristling with venomous spines, stingfish seldom inspire undying passion. Indeed, their Japanese name, *okoze*, derives from an old word meaning "ugly," while their genus, *Inimicus*, reflects a similarly dim view of their dubious charms.[1] By any objective standard, the title character of *The Stingfish*, probably composed sometime in the sixteenth or seventeenth century, possesses little more appeal than the rest of her kind, despite her high rank in the undersea court. Fatuous, pretentious, and downright ugly, Princess Stingfish falls short of virtually every feminine ideal—and therein lies the humor of the tale, which casts her in the role of romantic heroine, wooed by no less a suitor than the mountain god himself.

The narrator recounts the courtship of this odd couple with tongue firmly in cheek, employing copious poetic allusions to create an atmosphere of high sentiment, broken by only the occasional wink to the fundamental absurdity of the situation. However, the layers of parody and pastiche rest atop a deep mythical foundation. Viewed as a liminal realm where the ordinary gives way to the otherworldly, mountains loom as large in Japan's cosmology as they do in its geology. Their magic is embodied in the figure of the mountain god Yama-no-kami, who remains

---

The translation and illustrations are from the *Okoze* picture scroll (early seventeenth century) in the collection of the Tōyō University Library, typeset and annotated in Ōshima Tatehiko, ed., *Otogizōshi shū*, Nihon koten bungaku zenshū 36 (Tokyo: Shōgakukan, 1974), 475–85. There are three other extant manuscripts of *The Stingfish*, all of which were consulted: a captioned folding screen in the collection of Yukawa Tomisaburō, a book in the collection of Takayasu Rokurō, and an illustrated scroll owned by Aoyama Gakuin Women's Junior College.

1. Regarding the etymology of the word *okoze*, see Yoshida Kanehiko, *Ishokujū gogen jiten* (Tokyo: Tōkyōdō Shuppan, 1996), 51. An alternative theory holds that *okoze* derives from *oroka* ("foolish" or "absurd"). In either case, the root of the word is decidedly unflattering.

an object of veneration in rural areas throughout Japan, although his (or, in some cases, her) precise nature varies widely across regions.[2] However, almost all of this deity's diverse manifestations receive regular offerings of stingfish from their worshippers. Several explanations are given for this custom: some believers hold that the stingfish serves the mountain god, while others claim that they are husband and wife. In locations where the mountain god is in fact a goddess, she is imagined as an ugly woman who takes delight in the stingfish because it is even more hideous than she.[3]

Whatever bond may connect this mismatched pair, it has existed for centuries; the dictionary *Myōgoki* (thirteenth century) notes in its entry on stingfish that they are favored by the mountain god.[4] Ultimately, the association most likely derives from the legend of the marriage between the hunter Yamasachihiko and the dragon princess Toyotama-hime. The earliest version of the tale, found in *Kojiki* (*Record of Ancient Matters*, 712), makes no mention of the stingfish; however, some later variants identify this creature as the couple's go-between. *The Stingfish* thus represents a transformation of the original myth, in which Yamasachihiko—whose name means "Luck of the Mountains"—has merged with the gestalt figure of the mountain god, while the stingfish has been promoted from matchmaker to love interest.[5]

The blossoms of the mountain cherries are merely part of the scenery here, nothing special; when spring is in its splendor, most of the sights truly worth seeing are found on the seashore. The high waves and the low waves, each spilling over the other, washing across the glistening seaweed on the rocks; the plovers bobbing up and down in the water, and the music of their cries; the boats going out to sea, racing along with the gentle breezes in their sails, and the faint sound of voices singing . . . even if one glances at it without any particular attention, it is all quite elegant. There

---

2. The cult of the mountain god attracted the attention of many early-twentieth-century folklorists and ethnologists, among them Yanagita Kunio and Minakata Kumagusu. For a brief overview of contemporary mountain god worship, see Nagamatsu Atsushi, "Yama-no-kami shinkō no keifu," *Miyazaki kōritsu daigaku jinbungakubu kiyō* 12, no. 1 (2005): 213–19; for more in-depth analysis of specific regional practices, see Yamamura Minzoku no Kai, ed., *Yama no kami to okoze* (Tokyo: Entapuraizu, 1990).

3. Takaya Shigeo, "Suzuka Sanroku no yama no kami matsuri," in *Yama no kami to okoze*, ed. Yamamura, 159–60.

4. Ōshima Tatehiko, "Otogizōshi *Okoze* no haikei," in *Nihon bungaku no dentō to rekishi*, ed. Ronbunshū Henshū Iinkai (Tokyo: Ōfūsha, 1975), 606.

5. Ōshima, "Otogizōshi *Okoze* no haikei," 612–15. Yamasachihiko is abandoned by his dragon wife after he glimpses her true form. Unlike her forerunner, Princess Stingfish has no qualms about letting her husband see her as she is, scales and all.

The Stingfish

are a great many things here that one does not see in the mountains. The smoke from the salt makers' fires trailing into the sky—whose lovelorn tear tracks does it trace?[6] One can even look gently on the heartless fisher-girl who breaks off a bough of cherry blossoms while carrying brushwood down from the mountains.

The mountain god and his companions gathered here and composed verses on this and that as the fancy took them. They were rather odd poems, but the gist was something like this:

shibaki toru	The hearts of the fisher-girls
ama no kokoro	gathering brushwood—
haru nare ya	perhaps it is spring that has
kazasu sakura no	made them sweet, those sleeves bedecked
sode wa yasashi mo	with cherry blossoms.[7]

Reciting this verse, the mountain god wandered restlessly hither and yon.

Now among all the fish, Princess Stingfish was a lady of unrivaled elegance. Her face resembled that of the gurnard or the rockfish, with prominent bones, bulging eyes, and a wide mouth. Decked out in her twelve-layered robes and attended by many other fish, she floated atop the waves enjoying the spring.[8] She strummed her zither, and the mountain god heard a voice singing, faint but heavily accented:

hiku ami no	In every eye
megoto ni moroki	of the net as it pulls tight
waga namida	my tears
kakarazariseba	are not drawn to the surface—
kakaraji to	and if *I* am not drawn to the surface,
nochi wa kuyashiki	what regret shall follow
ryōshibune ka mo	for the fisherman's boat![9]

The shrill sound of nails plucking at strings rang out as she sang.

6. The traditional Japanese method of making salt involved boiling seawater. The smoke of the salt makers' fires became a stock poetic image suggesting lovelorn tears. The connotations of salt making connect to a larger complex of romantic associations surrounding the seashore and its inhabitants, many of which are alluded to in *The Stingfish.*

7. The poem plays on the double meaning of *yasashi,* translated here as "sweet." In the original Japanese, the word means both "elegant" (in reference to the cherry blossom–bedecked sleeves) and "gentle" (in reference to the fisher-girls' hearts).

8. Twelve-layered robes (*jūnihitoe*) constituted formal court dress for women.

9. In Japanese, the openings in a net are described as eyes, the basis for a pun on *kakaru,* which means both "to fall" (as tears) and "to catch" (as fish).

The mountain god watches Princess Stingfish play her zither in the waves. (From *Okoze*, courtesy of the Tōyō University Library)

The mountain god stood and listened raptly. His first sight of the stingfish had immediately planted a seed in his mind, and he wanted at least to move nearer to her—but since he could not swim, it was no use. When he crouched on the shore and beckoned with his hand, the stingfish cried, "How dreadful! Someone is watching us!" and slipped beneath the waves.

Nonetheless, the mountain god caught a glimpse of the hems of her skirts as she held them up, and he longed to see her again, if only for an instant. So he lingered there, staring at the place where she had been. However, she did not reappear. When at last the sun sank into the west, he trudged soddenly back to the mountains.[10]

Like Ariwara no Narihira in the distant past, the mountain god spent the night neither waking nor sleeping, unable to forget her face.[11] His chest felt heavy, and his

10. The word translated here as "soddenly," *shioshio*, more literally means "saltily," thus suggesting both seawater and tears.
11. The poet Ariwara no Narihira (825–880) gained fame for his romantic exploits, immortalized in *Ise monogatari* (*The Tales of Ise*, ca. tenth century). Here, the narrator quotes a poem from section 2 of this work:

oki mo sezu	I passed the night
ne mo sede yoru wo	neither waking
akashite wa	nor sleeping,
haru no mono tote	and I pass the day staring out
nagamekurashitsu	brooding on the spring.

The Stingfish

condition soon became worrisome; although he gathered nuts and pine seeds to eat, they would not get past his throat. Still, his love only continued to blossom—and though he wished to vanish like the dew on that blossom, he did not die.[12] When the day at last dawned, he again set out on the path to the shore, guided by his hopeful heart. Thinking that maybe, just maybe, Princess Stingfish would rise to the surface, he stared out at the open sea where the whitecaps broke over one another, but he did not so much as catch a glimpse of her shadow. Marking his trail with tears, the mountain god returned to his dwelling in a daze. If only some breeze would slip a message through the cracks in her jeweled blinds and let her know the strength of his feelings! Even after he died, if only she were to think of him in passing, surely the weight of his sins would be lightened in the next life.

As one who dwelled in the mountains, the mountain god did not know his way around the water at all, while those who dwelled in the water were at no less of a loss in the mountains, so there was no way for him to speak with her. Heaving a great sigh, he racked his brains over what to do. He made such a queer sight that even one glimpse of him would make you split your sides with laughter. It brings to mind the man who thought that the gargoyle roof tiles on Inaba Hall in the capital resembled the face of his wife back in his village—and even though he was in the capital, he was homesick from his journey, so he burst out sobbing.[13] No one could witness such a scene without snickering.

Just then, a river otter happened by, and the mountain god said, "Oh, good sir, you know how to swim! Such-and-such has happened, and I wish to send a letter; will you please deliver it for me?"

"The stingfish is extremely ugly," the river otter replied. "Her eyes bulge, her bones stick out, and her mouth is wide and red. The humans would be appalled if they were to hear that someone like *you*—a god of the mountains—was infatuated with someone like *her*. What a disgrace!"

"No, no—that's just your own prejudice," the mountain god said. "They say that a woman's eyes should have the shape of round bells;[14] it is the nature of beautiful women to have big eyes, just as it is the nature of those of noble blood to have

---

12. The original sentence hinges on the double meaning of *masari*, which not only means "increasing" but also forms part of the word for "chrysanthemum" (*masarigusa*). I have attempted to preserve some of this wordplay in my use of "blossom."

13. This is a reference to the *kyōgen* play *Oni-gawara* (*The Gargoyle Roof-Tile*), whose plot follows the summary in this sentence. See *The Gargoyle Roof-Tile* (*Oni-gawara*), in *The Kyōgen Book: An Anthology of Japanese Classical Comedies*, trans. Don Kenny (Tokyo: Japan Times, 1989), 96–100. Inaba Hall is the main worship hall of Byōdōji Temple in Kyoto.

14. Round bells (*suzu*) resemble Western sleigh bells in their design and are used in Shinto worship.

The mountain god entrusts the river otter with a letter for Princess Stingfish. (From *Okoze*, courtesy of the Tōyō University Library)

prominent bones, and a wide mouth shows intelligence. She is a flawless lady. No one could see her without losing his heart. And if there is gossip, well, that's just the way of the world." As they say, "Love makes even a harelip look like a dimple." Nonetheless, the mountain god's earnest demeanor was endlessly amusing.

343

"Write your letter, then, and I will deliver it for you," the river otter said.

The mountain god's joy was beyond words. He had neither brush nor inkstone with which to write, so he peeled a piece of bark from a tree and put down his thoughts on that: "Although you may find this unexpected, please permit me to send you this humble missive. Some time ago, I stole down to the seashore, and while I was gazing at the spring ocean, I saw you amusing yourself among the waves, strumming your zither, composing poetry, and singing airs.[15] I caught only a glimpse of you, but I could see that you were lovely and refined. If you were a flower, you would be a plum or a cherry blossom, delicate and graceful; you had all the elegance of a weeping willow tousled by the wind. I am bogwood from the deep mountains, doomed to helplessly rot away. What shall become of you when only my feelings linger on? I shall be overjoyed if you send me a reply, if only as proof that this letter has come into your hands." At the end, he added:

15. "Airs" is a translation of *rōei*, Chinese-style poems sung to set melodies.

The Stingfish

kanagashira	Although I may see
mebaru no oyogu	the rockfish and the grunion
nami no ue	swimming in the waves,
miru ni tsukete mo	I only have eyes for
okoze koishiki	my beloved stingfish.

After composing this poem, the mountain god handed the letter to the river otter.

His nose tickling with the urge to laugh, the river otter went to the seashore. With a splash, he paddled down to the bottom of the sea, where he obtained an audience with Princess Stingfish and told her everything. When she heard what he had to say, the stingfish was taken completely by surprise; her red face went even redder, and she would not even take the letter in her hands.

"How cold you are!" the otter exclaimed. "Like the little crabs living in the sea wrack, rack your heart and soak your sleeve with tears, for without compassion, how can we make our way in this world? Our way in this world is to honor even the bonds forged by a single night shared in a brushwood shelter—and *this* is no ordinary bond, but one that is fathomlessly deep. How can you ignore a heart drowning in love? The smoke from the salt makers' fires may drift in an unexpected direction, and when the wind blows through the spring willows, each trailing bough must twist and turn. Turn your thoughts to the plight of one whose heart, like the willow, is in knots."[16]

The river otter went on in this manner, while the stingfish furrowed her brow in thought. In the end, not being made of stone or wood (although there was a trace of embarrassment on her perpetually ruddy face), she wrote: "Although your letter was unexpected, I am moved by the depth of your emotion. Even if your words are trifles and your feelings are empty, such is the way of this sad world. When it comes time for the autumn grasses to wither, perhaps the wind-blown leaves on the bitter vines will not reveal their hidden faces—but then again . . . If we allow ourselves to grow close, what shall become of us afterward? In any case, if you can, it would be better

344

16. The river otter quotes from the anonymous poem 708 in *Kokin wakashū* (*Collection of Ancient and Modern Poems*, ca. 905):

Suma no ama no	The salt-burning smoke
shio yaku keburi	of the Suma fisher-girls,
kaze wo itami	wounded by the wind,
omowanu kata ni	has bent
tanabikinikeri	in an unexpected direction.

This entire passage consists of a patchwork of stock poetic conceits and allusions stitched together by *kakekotoba*, homophonous pivot-words chosen for their double meaning. I have attempted to mark their placement in the original text with English-language homophones.

for you to imagine that you never saw me—but still, as they say, 'compared with how I feel now . . .'—so perhaps it is all in vain. Now, I know that I am the boughs of the young willow, and you shall be the wind that enters me."[17] Then she composed a poem:

omoi araba	If it is your wish
tamamo no kage ni	let us sleep in the shadow
ne mo shinamu	of the glistening seaweed;
hijikimono ni wa	we shall take for our quilt
nami wo shitsutsu mo	the waves spreading beneath us.[18]

She handed this to the river otter, who happily returned and presented it to the mountain god. At first, the mountain god could only weep with joy, tears streaming down his face; but then he hastily opened the letter, and you can be certain that he was readily swayed by the words, "I am the boughs of the young willow, and you shall be the wind that enters me."

"This evening, I will go to Princess Stingfish," he announced. "You must be my guide."

"That is easy enough," the otter said. "I will go with you."

Meanwhile, the Octopus Lay-Priest had heard what had happened. "What a disgrace!" he cried. "I have sent letter after letter to the stingfish, but she would not even accept them. And just when I was beginning to resent her, she sends a reply to some mountain god who's never so much as held an ink brush or wielded a sword, saying that she will yield to his suit.[19] It's unbearable! She must look down on me because I'm a priest, if she gives in so easily to *him*. Brother Squid, are you here? Let's go get that Princess Stingfish and throttle her to death!" Ranting on in this manner, he spread his eight arms and crawled about restlessly.

"I feel the same way you do," said the Squid Lay-Priest, who happened to be nearby. "Please, call together all of our kinsmen and resolve to do what must be done."

"That's just what I'll do," the octopus said. Needless to say, the reed octopus, the long-arm octopus, the spider octopus, the cuttlefish, the gold-spot octopus, the bean

---

17. With its florid, breathless prose and barrage of poetic allusions, Princess Stingfish's letter is a deliberate parody of literary elegance.
18. The poem is a reworking of a verse in section 3 of *The Tales of Ise*. The word translated here as "quilt," *hijiki-mono*, puns on *hijiki*, a kind of seaweed.
19. The Octopus Lay-Priest disparages the mountain god for his lack of scholarly and military achievements. The two pursuits—known as *bun* and *bu*, respectively—were *sine qua non* for any cultured gentleman.

The Stingfish

Enraged that Princess Stingfish prefers the mountain god to him, the Octopus Lay-Priest speaks with a pair of squid. (From *Okoze*, courtesy of the Tōyō University Library)

The mountain god and Princess Stingfish live happily ever after. (From *Okoze*, courtesy of the Tōyō University Library)

octopus, the reef squid, and the flying squid all came, being members of his clan; and the other clans, both great and small, joined the assembly as well.

Upon hearing of this, the stingfish decided that rather than remain where she was, she ought to hide herself deep in the mountains. Accompanied by the rockfish and the grunion, she floated to the top of the waves and then made her way into the mountains—and on the way, who should she bump into but the mountain god, traveling down the narrow path to the seashore with the river otter in tow!

Overcome with joy, the mountain god did not know up from down and began babbling nonsense: "We have met on the mountain path! The surface of the sea lies deep in the mountains, and the river otter is the stingfish!" After that, they returned side by side to the mountain god's dwelling and vowed that they would be as two birds flying wing to wing or two trees with their branches intertwined. And so it is that whenever someone takes senseless delight in looking at something ugly, people say it is like "showing the stingfish to the mountain god."

TRANSLATION AND INTRODUCTION BY LAURA K. NÜFFER

The Stingfish

Lady Tamamo

There is an ancient thread of shared wisdom that can be expressed in four simple words: never trust a fox. In the European context, this infamous trickster most often assumes a masculine identity, as exemplified by Reynard of the medieval beast fables; East Asian traditions tend to take a different view, conflating vulpine cunning with feminine wiles. By the fourth century, the fox had carved out a niche in China's mythical bestiary as a shape-shifting femme fatale, and this archetype gained a relatively early hold in the Japanese imagination, first appearing in the Buddhist tale collection *Nihon ryōiki* (*Record of Miraculous Events in Japan*, ca. 822) and going on to inspire a vast body of lore and literature.[1] The foxes in Japanese tales do not always turn their powers to evil ends: they may perpetrate harmless mischief or even act as benefactors to deserving humans, as in *The Tale of Tamamizu*. But when they are bad, they are very bad indeed, and none is worse than Lady Tamamo, the arch-villainess of Japanese foxlore and the protagonist of *Lady Tamamo* (*Tamamo no mae sōshi* [*The Tale of Lady Tamamo*]), otherwise known as *Tamamo no sōshi* (*The Tale of Tamamo*). As Michael Bathgate has observed, the story of Tamamo's seduction and near-destruction of Cloistered Emperor Toba "appear[s] in virtually every genre and medium from the fifteenth century until the nineteenth," including more

---

The translation and illustrations are from *Tamamo no mae sōshi*, a set of two illustrated scrolls (sixteenth century) in the collection of the Nezu Art Museum, typeset in Okudaira Hideo, ed., *Otogizōshi emaki* (Tokyo: Kadokawa Shoten, 1982), 187–93. The translator also consulted the variant text published as *Tamamo no sōshi*, a woodblock-printed book (1653) in the collection of the Keiō University Library, typeset in Yokoyama Shigeru, Mori Takenosuke, and Ōta Takeyama, eds., *Muromachi jidai monogatari shū* (Tokyo: Ōokayama Shoten, 1940), 4:296–315.

1. For an overview of early Chinese representations of foxes as seductresses, see Xiaofei Kang, *The Cult of the Fox: Power, Gender, and Popular Religions in Late Imperial and Modern China* (New York: Columbia University Press, 2005), 17–21.

than a dozen variants of the *otogizōshi* translated here, which is the oldest of this particular textual lineage.[2]

Paradoxically, Tamamo's demonic nature manifests itself as superhuman perfection. She enthralls the cloistered emperor with her beauty and, worse yet, enraptures him with her seemingly endless knowledge. Her lectures to the throne on various esoteric subjects make up a sizable proportion of the text, not only delaying narrative resolution but also foregrounding the inversion of the proper hierarchy of ruler and subject. Although Tamamo is eventually unmasked as a fox-demon and slain by the archer Miura-no-suke, her death does not entirely restore the status quo. *Lady Tamamo* is set during a deliberately chosen historical moment, shortly before the rise of the first shogunate, and the story, like *The Demon Shuten Dōji*, operates on multiple levels to retroactively legitimize warrior rule.[3] It also expresses a more generalized patriotic sentiment: Tamamo topples dynasties in India and China before finally meeting her match in Japan. Later versions of the *otogizōshi* overlaid these secular messages with a spiritual one, appending a coda in which the Buddhist monk Gennō pacifies Tamamo's vengeful ghost.

349

During the reign of Emperor Konoe, in the spring of the first year of the Kyūju era, a creature in the guise of a young woman came to the palace of Cloistered Emperor Toba.[4] To describe her appearance: her jade hairpins were splendid, and her dazzling robes were exquisitely woven. A single flutter of her lotus-petal eyelids cast a hundred enchantments, and the half-moon arch of her blue-black eyebrows won her ten thousand hearts. Although she did not powder her face, her complexion was perfectly white, and although she used no rouge, her cheeks were naturally red. Her glistening lips were like a scarlet blossom, and her flawless skin was the same as white snow. Her arms resembled jewels, and her teeth seemed to be made of mother-of-pearl.

2. Michael Bathgate, *The Fox's Craft in Japanese Religion and Folklore: Shapeshifters, Transformations, and Duplicities* (New York: Routledge, 2004), 7.

3. For a discussion of political discourse in *Lady Tamamo*, see Hamanaka Osamu, "*Tamamo no mae* monogatari kō: Dakiniten to ōken" in *Otogizōshi hyakka ryōran*, ed. Tokuda Kazuo (Tokyo: Kasama Shoin, 2008), 528–44.

4. Emperor Konoe (1139–1155, r. 1142–1155) was the son of Emperor Toba (1103–1156, r. 1107–1123). Although Toba "retired" from the throne, he was the de facto monarch of Japan for twenty-seven years, from the death of Cloistered Emperor Shirakawa (1053–1129, r. 1073–1087) until his own death. The Kyūju era spanned the years 1154 to 1156.

She spoke little, but with great thoughtfulness; her voice was gentle, and her words insightful. Not only did she adorn herself in fine silks and perfume her robes with orchid incense,[5] but she surpassed even the cleverest persons, and there was nothing she did not know about matters both spiritual and secular. Everyone said that if this were the era of Tang Xuanzong, she would not envy even Yang Guifei; or if this were the time of Han Wudi, she would not be inferior to Li Furen.[6] Because of this, graced by a surfeit of imperial favor, she was permitted to approach the Jade Seat, and on occasion His Majesty would question her about matters of every sort.

"Now," he asked, "in the holy scriptures, is it not said that 'delusion is the same as enlightenment, and samsara the same as nirvana'?[7] If this is so, does it not signify that even if we do not cut off delusion, we will attain enlightenment, and even if we do not shun samsara, we will attain nirvana?"

The lady answered, "How can I, as one encumbered by the Five Obstructions and the Three Obediences, hope to grasp the principles of the one true Middle Way?[8] However, the concept at the heart of this verse is very simple. For example, delusion and enlightenment are like water and ice; the difference between samsara and nirvana is that between voice and its echo.

"However, if one is dragged along by the galloping of one's unbridled passions, the mountains of delusion are high, and the path of enlightenment is difficult to climb. If one obeys the monkey-like trickery of one's mind, the ocean of samsara is deep and the shore of nirvana is difficult to reach. Thus one must uphold the precepts with one's body and contemplate impermanence with one's heart. When one looks at the people of this world, they all seek the four elements with their flesh and chase after the five senses with their minds. Therefore, although they may go to the meditation hall now and again and attempt to rinse off the dirt of their sin with the water of wisdom,

5. Until this point, the description of Lady Tamamo borrows heavily from a description of a nobleman's daughter in *Shinsarugakuki* (*An Account of the New Monkey Music*, eleventh century), a collection of vignettes by Fujiwara no Akihira (989–1066). Akihira's description itself contains an allusion to the famous Tang poem *Song of Everlasting Sorrow* (*Chang hen ge*, 806); the poet, Bai Juyi (772–846), writes that the imperial concubine Yang Guifei "cast a hundred enchantments with her smile."

6. Yang Guifei (719–756) and Li Furen (second century B.C.E.) were Chinese imperial concubines famed for their beauty. Significantly, both were criticized by later historians for having undermined proper governance; in particular, Yang Guifei became the scapegoat for the disastrous An Lushan Rebellion.

7. This is a quotation from *Mohe zhiguan*, "a comprehensive treatise on soteriological theory and meditation" written by Zhiyi (538–597), the founder of the Tiantai school of Buddhism. See Robert E. Buswell Jr. and Donald S. Lopez Jr., *The Princeton Dictionary of Buddhism* (Princeton, N.J.: Princeton University Press, 2014), 546.

8. According to the Lotus Sutra, the Five Obstructions are five forms of rebirth precluded to women because of their gender, including, most importantly, rebirth as a buddha. The Three Obediences are specific to women and hail from Confucian rather than Buddhist philosophy; Confucian tradition holds that a woman must obey her father as a girl, her husband after she has married, and her son after she has been widowed.

the waves of consciousness surge up, and it is difficult to wash away even a single speck of dust. Or they may occasionally pay reverence to a statue of the Buddha and try to illuminate their deluded minds with the moon of awakening, but the clouds of ignorance lie thick, and it is difficult to brighten the darkness of the long night.

"To the enlightened mind, there is nothing that is not in keeping with Buddhist Law. Thus exoteric doctrine teaches that 'there is not a single color or scent that is not the Middle Way,'[9] while esoteric doctrine explains that 'whether lifting a foot or lowering a hand, everything is the place of enlightenment.'[10] Both the exoteric and the esoteric teachings are true teachings, and so there is no Buddhist Law that lies outside mundane phenomena. Alas! 'Dwelling every day in perfect enlightenment, betraying one's buddha-nature every night.'"[11]

Because the lady was truly enlightened, her response differed not at all from the teachings of the great patriarchs and ancient sages. When the cloistered emperor heard this, his confusion was dispelled and he cared for her even more dearly than before. The high-ranking nobles of the cloistered emperor's court all pricked up their ears, and there was not a tongue that did not wag.

Again, the cloistered emperor asked her a question: "There are a great many mysteries in the world, among them something that resembles a river in the sky. It is called the 'River of Heaven,' but could a river truly flow in the sky?"

She answered, "This is made clear on the surface of the Holy Teachings, so how can Your Majesty not know? You may think that this is entirely in jest, but the Kusha school and others hold that what we see in the sky is the breath of the great elephant on which the Buddha rides. In my opinion, I believe that all the myriad things have spirits, and what we see is the spirit of the clouds."

"So, if this is the case for the spirit of the clouds," the cloistered emperor asked, "then does everything else have a so-called spirit as well?"

She answered, "Among the four colors of the lotus, the blue lotus flower is the spirit; among the six perfumes, sandalwood is the spirit; among metals, gold; among jewels, the pearl. The spirit of the mountains is Mount Sumeru, and the spirit of the oceans is the Inland Sea. Among birds, it is the *garuda*; among dragons, it is Sāgara; among beasts, it is the lion; among fish, it is the *makara*. The spirit of the heavens is

---

9. This is another quotation from the writings of Zhiyi. See Jacqueline Stone, "Realizing This World as the Buddha Land," in *Readings of the Lotus Sutra*, ed. Stephen Teiser and Jacqueline Stone (New York: Columbia University Press, 2009), 211.

10. This is a misquotation of the fourth Chan patriarch Dao Xin (580–651), who wrote that "every aspect of the mind and body, [even] lifting your foot and putting it down, always is the place of enlightenment" (quoted in David W. Chappell, "The Teachings of the Fourth Ch'an Patriarch Tao-hsin," in *Early Ch'an in China and Tibet*, ed. Lewis Lancaster and Whalen Lai [Berkeley, Calif.: Asian Humanities Press, 1983], 108).

11. This seems to be a quotation, although the source is unclear.

Brahma Heaven, and the spirit of the kings is the Wheel-Turning King. Shakyamuni is the spirit of good people, and devils are the spirit of wicked people."

If you asked her one question, she would give ten answers. There was nothing in heaven and earth that this she-creature did not know. Soon, His Majesty's mind grew even more befogged, and he did not let her stray even an inch from his august body. Indeed, although she was ostensibly known as Lady Keshō, His Majesty inwardly thought of her as his empress.[12]

One year, sometime after the twentieth day of the ninth month, regretting the fading of autumn, the cloistered emperor arranged for a recital of poetry and music at the palace concert hall. During this occasion, a fierce storm arose in the courtyard and blew out the torches. At that moment, Lady Keshō, who was standing near His Majesty's seat, began to give off a bright glow, illuminating the interior of the palace. Wondering at this bizarre phenomenon, the courtiers cast their eyes about in all directions and saw the light coming from within the pearl-embroidered blinds like the morning sun. Hastily laying aside their instruments, they attempted to make the cloistered emperor understand how uncanny all this was. But His Majesty merely said, "How wondrous that the body of Lady Keshō should give off light!" and issued an imperial order that henceforth she should be known as Lady Tamamo.[13] In every way, it was just too appalling: his affection undiminished, the cloistered emperor took the threat lightly and was not in the least bit frightened. However, His Majesty's feelings being what they were, no one could speak without caution.

To make matters worse, the cloistered emperor had a fondness for music and poetry, and one day the courtier seated in the lowest seat came forward and said, "It is said that 'the Way of poetry extends to the lowest seat,' but the hidden meaning of this is difficult to apprehend. How am I to understand it and put it into practice?"

The lady answered, "What we call poetry, or *waka*, is the facilitator of the three bonds and the model of the five virtues.[14] Thus its way is to discern yin and yang in their entirety by looking at the utmost yin of all creation. As for its origins, the gods Izanagi and Izanami matched verses, and the god Susano'o composed the 'eight cloud' poem.[15] From then on, the Way of poetry has remained unbroken, stirring

---

12. The name Keshō is a double entendre. Taken in a Buddhist sense, the word means "avatar" or "miraculous birth," but it can also refer to other, more sinister supernatural manifestations.

13. The name Tamamo literally means "jeweled seaweed"; it is an ancient poetic epithet inspired by the glistening of wet seaweed on the shore. Although seaweed may not strike modern Anglophone readers as the most alluring of plants, it has sensual, even erotic, connotations in classical Japanese literature.

14. The three bonds are the bonds uniting ruler and subject, father and son, and husband and wife; the five virtues are benevolence, righteousness, decorum, wisdom, and integrity. Both concepts derive from Confucian teachings.

15. In Japanese mythology, Izanagi and Izanami were the primordial god and goddess who created the Japanese islands; here, "verses" refers to the ritual exchange of greetings during their marriage ceremony.

the ancient airs of Naniwa Bay and drawing from the stream of the Tomi River, extending to the *Man'yōshū*, the *Kokinshū*, and other books of verse up to the present day.[16] Beginning from that which pervades heaven and man and stretching even to the voices of the nightingale that sings in the flowers and the frog that dwells in the water, there is nothing that is not a poem."[17] She spoke all too cleverly, and everyone from the cloistered emperor down to the minister and the nobles all wondered if she were a reincarnation of Princess Sotoori or Ono no Komachi.[18]

When questioned further about the Way of music, she answered: "Broadly speaking, what we call the 'five notes' are the roots of the breath of the five organs. This breath is like a five-colored cloud. The resonance of the breath governs the five notes. The five notes can be divided into the six modes, which can then be classified as belonging to either the *ryo* or the *ritsu* scales.[19] The *ryo* scales are the voice of times of joy, and the *ritsu* scales are the voice of times of sorrow. The *sōjō, ōshiki*, and *ichikotsu* modes are all *ryo* scales, while the *hyōjō* and *banshiki* modes are *ritsu* scales. The *mujō* mode proceeds from both the *ryo* and the *ritsu* scales together. When speaking of *ryo* and *ritsu*, the term *mujō* is used in place of the term *fujō*. Generally, each of the modes has a first and second tone. The upper tone is known as the first tone, while the lower tone is known as the second. In terms of inhalation and exhalation, releasing breath produces the upper tone, while drawing breath produces the lower tone. One should approach the six modes with this understanding."[20]

After she said this, somebody then asked, "Why is it that the *sōjō, ōshiki*, and *ichikotsu* modes are known as 'the voice of joy' and classified as *ryo* scales, while the *hyōjō* and *banshiki* modes are known as 'the voice of sorrow' and classified as *ritsu* scales?"

Izanagi's son Susano'o is credited with composing the first *waka* (traditional thirty-one-syllable poem)—the "eight cloud" poem—which he is said to have recited after taking a wife.

16. The Tomi River and Naniwa Bay were locations frequently mentioned in classical poetry. *Man'yōshū* (*Collection of Myriad Leaves*, ca. 785) and *Kokin wakashū* (*Collection of Poems Ancient and Modern*, ca. 905) are generally recognized as the greatest of Japan's poetry anthologies.

17. This sentence paraphrases the opening of the famous preface to *Kokin wakashū* by Ki no Tsurayuki (872–945), the principal compiler of the anthology.

18. Princess Sotoori (Sotoorihime) was the consort of the quasi-historical Emperor Ingyō (traditionally 376–453, r. 411–453). Two verses attributed to her appear in *Nihon shoki* (*The Chronicles of Japan*, 720), and thanks to this she came to be regarded as the patron goddess of poetry. Ono no Komachi (ca. 825–ca. 900), said to be a descendant of Sotoori, was likewise renowned for her skill as a poet. In addition to their literary talents, both women were famous for their beauty.

19. Both *ryo* and *ritsu* are pentatonic scales used in traditional Japanese court music; they are roughly analogous to the major and minor scales, respectively. See János Kárpáti, "Tonality in Japanese Court Music," *Studia Musicologica* 25 (1983): 171–82.

20. The first half of Tamamo's disquisition on music closely parallels a passage from *Kakyō*, by the dramatist Zeami (ca. 1363–ca. 1443). See *On the Art of Nō Drama: The Major Treatises of Zeami*, trans. J. Thomas Rimer and Yamazaki Masakazu (Princeton, N.J.: Princeton University Press, 1984), 77–78.

Lady Tamamo

The lady answered, "Human existence intermingles both suffering and pleasure. The prosperous must inevitably decline, and all living beings must inevitably perish,[21] showing the impermanence of things, which does not wait for even the pause between one breath and the next. To explain further, first, the *sōjō* mode is the root of the breath that emanates from the liver. Among the four seasons, it corresponds with spring, and among the five phases, it corresponds with wood. Spring is the time when the trees and grasses come to life. Heaven bestows the seed, and earth nourishes it; thus all trees and grasses represent a fusion of yin and yang. Heaven and earth are like father and mother, while the trees and grasses are like their children. In this manner, the upper *mujō* mode is the father of the *sōjō* mode, and the lower *mujō* the mother. For this reason *sōjō* is written with characters meaning 'to harmonize together.' All things between heaven and earth rejoice in life; therefore, the *sōjō* mode is called 'the voice of joy' and classified as a *ryo* scale.

"Next, the *ōshiki* mode is the root of the breath that emanates from the heart. Among the four seasons, it corresponds with summer, and among the five phases, it corresponds with fire. Summer is the time when the trees and grasses flourish. Because all living beings rejoice in prosperity, the *ōshiki* mode is called 'the voice of joy' and classified as a *ryo* scale.

"Next, the *ichikotsu* mode is the root of the breath that emanates from the spleen. Among the four seasons, it corresponds with midsummer, and among the five phases, it corresponds with earth. Midsummer is the king of the four seasons. Thus this mode is called *ichikotsu*—*kotsu*, meaning 'to surpass,' to emphasize its power, and *ichi*, meaning 'one,' because it unites the four seasons. Earth is constant and does not decline; therefore, it causes rejoicing. Because of this, the *ichikotsu* mode is called 'the voice of joy' and classified as a *ryo* scale.

"The *ryo* scales abound in the masculine principle, which knows only joy and is without sorrow. Therefore, the *sōjō*, *ōshiki*, and *ichikotsu* modes are known as 'the voice of joy' and classified as *ryo* scales.

"Next, the *hyōjō* mode is the root of the breath that emanates from the lungs. Among the four seasons, it corresponds with autumn, and among the five phases, it corresponds with metal. In autumn, all things show signs of decline and have an aura of melancholy; therefore, the *hyōjō* mode is called 'the voice of sorrow' and classified as a *ritsu* scale.

---

21. This is a paraphrase of the famous opening line of *The Tale of the Heike* (thirteenth century), a military epic chronicling the Genpei War (1180–1185). The choice of allusion is significant, as *Lady Tamamo* foreshadows the events that would lead to this conflict.

354

"Next, the *banshiki* mode is the root of the breath that emanates from the kidneys. Among the four seasons, it corresponds with winter, and among the five phases, it corresponds with water. In winter, all things are at death's door; therefore, the *banshiki* mode is called 'the voice of sorrow' and is classified as a *ritsu* scale. The *ritsu* scales abound in the feminine principle, which waxes full of sorrow and is without joy. Therefore, both the *hyōjō* mode and the *banshiki* mode are known as 'the voice of sorrow' and classified as *ritsu* scales."

The courtiers questioned her still further, asking, "We have received a broad understanding of the Way of music and the Way of Japanese poetry, but who was the first person to play the koto?"

"It was Fuxi who invented the koto. The length of the koto, three feet and six inches, is modeled after the 360 days of the year; the five strings are modeled after the five phases. The *Book of Zhou* says that King Wen enjoyed the koto and added an extra string, which is known as 'Wen's string.' Later, King Wu added another string, which is known as 'Wu's string.'[22] For this reason, the seven strings of the koto are known as *gong, shang, jiao, zhi, yu, wen,* and *wu.* As for the large koto, it was invented by the Yellow Emperor. The panpipes were invented by Nuwa, the younger sister of Fuxi. The vertical flute was invented by Shun of Yu. The *sō no* koto was invented by Meng Tian. The *biwa* was invented by Fuxi. The transverse flute was invented by Qiu Zhong in the time of Han Wudi. The hand drum was invented by King Mu of Qin. The war drum was invented on the orders of Di Ku. The reed flute was created by Liu Zhou of Jin. Bells were first cast by a man known as Fushi. The bow and arrow were invented in the time of the Yellow Emperor. The ax was invented by Shennong. The wheel was invented by the Yellow Emperor. The boat was invented by a man known as Huo Di. Poetry was invented by a man known as Li Ling. The inkstone was invented by Zi Lu. The brush was invented by Meng Tian. Ink was first made by a man known as Xing Yi.[23] Paper was first made by Cai Lun. Fans were invented by Lady Ban. *Go* was invented by Prince Danzhu, the son of Emperor Yao. Backgammon was invented by Zijian. The crown was invented by the Yellow Emperor. Armor was invented by Chi You. The ball was invented by the Yellow Emperor. The first well was dug by Bo Yi. The first Buddhist temple was built during the time of Emperor Ming of Han."

---

22. This sentence is absent from the Nezu Art Museum text and is interpolated from the woodblock-printed edition of the tale.
23. The text names the inventor of ink as 那夢 (Na Meng), which appears to be an error for 邢夷 (Xing Yi). See Martina Siebert, "Making Technology History," in *Cultures of Knowledge: Technology in Chinese History,* ed. Dagmar Schäfer (Leiden: Brill, 2012), 272.

Lady Tamamo

Like this, even when the courtiers joined forces to question her about everything between heaven and earth, she answered without missing a single detail. And so the courtiers retreated, their tongues wagging.

Now as the cloistered emperor grew even more infatuated, his royal body began to grow unwell. He thought it nothing more than a common ailment, but as the days went by his illness worsened. He summoned the court physician, who conducted an examination. "Your Majesty's illness is caused by an evil spirit," he pronounced. "I am unable to cure it."

Now this court physician was a descendant of Waké no Akemochi; the Way of poisons and medicines and the methods of the healing arts held no secrets unknown to him. He was a god of treating disease and curing sickness, a buddha of acupuncture and moxibustion. He knew how to take the pulse of the five solid organs and the six hollow organs, and he excelled at diagnosing the root cause of the 404 diseases. He was a master of his craft, no different from Jivaka, the equal of Shen Nong and

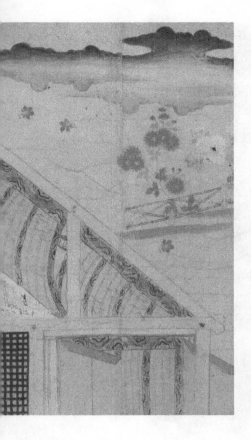

Lady Tamamo (*upper left*) answers questions from the cloistered emperor's courtiers. (From *Tamamo no mae sōshi*, courtesy of the Nezu Museum of Art)

Bian Que.[24] When he withdrew, the entire court at once turned their faces to heaven and lamented.

"Summon the head of the Bureau of Geomancy!" the cloistered emperor then declared, and so Abe no Yasunari was called and asked to perform a divination. He could not give any details, but he did say, "I discern that Your Majesty's illness has become exceedingly grave. Prayers should be begun immediately." Now, Lord Yasunari had mastered the magical techniques of Abe no Seimei.[25] When he divined the identity of a hidden object, it was as if he were seeing it with his own eyes, and when

24. The legendary Indian physician Jivaka was said to have treated the Buddha himself. The Chinese culture hero Shen Nong supposedly invented acupuncture and discovered the use of medicinal herbs, while Bian Que (fifth century B.C.E.), a quasi-historical physician, is credited with various miraculous feats of healing.

25. Abe no Seimei (921–1005) was a yin-yang master who became legendary for his feats of wizardry. He appears as a character in numerous tales, including, in this volume, *The Demon Shuten Dōji*, and is cited in *The Tale of the Mouse*.

Lady Tamamo

he guessed the nature of a possessing spirit, it was as if he were pointing to the palm of his hand. He could summon and dismiss the twelve heavenly generals; the thirty-six animals of the zodiac were at his beck and call. Thus although he had the outward form of a human, his soul was that of a god or a demon; and although his body resided in the mortal world, his spirit presided over heaven and earth.[26]

At that moment, all the courtiers, high- and low-ranking alike, were greatly astonished. High priests from Kōfukuji Temple and Enryakuji Temple were summoned, along with virtuous ascetics from various temples and mountains; they lined up rows of exoteric and esoteric altars, and joined their voices in chanting the Buddha's

26. Both the description of Abe no Yasunari and the preceding description of the court physician borrow extensively from *An Account of the New Monkey Music*. The thirty-six animals of the zodiac (*sanjūrokkin*) refers to the twelve principal animals of the zodiac and their twenty-four affiliated animals, which are employed in divination.

High priests pray for the cloistered emperor's recovery from a mysterious illness. (From *Tamamo no mae sōshi*, courtesy of the Nezu Museum of Art)

name and reciting sutras, praying with all their might. On the seventh day of prayer, the rituals reached their conclusion, but there was no sign of improvement. Even as his body grew weaker and weaker, the cloistered emperor continued to love Lady Tamamo beyond all reason, and now he spoke to her with tears in his eyes. "I knew already that one of us must cross the threshold of ceaseless change before the other," he lamented, "but when I think that we will be parted before much longer, I lose all concept of mortality and I forget that it is said that 'all those who meet must part.'"

Lady Tamamo replied, "Surely it is thanks to virtuous conduct in a past life that, pathetic though I am, I have been permitted to draw so near Your Majesty's august countenance. Alas, if only you could live for eighty thousand eons, like those who dwell in the highest heaven! This is my sole prayer. But if something were to happen to you, then I would not wish to linger in this world for even a day or a moment; I would wish only that we could remain together until we have both achieved perfect

Lady Tamamo

enlightenment." Grieving, she threw herself down beside the cloistered emperor and wailed. Lamenting that the week of prayer had produced no effect, the assembled priests withdrew.

Some time later, Yasunari made another report to the cloistered emperor. "I ought to give the details of my findings, but I fear I must refrain," he said, and did not state anything clearly. Speaking as one, the noblemen ordered him to say everything without hesitation. "There is nothing particularly mysterious about His Majesty's illness," Yasunari said. "It is the doing of that creature in human guise, Lady Tamamo. If His Majesty rids himself of this she-devil, his illness will be cured at once."

High and low, all who heard this stood aghast, too dumbfounded to speak. When discussion resumed, detailed inquiries were made into the particulars of the situation, and Yasunari said, "In the province of Shimotsuke, in a place called Nasu Moor, there is a fox that has lived for eight hundred years. This fox is seven arm-spans long, and it has two tails.[27] As to the origins of this fox . . . the Benevolent King Sutra tells us that there once was a king in the kingdom of Devala. This king had a single son, a prince called Kalmashapada.[28] Following the teachings of the heretic Radha, this prince intended to cut off the heads of a thousand kings and offer them to a tomb god, selfishly hoping to seize their thrones as well. He assembled tens of thousands of powerful warriors and demon kings and marched on the capitals of countries in every direction: north and south, east and west, near and far. As the conquests continued, he had captured 999 kings, and lacked only one. He held a council regarding what to do next, and the heretic advised him again: 'Ten thousand leagues to the north, there is a king known as Shrutasoma; capture this king to complete the count.'[29] The prince immediately sent powerful warriors to abduct this king. Now that he had the full thousand kings, he was just about to cut off their heads and offer them to the tomb god when Shrutasoma turned toward Kalmashapada and, pressing his hands together, pleaded, 'Grant me one day's leave so that I may pay homage to the Three Treasures and make offerings to itinerant monks.' And so he was given one day's leave.

"Now, King Shrutasoma, following the law of the Seven Buddhas of the Past, invited one hundred priests and asked them to give readings of the Perfection of Wisdom Sutra. The head priest chanted a verse on behalf of King Shrutasoma: 'In the fires of an eon's end, heaven and earth are thoroughly incinerated; Sumeru and its

27. In both Chinese and Japanese mythology, foxes were believed to grow additional tails as they aged, signaling their acquisition of supernatural powers. In some versions of *Lady Tamamo*, the fox has nine tails rather than two.
28. According to the ancient Indian epic *Mahabharata*, Prince Kalmashapada was cursed to become a flesh-eating demon in retribution for his mistreatment of holy ascetics.
29. Shrutasoma appears in the Buddhist Jātaka tales, where he is identified as a previous incarnation of the historical Buddha.

great oceans are all reduced to ashes.'[30] When King Shrutasoma heard these verses, he realized the four noble truths and the twelve-fold chain and understood the emptiness of self. Prince Kalmashapada, too, witnessed the truth of the emptiness of all phenomena, and he immediately repented of his wicked thoughts, turning to the thousand kings and saying, 'Guided by heresy, I brought about evil and committed atrocities. Now, quickly, return to your countries, practice wisdom, and carry out the Way of the Buddha.' The prince, too, had been awakened to the Way, and gained awareness that nothing arises or perishes.

"The tomb god to whom Prince Kalmashapada had intended to offer sacrifices so long ago is now this fox. This fox deceived Kalmashapada so he would cut off the heads of a thousand kings as a sacrifice, but through the might of the Buddhist teachings, he was awakened to the Way and did not cut off the heads of the thousand kings. When this happened, the tomb god vowed that however many ages and however many rebirths might go by, it would be born in the body of a wild fox and manifest itself in countries where Buddhism flourished, sometimes taking the form of a consort or a lady-in-waiting, other times becoming a serving woman or an attendant, but always drawing close to the emperor and working to destroy the Buddhist teachings. This fox manifested itself in China as the consort Bao Si, who begged favors of King You and at last destroyed him.[31] Although Japan is a small country, like a few grains of millet scattered on the edge of the earth, the Buddha's teachings have spread widely here; and so the fox vowed to destroy these teachings, steal the life of the ruler, and become king of Japan." Yasunari's voice grew quieter and quieter as he spoke.

Although the cloistered emperor heard all this, he did not believe it, and his illness worsened apace. A council was held regarding how to proceed, and Yasunari spoke again: "I will conduct a ceremony invoking the Lord of Mount Tai; when I do, have Lady Tamamo carry the sacred wand, and that which I have spoken of will be made manifest immediately."[32] And so all kinds of rare treasures were assembled as offerings, and twelve bushels of white rice were scattered in the courtyard. When the ceremony was about to begin and Lady Tamamo was asked to carry the sacred wand, her face suddenly went pale: "Pathetic though I am, I have been permitted the

30. Translation modified from Charles D. Orzech, *Politics and Transcendent Wisdom: The Scripture for Humane Kings in the Creation of Chinese Buddhism* (University Park: Pennsylvania State University Press, 1998), 163.

31. According to *Records of the Grand Historian* (*Shiji*, first century B.C.E.) by Sima Qian (ca. 145–ca. 85 B.C.E.), Bao Si was the beautiful but perpetually melancholy consort of King You (795–771 B.C.E., r. 781–771 B.C.E.). The only thing that made Bao Si smile was the beacon fires used to assemble the troops, and so the king repeatedly lit these fires in order to amuse her. When barbarian tribes invaded, the troops no longer recognized the beacon fires as a summons, and the Zhou dynasty fell.

32. Mount Tai, located in eastern China, served as a center of cultic worship for thousands of years, and its tutelary deity held a prominent place in the Daoist pantheon. The sacred wand (*gohei*) was a wooden staff with paper streamers used in Shinto rituals.

honor of drawing near His Majesty's august countenance. Carrying the sacred wand
at a purification ceremony is the duty of a low-ranking woman. Moreover, why
should I alone among all these people be humiliated in this fashion?" She went on in
this manner, speaking with resentment.

The man who was then serving as prime minister pleaded with her, saying, "Your
reservations notwithstanding, a master astrologer has determined the auspicious and
inauspicious times for the ceremony by examining the mutual compatibility of the five
phases. Our prayers have been determined to be auspicious because the officiant and
the patron are compatible, the year and the month are compatible, and the day and the
hour are compatible. Therefore, although there are many men and women in the cloistered emperor's court, the head of the Bureau of Geomancy has designated you as
the bearer of the sacred wand because you alone are compatible. If it is for the sake
of making His Majesty well, then what could be degrading about even the humblest
task? It is said that Emperor Shōmu's consort heated water for one hundred days
and washed the filth from one thousand beggars, and even in ancient times, no one
looked down on this as a humble task.[33] This invocation of the Lord of Mount Tai is

33. The prime minister refers to the legend of Empress Kōmyō (701–760), who, according to one medieval
source, is said to have sucked the puss from the suppurating sores of the thousandth beggar. See R. Keller

Lady Tamamo (*center*) is commanded to carry the sacred wand at a ceremony for the Lord of Mount Tai. (From *Tamamo no mae sōshi*, courtesy of the Nezu Museum of Art)

for the sake of curing His Majesty's illness; if you carry the sacred wand, everyone will admire the extent of your devotion, and even if it does become known, no one could possibly criticize you for it." His logic was infallible, and so Lady Tamamo agreed to carry the sacred wand.

Lady Tamamo was always a beauty without peer, but today, dressed in her formal robes, she was truly beyond words. She accepted the sacred wand, but midway through the ceremony, she could be seen shaking it frantically—and then she vanished, as if into thin air. Yasunari's prediction could not have been more accurate if he had been pointing to the palm of his own hand.

The courtiers held a council regarding how they should rid themselves of this fox, and two brilliant marksmen came forward. "It is said that in China, Yi shot down the nine suns, and in our own land, Yorimasa shot the *nue* in the palace.[34]

Kimbrough, *Preachers, Poets, Women, and the Way: Izumi Shikibu and Buddhist Literature of Medieval Japan* (Ann Arbor: University of Michigan Center for Japanese Studies, 2008), 217.

34. According to Chinese myth, there were once ten suns in the sky, threatening to set the world on fire. The great archer Yi prevented this destruction by shooting down all but one of them. The *nue*—a supernatural creature sometimes imagined as a bird, and sometimes as a monstrous hybrid of monkey, tiger, and snake—was supposedly driven from the imperial palace by Minamoto no Yorimasa (1106–1180). See Helen Craig McCullough, trans., *The Tale of the Heike* (Stanford, Calif.: Stanford University Press, 1988), 160–63.

Lady Tamamo

These men were truly divine masters of archery. Now, in our own land, how could anybody object to finding talented bowmen who wish to make a name for themselves and ordering them to shoot the fox?" All present agreed, and within a few days Kazusa-no-suke and Miura-no-suke of the eastern provinces had received an edict from the cloistered emperor that declared: "Regarding His Majesty's illness of this past autumn, the head of the Bureau of Geomancy, Abe no Yasunari, has offered the following diagnosis: 'In Nasu Moor in Shimotsuke Province, there is a fox possessing two tails and measuring seven arm-spans in length. If this fox is disposed of, His Majesty's illness will be cured posthaste.' Therefore, you are commanded to proceed thither and hunt the aforementioned fox."

When the edict from the cloistered emperor arrived, both Kazusa-no-suke and Miura-no-suke cleansed themselves, donned white robes, and knelt in the courtyard, bowing three times as they received it. They quickly gathered their households

Kazusa-no-suke and Miura-no-suke hunt the two-tailed fox on Nasu Moor. (From *Tamamo no mae sōshi*, courtesy of the Nezu Museum of Art)

together and held a council. "Although there are any number of famous warriors in the eastern provinces, we two alone have received an edict from the cloistered emperor," they said. "Honor in the present day and an example for future generations— what could be better than this? All you who are loyal to us, let us go to this place, leaving not a single man behind, and use all our skill with bow and arrow!" They set out without a moment's delay.

Kazusa-no-suke and Miura-no-suke arrived on the same day. Looking across the moor, they saw that it was vast and wild, with grass growing so deep that it seemed neither a horse nor a man could push through it. Nonetheless, making use of the force of their numbers, they managed to cut back the grass, and then they left the rest to their mounts. As soon as they entered the moor, a fox with two tails came running out of the deep grass, exactly as Yasunari had predicted. Kazusa-no-suke, Miura-no-suke, and their retainers all raced ahead, vying for the honor of shooting first, but

Lady Tamamo

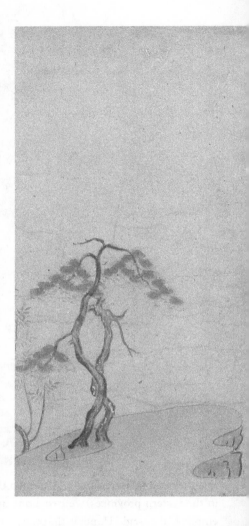

Lady Tamamo appears to Miura-no-suke in a dream. (From *Tamamo no mae sōshi*, courtesy of the Nezu Museum of Art)

their quarry was a monster with god-like powers. If their bow-hands held steady, then their string-hands slipped, and if their string-hands held steady, then their bow-hands slipped; if they searched for it above ground, it dove beneath the earth, and if they searched for it below ground, it ran through the sky. The fox raced every which way without so much as slowing, and no amount of skill could bring it down. After the fox had vanished to who-knew-where, they held a council. "With our current skill as archers, we will not be able to bring down this fox," they said. "Let us return to our province for a while and come up with a plan to train with our bows and arrows. Then we will hunt the fox." And so they all returned to their own homes.

This was Kazusa-no-suke's plan: he released balls from the back of an especially fleet-footed horse, and then used these balls as targets. This was Miura-no-suke's plan: because dogs are similar to foxes, he spent one hundred days chasing down dogs on horseback.

During their training, their arrows struck even the most impossible targets. Certain that they could not fail to hit the fox, they once more set out for Nasu Moor, intending to catch it once and for all—but they could not. For seven days and seven nights they camped there, until at last Kazusa-no-suke and Miura-no-suke climbed up to a high place and conferred.

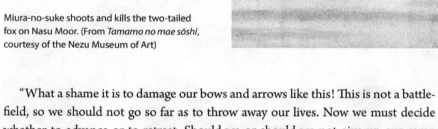

Miura-no-suke shoots and kills the two-tailed
fox on Nasu Moor. (From *Tamamo no mae sōshi*,
courtesy of the Nezu Museum of Art)

"What a shame it is to damage our bows and arrows like this! This is not a battle-field, so we should not go so far as to throw away our lives. Now we must decide whether to advance or to retreat. Should we or should we not give up our camp here? Either way, if we do not catch this fox, we cannot return to our home province. We will become vagrants and hide away in some mountain forest. Hail with highest reverence the Great Shrine of Amaterasu at Ise, protector of the nation! Hail with highest reverence the Triple Great bodhisattva Hachiman, guardian of a hundred kings! Hail with highest reverence the Nikkō Avatar of the Great Shrine at Utsu-nomiya! Please allow us to catch this fox tomorrow. Even if it is a demon with god-like powers, how could it fail to fear the royal authority? Although we may live in a degenerate age, the sun and the moon have not yet fallen to earth. Long ago, during the reign of Emperor Daigo, there was an imperial excursion to the pond in Shinsen Garden. There was a gray heron by the water's edge, and the emperor commanded a sixth-rank courtier to bring it to him. When the courtier moved forward, the heron began to spread its wings, and the courtier said, 'I do not seek to capture you for my

own sake, but by imperial command; do not fly away!' As soon as he spoke, the heron immediately settled itself, and the courtier captured it. The emperor said, 'Because you have made manifest Our royal authority, you shall be King of the Birds,' and he immediately conferred the fifth rank upon the heron, after which he released it. Because of this, the gray heron is known as the Fifth Rank Heron.[35] Such is the weight of the royal authority. How could this be any different now than it was in ancient times? Even if the royal authority is not so great as it once was, if it is combined with divine power, how could we fail to shoot down this fox?"

They prayed with utmost sincerity and then slept briefly. Miura-no-suke dreamed of a woman, no older than twenty and extremely beautiful, who turned to him with tears streaming down her face. "My wishes shall surely be fulfilled, and the longings

35. The episode involving Emperor Daigo (885–930, r. 897–930) and the heron is the subject of the noh play *Sagi* (*The White Heron*) and appears in *The Tale of the Heike* (Kakuichi text [1371]). See McCullough, trans., *Tale of the Heike*, 175.

Lady Tamamo

of the masses shall likewise be satisfied," she said.[36] "Are you wondering who I am? It is my life you seek. Please spare me if you can. If you do, I will watch over your children, your grandchildren, and all their descendants."

As she said this, Miura-no-suke started awake and immediately summoned his retainers. "I just had a miraculous dream," he said. "It should be easy enough to catch the fox now. Ride out, men!" They saddled their horses and set off on the hunt before dawn. Early in the hour of the dragon,[37] as the sun was coming up, the fox raced out of the moor toward the mountains. As it did, Miura-no-suke drew an arrow—iron-tipped and fletched with dyed feathers—nocked it to his bow, and brought down the fox with a single shot. Then he took the body and set out for the capital, traveling day and night so he could present it for the cloistered emperor's inspection.

Overcome with admiration for this extraordinary and unprecedented feat, the cloistered emperor decreed to Miura-no-suke, "You must reenact the hunt, wearing the same clothes that you wore on Nasu Moor." He then had a single red dog brought out. To this day, this is known as the "single-rider dog chase."[38]

Afterward, the fox's body was stored in the Uji Treasure House, where it remains to the present day. The details have been passed down in spoken legend. Inside the fox's belly, there was a gold jar that housed a relic of the Buddha; this was presented to the cloistered emperor. Its forehead held a white jewel that shone day and night; Miura-no-suke received this jewel, and it became the greatest treasure of his house. In the tips of the fox's tails, there were two needles—one white, one red—both of which were received by Kazusa-no-suke. He presented the red needle as an offering at his family temple, Seichōji; the white needle he gave to Minamoto no Yoritomo during his exile in Izu Province. It was because Yoritomo gained possession of this needle that he mounted a rebellion and chastised the Taira, washing away the shame of his father's defeat.[39] What a rare and marvelous working of karma! Even in these latter days, the royal authority carries weight, and the power of the gods and buddhas has not yet been exhausted, as all those who read this tale must know.

TRANSLATION AND INTRODUCTION BY LAURA K. NÜFFER

36. The fox-demon quotes from chapter 9 of the Lotus Sutra. See Burton Watson, trans., *The Lotus Sutra* (New York: Columbia University Press, 1993), 305.
37. The hour of the dragon is approximately 7:00 to 9:00 A.M.
38. The traditional dog chase involved teams of mounted archers competing to shoot multiple dogs.
39. Minamoto no Yoritomo (1147–1199) was the son of Minamoto no Yoshitomo (1123–1160), who was killed for his role in the Heiji Rebellion (1159). Yoritomo, then twelve years old, was exiled to Izu Province. He would later lead the Minamoto forces to victory in the Genpei War and become de facto ruler of the country as shogun.

The Tale of the Clam

The Tale of the Clam (*Hamaguri no sōshi*) chronicles the meeting, marriage, and eventual parting of two unlikely lovers: a poor middle-aged fisherman and the titular clam. As a testament to the enduring popularity of this odd couple, the tale survives in over a dozen variant texts produced over more than three centuries. The earliest of these, dated to 1526, bears the title *Shūyū no monogatari* (*The Tale of Shūyū*) after the hero of the same name. Shūyū became Shiyū and then Shishiu in subsequent retellings, but he is best known as Shijira, as he is called in roughly half the extant texts, including the version translated here.[1] Whatever his name, the male protagonist seems to have dropped out of the title relatively early in the tale's evolution, replaced by his mollusk wife. This change of namesakes is only fitting, given that the clam plays a far more active role in the story than does her hapless human husband.

Like so many animals in *otogizōshi*, the clam in *The Tale of the Clam* is not constrained by the limitations of her flesh-and-blood counterparts. She shifts easily from one identity to another, shedding her shell to become a beautiful maiden before at last revealing herself as a servant of the bodhisattva Kannon (Skt. Avalokiteśvara), sent to reward Shijira for his extraordinary filial piety. Much of the tale's interest derives from Shijira's ongoing failure to recognize his good fortune: he repeatedly attempts to throw the clam back into the water when it becomes snagged on his

The translation and illustrations are from the woodblock-printed *Hamaguri no sōshi* in the Osaka publisher Shibukawa Seiemon's *Companion Library* (*Otogi bunko*, early eighteenth century), typeset and annotated in Ichiko Teiji, ed., *Otogizōshi*, Nihon koten bungaku taikei 38 (Tokyo: Iwanami Shoten, 1958), 212–28.

1. Kobayashi Yuka, "Otogizōshi *Hamaguri no sōshi* no denpon ni tsuite no kōsatsu," *Koten bungaku kenkyū* 1 (1992): 38–39, 41–42; Matsumoto Ryūshin, *Eiin Muromachi monogatari shūsei* (Tokyo: Kyūko Shoin, 1970), 1:263. Nakano Maori (now Saitō Maori) suggests that the earliest forms of the tale likely gave the protagonist's name as Shijira, and that variants such as Shūyū are later corruptions, in "*Hamaguri no sōshi kō*," *Kokugo kokubun* 63, no. 3 (1994): 27–28. Shijira, a type of finely woven cotton fabric, does seem to be a particularly fitting name for the protagonist, who becomes fabulously wealthy thanks to his wife's skill as a weaver.

fishing line, and he shows little more enthusiasm for the woman who emerges from its shell. But for all his reluctance, Shijira allows himself to be led (and wed) by his unwanted guest, and so he makes his unwitting way to this-worldly prosperity and next-worldly bliss.

Like its shape-shifting heroine, *The Tale of the Clam* resists easy classification; it is simultaneously a Buddhist devotional tale, a tale of foreign lands (*ikoku monoga-tari*), and an interspecies tale (*irui monogatari*). The Buddhist themes of the story fit neatly with its exotic setting: the Indian kingdom of Magadha, where the historical Buddha lived and taught for many years. As one of the most enduringly popular figures in the Buddhist pantheon, Kannon appeared in dozens of distinct icono-graphic forms. Among them is the Clamshell Kannon (Kōri Kannon), first wor-shipped by Chinese fishermen; her introduction to Japan in the Muromachi period (1337–1573) doubtless provided the inspiration for *The Tale of the Clam*.[2]

In India, on the outskirts of the kingdom of Magadha,[3] there once lived a man named Shijira. He was an extraordinarily poor man. He had lost his father early and had only his mother to care for; but in those days, a terrible famine was sweeping India, and countless people wasted away and died. Shijira struggled to feed his mother and performed all manner of labor in order to support her, raising his eyes up to heaven and prostrating himself on the earth. But however much he labored, it was all to no avail.

Then an idea came to him: he would go to the bay with his pole and line so that he might support his mother by catching fish. And so he went to the bay and rowed a small boat out to the open sea, where he cast his line. He caught fish of all sorts, and so day after day he was able to feed his mother. Shijira was glad about this; but

2. The association between Kannon and clamshells may derive in part from the latter's resemblance to the female genitalia; although depicted as male in most canonical sources, Kannon attracted the greatest pop-ular devotion in feminine form. Japanese folklore seems to have gendered clams as female even in contexts unrelated to Buddhism, as is demonstrated by a widely distributed folktale known as *hamaguri nyōbō* (the clam-wife). In this story, a poor fisherman is visited by a mysterious woman who becomes his wife and serves him delicious meals every night. One day, the fisherman spies on his wife while she is cooking and catches her urinating into the pot; worse yet, he realizes that her urine tastes delicious because she is in fact a clam. Her identity discovered, the clam-woman disappears back into the ocean. The relationship be-tween the clam-wife folktale and *The Tale of the Clam* is unclear, although it is unlikely that they developed in isolation from each other.

3. Located in the Ganges River valley, Magadha ranked among the most powerful Indian kingdoms during the Buddha's lifetime and proved fertile ground for early Buddhism in subsequent centuries.

Shijira catches a clam. (From *Hamaguri no sōshi* [Shibukawa printing], courtesy of the University of Tokyo Library System, Katei Bunko)

then one day, when he went to the bay yet again and cast his line, he did not catch a single fish, even as the day wore on into evening. Shijira wondered if perhaps this was retribution for all the life he had taken to feed his mother. And later, when he still had not caught any fish, he thought, "How impatient my mother must be, waiting for me! She has not yet had anything to eat, and she must be growing fatigued." All thought of fishing slipped from his mind, for he could think only of his mother. But perhaps the fishing rod had a mind of its own, for just then—aha!—it seemed that Shijira had at last caught a fish. Carefully he pulled up his line, and when he looked, he saw that his hook was caught on a pretty little clam.

"What is this? What use could it possibly be?" Shijira thought, and tossed the clam into the sea. Well, clearly there were no fish to be had here, so he rowed his boat to the west and cast his line there—and when he did, there it was again, the same clam that he had caught in the waters to the south. "Hm, how strange!" Shijira thought, and once more he released it, tossing it into the sea.

After that, he rowed to the north and cast his line: and when he did, up once more came the clam that he had pulled up in the sea to the west. Then Shijira

The Tale of the Clam

The clam opens to reveal a beautiful young woman. (From *Hamaguri no sōshi* [Shibukawa printing], courtesy of the University of Tokyo Library System, Katei Bunko)

thought, "This is indeed something mysterious and strange, to pull up the same clam not once, not twice, but three times! I seem to have a three-fold bond with it." This time, he pulled it up all the way and tossed it into his boat. When he lowered his line again, the clam suddenly began to grow bigger. Oh, how strange! Shijira took it and tried to drop it into the sea, but just as he did, three rays of golden light shone out from inside the clam. What was this? Shijira's eyes widened, and his stomach dropped; terrified, he backed away. The shell of the clam swung open, and from it emerged a gorgeous lady, only seventeen or eighteen years of age.

When Shijira saw this, he scooped up seawater to rinse his face and hands[4] and said, "How strange that such a beautiful lady should rise up from the sea—a lady whose face is like a spring flower, whose countenance is like the autumn moon, perfect as a gem down to the very tips of her fingers! Are you perhaps a daughter of the Dragon King, or something of that nature?[5] I am ashamed to have you in this poor man's boat. Please return to your exalted dwelling."

4. Believing himself to be in the presence of a divine being, Shijira ritually purifies himself.
5. The Dragon King was believed to rule the sea from his underwater palace.

INTERSPECIES AFFAIRS

Then the lady said, "I do not know whence I came or whither I am going; please take me with you to your dwelling. Let us be of aid to each other, and make our way together in this sad world."

"Oh, no! I am afraid I cannot even think of such a thing. Although I am already forty years old, I still do not have a wife. My mother is over sixty; I worry that my heart would be distracted and I might neglect her if I married. So, even though I know it goes against my mother's wishes, I have no intention of taking a bride." He spoke as if the mere suggestion were outrageous.

"What an unfeeling man you are! This is the way of things, so listen carefully. Even brushing sleeves bespeaks a bond in another life; even the birds rest their wings on branches with which they have a bond. Just imagine the cruelty of telling me to go away, that it was meaningless for me to come to this boat, after I have begged you so much!" She spoke with heartfelt sincerity, choking back tears.

When he saw this, Shijira felt pity for her and thought, "In that case, I should at least let her go on land." Rowing quickly, he reached the beach ahead of the boats that were near the shore. "This is as far as I can take you, so I will say farewell," he said, and tried to return home—but the lady gripped his sleeve and wailed, "At least take me to your house and let me spend the night! When dawn comes, I will let my feet lead me where they will."

"What I call a 'house' is not even an ordinary house," Shijira said. "It is truly the hut of a poor man, a wretched place. There would be nowhere for you to sit; I would be ashamed to seat you on our everyday tatami. Please wait, and I will build a house for you."

To this the lady replied, "I have no wish to go elsewhere, even if it were to a house built of gold, silver, and precious gems. I will go to your dwelling."

"In that case, please wait a little. First I will ask my mother, and then I will come and fetch you." Shijira returned to his house; when he explained the situation to his mother, she was overjoyed and said, "Quickly! Clean the tatami, and then go and fetch her."

Shijira happily hurried down to the seashore to retrieve the lady. She had grown impatient with waiting and set out after him, so they met as she was going along the path. Shijira said, "It must be painful for you to walk on your bare feet; please allow yourself to be carried on the back of this poor and humble man." The lady gladly let him carry her. Arriving at his house, he let her down, and soon his mother came out to greet her. Ah, how ashamed she was! This was surely a heavenly maiden—how could she be in *their* house! She quickly set up a platform so that the lady's seat would be higher than hers, and treated her with boundless reverence.

The Tale of the Clam

Shijira introduces the clam-woman to his mother. (From *Hamaguri no sōshi* [Shibukawa printing], courtesy of the University of Tokyo Library System, Katei Bunko)

Then Shijira's mother said, "I am ashamed to make this request of you, but will you perchance consent to become Shijira's wife? My son is already forty years old, and he still has no wife or a single child, which grieves me day and night. I am already sixty years old and may not live to see tomorrow, and this alone is the one thing that worries me. Ah," she lamented, "what a perfect bride you would be for him!"

The lady said, "I do not know whence I came or whither I am going, but no matter; please let me be with Shijira. I will use skills unknown to other people, and we will make our way together in this sad world."

Shijira's mother was overjoyed. "Very well," she said, and she explained the situation to her son. Now Shijira was filial by nature, so he complied with his mother's wishes.

Even in India, people's curiosity is fierce, and everybody said, "There is a mysterious woman, fallen from heaven, at Shijira's place! Let us go and worship her." Monks and laypeople, men and women alike wrapped up offerings of polished rice and went to pay their respects. Within a day, they had accumulated three barrels and six half-bushels of white rice. The lady said to the women who came to visit her, "I have no clothing;[6] if you have any flax, please give it to me." And so the next day, they came bearing flax. Shijira rejoiced in his heart, overjoyed by the knowledge that he would be able to support his mother, thanks to the rice that had been brought to them the day before.

Meanwhile, the lady secretly began preparing the flax. Although Shijira never saw her combing it, she somehow combed a great amount nonetheless. When she said that she wanted a spindle, Shijira went to look for one. The sound of the flax being spun was most curious. If one listened closely and tried to put it into words, the sound when she pushed the spindle away from her was *namu-jōjū-butsu*, "Hail the Everlasting Buddha"; the sound when she pulled the spindle toward her was *namu-jōjū-hō*, "Hail the Everlasting Dharma"; and the sound when she wrapped the spindle was *anokutara-sanmyaku-sanbodai*, "Supreme Perfect Wisdom." Also, when she lifted up her bracer, it made a sound like *namu-myō*, "Hail the Wondrous . . . ," as she spun.

She spun for twenty-five days,[7] and then she said that she wanted a loom. Very well—Shijira began to build one for her. But then he looked at it and said, "An ordinary loom is no good. I will make alterations." He got out a book and made the loom as he wanted.

The lady was overjoyed, but then she thought, "How will I wrap it?" Immediately, divine beings became aware of her plight—for how could the principle of "vastly practicing the expedient means of wisdom" be wrong?[8]—and two complete strangers came and asked for a night's lodging. Together, they wrapped the loom. "How miraculous," Shijira's mother thought, not for the first time, and showed the lady ever more boundless reverence.

As for Shijira, after he had finished the loom, he once again resumed his labors. He was overjoyed that his mother could now live in comfort, and his heart was more at ease than ever before; he knew no suffering, although at this time the famine in Magadha was extraordinary. He rejoiced that they were at ease, and he had his mother sleep with her feet resting on his forehead.

At this time, Shijira's wife, who was sleeping beside him, asked Shijira, "Why are you crying?"

6. In some versions of the text, the lady describes herself as *sadaka* ("trustworthy" or "reliable") rather than *hadaka* (without clothing). I have elected to use the latter term, as it seems more logical in this context, following *Hamaguri no sōshi*, in *Otogizōshi*, ed. Ichiko, 218n.5.

7. The number twenty-five suggests chapter 25 of the Lotus Sutra, in which the bodhisattva Kannon vows to save all living beings.

8. This is a quotation from chapter 25 of the Lotus Sutra. See Burton Watson, trans., *The Lotus Sutra* (New York: Columbia University Press, 1993), 305.

The Tale of the Clam

Shijira said, "When my mother was younger, she was plump, and when I had her sleep with her feet on my forehead, they were heavy. But as the years passed, she grew thinner and thinner, and now she is so very light. There is nothing I can do but cry."

When Shijira's wife heard this, she said, "Ah, Shijira, your heart is truly admirable! How could you not have the blessings of the Buddha? Such filial piety is rare in this world." Then she told a tale: "Consider the birds of Yue, which build their nests in the south-facing branches.[9] They remember the shelter of their parents' wings, and when it comes time for them to leave the nest and all fly away together, mother and chicks alike cannot bring themselves to part. Although they are separated by clouds, their hearts are clouded by lingering attachment,[10] and so every day for one hundred days these filial birds return to the branches of the tree where they were born and rest their wings there, and their mother rejoices to have her chicks beside her." Consoling her husband, she said, "As miraculous proof of their filial conduct, however much a hunter may wish to catch these birds, set snares though he may, they will not be caught. Nor can they be caught by hawks or eagles. A person who has attained rebirth as a human but who does not obey his parents will receive great calamity in this world; he will meet with the seven misfortunes, and nothing will go as he wishes. But heaven will bestow blessings on a filial son, 'clearing away the seven misfortunes and giving rise to the seven fortunes'; all his wishes will be realized in a single day, and he will receive the reverence of the masses. In this life, he will progress on the path of seeking enlightenment and receive peace and pleasure; he will sit on a nine-tiered lotus throne beside the Eastern Pure Land of the Medicine King and the Western Pure Land of Amida and the highest Pure Lands of all the various buddhas; he will manifest divine powers; as long as he prays to Kannon, there is no doubt that this will be so." As she spoke, the fragrance of her breath carried the scent of otherworldly incense, which filled every nook and cranny of the house day and night.

Now Shijira's wife wished to weave, so she said to him, "This house is cramped and narrow; please build a room for my loom." Shijira immediately took some

9. The story of the birds of Yue comes from *Kongzi jiayu* (*The School Sayings of Confucius*). Despite its title, the book appears to be the invention of the scholar Wang Su (195–256), who lived more than six centuries after Confucius's death. See Paul Rakita Goldin, *Rituals of the Way: The Philosophy of Xunxi* (Chicago: Open Court Press, 1999), 135–36.

10. This passage contains wordplay that resists full translation. In the original text, *kumo* indicates both the figurative "clouds" of lingering attachment and the literal clouds that separate the mother bird from her chicks. Buddhist doctrine construed all worldly attachments, including those between a parent and a child, as impediments to enlightenment. Although *The Tale of the Clam* attempts to situate Confucian notions of filial piety within the framework of Buddhist soteriology, it cannot wholly suppress the tensions between the two philosophies.

Shijira's wife and her guest weave at the loom. (From *Hamaguri no sōshi* [Shibukawa printing], courtesy of the University of Tokyo Library System, Katei Bunko)

rough-hewn logs and built a room for her loom. Then his wife said, "When I am weaving, absolutely no one must enter."

"I understand," Shijira said, and told his mother as well. That evening, a young woman arrived from an unknown place and asked for lodging. Shijira's wife immediately offered her the room with the loom. Shijira's mother said, "You said that no one was to enter that room; why are you letting her stay there?"

"I do not mind having this particular woman here," Shijira's wife replied. The sound of them weaving together was marvelous indeed. The bodhisattva in the "Universal Gate" chapter of the Lotus Sutra weaves on a jeweled loom.[11] Truly it was a blessing to hear their voices as they wove all twenty-eight chapters of the Lotus Sutra, from the first volume to the eighth. Day and night, they wove for twelve

11. The bodhisattva in the "Universal Gate" chapter—chapter 25 of the Lotus Sutra—is Kannon. The Lotus Sutra makes no mention of Kannon using a loom; the connection derives from Japanese popular belief, specifically the legends surrounding Chūjōhime, an eighth-century noblewoman credited with weaving a miraculous tapestry depicting the Pure Land. For Chūjōhime's story, see R. Keller Kimbrough, trans., *Chūjōhime*, in *Traditional Japanese Literature: An Anthology, Beginnings to 1600*, ed. Haruo Shirane (New York: Columbia University Press, 2007), 1138–50.

The Tale of the Clam

Shijira's wife presents her husband with the woven cloth. (From *Hamaguri no sōshi* [Shibukawa printing], courtesy of the University of Tokyo Library System, Katei Bunko)

months. "Now it has been woven," Shijira's wife announced, and they folded up the cloth into a square the size of a *go* board, six inches thick and two feet on each side. Then she said to Shijira, "Tomorrow, take this to the market in Sarnath in the kingdom of Magadha and sell it."[12]

Shijira said, "What price should I ask for it?"

"Sell it for three thousand strings of gold coins," his wife replied.[13]

"What a strange idea!" Shijira said with laughter in his voice. "The cloth that is bought and sold nowadays is ordinarily quite cheap. That price is far too high."

"This is no ordinary cloth," his wife said. "There will certainly be someone at Sarnath who will recognize it. Its value is without bounds. Now, hurry and go—people will be arriving at the market soon."

So Shijira took the cloth to the market in Sarnath. "What on earth is this," some people scoffed, while others just looked at him suspiciously. He carried the cloth about for the whole day, but not a single person gave it a second look. "Just as I

12. Sarnath is said to have been the site of the Buddha's first sermon.
13. Typically, a string of coins consisted of one thousand perforated coins strung together.

INTERSPECIES AFFAIRS

expected," Shijira thought. He had been a fool indeed to bring this cloth to the market; how awful it was to have made a laughingstock of himself. Just as he was about to take the cloth back home, an elderly man came riding up the road on a dapple-gray horse, accompanied by thirty-three attendants.[14] He was a man of incomparably imposing appearance, more than sixty years of age, his beard and his hair pure white. "Who are you?" he asked, and Shijira replied, "I am called Shijira. I came to the market in Sarnath to sell this cloth, but no one bought it, so I am taking it back home."

"Ah, so you are the one I heard about," the old man said. "I'll have a look at that cloth." Shijira held it up toward the horse. When the thirty-three attendants unfolded the cloth, its length was thirty-three ells. "Cloth such as this is rare nowadays," the old man said. "I will buy it; what is the price?"

"Three thousand strings of gold coins," Shijira said.

"What a bargain! Now, let us go to my place." The old man invited Shijira to join him, and from there they traveled south.[15] They came to a gate with rows upon rows of high eaves towering into the clouds. Shijira's eyes widened in astonishment when he saw the agate base stones, the crystal pillars, the lapis lazuli rafters, and the seashell shingles. When they passed through the gate, the air was redolent with otherworldly incense, and flowers drifted down as the sound of music rose to the heavens. Shijira's heart felt young and ancient at the same time, and he forgot all about returning home.

The old man rode up to the edge of the veranda and dismounted before going inside. Soon, three men came out, carrying three thousand strings of gold coins. "How could any human be so strong?" Shijira wondered with some fear.

"Call our cloth merchant over here," the old man said, summoning Shijira inside. Legs trembling and heart racing, Shijira could not think where to stand. After having been summoned several times, he climbed the steps to the inner corridor. As he climbed, he felt as if he were walking across thin ice. Then the old man said, "Let him have some liquor of longevity." Shijira was by nature a man who loved his drink, so he tried a cup and found that it was a liquor beyond the power of words to describe, bursting with the flavor of sweet nectar. He could have drunk any amount of this liquor, but the old man said, "You must not drink more than seven cups." And so seven cups was all that he was given.

14. Here and elsewhere, the number thirty-three suggests the thirty-three manifestations of Kannon. According to the Lotus Sutra, Kannon will appear to each individual in whichever manifestation is best suited to guide him or her to salvation.

15. Kannon's Pure Land was believed to lie to the south. In some of the older variants of the story, the old man's residence is located in the west—the direction of the Pure Land of Amida (Skt. Amitābha) Buddha—suggesting that the original form of the tale may have incorporated elements of Amidism rather than focusing exclusively on Kannon.

The Tale of the Clam

Shijira drinks the liquor of longevity at the old man's palace. (From *Hamaguri no sōshi* [Shibukawa printing], courtesy of the University of Tokyo Library System, Katei Bunko)

Then the old man said, "I will have the three thousand strings of gold coins brought to your house," and he summoned three fearsome-looking men. Their names were Disciple Śravaka-Kaya, Disciple Vaiśravaṇa-Kaya, and Disciple Brahman-Kaya.[16] The old man bade them to bring all three thousand strings of gold coins to Shijira's house in a single journey.

When Shijira asked to take his leave, the old man said, "The liquor of longevity that you drank just now is the liquor of Kannon's Pure Land. One cup will preserve your life for a thousand years. Better still, you drank seven cups, so you will live for seven thousand years. From now on, even if you do not eat, you will feel no hunger; even if you have no clothes, you will feel no cold. This is the reward for your filial piety." After he had said this, the old man departed, riding on a cloud and radiating five-colored beams of light as he rose into the southern sky.

16. Śravaka literally means "hearer of the voice" and refers to a dedicated follower of the Buddha, Vaiśravaṇa (J. Bishamon or Bishamonten) is the guardian deity of the north, and a Brahman is a member of the Hindu priestly caste. All three number among the thirty-three manifestations (*kaya*) of Kannon.

Shijira returned to his home. He wanted to tell his wife what had happened, but when he could not find the words to describe what he had seen, she related the whole story without the slightest error. Shijira was terrified, and just as he was thinking that she must be some divine being in disguise, she announced, "Now I must take my leave."

"Oh, how sad!" Shijira's mother said when she heard this. "Not so long ago, I welcomed a daughter-in-law beyond my wildest expectations, and both Shijira and I knew joy beyond compare. And now you say that you are leaving—ah, my heart is breaking!" Raising her eyes up to the heavens and throwing herself down on the earth, she lamented endlessly.

Shijira's wife said, "Having stayed with you for so long, I wished to do something to earn my keep, and also to leave something for you to remember me by—although I do hope that you will one day forget what has passed—so I took pains to weave that cloth and sell it for three thousand strings of gold coins. This will support you for the rest of your life. However, you must not think that this is anything particularly extraordinary; it is nothing other than the result of Shijira's filial piety. I came here as a messenger from the Pure Land of Kannon. What do I have to hide now? I am Kumara-kumari-kaya, a servant of Kannon.[17] The place where you sold your cloth was Potala, the Pure Land of Kannon. After this, you shall live for seven thousand years, thanks to the seven cups of liquor that you drank. From now on, you shall prosper and receive the protection of the Three Treasures of the gods and buddhas. When you drank the liquor of longevity, three men came out to pour it for you; their names were Disciple Śravaka-Kaya, Disciple Vaiśravaṇa-Kaya, and Disciple Brahman-Kaya, and they are my comrades. Without a doubt, this, too, is because Kannon was moved to take pity on you by the virtue of your filial piety. Now, farewell." With these words, she set out from Shijira's house. At the gate, she begged her leave once more, like a bird leaving the nest.

Reluctant to part, Shijira looked up to the sky in the south and saw her rising upward on a white cloud. Music echoed in the air, the fragrance of otherworldly incense perfumed the four quarters, and flowers drifted down as all the various bodhisattvas came to greet her. Shijira stood dumbfounded for a long time, but because he could not imagine that they would ever meet again, he and his mother resolutely made their way home.

After that, Shijira did indeed prosper, and he was able to support his mother in perfect comfort. Now Shijira's karma destined him to attain buddhahood and

---

17. Kumara-kumari-kaya means "Youth-Maiden-Manifestation." In the "Universal Gate" chapter of the Lotus Sutra, Kannon vows to appear as a youth or a maiden to anyone able to hear the dharma from these manifestations. See Watson, trans., *Lotus Sutra*, 301–2.

The Tale of the Clam

achieve enlightenment, so he became a buddha and after seven thousand years ascended to heaven. At that time, lavender clouds trailed through the sky, the fragrance of otherworldly incense filled the four quarters, flowers drifted down, the wind of immortality blew, and the sound of music rang out endlessly as the twenty-five bodhisattvas, the thirty-three manifestations of Kannon, the twenty-eight attendants of Kannon, the three thousand buddhas, the sixteen Divine Youths, the four Heavenly Kings, and the five Wisdom Kings filled the sky, all utterly resplendent.[18]

Truly, this is the result of filial piety. Forever after, all those who read this tale and behave with filial piety will prosper like this; in this world and the next, all their wishes will be granted instantly. In this world, they shall be freed from the seven misfortunes, they shall experience no difficulties, they shall receive the reverence of the masses, and their descendants shall flourish. In the next world, they shall without a doubt attain buddhahood. Be filial and read this tale to others, read it to others!

TRANSLATION AND INTRODUCTION BY LAURA K. NÜFFER

384

18. The twenty-eight attendants of Kannon suggest the twenty-eight chapters of the Lotus Sutra. The three thousand buddhas comprise the buddhas of past, present, and future eons, while the sixteen Divine Youths serve as messengers to the buddhas. The four Heavenly Kings and the five Wisdom Kings are guardian deities of Buddhism associated with the cardinal directions. The twenty-five bodhisattvas accompany Amida when he welcomes the faithful to the Pure Land; their presence here hints at Amidist influences on the tale.

The War of the Twelve Animals

The Twelve Animals of the East Asian zodiac are familiar icons of modern Japanese visual culture, appearing everywhere from calendars and New Year's cards to best-selling manga series such as *Fruits Basket*. The cycle of twelve animals (mouse, ox, tiger, rabbit, dragon, snake, horse, goat, monkey, cock, dog, and boar), which could represent years, months, days, hours, or compass directions, originated in ancient China, where it began to appear in texts on divination in the third century B.C.E.; it was transmitted to Japan by at least the eighth century C.E. In Buddhist art, the Twelve Animals became associated with the Twelve Divine Generals who aid Yakushi (Skt. Bhaiṣajyaguru), the Medicine Buddha, in his battle against disease. The appearance of the Twelve Animals in a humorous set of fifteenth-century picture scrolls marks a midpoint in their progress from esoteric symbols associated with divination and secret rituals to the beloved popular figures of today.

The Picture Scrolls of the War of the Twelve Animals (*Jūnirui kassen emaki*), translated here as *The War of the Twelve Animals*, chronicles the struggle between the established forces of law and order, represented by the animals of the zodiac, and the rebellious non-zodiacal animals, led by the *tanuki* (raccoon dog, Japanese raccoon). As the earliest known example of a non-human tale (*irui-mono*) set entirely in the animal world, it cleverly parodies and plays off of, in both words and images, three standard genres of illustrated fiction: poetry exchanges, military tales, and stories of religious enlightenment. The first part, like *The Sparrow's Buddhist*

The translation is from the three-scroll *Jūnirui kassen* picture scrolls (fifteenth century) in the Kyoto National Museum, typeset in Umezu Jirō and Okami Masao, eds., *Obusama Saburō emaki, Haseo sōshi emaki, Eshi no sōshi, Jūnirui kassen emaki, Fukutomi sōshi emaki, Dōjōji engi emaki*, Nihon emakimono zenshū 18 (Tokyo: Kadokawa Shoten, 1968), 52–64. The illustrations are from the seventeenth-century copy of the fifteenth-century scrolls in the Chester Beatty Library, Dublin. The translator is grateful to Mr. Yasushi Zenno and Dr. Miyeko Murase for elucidating some especially difficult passages.

Awakening, relies heavily on animals composing classical poetry, in an *uta-awase* (poetry contest), a popular genre in which two poets composed on the same topic and received judgments (poetry evaluations) by the judge, who determined a winner or a draw. More than twenty versions have survived, the oldest of which (on which this translation is based) is a set of three scrolls that was designated an Important Cultural Property in 1961.

The first of the scrolls of *The War of the Twelve Animals* can be reliably dated to about 1451. However, documentary references indicate that there was an even older version of the work, perhaps as early as 1402. The location of the *tanuki*'s fortified burrow in the city of Sakai suggests a possible reference to the Ōei Rebellion (1399–1400), in which provincial daimyo rebelled against the shogun Ashikaga Yoshimitsu (1358–1408) and were defeated at Sakai. The story's antihero, the *tanuki*, may be a caricature of Imagawa Sadayo (also Imagawa Ryōshun; 1326–1420), a warrior and poet who was involved in the rebellion but managed to survive it and, like the *tanuki*, lived as a religious recluse thereafter.

Whatever the inspiration for the story may have been, the resulting tale was so successful in its own right that it continued to be widely enjoyed long after any covert political allusions had been forgotten. A number of copies of *The War of the Twelve Animals* were made in the seventeenth century, probably for sale in commercial picture shops, and a printed book version, *Kedamono Taiheiki* (*Record of Great Peace, the Animal Version*), was published in Kyoto in 1669.

Although the vows of the various buddhas and bodhisattvas are equal in merit, one whose benefit is especially outstanding in the Age of the Imitation Law is the prayer of Yakushi.[1] The promise of relief for body and spirit from the multitude of diseases, without exception, and the words concerning the quickly proven, unsurpassed, true spiritual awakening are indeed reliable, both in this world and the next.

Therefore, sculpting a statue of Shakyamuni Buddha and making it the main image of a hospital, Dengyō Daishi founded the Tendai sect and spread the Law of Mount

---

1. The Age of the Imitation Law is the second of three eras following the death of Shakyamuni Buddha. This phrase and several that follow appear in the Yakushi Sutra.

Tendai.[2] Not only that, Emperor Tenmu established a monastery and thereby preserved the imperial reign.[3] Priest Dōshō received the marvelous image and made manifest the benefits of devotion.[4] The pilgrims and believers exorcise the misfortunes of their lives, and services of worship fulfill the desires of their hearts. Moreover, since the Twelve Great Vows are for the sake of all living beings, the Twelve Divine Generals also graciously deign to protect us.[5]

As the messengers of the Twelve Divine Generals, the myriad animals, in order to guard the hours of the day and night, gathered together and amused themselves. They said to one another, "Since it is a form of entertainment in this country, let us hold a poetry contest." The time was already the eighth month,[6] and so they decided that they would take the moon as their subject and each of them would recite a poem.

Unexpectedly, a deer appeared, accompanied by that rascal, the *tanuki*.[7] The deer took a place at the side, neither to the left nor to the right,[8] and said: "I understand that this is a gathering for a poetry contest. How will you do it without a judge? In appearance, at least, I am one of the *kasen*, so I should be the judge."[9] When he spoke in this way, all the animals felt that their pleasure was spoiled, and they had nothing to say.

The dog, who was the guardian of the first hour of the night,[10] stepped forward and issued a challenge, saying, "We, as retainers of Yakushi, preside over the twelve hours. You are not one of our kind, and for that reason it is not desirable for you to be here on this occasion. Please go home immediately. If you are not of any use to us, then you are intruding. Don't do something that you will regret."

2. Dengyō Daishi is the posthumous name of Saichō (767–822), founder of the Tendai school of Buddhism in Japan. In this sentence, Shakyamuni seems to be a mistake for Yakushi.

3. Emperor Tenmu (631–686, r. 673–686) was known as a patron of Buddhism. The monastery referred to may be Yakushiji Temple, which was founded during his reign. Or Emperor Tenmu may be a mistake for Emperor Kanmu (737–806, r. 781–806), who was a patron of Saichō.

4. Dōshō (798–875) was a priest of the Shingon sect of Buddhism. Several stories of his dealings with miraculous statues of Yakushi are found in *Zoku Kojidan* (*Discussions of Ancient Matters, Continued*, thirteenth century), a collection of tales.

5. The Twelve Great Vows are the vows of Yakushi. According to the sutras, the Twelve Divine Generals are *yakṣa*, demons converted to Buddhism.

6. According to *Record of Great Peace, the Animal Version*, it was then the fifteenth day of the eighth month: mid-autumn and the night of a full moon in the lunar calendar. See *Kedamono Taiheiki*, in *Obusama Saburō emaki*, ed. Umezu and Okami, 78–82.

7. The *tanuki*, which is sometimes translated into English as "raccoon dog," is native to Japan.

8. The deer sat in the place of honor, appropriate to the judge.

9. The deer puns on the word *kasen*, which means both "Immortal of Poetry" and "Deer [*shika* or *ka*] Immortal."

10. The hour of the dog is approximately 7:00 to 9:00 P.M.

In the first illustration (not reproduced here), the Twelve Animals sit in two parallel rows representing the Left and Right teams for the poetry contest. The Left, seated above, represents the animals of the daytime hours: dragon, snake, horse, goat, monkey, and cock. The Right, seated below, comprises the animals of the nighttime hours: dog, boar, mouse, ox, tiger, and rabbit. Their comments, which contain various puns and allusions, are written beside their heads. At the far left, the dog and the dragon confront the deer and the *tanuki*. The following dialogue is inscribed:

COCK: We have set up a barrier, and we would hardly allow the likes of them to pass it.

MONKEY: What a strange intrusion that is!

RABBIT: Let me just put up my ears and listen to what you have to say.

GOAT: In any event, there must be a reason for this intrusion.

TIGER: Now then, let's seize them!

HORSE: How rude they are. Let's chase them away!

OX: Everyone is saying things in anger.

MOUSE (*dressed as a monk*): In the case of visitors like this, we should withdraw.

SNAKE (*dressed as a court lady*): What a long, long debate!

BOAR: How hateful! Let's charge them!

DOG: You shouldn't intrude when there's nothing to be gained! A place where people have no use for you is not the place to be. Make no mistake—you should get out of here now.

DEER: Master Dog, you have said things that I did not expect to hear. You could be said to resemble carnal desire, which will not leave even when beaten;[1] I may be compared to enlightenment, which comes when it is not expected. Between confusion and enlightenment there is no contest. How ill-mannered your words are.

I say to all of you, each of you guards one of the hours of the day. I myself have charge of a number of days in the month. The second, the third, the fourth, the fifth, the sixth, the seventh, the eighth, and the ninth, all are in my charge. And in addition, there is the twentieth.[2] Since I govern so much, how could I be left out? Please make use of me immediately.

DRAGON: What you have said truly has reason. Please forgive us at once. Without rising from your seat,[3] please be the judge.

1. The deer cites the Buddhist expression *bonnō no inu* (the dog of carnal desire), referring to the idea that desire follows a person like a dog, even when unwanted.
2. The deer puns on the word *ka* (deer), which is also the final syllable in the words for particular days of the month (*futsuka, mikka, yokka,* and so on). The deer has forgotten *tōka* (the tenth).
3. The dragon advises the deer to remain in the place of honor. There is a pun on *tatsu*, which means both "to rise" and "dragon."

When the dog said things of this kind, they saw that the deer seemed to be in danger, and each of them reconsidered. "It's only a game—let's just make him the judge, and see how it will be," they decided. "Take a seat," they said, "and judge."[11]

11. In *Record of Great Peace, the Animal Version*, it is the dragon who placates the other animals and offers to let the deer be the judge.

INTERSPECIES AFFAIRS

Left: Dragon

amatsu sora	Even the clouds that sadly float
ukitatsu kumo mo	across the heavenly skies
kokoro shite	have shown compassion—
tsuki wo ba saranu	the distant rainstorm
yoso no murasame	has stayed far from the moon.

Right: Dog

sato no inu no	When the village dog
tsuki miru aki no	views the moon on
yowa dani mo	an autumn night,
hoshi mamoru to ya	will people think
hito no omowamu	he is gazing in vain at the stars?[12]

The judge comments: "The poem of the Left speaks of letting the melancholy rain do as it pleases, for the sake of the moon. That is just as one would like it to be. The poem of the Right, in which the dog is mistakenly thought to be gazing in vain at the unattainable stars, sounds very regretful. Therefore, the victory is to the Left."

ROUND 2

Left: Snake

tsuki mireba	Gazing at the moon
usa mo wasururu	and forgetting sorrow—
aki no yo wo	surely there is no one
nagashi to omou	who would think
hito ya nakaramu	the autumn night too long.

Right: Boar

shinagadori	I gaze at the moon,
fusu i no toko no	undisturbed by the clouds
yamakaze ni	in the mountain wind
kumo mo sawaramu	that blows from the bed
tsuki wo miru ka na	of the sleeping boar.[13]

12. "The dog gazes at the stars" is an expression for longing for something that is beyond one's reach.
13. *Shinagadori* (grebe) is a fixed epithet for *i* (boar) and has not been translated.

The War of the Twelve Animals

The judge comments: "The poem of the Left speaks of looking at the moon, forgetting sorrow, and passing the autumn night without thinking it long. It is very nice. The poem of the Right, which also describes the heart of one wishing to see the moon, unobscured by the clouds in the mountain wind, is excellent. The two are difficult to distinguish, and so it must be called a tie."

ROUND 3

Left: Horse

Ausaka ya	Waiting for the full moon
seki no konata ni	on this side of the barrier
machiidete	at Ōsaka, Hill of Meeting,
yoru zo koenuru	I have passed the night
mochizuki no koma	with my Mochizuki pony.[14]

Right: Mouse

yomosugara	Throughout the night
aki no misora wo	I gaze at
nagamureba	the beautiful sky of autumn.
tsuki no nezumi to	Surely I have become
mi wa narinubeshi	the moon-mouse that gnaws away time.[15]

The judge comments: "The Mochizuki pony and the moon-mouse both have stories behind them. It is difficult to decide on victory or defeat. This must also be called a tie."

ROUND 4

Left: Goat

megurikite	With the turning of time,
tsuki miru aki ni	again it has become
mata narinu	moon-viewing autumn.

14. Mochizuki ponies are horses from the imperial farms at Mochizuki in Shinano Province; one of them was presented to the emperor in the eighth month of every year. The word *mochizuki* also means "full moon," hence the wordplay on which the poem is based.
15. "Moon-mouse" is a Buddhist term for the passage of time. It is derived from a parable in which a black and a white mouse gnaw at the roots of a tree in which a man is hiding from an elephant.

kore ya hitsuji no	Are these the footsteps of the sheep
ayumi naruramu	on its final road to death?[16]

Right: Ox

murakumo no	I look toward the moon
sora sadamaranu	in an unsettled sky
tsuki wo mite	with masses of clouds—
yowa no shigure wo	how sad I think it is:
ushi to koso omoe	rain in the dead of night.[17]

The judge comments: "In the poem of the Left, welcoming moon-viewing autumn sounds at first like something to celebrate, but the phrase about the 'footsteps of the sheep' suggests a heart that has become disillusioned with the world. The poem of the Right tells of a heart saddened by the rain in the dead of night, while watching the moon. It is truly fine. I felt myself becoming damp and crying alone. I believe it must be said that victory goes to the Right."

ROUND 5

Left: Monkey

tsuki wo nomi	Praying for the moon—
miyamaoroshi wa	that though the rain
shiguru to mo	blows down the mountain,
sora komorazaru	the sky may be unclouded
aki no yo mogana	even on an autumn night.

Right: Tiger

miru mama ni	The dew of my tears falls
namida tsuyu chiru	whenever I see
tsuki ni shi mo	the moon:
tora fusu nobe no	the sound of the autumn wind
akikaze no koe	on the moor where the tiger sleeps.

16. "The footsteps of the sheep" refers to the path of a sheep on its way to the slaughterhouse. Thus it is a Buddhist term for the approach of death. It also suggests the passage of time.
17. This poem puns on *ushi*, which means both "sad" and "ox." The last line of the poem could be translated as either "How sad I think it is" or "I think it is the hour of the ox" (1:00–3:00 A.M.).

The War of the Twelve Animals

The Twelve Animals of the zodiac hold a drinking party for the deer, who is seated to the far right. *Clockwise from the upper left*: monkey, snake, dragon, deer, *tanuki*, cock, dog, boar, and mouse. (From *Jūnirui kassen*, © The Trustees of the Chester Beatty Library, Dublin, and the HUMI Project, Keiō University)

The judge comments: "The poem of the Left pleads for mercy so that the moon not be clouded over even in the rain and autumn wind. My heart goes out to it. The poem of the Right mentions 'the moor where the tiger sleeps,' which makes one wonder how the tiger could go to sleep while gazing at the moon. Therefore, it must be said that the victory goes to the Left."

ROUND 6

Left: Cock

tsurenashi to	"Heartless!"
yūtsukedori no	cries the rooster,
naku nae ni	and faintly
kage honomekasu	a shadow appears—
ariake no tsuki	the moon at daybreak.

Right: Rabbit

akegata no	At dawn
tsuki no hikari ni	in the light of the moon,
shiro usagi	a rabbit as white as the moonlight—
mimi ni zo takaki	and loud in my ears,
matsukaze no koe	the sound of the wind in the pines.

INTERSPECIES AFFAIRS

The judge comments: "The poem of the Left, which tells of being cruelly kept waiting until the shadow of the moon appears faintly in the moonlight just before dawn, is unusually interesting. In the poem of the Right, the mention of the pine-wind loud in the ears sounds unpleasant. Therefore, I would like to say that the victory goes to the Left."

When the poetry contest was over, all the animals felt that they should treat the deer to a celebration. Each of them sought out some unusual delicacy, and they held a drinking party and a boisterous Dance of Longevity. The deer thanked them and said that while he regretted the need to say farewell, he had a long way to go on the mountain roads; and so he went home.

Two or three days after that, because it was difficult for them to forget their memories, all the Twelve Animals gathered together again. They established their meeting place in the foothills of the mountains of red maple leaves, and they asked the deer to serve as their judge once again. The deer considered that being present on that sort of occasion a second time was the kind of thing that the wise men of old warned against. He thought it over, and although he would have liked to, he did not go.[18]

The *tanuki*, who had accompanied the deer before, was envious of the hospitality to which the deer had been treated. When he imposed himself on them, the Twelve Animals became very angry, and they chased him away.

18. According to *Record of Great Peace, the Animal Version*, the deer sent a messenger to say that he had a cold.

The War of the Twelve Animals

In the second illustration (not fully reproduced here), the animals, with saké cups and plates of food, are seated in a circle around the dancing monkey. The dragon, who seems to be acting as host, gestures toward the monkey; beside him is the deer, who, as the guest of honor, is shown holding a saké cup. The following dialogue is inscribed:

TANUKI (*watching the deer*): Ah me! What good luck for the auspicious deer! If only I, the *tanuki*, were also to receive such divine fortune, then mightn't it be like this for me as well?
COCK: I have looked hard to find this coxcomb seaweed.
SNAKE: I drank my fill of saké, and now I think I'll shed what I am wearing and stretch out to nap.
DOG: This is pheasant of Katano.[1]
BOAR: I've dug up these mountain sweet potatoes.
MONKEY (*dancing and singing*):

> Among the myriad things, how splendid is the monkey!
> Thanks to the monkey,[2] in spring the blossoms do not fall;
> in autumn the moon is not clouded over;
> you are not parted from the one you love;
> and you do not meet with coldhearted women.
> "The apes of the Ba gorges cry three times;
> at daybreak the traveler's robe is dampened."[3]
> It is excellent! Mitsune also said in his poem,
> "Oh apes, do not cry so forlornly."[4] How nice it sounds!

The *tanuki*, having barely escaped with his life, hid in his burrow in a mound to recover from his wounds. Thinking about this sorrow, he felt that he must cleanse his shame. He conspired with myriad birds and beasts, and together, with gusto, they raised an army.

While a few of the soldiers gathered in the capital, there were also those who did not make the trip but simply inked their fur brushes and wrote letters. And so they plotted in secret. First were such creatures as the badger governor, of the same clan as the *tanuki*; the aged fox of Mount Inari; the young bear of the Kumano "Bear Field" Mountains; the wolf of Rendaino; the old kite of Mount Atago;[19] the white heron of Yurugi Wood; the village crows of the marketplace of Futsukaichi; and the owl, who loves treachery. All of them were in agreement. The subordinate generals included the cat, the marten, the weasel, the sparrow, and the horned owl.

A force of over three hundred warriors gathered in a fortress on the *tanuki*'s mound, and they all deliberated and took counsel. From among them, the impetuous

19. Mount Atago, northwest of Kyoto, was well known to be the home of *tengu*, which are often said to disguise themselves as kites.

I have been appointed the messenger of Sannō,[5]
and in the Rabbit Month of every year,
my day has been made the day of a royal outing.
The one known as Daigyōji in fact has my appearance.[6]
There's the Lotus Sutra Meeting at Jingoji, and the filial piety of the monkey;
and in the end the five hundred monkeys became self-realized buddhas.[7]
How auspicious, hey!

HORSE: These soybeans are what people call horse-feed beans.
RABBIT: I've brought these pastries because they have such a nice name; they're called "clover
flowers."

1. Katano was the site of an imperial game preserve, known for its pheasants and its cherry blossoms.
2. I have interpolated this phrase. The point of the passage is the repeated pun on *saru* (monkey) and *-zaru*, a negative verb ending. The same device was used in the monkey's poem in the poetry contest.
3. This is a couplet by Ōe no Sumiakira (d. 950), from a long Chinese poem in the Japanese poetic anthology *Honchō monzui* (*The Literary Essence of Our Court*, ca. 1040). Ba is an old name for Sichuan Province.
4. This is the first part of poem 1067 in *Kokin wakashū* (*Collection of Poems Ancient and Modern*, ca. 905), attributed to Ōshikōchi Mitsune (fl. ca. 898–922).
5. The Sannō Deity is the tutelary god of Mount Hiei, site of Enryakuji Temple of the Tendai sect.
6. Daigyōji Gongen, one of the twenty-one deities of the Hie (Sannō) shrines, is said to have a human body and the face of a monkey.
7. A "self-realized buddha" is a buddha that has attained enlightenment as a result of its own efforts. The story of the five hundred monkeys appears in a fragmentary text in the Japanese Imperial Household collection. See Ishizuka Kazuo, "Gosukō-in shinpitsu monogatari setsuwa dankan ni tsuite," *Shoryōbu kiyō* 17 (1965): 81–82.

The rabbit, horse, ox, and cock attack the *tanuki*. (From *Jūnirui kassen*, © The Trustees of the Chester Beatty Library, Dublin, and the HUMI Project, Keiō University)

In the third illustration (not fully reproduced here), the mouse, snake, boar, dog, and dragon glare angrily at the *tanuki* beside a red-leaved maple tree. The following dialogue is inscribed:

SNAKE: Let's surround him and beat him up!
BOAR: Let's knock him down and roll on him!
DRAGON: It has become my business. You strange, rude fellow, you should withdraw immediately. Do not disgrace yourself at the amusement of the young people.
DOG: You showed your skill on the last occasion, but now I'll break you.
TANUKI: What tedious things you gentlemen keep saying! Each of you guards only a single hour, and your former judge announced that he has charge of ten days in the month; but I govern two whole months. The reason is this: if you look at the words *tachinuru tsuki* [the month that has passed], there's a *ta* and a *nu* and a *ki*! It spells *tanuki*! How's that? You're looking so mean! Whenever there's a drinking party, I'm known for doing the *Tanuki* Dance, so we'll have fun. Quickly, treat me now!

In the scene that immediately follows, the *tanuki* has been knocked to the ground and is being attacked by the cock, ox, horse, and rabbit.

COCK: I'll kick him to the ground.
OX: Just gore him to death!
HORSE: I won't miss out on trampling him to death!
RABBIT: I'll knock him down with the rabbit pole![1]

---

1. The rabbit refers to an *uzue*, a decorated pole used in exorcism ceremonies on the first Rabbit Day of the New Year.

wolf came forward and said, "In order to achieve a victory in this matter, the best thing to do is as follows. It goes against the grain to let this month pass fruitlessly. However, the first day of the ninth month is an unlucky day. Let us advance on them on the evening of the second, toward the end of the hour of the dog, and make a night attack." When he said this, all of them agreed.

Now since the matter had become known throughout the land, the gist of it was reported to the Twelve Animals, and they were disturbed. To have acquired such a fellow as the *tanuki* as an enemy and to be about to be attacked by him was unspeakable. "Well then, let us counter-attack," they said to one another. Thinking that there was no time to lose, they soon set out.

Each of the Twelve Animals gathered many companions, both his own retainers and other useful persons. At dawn on the last day of the eighth month, with a force of over five hundred warriors, they besieged the fortress in Sakai where the enemy was entrenched.

The *tanuki*, taken by surprise, was flustered and panicked. However, being warriors who knew the meaning of honor, the troops who were gathered did not make

In the fourth illustration (not fully reproduced here), the conspirators sit in a circle in a rocky mountain landscape with containers of food and saké. Most of them hold weapons, and the *tanuki* has his armor beside him. The wolf (*upper right*) is the center of attention. The following dialogue is inscribed:

WOLF (*gesturing toward the* tanuki): Just attack; we will destroy them at once, and we will turn their homes into graveyards.

FOX: In a night attack, the road will probably be dark, so we will need to light torches.[1]

BEAR: I'll catch them with my bear-claw pitchfork and take them prisoner.

TANUKI: If they won't approach, I'll beat the attack drum.[2]

BADGER (*aside*): He's so fat that he won't be able to answer their challenge.

KITE: We speak of the Twelve Animals, but what are they, after all? The dragon, the monkey, the horse, the ox, and the dog, all were once beggars by the dry riverbed. The village crows saw them, so they will not dare to deny that.

OWL: For a night attack, it is best not to have clear weather, and there should not be starlight. Let's attack on a rainy night.

1. This is a reference to *kitsunebi* (fox fires), which were believed to be generated by magical foxes. In the scene of the night attack, the fox is shown holding a torch, just as he suggests here.
2. In folklore, *tanuki* have a habit of drumming on their bellies.

any fuss at all. They removed the barricade of branches, unfastened the ties of their quivers, and awaited the attacking force.

First, the cock crowed to announce the hour, whereupon the defenders responded with their own battle cry. After the ritual exchange of arrows, the barbs from both sides fell as thick as rain. The battle shouts resembled thunder; they made the heavens resound and the earth shake. Although time passed, it was not easy to see who would achieve the victory.

The mouse charged out from the side of the attackers. He held in his teeth the uppermost plate of the left sleeve of his armor, and he tilted back his neck plate.[20] From inside the fortress, the cat came out and chased him. The dog, from a distance, chased the cat back into the fortress.

At that time, the wolf, who from the beginning had been an impetuous warrior, came running out to grapple with the dog. From the side of the attackers, the tiger met with the wolf and slew the great wild dog. Within the fortress, they were deeply saddened because the wolf, whom they had relied on as a leader, had been killed.

20. This is possibly in order to dare the enemy to attack him, since tilting back the neck plate would leave the neck vulnerable. In the illustration, however, the mouse does not wear a helmet at all. Instead, he sports a *katō*, a kind of hood typically worn by warrior monks.

The War of the Twelve Animals

Despite his promises, the fox was of a deceptive nature.[21] Although he had sworn, "I'll come, I'll come," he did not appear on that day. Meanwhile, the kite, in *tengu*-like fashion, turned traitor and flew out of sight.

The attackers followed up on their victory and advanced. Countless numbers were killed. The vanguard was smashed, and as the remainder of the army had lost its cohesion, each and every member scattered and fled away.

Although the company of the Twelve Animals had won the battle, the *tanuki*, the ringleader of the rebels, had escaped them, and they were exceedingly resentful.

21. The fox is described as being *bakebakeshiki* (well transformed)—a play on words that refers to the fox's legendary shape-shifting abilities.

The wolf (*upper right*) points a folded fan at the *tanuki*, who sits beside his armor as he consults with the other non-zodiacal animals (fox, bear, cat, heron, owl, kite, badger, and others) about seeking revenge. (From *Jūnirui kassen*, © The Trustees of the Chester Beatty Library, Dublin, and the HUMI Project, Keiō University)

They decided that since it was already late in the day, it would be a good idea to bivouac for the night and take a rest. On the following morning at dawn, they would search once again in the surrounding burrows and hollow trees.

The *tanuki* felt that not only would he be unable to cleanse the shame of Kuaiji, but he had shown himself to be inferior to his teacher, and so had lost face.[22] He therefore disguised his appearance and fled the battlefield. He crawled into the

22. The "shame of Kuaiji" refers to an incident in the Warring States period of Chinese history. In the fourth century B.C.E., King Goujian of Yue was defeated by the king of Wu at Kuaiji Mountain. Years later, after much suffering, Goujian was finally able to kill the king of Wu and thus repair his pride. The story is recounted in the Japanese historical epic *Taiheiki* (*Record of Great Peace*, late fourteenth century). The *tanuki*'s teacher is likely the deer.

The War of the Twelve Animals

In the fifth illustration (not reproduced here), the Twelve Animals, attired in splendid armor, rush into battle from the right in a circular formation that echoes their cyclical order. The cock leads the way. In the battle that follows, the death of the wolf is depicted as the text describes it: the mouse is chased by the cat, who is chased by the dog, who is chased by the wolf, who is killed by the tiger. The laughing tiger, holding the wolf's head aloft on his sword, runs from the angry bear. The following dialogue is inscribed:

TIGER: I've taken his head! Anyone who wants to, come and fight me!
HERON (*flying overhead, shot by an arrow*): I have been here for so long and have come to such a sad state.

To the left, the *tanuki*'s forces are in retreat. They make their way up a rocky slope toward the *tanuki*'s headquarters. The circular entrance to his burrow can be seen at the far left.

UNIDENTIFIED BIRD (*trudging up the slope*): I said that they should have brought in provisions of rice, but they didn't listen. I'm so hungry.
KITE (*addressing the* tanuki): This battle is not as it should be, alas. I'd like to withdraw to Mount Atago, dig up the slopes, and have one more try at putting an obstacle in their way.

hollow of a tree, which he took to be his final stronghold, and rested there. He thought that he would like to fight an honorable battle one more time and to die in combat. The wolf, who had been his chief retainer among the soldiers with whom he had conspired, had been killed, and the rest of his army had scattered and fled. He was alone and without anyone to rely on, and he was at a loss as to what to do.

The old kite, who was a retainer of Tarōbō of Mount Atago, returned to the battlefield for a little while; but when he saw that the battle was hopeless, he cried *hyorori* and went away.[23] However, he still felt unsure about the entire matter. In a treetop in the wood near the fortress, he rested his wings and used his farseeing eyes. He saw that the *tanuki*, having lost the battle, had crept in abject misery into the hollow of a tree at the edge of the forest. Quickly, he flew there and inquired how things were going, and they discussed the matter, saying to each other, "Even though we have survived, it is pointless. What should we do next?"

The old kite said, "As was mentioned even on the battlefield, no one knows how it came about that from ancient times the Twelve Animals have taken the names of the Stems and Branches.[24] If only you build a fortress and take on the dog alone as

400

23. Tarōbō is a particularly famous *tengu* who appears, in this volume, in *The Palace of the Tengu* and *The Tale of the Handcart Priest*. *Hyorori* is most likely the cry of the kite. It may also be read as a variant of *hyorohyoro* ("haltingly," "falteringly," or "unsteadily"), in which case the phrase would read, "he cried falteringly and went away."
24. The Stems and Branches are the calendrical signs. Strictly speaking, the Twelve Animals represent the Twelve Earthly Branches, and the Ten Heavenly Stems are represented by the Five Elements doubled.

your enemy, then the good fortune of your escape may be made the turning point for your future. To rely on the fortress on the mound and to wait for your powerful enemies was shortsighted. But if, from a spacious place, you observe the weakness of your enemies and then attack and scatter them—and when the enemy is formidable, you withdraw and take a rest—you will always benefit. Within the narrow scope of a burrow, you were unable to strategically maneuver according to your desires, and for this reason many brave soldiers were lost. I think, however, that it was an act of fate. Hereafter, although we do not have much to depend on, let us finish it in this way.

"You are not the only one who holds a grudge; there is also the insult to your numerous like-minded companions. In this respect, there is a small fact that may mean considerable good luck for you. The company of the Twelve Animals is planning to search for you again tomorrow and is camping out tonight. They must surely be boasting of their victory in the battle, and they will have drunk large quantities of saké and be lying in a drunken sleep. If we launch an attack on their camp tonight, why should we not be able to kill some of their retainers? If we kill one or two of their best, then afterward, with the assistance of Tarōbō, we will withdraw to Mount Atago. If we dig up the slopes and entrench ourselves there, even the Twelve Animals will not easily overthrow us.

"It is the usual way in battles that even though one person may know his duty, if the rest of the force is divided in spirit, then they will disperse; and in this situation, they will be powerless. To judge by my own case, the remainder of our people are probably hiding in the vicinity, trying to find out whether or not you are still alive in order to make up their minds what to do. In a night attack, if there are too many people, they will fight among themselves, and it will be a bad thing. If we have only twenty or so of the best, then why shouldn't we succeed in an honorable vengeance? We should prepare quickly, before the night grows deeper." Saying this, he presently flew away.

Within moments, the old kite flew around and spread the word to the appropriate places. Just as expected, there were many companions who agreed that this was indeed what should be done, and many of them came out.

The badger, Gon no Kami, was returning to the backcountry of Tawara. The kite caught up with him just as he was about to cross Mount Kowata on foot; and when he spoke, the badger agreed to accompany him. The old fox of Mount Inari turned back from Kaerizaka. The young bear of Mount Kumano, since the way to his own mountain was so far, stopped for a while in the neighborhood of Imakumano and listened, and he too was in agreement.

Wild Dog Tarō, the son and heir of the wolf, had taken his father's remains and was planning to do his filial duty. But the Rendaino cemetery was still far away,

and thinking that one place would be the same as another for a mortuary temple, he was about to take the body to Ennenji Temple when he was informed of the situation. He rejoiced at the thought of meeting with his father's enemies a second time. Putting aside plans for the funeral service, he set out for Mitokoro. In addition, the eagle Washitarō joined them for the first time. He had been brought up in Twin Cedar Trees and thought that he could catch anything whatsoever in his claws.

A resident of Shinano Province, the hawk Takagorō of Whitebelly Nest was employed as a keeper in the imperial game preserve and so happened to be in the

The Twelve Animals of the zodiac celebrate their victory. (From *Jūnirui kassen*, © The Trustees of the Chester Beatty Library, Dublin, and the HUMI Project, Keiō University)

capital. The kite was his foster parent, so when he said to him, "This is the situation. Please join us," the hawk, who had always been a hot-blooded youth, set out at once and proceeded to take the lead. With the addition of other brave soldiers, a total of thirty-odd warriors banded together; and before the first bell of night, they gathered in the vicinity of the woods. When the *tanuki* looked out of the hollow tree and they told him why they were there, he was extremely happy.

Leaving a few members of the force behind, the *tanuki* and his companions attacked the enemy camp at midnight. The Twelve Animals were exhausted after the day's battle. Each of them had loosened his armor and was taking a rest. The drinkers

The War of the Twelve Animals

In the sixth illustration (not fully reproduced here), the Twelve Animals sit in a circle around the dancing cock in their outdoor camp. Helmets and weapons are on the ground or stacked against trees. To the left, animal retainers are preparing food. The following dialogue (not all of which is included in the seventeenth-century copy [shown here] of the fifteenth-century scrolls) is inscribed:

DOG: This spacious outdoor camp is especially enjoyable to me.[1]

MOUSE: If only this drinking party were not in travel lodgings, then I would have served pickled fish to eat with the saké.

DRAGON: I have won the battle, I have drunk saké, and my heart is carefree. All of you, relax and enjoy yourselves, too.

TIGER: We'll spend tonight singing and howling.

COCK (*singing and dancing*):

> "The Rooster Official announces the dawn;
> his voice awakens the wise king."[2]
> "When the rooster has crowed," I've heard,
> "the loyal ministers await the day."[3]
> In the service of the Prince of Huainan,
> my voice resounds in the clouds.[4]
> When the Lord of Mengchang was leaving Qin,
> I led his retainers on the barrier road, so the story goes.[5]
> What bird is it in whose very form
> the five virtues are displayed?[6]
> What creature is it that raises its voice
> in the unpeopled mountain village?
> "Ceaseless crowing," said the poet,
> sleeping on Mount Tatsuta;
> your comings and goings bewilder me
> at dawn on Mount Ōsaka.[7] I think it's lovely!

among them had not eaten any dinner but had drunk saké and were now sleeping it off, never imagining that their enemies were planning an attack.

The *tanuki*'s force split up and approached from the four directions. On three sides, they took up bows and arrows and set up the most skillful ones among them as archers. On the other side, they arrayed the attacking force, readied the points of their swords, and came in for the kill.

Since they were taken by surprise, the Twelve Animals were unable to take up arms. Many good warriors were wounded, and they scattered in four directions. The *tanuki*, having won the night attack, felt that his shame was somewhat cleansed. Sticking with the kite, he asked Tarōbō of Mount Atago to give him a fortress.

"Insofar as I shall render you assistance, even though I do not know the original history of this affair," Tarōbō said, "we must plan together where the fort will be. If

RABBIT: I'm tired. I think I'll just make some clover into a pillow and go to sleep.

HORSE: At our drinking party, there aren't any wind instruments, so I think I'll play the Horse Flute.[8]

MONKEY: This is better than when I danced. Oh, how interesting!

OX: The untalented ones like us regret that we have no name, and no cows either.[9]

BOAR: However many times the saké cup makes the rounds, one must drink. It's difficult.

To the left of the camp of the Twelve Animals is a wide band of mist, above which are the topmost branches of a pine tree in which the kite sits. The *tanuki* is hiding in the hollow tree and is conversing with the kite. Finally, at the far left, the kite flies away on his mission to reassemble the *tanuki*'s army.

1. This is a pun on *byōbyō taru*, which means "spacious" and suggests the bark of the dog (also *byōbyō* in this period).
2. These lines are from poem 524 in *Wakan rōeishū* (*Chinese and Japanese Poems to Be Sung*, ca. 1012), attributed to Miyako no Yoshika (d. 879). The Rooster Official wore a hat in the shape of a coxcomb and announced the hours.
3. The cock quotes from poem 63 in *Wakan rōeishū*, attributed to the Tang poet Jia Dao (779–849).
4. The Prince of Huainan (Liu An; d. 122 B.C.E.) was known for his interest in alchemy. According to legend, he drank an elixir of immortality and ascended to the heavens. The dogs and chickens in his courtyard licked the dregs of the elixir and became immortal, too, and it is said that they could be heard barking and crowing in the clouds.
5. The Lord of Mengchang (d. ca. 280 B.C.E.) was a prince of the state of Qi who was held prisoner in the state of Qin. While making his escape from Qin, he had to pass a barrier that opened only at dawn. One of his retainers imitated the crow of a rooster, causing all the real roosters in the neighborhood to crow. The barrier was opened, and he and his retainers passed safely through.
6. The cock refers to an anecdote in *Han shi waizhuan* (second century B.C.E.). See James Robert Hightower, trans., *Han Shih Wai Chuan: Han Ying's Illustrations of the Didactic Application of the Classic of Songs* (Cambridge, Mass.: Harvard University Press, 1952), 62.
7. This sentence contains indirect allusions to the anonymous poem 995 and to poem 740 in *Kokin wakashū* (*Collection of Poems Ancient and Modern*, ca. 905), attributed to Kan'in no Myōbu.
8. The horse puns on *komabue*, which means both "Korean flute" and "horse flute."
9. The ox puns on *myōji* (name) and *me-ushi* (cow).

we fail to build a citadel on this mountain, and we are overthrown by the enemy, how will that look? In time of war, as they always say, you should first assemble your forces and make use of them."

On the side of the Twelve Animals, the allies were unhappy that so many of their fine comrades had been wounded in the night attack on the field camp. They decided that they must call together their forces once again and attack the Atago fortress.

"On the previous occasion," the lower-ranking ones said, "the enemy were few in number, and the fortress was on level ground, so our army was victorious during the day. This time, the fortress is large, and since Tarōbō is assisting them, they will doubtless have a mighty force. Even if we attack from all sides, what will happen?"

The leader among them, the dragon Tatsudayū, came forward and said, "Even if Tarōbō of Mount Atago assists them, how could they be superior to our might? For

In the seventh illustration (not fully reproduced here), animals hurry forward and up a slope to join the *tanuki*, who is seen in a cave-like setting, wearing his armor again. As the scene moves to the left, the attackers, now led by the *tanuki*, rush out toward the outdoor camp of the Twelve Animals, where they attack their unprepared enemies. The following dialogue is inscribed:

TANUKI (*gesturing with a battle fan*): People are watching to see whether you will make any mistakes! Keep that in mind and don't do anything cowardly.

HAWK: Could there be anyone who is better than me? Any fearless, brave warriors on the side of the Twelve Animals, show me your skill!

BEAR (*attacking a foe with his* kumade): If we don't grapple here, then when can we expect to do it?[1] Come on!

The force of the Twelve Animals is shown being defeated. The tiger cowers behind a tree while the dragon tries in vain to rally them. A rabbit ties a bandage around the head of a dog.

DOG: I can't hear clearly, and my consciousness is fading away. Oh, how sad.

RABBIT: You're saying disgraceful things. If you die without taking revenge, it's a dog's death! Don't you want to survive somehow and achieve your true intention? This is not a serious wound. Take heart![2]

Pointing with an open fan, the *tanuki* (*right*) leads an attack on the Twelve Animals of the zodiac. (From *Jūnirui kassen*, © The Trustees of the Chester Beatty Library, Dublin, and the HUMI Project, Keiō University)

DRAGON: It's the enemies who weren't killed! What are they starting now? Let's not panic and go booming about.[3] I'm going to kill them all, without exception.

COCK (*standing over the ox*): Even though I'm yelling that we're being attacked and kicking him to wake him up, he won't get up. What can I do?

HORSE (*standing over the boar*): Even though I trample on him, trying to awaken him, he sleeps. It's ridiculous!

On the opposite side of the camp, archers fire at the Twelve Animals. We then see the *tanuki*'s victorious forces, with the kite in the lead, making their strategic withdrawal to Mount Atago, which is indicated by a label.

1. This is a pun on *kumade*, which means both "not to grapple" and "bearclaw pitchfork."
2. Modern commentators tend to identify the first speaker in this exchange (the wounded animal) as the rabbit and the second as the dog, probably because the second speaker's words pun on *omoitamainu* (don't [you] want?) and *inu* (dog). However, based on the illustration, it seems more likely that it is the dog who complains of his wound and the rabbit who urges him to endure.
3. This is a reference to the dragon's traditional association with lightning and thunder.

such a trivial matter as this, I need not bother to consult the Eight Great Dragon Kings. I shall merely call together the small dragons of the outer seas. When we come face to face with the enemy, who could stand against us? This time, send me to the rear gate. I'll go around by the Tanba Road, scale the peaks of Atago, force open the citadel, and finish them off." The rest of the force agreed that this was indeed what should be done, and they set a day and attacked from the front.

Hearing this, the defenders of the castle barred the way by digging up the slopes. They set up a wall of shields and waited. Since the fortress was strongly built, it was not likely to fall easily. From early morning until late afternoon, the armies were as evenly matched as the horns of an ox, and it was not possible to see who was winning or losing. Finally, when it reached the hour of the cock,[25] the defenders realized that the rear gate had been surrounded. There was turmoil within the castle. Inabikari "Lightning" was sent in first, with Raikō "Thunder Lord" thundering around him. In a short time, the central fortress had been breached.

25. The hour of the cock is approximately 5:00 to 7:00 P.M.

The dragons attack from the sky, while the owl and the kite (*left*) meet their ends on the ground. (From *Jūnirui kassen*, © The Trustees of the Chester Beatty Library, Dublin, and the HUMI Project, Keiō University)

How could even the faction of Tarōbō, on whom the *tanuki* had relied, withstand it? All the *tengu* ran away and hid themselves here and there under trees and between rocks. It was worse still for the rest of the force, and without firing a single arrow, they escaped into Shiwasu Valley. The *tanuki*, the ringleader, thought that if he stayed in his original form he would surely be killed; and so he transformed into a priest and hid under the altar of the Getsurin Hall.[26]

Having lost the battle, the *tanuki* felt that he could do nothing about the shame that he had now suffered twice. He fretted over how he might erase this humiliation and concluded that in his original form it would be all the more difficult to achieve. He thought that he would take the form of a demon to deceive his enemies; then, when they were in a state of confusion, he would seize all the Twelve Animals and gobble them up. He therefore secluded himself in "Black Mound" Kurozuka, where, just as he intended, he turned into a demon.[27]

26. Getsurinji was a temple on the western side of Mount Atago.
27. Kurozuka was a place in Musashi Province famous for being a home to demons.

The War of the Twelve Animals

In the eighth illustration (not fully reproduced here), animals rush forward to join the army of the Twelve Animals, who are gathered at the edge of a rocky ravine across from the *tanuki*'s fortress on Mount Atago. The following dialogue is inscribed:

DOG: We've surrounded the rear gate! Quick, let's attack the main gate, too. We'll capture the enemy general, Tanuki-tarō, before he escapes into his fortress-burrow.

COCK: You wretched country-bumpkin warriors were deceived by Tanuki-tarō, who has not even been to the capital. Who have you been hearing was your enemy? For you to ask now who is attacking you is disgusting. If you don't know, I'll tell you!

BOAR: It is our great honor to have been placed on the front of the armor of the Twelve Divine Generals.[1]

UNKNOWN SPEAKER: Don't you know that we have names that are used in acrostic poems?

HORSE (*largely illegible*): Those ignorant country-bumpkin warriors . . . Tora-saburō, the tiger . . . is Kitsune-maru, the notorious fox, trying to borrow the tiger's authority?[2]

TIGER (*largely illegible*): . . . an old friend.

UNKNOWN SPEAKER: Who is attacking? State your name!

TANUKI: Now, then, in the vanguard, that must be Nezumi-tarō, the mouse, who is in charge of the first of the twelve hours. If we put Neko-no-jūrō, the cat, in the front, how will that be? If you don't have a spare life, retreat quickly!

Inside the fortress, the *tanuki* sits surrounded by his allies.

BIRD: The enemy is already very close and is attacking. I'd like to try flying up and speaking with them.

TANUKI: Yes, that is what should be done. From above the wall of shields, let your beak resound and speak to them. If they still won't listen, then fly directly over the enemy's camp, look down on them, and speak to them.

UNKNOWN SPEAKER: Already the rear gate is surrounded. From the mountain to the west, outside the gate, I hear a great commotion, and furthermore, for your warriors at the main gate, the fight is hopeless. Quickly, let us withdraw to Kuwabara.[3] We should entrust ourselves to the teaching of the Saishōō-kyō—the Sutra of the Most Honored King—and chant the names of the Radiant Kings of the Four Directions.

UNKNOWN SPEAKER: Now, then, what should we do? However many our forces number, all of them are being routed. I think that at this point, you should dart into the fortress-burrow.

UNKNOWN SPEAKER: I hear that the general attacking the rear gate today is Tatsudayū. How fierce is the sound of his son, Ikazuchitarō, thundering all around! People who are used to living in a fortress-burrow may go into it, but where shall the rest of us hide? Let's flee to Kuwabara.

WILD DOG (?): Alas, the rear gate is already surrounded. Look at Inazuma in the lead!

Outside, on the far side of the fortress, the dragons are attacking from the sky. On the ground, the owl and the kite are dispatched by the horse and the ox, respectively.

HORSE: You hateful owl, you didn't know your place and were deceived by the lowly *tanuki*. You dared to make us your enemy, when we were exalted as palace Horse Officials. I'll put an end to this example of "the low oppressing the high."[4]

OWL: In their teachings, the men of old said not to fight. This must have been the kind of thing they warned against, though it is useless to say so now. Even if I have become involved in bad things and will end with the name of a traitor, the divine light of Amida's grace, which does not distinguish between the three aspirations for rebirth in the Pure Land, will not fail to shine upon me. Let me just call ten times on the name of Amida. Hail Amida Buddha, Hail Amida Buddha.

OX: When I lay sick for a year in the dry riverbed, you pecked at my sores. How resentful I felt! Since it was karmic retribution, I was powerless. But don't think that I am sad, you wretched old kite.[5]

KITE: I am an old kite and do not even know how many years are heaped upon me. I have lost too many feathers and I cannot fly, and furthermore I am wearing armor to which I am not accustomed, so I cannot make free use of my body.[6] In the past, by the stream in the moor, I would eat the flesh of horses and oxen; now, in retribution, I have had my back and wings broken by that cursed ox Ushi-jirō. Where are you now, strong-willed and reliable Taka-gorō? Bring along the eagle and the bear hawk, and before I die, let me see you pluck out and eat the two eyes of that cursed Ushi-jirō. If you do that, then I can go to the afterworld with my heart at ease. Alas, how sad, how sad!

Looking regretfully back over his shoulder, the *tanuki* makes his escape. At the far left is a temple building with a human priest seated on the veranda: the *tanuki* in disguise.

TANUKI (*in the guise of a priest*):

arite nao	Since my body,
fusuberarubeki	though alive, is already
mi nariseba	smoldering, I would rather
nobe no keburi to	disappear from thought
omoikiebaya	like the smoke on the moor.[7]

1. Medieval Japanese statues of the Twelve Divine Generals often depict the Twelve Animals on the generals' helmets.
2. "The fox borrows the tiger's authority" is a proverb akin to the English "ass in the lion's skin."
3. This is a response to the activity of the junior dragons. The name Kuwabara (literally, "Mulberry Field") was recited as a charm to avoid thunder and lightning.
4. Horse Officials (*uma no kami*) oversaw the stables in the imperial palace and the various imperial horse farms in the provinces. "The low oppressing the high" (*gekokujō*) was a phrase used to describe the social turmoil of the Muromachi period (1337–1573).
5. The ox's words contain a pun on *ushi*, which means both "sad" and "ox."
6. It is a little odd for the kite to be saying these things about himself. Komine Kazuaki interprets this passage as an interpolation to be spoken by a narrator reading the scroll aloud, in "Gachūshi no uchū: monogatari to kaiga no hazama," *Nihon bungaku* 41, no. 7 (1992): 31–33.
7. In addition to the apparent reference to cremation, there may be a play on the idea of smoking animals such as foxes and *tanuki* out of their burrows by burning leaves.

Feeling that he had already accomplished his objective, the *tanuki* set out for the place where the Twelve Animals were gathered. Just then, a dog barked at him on the road. He was frightened, and he barely escaped. His misery was immeasurable. He worried that if even a dog recognized him, then how much more so would such awesome beings as the dragon and the tiger! And so this plan, too, came to a fruitless end.

In the ninth illustration (partially reproduced on the book jacket), the *tanuki*, half-transformed into a demon, sits on a rocky ledge above a mountain stream and gazes into it. The following dialogue is inscribed:

TANUKI: Now that I have transformed myself, I'll use the water of this mountain stream as a mirror and see how terrifying I am.

On the road, the *tanuki* in demon form runs from a barking dog.

TANUKI: Oh, how sad! I have been recognized by even a wretched dog.

All in all, with one loss of face after another, the *tanuki* felt ashamed to be seen by anyone, and he hid himself deep in his burrow and reflected long and hard on the state of his life. In this world of illusion, he thought, we are bound by selfish attachments and pride; there would be no use in returning to that burning pit of hell.[28] What an impermanent, ever-changing world it is! The *tanuki* recalled the poem by Bai Juyi that asks, "The old grave—from what era is the man who lies there?" as well as the poem by Saigyō that speaks of adding a grave to the ancient graves.[29] He realized that even his nest in the burrow, which he cherished in his heart, had been inside the Burning House of the Three Worlds.[30]

"When the appointed time has come, and I am about to be burned," he thought, "and even the carriage drawn by great white oxen is on the side of my enemies, who will be waiting for me in front of the gate?[31] But if I can reverse the illusion of my attachment to this incarnation, then perhaps it may lead to enlightenment." He handed over to his wife and children the burrow in the mound where he had lived for so long and the garden grove that he had relied on as his land. With a stout heart, he left the house of carnal desire and entered on the path of spiritual awakening. His family grieved in farewell; they parted tearfully and were very sad.

Now that he had entered the religious path, the *tanuki* worried about which form of Buddhism he should study to achieve enlightenment.[32] "The teaching of Shingon

28. The *tanuki* has no wish to return to the troubled life that he has just experienced.
29. The *tanuki* remembers a line from the second of "Ten Poems in the Old Style" by Bai Juyi (772–846). The other verse is probably poem 820 in *Sankashū* (*Collection of a Mountain Home*), by Saigyō (1118–1190). The two poems are appropriate for the *tanuki* because his burrow lies in a grave-mound.
30. As the Lotus Sutra explains, the Burning House is the mundane world of desire. The Three Worlds are the past, the present, and the future.
31. According to the Lotus Sutra, a father who wished to entice his children out of a burning house promised them carts drawn by oxen, deer, and goats. When the children stepped outside, he gave each of them a carriage—the Single Vehicle of the Dharma—drawn by a great white ox. The *tanuki*, however, is not comforted by the thought of an ox cart, since the ox, as one of the Twelve Animals, is on the side of his enemies.
32. This paragraph and the next four paragraphs are missing from *The War of the Twelve Animals*. The translation is based on the corresponding passage in *Kedamono Taiheiki*, in *Obusama Saburō emaki*, ed. Umezu and Okami, 82b.

is the finest of the various sects," he thought. "Students of this school perform the practices of the Three Mysteries and live in contemplation of the Five Stages.[33] They become buddhas in this very life.

In the tenth illustration (not reproduced here), the *tanuki* says farewell to his wife and children inside his burrow. The smallest cub clings pathetically to his sleeve. Outside, he is seen walking away and looking back sadly.

"Then, again, there is the Lotus sect.[34] The purpose of the Buddha's incarnation on earth was for all living things to achieve buddhahood directly. When one enters this sect, one contemplates the doctrine of 'three thousand in a single thought.'[35] I could attain a state of purity of the six senses.

"On the other hand, when one inquires about the Hossō sect, one exposes one's eyes to such works as the Shinmitsukyō, the Sutra of Profound Understanding, and the Yugakyō, the Sutra on the Stages of Yoga Practice. I would toy with the flower of Five-Fold Consciousness-Only and polish the moon of the Bright Gate of the Hundred Teachings.[36]

"And then, again, when one practices mendicancy, one performs the rituals of Mount Ōmine, from which Zaō Gongen arises, and Mount Katsuragi, where the Diamond Boy is incarnated;[37] and one becomes an ascetic of a single dhāraṇī incantation. I would bow with the head of the wise man."[38]

The *tanuki* worried about all these things. He thought how very difficult it would be to follow the practices for achieving salvation through one's own efforts, and how, in these Latter Days of the Law—this evil world of the Five Defilements—there was only the Pure Land sect through which one could easily enter the Way.[39] He therefore decided that this teaching was the one for him.

413

33. The Three Mysteries (*sanmitsu*) are the body, speech, and mind of the Buddha. The Five Stages (*gosō*) are the five stages of Vairocana buddhahood.
34. Lotus sect is used as an alternative appellation for the Tendai school.
35. The doctrine of "three thousand in a single thought" is the notion that all things (represented by the number three thousand) are emanations of the human heart-mind.
36. Five-Fold Consciousness-Only (*gojū yuishiki*) refers to the five levels of realization of the Hossō doctrine of consciousness-only. The Bright Gate of the Hundred Teachings (*hyappō myōmon*) is a term for the comprehension of the multitude of Buddhist principles.
37. These are references to the practices of Shugendō, a mystical Shinto-Buddhist sect. The ferocious Zaō Gongen is the main deity of Shugendō, and the Diamond Boy (Kongō Dōji) is a guardian figure of esoteric Buddhism who is also worshipped in Shugendō.
38. Another possible translation is "I would carry out the ritual of the Skull of the Wise Man." This may refer to the heterodox practices of the Tachikawa sect of Buddhism. See James H. Sanford, "The Abominable Tachikawa Skull Ritual," *Monumenta Nipponica* 46, no. 1 (1991): 1–20.
39. According to Pure Land Buddhist doctrine, one can attain enlightenment in the Latter Days of the Law—the third of the three eras since the death of Shakyamuni Buddha—only by relying on the "other

Aided by two human priests, the *tanuki* receives the tonsure. (From *Jūnirui kassen*, © The Trustees of the Chester Beatty Library, Dublin, and the HUMI Project, Keiō University)

Having made up his mind, the *tanuki* sought out the followers of Priest Hōnen.[40] He joined the priesthood and took the name Kejōbō. In the end, he achieved his original intention of going to the capital, which he had not known as a layman, and he stayed in the practice hall of Badger Amida Buddha.[41] Night after night, he composed his heart, and beating time on his belly-drum, he performed the dancing *nenbutsu*.[42]

Because the *tanuki* thought that this dwelling away from the bustle of the city was not ideal, he built a grass hut in the neighborhood of Nishiyama. He picked flowers on the peaks and drew water in the valleys and worked toward salvation in the next life. But even as he avoided other things, it must have been difficult for him to abandon the lingering attachments of old. On moonlit nights and snowy mornings,

power" (*tariki*) of Amida (Skt. Amitābha) Buddha, which functions independently of any unenlightened being's power, practice, or achievement.

40. Hōnen (1133–1212) was the founder of the Pure Land (Jōdo) sect of Buddhism in Japan. He appears, in this volume, as a character in *Little Atsumori*.

41. The badger's name reflects a common practice among adherents of the Jishū "time sect" of Pure Land Buddhism of taking a religious name ending in -*ami*, -*amida*, or -*amidabutsu*.

42. The dancing *nenbutsu* is a kind of ecstatic dancing to the ritual incantation of the name of Amida Buddha, popularized by Priest Ippen (1234–1289) and his Jishū sect of Pure Land Buddhism.

In the eleventh illustration (not fully reproduced here), a human priest shaves the *tanuki*'s head while another one chants an appropriate passage from a sutra. The following dialogue is inscribed:

PRIEST (*chanting*): You are a beast, and your heart has opened to spiritual awakening.[1]

In another building, presumably the practice hall of Badger Amida Buddha, the *tanuki* drums on his belly as he performs the dancing *nenbutsu*.

TANUKI (*dancing and singing*):

uki koto wo	Swollen with thoughts
omoifukureshi	of sadness
kuyashisa mo	and frustration as well,
waga haratsuzumi	I beat my belly-drum
uchi zo odoroku	and am awakened.

1. This is a phrase from the Sutra of Brahma's Net (Bonmōkyō).

In the final illustration (not reproduced here), the *tanuki* is seen twice: first inside his mountain retreat, where his poetry appears on the sliding doors, and then descending a steep mountain path with buckets of water and a flowering branch. The following dialogue is inscribed:

TANUKI: In the old days, people referred to "the *tanuki* going to the capital" as an example of things that don't go well. Now, since the Capital of Absolute Truth is nowhere other than in myself, even the rays of the moon among the clouds and the tint of the snow on the palace do not disdain a dwelling such as this. As I continue thinking on it, my heart seems to become clearer and clearer.

inu no o wa	I look without concern on
usagi no sena to	the tail of the dog
yoso ni mite	and the back of the rabbit;
urayamareshi mo	my envy of them
mukashi narikere	is a thing of the past.
tsumi wa yuki	My sins are piled up like snow;
kokoro wa tsuki no	my heart has attachments like the moon.
satori koso	Enlightenment
noborikanenishi	is the capital
miyako narikere	that is difficult to reach.[1]

1. This poem contains puns on *tsumi*, which means both "sin" and "to pile up," and on *tsuki*, which means both "moon" and "attachments." Also, the moon is a traditional symbol of enlightenment, as it is here in the phrase *tsuki no satori* (the moon of enlightenment).

his heart was colored by worldly matters and his mouth was filled with poetry. And so he lived from day to day.

When the ascetic Iesato visited Mount Tai to escape from worldly entanglements, he dispelled five intoxications and overcame four demons. The only one that he did not defeat was the demon of poetry.[43] Minamoto no Shitagō has written this down.[44] Although China and Japan are different, this lingering attachment in our hearts is the same. How fine!

TRANSLATION AND INTRODUCTION BY SARAH E. THOMPSON

43. This probably is an intended pun on *shima*, or "the demon of poetry," and "the Four Demons (who hinder the practice of Buddhism)." Iesato defeated the latter, but not the former.
44. Minamoto no Shitagō (911–983) was the compiler of the dictionary *Wamyō ruijushō* (938) and an editor of *Gosen wakashū* (*Later Collection*, 951), an imperial anthology of Japanese poetry. It is unclear to what work of his this sentence refers.

The Sparrow's Buddhist Awakening

In his preface to *Kokin wakashū* (*Collection of Poems Ancient and Modern*, ca. 905), an imperial anthology of Japanese poetry, Ki no Tsurayuki (872–945) famously compared the sounds of birds and animals to human verse, declaring that "when we hear the twittering of the bush warbler in the blossoms and the voices of the frogs in the water, we realize that every living being has its song."[1] *The Sparrow's Buddhist Awakening* (*Suzume no hosshin*), also known as *The Tale of Kotōda* (*Kotōda monogatari*), imaginatively extends Tsurayuki's analogy by providing an illustrated record of the sad songs of more than a dozen birds and a single snake in the thirty-one-syllable *waka* form. The story is dominated by its poetry, much as *The War of the Twelve Animals* is. Even the *michiyuki* travelogue and other prose passages are replete with poetic wordplay. As the plucky sparrow-protagonist Kotōda wanders through the land as a Buddhist monk in the latter part of his tale, he seems to be cast in the role of an itinerant poet-priest in the manner of Saigyō (1118–1190), the famed *waka* poet.

As its title indicates, *The Sparrow's Buddhist Awakening* is also a religious fable, describing for readers how the devastating loss of a child inspired an avian husband and wife to take monastic vows. The work is playfully Amidist in its orientation, even claiming at its end that it was actually Kotōda who invented "*nenbutsu* dancing," a Pure Land devotional practice historically associated with the thirteenth-century Priest Ippen and his Jishū sect of Pure Land Buddhism. In its text and illustrations, the work depicts Kotōda's transformation from lay to monastic and, somewhat more subtly, from animal to human (the latter being a necessary stage on a non-human

The translation and illustrations are from the two-scroll *Suzume no hosshin* picture scrolls (sixteenth century) in the collection of the Suntory Museum of Art (former Akagi Bunko *emaki*), typeset in Yokoyama Shigeru and Matsumoto Ryūshin, eds., *Muromachi jidai monogatari taisei* (Tokyo: Kadokawa Shoten, 1979), 7:588–97. The first paragraph of the translation is from an early-Edo-period picture scroll in the Daitōkyū Kinen Bunko archive, typeset on page 581 of the same volume.

1. Ozawa Masao, ed., *Kokin wakashū*, Nihon koten bungaku zenshū 7 (Tokyo: Shōgakukan, 1971), 49.

being's path to enlightenment). In the first part of the story, Kotōda is portrayed as a bird fluttering in the trees; but upon taking monastic vows, he is shown in traditional Buddhist garb, and he walks instead of flies. By abandoning secular life, Kotōda seems to attain partial release from the animal realm, achieving a higher level of existence as a quasi-human monk, which he appears to recognize in the poem that he composes at Kiyomizu Temple.

Although the author of the story is unknown, an inscription on the paulownia box containing the scrolls from which this translation is derived attributes the calligraphy to Shin Naishi no Suke, the daughter of Asukai Masayasu (1436–1509). Alternatively, in his travel record *Kiryo manroku* (*Chronicle of Peregrinations*, 1802), Kyokutei Bakin suggested that the same scrolls should be credited to Kōtō no Naishi, whom he identified as one of the poets represented in the *renga* (linked-verse) anthology *Shinsen Tsukubashū* (*New Tsukuba Collection*, 1495).[2] *The Sparrow's Buddhist Awakening* was widely reproduced in the late Muromachi (1337–1573) and early Edo (1600–1867) periods, and it survives in multiple versions with major variations in the number and contents of its poems.

At a time not so long ago, something peculiar happened in Katayama Village in the Miya district of Yamato Province. There was an especially cheeky little fellow by the name of Kotōda the Sparrow. Seeking out a proper spouse, he told her of his love and sealed a bond with her for the rest of their lives and beyond. They shared a profound affection, like lovebirds with wings as one.

One spring, the wife found herself unusually out of sorts. Kotōda was distressed, but when her condition turned out to be nothing other than the pains of pregnancy, he, too, was overjoyed. He immediately built a birthing nest. The days eventually passed, and then, without incident, there was a child to raise.

Once when the couple was out seeking sustenance, a snake mercilessly swallowed their little bird. Never imagining what had occurred, they came home with some food. But when they looked around, their baby was gone. "What could have happened?" they cried. Their shock and confusion were beyond compare.

Thinking that it was the snake's doing, Kotōda addressed him, saying, "Listen here, Lord Snake! For what crime have you sought to repay us by murdering our

2. Matsumoto Ryūshin and Akai Tatsurō, "Sakuhin kaisetsu," in *Otogizōshi*, Shirīzu taiyō 19, Taiyō koten to emaki shirīzu 3 (Tokyo: Heibonsha, 1979), 147c.

child? You, too, have been blessed with life, and among all living creatures, are there any that don't love their children? Out of all the fifty-two species, you're the most odious in shape and form, which, indeed, seems to be the result of your wretched karma. Nevertheless, this land of ours is a Buddhist realm, and when you happen to have been born here, wouldn't you want to establish some kind of karmic link to achieve buddhahood this time around? Even if you haven't planted many good roots, if you were to make a single-hearted appeal, why wouldn't you be able to attain buddhahood by means of the other power of the Original Vows?[3] But until you do, if you just go on living and even adding to your karmic burden by killing things, when will you ever obtain release? It's pathetic!

"You may look down on us, but our bodies are built for flight, so if I were to tell Lord Stork, who can soar up and around in an instant, how far do you think you'd get? But it wouldn't do any good. Even with you gone, our little one could hardly come back. And what's more, due to the sin of having you killed, I'd fall even deeper into the Three Evil Realms.[4] Then, when would I ever obtain release? But if my wife and I were to take a lesson from our loss, seizing this chance to shave our heads, wrap ourselves in the dark-dyed robes of the clergy, and seek a link to enlightenment, we'd certainly be reborn in the Pure Land Paradise, where we could share a single lotus dais with our baby. When I think of it that way, I don't bear you any malice. Goodbye, Lord Snake."

In its shame and its fear of the stork, the snake was at a loss for words. It simply flicked its tongue and crawled off into the grass. As it left, the snake recited a poem:

iyashiku mo	Though despicable,
kuchi yue haji wo	it's to fill my mouth
kaku bakari	that I disgrace myself.
ukina wo nagasu	Oh, the misery of being
mi koso tsurakere	such a scandalous beast![5]

Now the sparrow couple spent the rest of the day and all that night lingering around the place where their nest had been. Yet the grief of that tragic separation! In a daze, they had no words to express their loss. They could only weep pitifully. All

3. The Original Vows (*hongan*) are Amida (Skt. Amitābha) Buddha's vows guaranteeing the possibility of rebirth in his Pure Land Paradise. The other power (*tariki*) is the power of Amida Buddha, which functions independently of any unenlightened being's power, practice, or achievement.

4. The Three Evil Realms are the realms of hell, animals, and hungry ghosts. As a bird, Kotōda already occupies the animal realm.

5. In Japanese, the word *kuchi* (mouth) combines with the syllables *na wo* (in *ukina wo*) to suggest *kuchinawa*, an old word for "snake."

the other birds heard the news, and feeling very sorry for the sparrows, they each composed a poem in mourning. The Bush Warbler Lesser Captain recited:

suzumeko no	Hearing of the death
naki zo to kikeba	of your sparrow child—
yosonagara	though not my loss,
koe mo oshimazu	I cry with sudden sorrow,
ne koso nakarure	holding nothing back.[6]

Kotōda replied:

omoiki ya	Did I ever think
imasara kakaru	that now I might grieve
nageki shite	like this—
yoso no tamoto wo	so much as to soak
nurasubeshi to wa	a stranger's sleeves?

6. The word *naki* has the triple meaning of "birdsong," "weeping," and "absence/death." Alternatively translated, the first two lines might read, "Hearing the chirps / of your sparrow child—."

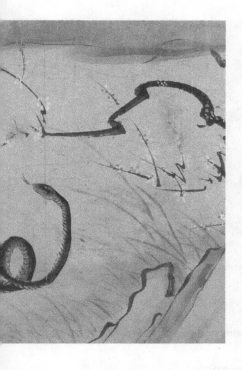

The sparrow Kotōda and his wife berate the murderous snake. (From *Suzume no hosshin*, courtesy of the Suntory Museum of Art)

Shinzaemon the Chickadee composed:

awaresa wo	Hearing such sadness,
kiku ni namida no	would that my own tears
susumebaya	flow freely,
itodo ukine no	adding yet another voice
kazu zo masareru	to the chorus of laments.[7]

Kotōda replied:

tare tote mo	What person,
shijū wa kaku to	cognizant of his life from
shirinagara	beginning to end,
ima towarubeki	could be unaware that now
mi to wa shirazu ya	was his time to be consoled?[8]

7. The poem contains the word "sparrow" (*susume / suzume*) embedded in its third line.
8. Kotōda's reply echoes the preceding verse by employing the word *shijū* (beginning to end) to suggest *shijūkara* (chickadee).

The Sparrow's Buddhist Awakening

Kotōda exchanges poems with the White Heron Commander of the Gate Guards. (From *Suzume no hosshin*, courtesy of the Suntory Museum of Art)

The Shrine Crow Assistant Chamberlain composed:

chihayaburu	Since I am one
kami ni tsukōru	who serves the mighty gods,
mi ni areba	even if I come and go,
yukite kō to mo	how could I not stop
towanu mono kana	to pay my sad respects?

Kotōda replied:

towarete ya	Even consoled,
nakanaka sode wo	I'll still soak my sleeves
nurasuran	in streams of tears,
waga kotonoha wo	my laments, like leaves,
yoso ni shirarete	all known to others.

The White Heron Commander of the Gate Guards composed:

ada nari to	For me, too,
waga mi no ue mo	the snake is a foe,

shirasagi no	which is why
yoso no aware ni	I wet my sleeves
sode nurasu kana	for a sorrow not my own.[9]

Kotōda replied:

kotowari wo	Though I thought
yomo shirasagi to	I couldn't see the sense of it,
omoishi ni	White Heron,
aware wo toishi	how kind of you
koto zo yasashiki	to inquire of my grief![10]

Nakatsukasa the Pheasant composed:

mi ni tsumite	Weighted with sorrow,
omoi koso yare	I send my thoughts out to you.
tarachine ga	How sad
sa koso wakare no	must be the parents
kanashikaruran	who have lost a child!

Kotōda replied:

nagekite mo	Though mourning
kaerubeki ni wa	won't bring our baby back,
aranedomo	it's still
sasuga ni oshiki	so very hard
ko no wakare kana	to bid a child farewell.

Shinzaemon the Heavy-Drinking Bulbul composed:[11]

9. The word *ada* can mean both "enemy" and "fleeting/evanescent." In addition, *shirasagi* (white heron) suggests *shira[zu]* (not knowing), so the first three lines might be translated, "I did not know / that for me, too, / life could be so fleeting."

10. As in the previous poem, *shirasagi* (white heron) suggests *shira[zu]* (not knowing).

11. Shinzaemon is identified as a *hiyodori-jōgo*, a name that puns on *hiyodori-jōgo* (*Solanum lyratum*, a vine-like plant native to East and Southeast Asia), and *hiyodori* (bulbul) and *jōgo* (heavy drinker). The plant is said to be so-named because of the bulbul's fondness for its berries.

The Sparrow's Buddhist Awakening

ōkata wa	Everyone calls me
hiyodori jōgo to	the Heavy-Drinking
iwaruredo	Bulbul,
kono nageki shite	but in this grief
sake mo nomarezu	I can't drink my wine.

Kotōda replied:

hito shirenu	Though I thought it was
nageki to koso wa	a grief that
omoishi ni	no one else could know,
samo toridori ni	how the birds all offer me
towarenuru kana	their respective sympathies![12]

Nakatsukasa the Crane composed:

tare tote mo	Now I understand
ko yue yamiji ni	how anyone, for a child,
mayou zo to	can wander lost
omoishirarete	on paths of darkness.
nururu sode kana	Ah, my teary sleeves![13]

Kotōda replied:

adashi yo to	Since I am one
omoinazorau	who thinks of this world
mi ni areba	as a fleeting realm,
sa made mo ware wa	I really haven't grieved
nagekazarikeri	to quite that extent!

---

12. The poem contains a pun on *toridori*, which means both "birds" and "respective."

13. The crane's poem alludes to poem 1102 in *Gosen wakashū* (*Later Collection*, 951), attributed to Fujiwara no Kanesuke (877–933):

hito no oya no	Though a parent's heart
kokoro wa yami ni	may not be mired
aranedomo	in darkness,
ko wo omou michi ni	one still wanders lost
madoinuru ka na	on paths of love for a child.

Hachirōzaemon the Bullfinch composed:

kono koto wo	People would
uso to ya hito no	surely think this
omouran	a bullfinch lie—
namida no fuchi ni	that I would sink and drown
shizumu waga mi wo	in a pool of tears.[14]

Kotōda replied:

nanigoto mo	In this world
uso to omoishi	in which I thought that
yo no naka ni	everything
kono koto bakari	was a bullfinch lie,
makoto narikeri	your words alone are true.

The Wild Goose Deputy of Computation composed:

suzume-ko no	The sparrow-child has
aki no inaba no	disappeared like the dew,
matazu shite	without awaiting
kiekemu tsuyu no	the ripe rice of autumn.
mi koso tsurakere	Oh the pain of a fleeting life!

Kotōda replied:

yo no naka wa	Though I know
kari no yadori to	that this world
shirinagara	is a temporary dwelling,
aki hitokoro wa	I'll still miss that dew-like life,
oshiki tsuyu no mi	especially in the autumn.[15]

The Rooster Deputy of Music composed:

14. Both this poem and its reply contain plays on *uso*, which means both "bullfinch" and "prevarication."
15. Kotōda's reply contains a play on *kari*, which means both "wild goose" and "temporary."

The Sparrow's Buddhist Awakening

Kotōda exchanges poems with the Rooster Deputy of Music. (From *Suzume no hosshin*, courtesy of the Suntory Museum of Art)

tarachine no	Such grieving
wakare wo sa nomi	for parents
nageku kana	who have lost a child!
ada naru yo to wa	Before now I never knew
kanete shirazu ya	what an uncertain world this is.

Kotōda replied:

omoiki ya	Did I ever think
ada naru yo to wa	this parting would really
shirinagara	be so hard,
sasuga ni oshiki	knowing as I did the
ko no wakare to wa	uncertainty of the world?

Shinroku the Quail said, "I feel so sorry for you, particularly since we're birds of a feather." And he composed:

omowaji to	Though I'd decided
omoedo itodo	not to feel, I'm affected
akugarete	all the more—
samo hoshikanuru	how difficult it is
waga tamoto kana	to dry my sleeves!

INTERSPECIES AFFAIRS

Kotōda replied:

> nakaji to wa   It seems there's
> iu mo nageki no   no one to tell us
> kotoba zo to   that declaring
> omoishirasuru   "I won't cry"
> hito wa araji na   is itself a lament!

The Cuckoo Cloud-Well Commander composed:

> yosonagara   Since I've heard
> kimi ga aware wo   about your sadness
> kiku kara ni   secondhand,
> waga naku ne wo ba   will anyone recognize
> hito ya shiruran   the grief within my cries?

Kotōda replied:

> iza saraba   In that case,
> namida kuraben   Cuckoo, let us
> hototogisu   compare our tears.
> ware mo ukiyo ni   I, too, can only cry my cry
> ne wo nomi zo naku   in this suffering world.

The Mandarin Duck Ginkgo Commander composed:

> izuko wo mo   I thought that
> mina oshidori to   everyone everywhere
> omoishi ni   was a mandarin duck,
> wakareshi toki no   for the waters of parting
> mizu ya musubitsu   take shape as tears![16]

Kotōda replied:

16. In the poem's second line, the word *oshidori* (mandarin duck) contains the word *oshi* (hard to relinquish), which suggests the pains of separation. Alternatively translated, the first part of the poem might read, "I thought that / everyone everywhere / begrudged their losses." The word *mizu* (water) is both a metonym for "tears" and an associated word (*engo*) echoing *oshidori*.

The Sparrow's Buddhist Awakening

mizudori no	To hear your kindness,
nasake wo kikeba	you water bird,
tanomoshi ya	is heartening indeed.
kusaba no kage ni	Now dwell in the shade
yadore waga ko yo	of the leaves, my child!

Kotōda addressed his wife, saying, "When I think hard about this world, it seems like a vision or a dream. Even if we were to live out our lives in it, what pleasure could we have? Indeed, if we were to compare ourselves to other things, we're like small boats that never dock at the shore or duckweed drifting off the jutting coast. Our lives are as uncertain as the dew atop a morning glory, vanishing before the twilight. If we cling to our fleeting lives and go on living in our self-contented ways, we'll be bound for the evil realms, where we'll be trapped for lives and ages to come. I think I'd like to take a lesson from what's happened, enter the monastic path, and pray for our baby in the afterworld. Then I, too, could escape from the cycle of birth and death. You're young, so you should make some kind of home for yourself in the lay world and never forget our child! When I think that our pledge to tread the same path through every sort of fire or flood was all in vain . . . that in this world in which those who meet are sure to part, and those who are born are sure to die, I should go on living out my days with you as my heart would wish . . . it's just too awful!"

Amid her tears, the wife recited a single verse:

futa oya wo	For the two parents
mata chirijiri ni	now to be torn asunder—
nasu koto mo	is this, too, because
kakego yue naru	of the child: a hanging tray
tamakushige kana	inside a jeweled comb box?[17]

Kotōda replied:

futa oya no	For the two parents
makoto no michi ni	to enter the True Path—
iru koto mo	this, too, is because
kakego yue naru	of the child: a hanging tray
tamakushige kana	inside a jeweled comb box.

17. The word *futa* (two) is a homonym of *futa* (lid), which is an associated word (*engo*) anticipating *tamakushige* (jeweled comb box). Also, *kakego* (hanging tray) contains the word *ko/go* (child).

Kotōda and his wife converse. (From *Suzume no hosshin*, courtesy of the Suntory Museum of Art)

After a while, the wife spoke: "It's just as you say. Even if we mourn, it won't bring our baby back, of course. I've loved you ever so much, but I'm deeply grateful for this decision you've made. It's a joy within my sorrow. Those who are born in the morning are taken away by the evening wind, and although we may gaze on the moon at night, it's concealed by the clouds at dawn. In this heartbreaking world in which the morning dew won't await the dusk, to set our hearts on anything is to invite chagrin. The ties between a husband and a wife transcend the present world, so even if this bond of ours is weak, we'll certainly be born on a single lotus in the world to come. Farewell, then, and goodbye." The wife flew away. But owing to the inevitable sorrow of parting, she returned and composed:

sakidataba	If you die first,
kusa no kage nite	then wait for me a while
mate shibashi	in the shady grass.
ware sakidataba	And if I go first,
machi mo koso seme	I'll wait for you, too.

Kotōda replied:

tare tote mo	Who at all
sakidatsu mi zo to	ought to think in terms of
omoubeshi	dying first?
yume miru hodo mo	Is this world any more
nokorubeki yo ka	lasting than a dream?

The Sparrow's Buddhist Awakening

Aided by the owl-monk Son'amidabu, Kotōda receives the tonsure. (From *Suzume no hosshin*, courtesy of the Suntory Museum of Art)

In tears, the sparrows flew their separate ways. The wife sought out a hermitage at "Nun's Point" Amagasaki, where, at the age of nineteen, she took religious vows. She chanted the *nenbutsu* with single-hearted devotion and eventually attained her long-standing desire for rebirth in the Pure Land.[18]

Kotōda ascended Amida Peak in the same province, where he sought out the abode of a priestly owl by the name of Son'amidabu and stated that he wished to take monastic vows. Moved by the sparrow's aspiration, the master called him in and said that there should be no difficulty. "The benefits of becoming a monk are enormous," he explained, "because to do so is superior even to making offerings to the eighty thousand buddhas." The owl conferred the verse about "transmigrating through the Three Worlds."[19] With that, in the twenty-third year since his birth, Kotōda finally came to uphold the monastic precepts. The owl shaved his head and gave him the Buddhist name of Jakuamidabu.[20] It was all most excellent!

Kotōda stayed on Amida Peak for some ten days, after which he took leave of the priestly owl and went to visit Mount Kōya.[21] From there, he traveled to the Kumano

18. The *nenbutsu* is the ritual invocation of the name of Amida Buddha.
19. This verse is traditionally recited when a person takes the tonsure.
20. Jakuamidabu can be written with characters that mean either "Sparrow Amida Buddha" or "Shaky-amuni Amida Buddha." The inclusion of Amida's name in Kotōda's own indicates Kotōda's devotion to the Pure Land cult. The owl's name, Son'amidabu, means "Reverend Amida Buddha."
21. Mount Kōya is the headquarters of the Shingon school of esoteric Buddhism.

Shrines, followed by a tour of the western provinces as far as Tsukushi.[22] Next, he visited Zenkōji Temple in Shinano Province. He made his way on to Kamakura, after which he wandered the six northern provinces. After that, he traveled to the capital.[23]

In the western mountains, Kotōda visited Atago, Takao, and Togano'o. He went to the temple on the Saga Plain,[24] where he bowed down and prayed to the sacred image of Shakyamuni carved by the craftsman-deity Viśvakarman. He traveled on to Tenryūji Temple and Rinsenji Temple, known for its waterwheel spinning through this suffering world. From atop the bridge at the Ōi River, where crowds of people come and go, he stared out at the boulder from which the lady Yokobue drowned her wretched self in longing for Takiguchi Tokiyori.[25] He was all the more moved to see it for himself.

At "stormy" Mount Arashi, bane of blossoms, Kotōda visited Hōrinji Temple, where he prayed for his fate in the world to come. He bowed down and prayed at Iwakura, Yoshimine, and other temples and buddha halls on peaks and in mountain valleys. He marveled at the sight of Mount Oshio, where Munesada once lived in seclusion, mourning the loss of his former emperor,[26] and he crossed the Katsura River where cormorant fishers pole their boats. Since quitting the secular world, his heart had never been so pure as he made his way to "Pure Water" Kiyomizu Temple, deeply inspired by the Kiyomizu Kannon's great merciful vow to save sentient beings.[27]

The place was more splendid than he had heard. With its soaring peak, Mount Otowa was suffused with the fragrance of the temple cherry blossoms borne on the spring breeze. Their petals lit on his monkish sleeves like a dusting of snow, lovely beyond the power of words to express or the mind to conceive. Gazing out at the trees, he composed a single verse:

431

---

22. Tsukushi is an old name for the island of Kyūshū. The three Kumano shrines are located on the Kii Peninsula, relatively near Mount Kōya.
23. The Kyoto capital, not far from where Kotōda first set out.
24. This is Seiryōji Temple, also known as the Saga Shakadō (Shakyamuni Hall of the Saga Plain). The phrase "western mountains" refers to the mountains immediately to the west of Kyoto.
25. According to the otogizōshi Yokobue sōshi (The Tale of Yokobue) and other sources, the seventeen-year-old Yokobue drowned herself in the Ōi River after her lover, Saitō Takiguchi Tokiyori, left her for the priesthood.
26. According to the noh play Munesada, the courtier Yoshimine Munesada (815–890), better known today as the poet-monk Henjō, renounced his secular life at Mount Oshio in the Ōhara district of the capital upon the death of Emperor Ninmyō (808–850, r. 833–850).
27. The Kiyomizu Kannon is the statue of the bodhisattva Kannon at Kiyomizu Temple in the eastern foothills of Kyoto.

Kotōda travels to Kiyomizu Temple. (From *Suzume no hosshin*, courtesy of the Suntory Museum of Art)

inishie wa	Though in the past
hana fumichirasu	I was one to trample and
mi naredomo	scatter the blossoms,
ima wa kozue wo	these days I view
yoso ni koso mire	the treetops from afar.

Upon leaving Kiyomizu Temple, Kotōda bowed down and prayed at Sōrinji Temple at Washino'o Sacred Eagle Peak.[28] The bell at Chōrakuji Temple in the deepening night echoed with the sound of impermanence, while in the Gion Forest, with his head pillowed on the root of a pine, he passed the endless hours until dawn. Setting out from the woods, he came to Awataguchi, meeting point for strangers and acquaintances alike,[29] and then to Mount Kachō, the "flowery summit" whose name is the same in winter, too. He bowed down and prayed at Hokkeji Temple; at "middle-of-the-mountains" Nakayama Temple, which is not in fact on a peak; and at Kamo Shrine, whose "righteous" Tadasu Deity rectifies the people's lies.

He continued on to "deep mud" Mizoro Pond, the bottom of which is actually

28. Washino'o, written with characters that mean "eagle's tail," is an area in the Higashiyama district of Kyoto. It is here identified with Sacred Eagle Peak (Skt. Gṛdhrakūṭa-parvata; J. Ryōjusen), where Shakyamuni is said to have preached the Lotus Sutra.

29. The author puns on the place-name Awataguchi, which contains a form of the verb *afu* (to meet).

pure, and then to Mount Kurama of the setting moon, where he earnestly prayed to the great merciful Tamonten to lead him to the Pure Land after death.[30] Returning to the capital, he made his way to Kitano Shrine, where he wholeheartedly prayed, "Hail, great sacred powerful heavenly deity! I ask that you please fulfill the requests in my heart!" It was toward the middle of the third month, and looking around the shrine grounds, he saw the tops of young and old trees alike enshrouded in clouds of blossoms. Pushing through snowy drifts in the shade of branches, he lost his way out. As he left the shrine, he composed:

kokoro seyo	Watch out,
kono miyashiro no	you glorious blossoms
hanazakari	around the shrine!
kaze no toga naru	The vengeance of the wind
oimatsu no kami	comes from the old pine god.

As Kotōda was wandering beyond the stables of the Right Imperial Guards, making his way through the Second Avenue region west of Uchino, a passing storm filled the sky with clouds. No rain fell, but in the manner of such storms, the sun was obscured. Because he had no fondness for any place over another, he was taken by a desire to build himself a hermitage there. Remembering that those who shelter in the shade of the same tree or drink from the same stream are linked by the bonds of former lives, he fashioned a hideaway in which to dwell for just a little while. But as he lived there from one day to the next, the year eventually came to an end, and he was still reluctant to leave. Looking in the sutras, he saw that there was no place where a person might abide. Still, he spent the rest of his life there, and since that time, those woods have been called the "Sparrow's Forest."

Now Kotōda—Jakuamidabu—made it his Buddhist practice to perform what is known as the dancing *nenbutsu*.[31] He did so with unwavering devotion until the age of one hundred. At the time of his death, he maintained right concentration and achieved his long-held desire for Great Pure Land Rebirth.

Although sparrows may live to be one hundred, the practice of dancing to the

30. Tamonten is another name for Bishamonten (also Bishamon, Skt. Vaiśravaṇa), one of the four Buddhist guardian deities. A famous statue of Bishamonten is enshrined at Kurama Temple in the mountains north of Kyoto.
31. The dancing *nenbutsu* is a kind of ecstatic dancing to the ritual incantation of the name of Amida Buddha, popularized by Priest Ippen (1234–1289) and his Jishū sect of Pure Land Buddhism.

nenbutsu began with Jakuamidabu. As you can see from this story, he behaved in just the proper way until death, which is why I have set down his tale in these bird tracks of letters.[32] Thus even birds can eschew this suffering world and hanker in their hearts for the Pure Land. In the face of their example, we humans should be ashamed! We should all do our best to embrace the Buddhist teachings and seek out ties to enlightenment.

TRANSLATION AND INTRODUCTION BY KELLER KIMBROUGH

32. The author puns on the phrase *tori no ato*, which means both "bird tracks" and "writing" (because written characters are said to resemble the footprints of birds).

English-Language Secondary Sources

General Sources

Araki, James T. "*Otogi-zōshi* and *Nara-ehon*: A Field of Study in Flux." *Monumenta Nipponica* 36, no. 1 (1981): 1–20.

Childs, Margaret. *Rethinking Sorrow: Revelatory Tales of Late Medieval Japan*. Ann Arbor: University of Michigan Center for Japanese Studies, 1991.

Keene, Donald. *Seeds in the Heart: Japanese Literature from Earliest Times to the Late Sixteenth Century*. New York: Holt, 1993.

Kimbrough, R. Keller. "Late Medieval Popular Fiction and Narrated Genres: Otogizōshi, Kōwakamai, Sekkyō, and Ko-jōruri." In *The Cambridge History of Japanese Literature*, edited by Haruo Shirane and Tomi Suzuki, with David Lurie, 355–69. Cambridge: Cambridge University Press, 2016.

Kimbrough, R. Keller. *Preachers, Poets, Women, and the Way: Izumi Shikibu and the Buddhist Literature of Medieval Japan*. Ann Arbor: University of Michigan Center for Japanese Studies, 2008.

Kimbrough, R. Keller, and Hank Glassman, eds. "Vernacular Buddhism and Medieval Japanese Literature." Special issue, *Japanese Journal of Religious Studies* 36, no. 2 (2009).

McCormick, Melissa. *Tosa Mitsunobu and the Small Scroll in Medieval Japan*. Seattle: University of Washington Press, 2009.

Mulhern, Chieko Irie. "*Otogi-zōshi*: Short Stories of the Muromachi Period." *Monumenta Nipponica* 29, no. 2 (1974): 181–98.

Nüffer, Laura K. "Of Mice and Maidens: The Ideology of Interspecies Romance in Medieval and Early Modern Japan." Ph.D. diss., University of Pennsylvania, 2014.

Ruch, Barbara. "Medieval Jongleurs and the Making of a National Literature." In *Japan in the Muromachi Age*, edited by John Whitney Hall and Toyoda Takeshi, 279–309. Berkeley: University of California Press, 1977.

Ruch, Barbara. "Origins of *The Companion Library*: An Anthology of Medieval Japanese Stories." *Journal of Asian Studies* 30, no. 3 (1971): 593–610.

Ruch, Barbara. "The Other Side of Culture in Medieval Japan." In *Medieval Japan*, edited by Kozo Yamamura, 500–543. Vol. 3 of *The Cambridge History of Japan*. Cambridge: Cambridge University Press, 1990.

Shirane, Haruo. "Cultures of the Book, the Parlor, and the Roadside: Issues of Text, Picture, and Performance." In *Japanese Visual Culture: Performance, Media, and Text*, edited by Kenji Kobayashi, Maori Saitō, and Haruo Shirane, 1–14. Tokyo: National Institute of Japanese Literature, 2013.

Shirane, Haruo, ed. *Traditional Japanese Literature: An Anthology, Beginnings to 1600*. New York: Columbia University Press, 2007.

Skord, Virginia. *Tales of Tears and Laughter: Short Fiction of Medieval Japan*. Honolulu: University of Hawai'i Press, 1991.

Work-Specific Sources

HASEO AND THE GAMBLING STRANGER (HASEO SŌSHI)

Reider, Noriko T. "*Haseo sōshi*: A Medieval Scholar's Muse." *Japanese Studies* 35, no. 1 (2015): 103–18.

Reider, Noriko T. *Japanese Demon Lore: Oni from Ancient Times to the Present*. Logan: Utah State University Press, 2010.

THE TALE OF THE DIRT SPIDER (TSUCHIGUMO ZŌSHI)

Reider, Noriko T. "*Tsuchigumo sōshi*: The Emergence of a Shape-Shifting Killer Female Spider." *Asian Ethnology* 72, no. 1 (2013): 55–83.

Takeuchi, Melinda. "Kuniyoshi's *Minamoto Raikō and the Earth Spider*: Demon and Protest in Late Tokugawa Japan." *Ars Orientalis* 17 (1987): 5–38.

THE DEMON SHUTEN DŌJI (SHUTEN DŌJI)

Kimbrough, R. Keller, trans. *The Demon Shuten Dōji* (Shibukawa text). In *Traditional Japanese Literature: An Anthology, Beginnings to 1600*, edited by Haruo Shirane, 1123–38. New York: Columbia University Press, 2007.

Kimbrough, R. Keller. "Sacred Charnel Visions: Painting the Dead in Illustrated Scrolls of *The Demon Shuten Dōji*." In *Japanese Visual Culture: Performance, Media, and Text*, edited by Kenji Kobayashi, Maori Saitō, and Haruo Shirane, 35–47. Tokyo: National Institute of Japanese Literature, 2013.

Kimbrough, R. Keller. "Shuten Dōji." In *The Ashgate Encyclopedia of Literary and Cinematic Monsters*, edited by Jeffrey Andrew Weinstock, 514–16. Burlington, Vt.: Ashgate, 2014.

Lin, Irene H. "The Ideology of Imagination: The Tale of Shuten Dōji as a *Kenmon* Discourse." *Cahiers d'Extrême-Asie* 13, no. 1 (2002–2003): 379–410.

Phillips, Quitman Eugene. "The Price *Shuten Dōji* Screens: A Study of Visual Narrative." *Ars Orientalis* 26 (1996): 1–21.

Reider, Noriko T. "Carnivalesque in Medieval Japanese Literature: A Bakhtinian Reading of *Ōeyama Shuten Dōji*." *Japanese Studies* 28, no. 3 (2008): 383–94.

Reider, Noriko T. *Japanese Demon Lore: Oni from Ancient Times to the Present*. Logan: Utah State University Press, 2010.

THE DEMON OF IBUKI (IBUKI DŌJI)

Kimbrough, R. Keller. "Late Medieval Popular Fiction and Narrated Genres: Otogizōshi, Kōwakamai, Sekkyō, and Ko-jōruri." In *The Cambridge History of Japanese Literature*, edited by Haruo Shirane and Tomi Suzuki, with David Lurie, 355–70. Cambridge: Cambridge University Press, 2016.

THE TALE OF TAWARA TŌDA (TAWARA TŌDA MONOGATARI)

Selinger, Vyjayanthi R. *Authorizing the Shogunate: Ritual and Material Symbolism in the Literary Construction of Warrior Order*. Leiden: Brill, 2013.

THE PALACE OF THE TENGU (TENGU NO DAIRI)

Kimbrough, R. Keller. "Bloody Hell! Reading Boys' Books in Seventeenth-Century Japan." *Asian Ethnology* 74, no. 1 (2015): 111–39.

Kimbrough, R. Keller. "Tourists in Paradise: Writing the Pure Land in Medieval Japanese Fiction." *Japanese Journal of Religious Studies* 33, no. 2 (2006): 269–96.

YOSHITSUNE'S ISLAND-HOPPING (ONZŌSHI SHIMA-WATARI)

Mills, D. E. "Medieval Japanese Tales: Part II." *Folklore* 84, no. 1 (1973): 58–74.

Thompson, Mathew W. "A Medieval Warrior in Early Modern Japan: A Translation of the *Otogizōshi Hōgan Miyako Banashi*." *Monumenta Nipponica* 69, no. 1 (2014): 1–54.

THE TALE OF AMEWAKAHIKO (AMEWAKAHIKO SŌSHI)

Reider, Noriko T. "A Demon in the Sky: *The Tale of Amewakahiko*, a Japanese Medieval Story." *Marvels & Tales: Journal of Fairy-Tale Studies* 29, no. 2 (2015): 265–82.

THE ORIGINS OF THE SUWA DEITY (SUWA NO HONJI)

Inoue Takami. "The Interaction Between Buddhist and Shinto Traditions at Suwa Shrine." In *Buddhas and Kami in Japan: Honji Suijaku as a Combinatory Paradigm*, edited by Mark Teeuwen and Fabio Rambelli, 287–312. London: Routledge Curzon, 2003.

Marra, Michele. *Representations of Power: The Literary Politics of Medieval Japan*. Honolulu: University of Hawai'i Press, 1993.

THE TALE OF THE FUJI CAVE (FUJI NO HITOANA SŌSHI)

Kimbrough, R. Keller. "Preaching the Animal Realm in Late-Medieval Japan." *Asian Folklore Studies* 65, no. 2 (2006): 179–204.

Kimbrough, R. Keller. "Tourists in Paradise: Writing the Pure Land in Medieval Japanese Fiction." *Japanese Journal of Religious Studies* 33, no. 2 (2006): 269–96.

Kimbrough, R. Keller. "Travel Writing from Hell? Minamoto no Yoriie and the Politics of *Fuji no hitoana sōshi*." *Proceedings of the Association for Japanese Literary Studies* 8 (2007): 112–22.

ISOZAKI (ISOZAKI)

Kimbrough, R. Keller. "Late Medieval Popular Fiction and Narrated Genres: Otogizōshi, Kōwakamai, Sekkyō, and Ko-jōruri." In *The Cambridge History of Japanese Literature*, edited by Haruo Shirane and Tomi Suzuki, with David Lurie, 355–70. Cambridge: Cambridge University Press, 2016.

Kimbrough, R. Keller. *Preachers, Poets, Women, and the Way: Izumi Shikibu and the Buddhist Literature of Medieval Japan*. Ann Arbor: University of Michigan Center for Japanese Studies, 2008.

THE TALE OF THE HANDCART PRIEST (KURUMA-ZŌ SŌSHI)

Kimbrough, R. Keller. "Battling *Tengu*, Battling Conceit: Visualizing Abstraction in *The Tale of the Handcart Priest*." *Japanese Journal of Religious Studies* 39, no. 2 (2012): 275–305.

ORIGINS OF THE STATUE OF KANNON AS A BOY (CHIGO KANNON ENGI)

Atkins, Paul S. "*Chigo* in the Medieval Japanese Imagination." *Journal of Asian Studies* 67, no. 3 (2008): 947–70.

Childs, Margaret H. "*Chigo Monogatari*: Love Stories or Buddhist Sermons?" *Monumenta Nipponica* 35, no. 2 (1980): 127–51.

Childs, Margaret H. *Rethinking Sorrow: Revelatory Tales of Late Medieval Japan*. Ann Arbor: University of Michigan Center for Japanese Studies, 1991.

Childs, Margaret H., trans. "The Story of Kannon's Manifestation as a Youth." In *Partings at Dawn: An Anthology of Japanese Gay Literature*, edited by Stephen D. Miller, 31–35. San Francisco: Gay Sunshine Press, 1996.

Faure, Bernard. *The Red Thread: Buddhist Approaches to Sexuality*. Princeton, N.J.: Princeton University Press, 1998.

Schmidt-Hori, Sachi. "The New Lady-in-Waiting Is a *Chigo*: Sexual Fluidity and Dual Trans-vestism in a Medieval Buddhist Acolyte Tale." *Japanese Language and Literature* 43, no. 2 (2009): 383–423.

LITTLE ATSUMORI (KO-ATSUMORI)

Kimbrough, R. Keller. "*Little Atsumori* and *The Tale of the Heike*: Fiction as Commentary, and the Significance of a Name." *Proceedings of the Association for Japanese Literary Studies* 5 (2004): 325–36.

Kimbrough, R. Keller. "Preachers and Playwrights: *Ikuta Atsumori* and the Roots of Noh." In *Like Clouds or Mists: Studies and Translations of Nō Plays of the Genpei War*, edited by Elizabeth Oyler and Michael Watson, 211–29. Ithaca, N.Y.: Cornell University East Asia Program, 2013.

THE CRONE FLEECE (UBAKAWA)

Dix, Monika. "*Hachikazuki*: Revealing Kannon's Crowning Compassion in Muromachi Fiction." *Japanese Journal of Religious Studies* 36, no. 2 (2009): 279–94.

Mulhern, Chieko Irie. "Cinderella and the Jesuits: An *Otogizōshi* Cycle as Christian Literature." *Monumenta Nipponica* 34, no. 4 (1979): 409–47.

Reider, Noriko T. " 'Hanayo no hime,' or 'Blossom Princess': A Late-Medieval Japanese Step-daughter Story and Provincial Customs." *Asian Ethnology* 70, no. 1 (2011): 59–80.

THE TALE OF THE MOUSE (NEZUMI NO SŌSHI)

Mills, D. E. "The Tale of the Mouse: *Nezumi no Sōshi*." *Monumenta Nipponica* 34, no. 2 (1979): 155–68.

Nüffer, Laura K. "Of Mice and Maidens: The Ideology of Interspecies Romance in Medieval and Early Modern Japan." Ph.D. diss., University of Pennsylvania, 2014.

THE CHRYSANTHEMUM SPIRIT (KIKU NO SEI MONOGATARI; KAZASHI NO HIMEGIMI)

McCormick, Melissa. "Flower Personification and Imperial Regeneration in *The Chrysanthemum Spirit*." In *Japanese Visual Culture: Performance, Media, and Text*, edited by Kenji

Kobayashi, Maori Saitō, and Haruo Shirane, 135–44. Tokyo: National Institute of Japanese Literature, 2013.

McCormick, Melissa. *Tosa Mitsunobu and the Small Scroll in Medieval Japan*. Seattle: University of Washington Press, 2009.

THE TALE OF A WILD GOOSE (KARI NO SŌSHI)

Nüffer, Laura K. "Of Mice and Maidens: The Ideology of Interspecies Romance in Medieval and Early Modern Japan." Ph.D. diss., University of Pennsylvania, 2014.

Shirane, Haruo. *Japan and the Culture of the Four Seasons: Nature, Literature, and the Arts*. New York: Columbia University Press, 2012.

THE STINGFISH (OKOZE)

Abe, Goh. "A Ritual Performance of Laughter in Southern Japan." In *Understanding Humor in Japan*, edited by Jessica Milner Davis, 37–50. Detroit: Wayne State University Press, 2006.

Blacker, Carmen. "The Mistress of the Animals in Japan: Yamanokami." In *The Concept of the Goddess*, edited by Sandra Billington and Miranda Green, 178–85. London: Routledge, 1996.

440

LADY TAMAMO (TAMAMO NO MAE SŌSHI)

Bathgate, Michael. *The Fox's Craft in Japanese Religion and Folklore: Shapeshifters, Transformations, and Duplicities*. New York: Routledge, 2004.

Smyers, Karen A. *The Fox and the Jewel: Shared and Private Meanings in Contemporary Japanese Inari Worship*. Honolulu: University of Hawai'i Press, 1999.

THE TALE OF THE CLAM (HAMAGURI NO SŌSHI)

Hakuin Zenji. "Inscription for a Painting of Clam Kannon." In *Poison Blossoms from a Thicket of Thorn*, translated and annotated by Norman Waddell, 428–30. Berkeley, Calif.: Counterpoint, 2014.

Kawai, Hayao. *The Japanese Psyche: Major Motifs in the Folklore of Japan*. Translated by Hayao Kawai and Sachiko Reece. Dallas: Spring, 1988.

Mayer, Fanny Hagin, ed. and trans. *Ancient Tales in Modern Japan: An Anthology of Japanese Folk Tales*. Bloomington: Indiana University Press, 1985.

THE WAR OF THE TWELVE ANIMALS (JŪNIRUI KASSEN EMAKI)

Thompson, Sarah E. "The War of the Twelve Animals (*Jūnirui kassen emaki*): A Medieval Japanese Illustrated Beast Fable." Ph.D. diss., Columbia University, 1999.

Permissions

Haseo and the Gambling Stranger
Haseo sōshi. Handscroll, late Kamakura period (ca. early fourteenth century). Important Cultural Property. Photos courtesy of the Eisei Bunko Museum. © Eisei Bunko Museum (Tokyo).

The Tale of the Dirt Spider
Traditionally attributed to Tosa Nagataka. *Tsuchigumo zōshi*. Handscroll, ca. early fourteenth century. Important Cultural Property. Images: TNM Image Archives. © Tokyo National Museum.

The Demon Shuten Dōji
Shuten Dōji e. Set of five handscrolls, ca. seventeenth century. Ibukiyama textual line. Photos courtesy of the Tōyō University Library. © Tōyō University Library.

The Demon of Ibuki
Ibuki Dōji. Set of three handscrolls, sixteenth or seventeenth century. Photos courtesy of The British Museum. © The Trustees of the British Museum.

The Tale of Tawara Tōda
Tawara Tōda monogatari. Set of three handscrolls, ca. seventeenth century. Photos courtesy of the Gakushūin University Department of Japanese Language and Literature. © Gakushūin University.

The Origins of Hashidate
Illustrated Story of the Origins of Hashidate (*Hashidate no honji*), the Shrine at Ama no Hashidate, early Edo period (mid-seventeenth century). Set of two handscrolls; ink, color, gold, and silver on paper; H. 32 × W. (entire scroll) 1132.9 cm (12⅝ × 446 in.), and H. 32 × W. (entire scroll) 1005.2 cm (12⅝ × 395¾ in.). Harvard Art Museums/Arthur M. Sackler Museum, Bequest of the Hofer Collection of the Arts of Asia, 1985.544.1 and 2. Figures on

pages 113 and 122: Imaging Department © President and Fellows of Harvard College; figures on pages 104, 106, 110, and 118: Melissa McCormick.

The Palace of the Tengu

Tengu no dairi. Set of two handscrolls, sixteenth century. Photos courtesy of the British Library. © The British Library Board, No. Or. 13839.

Yoshitsune's Island-Hopping

Onzōshi shima-watari. Handscroll, seventeenth century. Photos courtesy of the Akita Prefectural Library.

The Tale of Amewakahiko

Tosa Hirochika (ca. 1439–1492). *Amewakahiko sōshi.* Handscroll, fifteenth century. Ink and colors on paper; 32.1 × ca. 150–1046.8 cm (variable). Inv. 6536. Photos: Jürgen Liepe, courtesy of the Museum of Asian Art, Berlin, and Art Resource, NY. © Museum fuer Asiatische Kunst, Staatliche Museen, Berlin, Germany.

Isozaki

Isozaki. Nara ehon (Nara picture book), seventeenth century. Photos courtesy of the Keiō University Library.

The Tale of the Handcart Priest

Kuruma-zō emaki. Handscroll, seventeenth century. Photos courtesy of the Kyoto University Library.

Origins of the Statue of Kannon as a Boy

Chigo Kannon engi. Handscroll, late Kamakura period (ca. early fourteenth century). Important Cultural Property. Photos courtesy of the Kōsetsu Museum of Art (Kōbe). © Kōsetsu Museum of Art.

Little Atsumori

Ko-Atsumori emaki. Handscroll, sixteenth century. Photos courtesy of the Keiō University Library.

The Crone Fleece

Ubakawa. Nara ehon (Nara picture book), seventeenth or eighteenth century. Photos courtesy of the Jissen Women's University Library (Kurokawa Bunko). © Jissen Women's University Library.

The Tale of the Mouse

Nezumi no sōshi emaki. Set of five handscrolls, sixteenth century. Photos courtesy of the Suntory Museum of Art (Tokyo). © Suntory Museum of Art.

The Chrysanthemum Spirit
Traditionally attributed to Tosa Yukihide. Tale of the Chrysanthemum Spirit (*Kiku no sei no monogatari*, also known as *Kazashi no hime monogatari*), Muromachi period (sixteenth century). Handscroll; ink, color, and gold on paper; H. 17.2 × W. 748.7 cm (6¾ × 294¾ in.). Harvard Art Museums/Arthur M. Sackler Museum, Bequest of the Hofer Collection of the Arts of Asia, 1985.469. Photos: Imaging Department © President and Fellows of Harvard College. All rights reserved.

The Tale of Tamamizu
Tamamizu monogatari. Illustrated manuscript, ca. eighteenth or nineteenth century. Photos courtesy of the Kyoto University Library. © Kyoto University Library. All rights reserved.

The Tale of a Wild Goose
Kari no sōshi. Handscroll, monochrome ink, dated 1602. Photos courtesy of the Kyoto University Library. © Kyoto University Library. All rights reserved.

The Stingfish
Okoze emaki. Handscroll, early seventeenth century. Photos courtesy of the Tōyō University Library. © Tōyō University Library. All rights reserved.

Lady Tamamo
Tamamo no mae sōshi. Set of two handscrolls, sixteenth century. Photos courtesy of the Nezu Museum of Art (Tokyo). © Nezu Museum of Art. All rights reserved.

The Tale of the Clam
Hamaguri no sōshi. Woodblock-printed text with monochrome illustrations, early eighteenth century. Photos courtesy of the University of Tokyo Library System (Katei Bunko). © University of Tokyo. All rights reserved.

The War of the Twelve Animals
Jūnirui kassen. Set of three handscrolls, seventeenth century. CBL J 1154.1, 2, and 3. Photos courtesy of the Chester Beatty Library, Dublin, and the HUMI Project, Keiō University. © The Trustees of the Chester Beatty Library, Dublin, and the HUMI Project, Keiō University. All rights reserved.

The Sparrow's Buddhist Awakening
Suzume no hosshin. Set of two handscrolls, sixteenth century. Former Akagi Bunko scrolls. Photos courtesy of the Suntory Museum of Art (Tokyo). © Suntory Museum of Art. All rights reserved.

The Hermit and the Love-Thief: Sanskrit Poems of Bhartrihari and Bilhaṇa, tr. Barbara Stoler Miller 1978

The Lute: Kao Ming's P'i-p'a chi, tr. Jean Mulligan. Also in paperback ed. 1980

A Chronicle of Gods and Sovereigns: Jinnō Shōtōki of Kitabatake Chikafusa, tr. H. Paul Varley 1980

Among the Flowers: The Hua-chien chi, tr. Lois Fusek 1982

Grass Hill: Poems and Prose by the Japanese Monk Gensei, tr. Burton Watson 1983

Doctors, Diviners, and Magicians of Ancient China: Biographies of Fang-shih, tr. Kenneth J. DeWoskin. Also in paperback ed. 1983

Theater of Memory: The Plays of Kālidāsa, ed. Barbara Stoler Miller. Also in paperback ed. 1984

The Columbia Book of Chinese Poetry: From Early Times to the Thirteenth Century, ed. and tr. Burton Watson. Also in paperback ed. 1984

Poems of Love and War: From the Eight Anthologies and the Ten Long Poems of Classical Tamil, tr. A. K. Ramanujan. Also in paperback ed. 1985

The Bhagavad Gita: Krishna's Counsel in Time of War, tr. Barbara Stoler Miller 1986

The Columbia Book of Later Chinese Poetry, ed. and tr. Jonathan Chaves. Also in paperback ed. 1986

The Tso Chuan: Selections from China's Oldest Narrative History, tr. Burton Watson 1989

Waiting for the Wind: Thirty-Six Poets of Japan's Late Medieval Age, tr. Steven Carter 1989

Selected Writings of Nichiren, ed. Philip B. Yampolsky 1990

Saigyō, Poems of a Mountain Home, tr. Burton Watson 1990

The Book of Lieh Tzu: A Classic of the Tao, tr. A. C. Graham. Morningside ed. 1990

The Tale of an Anklet: An Epic of South India—The Cilappatikāram of Iḷaṅkō Aṭikaḷ, tr. R. Parthasarathy 1993

Waiting for the Dawn: A Plan for the Prince, tr. with introduction by Wm. Theodore de Bary 1993

Yoshitsune and the Thousand Cherry Trees: A Masterpiece of the Eighteenth-Century Japanese Puppet Theater, tr., annotated, and with introduction by Stanleigh H. Jones Jr. 1993

The Lotus Sutra, tr. Burton Watson. Also in paperback ed. 1993

The Classic of Changes: A New Translation of the I Ching as Interpreted by Wang Bi, tr. Richard John Lynn 1994

Beyond Spring: Tz'u Poems of the Sung Dynasty, tr. Julie Landau 1994

The Columbia Anthology of Traditional Chinese Literature, ed. Victor H. Mair 1994

Scenes for Mandarins: The Elite Theater of the Ming, tr. Cyril Birch 1995

Letters of Nichiren, ed. Philip B. Yampolsky; tr. Burton Watson et al. 1996

Unforgotten Dreams: Poems by the Zen Monk Shōtetsu, tr. Steven D. Carter 1997

The Vimalakirti Sutra, tr. Burton Watson 1997

Japanese and Chinese Poems to Sing: The Wakan rōei shū, tr. J. Thomas Rimer and Jonathan Chaves 1997

Breeze Through Bamboo: Kanshi of Ema Saikō, tr. Hiroaki Sato 1998

A Tower for the Summer Heat, by Li Yu, tr. Patrick Hanan 1998

Traditional Japanese Theater: An Anthology of Plays, by Karen Brazell 1998

The Original Analects: Sayings of Confucius and His Successors (0479–0249), by E. Bruce Brooks and A. Taeko Brooks 1998

The Classic of the Way and Virtue: A New Translation of the Tao-te ching of Laozi as Interpreted by Wang Bi, tr. Richard John Lynn 1999

The Four Hundred Songs of War and Wisdom: An Anthology of Poems from Classical Tamil, The Puṛanāṉūṛu, ed. and tr. George L. Hart and Hank Heifetz 1999

Original Tao: Inward Training (Nei-yeh) and the Foundations of Taoist Mysticism, by Harold D. Roth 1999

Po Chü-i: Selected Poems, tr. Burton Watson 2000

Lao Tzu's Tao Te Ching: A Translation of the Startling New Documents Found at Guodian, by Robert G. Henricks 2000

The Shorter Columbia Anthology of Traditional Chinese Literature, ed. Victor H. Mair 2000

Mistress and Maid (Jiaohongji), by Meng Chengshun, tr. Cyril Birch 2001

Chikamatsu: Five Late Plays, tr. and ed. C. Andrew Gerstle 2001

The Essential Lotus: Selections from the Lotus Sutra, tr. Burton Watson 2002

Early Modern Japanese Literature: An Anthology, 1600–1900, ed. Haruo Shirane 2002; abridged 2008

The Columbia Anthology of Traditional Korean Poetry, ed. Peter H. Lee 2002

The Sound of the Kiss, or The Story That Must Never Be Told: Pingali Suranna's Kalapurnodayamu, tr. Vecheru Narayana Rao and David Shulman 2003

The Selected Poems of Du Fu, tr. Burton Watson 2003

Far Beyond the Field: Haiku by Japanese Women, tr. Makoto Ueda 2003

Just Living: Poems and Prose by the Japanese Monk Tonna, ed. and tr. Steven D. Carter 2003

Han Feizi: Basic Writings, tr. Burton Watson 2003

Mozi: Basic Writings, tr. Burton Watson 2003

Xunzi: Basic Writings, tr. Burton Watson 2003

Zhuangzi: Basic Writings, tr. Burton Watson 2003

The Awakening of Faith, Attributed to Aśvaghosha, tr. Yoshito S. Hakeda, introduction by Ryūichi Abé 2005

The Tales of the Heike, tr. Burton Watson, ed. Haruo Shirane 2006

Tales of Moonlight and Rain, by Ueda Akinari, tr. with introduction by Anthony H. Chambers 2007

Traditional Japanese Literature: An Anthology, Beginnings to 1600, ed. Haruo Shirane 2007

The Philosophy of Qi, by Kaibara Ekken, tr. Mary Evelyn Tucker 2007

The Analects of Confucius, tr. Burton Watson 2007

The Art of War: Sun Zi's Military Methods, tr. Victor Mair 2007

One Hundred Poets, One Poem Each: A Translation of the Ogura Hyakunin Isshu, tr. Peter McMillan 2008

Zeami: Performance Notes, tr. Tom Hare 2008

Zongmi on Chan, tr. Jeffrey Lyle Broughton 2009

Scripture of the Lotus Blossom of the Fine Dharma, rev. ed., tr. Leon Hurvitz, preface and introduction by Stephen R. Teiser 2009

Mencius, tr. Irene Bloom, ed. with an introduction by Philip J. Ivanhoe 2009

Clouds Thick, Whereabouts Unknown: Poems by Zen Monks of China, Charles Egan 2010

The Mozi: A Complete Translation, tr. Ian Johnston 2010

The Huainanzi: A Guide to the Theory and Practice of Government in Early Han China, by Liu An, tr. and ed. John S. Major, Sarah A. Queen, Andrew Seth Meyer, and Harold D. Roth, with Michael Puett and Judson Murray 2010

The Demon at Agi Bridge and Other Japanese Tales, tr. Burton Watson, ed. with introduction by Haruo Shirane 2011

Haiku Before Haiku: From the Renga Masters to Bashō, tr. with introduction by Steven D. Carter 2011

The Columbia Anthology of Chinese Folk and Popular Literature, ed. Victor H. Mair and Mark Bender 2011

Tamil Love Poetry: The Five Hundred Short Poems of the Aiṅkuṟunūṟu, tr. and ed. Martha Ann Selby 2011

The Teachings of Master Wuzhu: Zen and Religion of No-Religion, by Wendi L. Adamek 2011

The Essential Huainanzi, by Liu An, tr. and ed. John S. Major, Sarah A. Queen, Andrew Seth Meyer, and Harold D. Roth 2012

The Dao of the Military: Liu An's Art of War, tr. Andrew Seth Meyer 2012

Unearthing the Changes: Recently Discovered Manuscripts of the Yi Jing (I Ching) *and Related Texts*, Edward L. Shaughnessy 2013

Record of Miraculous Events in Japan: The Nihon ryōiki, tr. Burton Watson 2013

The Complete Works of Zhuangzi, tr. Burton Watson 2013

Printed in the USA
CPSIA information can be obtained
at www.ICGtesting.com
JSHW021006160924
69943JS00002B/18

9 780231 184472